# THE BEST OF JERRY POURNELLE

**BAEN BOOKS by Jerry Pournelle**

*The Best of Jerry Pournelle* (edited by John F. Carr) • *Birth of Fire*
*Fires of Freedom* • *Oath of Fealty* (with Larry Niven)
*Fallen Angels* (with Larry Niven and Michael Flynn)
*Mutual Assured Survival* (with Dean Ing)
*Adventures in Microland*

**Heorot Series (with Larry Niven and Steven Barnes)**

*The Legacy of Heorot* • *Beowulf's Children*
*Starborn and Godsons* (forthcoming)

**Janissaries Series**

*Janissaries* • *Tran* • *Lord of Janissaries* (with Roland J. Green)
*Mamelukes* (forthcoming; edited and revised
by David Weber and Phillip Pournelle)

**THE CODOMINIUM UNIVERSE**

*King David's Spaceship*

**Falkenberg's Legion Series**

*West of Honor* • *The Mercenary* • *Prince of Mercenaries*
*Falkenberg's Legion*

**Falkenburg's Legion with S.M. Stirling**

*Go Tell the Spartans* • *A Prince of Sparta* • *The Children's Hour*
*The Prince* (omnibus)

**Laurie Jo Hansen Series**

*High Justice* • *Exiles to Glory* • *Exile—and Glory* (omnibus)

**The War World Series**

*The Burning Eye* • *Death's Head Rebellion* • *Sauron Dominion*
*Invasion* • *CoDominium: Revolt on War World*

**CoDominium Anthologies**
**(with Susan Shwartz, S.M. Stirling, Judith Tarr, and Harry Turtledove)**

*Blood Feuds* • *Blood Vengeance*

**Imperial Stars Series (with John F. Carr)**

*The Stars at War* • *Republic and Empire* • *The Crash of Empire*

**War World Anthology Series**
**(created by Jerry Pournelle, edited by John F. Carr)**

*War World* Volumes I–IV

**Man-Kzin Wars Series**

*The Children's Hour* (with S.M. Stirling)
*The House of the Kzinti* (with Dean Ing & S.M. Stirling)

**Far Frontiers (edited with Jim Baen)**

*Far Frontiers*, Volumes I–VII

# THE BEST OF JERRY POURNELLE

Edited by

John F. Carr

The Best of Jerry Pournelle



A Baen Books Original

Baen Publishing Enterprises
P.O. Box 1403
Riverdale, NY 10471
www.baen.com

ISBN: 978-1-9821-2417-5

Cover art by Stephen Hickman

First Baen printing November 2019

Distributed by Simon & Schuster
1230 Avenue of the Americas
New York, NY 10020

Library of Congress Cataloging-in-Publication Data

Names: Pournelle, Jerry, 1933-2017, author. | Carr, John F., editor.
Title: The best of Jerry Pournelle / edited by John F. Carr.
Identifiers: LCCN 2019028428 | ISBN 9781982124175 (trade paperback)
Subjects: GSAFD: Science fiction.
Classification: LCC PS3566.O815 A6 2019 | DDC 813/.54—dc23
LC record available at https://lccn.loc.gov/2019028428

Printed in the United States of America

10 9 8 7 6 5 4 3 2 1

**Acknowledgments**

Special thanks go to Alexander and Phillip Pournelle for their help with this project, and Larry Niven for his kind assistance.

I'd like to thank my copy editors, Victoria Alexander and Dwight Decker, for their dedication and hard work.

# CONTENTS

# THE BEST OF JERRY POURNELLE

# INTRODUCTION:
## What was Jerry Pournelle really like?
## by John F. Carr

I worked with Jerry Pournelle in his home/office in Studio City for over twenty years. During those two decades, I believe I got to know him better than anyone outside his family except for Larry Niven. I saw Jerry at his best, at home and relaxed, working feverishly to deadline, excited about a new project, scientific discovery or space flight, as well as down in the dumps when once again he and Larry were passed over for another Hugo Award. Does anyone today even remember the novel that beat *Lucifer's Hammer* and won the Best Novel Hugo of 1978?

There's even a Chilean heavy metal band named Lucifer's Hammer—although I suspect that Jerry wouldn't have viewed their homage as flattering.

Even Jerry realized that while he had many fans in the science-fiction community, there was a significant portion of fandom that disliked him—in part because of his politics and in part because of envy. If that hurt, Jerry never showed it. In fact, he reveled in it, calling himself out as being "somewhere to the right of Genghis Khan!"

I do know that every time I went to a science-fiction convention, Science Fiction Writers of America Nebula Award event or writer's gathering, people would come up to me and ask: "What is Jerry Pournelle *really* like?"

Before I answer that question, let's take a step backward and let me tell you a little about myself and my background. Jerry was an only child, while I came from a family of five children, four boys and one girl, with me the oldest. My father, John L. Carr, was born in

Philadelphia, Pennsylvania, and like Jerry was a veteran; he was stationed at the Desert Training Center in Indio, California, where he underwent extensive training with the US Army Tank Destroyers for the North African Campaign.

My dad never made it to the North African theater. During a ten-mile hike, with full backpack and kit, in 110 degree heat, my father collapsed—he'd had a heart attack. He was taken back to the base, revived and decommissioned. Until his dying day, my dad always felt as though he'd let his unit down. Before he joined up, he'd worked as a machinist; so in Philadelphia he went back to work making the tools of war. After the war, he ran into one of his fellow soldiers, who told him all their training in the heat had been in vain; instead his battalion had gone in first at Anzio, Italy, where they suffered losses approaching sixty percent.

I was born on Christmas Day in 1944, which leaves me thankful for my dad's heart attack! Life certainly has some odd twists and turns. My parents left Philly in 1948 for San Diego; three of my uncles had been in the merchant marines and based there. To them, compared to Philadelphia, it was paradise. My dad went to work for the Naval Electronics Lab in Point Loma and we moved to Pacific Beach. His next move was to Convair which was building the Atlas missile; his abilities were quickly noted and he was promoted to engineer without the prerequisite college degree. He continued working there even after Convair was bought out by General Dynamics.

I first went to work for Jerry on a trial basis in 1975. Jerry was looking for someone to help him organize his office; the growing success of *The Mote in God's Eye* had left him swamped with paperwork and demands on his time. He had hired the son of one of the professors at Pepperdine University, where Jerry had taught political science. At the University of Washington, Jerry had earned master's degrees in experimental statistics and systems engineering, as well as PhDs in psychology and political science. Jerry quickly determined he wasn't suited for academic life as a professor and left Pepperdine to work for the reelection committee of Sam Yorty, mayor of Los Angeles, as his speech writer. This gave him a lot of insight into the political world, which he later used in his books, but when the campaign was over and they promoted him to a desk job—he quit.

The professor's son turned out to be a dud. Instead of sorting Jerry's mail, he tossed it into banker boxes which he didn't even bother to label. Jerry got hold of me through Steven Goldin, the then editor of *The Science Fiction Writers of America Bulletin*. I was assisting Goldin as junior editor—which means I did most of the scut work, but I learned a lot. By this point, Jerry decided he needed help from someone who knew something about writing and the writing life. When Jerry called Goldin and asked if he wanted to work as his assistant, Steve turned him down as he had just signed contracts with Laser Books for several novels. He mentioned I was a published author—my first novel, *The Ophidian Conspiracy*, had just come out—and that I was helping Steven edit and publish the *SFWA Bulletin*; he told Jerry I was an ideal candidate for the job.

By this time, I had read *A Spaceship for the King* and some of Jerry's Falkenberg novellas and was a dedicated reader of *Galaxy Magazine* and very familiar with Jerry's "A Step Farther Out" columns. And, of course, *The Mote in God's Eye* had made quite a splash; many were calling it the best first-contact novel ever written. Plus, Jerry was heading up the Los Angeles area SFWA meetings and organized several outings to Pepperdine University in Malibu where we were given talks on campus by prominent scientists Jerry knew or had worked with. The clincher was lunch at a Malibu bistro which served deli sandwiches and Heinekens. No SF writer worth his salt has ever turned down a free lunch.

In those days, Jerry called himself a writer in the Hemingway tradition and he meant it. He typically wore a tan bush jacket and cargo pants, even around the house; he also smoked a pipe and was a two-fisted drinker. My favorite picture from that era was a large black & white photo of Jerry, dressed in his bush outfit, sitting in a rattan chair and cradling a Samurai sword.

Jerry was a large man, six feet two inches tall and just south of two hundred pounds; he dominated every gathering, especially the scientific and science-fiction circles he moved in. He spoke in a loud, booming voice with a trace of a Southern accent. With his encyclopedic knowledge, advanced degrees and great recall, he was completely at home whether talking about the latest scientific development, space research, publishing trend or political event. He was not a man to be trifled with; nor did he suffer fools gladly. His debating skills were second to none.

When Jerry called and asked if I was interested in helping him clean up his office for a few weeks, I immediately agreed and met him the next day. His office was a mess; overflowing banker boxes covering most of his office surfaces, including the floor! I went to work, sorting out the contracts, checks and critical correspondence from the "gubbage," as Jerry would call it, as well as the usual junk mail. During my stay, the professor's son showed up to pick up his unearned paycheck. I noted that his eyes were red and he carried the stench of a dedicated pot smoker, which explained a lot.

After several weeks of cleaning up the office mess, I went up into the attic—where Jerry kept his important files—and organized them as well. He had banker boxes stuffed with research papers with names like "Revolution Study," "Pepperdine," "Mars Study," "Mathoms," etc. I left on good terms and he said he'd call me again if he got into another bind.

Well, it only took about three weeks before chaos began to reign in Jerry's office once more. This time Jerry offered me a steady position as his assistant with an increase in salary. Jerry enjoyed having a staff, even a staff of one. As a beginning writer, I liked the financial security of a steady job; plus, it was a job with a writer who was going places. I figured I could learn a lot working with Jerry, and I was right. It was like getting paid while working toward a graduate degree.

It worked well right from the beginning: I opened all of Jerry's mail and, as a fellow writer, I knew automatically what was important and what wasn't. I even answered all of his noncritical mail, such as membership requests, speaking requests from con committees, letters from publicists and letters from his speaking bureau; all the things that eat up time. I became the master of the one-page letter. I started helping with the anthologies early on, managing the contracts for his *Black Holes* anthology. When the book was published, I took note of the advances to be paid, wrote out the checks for Jerry to sign and answered the publicity requests from the publisher.

Meanwhile, Jerry was working on *Inferno* with Larry and things were hopping. The interesting thing about *The Mote in God's Eye* was—while it never reached any bestseller lists—it just keep selling: like the Energizer Bunny it just kept going and going!

Before I started working for him, Jerry had signed a number of contracts with Laser Books, a new SF line under the Harlequin Romance imprint. Before the line went belly up, Laser Books published two of his books, *West of Honor* and *Birth of Fire*. They also held a contract for *Space Viking's Return*, the sequel to H. Beam Piper's *Space Viking*.

Jerry was having problems with the *Space Viking* sequel because it was a deceptively simple work: an action-adventure novel taking place in what Piper called the Old Federation. True, it was an action-packed space opera, but it was filled with military, historical and planetary details that had to be taken into consideration for the sequel to work. And, Jerry just didn't have the time to spend studying Piper's book.

So Jerry asked me to do a detailed study of the book, with notes and a detailed chronology. I'd always loved the book and getting paid to study and dissect it was like being given an early Christmas present. Of course, this fired up my collecting instincts and I went on a mission to locate every Piper story ever published, since many of them were part of the Space Viking future history, which I later named the Terro-Human Future History. This was before the Internet, and finding out-of-print books was a major chore. The Collector's Book Store in Hollywood, which was crammed to the rafters with movie memorabilia, rare books, photos, paintings and pulp fiction, was the answer to my prayers.

When I became *SFWA Bulletin* editor in 1978, Jerry realized that he not only had a valued employee but a fellow editor. Jerry edited books, not for the money, but because he wanted to pay forward the time and education about writing he'd been given by Robert A. Heinlein and H. Beam Piper and pass it forward to new writers. It also explains why Jerry was one of the judges of the Writers of the Future contest right up until his death.

From that point on I became his associate editor and we started editing a number of anthologies, The Endless Frontier series,

*Survival of Freedom*, the Imperial Stars series and the military SF series There Will Be War and War World.

So back to the original question: What was Jerry Pournelle really like? First of all, he was one of the most brilliant men I've ever met; he had an encyclopedic knowledge of the damndest things, both practical and fantastic. He didn't put up with nonsense from anyone, no matter what their reputation; he had an engineer's laser-like focus and was able chop logic like a butcher! You didn't want to debate Jerry—who had been on debate teams in college—unless you had all your ducks in a row, and even then you'd probably learn, to your chagrin, that some of them were dead ducks, when Jerry shot them down.

Jerry was well-aware of his "gifts" and he took full advantage of them. He used to sponsor parties at the annual meetings of the American Association of the Advancement of Science (AAAS) so that he could introduce scientists from different disciplines to each other. He was quite proud of this, and saw himself as sort of a bumble bee of science pollinating the different disciplines. With an open bar these soirees were always well attended; Jerry's sponsor for these meetings was the Vaughn Foundation.

Jerry first met James Vaughn when he was a professor of political science at Pepperdine University. Mr. Vaughn represented a group of Texas millionaires who, due to the political upheavals of the late sixties, were worried about the fate of the Republic and paid Jerry to do a study which he called "The Revolution Study." Jerry's final conclusion, as told to me when I asked, was that the Republic would survive the political issues of the day and that a successful left-wing revolution was unlikely.

Jerry's favorite Mr. Vaughn (he always referred to him as *Mister*) story was at one of the AAAS parties—Mr. Vaughn liked to rub shoulders with important and famous scientists—when Jerry introduced him to one of the scientists as a "Texas millionaire," and Mr. Vaughn quickly interrupted with, "No, I'm a Texas multimillionaire." We had a good laugh over that one.

Once of the things Jerry told me when I first went to work for him was that he was a terrible manager of people. In the past, underlings had complained he was a hard task-master and demanded perfection. Plus, he yelled a lot; not on purpose, but his hearing was bad due to spending too much time near ear-bursting artillery shells during the Korean War. Jerry left Boeing when his job of stress-testing the astronauts ended because they promoted him to a managerial position. "I'm the worst damn people manager you can find," he told me. "I'm hiring you because you know what I want, even before I do."

I took that as a high compliment, but it was a skill I'd developed while growing up with my own highly demanding father.

Jerry always treated me like a colleague, rather than an employee. He was the best boss I ever had: before working for Jerry I had worked as an assistant department store manager, a bookstore clerk, an expediter and record store manager. From the beginning, we got along like gangbusters. In the twenty years I worked for him, I can honestly say he *never* once either raised his voice to me, or got angry at me. And that's saying something!

I told this to fans, colleagues and friends, many of whom had a hard time reconciling this with what they had "heard" about Jerry and his larger than life public persona. But, when Jerry was at home in Chaos Manor, he was at his best, doing whatever it was he wanted to do. And I was at his side making sure he wasn't bothered by interruptions and nonsense.

When I learned that Harlan Ellison had just died in July of this year (2018), it hit me that the two most brilliant, outrageous and outspoken SF writers in the field had left us. Both of them, despite their opposing political viewpoints, respected each other a lot. In public they might spar for the benefit of the crowd, but in private they were friends. Our field is much smaller now with their loss. We will not see their like again.

# ECOLOGY NOW!

## by Jerry Pournelle

## Editor's Introduction

As Jerry recounted to me, he first tried selling short stories to John W. Campbell in the late fifties and early sixties, and earned a significant number of rejections over the years. However, Campbell liked to encourage new writers, especially those who were working scientists like Pournelle. And Jerry wrote stories and a number of novels over the next decade before Campbell bought his first story, "Peace with Honor." According to Jerry, he had a lot of help along the way. He sent his early stories to both H. Beam Piper and Robert Heinlein, who both encouraged him to keep writing. Heinlein took time to critique one of Jerry's early works. In his interview on the *Author Stories Podcast*, episode 161, Jerry says: "I once told Mr. Heinlein that once I got into Advance Plans at Boeing. I probably wrote more science fiction than he did, and I didn't have to put any characters in mine."

Asked by the interviewer of the *Authors Stories Podcast* when he decided to become a writer, Jerry replied:

Probably, sometime in the fifties, I was reading *Analog* and I read a story and I thought, God, I can write a better story than that. And at the same time I started going to a fan club, where I noticed the aristocrats were all pros who were actually published and everybody else was supposed to pay them homage—and that seemed like a good notion.

So I wrote a story and I sent it to John Campbell and he wrote back in a four-page letter telling me why he didn't like that story, but would I try again. I did that about four times and I'd get these long letters back, and then I didn't get a letter. And, I went: He didn't like that one either, so much that he didn't even say he didn't like it. And the next day I got a check.

After that I decided, how long has this been going on . . . ? At the time, I was an aerospace engineer, I ran the human factors lab for the Boeing Company in Seattle. I tended to be the team leader on almost any project I was on because I ended up writing the final report. In fact, I was the only engineer at Boeing who had his own typewriter. . . .

And I know, I was the only engineer who wrote on his own. I know you were supposed to dictate or write in longhand and the girls would type it up and you'd do all that. I can type faster than I can write in handwriting and I don't dictate. So I ended up writing the reports, but I never really coupled the fact that I was doing all that writing with writing for fiction until 1962–'61?

They had a convention in Seattle [the 19th World Science Fiction Convention in 1961 with Guest of Honor Robert A. Heinlein—Ed.] . . . and among the attendees were Robert Heinlein and Poul Anderson and Harlan Ellison and I got to know all of them, and I corresponded with Mr. Heinlein quite a lot after that because he was interested in the aerospace work I was doing and the engineering. . . . And Poul just became one of my best friends. I would stay at his house when I would go to the San Francisco area and that sort of thing. Poul read some of the . . . just junk I was writing and he said, "That ain't bad."

So eventually I wrote something and I kinda gulped hard and sent it to Mr. Heinlein, saying, "Is this any good?"

He wrote back. He said, "First, you will never tell anyone that I have read this 'til after I am dead." . . . He prefaced this with a thirty-five-page letter of detailed criticism all the way from things like misspelling—"You're a terrible speller"—and probably I am. The Boeing girls used to do the proofreading of my stuff so it never looked like that in the report. . . . I remember one remark stood out: Somewhere deep in his letter he said, "On page 41, there is a break in empathy—fix it." That's all he said.

And I looked at it, what does it mean "break in empathy" and I looked at it—and I realized that I had a clever phrase that made you admire the writing. And that takes you out of the story and makes you think "I'm reading a book by this writer and isn't that clever." That isn't what you want, at least, if you write like Mr. Heinlein did. What you want is for people to forget they're reading a story and just be in the story. Pay attention to the story; I did that and developed that kind of writing style, which is to say: I don't want you to know I'm writing it, I want you to read what I wrote—if you see what I mean.

Now, that is not the way to get literary reviews; the *New Yorker* people are all very clever and you read them—"and by Golly that's good"—but then you notice that the number of readers seems to be restricted to basically the *New Yorker* people. . . . That doesn't seem to be reasonable and certainly didn't work for science fiction, because in those days science fiction had a different slant.

In talking about *The Mote in God's Eye* on the *Author Story Podcast,* Jerry relates how he linked up with the Blassingame Agency.

I sent if off to my agent, who by the way was about the best agent in the business. Because when I'd written that first story, after Mr. Heinlein caused me to rewrite it. I did rewrite it and he said, "Nobody ever did that before! I mean, actually paid attention to what I said."

I had, of course, meticulously gone over everything. "Do you mind if I send it to my agent?"

"Don't throw me into that briar patch, Robert." So he did, and that's why I had the best agent in the business.

The Blassingame Agency was a big deal in the 1960s, representing science-fiction authors such as Heinlein and Frank Herbert, as well as literary maven John Barth. Lurton Blassingame took time out to critique Jerry's early works and to give him encouragement.

My first stories were action-adventure stories; the engineer sucked into the counter-spy business—that type of thing. I didn't write any science fiction at all really in those days. Eventually, I decided to write science fiction and tried it and I achieved the ambition I had ten years ago. I did write a better story than *Analog* was publishing, so I got it published in *Analog*. All by John Campbell, who promptly having bought one, bought four more from me and died.

And Miss Tarrant, who was the managing editor of *Analog*, did not buy new stories from anyone. . . . They offered the job of editor to Poul Anderson but he didn't want it. He didn't want to leave California. And, he suggested to the publisher that they consider me for it. And, when I realized what the salary was . . . I realized we'd have to leave California and go to New York. I couldn't live in New York on what they were paying him. I don't know how John did it. I couldn't do it, either.

Miss Tarrant made *Analog* up out of a lot of stuff. And one issue I had, let's see, a nonfiction science article in it, they were running my serial [*A Spaceship for the King*—Ed.], like episode 2 of the serial, and I had two other stories in there and they had to—one of them they could say was by me but the other one they made me make up a pen name [Wade Curtis—Ed.] which I used; which in fact was the pen name I'd used on the adventure stories. They all came out and Poul Anderson says to me: "You rascal, you've done everything but become the editor."

But that's how I got started.

"Ecology Now!" published in 1971 under the Wade Curtis pseudonym, was one of the first of Jerry's stories pitting large corporations against an increasingly socialist and bureaucratic United States government. These stories would later be collected together in *High Justice* for Pocket Books. Despite some confusion over the years, the stories in this collection were not a part of Jerry's CoDominium future history, but two separate series detailing the struggles of two dynasties: Laurie Jo Hansen, owner of the Hansen fortune, and Jeremy Lewis, owner of the Nuclear General Company.

This particular Nuclear General story, featuring Bill Adams (Jeremy Lewis's troubleshooter), was not included in *High Justice*; it appears here for the first time since its original publication in the December 1971 issue of *Analog Science Fiction*.

❁❁❁

**DR. ARTURO MARTINEZ** decided he wasn't as young as he used to be. It wasn't a completely new decision, and at this hour of the morning he didn't even regret it. At his age, a man had no business staying up all night, not when he had to get up early in the morning. But Dianne had enjoyed the company expense account night in Los Angeles; in fact, she enjoyed it so much that Art had to get his own breakfast.

And Martinez felt a perverse satisfaction in noting that his houseguest looked no better than he did despite being fifteen years younger than Martinez's forty-eight. Bill Adams might be a bright young fellow with accountant's ink instead of blood, but he sat gloomily across the breakfast table, staring with pale-blue eyes at his eggs and saying almost nothing. Arturo grinned.

"Feel all right?"

"About as well as you do," Adams answered. He managed a smile, smoothed back crew-cut sandy hair. "I don't suppose we've got time for much breakfast anyway?"

"No," Dr. Martinez hesitated. Adams was a friendly young Anglo, but you never could tell. . . . "Look, Bill I am not sure just what it is you want to do out there today—"

Adams shook his head, winced slightly at the exertion. "I keep telling you, don't worry about it. You're Acting Director and you're in charge. I'm just a visiting fireman with a hangover."

"Well, okay," Art answered. Bill Adams had flown in from Santa Barbara the night before. A likeable young fellow, quick to smile, interested in every aspect of Nuclear General's San Juan Capistrano Breeder and Power Reactor. He didn't act at all like one of the almost legendary people old man Lewis kept around him, the young fellows with no heart and eyes to see figures only. Adams carried a small pocket computer and had a habit of popping it out to make extrapolations from the figures he was given. He knew more about nuclear reactions than the accountants and more about the economics of power sale than the physicists, and he listened to everything with a genuine appearing smile.

The only trouble was that he *had* been sent down by Mr. Lewis, and the rumor was that Nuclear General only sent Adams where trouble was expected. Dr. Martinez tightened thin lips over slightly gapped teeth at the thought. There wasn't any trouble at the San Juan Reactor and there wasn't going to be any trouble. The physicists were happy with the reactor, the business manager satisfied with power sales, and Art himself supervised the ocean farms.

They finished their breakfast and Art led the way to the garage. He unplugged his Oldsmobile Electric and waited for Adams to comment as they got in. People always did.

"You like this?" Adams asked.

"It's all right, looks like a car and will out-accelerate anything you've got, I bet. Corners very well, too."

He settled in, buckled his safety belt. Adams ignored his.

"What about the range?"

"There you have exposed the weak point," Martinez admitted.

They drove through the quiet streets of a walled housing development. Dr. Martinez looked around with quiet satisfaction. When he was growing up, going to college, Chicanos did not live in places like this. Now he had a home as fine as anyone else, and he called no man "*Patron.*" It was a long time since he had— He eased the car over an enormous road hump, but wasn't gentle enough for Bill Adam's head.

"Sort of rough on cars, those things, aren't they?"

Art smiled. "Sure, if you are not careful you will lose some springs. Better than losing children to hot-rodders . . . about the electric car, Bill. I admit it is not as nice as a natural gas/gasoline vehicle such as the Jaguar we took to Los Angeles, but if the bossman ecologist in this town won't set a good example, who will?"

He took the road through the town of San Juan Capistrano, past the old Mission where he and Dianne and Henrietta attended mass. His son Candelario was at Nuclear General College and—Monsignor O'Malley was outside and waving to them. The men stopped work on the Mission to wave as well. All the workmen wore Nuclear General coveralls.

"Advertising?" Adams asked.

"You might call it that, but it comes from the Community Relations budget. The old Mission was hit very hard by the last earthquake. With Nuclear General construction technology this repair should be the last. The only difficult part is hiding the fiberglass and resilient bracing so the Mission looks as it used to."

"Pretty old building . . . eighteenth century?"

"Yes."

"You seem pretty proud of it."

"All of us in this town are proud of it," Martinez said. He didn't want to, but decided to explain. Dianne thought he should be very careful with this young man who was eyes and ears for *el patron* Lewis. The title his family used for the president brought a thin smile.

"Look, the men were not doing anything. We don't start construction on the new building for a month, and I do not need them for work at the plant. The earthquake did us no damage. Why should I not send them out to work on the Mission?"

"Easy," Adams protested. "I wasn't complaining. I keep trying to tell you. Art, you're the Acting Director. Until Mr. Lewis makes up his mind whether he can put a nonphysicist permanently in charge of a reactor, you're running the show. Personally, I think he's going to give it to you . . . if you want it. Do you?"

The question was casual but Art knew the answer would be important. What could he say? The Director was an important man, perhaps the most important man in the community. What would it mean to the Chicanos to have as top employer the son of a wetback bean picker? And not just the young men with education, but the dropouts, the militants might see hope. . . .

"Yes, I want it. But I will not resign if I do not get it."

"Good."

They stopped at a traffic light in Mission Square. There seemed to be more of the long-haired counterculture youths than usual. They called themselves strange names, such as hippies and yippies, which were two different things although Martinez didn't know which was which.

"You get many of those here?" Adams asked. "We're generally surrounded by them at Corporate Headquarters."

"San Juan is not much of a hangout for them," Arturo answered. "The Mission is not a state park, you know. Monsignor O'Malley will not put up with any nonsense on Mission grounds, throws them out for nudity, drugs—"

"There's one who's on your side." Adams indicated a young man wearing a large button proclaiming "ECOLOGY NOW!"

"Yes."

"You're not very enthusiastic."

"Should I be?" Dr. Martinez drove on through the old town, down toward the beach. His mouth tightened again as he spat the words out. "It took me ten years of study to become an ecological engineer, and even now I can see just how little I understand. It was not easy study, for me. And I did not go where they had a special program for Chicanos. I went to Cal Tech, and after that to Westinghouse. Now some *cabrone* with a major in 'brotherhood' pins on a green and white badge, and by God he is an ecologist fit to tell me how to operate the reactor."

"Easy," Bill Adams grinned. "That's the baby there, eh? Pretty, isn't it."

It was an impressive sight, although Arturo had seen it too often to notice unless someone called his attention to it. The reactor was built on an artificial island some fifty acres in extent, connected to the mainland by a wide causeway. A yacht harbor and fishing complex nestled in the sheltered bays the island had created, each boat swimming in a plastic bath to protect it from bottom growth. The sailboats were deserted, but Fishboat Harbor was a bustle of activity.

The reactor complex was large, but there was little to see. Three big blast retention domes housing two completed reactors and the skeleton of the new one under construction, two office buildings, a windowless fiberglass laboratory, all surrounded by wire fence. The generator dome was also windowless, a combination of pre-stressed concrete and more fiberglass. A circuit breaker farm stood outside the powerhouse, impressive with its crazy quilt of oil bath transformers, insulators hanging like Spanish moss from transmission towers, a jumble of wires but hardly unusual.

At the far end the island was being slowly expanded. When it was completed there would be a complex of pools with ordered rows of piping and values in geometric perfection, the desalinization plant. Its construction had been delayed because of the voracious demand for power in Southern California outstripped even the need for water, and the fresh water facility would have to wait until the new reactor was complete. When it was done—provided it wasn't needed as power again—fifty million gallons of water a day would be available for Imperial Valley farms.

The most spectacular sight at the San Juan Reactor complex was offshore. Arturo pointed proudly; this was his, and it was unique in all the world.

"The colored areas are the plankton blooms," he explained. "We take raw sewage from San Juan Capistrano, part of San Diego, San Clemente and other beach cities. It is treated in special underground vertical holding tanks, and we are able to use waste heat from the reactor to speed up the process. Then we take the effluent, heat it again with more so-called waste heat, and dump it onto the bottom along five miles of pipe. Because it is warm it rises through the baffles and is eaten by the plankton strains we have developed. It is very warm out there; 100 degrees Fahrenheit, and that means the diatoms and rotifers have a very high metabolic rate."

"Pretty impressive," Adams said. He shaded his eyes with one hand, stared at the water, ignoring the pain the bright morning sun was causing. "What brings about all the colors? It looks like a rainbow."

"Those are different temperature areas, each feeding a different predominant species. Now look out to the edge of the bloom areas, where the boats are. That is heated water also. We have special species of herring, smelt, sardine and cod living out there. The heated water keeps predators away, and we harvest over six hundred tons of protein to the square mile."

"That's pretty good," Adams said. Then he laughed. "Actually I don't know if it's good or not. Nothing to compare it with."

Art smiled. He could like this man. "Ordinary pasture ashore will yield about fifty tons to the square mile. The best natural fishing waters in the world, which are off Peru, give four hundred or so."

"I am impressed." Adams whipped out his pocket computer and his fingers dashed over the tiny keyboard. He put it back in his pocket and whistled.

"Yes." Martinez drove down toward the reactor island. "And we are only just starting. We have planted oysters on rafts also. In other places they harvest yields of tons of protein to the square mile that way."

"But you don't get that yet?"

"We have had trouble developing strains that will survive and breed in high temperatures."

"Give them cooler water," Adams said. He caught himself and laughed.

"Sure." Martinez grinned cheerfully. "It gets to me that way, too. There is such a protein shortage you start thinking of what to do and forget the whole project is intended to use the waste heat from the reactor. But we are planting high temperature tolerant strains of mussels now, they grew well in the laboratory and we have hopes. Many countries are watching us."

The guards saluted as they passed through the outer gates. Art drove to his parking slot by the gleaming white main office building. The number two tombstone had his name painted on it. It had been a great day when that was painted, but now number one stood ominously blank. Martinez could have taken number one, but if he didn't make director he'd have to give it up.

It would be all right if he never became director, but to take complete charge and lose it would be intolerable. They walked silently inside, took film badges and dosimeters from the rack. Directors of reactor facilities are always physicists. *And Anglos*, he added to himself, but angrily dismissed the thought as unfair. Mr. Lewis was dedicated to profits, and could hardly care if a man were Chicano or purple if the two magic numbers came out right. ROI and PII, Return on Investment and Position in the Industry, these were Lewis's gods and his worship of them pushed out lesser prejudices.

And why do I want it? he asked himself. No one interferes with me, and being director is sorrow, a worry with sales rates and personnel and administration, the ruin of a good scientist. He'd told himself that a thousand times—

He'd kept his old offices, but he took Adams to the director's control desk. Three walls of the tower room were covered with functional diagrams of the reactors and powerhouse/ecological complexes that served them. Lights winked, dials showed temperatures and flows, water and steam and liquid sodium, power output, sewage flow rates, sea temperatures and always the winking green lights for safe temperature in the reactor cores. Models of the control rods hung above the plastic representation of the breeders, suspended by a magnetic field exactly as their real life counterparts were poised to plunge at the touch of a scram button.

A duty officer in another building had duplicates of the intricate console system. In practice the director never used his magnetic keys to unlock his desk and override his operating engineers' decisions, and the engineers themselves had little to do but watch the computer-controlled operations. Still, the director's tower was the symbol of power and authority. From here everything could be done, provided the computer did not disagree and scram the reactors regardless of the director's will.

"Childe Harolde will be impressed with this," Arturo said. "Have a seat. Susie will bring us some coffee."

"You take Senator McGehee a bit too lightly," Adams warned. "He's after Nuclear General because Mr. Adams supported Garner last year. And that children's crusade of McGehee's isn't the joke some columnists want to make of it. The man's dangerous."

"We have no government support," Martinez protested. "This whole complex was built on company funds. Lewis and Van Cott gambled everything they own on it after the AEC lost the appropriation for a fast breeder—"

"Easy," Adams laughed. "I know the story, Art." He chuckled and after a moment Art relaxed, laughed with him. "Sure it was a legendary gamble that paid off," the troubleshooter continued. "A new breeder process and power reactor without an experimental prototype. But your power sales are all that keeps this facility out of the hands of its creditors, and with Senator McGehee on the warpath, we're worried."

"So that is why you are down here?"

"Sure. We're not worried about technical questions. You've done well, as well as Gladstone, maybe better now that the fishing is making money and you've got sewage disposal payments from San Diego. We can't complain about any of that, but—"

Adams was interrupted by the arrival of Martinez's secretary. Adams grinned at her while Martinez hid his amusement. Last week she'd worn shorts, now she sported a thin nearly transparent skirt reaching within inches of her knees. Art's wife paid little attention to style changes and Henrietta took after her mother, but Susie followed them slavishly. She smiled, set out the coffee, and saw the men were busy, then vanished quickly in a flurry of bright blue and red-checked stockings. Adams continued to grin after she was gone, then swiveled to face Martinez.

"Look, Art, get it through your head I'm not here about your job. Secretary, maybe, but not your job—" He winked. "The Old Man was scared of this McGehee thing, sent me down to be on hand just in case. That's all, now relax."

He sipped coffee, looked around the room. "Does this place explain the ecology system you've developed? Frankly I've seen reactors, we've got three more complexes, but this sewage disposal through protein production is unique."

"Surprised you don't know about it," Art said. He was gruff. "I've briefed corporate headquarters often enough."

Adams laughed again. "You keep misunderstanding, Art. I'm not one of the financial whiz kids, I'm not a management supervisory VP, I'm a troubleshooter. You've never had trouble, so there's a lot about your operation I don't know. I see I ought to learn more, since the company's new seacoast reactors will probably have to use your systems."

Senator McGehee's helicopter arrived at eleven. Dr. Martinez, his dark hair disarranged by the whirling winds of the jet chopper, anxiously shook hands with the thin-faced senator. He's even younger than his pictures, Martinez decided. Of course he inherited his seat, as nearly as anyone can inherit a Senate seat in this country.

"This is Jim Reilly," McGehee was saying. His voice was a mixture of Harvard and his native Midwest. "My Administrative Assistant." He made it sound as if he'd just introduced the President.

McGehee wore his hair in the tangled forward sweep made famous by his father, but unlike most of the McGehee official family Reilly made no attempt to copy his boss. He wore a drooping bandito mustache, long sideburns and flowing locks. It was difficult to tell how old Reilly was, but Martinez decided he wasn't over twenty-five. McGehee was just over thirty, of course, barely eligible to be a senator of the United States.

"ECOLOGY NOW! POWER TO THE PEOPLE!" As the

helicopter engines quieted they heard the shouts. A group of hippies and yippies was clamoring at the main gate. Dr. Martinez saw at least fifty, and more padding barefoot over the causeway from the mainland. McGehee grinned boyishly and raised his fist in a waving salute his family affected. The bearded youths outside cheered.

"A MAN OF THE PEOPLE! POWER TO THE PEOPLE!"

"My public," McGehee said. "I suppose you have to keep them locked out of here?"

"I . . . un—" Arturo Martinez had no words.

"The Atomic Energy Commission insists that all visitors register in advance," Bill Adams said smoothly. "Shall we go inside, Senator?"

The young female technicians who zeroed their dosimeters giggled loudly, obviously enraptured at the chance to touch the senator. No question about it, Martinez decided, this fellow is as near to an idol as the kids have today. Susie had barely been able to contain herself when she found he was coming, even Henrietta had wanted to come out to the plant . . . I wonder if he's earned it. They turned to go inside, and Arturo caught himself.

"You didn't register mine," he told the technician. There was an embarrassed silence before the girl took the proffered pencil-like instrument, inserted it into the computer reader. In less than a second the instrument was reset, the dose reading registered in Dr. Martinez's permanent records. They went inside the reactor dome.

"What would have happened if you'd forgotten?" McGehee asked.

"The computer would have caught it; with its detectors it can spot an unregistered dosimeter."

"Would you have fired that nice young lady?" the senator insisted.

"Nuclear General doesn't operate that way," Adams said quickly. "Mr. Lewis thinks that if an employee isn't interested in doing a good job, he shouldn't be with the company, and if he is, threats aren't needed."

Art nodded to himself. It was only because of that policy that he could ever be director. Of course, the incident was already noted by the computer and now in the girl's training record. There was no need for her at that station, the computer and a guard would be enough, but all health physics trainees got a tour of gate watching as a probationary test of attitude and thoroughness.

The reactor itself wasn't impressive since it was hidden behind layers of concrete and shielding, an enormous regular octagon in the middle of the huge white floor. Above the reactor the safety rods looked like thick javelins perpetually falling to earth. Martinez tried to explain the reactor operation, though he could see that the senator was paying little attention.

"The reactor burns Plutonium-239 in long stainless steel rods we call needles," Martinez said. "The plutonium fissions to give us residual fission products and neutrons. One of the neutrons is used in another plutonium fission reaction, while the others are free to hit the Uranium-238 blanket surrounding the core. When Uranium-238 captures a neutron it becomes Plutonium-239 after going through some intermediate stages. We can double our original fuel supply in about four years, meanwhile producing over 2,000 megawatts of power."

"That's slightly more than Hoover Dam," Adams told the senator with a grin. "I can never keep these numbers straight. The power is sold to Southern California electric companies, of course."

McGehee nodded. "The plutonium you produce. Will it make bombs?"

"Yes," Martinez answered. "We sell some of it to the AEC."

"I thought so," McGehee said. "Make a note of that, Jim."

Reilly nodded vigorously.

"We sell it to the AEC because the government requires us to do so," Bill Adams pointed out smoothly. "Actually, the world market price for fuel plutonium is well above what the Atomic Energy Commission pays us."

"You don't lose money on it," McGehee said.

"No, sir, but we don't make nearly as much on weapons grade as we could on fuel grade." Adams spoke rapidly, but the senator was whispering something to his assistant. They went through the reactor building, past radiation monitor stations where they inserted their dosimeters, to the next dome.

"This is another breeder reactor," Martinez told them. "It is shut down now for routine servicing and recovery of fissionables. This one has several experimental features including an auxiliary breeding cycle to convert Thorium-232 into Uranium-233. There is no other like it in the world."

"It looks like a lump of concrete to me," McGehee sniffed.

"Well, yes, sir, they all do," Martinez answered. *Tonto Anglo*, he thought to himself, but growing up in an Anglo world had taught him control over his voice if not his thoughts. "If you would like, we can put on radiation armor and go inside the shielding. There are men working there now and it would be safe enough."

"No, thank you." McGehee turned to his assistant. "You have noted the elaborate precautions they take, even for a routine visit like this. Obviously a very dangerous place."

"Wait a minute, sir," Martinez protested. Bill Adams shook his head in warning, but Art persisted. "We take precautions here because anyone working around a reactor would be loco if he did not, but we have safer working conditions than steam generators."

"Certainly, certainly. And nuclear power is always safe, can't harm anyone," McGehee said caustically. "You needn't give me your standard snow job, Dr. Martinez. I've heard it all before. Next you'll tell me the Santa Fe disaster didn't happen."

"It did not happen to a Nuclear General plant," Martinez insisted. He felt his voice rising out of control, fought to remain calm and polite to this *hijo de cientos padres*. . . . "We learned much from that blowup, with what we have learned . . ."

"With what we have learned, we still go on building these pollution sources," McGehee said. "But I think we can put a stop to that. . . ."

"DIRECTOR MARTINEZ, DIRECTOR MARTINEZ. 771, 771. DIRECTOR MARTINEZ."

"Excuse me," Arturo said. He went to one of the many telephone stations, dialed 771.

"Pulaski, Security," the phone said. "Hate to bother you, sir, but there's a big ugly crowd at the main gate. Insist they talk to Senator McGehee. I think they're going to break in."

"I see. Have you called the local sheriff's station?"

"Yes, sir, we've got a couple of carloads of deputies standing by, but them boys ain't going to do much, Dr. Martinez. Not since two of 'em got sent to jail by the Feds for violating the civil rights of them rioters at the Irvine University, they ain't. Deputies are scared of the Feds, and between you and me, Doctor, I'm scared, too."

"Yes. All right, Pulaski. Thank you." He turned back to the group. "There is trouble at the main gate. I think we had better go there."

The crowd was shouting. Some held up banners. "ECOLOGY NOW! END THERMAL POLLUTION! NO MORE DEFORMED CHILDREN! SHUT IT DOWN, SHUT IT DOWN, SHUT IT DOWN!" The shouts were random, but when Martinez and the others appeared the chanted in unison.

"ECOLOGY NOW, SHUT IT DOWN! ECOLOGY NOW, SHUT IT DOWN!" The crowd surged forward pushing against the main gates. Someone flashed a wire cutter, and the gates flew open.

"What do we do, sir?"

Martinez turned to see Captain Pulaski. His company police were falling back, facing the crowd. "Should we throw them out?"

"You'll do no such thing!" McGehee snapped. "They aren't hurting anything. Have you got a bullhorn?"

"Yes, sir."

"Give it here." McGehee took the speaker, turned to the crowd. "HELLO, I'M SENATOR MCGEHEE."

The chant stopped. Someone cheered, then all yelled approval. "POWER TO THE PEOPLE, POWER TO THE PEOPLE." The McGehee family slogan.

"YOU CAN BE SURE THAT WE WILL ACCOMPLISH SOMETHING HERE TODAY," McGehee told them. "NO LONGER CAN THESE MONOPOLY COMPANIES GET AWAY WITH IGNORING THE ENVIRONMENT. BUT THIS IS NOT THE WAY TO DO IT. VIOLENCE IS NOT THE ANSWER. PLEASE BE PATIENT WHILE I SPEAK WITH DIRECTOR MARTINEZ."

"NO JIVE. SHUT IT DOWN. ECOLOGY NOW, SHUT IT DOWN! ECOLOGY NOW, SHUT IT DOWN!" The chant resumed, but the crowd seemed held in place near the main gates. Then suddenly a small group charged forward to the doors of the reactor dome.

"Pulaski, keep them out of there!" Martinez ordered. "*Maria sanctissima*, if they get in that building—"

"Shall we go inside?" Bill Adams said quietly. "They don't seem anxious to break into the reactor just yet—"

"ECOLOGY NOW, SHUT IT DOWN! ECOLOGY NOW, SHUT IT DOWN!"

"Senator, you don't understand, we can't shut the system down," Martinez pleaded again. From the big control room in the director's tower they could see hundreds of counterculture students surging through the plant yards. Police held the doors of the reactor and laboratory buildings, but already the students were inside some of the offices and annexes. And where is Adams now that I need him? Martinez thought. Where has the great Anglo troubleshooter gone now that trouble has found us?

"They have trashed two offices in the biology annex," Pulaski reported. "Dr. Martinez, I'm willing to take the chance on a San Juan Capistrano jury acquitting me. Let me clear out those buildings."

"They have threatened to break into the reactor if you do; you would have to shoot someone to prevent that," Martinez said thoughtfully.

"Repression!" McGehee snorted. "Your only answer. Have you tried listening to them?"

"*Si*, we have tried, but they are not reasonable, they only chant," Arturo answered. "Ecology now, shut it down . . . end thermal pollution . . . end birth defects. When I try to explain they chant louder. They will not listen to me."

"They've had to listen to people like you all their lives," McGehee said. "They don't see any point in it now. Dr. Martinez, these are intelligent students. They've heard all the arguments, they know what you're going to say, why should they hear it again? Listening just puts off action, and they want action, not rhetoric. If you really want them to leave, shut down the reactor!"

"But I have told you, we cannot shut down the reactor—"

"Oh, come off it," Reilly said. Martinez looked up in amazement. The Administrative Assistant had hardly spoken, never except in response to the senator. "Look," Reilly continued smugly. "You jokers put out two thousand megawatts and sell the stuff for three cents a kilowatt hour. That's about thirty grand an hour. You can afford that."

"Thank you," McGehee said. "You see, Dr. Martinez, all you have to do is shut down the plant for today. The students will see that you have listened to them and go home. Certainly a third of a million dollars is a lot of money, but I'm sure Nuclear General will survive the loss."

"But that is not the important loss at all," Martinez insisted. Where was Adams, he was good at talking, they might listen to him. But the troubleshooter had vanished when they came into the office, hadn't been seen for an hour. "Senator, I have tried to explain before. If the reactor is shut down there is a buildup of certain fission byproducts. The most important is Xenon-135. These poison the nuclear reactions so that the reactor cannot be restarted until it has been flushed."

He strode rapidly around the room, his hands moving in flowing gestures. *Madre de Dios*, give me strength to convince them. Arturo stopped by the window, pointed out to the sea.

"Out there in the Pacific we have an ecological balance, Senator. It is maintained by high temperatures in the water. If we shut down the plant, before it can be restarted the water will cool. Our tropical strains will die from thermal shock. Predators will move into the rich seas. It will take months, perhaps years, to bring the system back to balance because meanwhile the sewage has to go *somewhere*. Without the reactor there is no treatment and our farms will be polluted with raw sewage."

"Then this misplanned facility ought to be closed," McGehee snapped. "If the balance is that delicate, it should never have been started in the first place. We're better off without it, which is what I've always maintained."

"But—" Arturo tried again to explain that the secondary reactor was usually in operation and could provide enough heat to keep the thermal bio-system operative in this case of primary reactor scram. That the cities produced sewage no matter what and— It was no use. McGehee had picked up the phone and was talking to newsmen.

"And that's not satisfactory," the senator was saying. "Repression is never satisfactory in America. We will have no KKK tactics here, not while I am on the scene. We will show everyone it is time for the monopolies to listen to the people."

***

Susie came into the room, touched Martinez on the shoulder. "Bill . . . uh, Mr. Adams would like to see you outside, Dr. Martinez," she whispered. Did she whisper to keep it a secret from McGehee or because she was reverent in the great man's presence?

McGehee was busy on the phone, and young Reilly had plugged his attaché case into the terminals of another phone and was punching data into the small console. Probably getting speech material for the senator from the lawmaker's office back east, Martinez thought. Neither was paying attention to him.

Adams was outside sitting on the edge of Susie's desk. "How's it going?" the troubleshooter asked. He seemed calm as ever, maddeningly calm.

"Not well," Arturo answered. "They have given us two hours to shut down the reactor before they break in and do it. Of course, if they get into the reactor dome we will have no choice but to scram, otherwise there could be an accident. I have alerted Southern California Edison about the possible power loss."

Adams nodded. "I've talked to Mr. Lewis and the Governor, in that order. The Governor's willing to send in the National Guard, but he'd rather not."

Martinez laughed, a hard bitter sound. "I suppose it would not be good for his chance of being President if the Guard fired on those *cabrones*."

"That's part of it," Adams agreed. "But Senator McGehee could get those kids out of here just by asking them to go. They listen to him."

"Sure, but he will not do so," Martinez said. "I have pleaded with him, and he says he cannot."

"Won't, not can't. He wants to keep what he calls his credibility with them. McGehee's in more trouble politically than you might think. The only national support he's got is from the hippies and yippies, and they're losing enthusiasm, demanding action."

Adams took a battered pack of Camels from his jacket, lit one and puffed slowly. "I think this whole thing was planned, Art. The reactor's not well understood, people are still afraid of nuclear energy. The earthquake and Santa Fe mess scared them even more, so the 'nuclear pollution' war cry's got a lot of strength. McGehee's trying to ride the wave, hopes to make points by being the people's champ against the giants like Nuclear General. Did you know the underground papers have been urging their people to come here for the senator's visit? For the past three weeks?"

"Three weeks! But we only knew he was coming a week ago ourselves!"

Adams nodded. "Precisely. Anyway, we've got a couple of hours. Stall."

"Stall? But we must do something! Call in the Guard, we must protect the plant! Do you know how important this sea farm is to the world? We must act!"

"Yeah, but I've got a secret weapon coming. I hope."

"But—no! We must take action," Arturo said.

Adams sighed deeply. What he was about to say was distasteful. "Dr. Martinez, on Mr. Lewis's authority you will do nothing without my okay. I don't like to put it that way, but is it understood?"

"*Si, Patron.*"

Adams looked pained, but the door was opening and they saw Senator McGehee come out. "Right. Sorry you feel that way, but that's it. Take any precaution you want, but before you move against those kids you check with me. And get hold of yourself, man, it's going to be a long wait for both of us."

"ECOLOGY NOW, SHUT IT DOWN! ECOLOGY NOW, SHUT IT DOWN!"

"Time's almost up," McGehee observed. "What are you going to do, Director Martinez?"

"I still ask you to speak to them, Senator. You can persuade them to leave, and no one will be hurt."

"No. I couldn't, and I'm not interested anyway. I don't really care if your facility is destroyed, Martinez. I've no use for private nuclear reactors, I think they are dangerous and absurd. Why should the Lewises and Van Cotts make money from atomic energy when the research investment was made by all of the people?"

"But it wasn't, Senator?" Adams said carefully.

"Are you trying to tell me the Manhattan Project was privately financed?" McGehee snapped.

"I wasn't referring to the Manhattan Project at all," Adams said. "That was years before you were born. I'm talking about private research, which was significant even back in the sixties, and the risk investment that built this plant. If Lewis and Van Cott hadn't put up their fortunes and borrowed every nickel they could get, these breeder techniques would never have been developed, not to mention Dr. Martinez's eco-systems which you won't even take the trouble to learn about."

"Humph." McGehee ran tapering fingers through his thick hair. He was not accustomed to being spoken to in that tone of voice and he resented it. "In any event I notice you are willing to commit murder. I see you have brought in National Guardsmen by sea."

"But we must protect the plant, Senator," Martinez insisted. "Don't you understand, Senator, the technology we are developing here can prevent famines, malnutrition, can—"

"No, I don't understand how further pollution of the environment is going to do all that," McGehee sniffed.

"But if you'd only listen," Martinez said despairingly. He was interrupted by a comment from outside the office door, a thick drawl.

"That always was Johnny's problem in a nutshell, he never did listen to anybody."

They swiveled to face the newcomer. He was short, almost dumpy, with a swelling paunch that forced out his bright-colored flowered vest. His white hair and wispy white moustache were alike uncombed and with his dark coat he seemed almost a parody of the elderly politician, but there was nothing amusing about his eyes.

Martinez recognized him now, Representative Craig, Chairman of the joint Senate-House Committee on Atomic Energy.

Adams got hastily to his feet and grinned. "Glad to see you, sir. You're just in time, but just barely—"

"Saw the trouble outside." Craig faced Senator McGehee. "Understand you won't talk to that rabble, Senator."

"Don't use your imperial tone on me," McGee snapped. "I don't have to take orders from you. Besides, you don't know any more about nuclear reactors than I do. I've heard you admit it."

"Maybe not," Craig drawled. He hitched his vest more comfortably over his spreading middle and looked around for a chair. "I never was much good at technical details, but I sure spend a lot of time looking at results. Now this plant turns out more power, produces nuclear fuel and gets rid of sewage. Last year, and the year before that, the Southern California Chamber of Commerce had me out here to present San Juan Reactor with a reward for the fewest lost-time accidents of any industry in the district. I understand that kind of result, boy."

"Competent scientists have assured me this place is unsafe," McGehee said. "Men from the Atomic Energy Commission labs."

"Why sure they did," Craig chuckled. "Did you understand a word they said or just hear what you wanted to? Those bureaucrats have a powerful motive for wanting their agency to take control of a successful operation like this one, and that's what they're after, Johnny. No way is this place going to be closed, the power's needed too much. Now, like I told you, look at results. It seems to me it was the AEC boys who had the only serious accident with reactors so far."

"The whole idea of nuclear power is dangerous and unnecessary!" McGehee shouted. The strain showed in his voice now, and something more as well. Martinez watched in fascination, remembering McGehee's precise self-control when they were in the reactor domes, his studied disinterest but strange nervousness—the man was pathologically afraid of nuclear energy! There were a lot like him, but most were not senators.

"Lord love you, civilization's dangerous," Craig was saying. He took off his old-fashioned spectacles and polished them with his handkerchief. "You pack this many people in this small space, give 'em all the gadgets they think they got to have to stay alive and happy, of course, it's going to be dangerous. Without the best technology we can develop, though, we won't live in danger. We just won't live at all."

McGehee started to say something, but Craig held up his hand, palm outward. "You just listen to me for a second, boy. What you're about to say is there're too many people and we have to do something about that, right? All I can say to that is anybody who uses a slogan like 'power to the people' sure looks funny with thoughts like that. Who are you going to kill? The ones that voted for you, or the ones that didn't?"

McGehee sighed heavily and went to the window, pointedly watched the crowd below.

"Now, you've stopped listening," Craig chuckled. "I don't blame you much, and maybe you've heard it before. But that's always been your trouble, you know, you never had to listen to anybody. You reach thirty years and your father's brother-in-law resigns the seat he's kept warm for you, and with all that money you never have to go out and campaign, don't listen to your constituents. And those Harvard professors of yours are scared to death of your name, hoping if you liked 'em you'd appoint 'em to the cabinet, and you never listened to them. Or me, either. You know, it's no wonder you're an arrogant little squirt not worth the powder to blow you up."

"You can't talk to the senator like that!" Reilly protested.

Craig laughed. It wasn't his usual chuckle, but a big hearty laugh, full of amusement, and somehow indicating a decision. "Why I sure can, and he's going to listen, too. You keep your long nose out of this, boy, before I get mad. Now I think I was talking, let's see, where was I?" He stared around the room at the clutter of dials, screens, moving pens and winking lights, instruments recording the smooth flow of as much power as the great falls of Hoover Dam.

"I think I was explaining why you're going to make a speech, wasn't I, Johnny?" He sighed, almost wistfully. "You know, when your father first came into Congress I'd been there a while. We got to be good friends, your father and I. And he always thought he wouldn't live out his three score and ten, so he asked me to keep a sort of political eye on you if anything happened to him. I did it, too; all the time wondering if you'd ever be half the man your father was, 'cause half that much man would still be a lot more than most of us. And boy, *you have got a long way to go!*"

The smile vanished from the elderly man's face. "I'd never do anything to hurt you, Johnny, but this time it's come to the crunch. Now will you go out and make that speech 'cause I'm asking you to speak to them?"

McGehee licked his lips nervously, brushed his hair back again and again, as if he didn't know he was doing it. "I can't. Those people are expecting—"

Craig sighed heavily. "I know about that, too, Johnny. Know about a lot of things I never mentioned. Now, you and I, we better go into the next room and discuss what you're going to say to those hippies down there, or unless the women in your state are more broadminded than I think they are, you are going to be the shortest term senator ever to come out of the Midwest."

"What do you mean?" McGehee asked. There was panic in the question.

"You know what I mean, boy. I'm talking about a secretary name of Alicia Ann for a start. There's more I could say, but not in front of these people. Now are you coming with me, or should this hot-blooded assistant of yours start writing your resignation speech?"

"You've got to give me a little more time—"

"No. **GET OFF THE DIME!**"

McGehee stared at the older man, saw the congressman breathing hard, his lips fattened in determination. The senator looked at Craig for a long time, then carefully went to the desk phone and took the plug out of Reilly's briefcase console. "All right, Uncle Boyd. Let's go. When you're beaten, give up and save what you can. I guess you taught me that."

Martinez watched in amazement as the legislators left the office.

"You can leave, too, Mr. Reilly," Bill Adams said. He spoke quietly but his voice sounded loud in the suddenly still office. "You can wait in the lobby."

Reilly nodded and left without a word.

"Ought to reinforce those gates," Adams said cheerfully. "Well, did you learn something from all this?"

"I have learned . . ." Martinez hesitated. Trivial thoughts conflicted with the more significant. He felt emotionally drained. "I have learned we must increase the advertising budget to get the importance of our work before the public," Martinez answered. "And that I am not really able . . . are you the new director?"

"No. I told Mr. Lewis that we had a perfectly good man in charge, and he agreed. Besides, I'd be of no use at all. I don't know either physics or ecology."

"Just what is your specialty?" Arturo asked. He should be shouting with joy, but somehow the promotion didn't mean quite as much as he'd thought it would. But Dianne would be pleased—

" . . .of things, but I majored in political science," Adams was saying.

"Yes." Art laughed hard.

"What?" Bill Adams asked.

"Ecology. I have degrees in the field, but it is not enough to know only this." He waved toward the Pacific, blue with patches of reds and greens rising and falling in the gentle swells. "Today I find that politics may be the most important sub-system of them all."

They laughed together as below them Senator McGehee went out into the plant yard and raised the bullhorn.

# SURVIVAL WITH STYLE

### by Jerry Pournelle

## Editor's Introduction

After the hasty troop evacuation of Saigon, the impeachment of President Nixon, the Manson murders and the ensuing chaos, the seventies were a time of growing cynicism, hedonism and fear of the future. Environmental activists, like Stanford professor Paul Ehrlich, who wrote *The Population Bomb* in 1968, were proclaiming doom and gloom, foretelling of the death of the oceans and even mother Earth. I saw Dr. Ehrlich speak at San Diego State University in the late sixties; there he gave his doom and gloom speech before thousands of impressionable students. He preyed on fear, predicting there would be widespread famines in the United States in the seventies.

He further claimed in *The Population Bomb* that "[b]y the year 2000 the United Kingdom will be simply a small group of impoverished islands, inhabited by some 70 million hungry people." And that India was foredoomed to starvation and catastrophe. "The battle to feed all of humanity is over. In the 1970s and 1980s hundreds of millions of people will starve to death in spite of any crash programs embarked upon now."

The Club of Rome forecast *The Limits to Growth* claimed that "[w]e are running out of the essentials for modern civilization: oil, metals, lumber—just about everything." Stewart Brand was championing "Small is Good" and the end of Western Civilization as we know it. To top it off, we were engaged in an arms race with the Soviet Union that looked as if it at any moment it was going to end in a thermonuclear holocaust that would extinguish civilization, if not mankind.

Jerry Pournelle's early *Galaxy Magazine* science columns were a beacon of light during the Jimmy Carter era of malaise and the OPEC Oil Crisis. The Apollo space program days were over and inflation was on the rise. Jerry was one of a few optimistic voices in the land, promising a better future and wealth for everyone. Unlike most prophets, Jerry had detailed plans on how to do everything he claimed—good plans that he was willing to shout from the rooftops.

Jim Baen and Jerry Pournelle always had a great writer/editor relationship. Jim became managing editor at *Galaxy* in 1973. He succeeded Ejler Jakobsson as editor of *Galaxy* and *If* in 1974. Baen was very knowledgeable about science and he loved to throw ideas out to Jerry who would then run with them. Both men had similar political views and shared the same taste in science fiction.

Jim Baen, through diligent hard work (certainly not with *Galaxy*'s financial clout, since the magazine paid both poorly and slowly), managed to turn the magazine around; he not only doubled the readership, but published quality stories from new and established authors.

In the first issue of *Far Frontiers*, Jerry describes how he became a columnist for *Galaxy* and met Jim Baen:

Way back when I decided to make a career out of writing, the traditional route was to build a reputation by writing for the magazines, and when you became well known enough, go for the real money by getting a book contract. It was true then, as now, that you can't make a living writing short fiction.

That hadn't always been true. Stuart Cloete (*Rags of Glory*) once told me that *The Saturday Evening Post* paid him $4,500 for a short story—and that was in 1948, when a graduate chemist's annual starting salary was no more than that. In those times writers could support themselves from sales of short works; but in the 1970s those days were long gone. By the time I was trying to break in to this business, everyone knew that the object was to build a reputation fast, then get book contracts.

Of course, it took time to build a reputation. People—and

contrary to rumor, editors are people—remember stories, but not authors. You have to write a lot of stories, or articles, before anyone knows who you are. However, it's different with columns. People often remember who wrote a column even though only one has been printed. Short of winning several awards, the fastest way to build name recognition in the science fiction field is to do a column.

The next step was to find someone who'd let me write one. It didn't take long to decide: *Galaxy Science Fiction* under Ejler Jakobsson didn't enjoy all the glory it once held when Horace Gold founded it, but it was important to the science fiction field—and it didn't have a science column. Willy Ley had been the science columnist, and he had died (absurdly, only a few months before Apollo 11).

Somehow I convinced Jakobsson to let me give it a try. Alas, it was nearly a disaster. Ejler wanted rewrite after rewrite, change after change, each accompanied by hours of telephone discussion. I was grateful for the chance to do the column, and indeed I was learning quite a lot about magazine style and procedure; Ejler was a good teacher. However, he couldn't leave well enough alone, and the endless rewrites were driving me batty.

Suddenly everything changed. Ejler Jakobsson left *Galaxy*. The managing editor, a newcomer virtually unknown in the science fiction, took over the post. He wanted me to continue the column.

That's how I met Jim Baen.

Some partnerships click. Larry Niven and I have known from the very first story conference that we ought to work together.

It was the same with Jim Baen. He had suggestions for changes that obviously improved the column. He also made editorial changes in my style—and did it so well that it was only by accident that I discovered he was making any changes at all.

The really fun part, though, was putting the column together. Usually I'd choose the topic, although sometimes Jim would suggest something. After we agreed on the subject, we'd spend a couple of hours on the phone discussing it. The result was wonderful. By the time we were done, I'd understand the subject—often through the need to explain it to Jim.

I needn't pile Pelion on Ossa. Baen and I hit it off, and working together we produced what many reviews said was the best science column in the business.

When Jim left *Galaxy* to become the science fiction editor at Ace Books, he missed the magazine world; thus was born *Destinies*, a magazine that looked a lot like *Far Frontiers*.

Then Jim left Ace Books, and *Destinies* died as well. For over four years I did a column for *Analog*, but my heart wasn't in it and eventually I excused myself—

And came the day that Jim Baen called to tell me he had become Jim Baen Inc., and had his own publishing company.

"Doing a magazine?" I asked.

"Well, I wouldn't have time. . . ."

"Alas. If you did, I could do the science column. I confess to missing our long conversations on the state of the sciences."

"I miss them too." Jim sounded thoughtful. "I don't have time to do it alone. Want to co-edit with me?"

It wasn't quite that simple. Even together we don't have time to do a magazine; but we solved that problem by enlisting the aid of Managing Editor John Carr, and Senior Editor Betsy Mitchell.

Thus was born Far Frontiers (later changed to *New Destinies*) and thus was reborn "A Step Farther Out."

❂ ❂ ❂

**THE VIEW THAT WE ARE DOOMED** has taken over a large part of the American intellectual community, and has been passed on to a generation of students. If accepted, it is a profound change in the traditional philosophy of the West which looked forward to progress.

According to *Future Shock*, we are afraid of our future. It remains to ask—should we be? There is another view: that we cannot only survive, but survive with style.

Suddenly we're all going to die. Look around you: a spate of works, such as *The Population Bomb, Eco-Doom*, and the like, and organizations such as "Friends of the Earth," and "Concerned Citizens" for one cause or another. All have the same message: Western Civilization has been on an energy resources spree, and it is time to call a halt.

The arguments are largely based on a book called *The Limits to Growth*. Written by a management expert for a group of industrialists calling themselves The Club of Rome, *Limits to Growth* may be the most influential book of this century. Its conclusions are based on a complex computer model of the world-system. The variables in the model are population, food production, industrialization, pollution, and consumption of nonrenewable resources.

The results of the study are grim and unambiguous: unless we adopt a strategy of Zero-Growth and adopt it now, we are doomed. Western Civilization must learn to make do, or do without; unlimited growth is a delusion that can only lead to disaster; indeed, any future growth is another step toward doom.

Doom takes any of several forms, each less attractive than the others. In each case population rises sharply, then falls even more sharply in a massive human die-off. "Quality of Life" falls hideously. Pollution rises exponentially. All this is shown in Figure 1, which is taken from one of the computer runs.

According to Meadows and many others, Earth is a closed system, and we cannot continue to rape her as we have in the past. If we do not learn restraint, we are finished.

Nor can technology save us. Perhaps the worst tendency of the modern era is our reliance on technological "fixes," the insane delusion that what technology got us into, it can take us out of. No; according to the ecodisaster view technology not only will not save us, but will hasten our doom. We have no real alternative but Zero-Growth. As one ZG advocate recently said, "We continue to hold out infinite human expectations in a finite world of finite resources. We continue to act as if what Daniel Bell calls 'the revolution of rising expectations' can be met when we all know they cannot."

Jay Forrester, whose MIT computer model was the main inspiration for the zero-growth movement, goes much further. Birth control, he strongly implies, cannot alone do the job. It is a clear deduction from Forrester's model that only drastic reductions in health services, food supply, and industrialization can save the world-system from disaster.

It is important to recognize the severe consequences of a policy of Zero-Growth. For Western Civilization, ZG means increasing unemployment and a falling standard of living; worse than inconvenient, but not quite a total catastrophe. For the rest of the world things are not so simple. Behind all the number and computer programs there is a stark reality: millions in the developing countries shall remain in grinding poverty—forever.

*Figure 1*

**FOUR DOOMS AS POSTULATED BY THE MIT WORLD MODELS**

***FAMINE . . . POLUTION . . . OVERCROWDING . . .***

***DEPLETION OF NON-RENEWABLES***

*Figure 2*

**. . . AND THIS IS THE WAY THE WORLD ENDS . . .**

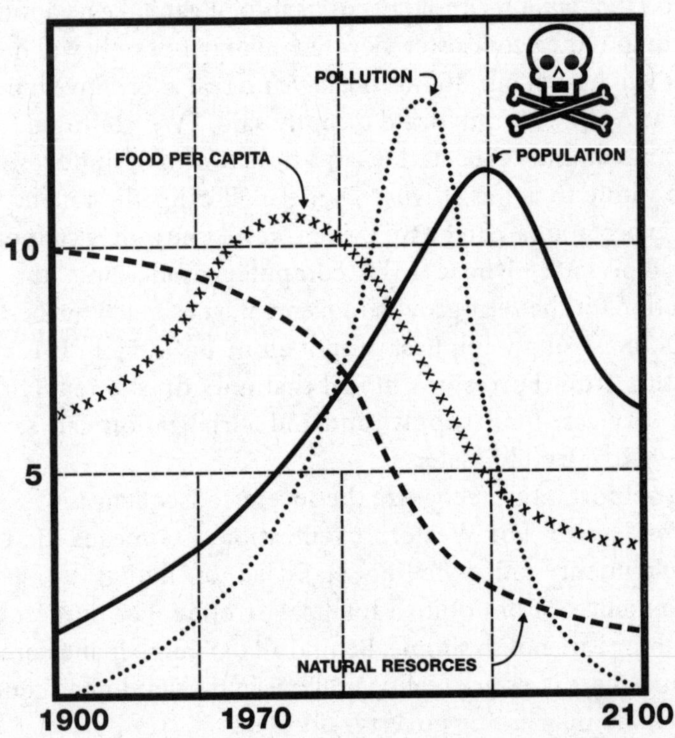

***The "standard" model of World Three. The projection assumes no major changes in the physical, economic, or social relationships (as modeled in World Three). Population growth is finally halted "by a rise in death rate due to decreased food and medical services." "THE LIMITS TO GROWTH"***

---

They may be unwilling to accept this. There is then the decision to be made—must they be forced to accept? The advocates of Zero-Growth also advise, on both practical and moral grounds, massive sharing with the developing world. Indeed, under the ZG strategy, the West has only two choices: massive sharing with the developing world, or to retain wealth while most of the world remains at the end of the abyss. Neither alternative is attractive, but there is nothing for it: failure to adopt Zero-Growth is no more than selfishness, robbing children and grandchildren for our own limited and temporary pleasures.

So say the computers.

I don't accept that. I want Western Civilization to survive; not only survive but survive with style.

I want to keep the good things of our high-energy technological civilization: penicillin, stereo, rapid travel, easy communications, varied diet, plastic models, aspirin, freedom from toothache, science fiction magazines, libraries, cheap paperback books, pocket computers, fresh vegetables in mid-winter, lightweight backpacks and sleeping bags—the myriad products that make our lives so much more varied than our grandfathers.

Moreover, I want to feel right about it. I do not call it survival with style if we must remain no more than an island of wealth in the midst of a vast sea of eternal poverty and misery. Style, to me, means that everyone on Earth shall have hope of access to most of the benefits of technology and industry—if not for themselves, then certainly for their children.

This is a tall order. Economists say it cannot be done. My wishes are admirable, but irrelevant. The universe cares very little what we want; there are inherent limits, and the models of the world-system prove that what I want cannot be brought about.

Their view is not so thoroughly proved as all that. Computers and computer models are very impressive, but a computer can give you no more information than you have put into it. It may be that Forrester and the other eco-doomsters have modeled the wrong system. At least it is worth taking a look; surely it is against man's very nature simply to roll over and die without a struggle.

Arthur Clarke once said that when a gray-bearded scientist tells you something is possible, believe him; but when he says it's impossible, he's very likely wrong. That has certainly been true in the past. Surely we are justified in examining the assumptions of those models which tell us we are doomed, and which dictate a policy of Zero-Growth.

The economists' models warn of four dooms: inadequate food supply; increasing pollution; depletion of nonrenewable resources; and overcrowding through uncontrolled rise in population. Let us examine each in turn.

The first, food production, is surprisingly less critical than is generally supposed. This is hardly to deny that there is hunger and starvation in the world. However, given sufficient energy resources, food production is relatively simple. The UN's Food and Agricultural Organization reports that there are very few countries that do not, over a ten-year average period, raise enough food to give their populations more than enough to eat.

There are two catches to this. First, even in the West, birds, rodents, and fungi eat more of man's crops than ever does man. True we harvest more than most nations; but to do so requires high technology.

The second catch is the "over a ten-year period" part. The average crop production is sufficient, but drought, flood, and other natural disasters can produce famine through crop failures over a one-, two-, or three-year period. In much of the world there is no technology for storing surpluses. The West has known for a long time about the seven fat years followed by seven lean years, but it took us centuries to come up with reliable ways to meet the problem of famine.

Our solutions have been three-fold: increased production, better food storage, including protection from vermin; and weaving the entire West into a single area through efficient transportation. Drought-stricken farmers in Kansas can be fed wheat from Washington state, beef from the Argentine and lettuce from California.

All this takes industrial technology on a large scale. Western farming methods use fertilizers. The transportation system is clearly a high-energy enterprise. Even providing Mylar linings for traditional dung-smeared grain storage pits (animal dung is often the only waterproofing material available) requires high-energy technology.

And in the West we waste land because we have land to waste; our agricultural technology produces surpluses.

A hardworking person needs about 7,000 large calories, or 7 million gram-calories per day. The sun delivers nearly 2 gram-calories per square centimeter per minute; assume about 10% of that gets through the atmosphere and that the sun shines about five hours (three hundred minutes) per day on the average. Further assume that our crops are about 1% efficient in converting sunlight to edible energy. Simple multiplication shows that a patch 35 meters on a side—about a quarter of an acre—will feed one human being.

Granted, that's an unfair calculation; but it isn't *that* far off from reality. My greenhouse, 2.5 meters on a side, can produce enormous quantities of squash and beans and tomatoes in hydroponics tanks and there's no energy wasted in transportation Again I see no point in belaboring the obvious. Given the energy resources, pollution is not a real problem. Certainly pollution cannot be the limiting factor in industrial growth. It is another aspect of the energy shortage.

If famine and pollution do not define the limits to growth, then what of rising population? The view that we shall in the near future become so overcrowded that we will die of the resulting stresses is examined in detail in another chapter; for now let us look at the long-term prospects.

Throughout history there has been only one means of controlling population growth. It is not war; populations often rise in wartime. Famine and pestilence have of course reduced populations drastically, but the recovery from even these horsemen is often quite rapid, with birth rates sky rocketing so that within a generation population is higher than it was before the catastrophe. No: the only reliable means of limiting population is wealth.

The United States has a fertility rate below the replacement value; were it not for immigration the US population would begin to decline. There is a "bow wave" effect from the WWII "baby boom" that distorts the picture, but the "boom babies" are rapidly reaching the end of their fertility epoch.

France, Ireland, Japan, Britain, West Germany, Netherlands; where there is wealth there is decline in the birth rate. David Riesman in his *The Lonely Crowd* pointed out many years ago that the Western nations were probably best described as in a condition of "incipient population decline," and it seems his prophecy was true. Now it's true enough that if we manipulate exponential curves and thus mindlessly project population growth ahead, we will come to a point at which the entire mass of the solar system (indeed, of the universe) has been converted into human flesh. So what? It isn't going to happen, and no one seriously believes that it will. Obviously *something* will stop population growth *long* before that.

On a slightly more realistic scale, I have calculated how long it takes, at various growth rates, to reach "standing room only" on the Earth: that point at which there are four of us on each square meter of the Earth's surface (even counting the oceans and polar areas as "standable" surface). Figure 3 shows that those times are surprisingly near—if we have unlimited population growth. Yet the fact remains that as societies get wealthier; their ability to sustain larger populations increases—but their actual population growth declines or even halts.

Of course there are powerful religions whose adherents control large portions of the globe, and which condemn birth control and seemingly all other usable means of population limitation.

Yes. And I'm no theologian. But I cannot believe that any rational interpretation of scripture commands us to breed until we literally have no place to sit. Realistically we are not going to increase our numbers to that point; and, realistically, no religious leader is going to order it done.

"So God created man in his own image, in the image of God created he him; male and female created he them. And God blessed them, and God said unto them, Be fruitful and multiply, and replenish the earth and subdue it; and have dominion over the fish of the sea and the fowl of the air, and over every living thing that moveth upon the earth."

I will leave theology to the theologians; but the command was "Multiply and replenish the earth, and subdue it"; and surely there must come a time when that has been *done*? When there can be no doubt that we have been sufficiently fruitful? And surely dominion over the wild things of the Earth does not mean that we are to exterminate and replace them? Surely even those of the deepest faith may without blasphemy wonder if we are not rapidly approaching a time when we shall indeed have replenished and subdued the Earth.

## *Figure 3*

"So God created man in his own image, in the image of God created he him; male and female created he them. And God blessed them, and God said unto them, Be fruitful, and multiply, and replenish the earth, and subdue it; and have dominion over the fish of the sea, and over the fowl of the air, and over every living thing that moveth upon the earth."

Area, sphere: $A = 4 \Pi R^2$
Radius, Earth: $6.371 \times 10^8$ cm.
Area, Earth: $1.700215 \times 10^{18}$ $cm^2$

Standing room area requirement: $50\ cm^2$ = 2500 sq. cm.
(about 4 people/sq. yard)

Number of people when Standing Room Only:
$6.80086 \times 10^{14}$
Present population: $4 \times 10^9$ (4 billion)

Assuming growth rate of 2% a year, it's SRO in 2584
At 1% growth, we get there in 3186 AD
At 4%, we get there in 2283

QUERY: At what point will the command be fulfilled?

## *Figure 4*

# Little Bugs to Big Bang: Some Energy Events

Exponential Notation: $10^2 = 100$, i.e. 1 followed by two zeroes; $10^3 = 1{,}000$; $10^6 = 1{,}000{,}000$; etc.

| EVENT: | ERGS: |
|---|---|
| Mosquito taking flight | 1 |
| Man climbing one stair | $10^9$ |
| Man doing one day's work | $2.5 \times 10^{14}$ |
| One ton of TNT exploding | $4.2 \times 10^{16}$ |
| US *per capita* energy use, 1957 | $2.4 \times 10^{18}$ |
| Converting one gram hydrogen to helium | $6.4 \times 10^{18}$ |
| Saturn 5 rocket | $10^{22}$ |
| One megaton, as in bombs | $4.2 \times 10^{22}$ |
| Total annual energy use, Roman Empire | $10^{24}$ |
| Krakatoa | $10^{25}$ |
| Annual output, total US installed electric power system, 1969 | $5.4 \times 10^{25}$ |
| Thera explosion (largest single energy event in human history) | $10^{26}$ |
| Total electric power produced world, 1969 | $1.6 \times 10^{26}$ |
| Total present annual energy use, world | $10^{29}$ |
| One Solar Flare | $10^{31}$ |
| Annual Solar Output | $2 \times 10^{39}$ |
| Nova | $10^{44}$ |
| Quasar, lifetime output | $10^{61}$ |
| BIG BANG | $10^{80}$ |

Thus we see that of our four dooms, three are aspects of the energy crisis: given sufficient energy we will not be overwhelmed by problems of food, pollution, or even over-population. But can we find the energy? Will not generating energy itself pollute the Earth beyond the survival level?

At this point I must introduce some elementary mathematics. I will try to keep them simple and work it so that you don't have to follow them to understand the conclusions, but if I am to halfway prove what I assert I simply must resort to quantitative thinking. Failure to calculate actual values, blind qualitative assertion without quantity, has been the genesis of a very great deal of misunderstanding and I don't care to add to that storehouse of misinformation. Besides, only through numbers can you get any kind of "feel" for the energy problem.

The basic energy measurement is the erg. It is an incredibly tiny unit: about the amount of energy a mosquito uses when she jumps off the bridge of your nose. In order to deal with meaningful quantities of energy we will have to resort to powers-of-ten notation. Example: $10^2 = 100$; $2 \times 10^2 = 200$; $10^3 = 1000$; and $10^{28}$ is 1 followed by 28 zeroes.

Some basic energy events are shown in Figure 4. Note that a number of natural events are rather large compared to man's best efforts. It takes a billion ergs to climb a stair, and a day's hard work uses 100,000 times more; yet a ton of TNT exploding contains a hundred day's work and more, while converting one gram of hydrogen to helium will yield more energy than each of us used in a year—and by "used" I don't mean each of us directly, but our share of all the energy used that year in the United States: dams, factories, mines, automobiles, etc. I need hardly point out that there are a lot of grams (a gram is one cubic centimeter) of water in the oceans. Nor need we worry about "lowering the oceans" when we extract hydrogen for fusion power. True, some rather silly stories have asserted that we might, but a moment's calculation will show that if we powered the Earth with each of 20 billion people consuming more energy than we in the United States do now, the oceans would not be lowered an inch in some millions of years.

Of course fusion might not work. Given the present funding levels we may never achieve it, or the concept itself may be flawed, or the pollution associated with successful fusion may be unacceptable. Are there other methods? One possible system is pictured in Figure 5. It is an Earth-based solar power system, and the concept is simple enough. All over the Earth the sun shines onto the seas, warming them. In many places—particularly the Tropics—the warm water lies above very cold depths. The temperature difference is in the order of 50 degrees F, which corresponds to the rather respectable water-pressure of 90 feet. Most hydro-electric systems do not have a 90 foot pressure head.

The system works simply enough. A working fluid—such as ammonia—which boils at a low temperature is heated and boiled by the warm water on the surface. The vapor goes through a turbine; on the low side the working fluid is cooled by water drawn up from the bottom. The system is a conventional one; there are engineering problems with corrosion and the like, but no breakthroughs are needed, only some developmental work.

The pollutants associated with the Ocean Thermal System (OTS) are interesting: the most significant is fish. The deep oceans are deserts, because all the nutrients fall to the bottom where there is no sunlight; while at the top there's plenty of sun but no phosphorus and other vital elements. Thus most ocean life grows in shallow water or in areas of upwelling, where the cold nutrient-rich bottom water comes to the top.

More than half the fish caught in the world are caught in regions of natural upwelling; such as off the coasts of Ecuador and Peru. The OTS system produces artificial upwelling; the result will be increased plankton blooms, more plant growth, and correspondingly large increases in fish available for man's dinner table. The other major pollutant is fresh water, which is unlikely to harm anything and may be useful.

Certainly there are some engineering problems; but not so many as you might expect. The volumes of water pumped are comparable to those falling through the turbines at a large dam, or passing through the cooling system of a comparable coal-fired power plant. The energy itself can be sent ashore by pipeline after electrolysis of water into hydrogen and oxygen; or a high-voltage DC power line can be employed; or even used to manufacture liquid hydrogen for transport in ships as we now transport liquid natural gas.

## Figure 5

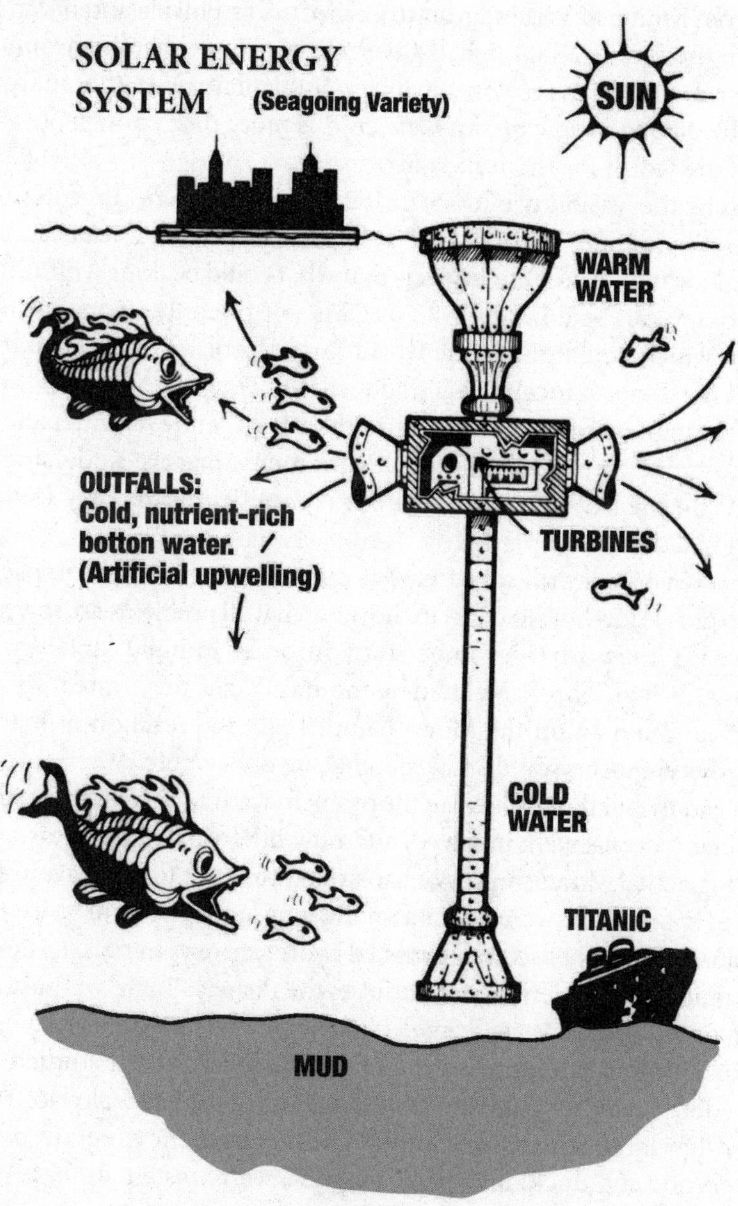
SOLAR ENERGY
SYSTEM (Seagoing Variety)
SUN
WARM
WATER
OUTFALLS:
Cold, nutrient-rich
botton water.
(Artificial upwelling)
TURBINES
COLD
WATER
TITANIC
MUD

As to the quantity of power available: if you imagine the continental United States being raised ninety feet, forming a sheer cliff from Maine to Washington to California to Florida and back to Maine; then pour Niagara Falls over every foot of that, all around the perimeter forever; you have a mental picture of the energy available in one Tropic of, say, Cancer. It is more than enough power to run the world for thousands of years.

Finally the feasibility of OTS: in 1928 Georges Claude, inventor of the neon light, built a 20 kW OTS system for use in the Caribbean. It worked for two years. One suspects that what could be done with 1928 technology can be done in 1988. OTS is not the only nonpolluting system which could power the world forever. Solar Power Satellites would do the task nicely. Few doubt that they could provide more than enough energy to industrialize the world, and we understand how to build them far better at this moment than we understood rockets on the day President Kennedy committed us to going to the Moon in a decade.

That is a point worth repeating: We can power the Earth from space. We do not "know how to do it" in the sense that all problems are solved; but we do know what we must study in order to build large space systems. When John F. Kennedy announced that the United States would land a man on the Moon before 1970, the reaction of many aerospace engineers was dismay: not that anyone doubted we could get to the Moon, but those closest to the problem were acutely aware of just how many details were involved, and how little we had done toward building actual Moon ships. We had at that time yet to rendezvous or dock in space; there were no data on the long-term effects of space on humans; we had not successfully tested hydrogen-oxygen rockets; there were guidance problems; etc., etc. Thus the dismay: There was just so much to do, and ten years seemed inadequate time in which to do it.

Solar Power Satellites, on the other hand, have been studied in some detail; and we have the experience of Apollo and Skylab. We know that large structures can be built in space; they require only rendezvous and docking capabilities, and we've tested all that. We know we can beam the power down from space; the system has been tested at JPL's Goldstone, and the DC to DC efficiency was 85%. There are other problem areas, but in each case we know far more now than we knew of Mooncraft in 1961.

## *Figure 6*

### METALS FOR THE WORLD. . . .

In 1967, the United States produced 315 million tons of iron, steel, rolled iron, aluminum, copper, zinc, and lead.

Total metal produced, USA, 1967: $2.866 \times 10^{14}$ grams.

Assume 3% ore, of density 3.5 gm/cm$^3$, and the USA produced the equivalent of a sphere 1.7 kilometers in diameter.

At 230,000,000 population, we produced $1.25 \times 10^6$ grams *per capita*. To supply the world with that much requires $5 \times 10^{15}$ grams or FIVE BILLION TONS.

Assuming 3% ore at 3.5 gm/cm$^3$, five billion tons of ore is a sphere 2.25 kilometers in radius or 4½ kilometers in diameter.

There are 40,000 or more asteroids larger than 5 km in diameter.

We may not run out of metals after all. . . .

Ocean Thermal and Solar Power Satellites: either would power the world. I could show other systems, some not so exotic. My engineering friends tell me that OTS and SPS may even be the hard way, and there are much more conventional ways to supply Earth with energy.

No matter. My point is that we can find the energy. The method used is unimportant to the argument I make here: that we can survive, and survive with style.

Given energy we will not starve; we will lick the pollution problem; and we will generate the wealth which historically has brought about population limits. At least three of the dooms facing us can be avoided.

That brings us to the fourth doom: depletion of nonrenewable resources. Can we manufacture the materials needed for survival with style? And can we do it without polluting the Earth?

Assuming 3% ore at 3.5 gm/cm$^3$, 5 billion tons of ore is a sphere 2.25 kilometers in radius or 4.5 kilometers in diameter.

There are 40,000 or more asteroids larger than 5 km in diameter.

We may not run out of metals after all. . . .

In 1967, a year for which I happen to have figures, the Unites States produced 315 million tons of iron, steel, rolled iron, aluminum, copper, zinc, and lead. (I added up all the numbers in the almanac to get that figure.) It comes to 2.866 x 10$^{14}$ grams of metal. Assume we must work with 3%-rich ore, and we have 9.6 x 10$^{15}$ grams of ore, or 10.5 billion tons.

It sure sounds like a lot. To get some feel for the magnitude, let's put it all together into one big pile. Assuming our ore is of normal density, we end up with a block less than 1.5 kilometers on a side: something more than a cubic kilometer, something less than a cubic mile. Or, if you like a spherical rock, it's less than 2 kilometers in diameter.

There are 40,000 or more asteroids larger than 5 km in diameter.

We may not run out of metals after all. . . .

But the title is "Survival with Style." Style to me does not consist of the West as an island of poverty in the midst of a vast sea of misery.

Style, to me, means that everyone on Earth has a chance at wealth—or at least at a decent life.

## *Figure 7*

**CALL SMYTHE, THE SMOOTHER MOVER . . .**

Take one each, FIVE BILLION TON asteroid.
Move from the Belt to Earth orbit.

Requires a velocity change of 7 kilometers a second.

$$KE = \tfrac{1}{2} M V^2$$

Or, we need $1.225 \times 10^{27}$ ergs.

For reference, the world annual energy use is $10^{29}$ so we're using about 1% of it. . . .

That's also 30,000 megatons.
And 30,000 one-megaton bombs might just do it.

For a slightly more efficient system,
we can get the energy by converting 2,000 tons of hydrogen to helium . . .

Once we have the rock in Earth orbit, it's simple to get the metal out. We merely boil the entire rock. Of course that takes rather large mirrors, but what the heck. . . .

# PEACE WITH HONOR

## by Jerry Pournelle

## Editor's Introduction

"Peace With Honor" is the first published story of Jerry Pournelle's crowning literary creation, the CoDominium/Empire of Man future history. It appeared in the May 1971 issue of *Analog Science Fiction*. The CoDominium is a pieced-together super-national alliance of the United States of America and the Union of Soviet Socialist Republics, which Jerry created during the period of détente between the US and USSR. It is governed by a Grand Senate which is based on the Moon, safe from earthly powers. The CoDominium controls egress and ingress to Earth's landmass from space through ballistic missiles, beam weapons and armed spacecraft.

Grand Senators are selected from only the two superpowers. Much like the early post-Roman Republic alliances, it's a makeshift governing body that imposes peace. After an interstellar drive is discovered, the CoDominium establishes colonies on planets of nearby stars. Through its control of off-Earth space, the CoDominium becomes the planetary government. Its control is resented by the other nations of Earth, but the alliance is powerful enough no other country can act against its will or military might.

Here's what Jerry had to say about the creation of the CoDominium in *There Will Be War, Volume V*:

In 1970 Stefan Possony and I published *The Strategy of Technology*. In the introductory chapter of this series, we argued that technology can be thought of as an impersonal force much like a stream. Those who doubt that will probably find illuminating a close reading of James Burke's wonderful book *Connections*. What one tinkerer does not invent, another will.

At the same time, the analogy can be carried too far. Technology is created by people, and the technological stream can be directed—or diverted. Possibly it can be dammed.

Given the present international situation, suppression of technological development is highly unlikely. Neither the US nor Soviet Union would trust the other without the most stringent verification measures: measures that I doubt even the US would submit to, while Soviet resistance to any inspection amounts almost to an obsession. Moreover, even if bilateral agreements were implemented and worked smoothly, even if NATO and Warsaw Pact nations were brought under the agreement, there remains the rest of the world. China, Japan, Israel, South Africa, India, Pakistan—the list goes on and on. All these nations are capable of developing, implementing and deploying high technology weapons; and as Possony and I argued (I hope persuasively) in *The Strategy of Technology*, the Technological War could be bloodlessly decisive.

Suppose, though, that the United States and the Soviet Union formed a CoDominium, and through that structure brought the entire world under their joint control. The two superpowers need not care for each other. It is only needful that they be dedicated to the notion that it is better that they rule jointly than for anyone else to rule at all.

Under those circumstances technology might be suppressed by sufficiently ruthless action by the FBI, KGV and CoDominium intelligence services; nothing less would do the job. Given that cooperation, though, science and technology could be slowed if not halted so long as the alliance held.

It seems arguable, anyway; and this was the premise of my first science fiction stories. The CoDominium takes us from the turn of the [twentieth—Ed.] century to the far future, and includes *The Mercenary*, *The Mote in God's Eye* and *King David's Spaceship*.

❂ ❂ ❂

**THE MAN ON THE TRI-V** was in full form. His speech had started quietly enough, as Harmon's speeches always did, full of resonant tones and appeals to reason, the quiet voice speaking so softly that you had to listen closely to be sure of hearing him. But slowly, oh so slowly, the background changed subtly until now Harmon stood before the stars and stripes covering the hemisphere, an American Eagle splendid over the Capitol, and the speaker had worked himself into one of his famous frenzies, his former calm and detachment obviously overcome with emotion.

"Honor? It is a word Lipscomb no longer knows. Whatever he might have been—and my friends we all know what he was—he is no longer one of us! His cronies, the dark little men who whisper to him, they have corrupted even so great a man as President Lipscomb! And what of our country? She bleeds! People of America, she bleeds from the running sores of these men and their CoDominium!

"They say that withdrawal from the CoDominium would mean war. I pray God it would not, but if it did, why these are hard times. Many of us would be killed, but we would die as men! And today our friends, our allies, the people of Hungary, the people of Romania, the Czechs, the Slovaks, the Poles, they groan under the oppression of their communist masters, and who keeps them there? Our CoDominium! We do! We have become slave masters! Better to die as men.

"But it will not come to that. The Russians would never fight. They are soft, soft as we, their government as riddled with corruption as ours. People of America, hear me! People of America, listen!"

The Honorable John Rogers Grant spoke softly and the Tri-V turned itself off, a walnut panel sliding over the darkening screen. Grant grimaced, spoke again, and the servitor brought him a small bottle of milk. With all the advances in medical science, there was nothing Grant could afford to have done for an ulcer. Money was no problem, but when in God's Name would he find time?

He glanced at the papers on his desk, reports with bright red Security covers, closed his eyes for a moment. Harmon's speech was an important one, and would undoubtedly have an effect on the coming elections. The man was getting to be a menace, Grant thought. He put the thought aside; John Grant liked Harmon, at one time they had been friends. Lord, what have we come to? He opened the first report.

There had been a riot at the International Federation of Labor convention. Three killed, and the smooth plans for the re-election of Matt Brady thrown into confusion. Grant grimaced again and drank more milk. The intelligence people had assured him that this one would be easy. Digging through the reports he found that some of Harvey Bertram's child crusaders were responsible. They'd bugged Brady's suite, got enough evidence of sell-outs and deals to inflame sentiment on the floor. The report ended with the recommendation that the government drop Brady, concentrate support on MacKnight who had a good reputation, but whose file in the CIA building bulged with information. MacKnight would be easy to control. Grant nodded to himself, scrawled his initials on the action form, dropped it in the TOP SECRET OUT slot. No point in wasting time, but he wondered what would happen to Brady. Matt Brady had been a good friend to the Unity Party, blast Bertram's people anyway.

He took up the next file, but before he could open it his secretary came in. He looked up and smiled gently, glad of his decision to ignore the stupid telecom. Some executives never saw their secretaries from the moment they came in until they were ready to leave.

"Your appointment, sir," she said. "Almost time. And it's time for your nerve tonic."

He grunted. "I'd rather die." But he let her pour a shot glass of the evil-tasting stuff, and he tossed it off and chased it with milk before glancing at his watch. Not that the watch was needed, he thought. Miss Ackridge knew the travel time to every Washington office. There'd be no time to start another report, which suited Grant fine.

He let her help him into his black coat, brush off a few silver hairs. He didn't feel fifty-five, but he looked it now. It happened all at once. Five years ago he could pass for forty. John saw the girl in the mirror behind him and knew that she loved him, but it wouldn't work. Why the hell don't you get married again, John Grant? It isn't as if you're pining away for Priscilla. By the time she died you were praying it would happen. You can even admit that now. Why do you go on acting as if the great love of your life has departed forever? All you'd have to do is turn around, say five words, she'd . . . she'd what?

She wouldn't be the perfect secretary any longer, and secretaries are harder to find than mistresses. Let it alone.

She stood there for a moment, then moved away. "Your daughter wants to see you this evening," she told him. "She's driving down this afternoon. Says it's important."

"Know why?" Grant asked. Ackridge knew more about Sharon than Grant did. A whole lot more, probably.

"I can guess. I think her young man has asked her."

John nodded. It was hardly unexpected, but it hurt. So soon, so soon. They grow so fast, and there's so little time. John Jr. was with the Calisto Squadron, first lieutenant of a CoDominium Navy frigate, due for a command of his own any year now. Frederick was dead in the accident with his mother, and now Sharon had found another life . . . that she hadn't before. Since he became Honorable Deputy Secretary he might as well have died for as often as they had time together.

"Run his name through CIA, Flora, meant to do that months ago, can't think of why I didn't get around to it. They won't find anything, but we'll need it for the records."

"Yes, sir. You'd better be on your way, now. Your drivers are outside."

He glanced around the office, scooped up his briefcase. "I won't be back today, have my car sent around to the White House, will you? I'll drive myself home tonight."

"Yes, sir. You can send the briefcase back with your driver, then," she said carefully, reminding him of his own regulations. Too many papers turned up missing from too many houses lately. If you want to work nights, stay at the office.

He acknowledged the salutes of the driver and armed "mechanic" with a cheery wave, led them to the elevator at the end of the long corridor. Paintings and photographs of ancient battles hung along both sides of the hall, and there was carpet on the floor, but otherwise it was like a cave. Blasted Pentagon, he thought for the hundredth time. Silliest building ever constructed. Nobody can find anything, and it can't be guarded at any price. Why couldn't someone have bombed it?

They took a surface car to the White House. He could have made his own clearance for a flight, but it would have been another detail, and why bother? Besides, this way he got to see the cherry trees and flower beds around the Jefferson. The Potomac was a sludgy brown mess despite the latest attempt to clean it up. You could swim in it if you had a strong stomach, but the Army Engineers had "improved" it a few administrations back, giving it concrete banks . . . why the devil would anyone want to make a concrete ditch out of a river, he wondered. Now the workmen were tearing the lining out, which kept the water perpetually muddy. One day they'll be through with it.

They drove through rows of government buildings, some of them abandoned. Urban Renewal had given Washington all the office space the government needed, more, until there were empty buildings, big relics of the time when Washington was the most crime-ridden city in the world. Back around the turn of the century, maybe more, they'd torn everything down, hustled everyone out of Washington who didn't belong there, the bulldozers quickly following to demolish the tenements. For some political reason it was thought desirable to put up offices as quickly as the other buildings were torn down, to make the displaced people think it was all necessary, and now there were these empty tombs.

They passed the Population Control Bureau, two square block of humming activity, then around the Ellipse and past Old State to the gate. The guard checked his identity carefully, using the little scanning plate on his palm-print, although blast it, that guard knew John Grant as well as he knew his own mother. Grant sighed and waited until the computer flashed back the "all right," was driven into the White House basement and escorted quickly up to the Oval Office. He got there one minute early for his appointment.

The President stood when Grant entered, and the others shot to their feet as if they had ejection charges under them. Grant shook hands around, but looked closely at Lipscomb. The President was feeling the strain, no question about it. Well, they all were. Too bad about the Chief, but they had to have him.

"Sorry the Secretary couldn't make it, Mister President," Grant announced ritually. Lipscomb made a wry face but said nothing. The Secretary of Defense was a political hack who controlled a bloc of Aerospace Guild votes and an even larger bloc of aerospace industry stocks. As long as government contracts kept his companies busy employing his men, he didn't give a damn about policy, and since he couldn't keep his big mouth shut it was best not to tell him about the meetings. He could sit in on formal Cabinet sessions where nothing was ever said and would never know the difference anyway.

Grant kept his attention on the President. Lipscomb didn't like to be reminded of the incompetence of his cabinet, the political deceptions that divorced power from its appearance. The ritual was getting old, why not just sit down and say nothing? Silently, Grant took his place at the center of the table across from the President.

Except for Lipscomb, none of the men in the Oval Office were well-known to the public. Any one of them could have walked down the streets of any city except Washington without fear of recognition. But the power they controlled, as assistants and deputies, clerks even, was immense and they all knew it. There was no need to pretend to each other.

The servitor brought drinks and Grant accepted a small Scotch. Some of the others didn't trust a man who wouldn't drink with them. His ulcer would give him hell, and his doctor more, but doctors and ulcers didn't understand the realities of power. Neither, Grant thought, do I or any of us. But understand it or not, we've got it, and we've got to do something with it.

"Mr. Karins, would you begin?" the President asked. Heads swiveled to the west wall where Karins had set up a briefing screen. A polar projection of Earth glowed behind him, lights blinking the status of forces which the President ordered, but Grant controlled.

Karins stood confidently, his paunch spilling out over his belt, an obscenity in so young a man. Herman Karins was the second youngest man in the room, Assistant Director of the Bureau of Budget and said to be one of the most brilliant economists Yale had ever produced. He was certainly one of the best political technicians in the country, but that didn't show in his résumé, or degrees.

He took off the cover sheet to show a set of figures. "I have the latest poll results," Karins said too loudly. "This is the real stuff, gentlemen, not what we hand out to the papers. It stinks."

It certainly did stink. The Unity Party was hovering around thirty-eight percent, just about evenly divided between the Republican and Democratic wings. Harmon's Patriot Party had just over twenty-five. Millington's violently left wing Liberation Party had its usual ten, but the real shocker was Bertram's Freedom Party. Bertram's popularity stood at an unbelievable twenty percent of the population.

"These are figures for those who have an opinion and might vote," Karins said. "The usual. 'Course there're about half who don't give a damn about anything, but they vote by who got to 'em last anyway; we know how they split off. You see the bad news."

"You're sure of this?" the Assistant Postmaster General asked. He was the leader of the Republican wing of Unity, and it hadn't been six months since he had told them they could forget Bertram and his bleeding hearts.

"Yes, sir, I'm sure of it," Karins said. "And it's growing. Those riots at the labor convention probably gave 'em another five points, but we don't show that yet. Give Bertram another six months and he'll be ahead of us. How you like them apples, boys and girls?"

"There is no need to be flippant, Mr. Karins," the President said.

"Sorry, Mister President." Karins wasn't sorry at all and he glared at the Assistant Postmaster General with triumph. Then he flipped the pages of the chart to show new results.

"This is the soft and hard vote, gentlemen. You'll notice Bertram's vote is pretty soft, but solidifying. Harmon's is so hard you couldn't get 'em away from him without using nukes. And ours is getting a little like butter. Mister President, I can't even guarantee we'll be the largest party after the election, much less that we can hold a majority."

"Incredible," the Chairman of the Joint Chiefs muttered.

"Worse than incredible," Grand Senator Bronson agreed. "A disaster. Who will win?"

Karins chuckled. Bronson's appointment to the CoDominium Grand Senate expired just after the election. Unless Unity won, he wouldn't be going back to Luna Base next year. "Toss-up, Senator. Some of our support is drifting to Harmon, some to Bertram. I'd say Bertram if I had to call it, though."

"You've been quiet, John," the President said. "You have no observations?"

"No, sir," Grant answered. "It's fairly obvious what the result will be if we lose, no matter who wins. If Harmon takes over, he pulls out of the CoDominium and we have war. If Bertram takes over, he relaxes security, Harmon drives him out with his storm troopers, and we have war anyway."

Karins nodded. "I don't figure Bertram could hold power more'n a year, probably not that long. Man's too honest."

The President sighed loudly. "I can recall a time when men said that about me, Mr. Karins."

"It's still true, Mister President," Karins said hurriedly. "But you're realistic enough of a realist to let us do what we have to do. Bertram won't."

"So what do we do about it?" the President asked gently.

"Rig the election," Karins answered quickly. "I give out the popularity figures here." He showed another chart indicating that the Unity Party had well over a majority popularity. "Then we keep pumping out more faked stuff, while Mr. Grant's people work on the computers. Hell, it's been done before."

"Won't work this time." They turned to look at the youngest man in the room. Larry Moriarty, assistant to the President, and sometimes called the "resident heretic," blushed at the attention. He was naturally shy, hated to be noticed until he got worked up. When he was fully committed to an argument, though he could shout with the best of them. "The people know better. Bertram's people are already getting jobs in the computer centers, aren't they, Mr. Grant? They'll see it in a minute."

Grant nodded. He'd sent the report over the day before; interesting that Moriarty had digested it already.

"You make this a straight old rigged election, you'll have to use CoDominium Marines to keep order," Moriarty continued.

"The day I need CoDominium Marines to put down riots in the United States is the day I resign," the President said coldly. "I may be a realist, but there are limits to what I will do. You'll need a new chief."

"That's easy to say, Mr. President," Grant said. He wanted his pipe, but the doctors had forbidden it. To hell with them, he thought, and took a cigarette from the pack on the table. "It's easy to say, but you can't do it. What happens after you resign?"

"I don't think I care," the President answered.

"But you do, sir. The Unity Party supports the CoDominium, and the CoDominium keeps the peace. An ugly peace, but by God, peace.

I wish . . . Lord, how I wish . . . that support for the CoDominium treaties wasn't tied so thoroughly to the Unity Party, but it is and that's that. And you know damn well that even in the Party it's only a thin majority that supports the CoDominium. Right, Harry?"

The Assistant Postmaster General nodded. "But don't forget, there's support for the CD in Bertram's group."

"Sure, but they hate our guts. Call us corrupt," Moriarty said. "They're right, too."

"So flipping what if they're right?" Karins snapped. "We're in, they're out. Anybody who's in for long is corrupt. If he isn't, he ain't in."

"I fail to see the point of this discussion," the President interrupted. "I for one do not enjoy being reminded of all the things I have done to keep this office, and I am sure most of you like it no better than I do. The question is, what are we going to do? And I feel I must tell you that as far as I'm concerned, nothing would make me happier than to have Mr. Bertram sit in this chair. I'm tired, gentlemen. I've been President for eight years, and I don't want it anymore."

Everyone spoke at once, shouting to the President, murmuring to their neighbors, until Grant cleared his throat loudly. "Mister President," he said using the tone of command he'd been taught during his brief tour in the Army Reserve. "Mister President, that is, if you will pardon me, sir, a ludicrous suggestion. There is no one else in the Unity Party who has even a ghost of a chance of winning. You remain popular. The people trust you. Even Mr. Harmon speaks as well of you as he does of anyone not in his group. Mr. Bertram thinks highly of you personally. You cannot resign without dragging the Unity Party with you, and you cannot give that chair to Mr. Bertram. He couldn't hold it six months."

"And would that really be so bad, John?" Lipscomb was using all the old charm now, the fireside manner that the voters loved, the tones and warmth and expressions that won ambassadors and voters, senators and taxpayers. "Are we really so sure that only we can save the human race, John? Or are we merely only interested in keeping our own power?"

"Some of both, I suppose," Grant answered. "Not that I wouldn't mind retiring."

"Retire!" Karins snorted. "You let Bertram's clean babies in the files for two hours, and none of us will retire to anything better'n a CD prison planet. You got to be kidding, retire."

"That may be true," the President said, "but there are other ways. General, what does happen if Harmon takes power and starts a war?"

"Mr. Grant knows better than I do," General Carpenter said. When the others looked at him with amazement, Carpenter continued. "Nobody's ever fought a nuclear war. Why should the uniform make me more of an expert than you? But I'd say we could win. Heavy casualties, but our defenses are good." He gestured at the moving lights on the wall projection. "Better technology than the Russkis. The laser guns ought to get most of their missiles. CD Fleet won't let either one of us use space weapons. We might win."

"We might." Lipscomb was grim. "John?"

"We might not win. And we might succeed in killing about half the human race. We might get more. How in God's Name do I know what happens if we start throwing nuclear weapons around?"

"But the Russians aren't prepared," a commerce official said. "If we hit them without warning—people never change governments in the middle of a war."

President Lipscomb sighed. "I am not going to start a nuclear war to retain power. Whatever I have done, I have done to keep peace. That's my last excuse. I could never live with myself if I sacrifice peace to keep power. I'd rather sacrifice my power to keep peace."

Grant cleared his throat gently. "We couldn't do it anyway. If we start converting defensive missiles to offensive, CoDominium Intelligence would hear about it in ten days. The Treaty prevents that, you know." He lit another cigarette. "Of course, we could denounce the CoDominium. That would just about assure us of losing the election. And probably put Kaslov's people in power in the Soviet Union."

Kaslov was a pure Stalinist, who wanted to liberate Earth for communism. Some called him the last communist, but of course he wasn't the last. He had plenty of followers. Grant could remember a secret conference with Ambassador Chernikov only weeks ago. The Soviet was a polished diplomat, but it was obvious that he wanted something desperately. He wanted the United States to keep the pressure on, not relax her defenses at the borders of the US sphere of influence, because if the communist probes took anything out of the US sphere without a hard fight, Kaslov would gain more influence at home. Telling Grant about it was as close to playing politics as a professional like Chernikov would ever come; and it meant that Kaslov was gaining influence, not losing it.

"This is all nonsense," the Assistant Postmaster announced. "We aren't going to quit, we won't start the war. Now what does it take to get the support away from Mr. Clean Bertram and funnel it back to us? A good scandal, right? Find Bertram's dirtier than we ever thought of being, right? Catch some of his boys plotting something really bad, right? Working with the Japs, maybe. Giving the Japs nukes. I'm sure Mr. Grant can arrange something like that."

Karins nodded vigorously. "That would do it. Disillusion his organization, drive his followers out. The pro-CoDominium people in his outfit would come to us like a shot." He paused, chuckled evilly. "'Course some of 'em will head for Millington's Liberation bunch." Karins laughed again. No one worried about Millington's Liberation Party very much. Without his madmen to cause riots and keep the taxpayers afraid, other measures the Unity Party had to take would never be accepted. Millington's people gave the police some heads to crack, a nice riot for Tri-V to keep the Citizens amused and the taxpayers happy.

"I think we can safely leave the details to Mr. Grant," Karins grinned.

"What will you do, John?" the President asked.

"Do you really want to know, Mister President?" Moriarty interrupted. "I don't."

"Nor do I, but if I can condone it, I can at least find out what it is. What will you do, John?"

"Frame-up, I suppose. Get a plot going, then uncover it."

"That?" Moriarty shook his head. "Man, it's got to be better than that. The people are beginning to wonder about all these plots."

Grant nodded. "There will be evidence. Hard-core, cast-iron evidence. Such as a secret arsenal of nuclear weapons."

There was a gasp. Then Karins grinned widely, laughed. "Oh, man, that's torn it. Hidden nukes. Real ones, I suppose?"

"Of course." Grant looked with distaste at the fat youth. What would be the point of fake nuclear weapons? But Karins lived in a world of deception, so much so that fake weapons would be appropriate of this nightmare scene.

Karins chuckled again. "Better have lots of cops when you break that story. People hear that, they'll tear Bertram apart."

True enough, Grant thought. It was a point he'd have to remember. Protection of those kids wouldn't be easy. Not since a militant group A-bombed a Mississippi town, and a criminal syndicate tried to hold San Francisco for a hundred million dollars ransom. People no longer thought of private stocks of atomic weapons as something to laugh at. They'd kill anyone they believed had some.

"We won't involve Mr. Bertram personally," the President said grimly. "Not at any price and under no circumstances. Is that understood?"

"Yes, sir," John answered quickly. He hadn't liked the idea either, was eager to agree. "Just some of his top aides." Grant stubbed out the cigarette. It, or something, had left a foul taste in his mouth. He turned to Grand Senator Bronson. "Senator, the CoDominium will end up with final custody. I'll see they are sentenced to transportation for life. I'd prefer if they didn't have too hard a sentence to serve."

Bronson nodded, his hands clasped over his vest, a satisfied smile breaking through the doubts he'd had before. He could probably not have made a deal with Bertram, this was better. "Oh, certainly, whatever you like. Let them be planters on Tanith if they'll cooperate. We can see they don't suffer."

Like hell we can, Grant thought. Even as an independent planter, life on Tanith was no joy. He shook his head wearily and lit another cigarette.

Grant left the meeting a few minutes later. The others could continue in endless discussion, but for Grant there was no point to it. The action they had to take was clear, and the longer they waited the more time Bertram would have to assemble his supporters and harden his support. If something were to be done, it might as well be now while Bertram's vote was soft. Give them a reason to leave his camp while they still were unsure. Grant had found all his life that the wrong action taken decisively and in time was often better than the right action taken later.

He thought about the situation on his way back to his office, and after he reached the Pentagon summoned his deputies and issued orders. The whole thing took no more than an hour. The machinery was already in motion.

Grant's colleagues always said he was rash, too quick to take action without looking at all the consequences. They also conceded that he was lucky, that what he did usually worked out well, but they complained that he didn't think it over enough. John Grant saw no point in enlightening them: he did think things over, but by anticipating them rather than reacting to crises. He had known that Bertram's support was growing alarmingly for weeks, had made contingency plans for the event in case Karins's polls turned out badly. He hadn't expected them to come out *that* bad, but it only indicated that the drastic actions Grant had already planned were needed immediately.

Within days there would be a leak from the conference; there always was. Not a leak about the actions to be taken, but about the alarm and concern. Some secretary would notice that Grant had come back to the Pentagon after dismissing his driver. Another would see that Karins chuckled more than usual when he left the Oval Office, that Senator Bronson and the Assistant Postmaster General went off to have a drink together. Another clerk would add that Karins was reporting on political trends, and another would overhear a remark about Bertram. . . .

No. If they had to take action, take it now while it might work. Grant dismissed his aides with a sense of satisfaction. He had been ready, and the crisis would be over before it began. It was only after they left that he crossed the paneled room to the teak cabinet, opened it and poured a double Scotch.

He laughed at himself as he drank it. That's the boy, Grant. Tear hell out of your ulcer. Punish yourself, you can atone for what you're doing. What you need is a good wife. Somebody who doesn't know a damn thing about politics, who'll listen and tell you that you had to do it, that you're still a good man. Everybody ought to have a source of comfort like that. He envied the statesmen of the old days when there would be a Father Confessor trained in statecraft that you could go to for reassurance. Reassurance and maybe a little warning, do this or that or you won't be forgiven.

⁂

The Maryland countryside slipped past far below as the Cadillac cruised along on autopilot. A ribbon antenna ran almost to Grant's house, and he watched the twilight scene, house lights blinking, a few surface cars runing along the roads. Behind him was the sprawling mass of Columbia Welfare Island where most of those displaced from Washington had ended up, lumps of poured concrete buildings and roof parks, the seething resentment of useless life kept placid by government-furnished supplies of Tanith hashpot and *borloi* and cheap booze. A man born in one of those complexes could stay there all his life if he wanted to and some did. Grant tried to imagine what it would be like there, but he couldn't. Reports from his agents gave an intellectual picture, but there was no way to identify with those people, the hopelessness and dulled senses, burning hatreds and terrors. Karins knew, though. Karins had begun his life on a welfare island somewhere in the Midwest, clawing his way through the schools to a scholarship, refusing stimulants and dope and never watching Tri-V . . . was it worth it?

The speaker on the dash suddenly came to life, cutting off Beethoven in mid bar. "**WARNING. YOU ARE APPROACHING A GUARDED AREA. UNAUTHORIZED CRAFT WILL BE DESTROYED WITHOUT FURTHER WARNING. IF YOU HAVE LEGITIMATE ERRANDS IN THIS RESTRICTED AREA, FOLLOW THE GUIDE BEAM TO THE POLICE CHECK STATION. THIS IS A FINAL WARNING.**"

The Cadillac automatically turned off course, riding the beam down to State Police headquarters, and Grant cursed. He fumbled with switches on the dash, spoke softly. "This is John Grant, resident in Peachem's Bay. Something seems to be wrong with my transponder."

There was a short wait, then the mechanical voice on the speaker was replaced by a soft feminine one. "We are very sorry, Mr. Grant. Your signal is correct. Our identification unit is out of order. You may proceed, of course."

"You'd better get that thing fixed before it shoots down a taxpayer," Grant said irritably. Anne Arundel County was a Unity Party stronghold, how long would be before there was an accident like that? The taxpayers would begin to listen to Bertram and his Freedom Party cant.

"We'll see to it immediately, sir," the girl answered. "Good evening."

"Yeah. All right, I'm going home." He took the manual controls and cut across country, ignoring regulations. If they wanted to give him a ticket—all they could do now that they knew who he was—let them. His banking computer would pay the fine without Grant ever being aware of it. It brought a wry smile to his face—traffic regulations were broken, computers noted it in their memories, other computers paid the fines, and no human ever became aware of them. Until finally there were enough tickets that a warning of license suspension would be issued. Since that could never happen to Grant, there was no way he'd ever find out about the violations.

There was his home ahead, a big rambling early twentieth century place on the cove, his yacht was anchored offshore, wooded grounds. Be nice to stay there a few weeks. He wondered if he wanted to retire. The President certainly did, and most of his colleagues said much the same. The thought of a long rest, repair to his ulcer, sailing out to Bermuda, that was intriguing, but years of inactivity? He couldn't imagine life without responsibilities, and the thought of retirement was vaguely frightening. He's seen too many old friends come apart just when it looked like they ought to be happiest.

Carver, the chauffeur, rushed out to help Grant down from the Cadillac and take it to the garage; Hapwood was waiting with a glass of sherry in the big library. Prince Bismarck, shivering in the presence of his god, put his Doberman head on Grant's lap and stared into his eyes, ready to leap into the fire at command. There was irony in the situation. At home Grant enjoyed the power of a feudal lord, but it was a power that many wealthy men could command, and it was limited by how strongly the staff wanted to stay out of Welfare. But he only had to lift the Security phone in the corner, and his real power, completely invisible and limited only by what the President wanted to find out, would operate. An interesting thing, power. Wealth gave him the visible power, heredity gave him the power over the dog . . . what gave him the real power of the Security phone?

"What time would you like dinner, sir?" Hapwood asked. "And Miss Sharon is here with a guest."

"A guest?"

"Yes, sir. A young man, Mr. Allan Torrey, sir."

"Have they eaten?"

"Yes, sir. Miss Ackridge called to say that you would be late for dinner."

"All right, Hapwood. I'll eat now and see Miss Grant and her guest afterward."

"Very good, sir. I will inform the cook." Hapwood left the room invisibly.

Grant smiled again. Hapwood was another figure from Welfare, a man who grew up speaking a dialect Grant would never recognize. What had possessed him to study the manners of English butlers of a hundred years before, perfecting his style until he was known all over the country as the perfect household manager? Why would a man do that?

Certainly there was money in it. Hapwood didn't know it, but Grant had a record of every cent his butler took in, kickbacks from grocers and caterers, "contributions" from the gardeners, and the surprisingly well-managed investment portfolio. Hapwood could have retired to his own house years ago, but instead here he was, still the perfect butler. It had intrigued Grant enough to have his agents look into Hapwood very carefully, but the man had no politics other than staunch support for Unity, and the only suspicious thing about his contacts was the refinement with which he extracted money from every transaction involving Grant's house. The man had no children, and whatever sexual needs he experienced were satisfied by infrequent visits to the fringe areas around Welfare.

Grant ate mechanically, hurrying to be through and see his daughter, yet afraid to meet the boy she had brought home. For a moment he thought of using the Security phone to find out more about him, but he shook his head angrily. Too much security thinking wasn't good, for once he was going to be a parent meeting his daughter's intended. He left half his steak uneaten and went to the high-ceilinged library, sat behind the massive Oriental fruitwood desk with its huge bronze fitting. Behind him and to both sides the walls were lined with bookshelves, immaculate dust-free accounts of the people of dead empires. It had been years since he took one down. Now, all his reading was confined to typescript reports, some copied by human secretaries but most generated by computers. They told a live story about living people, but sometimes, late at night, as Grant sat in the huge library he wondered if his country were not as dead as the empires in his books. He loved his country but hated her people, all of them: Karins and the new breed, the tranquilized Citizens in their welfare islands, the smug taxpayers who grimly held their privileges. . . . So what was it that he loved? Only history, and stories of the greatness that once had been the United States, something found only in those books and not in the neat reports with their bright red Security folders.

But then Sharon came in, a lovely girl, far prettier than her mother had ever been, but she lacked her mother's poise. She ushered in a tall boy in his early twenties. As they crossed the room Grant studied him closely. Nice-looking. Long hair, neatly trimmed, conservative mustache for these times although it would have been pretty wild in Grant's day. Blue and violet tunic, red scarf . . . a little flashy, but even John Jr. went in for clothes like that whenever he got out of CoDominium uniform.

The boy walked hesitantly, almost timidly, and Grant wondered if it were fear of him and his position in the government, or just the natural nervousness of a young man about to talk to his fiancée's father. The tiny diamond on Sharon's hand sparkled in the yellow light from the fireplace, and she held the hand unnaturally, not sure of herself with the unfamiliar ring.

"Daddy, I . . . I've talked so much about him, this is Allan. He's just asked me to marry him! I am so happy!" Trustingly, sure of his approval, never thinking for a second—Grant wondered if Sharon wasn't the only person in the country who didn't fear him. Except for John Jr., who thank God was beyond the reach of Grant's Security phone. The CD Fleet took care of its own.

"Hello, Allan." Grant stood and extended his hand. Torrey's grip was firm, but his eyes avoided Grant's. "So you want to marry my daughter." He glanced pointedly at her left hand. "Looks like she approves the idea, anyway."

"Yes, sir. Uh, sir, she wanted to wait and ask you before she put the ring on, but well . . . it's my fault, sir." Torrey looked up at him this time, almost in defiance.

"Yes. Well . . . Sharon, as long as you're home for the evening, I wish you'd speak to Hapwood about Prince Bismarck. I don't think the animal is properly fed."

"You mean right now?" she asked. She tightened her small mouth into a pout. "Really, Daddy, this is Victorian! Sending me out of the room while you talk to my fiancé!"

"Yes, it is, isn't it?" Grant said nothing else, and finally she turned away.

Then impishly: "Don't let him frighten you, Allan. He's about as dangerous as that . . . as that moose head in the trophy room!" She fled before there could be any reply.

They sat awkwardly. Grant coming out from behind his desk to sit near the fire with Torrey. Drinks, offer of a smoke, all the usual amenities—anything to avoid saying something important, but finally Hapwood had brought their refreshments and the door was closed.

"All right, Allan," John Grant began. "Let's be trite and get it over with. How do you intend to support her?"

Torrey looked straight at him this time, his eyes dancing with what Grant was certain was concealed amusement. "I expect to be appointed to the Department of the Interior. I'm a trained engineer."

"Interior?" Grant thought for a second. The answer surprised him—he hadn't thought the boy was just another office seeker. Well, why not? "I suppose it could be arranged."

Torrey grinned. It was an infectious grin, and Grant liked it. "Well, sir, it's already arranged. . . . I wasn't asking for a job."

"Oh?" Grant shrugged. "I hadn't heard anything—you'll be Civil Service."

"No, sir, Deputy Assistant Secretary, Natural Resources Control. Environments. I took a master's in ecology with my engineering degree."

"That's interesting, but I can't recall seeing anything about the appointment. . . ."

"It won't be official yet, sir. Not until Mr. Bertram is elected President. For the moment I'm on his staff." The grin was still there, and it was friendly, not hostile, not mocking. The boy thought politics was a game, wanted to win.

He's seen the polls, Grant thought. God knows—Allan Torrey?

Just who was he on Bertram's staff? "Give my regards to Mr. Bertram when you see him. What is it you do for him?"

Allan shrugged. "Write speeches, carry the mail, run the Xerox—you've been in campaign headquarters. I'm the guy who gets the jobs no one else wants."

Grant laughed. "Yeah. Started that way myself. Only staffer they could afford to use as a gopher, they didn't have to pay me. I soon put a stop to that, though. Hired my own gopher out of what I used to contribute. I guess that's not open to you?"

"No, sir. My father's a taxpayer, but . . . well, paying taxes is pretty tough right now."

"Yes." Well, at least he wasn't from a Citizen family. Torrey, now just who the hell . . . he could find out when Flora had the Security report. Important thing now was to get to know the boy.

It was hard to do. Allan was frank, open, more relaxed after Hapwood brought his third drink. Grant was pleased to see that the boy refused a fourth. But there was nothing of substance to talk about. No consciousness of the realities of politics. One of Bertram's child crusaders, out to save the United States from people like John Grant although he was too polite to say so. John could remember when he was that young, wanted to save the word, but then it was so different. No one wanted to end the CoDominium then, they were too happy to have the Cold War under control at last. What happened to the great sense of relief when we could stop worrying about atomic wars? It was all anybody could think of when Grant was young, how this might be the Last Generation . . . now they took it for granted that there would always be peace. Was peace, then, such a little thing? He realized Torrey was speaking.

"Take the Baja Project, for example. All those nuclear plants. And all the artificial harbors. Thermal pollution of the Sea of Cortez! They'll kill off a whole ecology just for their cities. And it isn't necessary, sir. I know we have to have living space for cities. God knows I don't want the Citizens cooped up in their welfare islands, but that isn't what the government is planning. What they're going to build will be more estates for taxpayers, not a decent place for Citizens." He was speaking intently, trying to burn past Grant's gentility, to get to the man underneath.

"I know it isn't part of your department, sir. You probably don't even know what they're doing. But it is so wrong . . . I'm sorry, sir, but I really believe it. The Lipscomb government has been in too long. It's got away from the people, and . . . and I'm sure you're not aware of it, but the corruption! Sir, I wish you could see some of the reports we have, some of the dirty things the government's done just to stay in power. It's time for a change, and Mr. Bertram is the man, I know he is."

Grant's smile was thin, but he managed to bring it off. "Maybe you're right. I wouldn't mind living in this house instead of the Pentagon. Might as well live in Washington for all the time I manage to get out here." What was the point of it? He wouldn't convince this boy, and Sharon wanted him . . . he'd drop Bertram after the scandals broke. And how could Grant explain that the Baja Project was developed to aid a syndicate of taxpayers that without their support the government wouldn't last a week? The damn fools, of course they were wrecking the Gulf of California—oh hell, the Sea of Cortez. Call it that, it made the six states which were formerly the Republic of Mexico happier. Of course, they were wrecking it, through sheer shortsighted idiocy, but what could the government do? You might get the Citizens to huddle around their Tri-V in their welfare islands, smoke *borloi*, but without taxpayers. . . . There was no point in explanations. At that boy's age, Grant wouldn't have believed it either.

Finally, painfully, the interview was over. And there was Sharon, grinning sheepishly because she was engaged to one of Bertram's people, understanding what that meant no better than Allan Torrey. It was only a game. Bertram would be in government and Lipscomb, the Unity Party, would be the opposition, just the game that the Republicans and Democrats used to play.

How could he tell them that if Unity ever went out, the rules would change, there wouldn't be an alternative anymore. You'd get Bertram against Harmon, or Bertram against the Liberation Party, or worse, Harmon and the Liberation people working together against Bertram, and somebody would try to mobilize the Citizens, get them involved, and the whole structure would come crashing down . . . and then? Then the Leader, the Man with a Cause, the Friend of the People. It was all there, told time and time again in those aseptically clean books all around him.

BERTRAM AIDES ARRESTED BY
INTERCONTINENTAL BUREAU OF INVESTIGATION!!
IBI RAIDS SECRET WEAPONS CACHE.
NUCLEAR WEAPONS HINTED!!!

> CHICAGO, MAY 15, (UPI)—IBI agents here have arrested five top aides to Senator Harvey Bertram in what government officials call one of the most despicable plots ever discovered. . . .

Grant read the transcript of the *extra* Tri-V newscast without satisfaction. It had all gone according to plan, and there was nothing left to do. The evidence was there. He could let Bertram's people wiggle all they wanted to, challenge jurors, challenge judges. The Attorney General, in a spirit of fairness, would even waive the government's rights under the Thirty-first Amendment, let the case be tried under the old adversary rules. It wouldn't matter.

Then, in small type, there it was, and he gasped. "Arrested were Gregory Kalamintor, 19, press secretary to Bertram; Timothy Giordano, 22, secretary; Allan Torrey, 22, executive assistant . . ." The rest of the page blurred. "Oh, My God, what have we done?" Grant asked. He sat with his head in his hands.

He hadn't moved when Miss Ackridge buzzed. "Your daughter on Four, sir. She seems upset."

"Yes." Grant punched savagely at the button. Sharon's face swam into view, her makeup was ruined by long streaks of tears. She looked ten years older, much like her mother during one of . . .

"Daddy! They've arrested Allan! And I know it isn't true, I was in that house in Chicago two days ago, they didn't have nuclear weapons! A lot of Mr. Bertram's people said you'd never let the country have an honest election. They said John Grant would see to it, and I told him they were wrong. . . . Daddy, what happened? It's true, isn't it? You've done this to stop the election."

He tried to say something, but there was nothing to say. She was right. But where was she calling from, who might be listening in? "I don't know what you're talking about. I saw the newscast about

Allan's arrest, but I know nothing more. Come home, kitten, and we'll talk about it there."

"Oh no! You're not getting me in that big house. Have Dr. Pollard come over, give a nice friendly little shot, and I forget all about Allan. . . . No! I'm staying right here until . . . I guess I just won't be coming home. And when I go to the newspapers, I think they'll listen to me. I don't know what to tell them, but I'm sure Mr. Bertram's people can write something for me. How do you like that, Mister God?"

"Anything you tell the press about the government will be a lie, Sharon. You don't know anything." He fought to stay calm, but he couldn't think what to do. He noticed his assistant get up and leave the office.

"Lies? Where did I learn to lie? I'm only following your example, Daddy dear." The screen went blank. She had hung up on him.

Was it that thin? he thought. The trust she'd had in him, the love, whatever it was . . . was it that thin?

"Sir?" It was Hartman, his assistant.

"Yes?"

"She was calling from Champaign, Illinois. A Bertram headquarters they think we don't know about. The phone had a guaranteed no-trace device on it."

"Trusting lot, aren't they?" Grant said. "Have some good men watch that house, but leave her alone." He stood, felt a wave of something, dizziness and something else, so that he had to hold the edge of the desk. "MAKE DAMNED SURE THEY LEAVE HER ALONE. DO YOU UNDERSTAND?" he shouted.

Hartman went as pale as Grant. The chief hadn't raised his voice to one of his own people in five years. "Yes, sir, I understand."

"And get out of here." John spoke carefully, in low tones, and the cold mechanical voice was more terrifying than the shout.

Alone he sat staring at the blank telephone, sitting at the seat of power. Now what, he thought. It wasn't generally known that Sharon was engaged to the boy, in fact hardly anyone knew about it. He'd talked them out of making it formal until the banns could be announced in the National Cathedral, all the requirements of the Church satisfied. At the time it was just something they should do, but . . .

But what? He couldn't have the boy released. Not that boy. He wouldn't keep silent even as the price for his own freedom. He'd be at a newscaster's booth within five minutes. And then the headlines: BERTRAM AID ACCUSES GOVERNMENT. DAUGHTER OF DEPUTY SECRETARY OF DEFENSE SAYS SECRET NUKE CACHE A PLANT ARRANGED BY HER FATHER.

Or something more clever. Of course, Bertram's people would say it was a plant, but that didn't matter. Anyone accused of what was nearly the ultimate crime would say that. But if the daughter of the top secret policeman in the country said it . . . He punched the communicator.

Grand Senator Bronson appeared on the screen, looked up in surprise. "Oh hello, John. Need something?" Bronson asked nervously. Whenever John Grant called on the special scrambled circuit, interrupting all other conversations, it was likely to be unpleasant.

"Are you alone?"

"Yes."

"When's the next CD warship going outsystem? Not a colony ship, and most especially not a prison ship. A warship."

"Why . . . I don't know. I suppose anything could be arranged, if you'd . . . what's on your mind, John?"

"I want—" Grant hesitated. But there was no time to be lost. None. "I want space for two very important prisoners. A . . . a married couple. The crew is not to know their identity, and anyone who does learn their identity must stay outsystem for at least five years. I want these people put down on a good colony world, something decent. Like Sparta, where they can't get back again. Nobody comes here from Sparta, do they?"

"But . . . yes, I suppose it can be arranged."

Grant's expression discouraged debate.

"It will be arranged. And for tonight. I'll have the prisoners brought to you tonight. You have that CD ship ready. And . . . it better not be the *Saratoga*. My son's on that one, he'll know one of the prisoners." Grant reached for the phone. "Make sure there's a chaplain aboard, the kids will be getting married."

Bronson frowned into the telephone lens. "John, are you sure you're all right?"

"Yes. One other thing. They're to have a good estate on Sparta, but they're not to know who arranged it. Just take care of it for me and I'll pay."

It was all so very simple. Direct his agents to arrest Sharon and conduct her to CD Intelligence. No, he wouldn't want to see her first. Have the Attorney General send young Torrey to the same place, let it out he'd escaped, try him in *absentia*. It wasn't as neat as having all of them convicted in open court, but there'd be enough convictions.

Inside, something screamed at him, screamed again and again, this was his daughter, his pretty little girl, the only person in the world who wasn't afraid of him . . . calmly, almost gently, Grant leaned back in his leather chair. What world would it be for her if the government fell?

He dictated instructions for his agents, took the flimsy order sheet from the writer. His hand didn't tremble at all as he signed it. Then, slowly, carefully, he leaned back again, tasting the blood and bile that he knew would be in his throat the rest of his life: tasting the price of peace.

# JERRY POURNELLE'S FUTURE HISTORY

## by Larry King

### Editor's Introduction

Jerry Pournelle created one of the most interesting and well-developed future histories in the SF field, following in the footsteps of his two favorite authors, H. Beam Piper and Robert A. Heinlein. In the following essay, Larry King—the author of one of the Internet's most thorough and well-researched author sites—dedicated to the worlds of Jerry Pournelle, Larry Niven, E.E. "Doc" Smith, Tolkien and the *Babylon 5* TV series—gives us a fascinating overview of Jerry's CoDominium/Empire of Man future history.

**THE SCIENCE FICTION FUTURE HISTORY** was invented by Robert Heinlein. Of course, science fiction authors had been creating possible futures long before 1939, but these had been used either for a single tale (Wells, Stapledon) or for a series of novels (Smith, Williamson). Heinlein's future history was a playing field for dozens of *unrelated* stories—indeed, it was big enough to contain multiple *series*. You don't have to read Heinlein's D. D. Harriman stories to understand his Lazarus Long novels: they occur in the same universe, but share no characters or plot elements. You don't have to read Larry Niven's Gil Hamilton stories to understand his

Ringworld novels. And you don't have to read Jerry Pournelle's Falkenberg stories to understand *The Mote in God's Eye.*

So why do science fiction fans love to read all the stories in a future history? Why do they immerse themselves in an imaginary world, eagerly devouring every new story of the Technic Civilization, or Darkover or the Alliance-Union universe? Perhaps these readers recognize that a fictional universe is itself a kind of character—a creation that is revealed, bit by bit, in each story that uses it as a setting.

Some future histories are created haphazardly: each time a new story is written, bits of backstory are created to justify the plot. (The *Star Trek* universe is a good example of this.) The resulting timeline is devoid of any coherence. Pournelle's future history, on the other hand, is extremely coherent: even a cursory glance at the timeline shows how much thought he put into how humanity's future might develop, drawing on his study of sociology, history and politics.

Pournelle's saga begins by positing two developments. Given these two hypotheses, human history unfolds over ten centuries in a reasonable—almost *inevitable*—fashion. (Until the Moties show up!)

The first development is the CoDominium. An American/Soviet military alliance may seem a strange idea in hindsight, but recall the state of the Cold War when Pournelle published the first CoDominium story ("Peace With Honor," *Analog*, May 1971). The USA and the USSR were steadfast in their determination to avoid a nuclear exchange. Nixon and Brezhnev were negotiating an arms-control treaty under the banner of "detente." The two superpowers seemed intent on avoiding a direct conflict, and yet they were waging a proxy war in Vietnam. Every time a regional conflict arose—India versus Pakistan, Israel versus the Arab states, Iraq versus the Shah's Iran—the two superpowers chose sides. It was easy to see that the most likely route to nuclear holocaust would involve a regional conflict that spiraled out of control. After all, in 1962 it had been Khrushchev who decided to remove the missiles from Cuba; Castro had been willing to start a war.

How could the USA and the USSR guarantee that their Third World allies would never drag them into a real war? In "Peace With Honor," Pournelle proposed a brilliantly unorthodox answer. The two superpowers form a pact with each other, and declare to the world that this new alliance—the CoDominium—possesses sole power to wage war on Earth and in space. No longer will Third World countries be able to call on the Americans or the Soviets to aid them in their regional conflicts. From now on, such conflicts will be suppressed by the combined power of the USA and the USSR, and any nation on Earth that dares defy this alliance will regret it. The rest of the world is profoundly unhappy with this development, but what can they do? Fight *both* superpowers at once? The result is a century of peace, albeit a very uncomfortable one.

The USA and the USSR remain two separate countries, with radically different political and economic systems. They don't fully trust each other, but they trust the volatile Third World less. Each preserves a nominal national military force, but the bulk of their power is poured into the CoDominium Armed Services. The CD is governed by the Grand Senate, half of whose members are elected from the United States, and half appointed by the Soviet Union. In the USA, these changes require constitutional amendments and treaties, which are passed with the support of the Republicans and the Democrats; in the USSR, these changes are mandated by Communist Party fiat.

The second hypothetical development is human settlement of numerous nearby planets. At the beginning of the twenty-first century, an FTL drive is discovered. Each pair of neighboring stellar systems is connected by an "Alderson tramline," which allows instantaneous travel between two fixed points in space. (Travel within a system must still be done the old-fashioned way.) When humans begin to explore the nearby star systems, they discover dozens of planets with breathable atmospheres and soil that will support Terran plants—and often edible native plants as well. With all this real estate available, there is no need to compete over territory. The most pleasant planets are the most desirable. The United States and the Soviet Union occupy many worlds, and other rich Earth nations establish colonies of their own on pleasant planets: Meiji (Japan), Churchill (Britain), Friedland (Germany), Dayan (Israel), Xanadu (China). Less pleasant worlds that can become hospitable with hard work are settled by eccentric groups of motivated colonists: Covenant by Scottish Presbyterian separatists, Ararat by conservative Christian churches, Sparta by university professors who draw on classical models to create a constitutional dual monarchy. And unpleasant planets with valuable resources are gobbled up by mining companies that lobby the CoDominium to "reform" the prison system, sentencing criminals to involuntary servitude on sweltering Tanith or frozen Fulson's World. Thus the "Great Exodus" of the early twenty-first century resembles the colonization of the New World in the sixteenth and seventeenth centuries.

For much of the twenty-first century, there are no interstellar conflicts. The CD Navy has a monopoly on armed spaceships, and the CD Marines stamp out insurrections on the colonies.

However, as the decades pass, it becomes more and more difficult for the American/Soviet alliance to maintain control over the entire Earth. The CD military has a near-monopoly on *existing* weapons of mass destruction, but what if some nation develops a new kind of weapon? To forestall that possibility, the CoDominium begins suppressing scientific research. When ethnic minorities within the Soviet Union demand autonomy, entire peoples are deported to colony planets. Some disgruntled American Indian tribes are deported as well. The United States begins to supply free drugs to welfare recipients to reduce violent crime. But none of these measures fix the long-term instability in the CoDominium.

Moreover, mass deportations do not solve the problem of unrest: they merely export the problem to the colonies. When violent criminals are deported to an agricultural planet, they refuse to become farmers and choose brigandage instead. When life-long welfare recipients are deported to a planet with a subsistence-level economy, they expect to have their needs met without having to work. The results are often disastrous. A common theme in Pournelle's stories is that cataclysm and misery are often caused not by deliberate evil, but by the unintended results of regulations made by inattentive bureaucrats.

In many science fiction stories, human expansion into the galaxy continues without interruption. But Pournelle, who had spent years dealing with real-life politics, was aware of the many reasons such expansion might end. As with the British Empire two centuries earlier, the expenses of the CoDominium's colonization are borne by the taxpayers, while the profits flow to private corporations. So when the economy goes into a downturn and voters demand lower taxes, the Grand Senate makes drastic cuts to anything space related. The CD Navy and Marines are forced to abandon many planets. Now, when a colony is threatened by civil war or besieged by violent transportees, they can no longer call on the CD to help them. An era of mercenary armies begins. For a price, a colonial government can hire an armor brigade from Friedland, infantry from Covenant, or cyber-warfare experts from Meiji. When Colonel John Christian Falkenberg of the 42nd Regiment of Line Marines is cashiered for stepping on the wrong Grand Senator's toes, he too becomes a mercenary, and most of his former regiment joins him.

These events form the backdrop for Pournelle's tales of the twenty-first century. *West of Honor*, "He Fell Into a Dark Hole," and "Peace With Honor" take place when Falkenberg is a CD officer. His mercenary career is chronicled in "The Mercenary," "His Truth Goes Marching On," "Silent Leges," the new portions of *Prince of Mercenaries*, and "Sword and Scepter." When these stories were published in paperback, "Peace With Honor," "The Mercenary," and "Sword and Scepter" were combined together as *The Mercenary*. Later, *West of Honor*, *The Mercenary*, and some additional material became *Falkenberg's Legion*. *Prince of Mercenaries* incorporated "Silent Leges" and "His Truth Goes Marching On," but was mostly new.

In 1988, Pournelle's future history became a "shared universe" with the inauguration of the *War World* series of short story collections (and later, novels) set on Haven, one of the more distant worlds settled by the CoDominium. The *War World* stories exhibit every facet of Pournelle's universe on one planet: Haven's settlers include an insular religious group, involuntary transportees from Earth, venal politicians, mining corporations eager to make a quick buck and a regiment of CD Marines vainly trying to keep order. Pournelle initiated the *War World* project, but much of the work was done by Poul Anderson, Roland Green, Steven Shervais, John F. Carr and Don Hawthorne. After Pournelle went into semiretirement in the late 1990s he put Carr in charge of the entire project.

As the CoDominium becomes weaker in the late twenty-first century, unrest among Third World nations grows. The USA and

USSR begin drifting apart, with hardliners in both superpowers agitating to end the alliance and resume the great struggle between capitalism and communism. A few forward-thinking individuals, led by Grand Admiral Sergei Lermontov, conclude that nuclear war is inevitable, and therefore the survival of the human race hinges on whether enough extrasolar colonies can become self-sustaining before Earth destroys itself. Two novels written by Pournelle and S. M. Stirling, *Go Tell the Spartans* and *Prince of Sparta*, narrate how Prince Lysander of Sparta, aided by several of Lermontov's allies and one brigade from Falkenberg's Legion, manages to establish a regime that can survive after Earth is gone. (These novels, along with all of the Falkenberg stories mentioned above, were reprinted in the hardcover omnibus *The Prince*; only "He Fell Into a Dark Hole" was omitted.)

In 2103, the CoDominium government collapses and the Great Patriotic Wars erupt on Earth. The majority of its inhabitants perish. Earth will never again play an important role in humanity's story.

For the next century and a half, Earth's former colonies join together in various alliances and fight occasional wars. The most durable federation is led by Sparta and the Russian colony of St. Ekaterina. Their stable government—in which rights and duties are carefully balanced—helps them win the allegiance of much of the former CoDominium Navy. In 2250, after uniting all humanity under one government, Leonidas I of Sparta proclaims the "Empire of Man."

Three and a half centuries of peace ensue. The Empire of Man expands to include hundreds of human worlds. Scientists achieve a profound understanding of physics; engineers create tethered space stations and other marvels; biologists are able to design vaccines by analyzing the genetic structure of a virus. And in what may be the Empire's greatest achievement, the planets New Scotland and New Ireland are rendered habitable after a century of terraforming.

But the planet Sauron has been breeding a race of genetic supermen, and has created an army of cyborgs. In 2603, they launch a surprise attack on St. Ekaterina. Sauron and its allies wreak tremendous carnage in the Secession Wars: battle cruisers are destroyed as fast as they can be built, dozens of worlds are completely depopulated. But eventually the secessionist advances are halted. In the final counterattack of 2640, the Imperial Navy destroys the rebel navy, and bombards the Sauron homeworld until magma begins to seep through the planetary crust.

The war is over. The secessionists have lost, but so has the Empire. Sparta is forced to abandon all but a small core of nearby planets, and some of their technology and scientific knowledge is lost. (In classic SF, lost information was a common trope. In Asimov's and Herbert's future histories, the galactic civilization does not even recall which planet humans evolved on! Given recent advances in digital storage technologies, it's hard to imagine this happening.) Some isolated planets retain their industry, infrastructure, and even spacefaring capability. But many others, damaged by decades of bombardment and cut off from interstellar trade, regress to a pre-industrial stage—and sometimes outright barbarism.

Many parsecs from the core of the fallen empire, a lone Sauron ship has survived. They reach Haven, destroy all of its spacefaring capability, and make themselves masters of the planet. John F. Carr and Don Hawthorne's *War World* novels *The Lidless Eye* and *Cyborg Revolt* tell of the Sauron occupation and the native peoples' resistance. Over the next three centuries, the Saurons—despite their dominance—gradually become just one more of Haven's tribal societies. In the novels *Blood Feuds* and *Blood Vengeance*, co-authors S. M. Stirling, Judith Tarr, Susan Shwartz, and Harry Turtledove transplant the classic tragedies of Sophocles and Aeschylus to Sauron-occupied Haven, with the last functioning Sauron computer playing the role of the blind prophet Tiresias.

Despite the loss of their empire, Sparta and its allies St. Ekaterina and Crucis have preserved their civilization. After two centuries of gradual recovery, they once again begin to expand their influence. In 2903, Leonidas IV proclaims the "Second Empire of Man." Yet the Second Empire lives in the shadow of the First. There is no need to settle new planets; instead, they seek out existing human worlds that were settled long ago. Whenever they encounter a civilized planet with spacefaring capability, they invite it to join the Empire. Whenever they discover a world that has regressed into a pre-spaceflight state, they annex it and impose colonial rule. The Second Empire's greatest fear is spacefaring worlds that refuse to join them; these "Outies" are often hostile, and must not be ignored—for the Empire has sworn that interstellar war must never come again.

Pournelle set no stories between the early twenty-second and the mid-twenty-ninth centuries. This entire period, which includes nuclear war on Earth, the rise of the First Empire of Man, centuries of peace during its height, the Secession Wars, the destruction of the Saurons, and the prehistory of the Second Empire were never directly treated. Instead, these events form the backdrop for his tales of the Second Empire. Why this chronological gap? Perhaps Pournelle found the Second Empire more interesting than the first, for it allows imperial rule to be seen from many perspectives at once. Inhabitants of primitive planets are in awe of the Second Empire, with its irresistible weapons and inexplicable scientific marvels. Yet the Empire's ruling class know that their science is dwarfed by that of the First Empire, and yet they also remember that science and civilization were not able to save the First Empire from utter destruction. These complex dynamics are seen in the story of Prince Samual's World and Makassar (Pournelle's novel *A Spaceship for the King*, expanded into *King David's Spaceship*) and the tales set on New Scotland ("Motelight" and early chapters of *The Mote in God's Eye*, as well as the unpublished "First Patrol").

*The Mote in God's Eye*, which began Larry Niven and Jerry Pournelle's famed collaboration, is set in this timeline. Niven found Pournelle's future history interesting, but suggested they add a new element: intelligent aliens. The "Moties" they created for the book are one of the most ingenious and carefully designed alien species in science fiction. *The Mote in God's Eye* is a drama in which the humans must deal with the tension between their political, religious, and familial obligations. It is also the best "first contact" story ever written, in which the reader sees the Moties as terrifying yet endearing aliens, while also seeing the humans as profoundly alien through the eyes of the Moties.

Niven and Pournelle sent the first draft to Robert Heinlein, who suggested that—given the complexity of the backstory—the book should include a timeline. He suggested it might begin with something like "1969: Neil Armstrong sets foot on Earth's Moon" (Letter to Niven and Pournelle, 7/20/1973, reprinted in *The Virginia Edition: The Complete Works of Robert A. Heinlein*). The authors agreed, and from that point forward, every book in Pournelle's future history has contained a timeline that begins with Heinlein's seven words. When I discovered *The Mote in God's Eye* at the library in the 1970s, the timeline fascinated me, with its rises and falls of civilization as humans expanded into the galaxy.

Two decades after *Mote*, Niven and Pournelle published a sequel, entitled *The Gripping Hand* (in the UK, *The Moat Around Murcheson's Eye*). This book examined the repercussions of the decision made at the end of *Mote*, and described the asteroid civilization in the Mote system that had only been hinted at in the first book. It also contained the first scenes set on Sparta, the Imperial capital, since the CoDominium stories set almost a millennium earlier.

Jerry Pournelle has a reputation for being a "political" author. If this is taken to mean that he puts a lot of thought into the implications of political systems in his stories, that's quite true. But this does not mean that his books offer simplistic responses to difficult questions. When John Grant, John Christian Falkenberg, and Rod Blaine are forced to make difficult decisions, they continue to agonize over them afterward. Pournelle's future history stories address some very difficult moral questions: If you are convinced that victory for a certain candidate will precipitate nuclear war, are dirty tricks and ballot-stuffing justified? Is it permissible to preemptively kill thousands to save hundreds of thousands? Could there ever be a justification for slaughtering an entire intelligent species? Does a soldier owe loyalty to a commanding officer who has abandoned the purpose for which they were fighting? Even when his characters answer these questions, one cannot be certain that their answer is Pournelle's answer.

Some pundits objected to *The Mote in God's Eye* for depicting an aristocratic society. In the essay "Building the Mote in God's Eye," Niven and Pournelle responded to these critics. "Do we, they ask, really *believe* in imperial government? And *monarchy*? That depends on what they mean by 'believe in.' Do we think it's desirable? We don't have to say. Inevitable? Of course not. Do we think it's *possible*? Damn straight." If these pundits had read more carefully, they would have seen that if Pournelle's stories share a central political thesis (which is a very debatable point), it is certainly not that monarchy is the best form of government. Rather, it is that the way to create a just and stable regime is to ensure that rights correspond to duties. In the Second Empire, the imperial heir is required to serve in the armed forces before he ascends to the throne. In *The Mote in God's Eye*, Rod Blaine recalls hearing that Admiral Plekhanov "had the Crown Prince—now Emperor—stretched over a mess table and whacked with a spatball paddle when His Highness was serving as a midshipman in *Plataea*." A generation later, when Kevin Renner visits Sparta in *The Gripping Hand*, he eavesdrops on the aristocracy in order to determine whether they are focusing on their duties or only on their privileges. The price of civilization is eternal vigilance.

The earliest stories set in this universe were published in the 1970s; they placed the founding of the CoDominium in the year 1990. *Falkenberg's Legion* (1990) pushed its founding back to sometime "between 1990 and 2000." Then in 1991, the Soviet Union collapsed. The fall of history's longest-lasting totalitarian state was certainly welcome news to Pournelle—but it rendered the CoDominium impossible. Pournelle and Stirling responded in *Prince of Sparta* (1993) by proposing that the USSR's collapse was followed by years of economic turmoil, leading to the USSR's rebirth and then the creation of the CoDominium around the turn of the century. A decade later, Pournelle—rather than revising the timeline again—declared that the CoDominium "has moved into the 'alternate history' category" (*The View from Chaos Manor*, View 202, 4/22/2002).

Yet the future history created by Pournelle is still alive. *War World* novels and stories continue to appear; Falkenberg even makes an appearance in *War World: Jihad*. Jerry's daughter Jennifer Pournelle wrote *Outies*, a sequel to *Mote* and *Gripping Hand* that delves into the religious and political currents in the Trans-Coalsack Sector, as well as presenting new Motie subspecies in a very unexpected setting.

A bibliography, reading order, and timeline of this universe can be found at www.chronology.org/pournelle.

The following story is the first published tale of John Christian Falkenberg ("The Mercenary," *Analog*, July 1972). Pournelle would subsequently write stories set chronologically earlier and later than this one. "The Mercenary," set soon after Falkenberg has been cashiered from the CD Marines and begun his mercenary career, is an excellent introduction to this famous character.

# THE MERCENARY

## by Jerry Pournelle

### Editor's Introduction

All of Jerry's early John Christian Falkenberg stories appeared in John W. Campbell's *Analog Science Fiction and Science Fact*, the top SF magazine of the time. They quickly established Jerry as the premier science-fiction military writer in the field. The Falkenberg stories were popular and controversial—many in the anti-war faction decried them as "glorifying war." In truth, the Falkenberg stories did not glorify war, but showed the horrors that came when peace was broken and had to be restored.

Jerry was a veteran of the Korean War; he knew all about war, from its glories to its miseries. After graduating from a Christian Brothers High School, Jerry gained an appointment to West Point; he didn't finish, though. The Army needed bodies on the ground in Korea and he was yanked from West Point and made one of the ninety-day OCS commissioned officers and assigned to the artillery corps. Jerry served in Korea from 1950 to 1952.

Jerry once wistfully mentioned to me that "The Mercenary" was one of the last stories of his John W. Campbell bought before he died. It was in the pages of *Astounding Science Fiction* that Jerry discovered the wonder and limitless possibilities of science fiction and honed his craft from Campbell's insightful letters of rejection. It was only fitting that Jerry was not only Campbell's last authorial discovery, but won the first John W. Campbell Award for Best New Writer of 1973.

This is the story that started it all. It begins shortly after Falkenberg is cashiered from the CoDominium Marines and sets out to recruit a mercenary regiment.

I

**THE LANDING BOAT FELL AWAY** from the orbiting warship, drifted to a safe distance and fired retros. When it entered the thin reaches of the planet's upper atmosphere, scoops opened in the bows, drew in until the stagnation temperature in the ramjet chamber was high enough for ignition. Engines lit with a roar of flame. Wings swung out slightly, enough to provide lift at hypersonic speeds, and the spaceplane turned, streaked over empty ocean toward the continental land mass two thousand kilometers away.

It circled over craggy mountains twelve kilometers high, then dropped low over thickly forested plains. It slowed until it was no longer a danger to the thin strip of inhabited lands along the ocean shores. The planet's great ocean was joined to a smaller sea by a nearly landlocked channel no more than five kilometers across at its widest point, and nearly all of the colonists lived near the junction of the waters.

Hadley's capital city nestled on a long peninsula at the mouth of that channel, and the two natural harbors, one in the sea, the other in the ocean, gave the city the fitting name of Refuge. The name suggested a tranquility the city no longer possessed.

The ship extended its wings to their fullest reach and floated low over the calm water of the channel harbor. It touched and settled in. Tugboats raced across clear blue water. Sweating seamen threw lines and towed the landing craft to the dock where they secured it.

A long line of CoDominium Marines in garrison uniform marched out of the boat. They gathered on the gray concrete piers into neat brightly colored lines. Two men in civilian clothing followed the Marines from the flyer.

They blinked at the unaccustomed blue-white of Hadley's sun. The sun was so far away that it would have been only a small point if either of them were foolish enough to look directly at it. The apparent small size was only an illusion caused by distance; Hadley received as much illumination from its hotter sun as Earth does from Sol.

Both men were tall and stood as straight as the Marines in front of them, so that except for their clothing they might have been mistaken for a part of the disembarking battalion. The shorter of the two carried luggage for both of them, and stood respectfully behind; although older he was obviously a subordinate. They watched as two younger men came uncertainly along the pier. The newcomers' unadorned blue uniforms contrasted sharply with the bright reds and golds of the CoDominium Marines milling around them. Already the Marines were scurrying back into the flyer to carry out barracks bags, weapons, and all the other personal gear of a light infantry battalion.

The taller of the two civilians faced the uniformed newcomers. "I take it you're here to meet us?" he asked pleasantly. His voice rang through the noise on the pier, and it carried easily although he had not shouted. His accent was neutral, the nearly universal English of non-Russian officers in the CoDominium Service, and it marked his profession almost as certainly as did his posture and the tone of command.

The newcomers were uncertain even so. There were a lot of ex-officers of the CoDominium Space Navy on the beach lately. CD budgets were lower every year. "I think so," one finally said. "Are you John Christian Falkenberg?"

His name was actually John Christian Falkenberg III, and he suspected that his grandfather would have insisted on the distinction. "Right. And Sergeant Major Calvin."

"Pleasure to meet you, sir. I'm Lieutenant Banners, and this is Ensign Mowrer. We're on President Budreau's staff." Banners looked around as if expecting other men, but there were none except the uniformed Marines. He gave Falkenberg a slightly puzzled look, then added, "We have transportation for you, but I'm afraid your men will have to walk. It's about eleven miles."

"Miles." Falkenberg smiled to himself. This *was* out in the boondocks. "I see no reason why ten healthy mercenaries can't march eighteen kilometers, Lieutenant." He turned to face the black shape of the landing boat's entry port and called to someone inside. "Captain Fast. There is no transportation, but someone will show you where to march the men. Have them carry all gear."

"Uh, sir, that won't be necessary," the lieutenant protested. "We can get—well, we have horse-drawn transport for baggage." He looked at Falkenberg as if he expected him to laugh.

"That's hardly unusual on colony worlds," Falkenberg said. Horses and mules could be carried as frozen embryos, and they didn't require high-technology industries to produce more, nor did they need an industrial base to fuel them.

"Ensign Mowrer will attend to it," Lieutenant Banners said. He paused again and looked thoughtful as if uncertain how to tell Falkenberg something. Finally he shook his head. "I think it would be wise if you issued your men their personal weapons, sir. There shouldn't be any trouble on their way to barracks, but—anyway, ten armed men certainly won't have any problems."

"I see. Perhaps I should go with my troops, Lieutenant. I hadn't known things were quite this bad on Hadley." Falkenberg's voice was calm and even, but he watched the junior officers carefully.

"No, sir. They aren't, really. . . . But there's no point in taking chances." He waved Ensign Mowrer to the landing craft and turned back to Falkenberg. A large black shape rose from the water outboard of the landing craft. It splashed and vanished. Banners seemed not to notice, but the Marines shouted excitedly. "I'm sure the ensign and your officers can handle the disembarkation, and the President would like to see you immediately, sir."

"No doubt. All right, Banners, lead on. I'll bring Sergeant Major Calvin with me." He followed Banners down the pier.

There's no point to this farce, Falkenberg thought. Anyone seeing ten armed men conducted by a presidential ensign will know they're mercenary troops, civilian clothes or not. Another case of wrong information.

Falkenberg had been told to keep the status of himself and his men a secret, but it wasn't going to work. He wondered if this would make it more difficult to keep his own secrets.

Banners ushered them quickly through the bustling CoDominium Marine barracks, past bored guards who half saluted the Presidential Guard uniform. The Marine fortress was a blur of activity, every open space crammed with packs and weapons; the signs of a military force about to move on to another station.

As they were leaving the building, Falkenberg saw an elderly Naval officer. "Excuse me a moment, Banners." He turned to the CoDominium Navy captain. "They sent someone for me. Thanks, Ed."

"No problem. I'll report your arrival to the admiral. He wants to keep track of you. Unofficially, of course. Good luck, John. God knows you need some right now. It was a rotten deal."

"It's the way it goes."

"Yeah, but the Fleet used to take better care of its own than that. I'm beginning to wonder if anyone is safe. Damn Senator—"

"Forget it," Falkenberg interrupted. He glanced back to be sure Lieutenant Banners was out of earshot. "Pay my respects to the rest of your officers. You run a good ship."

The captain smiled thinly. "Thanks. From you that's quite a compliment." He held out his hand and gripped John's firmly. "Look, we pull out in a couple of days, no more than that. If you need a ride on somewhere I can arrange it. The goddam Senate won't have to know. We can fix you a hitch to anywhere in CD territory."

"Thanks, but I guess I'll stay."

"Could be rough here," the captain said.

"And it won't be everywhere else in the CoDominium?" Falkenberg asked. "Thanks again, Ed." He gave a half salute and checked himself.

Banners and Calvin were waiting for him, and Falkenberg turned away. Calvin lifted three personal effects bags as if they were empty and pushed the door open in a smooth motion. The CD captain watched until they had left the building, but Falkenberg did not look back.

"Damn them," the captain muttered. "Damn the lot of them."

"The car's here." Banners opened the rear door of a battered ground effects vehicle of no discoverable make. It had been cannibalized from a dozen other machines, and some parts were obviously cut-and-try jobs done by an uncertain machinist. Banners climbed into the driver's seat and started the engine. It coughed twice, then ran smoothly, and they drove away in a cloud of black smoke.

They drove past another dock where a landing craft with wings as large as the entire Marine landing boat was unloading an endless stream of civilian passengers. Children screamed, and long lines of men and women stared about uncertainly until they were ungently hustled along by guards in uniforms matching Banners's. The sour smell of unwashed humanity mingled with the crisp clean salt air from the ocean beyond. Banners rolled up the windows with an expression of distaste.

"Always like that," Calvin commented to no one in particular. "Water discipline in them CoDominium prison ships bein' what it is, takes weeks dirtside to get clean again."

"Have you ever been in one of those ships?" Banners asked.

"No, sir," Calvin replied. "Been in Marine assault boats just about as bad, I reckon. But I can't say I fancy being stuffed into one cubicle with ten, fifteen thousand civilians for six months."

"We may all see the inside of one of those," Falkenberg said. "And be glad of the chance. Tell me about the situation here, Banners."

"I don't even know where to start, sir," the lieutenant answered. "I—do you know about Hadley?"

"Assume I don't," Falkenberg said. May as well see what kind of estimate of the situation the President's officers can make, he thought. He could feel the Fleet Intelligence report bulging in an inner pocket of his tunic, but those reports always left out important details; and the attitudes of the Presidential Guard could be important to his plans.

"Yes, sir. Well, to begin with, we're a long way from the nearest shipping lanes—but I guess you knew that. The only real reason we had any merchant trade was the mines. Thorium, richest veins known anywhere for a while, until they started to run out.

"For the first few years that's all we had. The mines are up in the hills, about eighty miles over that way." He pointed to a thin blue line just visible at the horizon.

"Must be pretty high mountains," Falkenberg said. "What's the diameter of Hadley? About eighty percent of Earth? Something like that. The horizon ought to be pretty close."

"Yes, sir. They are high mountains. Hadley is small, but we've got bigger and better everything here." There was pride in the young officer's voice.

"Them bags seem pretty heavy for a planet this small," Calvin said.

"Hadley's very dense," Banners answered. "Gravity nearly ninety percent standard. Anyway, the mines are over there, and they have their own spaceport at a lake nearby. Refuge—that's this city—was founded by the American Express Company. They brought in the first colonists, quite a lot of them."

"Volunteers?" Falkenberg asked.

"Yes. All volunteers. The usual misfits. I suppose my father was typical enough, an engineer who couldn't keep up with the rat race and was tired of Bureau of Technology restrictions on what he could learn. They were the first wave, and they took the best land. They founded the city and got an economy going. American Express was paid back all advances within twenty years." Banners's pride was evident, and Falkenberg knew it had been a difficult job.

"That was, what, fifty years ago?" Falkenberg asked.

"Yes."

They were driving through crowded streets lined with wooden houses and a few stone buildings. There were rooming houses, bars, sailors' brothels, all the usual establishments of a dock street, but there were no other cars on the road. Instead the traffic was all horses and oxen pulling carts, bicycles, and pedestrians.

The sky above Refuge was clear. There was no trace of smog or industrial wastes. Out in the harbor tugboats moved with the silent efficiency of electric power, and there were also wind-driven sailing ships, lobster boats powered by oars, even a topsail schooner lovely against clean blue water. She threw up white spume as she raced out to sea. A three-masted, full-rigged ship was drawn up to a wharf where men loaded her by hand with huge bales of what might have been cotton.

They passed a wagonload of melons. A gaily dressed young couple waved cheerfully at them, then the man snapped a long whip at the team of horses that pulled their wagon. Falkenberg studied the primitive scene and said, "It doesn't look like you've been here fifty years."

"No." Banners gave them a bitter look. Then he swerved to avoid a group of shapeless teenagers lounging in the dockside street. He had to swerve again to avoid the barricade of paving stones that they had masked. The car jounced wildly. Banners gunned it to lift it higher and headed for a low place in the barricade. It scraped as it went over the top, then he accelerated away.

Falkenberg took his hand from inside his shirt jacket.

Behind him Calvin was inspecting a submachine gun that had appeared from the oversized barracks bag he'd brought into the car with him. When Banners said nothing about the incident, Falkenberg frowned and leaned back in his seat, listening. The Intelligence reports mentioned lawlessness, but this was as bad as a welfare island on Earth.

"No, we're not much industrialized," Banners continued. "At first there wasn't any need to develop basic industries. The mines made everyone rich, so we imported everything we needed. The farmers sold fresh produce to the miners for enormous prices. Refuge was a service industry town. People who worked here could soon afford farm animals, and they scattered out across the plains and into the forests."

Falkenberg nodded. "Many of them wouldn't care for cities."

"Precisely. They didn't want industry, they'd come here to escape it." Banners drove in silence for a moment. "Then some blasted CoDominium bureaucrat read the ecology reports about Hadley. The Population Control Bureau in Washington decided this was a perfect place for involuntary colonization. The ships were coming here for the thorium anyway, so instead of luxuries and machinery they were ordered to carry convicts. Hundreds of thousands of them, Colonel Falkenberg. For the last ten years there have been better than fifty thousand people a year dumped in on us."

"And you couldn't support them all," Falkenberg said gently.

"No, sir." Banners's face tightened. He seemed to be fighting tears. "God knows we try. Every erg the fusion generators can make goes into converting petroleum into basic protocarb just to feed them. But they're not like the original colonists! They don't know anything, they won't *do* anything! Oh, not really, of course. Some of them work. Some of our best citizens are transportees. But there are so many of the other kind."

"Why'n't you tell 'em to work or starve?" Calvin asked bluntly. Falkenberg gave him a cold look, and the sergeant nodded slightly and sank back into his seat.

"Because the CD wouldn't let us!" Banners shouted. "Damn it, we didn't have self-government. The CD Bureau of Relocation people told us what to do. They ran everything. . . ."

"We know," Falkenberg said gently. "We've seen the results of Humanity League influence over BuReloc. My sergeant major wasn't asking you a question, he was expressing an opinion. Nevertheless, I am surprised. I would have thought your farms could support the urban population."

"They should be able to, sir." Banners drove in grim silence for a long minute. "But there's no transportation. The people are here, and most of the agricultural land is five hundred miles inland. There's arable land closer, but it isn't cleared. Our settlers wanted to get away from Refuge and BuReloc. We have a railroad, but bandit gangs keep blowing it up. We can't rely on Hadley's produce to keep Refuge alive. There are a million people on Hadley, and half of them are crammed into this one ungovernable city."

They were approaching an enormous bowl-shaped structure attached to a massive square stone fortress. Falkenberg studied the buildings carefully, then asked what they were.

"Our stadium," Banners replied. There was no pride in his voice now. "The CD built it for us. We'd rather have had a new fusion plant, but we got a stadium that can hold a hundred thousand people."

"Built by the GLC Construction and Development Company, I presume," Falkenberg said.

"Yes . . . how did you know?"

"I think I saw it somewhere." He hadn't, but it was an easy guess: GLC was owned by a holding company that was in turn owned by the Bronson family. It was easy enough to understand why aid sent by the CD Grand Senate would end up used for something GLC might participate in.

"We have very fine sports teams and racehorses," Banners said bitterly. "The building next to it is the Presidential Palace. Its architecture is quite functional."

The Palace loomed up before them, squat and massive; it looked more fortress than capital building.

The city was more thickly populated as they approached the Palace. The buildings here were mostly stone and poured concrete instead of wood. Few were more than three stories high, so that Refuge sprawled far along the shore. The population density increased rapidly beyond the stadium-palace complex. Banners was watchful as he drove along the wide streets, but he seemed less nervous than he had been at dockside.

Refuge was a city of contrasts. The streets were straight and wide, and there was evidently a good waste-disposal system, but the lower floors of the buildings were open shops, and the sidewalks were clogged with market stalls. Clouds of pedestrians moved through the kiosks and shops.

There was still no motor traffic and no moving pedways. Horse troughs and hitching posts had been constructed at frequent intervals along with starkly functional street lights and water distribution towers. The few signs of technology contrasted strongly with the general primitive air of the city.

A contingent of uniformed men thrust their way through the crowd at a street crossing. Falkenberg looked at them closely, then at Banners. "Your troops?"

"No, sir. That's the livery of Glenn Foster's household. Officially they're unorganized reserves of the Presidential Guard, but they're household troops all the same." Banners laughed bitterly. "Sounds like something out of a history book, doesn't it? We're nearly back to feudalism, Colonel Falkenberg. Anyone rich enough keeps hired bodyguards. They *have* to. The criminal gangs are so strong the police don't try to catch anyone under organized protection, and the judges wouldn't punish them if they were caught."

"And the private bodyguards become gangs in their own right, I suppose."

Banners looked at him sharply. "Yes, sir. Have you seen it before?"

"Yes. I've seen it before." Banners was unable to make out the expression on Falkenberg's lips.

They drove into the Presidential Palace, were saluted by the blue uniformed troopers. Falkenberg noted the polished weapons and precise drill of the Presidential Guard. There were well-trained men on duty here, but the unit was small. Falkenberg wondered if they could fight as well as stand guard. They were local citizens, loyal to Hadley, and would be unlike the CoDominium Marines he was accustomed to.

He was conducted through a series of rooms in the stone fortress.

Each had heavy metal doors, and several were guardrooms. Falkenberg saw no signs of government activity until they had passed through the outer layers of the enormous palace into an open courtyard, and through that to an inner building.

Here there was plenty of activity. Clerks bustled through the halls, and girls in the draped togas fashionable years before on Earth sat at desks in offices. Most seemed to be packing desk contents into boxes, and other people scurried through the corridors. Some offices were empty, their desks covered with fine dust, and there were plastiboard moving boxes stacked outside them.

There were two anterooms to the President's office. President Budreau was a tall, thin man with a red pencil mustache and quick gestures. As they were ushered into the overly ornate room the President looked up from a sheaf of papers, but his eyes did not focus immediately on his visitors. His face was a mask of worry and concentration.

"Colonel John Christian Falkenberg, sir," Lieutenant Banners said. "And Sergeant Major Calvin."

Budreau got to his feet. "Pleased to see you, Falkenberg." His expression told them differently; he looked at his visitors with faint distaste and motioned Banners out of the room. When the door closed he asked, "How many men did you bring with you?"

"Ten, Mister President. All we could bring aboard the carrier without arousing suspicion. We were lucky to get that many. The Grand Senate had an inspector at the loading docks to check for violation of the antimercenary codes. If we hadn't bribed a port official to distract him we wouldn't be here at all. Calvin and I would be on Tanith as involuntary colonists."

"I see." From his expression he wasn't surprised. John thought Budreau would have been more pleased if the inspector had caught them. The President tapped the desk nervously. "Perhaps that will be enough. I understand the ship you came with also brought the Marines who have volunteered to settle on Hadley. They should provide the nucleus of an excellent constabulary. Good troops?"

"It was a demobilized battalion," Falkenberg replied. "Those are the troops the CD didn't want anymore. Could be the scrapings of every guardhouse on twenty planets. We'll be lucky if there's a real trooper in the lot."

Budreau's face relaxed into its former mask of depression. Hope visibly drained from him.

"Surely you have troops of your own," Falkenberg said.

Budreau picked up a sheaf of papers. "It's all here. I was just looking it over when you came in." He handed the report to Falkenberg. "There's little encouragement in it, Colonel. I have never thought there was any military solution to Hadley's problems, and this confirms that fear. If you have only ten men plus a battalion of forced-labor Marines, the military answer isn't even worth considering."

Budreau returned to his seat. His hands moved restlessly over the sea of papers on his desk. "If I were you, Falkenberg, I'd get back on that Navy boat and forget Hadley."

"Why don't you?"

"Because Hadley's my home! No rabble is going to drive me off the plantation my grandfather built with his own hands. They will not make me run out." Budreau clasped his hands together until the knuckles were white with the strain, but when he spoke again his voice was calm. "You have no stake here. I do."

Falkenberg took the report from the desk and leafed through the pages before handing it to Calvin. "We've come a long way, Mister President. You may as well tell me what the problem is before I leave."

Budreau nodded sourly. The red mustache twitched and he ran the back of his hand across it. "It's simple enough. The ostensible reason you're here, the reason we gave the Colonial Office for letting us recruit a planetary constabulary, is the bandit gangs out in the hills. No one knows how many of them there are, but they are strong enough to raid farms. They also cut communications between Refuge and the countryside whenever they want to."

"Yes." Falkenberg stood in front of the desk because he hadn't been invited to sit. If that bothered him it did not show. "Guerrilla gangsters have no real chance if they've no political base."

Budreau nodded. "But, as I am sure Vice President Bradford told you, they are not the real problem." The President's voice was strong, but there was a querulous note in it, as if he was accustomed to having his conclusions argued against and was waiting for Falkenberg to begin. "Actually, we could live with the bandits, but they get political support from the Freedom Party. My Progressive Party is larger than the Freedom Party, but the Progressives are scattered all over the planet. The FP is concentrated right here in Refuge, and they have God knows how many voters and about forty thousand loyalists they can concentrate whenever they want to stage a riot."

"Do you have riots very often?" John asked.

"Too often. There's not much to control them with. I have three hundred men in the Presidential Guard, but they're CD recruited and trained like young Banners. They're not much use at riot control, and they're loyal to the job, not to me, anyway. The FP's got men inside the guard."

"So we can scratch the Presidential Guard when it comes to controlling the Freedom Party," John observed.

"Yes." Budreau smiled without amusement. "Then there's my police force. My police were all commanded by CD officers who are pulling out. My administrative staff was recruited and trained by BuReloc, and all the competent people have been recalled to Earth."

"I can see that would create a problem."

"Problem? It's impossible," Budreau said. "There's nobody left with skill enough to govern, but I've got the job and everybody else wants it. I might be able to scrape up a thousand Progressive partisans and another fifteen thousand party workers who would fight for us in a pinch, but they have no training. How can they face the FP's forty thousand?"

"You seriously believe the Freedom Party will revolt?"

"As soon as the CD's out, you can count on it. They've demanded a new constitutional convention to assemble just after the CoDominium Governor leaves. If we don't give them the convention they'll rebel and carry a lot of undecided with them. After all, what's unreasonable about a convention when the colonial governor has gone?"

"I see."

"And if we do give them the convention they want, they'll drag things out until there's nobody left in it but their people. My party is composed of working voters. How can they stay on day after day? The FP's unemployed will sit it out until they can throw the Progressives out of office. Once they get in they'll ruin the planet. Under the circumstances I don't see what a military man can do for us, but Vice President Bradford insisted that we hire you."

"Perhaps we can think of something," Falkenberg said smoothly. "I've no experience in administration as such, but Hadley is not unique. I take it the Progressive Party is mostly old settlers?"

"Yes and no. The Progressive Party wants to industrialize Hadley, and some of our farm families oppose that. But we want to do it slowly. We'll close most of the mines and take out only as much thorium as we have to sell to get the basic industrial equipment. I want to keep the rest for our own fusion generators, because we'll need it later.

"We want to develop agriculture and transport, and cut the basic citizen ration so that we'll have the fusion power available for our new industries. I want to close out convenience and consumer manufacturing and keep it closed until we can afford it." Budreau's voice rose and his eyes shone; it was easier to see why he had become popular. He believed in his cause.

"We want to build the tools of a self-sustaining world and get along without the CoDominium until we can rejoin the human race as equals!" Budreau caught himself and frowned. "Sorry. Didn't mean to make a speech. Have a seat, won't you?"

"Thank you." Falkenberg sat in a heavy leather chair and looked around the room. The furnishings were ornate, and the office decor had cost a fortune to bring from Earth; but most of it was tasteless—spectacular rather than elegant. The Colonial Office did that sort of thing a lot, and Falkenberg wondered which Grand Senator owned the firm that supplied office furnishings. "What does the opposition want?"

"I suppose you really do need to know all this." Budreau frowned and his mustache twitched nervously. He made an effort to relax, and John thought the President had probably been an impressive man once. "The Freedom Party's slogan is 'Service to the People.' Service to them means consumer goods now. They want strip mining. That's got the miners' support, you can bet. The FP will rape this planet to buy goods from other systems, and to hell with how they're paid for. Runaway inflation will be only one of the problems they'll create."

"They sound ambitious."

"Yes. They even want to introduce internal combustion engine economy. God knows how, there's no support technology here, but there's oil. We'd have to buy all that from off planet, there's no heavy industry here to make engines even if the ecology could absorb them, but that doesn't matter to the FP. They promise cars for everyone. Instant modernization. More food, robotic factories, entertainment . . . in short, paradise and right now."

"Do they mean it, or is that just slogans?"

"I think most of them mean it," Budreau answered. "It's hard to believe, but I think they do."

"Where do they *say* they'll get the money?"

"Soaking the rich, as if there were enough wealthy people here to matter. Total confiscation of everything everyone owns wouldn't pay for all they promise. Those people have no idea of the realities of our situation, and their leaders are ready to blame anything that's wrong on the Progressive Party, CoDominium administrators, anything but admit that what they promise just isn't possible. Some of the party leaders may know better, but they don't admit it if they do."

"I take it that program has gathered support."

"Of course it has," Budreau fumed. "And every BuReloc ship brings thousands more ready to vote the FP line."

Budreau got up from his desk and went to a cabinet on the opposite wall. He took out a bottle of brandy and three glasses and poured, handing them to Calvin and Falkenberg. Then he ignored the sergeant but waited for Falkenberg to lift his glass.

"Cheers." Budreau drained the glass at one gulp. "Some of the oldest families on Hadley have joined the damned Freedom Party. They're worried about the taxes *I've* proposed! The FP won't leave them anything at all, but they still join the opposition in hopes of making deals. You don't look surprised."

"No, sir. It's a story as old as history, and a military man reads history."

Budreau looked up in surprise. "Really?"

"A smart soldier wants to know the causes of wars. Also how to end them. After all, war is the normal state of affairs, isn't it? Peace is the name of the ideal we deduce from the fact that there have been interludes between wars." Before Budreau could answer, Falkenberg said, "No matter. I take it you expect armed resistance immediately after the CD pulls out."

"I hoped to prevent it. Bradford thought you might be able to do something, and I'm gifted at the art of persuasion." The President sighed. "But it seems hopeless. They don't want to compromise. They think they can get a total victory."

"I wouldn't think they'd have much of a record to run on," Falkenberg said.

Budreau laughed. "The FP partisans claim credit for driving the CoDominium out, Colonel."

They laughed together. The CoDominium was leaving because the mines were no longer worth enough to make it pay to govern Hadley. If the mines were as productive as they'd been in the past, no partisans would drive the Marines away.

Budreau nodded as if reading his thoughts. "Well, they have people believing it anyway. There was a campaign of terrorism for years, nothing very serious. It didn't threaten the mine shipments, or the Marines would have put a stop to it. But they have demoralized the capital police. Out in the bush people administer their own justice, but here in Refuge the FP gangs control a lot of the city."

Budreau pointed to a stack of papers on one corner of the desk. "Those are resignations from the force. I don't even know how many police I'll have left when the CD pulls out." Budreau's fist tightened as if he wanted to pound on the desk, but he sat rigidly still. "Pulls out. For years they ran everything, and now they're leaving us to clean up. I'm President by courtesy of the CoDominium. They put me in office, and now they're leaving."

"At least you're in charge," Falkenberg said. "The BuReloc people wanted someone else. Bradford talked them out of it."

"Sure. And it cost us a lot of money. For what? Maybe it would have been better the other way."

"I thought you said their policies would ruin Hadley."

"I did say that. I believe it. But the policy issues came after the split, I think." Budreau was talking to himself as much as to John. "Now they hate us so much they oppose anything we want out of pure spite. And we do the same thing."

"Sounds like CoDominium politics. Russkis and US in the Grand Senate. Just like home." There was no humor in the polite laugh that followed.

Budreau opened a desk drawer and took out a parchment. "I'll keep the agreement, of course. Here's your commission as commander of the constabulary. But I still think you might be better off taking the next ship out. Hadley's problems can't be solved by military consultants."

Sergeant Major Calvin snorted. The sound was almost inaudible, but Falkenberg knew what he was thinking. Budreau shrank from the bald term "mercenary," as if "military consultant" were easier on his conscience. John finished his drink and stood.

"Mr. Bradford wants to see you," Budreau said. "Lieutenant Banners will be outside to show you to his office."

"Thank you, sir." Falkenberg strode from the big room. As he closed the door he saw Budreau going back to the liquor cabinet.

Vice President Ernest Bradford was a small man with a smile that never seemed to fade. He worked at being liked, but it didn't always work. Still, he had gathered a following of dedicated party workers, and he fancied himself an accomplished politician.

When Banners showed Falkenberg into the office, Bradford smiled even more broadly, but he suggested that Banners should take Calvin on a tour of the Palace guardrooms. Falkenberg nodded and let them go.

The Vice President's office was starkly functional. The desks and chairs were made of local woods with an indifferent finish, and a solitary rose in a crystal vase provided the only color. Bradford was dressed in the same manner, shapeless clothing bought from a cheap store.

"Thank God you're here," Bradford said when the door was closed. "But I'm told you only brought ten men. We can't do anything with just ten men! You were supposed to bring over a hundred men loyal to us!" He bounced up excitedly from his chair, then sat again. "Can you do something?"

"There were ten men in the Navy ship with me," Falkenberg said. "When you show me where I'm to train the regiment I'll find the rest of the mercenaries."

Bradford gave him a broad wink and beamed. "Then you did bring more! We'll show them—all of them. We'll win yet. What did you think of Budreau?"

"He seems sincere enough. Worried, of course. I think I would be in his place."

Bradford shook his head. "He can't make up his mind. About anything! He wasn't so bad before, but lately he's had to be forced into making every decision. Why did the Colonial Office pick him? I thought you were going to arrange for me to be President. We gave you enough money."

"One thing at a time," Falkenberg said. "The Undersecretary couldn't justify you to the Minister. We can't get to everyone, you know. It was hard enough for Professor Whitlock to get them to approve Budreau, let alone you. We sweated blood just getting them to let go of having a Freedom Party president."

Bradford's head bobbed up and down like a puppet's. "I knew I could trust you," he said. His smile was warm, but despite all his efforts to be sincere it did not come through. "You have kept your part of the bargain, anyway. And once the CD is gone—"

"We'll have a free hand, of course,"

Bradford smiled again. "You are a very strange man, Colonel Falkenberg. The talk was that you were utterly loyal to the CoDominium. When Dr. Whitlock suggested that you might be available I was astounded."

"I had very little choice," Falkenberg reminded him.

"Yes." Bradford didn't say that Falkenberg had little more now, but it was obvious that he thought it. His smile expanded confidentially. "Well, we have to let Mr. Hamner meet you now. He's the Second Vice President. Then we can go to the Warner estate. I've arranged for your troops to be quartered there, it's what you wanted for a training ground. No one will bother you. You can say your other men are local volunteers."

Falkenberg nodded. "I'll manage. I'm getting rather good at cover stories lately."

"Sure." Bradford beamed again. "By God, we'll win this yet." He touched a button on his desk. "Ask Mr. Hamner to come in, please." He winked at Falkenberg and said, "Can't spend too long alone. Might give someone the idea that we have a conspiracy."

"How does Hamner fit in?" Falkenberg asked.

"Wait until you see him. Budreau trusts him, and he's dangerous. He represents the technology people in the Progressive Party. We can't do without him, but his policies are ridiculous. He wants to turn loose of everything. If he has his way, there won't be any government. And his people take credit for everything—as if technology was all there was to government. He doesn't know the first thing about governing. All the people we have to keep happy, the meetings, he thinks that's all silly, that you can build a party by working like an engineer."

"In other words, he doesn't understand the political realities," Falkenberg said. "Just so. I suppose he has to go, then."

Bradford nodded, smiling again. "Eventually. But we do need his influence with the technicians at the moment. And of course, he knows nothing about any arrangements you and I have made."

"Of course." Falkenberg sat easily and studied maps until the intercom announced that Hamner was outside. He wondered idly if the office was safe to talk in. Bradford was the most likely man to plant devices in other people's offices, but he couldn't be the only one who'd benefit from eavesdropping, and no place could be absolutely safe.

There isn't much I can do if it is, Falkenberg decided. And it's probably clean.

George Hamner was a large man, taller than Falkenberg and even heavier than Sergeant Major Calvin. He had the relaxed movements of a big man, and much of the easy confidence that massive size usually wins. People didn't pick fights with George Hamner. His grip was gentle when they shook hands, but he closed his fist relentlessly, testing Falkenberg carefully. As he felt answering pressure he looked surprised, and the two men stood in silence for a long moment before Hamner relaxed and waved to Bradford.

"So you're our new colonel of constabulary," Hamner said. "Hope you know what you're getting into. I should say I hope you *don't* know. If you know about our problems and take the job anyway, we'll have to wonder if you're sane."

"I keep hearing about how severe Hadley's problems are," Falkenberg said. "If enough of you keep saying it, maybe I'll believe it's hopeless, but right now I don't see it. So we're outnumbered by the Freedom Party people. What kind of weapons do they have to make trouble with?"

Hamner laughed. "Direct sort of guy, aren't you? I like that. There's nothing spectacular about their weapons, just a lot of them. Enough small problems make a big problem, right? But the CD hasn't permitted any big stuff. No tanks or armored cars, hell, there aren't enough cars of any kind to make any difference. No fuel or power distribution net ever built, so no way cars would be useful. We've got a subway, couple of monorails for in-city stuff, and what's left of the railroad . . . you didn't ask for a lecture on transportation, did you?"

"No."

Hamner laughed. "It's my pet worry at the moment. We don't have enough. Let's see, weapons . . ." The big man sprawled into a chair. He hooked one leg over the arm and ran his fingers through thick hair just receding from his large brows. "No military aircraft, hardly any aircraft at all except for a few choppers. No artillery, machine guns, heavy weapons in general. Mostly light-caliber hunting rifles and shotguns. Some police weapons. Military rifles and bayonets, a few, and we have almost all of them. Out in the streets you can find anything, Colonel, and I mean literally anything. Bows and arrows, knives, swords, axes, hammers, you name it."

"He doesn't need to know about obsolete things like that," Bradford said. His voice was heavy with contempt, but he still wore his smile.

"No weapon is ever really obsolete," Falkenberg said. "Not in the hands of a man who'll use it. What about body armor? How good a supply of Nemourlon do you have?"

Hamner looked thoughtful for a second. "There's some body armor in the streets, and the police have some. The Presidential Guard doesn't use the stuff. I can supply you with Nemourlon, but you'll have to make your own armor out of it. Can you do that?"

Falkenberg nodded. "Yes. I brought an excellent technician and some tools. Gentlemen, the situation's about what I expected. I can't see why everyone is so worried. We have a battalion of CD Marines, not the best Marines perhaps, but they're trained soldiers. With the weapons of a light infantry battalion and the training I can give the recruits we'll add to the battalion, I'll undertake to face your forty thousand Freedom Party people. The guerrilla problem will be somewhat more severe, but we control all the food distribution in the city. With ration cards and identity papers it should not be difficult to set up controls."

Hamner laughed. It was a bitter laugh. "You want to tell him, Ernie?"

Bradford looked confused. "Tell him what?"

Hamner laughed again. "Not doing your homework. It's in the morning report from a couple of days ago. The Colonial Office has decided, on the advice of BuReloc, that Hadley does not need any military weapons. The CD Marines will be lucky to keep their rifles and bayonets. All the rest of their gear goes out with the CD ships."

"But this is insane," Bradford protested. He turned to Falkenberg. "Why would they do that?"

Falkenberg shrugged. "Perhaps some Freedom Party manager got to a Colonial Office official. I assume they are not above bribery?"

"Of course not," Bradford said. "We've got to do something!"

"If we can. I suspect it will not be easy." Falkenberg pursed his lips into a tight line. "I hadn't counted on this. It means that if we tighten up control through food rationing and identity documents, we face armed rebellion. How well organized are these FP partisans, anyway?"

"Well organized and well financed," Hamner said. "And I'm not so sure about ration cards being the answer to the guerrilla problem anyway. The CoDominium was able to put up with a lot of sabotage because they weren't interested in anything but the mines, but we can't live with the level of terror we have right now in this city. Some way or other we have to restore order—and justice, for that matter."

"Justice isn't something soldiers ordinarily deal with," Falkenberg said. "Order's another matter. *That* I think we can supply."

"With a few hundred men?" Hamner's voice was incredulous. "But I like your attitude. At least you don't sit around and whine for somebody to help you. Or sit and think and never make up your mind."

"We will see what we can do," Falkenberg said.

"Yeah." Hamner got up and went to the door. "Well, I wanted to meet you, Colonel. Now I have. *I've* got work to do. I'd think Ernie does too, but I don't notice him doing much of it." He didn't look at them again, but went out, leaving the door open.

"You see," Bradford said. He closed the door gently. His smile was knowing. "He is useless. We'll find someone to deal with the technicians as soon as you've got everything else under control."

"He seemed to be right on some points," Falkenberg said. "For example, he knows it won't be easy to get proper police protection established. I saw an example of what goes on in Refuge on the way here, and if it's that bad all over—"

"You'll find a way," Bradford said. He seemed certain. "You can recruit quite a large force, you know. And a lot of the lawlessness is nothing more than teenage street gangs. They're not loyal to anything. Freedom Party, us, the CD, or anything else. They merely want to control the block they live on."

"Sure. But they're hardly the whole problem."

"No. But you'll find a way. And forget Hamner. His whole group is rotten. They're not real Progressives, that's all." His voice was emphatic, and his eyes seemed to shine. Bradford lowered his voice and leaned forward. "Hamner used to be in the Freedom Party, you know. He claims to have broken with them over technology policies, but you can never trust a man like that."

"I see. Fortunately, I don't have to trust him."

Bradford beamed. "Precisely. Now let's get you started. You have a lot of work, and don't forget now, you've already agreed to train some party troops for me."

The estate was large, nearly five kilometers on a side, located in low hills a day's march from the city of Refuge. There was a central house and barns, all made of local wood that resembled oak. The buildings nestled in a wooded bowl in the center of the estate.

"You're sure you won't need anything more?" Lieutenant Banners asked.

"No, thank you," Falkenberg said. "The few men we have with us carry their own gear. We'll have to arrange for food and fuel when the others come, but for now we'll make do."

"All right, sir," Banners said. "I'll go back with Mowrer and leave you the car, then. And you've the animals . . ."

"Yes. Thank you, Lieutenant."

Banners saluted and got into the car. He started to say something else, but Falkenberg had turned away and Banners drove off the estate.

Calvin watched him leave. "That's a curious one," he said. "Reckon he'd like to know more about what we're doing."

Falkenberg's lips twitched into a thin smile. "I expect he would at that. You will see to it that he learns no more than we want him to."

"Aye, aye, sir. Colonel, what was that Mr. Bradford was saying about Party troopers? We going to have many of them?"

"I think so." Falkenberg walked up the wide lawn toward the big ranch house. Captain Fast and several of the others were waiting on the porch, and there was a bottle of whiskey on the table.

Falkenberg poured a drink and tossed it off. "I think we'll have quite a few Progressive Party loyalists here once we start, Calvin. I'm not looking forward to it, but they were inevitable."

"Sir?" Captain Fast had been listening quietly.

Falkenberg gave him a half smile. "Do you really think the governing authorities are going to hand over a monopoly of military force to us?"

"You think they don't trust us."

"Amos, would *you* trust us?"

"No, sir," Captain Fast said. "But we could hope."

"We will not accomplish our mission on hope, Captain. Sergeant Major."

"Sir."

"I have an errand for you later this evening. For the moment, find someone to take me to my quarters and then see about our dinner."

"Sir."

Falkenberg woke to a soft rapping on the door of his room. He opened his eyes and put his hand on the pistol under his pillow, but made no other movement.

The rap came again. "Yes," Falkenberg called softly.

"I'm back, Colonel," Calvin answered.

"Right. Come in." Falkenberg swung his feet out of his bunk and pulled on his boots. He was fully dressed otherwise.

Sergeant Major Calvin came in. He was dressed in the light synthetic leather tunic and trousers of the CD Marine battledress. The total black of a night combat coverall protruded from the war bag slung over his shoulder. He wore a pistol on his belt and a heavy trench knife was slung in a holster on his left breast.

A short wiry man with a thin brown mustache came in with Calvin.

"Glad to see you," Falkenberg said. "Have any trouble?"

"Gang of toughs tried to stir up something as we was coming through the city, Colonel," Calvin replied. He grinned wolfishly. "Didn't last long enough to set any records."

"Anyone hurt?"

"None that couldn't walk away."

"Good. Any problem at the relocation barracks?"

"No, sir," Calvin replied. "They don't guard them places. Anybody wants to get away from BuReloc's charity, they let 'em go. Without ration cards, of course. This was just involuntary colonists, not convicts."

As he took Calvin's report, Falkenberg was inspecting the man who had come in with him. Major Jeremy Savage looked tired and much older than his forty-four years. He was thinner than John remembered him.

"Bad as I've heard?" Falkenberg asked him.

"No picnic," Savage replied in the clipped accents he'd learned when he grew up on Churchill. "Didn't expect it to be. We're here, John Christian."

"Yes, and thank God. Nobody spotted you? The men behave all right?"

"Yes, sir. We were treated no differently from any other involuntary colonists. The men behaved splendidly, and a week or two of hard exercise should get us all back in shape. Sergeant Major tells me the battalion arrived intact."

"Yes. They're still at Marine barracks. That's our weak link, Jeremy. I want them out here where we control who they talk to, and as soon as possible."

"You've got the best ones. I think they'll be all right."

Falkenberg nodded. "But keep your eyes open, Jeremy, and be careful with the men until the CD pulls out. I've hired Dr. Whitlock to check things for us. He hasn't reported in yet, but I assume he's on Hadley."

Savage acknowledged Falkenberg's wave and sat in the room's single chair. He took a glass of whiskey from Calvin with a nod of thanks.

"Going all out hiring experts, eh? He's said to be the best available. . . . My, that's good. They don't have anything to drink on those BuReloc ships."

"When Whitlock reports in we'll have a full staff meeting," Falkenberg said. "Until then, stay with the plan. Bradford is supposed to send the battalion out tomorrow, and soon after that he'll begin collecting volunteers from his party. We're supposed to train them. Of course, they'll all be loyal to Bradford. Not to the Party and certainly not to us."

Savage nodded and held out the glass to Calvin for a refill.

"Now tell me a bit about those toughs you fought on the way here, Sergeant Major," Falkenberg said.

"Street gang, Colonel. Not bad at individual fightin', but no organization. Hardly no match for near a hundred of us."

"Street gang." John pulled his lower lip speculatively, then grinned. "How many of our battalion used to be punks just like them, Sergeant Major?"

"Half anyway, sir. Includin' me."

Falkenberg nodded. "I think it might be a good thing if the Marines got to meet some of those kids, Sergeant Major. Informally, you know."

"Sir!" Calvin's square face beamed with anticipation.

"Now," Falkenberg continued. "Recruits will be our real problem. You can bet some of them will try to get chummy with the troops. They'll want to pump the men about their backgrounds and outfits. And the men will drink, and when they drink they talk. How will you handle that, Top Soldier?"

Calvin looked thoughtful. "Won't be no trick for a while. We'll keep the recruits away from the men except drill instructors, and DIs don't talk to recruits. Once they've passed basic it'll get a bit stickier, but hell, Colonel, troops like to lie about their campaigns. We'll just encourage 'em to fluff it up a bit. The stories'll be so tall nobody'll believe 'em."

"Right. I don't have to tell both of you we're skating on pretty thin ice for a while."

"We'll manage, Colonel." Calvin was positive. He'd been with Falkenberg a long time, and although any man can make mistakes, it was Calvin's experience that Falkenberg would find a way out of any hole they dropped into.

And if they didn't—well, over every CD orderly room door was a sign. It said, "You are Marines in order to die, and the Fleet will send you where you can die." Calvin had walked under that sign to enlist, and thousands of times since.

"That's it, then, Jeremy," Falkenberg said.

"Yes, sir," Savage said crisply. He stood and saluted. "Damned if it doesn't feel good to be doing this again, sir." Years fell away from his face.

"Good to have you back aboard," Falkenberg replied. He stood to return the salute. "And thanks, Jeremy. For everything . . ."

The Marine battalion arrived the next day. They were marched to the camp by regular CD Marine officers, who turned them over to Falkenberg. The captain in charge of the detail wanted to stay around and watch, but Falkenberg found an errand for him and sent Major Savage along to keep him company. An hour later there was no one in the camp but Falkenberg's people.

Two hours later the troops were at work constructing their own base camp.

Falkenberg watched from the porch of the ranch house. "Any problems, Sergeant Major?" he asked.

Calvin fingered the stubble on his square jaw. He shaved twice a day on garrison duty, and at the moment he was wondering if he needed his second. "Nothing a trooper's blast won't cure, Colonel. With your permission I'll draw a few barrels of whiskey tonight and let 'em tie one on before the recruits come in."

"Granted."

"They won't be fit for much before noon tomorrow, but we're on schedule now. The extra work'll be good for 'em."

"How many will run?"

Calvin shrugged. "Maybe none, Colonel. We got enough to keep 'em busy, and they don't know this place very well. Recruits'll be a different story, and once they get in we may have a couple take off."

"Yes. Well, see what you can do. We're going to need every man. You heard President Budreau's assessment of the situation."

"Yes, sir. That'll make the troops happy. Sounds like a good fight comin' up."

"I think you can safely promise the men some hard fighting, Sergeant Major. They'd also better understand that there's no place to go if we don't win this one. No pickups on this tour."

"No pickups on half the missions we've been on, Colonel. I better see Cap'n Fast about the brandy. Join us about midnight, sir? The men would like that."

"I'll be along, Sergeant Major."

Calvin's prediction was wrong: the troops were useless throughout the entire next day. The recruits arrived the day after.

The camp was a flurry of activity. The Marines relearned lessons of basic training. Each maniple of five men cooked for itself, did its own laundry, made its own shelters from woven synthetics and rope, and contributed men for work on the encampment revetments and palisades.

The recruits did the same kind of work under the supervision of Falkenberg's mercenary officers and NCOs. Most of the men who had come with Savage on the BuReloc colony transport were officers, centurions, sergeants, and technicians, while there was an unusual number of monitors and corporals within the Marine battalion. Between the two groups there were enough leaders for an entire regiment.

The recruits learned to sleep in their military great-cloaks, and to live under field conditions with no uniform but synthi-leather battledress and boots. They cooked their own food and constructed their own quarters and depended on no one outside the regiment. After two weeks they were taught to fashion their own body armor from Nemourlon. When it was completed they lived in it, and any man who neglected his duties found his armor weighted with lead. Maniples, squads, and whole sections of recruits and veterans on punishment marches became a common sight after dark.

The volunteers had little time to fraternize with the Marine veterans. Savage and Calvin and the other cadres relentlessly drove them through drills, field problems, combat exercises, and maintenance work. The recruit formations were smaller each day as men were driven to leave the service, but from somewhere there was a steady supply of new troops.

These were all younger men who came in small groups directly to the camp. They would appear before the regimental orderly room at reveille, and often they were accompanied by Marine veterans. There was attrition in their formations as well as among the Party volunteers, but far fewer left the service—and they were eager for combat training.

After six weeks Vice President Bradford visited the camp. He arrived to find the entire regiment in formation, the recruits on one side of a square, the veterans on the other.

Sergeant Major Calvin was reading to the men.

"Today is April 30 on Earth." Calvin's voice boomed out; he had no need for a bullhorn. "It is Camerone Day. On April 30, 1863, Captain Jean Danjou of the Foreign Legion, with two officers and sixty-two legionnaires, faced two thousand Mexicans at the farmhouse of Camerone.

"The battle lasted all day. The legionnaires had no food or water, and their ammunition was low. Captain Danjou was killed. His place was taken by Lieutenant Villain. He also was killed.

"At five in the afternoon all that remained were Lieutenant Clement Maudet and four men. They had one cartridge each. At the command each man fired his last round and charged the enemy with the bayonet.

"There were no survivors."

The troops were silent. Calvin looked at the recruits. They stood at rigid attention in the hot sun. Finally Calvin spoke. "I don't expect none of you to ever get it. Not the likes of you. But maybe one of you'll someday know what Camerone is all about.

"Every man will draw an extra wine ration tonight. Combat veterans will also get a half liter of brandy. Now attention to orders."

Falkenberg took Bradford inside the ranch house. It was now fitted out as the Officers' Mess, and they sat in one corner of the lounge. A steward brought drinks.

"And what was all that for?" Bradford demanded. "These aren't Foreign Legionnaires! You're supposed to be training a planetary constabulary."

"A constabulary that has one hell of a fight on its hands," Falkenberg reminded him. "True, we don't have any continuity with the Legion in this outfit, but you have to remember that our basic cadre are CD Marines. Or were. If we skipped Camerone Day, we'd have a mutiny."

"I suppose you know what you're doing." Bradford sniffed. His face had almost lost the perpetual half smile he wore, but there were still traces of it. "Colonel, I have a complaint from the men we've assigned as officers. My Progressive Party people have been totally segregated from the other troops, and they don't like it. I don't like it."

Falkenberg shrugged. "You chose to commission them before training, Mr. Bradford. That makes them officers by courtesy, but they don't know anything. They would look ridiculous if I mixed them with the veterans, or even the recruits, until they've learned military basics."

"You've got rid of a lot of them, too—"

"Same reason, sir. You have given us a difficult assignment. We're outnumbered and there's no chance of outside support. In a few weeks we'll face forty thousand Freedom Party men, and I won't answer for the consequences if we hamper the troops with incompetent officers."

"All right. I expected that. But it isn't just the officers, Colonel. The Progressive volunteers are being driven out as well. Your training is too hard. Those are loyal men, and loyalty is important here!"

Falkenberg smiled softly. "Agreed. But I'd rather have one battalion of good men I can trust than a regiment of troops who might break under fire. After I've a bare minimum of first-class troops, I'll consider taking on others for garrison duties. Right now the need is for men who can fight."

"And you don't have them yet—those Marines seemed well disciplined."

"In ranks, certainly. But do you really think the CD would let go of reliable troops?"

"Maybe not," Bradford conceded. "Okay. You're the expert. But where the hell are you getting the other recruits? Jailbirds, kids with police records. You keep them while you let my Progressives run!"

"Yes, sir." Falkenberg signaled for another round of drinks. "Mister Vice President—"

"Since when have we become that formal?" Bradford asked. His smile was back.

"Sorry. I thought you were here to read me out."

"No, of course not. But I've got to answer to President Budreau, you know. And Hamner. I've managed to get your activities assigned to my department, but it doesn't mean I can tell the Cabinet to blow it."

"Right," Falkenberg said. "Well, about the recruits. We take what we can get. It takes time to train green men, and if the street warriors stand up better than your party toughs, I can't help it. You can tell the Cabinet that when we've a cadre we can trust, we'll be easier on volunteers. We can even form some kind of part-time militia. But right now the need is for men tough enough to win this fight coming up, and I don't know any better way to do it."

After that Falkenberg found himself summoned to report to the Palace every week. Usually he met only Bradford and Hamner; President Budreau had made it clear that he considered the military force as an evil whose necessity was not established, and only Bradford's insistence kept the regiment supplied.

At one conference Falkenberg met Chief Horgan of the Refuge police.

"The chief's got a complaint, Colonel," President Budreau said.

"Yes, sir?" Falkenberg asked.

"It's those damned Marines," Horgan said. He rubbed the point of his chin. "They're raising hell in the city at night. We've never hauled any of them in because Mr. Bradford wants us to go easy, but it's getting rough."

"What are they doing?" Falkenberg asked.

"You name it. They've taken over a couple of taverns and won't let anybody in without their permission, for one thing. And they have fights with street gangs every night.

"We could live with all that, but they go to other parts of town, too. Lots of them. They go into taverns and drink all night, then say they can't pay. If the owner gets sticky, they wreck the place. . . ."

"And they're gone before your patrols get there," Falkenberg finished for him. "It's an old tradition. They call it System D, and more planning effort goes into that operation than I can ever get them to put out in combat. I'll try to put a stop to System D, anyway."

"It would help. Another thing. Your guys go into the roughest parts of town and start fights whenever they can find anyone to mix with."

"How are they doing?" Falkenberg asked interestedly.

Horgan grinned, then caught himself after a stern look from Budreau. "Pretty well. I understand they've never been beaten. But it raises hell with the citizens, Colonel. And another trick of theirs is driving people crazy! They march through the streets fifty strong at all hours of the night playing bagpipes! Bagpipes in the wee hours, Colonel, can be a frightening thing."

Falkenberg thought he saw a tiny flutter in Horgan's left eye, and the police chief was holding back a wry smile.

"I wanted to ask you about that, Colonel," Second Vice President Hamner said. "This is hardly a Scots outfit, why do they have bagpipes anyway?"

Falkenberg shrugged. "Pipes are standard with many Marine regiments. Since the Russki CD outfits started taking up Cossack customs, the Western bloc regiments adopted their own. After all, the Marines were formed out of a number of old military units. Foreign Legion, Highlanders—a lot of men like the pipes. I'll confess I do myself."

"Sure, but not in my city in the middle of the night," Horgan said.

John grinned openly at the chief of police. "I'll try to keep the pipers off the streets at night. I can imagine they're not good for civilian morale. But as to keeping the Marines in camp, how do I do it? We need every one of them, and they're volunteers. They can get on the CD carrier and ship out when the rest go, and there's not one damned thing we can do about it."

"There's less than a month until they haul down that CoDominium flag," Bradford added with satisfaction. He glanced at the CD banner on its staff outside. Eagle with red shield and black sickle and hammer on its breast; red stars and blue stars around it. Bradford nodded in satisfaction. It wouldn't be long.

That flag meant little to the people of Hadley. On Earth it was enough to cause riots in nationalistic cities in both the US and the Soviet Union, while in other countries it was a symbol of the alliance that kept any other nation from rising above second-class status. To Earth the CoDominium Alliance represented peace at a high price, too high for many.

For Falkenberg it represented nearly thirty years of service ended by court-martial.

Two weeks to go. Then the CoDominium governor would leave, and Hadley would be officially independent. Vice President Bradley visited the camp to speak to the recruits.

He told them of the value of loyalty to the government, and the rewards they would all have as soon as the Progressive Party was officially in power. Better pay, more liberties, and the opportunity for promotion in an expanding army; bonuses and soft duty. His speech was full of promises, and Bradford was quite proud of it.

When he had finished, Falkenberg took the Vice President into a private room in the Officers' Mess and slammed the door.

"Damn you, you don't *ever* make offers to my troops without my permission." John Falkenberg's face was cold with anger.

"I'll do as I please with my army, Colonel," Bradford replied smugly. The little smile on his face was completely without warmth. "Don't get snappy with me, *Colonel* Falkenberg. Without my influence Budreau would dismiss you in an instant."

Then his mood changed, and Bradford took a flask of brandy from his pocket. "Here, Colonel, have a drink." The little smile was replaced with something more genuine. "We have to work together, John. There's too much to do, even with both of us working it won't all get done. Sorry, I'll ask your advice in future, but don't you think the troops should get to know me? I'll be President soon." He looked to Falkenberg for confirmation.

"Yes, sir," John took the flask and held it up for a toast. "To the new president of Hadley. I shouldn't have snapped at you, but don't make offers to troops who haven't proved themselves. If you give men reason to think they're good when they're not, you'll never have an army worth its pay."

"But they've done well in training. You said so."

"Sure, but you don't tell *them* that. Work them until they've nothing more to give, and let them know that's just barely satisfactory. Then one day they'll give you more than they knew they had in them. That's the day you can offer rewards, only by then you won't need to."

Bradford nodded grudging agreement. "If you say so. But I wouldn't have thought—"

"Listen," Falkenberg said.

A party of recruits and their drill masters marched past outside. They were singing and their words came in the open window.

"Double time, heaow!" The song broke off as the men ran across the central parade ground.

Bradford turned away from the window. "That sort of thing is all very well for the jailbirds, Colonel, but I insist on keeping my loyalists as well. In future you will dismiss no Progressive without my approval. Is that understood?"

Falkenberg nodded. He'd seen this coming for some time. "In that case, sir, it might be better to form a separate battalion. I will transfer all of your people into the Fourth Battalion and put them under the officers you've appointed. Will that be satisfactory?"

"If you'll supervise their training, yes."

"Certainly," Falkenberg said.

"Good." Bradford's smile broadened, but it wasn't meant for Falkenberg. "I will also expect you to consult me about any promotions in that battalion. You agree to that, of course."

"Yes, sir. There may be some problems about finding locals to fill the senior NCO slots. You've got potential monitors and corporals, but they've not the experience to be sergeants and centurions."

"You'll find a way, I'm sure," Bradford said carefully. "I have some rather, uh, special duties for the Fourth Battalion, Colonel. I'd prefer it to be entirely staffed by Party loyalists of my choosing. Your men should only be there to supervise training, not as their commanders. Is this agreed?"

"Yes, sir."

Bradford's smile was genuine as he left the camp.

Day after day the troops sweated in the bright blue-tinted sunlight. Riot control, bayonet drill, use of armor in defense and attacks against men with body armor; and more complex exercises as well. There were forced marches under the relentless direction of Major Savage, the harsh shouts of sergeants and centurions, Captain Amos Fast with his tiny swagger stick and biting sarcasm . . . but the number leaving the regiment was smaller now, and there was still a flow of recruits from the Marine's nocturnal expeditions. Falkenberg was able to be more selective in his recruiting.

Each night groups of Marines sneaked past sentries to drink and carouse with the field hands of nearby ranchers, gambled and shouted and paid little attention to their officers. But they always came back, and when Bradford protested about their lack of discipline off duty he would get the same answer. "They don't have to stay here," Falkenberg told him. "How do you suggest I control them? Flogging?"

The constabulary army had a definite split personality. And the Fourth Battalion grew larger each day.

II

George Hamner tried to get home for dinner every night, no matter what it might cost him in night work later. His walled estate just outside the Palace district was originally built by his grandfather with money borrowed from American Express and paid back before it was due; a big comfortable place which cunningly combined local materials and imported luxuries, George was always glad to return there.

It was less than a week until the CoDominium governor departed, one week before complete independence for Hadley. That should be a time of hope, but George Hamner dreaded it. Problems of public order weren't officially part of his Ministry of Technology assignment, but he couldn't ignore them. Already half of Refuge was untouched by government, an area where the police went only in squads and maintenance crews performed their work as quickly as possible under the protection of CD Marines. What was it going to be like when the CD was gone?

Hamner sat in the paneled study watching lengthening shadows in the groves outside make dancing patterns across neatly clipped lawns. The outside walls spoiled the view of Raceway Channel below, and Hamner cursed them, cursed the necessity of walls and a dozen armed men to patrol them, remembering a time as a boy when he'd sat in this room with his father, listening to the great plans for Hadley. A paradise planet, and Lord, Lord, what have we made of it?

An hour's work didn't help. There weren't any solutions, only chains of problems that brought him back to the same place each time. A few years—that's all they needed, but he didn't see how they could get them.

The farms could support the urban population if they could move people out to the agricultural interior and get them working, but they won't leave Refuge. If only they would—if the city's population could be thinned, the power now diverted to food manufacture could be used to build transportation net to keep people in the interior or bring food from there to the city. They could manufacture things needed to make country life pleasant enough that people would be willing to leave Refuge to live there. But there's no way to the first step. The people wouldn't move and the Freedom Party promised they wouldn't have to.

George shook his head, thought about Falkenberg's army. If there were enough soldiers, could they forcibly evacuate part of the city? But there'd be resistance, civil war, slaughter. Hamner laughed bitterly. Not only Budreau, but I can't do it. Bradford would . . . but what then? Besides, there weren't enough soldiers. There was no military answer.

His other problems were of the same kind. He could see that all the government was doing was putting bandages on Hadley's wounds, treating symptoms because there was never enough control over events to treat causes. He picked up an engineering report on the fusion generators.

Spare parts needed . . . how long can we keep things running even at this crazy standoff, he wondered. A few years. After that famine, because the transport net couldn't be built fast enough, and when the generators failed, the city's food supplies would be gone. Sanitation services crippled, too; there would be plague despite the BuReloc inoculations.

He set his slide rule down on the desk, wishing for one of the computers that were common on planets closer to Earth. The Freedom Party leader had one. George had talked to him about the fusion generators only two days before, and it seemed as if the Freedom Party didn't care that the generators wouldn't last forever. The FP leader's attitude was that Earth wouldn't allow famine, that Hadley could use her own helplessness as a weapon against the CoDominium. The concept of real independence from the CD didn't interest him. Hamner thought about that and swore, went back to engineering. He liked problems he could get his hands on and know he'd solved them, not political troubles that kept coming back no matter what he did.

Laura came in with a pack of shouting children. Was it already time for them to go to bed? The four-year-old picked up his father's slide rule, played with it carefully before climbing into his father's lap. George kissed the boy, hugged the others and sent them out, wondering as he did every night what would happen to them. Get out of politics, he told himself. You can't do Hadley any good, and you're not cut out for the game. You'll only get Laura and the kids finished along with yourself. But what happens if we let go, if we can't succeed, another part of his mind asked, and he had no answer to that.

But it doesn't matter . . . you'll get your family killed, and for what? Debts, inadequate pay, temptation after temptation to give in, compromise, look after Number One, swim with the stream until you become somebody you don't even want to know. . . .

"You look worried," Laura said after she'd seen the children to bed. "It's only a few days. . . . What happens George? What really happens when the CoDominium leaves for good? It's going to be bad, isn't it?"

He pulled her to him, feeling her warmth, tried to draw comfort from her nearness and at the same time distract her, but she knew that trick. "Shouldn't we take what we can and go east?" she asked. "We wouldn't have much, but you'd be alive."

"It won't be *that* bad," he told her. He tried to chuckle, as if she'd said something funny, but the sound was hollow. "We've got a planetary constabulary . . . at the worst it should be enough to protect the government. But I am moving all of you into the Palace in a couple of days."

"The Army," she said with plenty of contempt. "Some Army, Georgie. Bradford's volunteers who'd kill you just to make that horrible little man happy—and those Marines! You said yourself they were the scrapings."

"I said it. I wonder if I believe it. There's something strange happening here, Laura. Something I don't understand. I went to see Karantov the other day, thought I'd presume on an old friend to get a little information about this man Falkenberg. Boris wasn't in his office, but one of the junior lieutenants. The kid was green, only been on Hadley a few months. . . . We got into a conversation about what happens after independence. Discussed street fighting, mob suppression, and how I wished we had some reliable Marines instead of the people they were getting there. He looked funny and asked just what did I want, the Grand Admiral's Guard?

"But then Boris came in and I asked what the lieutenant meant, he said the kid was new and didn't know what he was talking about."

"And you think he did?" Laura asked. "But what could he have meant? Stop that!" she added hastily. "You have an appointment."

"It can wait."

"With only a couple of dozen cars on this whole planet and one of them coming for you, you will not keep it waiting while you make love to your wife, George Hamner!" Her eyes flashed, but not with anger. "Besides, I want to know what Boris told you." She danced away from him, and he went back to the desk. "What *do* you think he meant?"

"I don't know . . . but those troops don't look like misfits to me. Not on training exercises. Off duty they drink and shout and they've got the field hands locking their daughters but come morning they muster out on that parade ground like . . . And there's more. The officers. They're not from Hadley, and I don't know who they are!"

"Why don't you ask?"

"I took it up with Budreau, and he gave me a stall about it being in Bradford's ministry, so I asked him and Ernie told me they were Progressive volunteers. I'm not that stupid, Laura. I may not notice everything, but if there were men with military experience in the Party I'd know. So why would Bradford lie?"

Laura looked thoughtful, pulled her lower lip in a gesture so familiar that Hamner hardly noticed it any longer. He'd kidded her about it before they married. . . . "He lies just for practice," she said. "But his wife has been talking about independence, and she seems to think Ernest will be President. Not someday, but soon . . . Why would she think that?"

George shook his head. "Maybe—no, he hasn't the guts for that. Ernie would never oust Budreau. He knows half the party wouldn't stand for it. . . . The technicians would walk out in a second, they can't stand him and he knows it."

"Ernest Bradford has never yet admitted any limitations," Laura reminded him. She glanced back at the clock behind George. "It's getting late and you haven't told me what Boris said about Falkenberg?"

"Said he was a good Marine commander. Started as a Navy man, transferred to Marines became a regimental commander with a good combat record. That's all in the reports we have. . . . I got the scoop on the court-martial. There weren't any slots for promotion. But when a review board passed Falkenberg over for a promotion that the admiral couldn't have given him in the first place, Falkenberg made such a fuss about it that he was dismissed for insubordination."

"Can you trust him to command here?" she asked. "His men may be the only thing keeping you alive. . . ."

"I know. And keeping you alive, and Jimmy, and Christie, and Peter. . . . I asked Boris. He said there's not a better man available. You can't hire CD men from active duty, or even retired officers. . . . Boris says that Falkenberg's really better than anyone we could get anyway. Troops love him, brilliant tactician, experience in troop command and staff work as well. . . . Laura, if he's that good, why did they boot him out? My God, fussing about promotions should be pretty trivial and besides, it's not smart. Falkenberg would have to know it couldn't get him anywhere. None of it. . . ."

The interphone buzzed, and Hamner answered it absently. It was the butler to announce that his car and driver were waiting. "I'll be late, sweetheart. Don't wait up for me. But you might think about . . . I swear that Falkenberg is the key to something. I wish I knew what."

"Do you like him?" Laura asked.

"He isn't a man who tries to be liked."

"I said, do *you* like him."

"Yes. And there's no reason to. I like him, but can I trust him?" As he went out he thought about that. Could he trust Falkenberg? With Laura's life . . . and the kids, for that matter . . . with a whole planet that seemed headed for hell with no way out.

The troops were camped in an orderly square, earth ramparts thrown up around the perimeter, tents in lines that might have been laid with a transit. Equipment was scrubbed and polished, blanket rolls tight, each item in the same place inside the two-man tents . . . yet the men were milling about, shouting, gambling openly in front of the campfires. There were plenty of bottles in evidence even from the outer gates.

"Halt! Who's there?"

Hamner started. He hadn't seen the sentry. This was his first visit to the camp at night, and he was edgy. "Vice President Hamner," he answered.

A strong light played on his face from the opposite side of the car. Two sentries, then, and both invisible until he'd come on them. "Good evening, sir," the first sentry said. "I'll pass the word you're here. Corporal of the Guard, Post Number Five!" The call rang clearly in the night. A few heads around campfires turned toward the gate, then went back to their other activities.

Hamner was escorted across the camp to officers' row. The huts and tent stood across a wide parade ground from the densely packed company streets of the troops, and Hamner saw another set of guards posted around these tents. Falkenberg came out of his hut. "Good evening, sir. What brings you here?"

I'll just bet you'd like to know, Hamner thought. "I have a few things to discuss with you, Colonel. About the organization of the constabulary."

"Certainly." Falkenberg was crisp and he seemed slightly nervous. "Let's go to the Mess, shall we? More comfortable there. Haven't got my quarters made up for visitors."

Or you've got something here I shouldn't see, George thought. . . . God, can I trust him? Can I trust anyone? Falkenberg led the way to a building in the center of officers' row. There were troops milling around the parade ground, most wearing the blue and yellow duty uniforms Falkenberg had designed, but others trotted past in synthileather battledress, carrying heavy packs.

"Punishment detail," Falkenberg commented. "Not as many of those as there used to be."

Sound crashed from the Officers' Mess building, drums and bagpipes, a wild sound of war mingled with shouted laughter. Inside, two dozen men sat at a long table as white-coated stewards moved briskly about with whiskey bottles and glasses. Kilted bandsmen marched around the table with pipes, drummers stood in one corner. The deafening noise stopped as Falkenberg entered, and everyone got to his feet, some unsteadily.

"Carry on," Falkenberg said automatically, but no one did. They eyed Hamner nervously, and at a wave from the mess president at the head of the table the pipers went outside, followed by drummers and several stewards with bottles.

"We'll sit over here, shall we?" the colonel asked. He led Hamner to a small table in one corner. A steward brought a whiskey bottle and two glasses.

George looked at the officers carefully. Most of them were strangers, but he recognized half a dozen Progressives, the highest rank a first lieutenant. Hamner waved at the ones he knew, received brief smiles that seemed almost guilty before they turned back to their companions.

"Yes, sir?" Falkenberg prompted.

"Who are these men?" George demanded. "I know they're not native to Hadley. Where did they come from?"

"CoDominium officers on the beach," Falkenberg answered simply. "Reduction in force. Lots of good men got riffed into early retirement. Some of them heard I was coming here, chose to give up their reserve ranks and come out on the colony ship on the chance I'd hire them. Naturally I jumped at the opportunity to get experienced men at prices we could afford. Vice President Bradford knows all about it."

I'm sure he does, Hamner thought. I wonder what else that little snake knows about. Without his support Falkenberg would be out of here in a minute . . . but then what would we do? "I see. I've been looking at the organization of troops, Colonel. You've kept all the Marines in one battalion with, uh, with these newly hired officers. Then you've got three battalions of locals, but all the Party stalwarts are in the fourth, your second and third are locals but again under your own men."

"Yes, sir?" Falkenberg nodded agreement, gave Hamner a look of puzzlement. Hamner had noticed that particular trick of Falkenberg's before.

And you know my question, George thought. "Why, Colonel? A suspicious man would say you've got your own little army here, with a structure set so that you can take complete control if there's ever a difference of opinion between you and the government."

"A suspicious man might say that," Falkenberg agreed. He lifted one glass of whiskey, waited for George, then drained it. A steward immediately brought freshly filled glasses.

"But a practical man might say something else," Falkenberg continued. "You wouldn't expect me to put green officers in command of those guardhouse troops, would you? Or your good-hearted Progressives in command of green recruits? By Mr. Bradford's orders I've kept the Fourth Battalion as free of my mercenaries as possible, which isn't helping their training any. He seems to have the same complaint as you do, and wants his own Party force, I suspect to control me. Which is silly, Mr. Hamner. You have the purse strings. Without your supplies and money to pay these men, I couldn't hold them an hour."

"Troops have found it easier to rob the paymaster than fight before now," Hamner observed. "Cheers." He drained the glass, then suppressed a cough. The stuff was strong, and he wasn't used to neat whiskey.

Falkenberg shook his head. "I might have expected that remark from Bradford, but not you."

Hamner nodded. Bradford was always suspicious of something. There were times when George wondered if the Vice President were quite sane, but that was absurd. Still, when the pressure was on, Ernie did manage to get on people's nerves, always trying to control everything. Bradford would rather have nothing done than allow action he didn't control.

"Just how am I supposed to organize this coup?" Falkenberg asked. "You can see, I've no more than a handful of men loyal directly to me. The rest are mercenaries, and your locals make up the majority of our forces. Mr. Hamner, you've paid a large price to bring my staff and me to your planet. We're expected shortly to fight impossible odds with nonexistent equipment. If you also insist on your own organization of the forces, I cannot accept the responsibility. . . . If President Budreau so orders, I'll turn command over to anyone he names."

Neatly said, Hamner thought. And predictable too. Who would Budreau name. Bradford, of course, and George trusted Falkenberg more than Ernie. Nothing wrong with Falkenberg's answers, nothing you could put your finger on. . . . "What do you want out of this, Colonel Falkenberg?"

"Money. A little glory, perhaps, although that's not a word not much used outside the military nowadays. A position of responsibility commensurate with my abilities. I've always been a soldier, Mr. Hamner. You do know why I'm no longer in CD service."

"No, I don't." Hamner was calm, but the whiskey was enough to make him bold, even in this camp surrounded by Falkenberg's men. . . . Who is this man we're going to entrust our lives to? For that matter, haven't we already done that? "I don't know at all. It makes no sense for you to have complained about promotion, Colonel, and the admiral wouldn't have let you be dismissed if you hadn't wanted. Why did you have yourself cashiered?"

Falkenberg inspected him closely, his lips tight, gray eyes boring into Hamner. "I suppose you are entitled to an answer. Grand Senator Bronson has sworn to ruin me, Mr. Hamner, for reasons I won't tell you. If I hadn't been dismissed for a trivial charge of technical insubordination, I'd have had to face an endless series of trumped-up charges. This way I'm out with a clean record."

"And that's all there is to it?"

"That's all."

It was plausible. So was everything. And Hamner was sure that the story would check out. Yet—yet the man was lying, for no reason George could imagine. Not lying directly, not refusing to answer, but not telling it all . . . if he only knew the right questions.

The pipers came back in, looked at Falkenberg. "Something more?"

"No."

"Thank you." The colonel nodded to the pipe major, who raised his baton. The pipers marched to the crash of drums, an incredibly marital sound, and the younger officers glanced around, picked up their drinks again. Someone shouted and the party was on again.

The Progressives were drinking with Falkenberg's mercenaries . . . every one of the partisans in the room was one of his own wing. There wasn't one of Bradford's people in the lot. He rose, signaled to a Progressive lieutenant to follow him. "I'll let Farquahar escort me out, Colonel," Hamner said.

"As you please."

The noise followed them outside. "All right, Jamie, what's going on here?" Hamner demanded.

"Going on, sir? Nothing that I know of . . . you mean the party. Ah, we're celebrating the men's graduation from elementary training, tomorrow they start advanced work. Major Savage thought a regimental dining in would help knit the troops together, be good for morale. . . ."

"I do not mean the party." They were at the edge of officer's row now, and Hamner stopped their stroll. Hadley's third moon, the bright one called Klum, cast weird shadows around them. "Maybe I do mean the party. Where are the other officers, Mr. Bradford's people?"

"Ah, they had a field problem that kept them out of camp until late, sir. Mr. Bradford came around about dinnertime and took them with him and took them to the ranch house. He spends a lot of time with them, sir."

"You've been around the Marines, Jamie. Where are the men from? What CD outfits?"

"I really don't know, sir. Colonel Falkenberg has forbidden us to ask. He told the men no matter what their record says before, they start new here. I get the impression that some of them have served with the colonel before. They don't like him, curse him quite openly. But they're afraid of that big sergeant major of his. . . . Calvin has offered to whip any two men in the camp, they choose the rules. None of the Marines would try it. After the first couple of times, none of the recruits would either."

"Not popular." Hamner brushed his hair back from his brows, remembered what Major Karantov had told him. Whiskey buzzed in his head. "Who is popular?"

"Major Savage, sir. The men like him. And Captain Fast, the Marines particularly respect him. He's the colonel's adjutant."

"All right. Look, can this outfit fight? Have we got a chance?" They stood and watched the scenes around the campfires, men drinking, shouting. There was a fist fight in front of one tent, and no officer moved to stop it. "Do you permit that?"

"No—we only stop the men if we officially see something, sir. See, the sergeants have broken up the fight. As to their abilities, really, how would I know? The men are tough, Mr. Hamner, and they obey orders."

Hamner nodded. "All right, Jamie. Go back to your party." He strode to his car. As he was driven away, he knew something was wrong, but still had no idea what.

The stadium had been built to hold 100,000 people. There were at least that many jammed inside, and an equal number swarmed about the market squares and streets adjacent to it. The full CoDominium Marine garrison was on duty to keep order, but they weren't needed. The celebration was boisterous but peaceful, with Freedom Party gangs as anxious to avoid an incident as the Marines on this, the greatest day for Hadley since the planet's discovery.

Hamner and Falkenberg watched from the upper tiers of the stadium. Row after row of plastisteel seats cascaded down from their perch to the central grassy field below. Across from them President Budreau and Governor Flaherty stood in the presidential box surrounded by the blue-uniformed Presidential Guard. Vice-President Bradford, Freedom Party leaders, Progressive officials, officers of the retiring CoDominium government were also there, and George knew what some of them were thinking: Where did Hamner get off to? Bradford would particularly notice his absence, probably thought Hamner was out stirring up rebellion. Lately Bradford had accused George of every kind of disloyalty to the Progressive Party.

To the devil with the little man! George thought. He hated crowds, and the thought of standing there and listening to all those speeches, being polite to the party officials was appalling. When he'd suggested watching from another vantage point, Falkenberg quickly agreed. As George suspected, the soldier disliked civilian ceremonies.

The ritual was almost over. The CD Marine bands had marched through the field, the speeches had been made, presents delivered and accepted. A hundred thousand people had cheered, an awesome sound, frightening in its potential power. Hamner glanced at his watch, and as he did the Marine band broke into a roar of drums. The massed drummers ceased to beat one by one until there was but a single drum roll that went on and on and on, until it too, stopped. The entire stadium waited.

One trumpet, no more. A clear call, plaintive but triumphant, the final salute to the CoDominium banner above the Palace. The notes hung in Hadley's crystal air like something tangible, and slowly, deliberately, the crimson and blue banner floated down from the flagpole as Hadley's blazing gold and green arose.

Across the city uniformed men saluted these flags, one rising, the other setting. The blue uniforms of Hadley saluted with smiles, the red-uniformed Marines with indifference. The CoDominium banner rose and fell across two hundred light-years and seventy worlds in this year of Grace 2079; what difference would one minor planet make?

Hamner glanced at John Falkenberg. The colonel had no eyes for the rising banners of Hadley. His rigid salute was given to the CD flag, and as the last note of the final trumpet salute died away Hamner thought he saw Falkenberg wipe his eyes. The gesture was so startling that George looked again, but there was nothing more to see.

"That's it, then," Falkenberg snapped. His voice was crisp, gruff even. "I suppose we ought to join the party. Can't keep His Nibs waiting."

Hamner nodded. The presidential box connected directly to the Palace, and the officials would arrive at the reception quickly while Falkenberg and Hamner had the entire width of the stadium to traverse. People were streaming out to join the festive crowds outside and it would be impossible to cross it directly. "Let's go this way," George said. He led Falkenberg to the top of the stadium and into a small alcove where he used a key to open an inconspicuous door. "Tunnel system takes us right into the Palace, across and under the stadium," he told Falkenberg. "Not exactly secret, but we don't want the people to know about it because they'd demand we open it to the public. Designed for maintenance crews, mostly." He locked the door behind them, looked around at the wide interior corridor. "Building was designed pretty well, actually."

The grudging tone of admiration wasn't natural to him. If a thing was well done, it was well done . . . but lately he found himself talking more and more that way, especially when the CoDominium was discussed. He resented the whole CD administration, the men who'd dumped the job of governing after creating problems no one could solve.

They wound down stairways, through more passages, up to another set of locked doors, finally emerging into the Palace courtyard. The celebrations were already under way, and it would be a long night; and what after that? Tomorrow the last CD boat would rise, and the CoDominium would be gone. Tomorrow, Hadley would be alone with her problems.

* * *

"Tensh-Hut!" Sergeant Major Calvin's crisp command cut through the babble.

"Please be seated, gentlemen," Falkenberg said. He took his place at the head of the long table in the command room of what had been the central headquarters for the CoDominium Marines. Except for the uniforms and banners there were few changes from what people already called the old days. The officers were seated in the usual places for a regimental staff meeting, maps displayed on the walls behind them, white-coated stewards brought coffee and discretely retired past the sentries outside. The constabulary had occupied the Marine barracks for two days, and the Marines had been there twenty years.

There was another difference from the usual protocol of a council of war. A civilian lounged in the seat reserved for the regimental intelligence officer; his tunic was a riot of colors. He was dressed in current Earth fashions, brilliant cravat and baggy sleeves, long sash took the place of a belt. Hadley's upper classes were only just beginning to acquire such finery. When he spoke it was with the lazy drawl of the American South, not the more clipped accents of Hadley.

"You all know why we're here," Falkenberg told the assembled officers. "Those of you who've served with me before know I don't hold many staff councils, but they are customary among mercenaries. Sergeant Major Calvin will represent the enlisted personnel of the regiment."

There were faint titters. Calvin had been associated with John Falkenberg for eighteen standard years. Presumably they had differences of opinion, but no one could remember one. The idea of the RSM opposing his colonel in the name of the troops was amusing.

Falkenberg's frozen features relaxed slightly, as if he appreciated his own joke. He looked around the room at his officers. They were all men who had come with him, all former Marines. The Progressive officers were on duty elsewhere—and it had taken careful planning by the adjutant to accomplish that.

"Dr. Whitlock, you've been on Hadley sixty-seven days. That's not very long to make a planetary study, but you had access to Fleet data as well. Have you reached any conclusions?"

"Yeah. Not from Fleet's evaluation, Colonel. Can't think why you went to the expense of bringin' me out here. Your intelligence people know their jobs 'bout as well as I know mine." Whitlock leaned back in his seat, relaxed and casual in the midst of the others' military formality, but there was no contempt in his manner. The military had one set of rules, he had another, both probably right for the jobs they did.

"Your conclusions are similar to Fleet's, then," Falkenberg prompted.

"With the limits of analysis, yes, suh. Doubt any competent man *could* reach a different conclusion. This planet's headed for barbarism within a generation." Whitlock produced a cigar from a sleeve pocket, then inspected it carefully. "You want the analysis or just the conclusion?"

There was no sound from the other officers, but Falkenberg knew that some of them were startled. Good training kept them from showing it. He examined each face in turn. Major Savage knew and Captain Fast was too concerned with regimental affairs to care. . . . Calvin knew, of course. Who else? "If you could summarize your efforts briefly, Dr. Whitlock?"

"Simple enough. There's no self-sustaining technology for a population half this size. Without imports the standard of livin's going to fall, and when that happens, 'stead of working, the people here in Refuge will demand the guv'mint do something about it. Guv'mint's in no position to refuse. Not strong enough. Have to divert investment resources into consumer goods. Be a decrease in technological efficiency, fewer goods, more demands, lead to a new cycle of the same. Hard to predict just what comes after that, but it can't be good. Afore long they won't have the technological resources even if they get better organized. Not a new pattern, Colonel. Surprised you didn't take Fleet's word for it."

Falkenberg nodded. "I did, but with something this important I thought I better get an expert. You've met the Freedom Party leaders, Dr. Whitlock. Is there any chance they could, ah, save civilization here?"

Whitlock laughed. It was a long drawn-out laugh, relaxed, totally out of place in a military council. "'Bout as much chance as for a 'gator to turn loose of a hog, Colonel. Even did they want to, what are they goin' to do? Suppose they get a vision, try to change their policies? Somebody'll start a new party along the lines of the one they got now. You *never* going to convince all them people there's things the guv'mint just *cain't* do. They don't want to believe that, and there's always going to be slick talkers willing to say it's all a plot. Now, if the Progressive Party was able to set up along the lines of the communists, *they* might be able to keep something going a while longer."

"Do you think they can?" Major Savage asked.

"Nope. They might have fun tryin'," Whitlock answered. "Problem is the countryside's pretty independent. Not enough support for that kind of thing in the city, either. Eventually it'll happen, but the revolution that gives this country a real powerful guv'mint's going to be one bloody mess, I can tell you. A long drawn-out bloody mess at that."

Whitlock sighed. "No matter where you look, you see problems. City's vulnerable to any sabotage that stops the food plants . . . and you know them fusion generators ain't exactly eternal; I don't give them a lot of time before they slow down the way they're runnin' 'em. This place is operating on its capital, not its income, and pretty soon that's going to be gone." Whitlock stood up, stretched elaborately. "So the answer is I can, but they always come out the same. This place ain't about to be self-sufficient without a lot of blood spilled."

"Could they ask for help from American Express?" The question was from a junior officer near the foot of the table.

"Sure they could," Whitlock drawled. "Wouldn't get it, but they could ask. Son, the Russians aren't going to let a US company like AmEx get hold of a planet and add it to the US sphere, same as the US won't let the commies come in and set up shop. Grand Senate would order a quarantine on this system just like that." The historian snapped his fingers. "Whole purpose of the CoDominium."

"One thing bothers me," Captain Fast said. "You've been assuming that the CD will simply let Hadley revert to barbarism. Won't BuReloc and the Colonial Office come back if things get that desperate?"

"Might, if they was around to do it," Whitlock answered. This time there was a startled gasp from some of the junior officers. "Haven't told them about that, Colonel? Sorry."

"Sir, what does he mean?" the lieutenant asked. "What could happen to the Bureau of Relocation?"

"No budget," Falkenberg answered. "Gentlemen, you've seen the tensions back on Earth. Kaslov's people are gaining influence in the Presidium, Harmon's gang have won some minor elections in the States, and both want to abolish the CD. They've had enough influence to get everyone's appropriations cut to the bone—I shouldn't have to tell you that, you've seen what's happening to the Navy and the civilian agencies get the same.

"Population control has to ship people to worlds closer to Earth whether they can hold them or not. Marginal exploitation ventures like Hadley's mines are to be shut down. This isn't the only planet the CD's abandoning this year—excuse me, granting independence," he added ironically. "No, Hadley can't rely on the CoDominium to help. If this world's to reach takeoff, it's going to have to do it on its own."

"Which Dr. Whitlock says is impossible," Major Savage observed. "John, we've got ourselves into a cleft stick, haven't we?"

"Ah said it was unlikely, not that it was impossible," Whitlock reminded them. "It'll take a guv'mint stronger than anything Hadley's liable to get, and some pretty smart people making the right moves. Or maybe there'll be some luck. Like a good, selective plague. Now that'd do it. Plague to kill about a hundred thousand, leave the right ones . . . course if it killed a lot more'n that, probably wouldn't be enough left to take advantage of the technology. Reckon a plague's not the answer at that."

Falkenberg nodded grimly. "Thank you, Dr. Whitlock. Now, gentlemen, I want battalion commanders and headquarters officers to read Dr. Whitlock's report. Meanwhile, we have other actions. Major Savage will shortly make a report to the Cabinet. I want you to pay attention to that report. Jerry?"

Savage stood, strode briskly to the wall chartboard, uncovered briefing charts. "Gentlemen. The regiment consists of approximately two thousand officers and men. Of these, five hundred are former Marines. Another five hundred, approximately, are Progressive partisans, who are organized under officers appointed by Mr. Bradford. The other thousand are general recruits, including youngsters who want to play soldier. All locals have received basic training comparable to CD Marine ground basic without assault, fleet, or jump schooling. Their performance has been somewhat better than we might expect from a comparable number of Marine recruits in CD service.

"This morning, Mr. Bradford ordered the colonel to remove the last of our officers and noncoms from the Fourth Battalion, and as of this P.M. the Fourth will be totally under the control of the First Vice President, for what purpose he has not informed us."

Falkenberg nodded. "In your estimate, Major, are the troops ready for combat duties?" John sipped his coffee, listened idly. The briefing was rehearsed, and he knew what Savage would answer. The men were trained, but not yet a combat unit. He waited until Savage had completed that part of the presentation. "Recommendations?"

"Recommended that the Second Battalion be integrated with the First, sir. Normal practice is to have one recruit, three privates, and a monitor to each maniple. With equal numbers of new men and veterans we'll have a higher proportion of recruits, of course, but this will give us two battalions of men under our veteran Marines, with Marine privates for leavening. We will thus break up the provisional training organization and set up the regiment with a new permanent structure, First and Second Battalions for combat duties, Third composed of locals with former Marine officers to be held in reserve. The Fourth will not be under our command."

"Your reasons for this organization?" Falkenberg asked.

"Morale, sir. The new troops feel discriminated against. They're under harsher discipline than the former Marines, and they resent it. Putting them in the same maniples with the Marines will stop that."

"You have the new organization plan there, Major?"

"Yes, sir." Savage turned the charts from their wall recess. The administrative structure was a compromise between the present permanent garrison standard of CD Marines and the national army of Churchill, so arranged that all of the key positions had to be held by Falkenberg's mercenaries. The best officers of the Progressive forces were either in the Third or Fourth Battalions, and there were no locals with the proper command experience. . . .

John looked at it carefully, listened to Savage's explanation. It ought to work. It looked very good and there was no sound military reason to question the structure. . . .

He didn't think the President would object. Bradford would be pleased about the Fourth, hardly interested in the other battalions now, although give him time.

When Savage was finished, Falkenberg thanked him and stood up again at the head of the table. "All right. You've heard Major Savage give the briefing, if you have any critiques, let's have them. We want this smooth, without problems from the civilians. Another thing, Sergeant-Major!"

"Sir!"

"As of reveille tomorrow, this entire regiment is under normal discipline. Tell the Forty-second the act's over, we want them back on behavior. From here on recruits and old hands will be treated the same, and the next man who gives me trouble will wish he hadn't been born."

"Sir!" Calvin smiled happily. The last months had been a strain for everyone. Now the old man was taking over again, thank God. The men had lost some of their edge, but he'd soon put it back again. It was time to take off the masks, and Calvin for one was glad of it.

## III

The sound of fifty thousand people shouting in unison can be terrifying. It raises fears at a level below thought, a panic older than the fear of nuclear weapons and the whole panoply of technology, raw naked power, a cauldron of sound. Everyone in the Palace listened to the chanting crowd, and if most of the government officials were able to appear calm, they were afraid nonetheless.

The Cabinet meeting started at dawn, went on until late in the morning, on and on without settling anything. It was getting close to when Vice President Bradford stood at his place at the council table, the thin smile gone, his lips tight in rage. He pointed a trembling finger at George Hamner.

"It's your fault!" Bradford shouted. "Now the technicians have joined in the demand for a new constitution, and you control them. I've always said you were a traitor to the Progressive Party!"

"Gentlemen, please," President Budreau insisted tiredly. "Come now, that sort of language—"

"Traitor?" Hamner demanded. "If your blasted officials would pay a little attention to the technicians, this wouldn't have happened. In three months you've managed to convert the techs from the staunchest supporters of this party into allies of the rebels, despite everything I could do." George made a conscious effort to control his own anger. "You've herded them around the city like cattle, worked them overtime for no increase in pay, and set those damned soldiers of yours on them when they protested. It's worth a man's life to have your constabulary mad at him. I know of cases where your troops have beaten my people to death! And you've got the nerve to call me a traitor! I ought to wring your goddamn neck."

"This isn't getting us anywhere," Budreau protested. There was a roar from the stadium. The Palace seemed to vibrate to the shouts of the constitutional convention. Wearily, Budreau rose to his feet. The others remained sitting, something they wouldn't have done even a month earlier. "We adjourn for half an hour to allow tempers to cool," Budreau insisted. "And I want no more accusations when we convene again."

Bradford left the room with a handful of his closest supporters. Other ministers followed him, afraid not to be seen with the First Vice President. It could be dangerous to oppose him. . . .

Outside in the hall he was joined by Lieutenant Colonel Cordova, commander of the Fourth Battalion of constabulary, a fanatic Bradford supporter. They whispered together until they were out of Hamner's sight.

"Buy you some coffee?" The voice came from behind and startled George. He turned to see Falkenberg.

"Sure. Not that it's going to do any good . . . we're in trouble, Colonel."

"Anything decided?" Falkenberg asked. "It's been a long wait."

"And a useless one. They ought to invite you into the Cabinet meetings, or let you go, there's certainly no reason to keep you waiting in an anteroom while we yell at each other. I've tried to change the policy, but I'm not too popular right now. . . ."

There was another shout from the stadium.

"Whole government's not too popular," Falkenberg observed. "And when that convention gets through. . . ."

"Another thing I tried to stop last week," George told him. "But

Budreau didn't have the guts to stand up to them. So now we've got fifty thousand drifters, with nothing better to do, sitting as an assembly of the people. That ought to produce quite a constitution."

Falkenberg shrugged. He seemed about to say something, changed his mind. They reached the executive dining room, took seats near one wall. Bradford's group had a table across the room from them. All of Bradford's people looked at them suspiciously.

"You'll get tagged as a traitor for sitting with me, Colonel." Hamner laughed, grew serious. "I think I meant that, you know. Bradford's blaming me for our problems with the techs, and between us he's also insisting that you aren't doing enough to restore order in the city."

Falkenberg ordered coffee. "Do I need to explain to you why we haven't?"

"No." George shook his head slowly. "God knows you've been given almost no support the last two months. Impossible orders, never been allowed to do anything decisive . . . I see you've stopped the raids on rebel headquarters."

Falkenberg nodded. "We weren't catching anyone. Too many leaks in the Palace, too often the Fourth Battalion had already muddied the waters. If they'd let us do our job instead of having to ask permission through channels for every operation we undertake, maybe the enemy wouldn't know as much about what we're going to do. I've quit asking."

"You've done pretty well with the railroad."

Falkenberg said, "That's one success, anyway. Things are pretty calm in the country where we're on our own. Odd, isn't it, that the closer we are to the expert supervision of the government, the less effective my men seem to be?"

"But can't you control Cordova's men? They're causing more people to join the Freedom Party than you can count. I can't believe unrestrained brutality is useful."

"Mr. Bradford has removed all command over the Fourth from me," Falkenberg answered. "Expanded it pretty well, too. That battalion's nearly as large as the rest of the regiment."

"He's accused me of being a traitor," Hamner said carefully. "With his own army, he might have something planned. . . ."

Falkenberg smiled grimly. "I wouldn't worry about it too much."

"You wouldn't? Well, I'm scared, Colonel. And I've got my family to think about. I'm plenty scared."

"Would you feel safer if your family were in our regimental barracks?" Falkenberg looked at Hamner critically. "It could be arranged."

"It's about time we had something out," George said. "Yes, I'd feel safer with my wife and children under your protection. But I want you to level with me. Those Marines of yours—those aren't penal battalion men. I've watched them. And those battle banners they've got on the regimental standard . . . they didn't win those in any peanut actions in three months on this planet! Just who are those troops, Colonel?"

John smiled thinly. "Wondering when you'd ask. Why haven't you brought this up with Budreau?"

"I don't know. Trust you more than I do Bradford, maybe . . . if the President dismissed you there'd be nobody able to oppose Ernie. Hadley's going downhill so fast another conspirator more or less can't make any difference anyway. . . . You still haven't answered my question."

"The battle banners are from the Forty-second CD Marine Regiment," Falkenberg answered slowly. "Decommissioned as part of the budget cuts."

"Forty-second." Hamner thought for a second, remembered the files he'd seen on Falkenberg. "Your regiment."

"A battalion of it," John agreed. "Their women are waiting to join them when we get settled. When the Forty-second was decommissioned, the men decided to stay together if they could."

"So you brought not only the officers, but the men as well. What's your game, Colonel? You want something more than just pay for your troops. What is it? I wonder if I shouldn't be more afraid of you than of Bradford."

Falkenberg shrugged. "Decision you have to make, Mr. Hamner. I could give you my word that we mean you no harm, but what would that be worth? I will pledge to take care of your family. If you want us to."

There was another shout from the stadium. Bradford and Lieutenant Colonel Cordova left their table, still talking in low tones. The conversation was animated, with violent gestures, as if Cordova were trying to talk Bradford into something. As they left, Bradford agreed.

George watched them leave the room, then nodded thoughtfully to Falkenberg. "I'll send Laura and the kids over to your headquarters this afternoon. Whatever you've got planned, it's going to have to be quick."

John shook his head slowly. "You seem to think I have some kind of master plan, Mister Vice President. I'm only a soldier in a political situation."

"With Professor Whitlock to advise you," Hamner reminded him. "That cornball stuff doesn't fool me. I looked him up. He's another part of the puzzle I don't understand. Why doesn't he come to the President instead of moving around the city like a ghost? He must have fifty political agents out there." Hamner watched Falkenberg's face closely. "Surprised you with that one, didn't I? I'm not quite so stupid as I look . . . but I can't fit the pieces together. Maybe I ought to use whatever influence I have left to get you out of the picture entirely."

"Go ahead." Falkenberg's smile was cold. "Who watches your wife for you after that? The chief of police? Listen." The stadium roared again, an angry sound that swelled in volume.

"You win." Hamner left the table and walked slowly back to the council room, his head swirling with doubts. One thing stood out clearly: John Christian Falkenberg controlled the only military force on Hadley that could oppose both Bradford's people and the Freedom Party gangsters. He kept that firmly in mind as he turned, went downstairs to the apartment he'd been assigned.

The sooner Laura was in the Marine barracks, the safer he'd feel. . . . Was he sending her to another enemy? But what could Falkenberg use her for? Mercenary or not, the man was an honorable man. Boris Karantov had been emphatic about that. And he hadn't any reason to hate George Hamner. Keep remembering that and try not to remember the rest of it. The crowd screamed again. "POWER TO THE PEOPLE!" George heard and walked faster.

Bradford's grin was back. It was the first thing George noticed as he came into the council chamber. The little man stood at the table with an amused smile.

"Ah, here is our noble Minister of Technology and Second Vice President," Bradford grinned. "Just in time, Mister President, that gang out there is threatening the city. I'm sure you will all be pleased to know that I've taken steps to end the situation. At this moment, Colonel Cordova is arresting the leaders of the opposition. Including, Mister President, the leaders of the Engineers' and Technicians' Association who have joined them. This rebellion will be over within the hour."

Hamner stared at the man. "You fool! You'll have every technician in the city joining the FP! And they control the power plants, our last influence over the crowd. You bloody damned fool!"

Bradford's smirk widened as he spoke with exaggerated politeness. "I thought you'd be pleased, George. And naturally I've sent men to the power plants. Ah, listen."

The crowd outside wasn't chanting anymore. There was a confused babble, then a welling of sound that turned ugly, but nothing coherent. Then a rapid fusillade of shots.

"My God!" President Budreau stared wildly in confusion. "Who are they shooting at? You've started open war?"

"It takes stern measures, Mister President," Bradford said calmly. "Perhaps too stern for you?" He shook his head slightly. "The time has come for harsh measures, Mister President. Hadley cannot be governed by weak-willed men. Our future belongs to those who have the will to grasp it!"

Hamner stood, went to the door. Before he reached it, Bradford called to him. "Please, George," he said pleasantly. "I'm afraid you can't leave just yet. It wouldn't be safe for you. I took the liberty of ordering Colonel Cordova's men to, uh, guard this room while my troops restore order."

An uneasy quiet had settled on the stadium, and they waited for a long minute. Then there were screams and more shots, and the sounds were moving closer, as if they were outside the stadium. Bradford frowned, but no one said anything. They waited for what seemed a lifetime as the firing continued, guns, shouts, screams, sirens and alarms.

The door burst open. Cordova, now wearing the insignia of a full colonel, came in, glanced about wildly. "Mr. Bradford, could you come outside, please?"

"You will make your report to the Cabinet," Budreau ordered. "Now, sir."

Cordova still looked to Bradford, who nodded. "Yes, sir," the young officer said. "As directed by Vice-President Bradford, elements of the Fourth Battalion proceeded to the stadium and arrested some forty leaders of the so-called constitutional convention. Our plan was to enter quickly and take the men out through the presidential box and into the Palace. However, when we attempted to make the arrests we were opposed by armed men, many in the uniforms of household guards. There were not supposed to be any weapons in the stadium, but this was in error. The crowd overpowered my officers and released their prisoners. When we attempted to recover them, we were attacked by the mob and forced to fight our way out of the stadium."

"Good Lord," Budreau sighed.

"The power plants! Did you secure them?" Hamner demanded.

Cordova looked miserable. "No, sir. My men were not admitted. A council of technicians and engineers holds the power plants, and they threaten to destroy them if we attempt entry. We will try to seal them off from outside support, but I don't think that will be possible with only my battalion. In my judgment, we will require the full complement of the constabulary to restore order."

Hamner sat heavily, tried to think. A council of technicians. He'd know most of them, they'd be his friends . . . but did they trust him now? Was this good or bad? At least Bradford didn't control the plants.

"What is the current status outside?" Budreau demanded. They could still hear firing in the streets.

"Uh, there's a mob barricaded in the market, another in the theater across from the Palace, sir. My troops are trying to dislodge them."

"Trying. I take it they weren't able to succeed." Budreau struck his hands together, suddenly rose and went to the anteroom door. "Colonel Falkenberg?" he called.

"Yes, sir?" John entered the room as the President beckoned.

"Colonel, are you familiar with the situation outside?"

"Yes, sir."

"Damn it, man, can you do something?"

"What does the President suggest I do?" Falkenberg looked at the

Cabinet members. "For three months we have attempted to restore order in this city. Even with the cooperation of the technicians we have been unable to do so for reasons which ought to be obvious. Now there is open rebellion and you have alienated one of the most powerful blocs within your party. We no longer control either the power plants or the food processing centers. I repeat, what does the President suggest I do?"

Budreau nodded. "A fair enough criticism."

He was interrupted by Bradford. "Drive that mob! Use those precious troops of yours to fight!"

"Will the President draw up a proclamation of martial law?" Falkenberg asked.

Budreau nodded reluctantly. "I have to."

"Very well," John continued. "But I want to make something very clear. If I am to enforce martial law I must have command of all government forces, including the Fourth Battalion. I will not attempt to restore order when some of the troops are not responsive to my policies."

"No!" Bradford stared wildly at Falkenberg. "I see what you're doing! You're against me, too! You always have been. That's why it was never time to make me President, you're planning to take over this planet! You want to be dictator. Well, you won't get away with it. Cordova, arrest that man!"

Cordova licked his lips and looked at Falkenberg. "Lieutenant Hargreave!" he called. The door to the anteroom opened fully but no one came in. "Hargreave!" Cordova shouted again. He put his hand to his pistol. "You're under arrest, Colonel Falkenberg."

"This is absurd," Budreau shouted. "Colonel Cordova, take your hand off that weapon! I will not have my Cabinet meeting turned into a farce."

Bradford stared intently at the President. "You too, huh? Arrest Mr. Budreau, Colonel Cordova. As for you, Mr. Traitor George Hamner, you'll get what's coming to you. I've got men all through this Palace, I knew I might have to do this."

"What is this, Earnest?" President Budreau asked. He seemed bewildered. "Are you serious?"

"Oh, shut up, old man," Bradford snarled. "I suppose you'll have to be shot as well."

"I think we've heard enough," Falkenberg said carefully. His voice rang through the room, although he hadn't shouted. "And I refuse to be arrested."

"Kill him!" Bradford shouted. He reached under his tunic.

Cordova put his hand back on his pistol. There were shots from the doorway, impossibly loud, filling the room. Hamner's ears rang from the muzzle blast. Bradford spun toward the door, a surprised look on his face, then his eyes glazed and he slid to the floor, the half smile still on his lips. More shots, a crash of automatic weapons, and Cordova was flung against the wall of the council chamber, held there for an incredibly long moment. Bright red blotches spurted across his uniform.

Sergeant Major Calvin came into the room with three Marines in battle dress, leather over bulging body armor, their helmets dull in the bright blue-tinted sunlight streaming from the chamber's windows.

Falkenberg nodded and holstered his pistol. "All secure, Sergeant Major?"

"Sir!"

Falkenberg nodded again. "Like Mr. Bradford said, I took the liberty of securing the corridors, Mister President. Now, sir, if you will issue that proclamation, I'll see to the situation in the streets outside. I believe that Captain Fast has already drawn it up for your signature."

"But—" Budreau's tone was hopeless. "All right. Not that there's much chance." The President sat at the head of the table, still bewildered by the rapid turn of events. Too much had happened, too much to do. The battle sounds outside were louder, and the room was filled with the sharp copper odor of blood.

"You'd better speak to the Presidential Guard," Falkenberg said. "They won't know what to do."

"Aren't you going to use them in the street fight?"

Falkenberg shook his head. "I doubt if they'd fight. They live here in the city, too many friends on both sides. They'll protect the Palace, but they won't be reliable for anything else."

"Have we got a chance?"

"Depends on how good the people we're fighting are. If they've got a commander half as good as I think, we won't win this battle."

⌘⌘⌘

Two hours proved him right. Fierce attacks drove the rioters away from the immediate area of the Palace, but Falkenberg's regiment paid for every yard they gained. Whenever they took out a building, the enemy left it blazing. When the regiment trapped one large group of rebels, Falkenberg was forced to abandon the assault to aid in evacuating a hospital that the enemy torched. In three hours, fires were raging all around the Palace.

There was no one in the council chamber with Budreau and Hamner when Falkenberg came back to report.

"They've got good leaders," John told them. "When they left the stadium, immediately after Cordova's assault, they stormed the police barracks. Took the weapons, distributed them to their allies, and butchered the police. And we're not fighting just the mob out there. We've repeatedly run up against well-armed men in household forces uniform. I'll try again in the morning, but for now, Mister President, we don't hold much more than half a kilometer around the Palace."

The fires burned all night, but there was little fighting. In the morning the regiment sallied out again, moved northward toward the concentration points of the rioters. Within an hour they were heavily engaged against rooftop snipers, barricaded streets, and everywhere burning buildings.

The Fourth Battalion, Bradford's former troops, were decimated in repeated assaults against the barricades. Hamner accompanied the soldiers to Falkenberg's field headquarters, watched the combat operations.

"You're using up those men pretty fast," he said.

"Not by choice," Falkenberg said. "The President has ordered me to break the enemy resistance. That squanders soldiers. I'd as soon use the Fourth Battalion to blunt the fighting edge of the rest of the regiment."

"But we're not getting anywhere."

"No. The opposition's too good, and there are too many of them. We can't get them concentrated for an all-out battle, they simply set fire to part of the city and retreat under cover of the flames." He stopped, listened to a report from a runner, then spoke quietly into a communicator. "Fall back to the Palace."

"You're retreating?" Hamner demanded.

"I have to. I can't hold this thin a perimeter. I've only two battalions—and what's left of the Fourth."

"Where's the Third? The Progressive partisans? My people?"

"Out at the power plants and food centers," Falkenberg answered. "We can't get in without giving the techs time to wreck the place, but we can keep any of the rebels from getting in. The third isn't as well trained as the rest of the regiment—and besides, the techs may trust them."

They walked back through burned-out streets, the sounds of fighting followed them as the regiment retreated. Worried Presidential Guards let them into the palace, swung heavy doors shut behind them.

President Budreau was in his ornate office with Lieutenant Banners. "I was going to send for you," Budreau said. "We can't win this, can we?"

"Not the way it's going."

"That's what I thought. Pull your men back to barracks, Colonel. I'm going to surrender."

"But you can't," George protested. "Everything we've dreamed of. . . . You'll doom Hadley. The Freedom Party can't govern. . . ."

"Precisely. You've seen it too, haven't you? How much governing are we doing? Before it came to an open break, perhaps we had a chance. Not now. Bring your men back to the Palace, Colonel Falkenberg. Or are you going to resist my commands?"

"No, sir. The men are retreating already. They'll be here in a few minutes."

Budreau sighed loudly. "I told you the military answer wouldn't work here, Falkenberg."

"We might have accomplished something in the past months if we'd been given the chance."

"You might. You might not, also. It doesn't matter now. This isn't three months ago. It's not even yesterday. I might have bargained with them then. But it's today, and we've lost. You're not doing much besides burning down the city . . . at least I can spare Hadley that. Banners, go tell the Freedom Party leaders I can't take anymore." The Guard officer saluted and left, his face an unreadable mask.

"So you're resigning," Falkenberg said slowly.

Budreau nodded.

"Have you resigned, sir?" Falkenberg asked deliberately.

"Yes, blast it. Banners has promised to get me out of here. On boat, I can sail up the coast, cut inland to the mines. There'll be a starship come in there sometime. I can get out on it. You'd better come with me, George." He put his face to his hands for a moment, then looked up. "What will you do, Colonel Falkenberg?"

"We'll manage. There are plenty of boats in the harbor. For that matter, the new government will train soldiers."

"The perfect mercenary," Budreau said with contempt. He sighed, then looked around the office. "It's a relief. I don't have to decide things anymore." He stood and his shoulders were no longer stooped. "I'll get the family. You'd better be moving too, George."

"I'll be along, sir. Don't wait for us—as the colonel says, there are plenty of boats." He waited until Budreau had left the office. "All right, what now?"

"Now we do what we came here to do," Falkenberg snapped. "You haven't been sworn in as president yet, and you won't get the chance until I've finished. And there's nobody to accept your resignation, either."

Hamner looked at him carefully. "So you do have an idea. Let's hear it."

"Under Budreau's proclamation of martial law, I am to take whatever actions I deem necessary to restore order in Refuge. That order is valid until a new president rescinds it. And at the moment there's no president."

"But—Budreau's surrendered! The Freedom Party will elect one!"

"Under Hadley's constitution only the Senate and Assembly in joint session can alter the order of succession. They're scattered across the city and their meeting chambers have been burned . . . to play jailhouse lawyer, Mr. Hamner, Budreau doesn't have the authority to appoint a new president. With Bradford dead, you're in charge here—but not until you appear before a magistrate and take the oath of office."

"I see . . . and there aren't any magistrates around. How long do you think you can stay in control here?"

"As long as I have to." Falkenberg turned to an aide. "Corporal, I want Mr. Hamner to stay with me. You're to treat him with respect but he goes nowhere and sees no one without my permission. Understood?"

"Sir!"

"And now what?" Hamner asked.

"And now we wait," John said softly. "But not too long. . . ."

Hamner and Falkenberg sat at the council chamber's table. Communications gear had been spread across one side table, but there was no situation map; Falkenberg had not moved his command post here. When Captain Fast came in periodically to give reports on the combat situation, Falkenberg didn't seem interested; but when Dr. Whitlock's agents came in from time to time, the soldier was attentive. After a long wait the regiment was assembled in the Palace courtyard, while the Presidential Guard still held the Palace entrances, refusing to admit the rioters. The rebels were obviously instructed to leave the guardsmen alone so long as they took no action against them, giving an uneasy truce.

After Banners reported the President's surrender, the crowd began to flow into the stadium, shouting with triumph. Still they waited, Falkenberg with outward calm.

An hour later Dr. Whitlock came to the council room. He looked at Falkenberg and Hamner, then sat easily in the president's chair. "Don't reckon I'll have another chance to sit in the seat of the mighty," he grinned. "It's 'bout like you figured, Colonel. Mob's moved right into the stadium. Nobody wants to be left out now they think they've won. Got some senators out there on the field, fixin' to elect themselves a new president."

"The election won't be valid," Hamner said.

"Naw, suh, but that don't seem to stop 'em none. They figure they've won the right, it seems. And the Guard has already said they're goin' to honor the people's choice." Whitlock smiled ironically.

"How many of my technicians are out there in that mob?" Hamner asked. "They'd listen to me, I know they would."

"Not as many as there used to be," Whitlock replied. "Most of 'em couldn't stomach the burnin' and looting. Still, there's a fair number."

"Can you get them out?" Falkenberg asked.

"Doin' that right now," Whitlock grinned. "Got some of my people goin' round tellin' them they already got Mr. Hamner as president, why they want somebody else? Seems to be working, too. Should have all that's goin' out of there in a half hour or so."

Falkenberg nodded. "Let's speed them on their way, shall we?" He strode to the control wall of the council chamber, opened a panel. "Mr. Hamner, I can't give you orders, but I suggest you make a speech. Say you're going to be president and things are going to be different. Then order them to go home or face charges as rebels."

Hamner nodded. It wasn't much of a speech, and from the roar outside the crowd did not hear much of it anyway. He promised amnesty for anyone who left the stadium and tried to appeal to the Progressives who were caught up in the rebellion. When he put down the microphone, Falkenberg nodded.

"Half an hour, Dr. Whitlock?" he asked.

"About that," the historian agreed.

"Let's go, Mister President." Falkenberg was insistent.

"Where?" Hamner asked.

"To see the end of this. Do you want to watch, or would you rather join your family? You can go anywhere you like except to a magistrate or to someone who might accept your resignation."

"Colonel, this is ridiculous! You can't force me to be president! And I don't understand what's going on."

Falkenberg's smile was grim. "Nor do I want you to. You'll have enough trouble living with yourself anyway. Let's go."

The First and Second Battalions were assembled in the Palace courtyard. The men stood in ranks, synthi-leather battledress stained with dirt and recent street fighting. Their armor bulged under the uniforms of impassive men. Hamner thought they might have been carved from stone.

Falkenberg led the way to the stadium entrance. Lieutenant Banners stood in the doorway.

"Halt," he commanded.

"Really, Lieutenant? Would you fight my troops?" Falkenberg indicated the grim lines behind him.

"No, sir," Banners protested. "But we have barred the doors. The emergency meeting of the Assembly and Senate is electing a new president out there. When he's sworn in, the Guard will be under his command—until then, we can't permit your mercenaries to interfere."

"I have orders from Vice-President Hamner to arrest the leaders of the rebellion, and a valid proclamation of martial law," Falkenberg insisted.

"I'm sorry, sir." Banners seemed to mean it. "Our council of officers has decided that President Budreau's surrender is valid. We intend to honor it."

"I see." Falkenberg withdrew. "Hadn't expected this," he said.

"It would take a week to fight through those guardrooms. . . ." Falkenberg thought for a moment. "Give me your keys!" he snapped at Hamner.

Bewildered, George took them out. Falkenberg examined them, grinned. "There's another way into there, you know. . . . Major Savage! Take G and H Companies of Second Battalion to secure the stadium exits. Place anyone who comes out under arrest. And you'd better dig the men in pretty good, they'll be coming out fighting. But I don't expect them to be well organized."

"Yes, sir. Do we fire on armed men?"

"Without warning, Major. Without warning." Falkenberg turned to the assembled soldiers. "Follow me."

He led them to the tunnel entrance, unlocked the doors. Hamner trailed behind him as they wound down stairways, across, under the field. He could hear the long column of armed men tramp behind him. They moved up stairways on the other side, marching briskly until Hamner was panting, but the men didn't seem to notice. Gravity difference, Hamner thought. And training.

They reached the top, and deployed along the passageways. Falkenberg stationed men at each exit and came back to the center doors. "MOVE OUT!" he commanded.

The doors burst open. The armed troopers moved quickly across the top of the stadium. Most of the mob was below, and a few unarmed men were struck down when they tried to oppose the regiment. Rifle butts swung, then there was a moment of calm. Falkenberg took a speaker from a corporal attendant.

**"ATTENTION. ATTENTION. YOU ARE UNDER ARREST BY**

**THE AUTHORITY OF THE MARTIAL LAW PROCLAMATION OF PRESIDENT BUDREAU. LAY DOWN ALL WEAPONS AND YOU WILL NOT BE HARMED. IF YOU RESIST, YOU WILL BE KILLED."**

Someone below fired at them. Hamner heard the flat snap of the bullet as it rushed past, then the crack of the rifle.

One of the leaders on the field below had a speaker, shouted orders. **"ATTACK THEM! THERE AREN'T MORE THAN A THOUSAND OF THEM, WE'RE THIRTY THOUSAND STRONG. ATTACK, KILL THEM!"** There were more shots. Several of Falkenberg's men fell.

**"PREPARE FOR VOLLEY FIRE!"** Falkenberg called. **"MAKE READY. TAKE AIM. IN VOLLEY, FIRE!"**

Seven hundred rifles crashed as one.

**"FIRE!"** Someone screamed, a long drawn-out cry, a plea without words.

**"FIRE!"**

The line of men clambering up the seats toward them wavered, broke. Men screamed, some pushed back, tried to get behind someone, anywhere but under the unwavering muzzles of the rifles.

**"FIRE!"**

It was like one shot, very loud, lasting far longer than a rifle shot ought to, but impossible to hear individual weapons.

**"THE FORTY-SECOND WILL ADVANCE. FIX BAYONETS. FORWARD, MOVE. FIRE. FIRE AT WILL."**

Now there was a continuous crackle of weapons. The leather-clad lines moved forward, down the stadium seats, inexorably toward the press below on the field.

**"SERGEANT MAJOR!"**

**"SIR!"**

**"MARKSMEN AND EXPERTS FIRE ON ALL ARMED MEN."**

**"SIR!"**

Calvin spoke into his communicator. Two sections fell out of the advancing line, took cover behind seats. They began to fire, carefully but rapidly. Anyone below who raised a weapon died.

Hamner was sick. The screams of the wounded could be heard everywhere.

**"GRENADIERS WILL PREPARE TO THROW."** Falkenberg ordered. **"THROW!"**

A hundred grenades arched out, down into the milling crowds below. Their muffled explosions were masked by the screams of terror. **"IN VOLLEY, FIRE!"**

The regiment advanced, made contact with the mob below. There was a brief struggle. Rifles fired, and bayonets flashed red, the line halted momentarily. Then it moved on, leaving behind a ghastly trail.

Men were jammed at the stadium exits, trampling each other in a scramble to escape. There was a rattle of gunfire from outside.

"You won't even let them out!" he screamed at Falkenberg.

"Not armed. And not to escape." The colonel's face was hard, cold, his eyes narrowed to slits as he peered down at the battle.

"Are you going to kill them all?"

"All who resist."

"But they don't deserve this!" Hamner insisted.

"No one does, George. Sergeant Major!"

"Sir!"

"Half the marksmen may concentrate on the leaders now."

"Sir!" Calvin spoke quietly into his command set. As Hamner watched, the snipers began concentrating their fire on the presidential box across from them. Centurions ran up and down the line of hidden troops, pointing out targets. The marksmen kept up a steady fire.

The leather lines of armored men advanced inexorably. They had almost reached the lower tier of seats. There was less firing now, but the scarlet-painted bayonets could be seen everywhere. A section fell out of the line, moved to guard a tiny number of prisoners at the end of the stadium. The rest of the line moved on.

When the regiment reached ground level, their progress was slower. There was not much opposition, but the sheer mass of people in front of them held the troopers. In some places there were pockets of armed fighting, which held for long moments until flying squads rushed up to reinforce the line.

A company of troopers formed, rushed up a stairway on the opposite side of the stadium, fanned out across the top. Then their rifles leveled, crashed in another terrible series of volleys.

Suddenly it was over. There was no opposition, only screaming crowds, men throwing away weapons to run with their hands in the air, others falling to their knees to beg for quarter. A final volley crashed out, then a deathly quiet fell over the stadium.

But it wasn't quiet, Hamner discovered. The guns were silent, men no longer shouted, but there was sound. Screams of wounded men.

Falkenberg nodded grimly. "Now we can find a magistrate, Mister President. Now."

"I—Oh my God!" Hamner stood at the top of the stadium, held a column to steady his weakened legs. The scene below seemed unreal. There was too much of it, too much blood, rivers of blood, blood cascading down the steps, pouring down stairwells to soak the grassy field below.

"It's over," Falkenberg said gently. "For all of us. The regiment will be leaving as soon as you're properly in command. You shouldn't have any trouble with your power plants. Your technicians will trust you now that Bradford's gone. And without their leaders, the city people won't resist. You can ship as many as necessary out to the interior, disperse them among the loyalists where they won't do you any harm. That amnesty of yours—it's only a suggestion, but I'd keep it."

Hamner turned dazed eyes toward Falkenberg. "Yes. There's been too much slaughter today. . . . Who are you, Falkenberg?"

"A mercenary soldier, Mister President. Nothing more."

"But—who are you working for?"

"That's the question nobody asked before. Grand Admiral Lermontov."

"Lermontov—but you've been drummed out of the CoDominium! You mean that—you were hired by the admiral? As a mercenary?"

Falkenberg nodded coldly. "More or less. The Fleet's a little sick of being used to mess up people's lives without having a chance to—to leave things in working order."

"And now you're leaving?"

"Yes. We couldn't stay here, George. Nobody is going to forget this. You couldn't keep us on and build a government that works. I'll take First and Second Battalions, there's more work for us. The Third will stay here to help you. We put all the married locals, the solid people, in Third and sent it off to the power plants where they wouldn't have to fight." He looked across the stadium, turned back to Hamner.

"Blame it all on us, George. You weren't in command. You can say Bradford ordered the slaughter, killed himself in remorse . . . people will want to believe that. They'll want to think somebody was punished for—for this." He waved expressively. A child was sobbing out there somewhere.

"It had to be done," Falkenberg insisted. "Didn't it? There was no way out, nothing you could do to keep civilization . . . Dr. Whitlock estimated a third of the population would die when things collapsed. Fleet Intelligence put it higher than that. Now you have a chance." Falkenberg was speaking rapidly, and George wondered whom he was trying to convince.

"Move them out," Falkenberg said. "Move them out while they're still dazed . . . you won't need much help for that. We've got the railroad running again, use it fast and ship them out to the farms. It'll be rough with no preparation, but it's a long time until winter—"

Hamner nodded. "I know what to do." He leaned against the column, gathered new strength from the thought. "I've known all along what had to be done. Now we can get to it. We won't thank you for it, but—you've saved a whole world, John."

Falkenberg looked at him grimly, then pointed to the bodies below. "Damn you, don't say that!" he shouted. "I haven't saved anything. All a soldier can do is buy time. . . . I haven't saved Hadley. You have to do that. God help you if you don't."

# THE HOSPITAL VISIT

## by David Gerrold

### Editor's Introduction

When I told my friend, William F. Wu, that I was editing this book, he asked me whether or not I knew that Jerry and Harlan had been good friends. I replied that I did know, having seen them together on several occasions as well as being privy to their generosity toward older science fiction notables in financial trouble, such as H. L. Gold.

Bill then told me he had read about a meeting between the two of them on David Gerrold's web site that I ought to include in the book.

I got in touch with David and he was gracious enough to give me permission to include this fascinating piece about the Ellison/Pournelle friendship.

**HARLAN ELLISON HAD A STROKE** a couple years back and he was recuperating at St. Joseph's hospital in Burbank, just around the corner from Disney. I went over to visit him and we were having one of those old-friend talks that meandered everywhere and nowhere.

Harlan pointed to a laminated page hanging over something on the wall. Behind it was a crucifix. He said he'd told the nurses at St. Joseph's that he found it counterproductive to his recovery, having to see a Jew nailed to the opposite wall. Right there, I knew that his mind was as sharp as ever.

About a half hour in, a nurse came to the room to inform us that Jerry Pournelle and John DeChancie were on their way up. Harlan rolled his eyes, the kind of expression that suggested he was going to have to put up with something unpleasant.

A little context. I'd known both men since 1968. They had known each other longer. And in the half century that the two of them had known each other, they had never been on the same side of an argument. They had often been ferocious opponents—especially on political issues. (And in the sixties, Jerry had said some things that were especially unkind. Not that Harlan hadn't also drawn blood . . . so it was probably a fair fight.) It was no secret that there had been long-lasting enmity between them, possibly mellowed by time, but just as possibly not forgotten.

But here was Jerry and John DeChancie toddling into the room—and it was like a gathering of long-lost friends. I don't remember if Jerry was using his walker or a cane, he always made those things irrelevant, but here's what happened:

Jerry came in and both he and Harlan lit up immediately, truly happy to see each other. They spent the next half hour swapping tales of their military experiences—Jerry's experience was considerable, of course. Harlan's stories were about how he managed to get honorably discharged instead of hauled up before a firing squad. The wealth of information and anecdote was enormous. I wish I had recorded that conversation, because if you didn't know the history, you would have assumed these two were long-lost brothers. I just sat and listened, so did John. You don't often get a first-row seat to watch two giants enjoying each other's company.

Now, Harlan was famous for having fannish Alzheimer's—he can forget everything but the grudge. But in that moment, it was clear to me (and likely John as well) that these two men had earned each other's true respect, and as a result, there was an enormous affection between them. It was probably one of Harlan's better visits while he was in the hospital. After Jerry and John left, I could see that Harlan was emotionally energized.

What that afternoon demonstrated to me was something I had learned many years before—that Jerry Pournelle had one of the biggest hearts of anybody in the SF community. And Harlan as well. It's just not immediately apparent to the casual observer. It's kind of like a slightly overbaked apple pie—you gotta get through the hard crust to find the sweetness. But it's well worth the effort.

They're both gone now and I cannot begin to say how much I will miss them both. They were giants, each in their own way.

# MANUAL OF OPERATIONS

by Jerry Pournelle

❁

## Editor's Introduction

"Manual of Operations" is the only humorous story that Jerry ever wrote. Not that he couldn't be funny, many of his novels are laced with a wry wit, reminiscent of H. Beam Piper. However, no one has ever accused Jerry of writing trifles.

In his *There Will Be War* introduction to "Manual of Operations," Jerry has this to say:

In the bad old days of science fiction, a John W. Campbell editorial was liable to have one result: a dozen writers would turn out stories illustrating the point Mr. Campbell had made. Sometimes these were good stories; sometimes they were bloody awful since they'd been churned out quickly in hopes of catching John W. Campbell with his checkbook open.

There is a sense in which I wrote this story in response to a Campbell editorial: John once said that our attempts to understand truly advanced alien science were likely to be no more successful than a medieval monk's attempts to understand television were a TV to suddenly appear in his cloister. That intrigued me enough to want to write a story on the theme.

On the other hand, it took me five years and the result turned out quite differently from what I had first conceived.

❁ ❁ ❁

**"HARRY LOGAN,** stop messing around with that junk and Get a Job!"

"Yes, dear." It used to be a daily ritual. Now it was three or four times a day. If he'd been musically inclined, Harry could have set it to music: Chorale and concerto for percussion and nagging wife. GET A JOB, BOOM BOOM, YES DEAR, YES DEAR, GET A JOB, BOOM BOOM, YES DEAR, YES DEAR . . .

"I mean it, Harry. I can't pay the grocery bills, there's the doctor, and Shirley's orthodontist, and J.C. Penny's is sending our account to a collection agency. You've got to Do Something Before I Go Out of My Mind!"

"Yes, dear." He didn't raise his eyes from the microscope ($65.00 surplus from Los Angeles City College, a good buy, I *need* it, Ruth. I can use it to make some money.) After a while he heard her retreating footsteps.

This was a preliminary skirmish. She'd be back with the main force attack later. But for now . . . Outside, the rooster squawked loudly and drove a young opossum away from his harem. The dog barked and ran ashamedly to help the scrappy little cock. The dog got a piece bit out of his ear for reward. Harry gratefully left the microscope with its dirty slide and listened to the sounds of peace.

The letters from his last job enquiries were on his desk, but he'd been afraid to tell Ruth. They all said the same thing. *Dear Mr. Logan, we are very pleased that you have considered our company as a possible employer. However, at this time we have no position suitable for a man of your unique talents. Please be assured that we will keep your application on file. . . .*

Harry knew why they didn't want him. He had no college degrees. In fact, he'd never been inside a college in his life, and there were dozens, hundreds, thousands of new engineering graduates looking for work. What chance did a company-trained engineer have for a professional position? He'd tried starting over, but that was no good either: with three published papers on solid-state physics and four patents to his credit he was overqualified to be a technician. No engineer wanted a lab tech who knew more than his boss.

Harry was sure that the constant fights he'd had with company administrators had nothing to do with his rejections. He'd been *right* every time. But somehow, after the companies *learned* that, they still wouldn't hire him back. . . .

His research wasn't going well. His papers were rejected by reputable journals as too far out and he couldn't write down for the popular science magazines. Nothing was going well, and the cold reality gnawed at his guts. What in hell *am* I going to do? he thought. It was a moment of panic.

The house was paid for. (Harry, you should have kept title to that patent, not sold it outright! Harry, you have no business sense at all! But Ruth, I wanted to keep the patent and you said we have to have a house.) At least they couldn't take the house. But he couldn't raise chickens out here in Tujunga Wash anymore. The Los Angeles City Department of Health had sent a complaint. His house was miles from any other habitation, but somehow it was inside the city limits. . . .

He stood for a moment by the desk, then paced nervously to his work bench. The blasted circuit ought to work, why didn't it? But growing integrated circuitry was a tricky thing and he had only the most primitive equipment to work with. He thought about that. Sometimes, Ruth took off her wedding ring to do the dishes, and he could pawn it for—

He didn't finish the thought. There was a knock on the workroom door and Logan looked up in surprise.

"Harry Logan?" the man asked. There was an accent to the voice, probably Canadian. An ordinary man: big framed, going bald, dark hair where he had any. Stocky and tough, but well dressed. "You are Harry Logan, aren't you?"

"Yes," Harry admitted. It was an admission: The last guy who came to see him had been a bill collector and this guy was built like one.

"May I come in?"

"You're already in. I don't think I know you."

"David McClellan. Before we waste each other's time, are you the man who published that far-out thing about the future of solid-state physics in *Tele-Tech*? Also the article speculating about unknown forces?"

"Yes." The unknown forces article had got him fired from his last job. His descriptions of equipment he used in the research made it plain he was working on that problem despite orders to abandon it. Who'd have thought the director would read a thing like that? "Yeah, I wrote them that."

"Good. I've got a consulting job for you."

"What kind of work?" Harry asked. No good to sound too eager. "I'm a little busy, but—"

"You'll be well paid. Besides, you'll learn something new. I guarantee it." The man was assured, and his confidence was infectious. Logan found himself looking forward to whatever McClellan had in mind. What did "well paid" mean? Anything was good pay now. . . .

McClellan was still talking. "But you don't have a working telephone so I couldn't call for an appointment. Glad to find you in."

"Eh—oh, sure." Damn phone company. He'd always paid his bills eventually. . . . "Where is this work?"

"Canada. I want you to come with me right away."

Logan brought up the subject of money. It wasn't any problem. McClellan took a thousand dollars from his wallet and handed it over. It was an expensive wallet, and it looked full.

Ruth exploded as expected. McClellan wouldn't say where they were going. He seemed obsessed with secrecy about the whole project, and Ruth took Harry's inability to be precise for deviousness.

"Off to Canada with some bum you just met! Can't say where! Harry Logan, you're Up To Something! You're going off to drink again, and I won't put up with it, Harry Logan, now you listen to me, you take one drink and you can't stop, I know all about you, you're not going off to any . . ."

She was speechless for the first time in years as Harry shoved a thousand dollars at her. He was tempted to stuff it into her mouth.

"Where in hell are we going?" Harry asked. It seemed a reasonable question. They'd landed in Vancouver, taken a small turbo-prop north to Dawson, and immediately drove away from the airport in a Rover. Now they'd left the highway and started off into rugged hill country. McClellan hadn't said three hundred words since they left Tujunga Wash.

"You'll see soon enough." The country got wilder, pine trees and scrub brush, and they turned off the gravel road onto an unmarked dirt track. Harry had to hold on to keep from being jounced out of his seat. After they were a half mile in, the trail vanished. McClellan swung off into the forest, driving over dried pine needles that blew over their tracks in the stiff breeze.

"Timber country," McClellan said. "Nobody comes here but me. I own it."

They passed weathered No Trespassing signs, forded a small creek, bounced across another rocky flat, and plunged into more thick woods; then they topped a small rise at the edge of a tiny clearing, and there it was.

Logan had a brief impression of a logging camp. Log shack covered with mud. A generator trailer. A camp fire, with a wiry bearded man squatting in front of it. None of these really registered, because the little clearing was dominated by an alien shape.

That was the first thing Harry was sure of. It was wrong. Alien. The color was wrong, the shape was wrong, everything about it. Then he looked for details.

The ship was round, about twenty feet in diameter, and swept up in thickness from infinitesimal at the edges to about seven feet in the center. The cross-section shape was part of the alien impression: it thickened in a series of compound curves not smoothly blended into each other.

It wasn't perfectly round. From above it would have looked like a distorted circle, but there was no conic section that could describe it. One end was elongated and flattened, with its thin edge stretching out another four or five feet, no thicker than a man's hand at the greatest dimension, undulating in waves of curved sections that made no sense.

The whole ship was a dull metallic gray-green, and it shined, not brightly, and not evenly over its surface; when he tried to look closely Harry saw that it was the light pattern that gave an illusion of motion to the hull sections. The ship didn't change shape, but the glowing areas moved in rippling patterns across the surface.

Harry turned to his companion. The man was watching Logan curiously. "A flying saucer," Harry said. "Yours?"

McClellan laughed. "It is now." He raised his voice to shout. "Al, he thinks we're little green men! He asked if it was mine!"

The bearded man laughed with them as he came to the Rover. "I'm Al Parish, Mr. Logan." Parrish held out a lumberjack's hand and crushed Harry's. "Do we look like we could build that thing?"

"No. All right, what's the story?"

"Come sit by the fire and have a drink," McClellan answered. "We're going to tell you."

David McClellan owned timber lands. He'd inherited them and was happy to live off the income. He also liked to hike in his woods. "And one day—there it was," he finished.

"But—who brought it here? What about the crew?"

McClellan shrugged. "Nothing. It was like you see it here. And there's no strange bones around, nothing here at all. Maybe the crew got killed by rattlers and dragged off by scavengers. Maybe anything, but they're gone. After I poked around for a week I went and got Al."

"I'm an engineer," Parrish added. "Not much of one, maybe, but the only engineer Dave knew. And this thing is driving me crazy. When I talked to the professors at the university about some of the effects I got they told me I'd been drinking. Nothing like that could ever work. So I remembered the articles you wrote and Dave went to get you."

"Thanks," Logan said. He meant it. "But aren't you going to tell the government?"

"Hell no!" McClellan exploded. "They'd thank us and never let us near it again." He spat into the fire. "I want that ship, Logan. It's mine."

Harry could understand that. He'd had his problems with administrators. He didn't care if the government never found out about it. "You think it uses advanced solid-state devices, huh?"

"Has to be something like that," Parrish answered. "I can't even find the power source. It's got one, you see things work, but no power. No wires, nothing, just blocks of glop. Lots of those, but I can't see what they connect to or even how they connect." Al poured an enormous mug of coffee, drank half, and filled it to the top with Christian Brothers brandy. Harry looked at it hungrily, but he knew better. Ruth was right more often than he wanted to admit.

"Near as I can figure," Parrish said, "this thing operates with some force nobody on Earth ever heard of. And you wrote about that, and about the future of solid-state work—hell, at least you'll admit it's possible for the ship to work!"

"Can I look at it?"

"Yeah." McClellan seemed reluctant. "But be careful. We don't know what does which to what. You might put us out in the orbit of Saturn."

It seemed as strange inside as out. The entrance was two doors four feet high with a two foot space between them, an obvious airlock that a man might just barely have crammed himself into. Both sliding doors were open, and somebody had wedged them into their recesses with pine logs.

"Haven't been able to close this ship up," Parrish explained, "but I didn't want to take any chances. Be hell to be trapped in here."

The inside was one big chamber about the shape of the outside of the ship. Three chairs which would have been perfect for small human children were bolted to the steel-gray deck. The chairs swiveled and were equidistant around a circular console in the center of the ship. The console had a shelf two feet off the floor and a sloping panel inboard of that rose nearly to the top of the cabin. The panel was a jumble of translucent plates, many of them marked with squiggles that might have been Arabic but Logan was sure it wasn't.

"Near as I can figure, the panels above the console are some kind of screens," Parrish told him. "But there ain't nothing behind them, so I don't know. Course, they might be kids' greasepaint boards for all I know."

"Kids?"

"Sure. Whole thing could be a toy. Look at the size. Like a doll house. Admit it isn't likely, but then the ship isn't likely either."

"That's for sure." Harry was just able to stand in the space next to the console. Everywhere else the ceiling was too low and he had to crouch.

Parrish showed him around the ship. Under one chair was a gizmo with an air scoop sticking out of a solid box to a tank, and a steady stream of air flowed from the tank.

"What kind of air does it make?" Logan asked.

"About like ours, only feel. Hot, and wet as hell. Little more oxygen too."

"What else works?"

"Funny about that," Parrish said. "Sometimes lights flash. Sometimes we hear noises. Nothing predictable, and no way to control any of it. Look, there's not even controls to work, no knobs or switches. Least, nothing we can recognize as a control," he added thoughtfully. "Maybe it's like somebody in the Middle Ages finding a radio—he'd never know what switches and knobs were."

They went back outside, although Logan wanted to remain in the ship. The others persuaded him; he'd have plenty of time to look at it, and it gave them the creeps in the dark. Before they left Parrish lifted a deck plate. The thin gray metal section came away easily to reveal a mass of brightly colored rectangular shapes varying in size from larger than an attaché case to smaller than a matchbox. The blocks fitted together perfectly and couldn't be pulled out, but when Parrish touched one corner with a steel screwdriver they popped out easily. There weren't any connections Harry Logan could see; the blocks were of uniform texture, like hardened epoxy. When replaced they fitted together again like a parquet floor, and couldn't be removed by force.

"See what I mean about advanced solid state?" McClellan asked. They sat around the campfire and ate shish kabob while Parrish told what he had tried.

He had used every detection device he could think of with no result whatsoever. Oscilloscope, voltmeter, electroscope, they all gave the same result. "That ship's electromagnetically dead," Parrish said. "It's all at ground potential. Except for one thing, that flat surface dead aft—well, I think it's aft, but what the hell, there being no windows or anything, how would I know? Anyway, that flat place is a south pole. Damn strong one, I had to use the Rover to pull my magnet off it. But it only attracts north poles, repels south ones, and has no effect on nonmagnetized iron. It's directional, and there isn't a north pole on the ship. How's that grab you?"

"A monopole?" Harry asked. "Could it be the drive?"

"Damned if I know. I don't think it's strong enough to lift the ship. For that matter, nothing I think of can lift that ship."

"What do you mean?"

Parrish shrugged and pulled another chunk of steak off the skewer. "It's heavy. Or it's rooted in place, take your choice. Tried jacking it up and broke the Rover's jack. Got a big fifty-ton hydraulic job and managed to push the jack down into the ground. That ship doesn't lift. It's enough to drive me crazy."

"Yeah." Logan stared into the campfire.

Parrish took the dirty dishes and put them in a bucket to soak. "Wash up in the morning. Now for something I've been waiting for since we found that thing," he said. He went to the Rover and got out a case of brandy. "Didn't have but a couple of bottles to last me and had to stay sober while you were gone . . . after playing with that thing, I want to get drunk." He looked at the brandy with affection. "Have a drink, Harry Logan. You too, McClellan, you old stick."

Why not? Harry thought. One drink wouldn't hurt. Might open up his subconscious. Parrish had tried every test Harry could think of, maybe something would come to him. One drink.

By midnight they were all singing. At one in the morning, McClellan was making speeches denouncing the government, which he suspected of wanting to take his ship for income taxes. By two they went over to be sure the ship was still there.

They squeezed into the cabin, and Harry was just able to sit in one of the chairs. The others were too big. It was dark, and Harry couldn't see a thing. "Wish there was some light."

The lights came on, a soft glow from the walls with no bright spots.

"What the hell did you do?" McClellan demanded.

"I thought at it," Logan answered. "Shee, it's simple, you think at it and she does what you want. Watch." He thought at the screens. A globe sprang into view on the panel above him. It was a holograph somehow projected into a piece of plastic a half inch thick.

McClellan and Parrish crowded against Logan's chair. "But how could it work?" Parrish asked.

"Who cares?" Harry answered thickly. "Let's get her moving!" He shouted at the ship. "Lift off!"

Nothing happened.

Logan made a face, then formed a mental picture of the ship rising from the ground.

Harry didn't feel a thing. McClellan and Parrish shouted something. A cold wind blew on his neck and Harry looked around.

The cabin was empty, the wedged doors gaping behind him, and through them he saw the lights of a small town rapidly falling away below. "Jesus Christ!" he shouted. A bearded face appeared on the screen.

"I've got to get down! Take me down!" He thought of descending. The ship plummeted. "Gently." He pictured that. The rapid descent slowed.

He tried to think of places to take the ship. Crazy thoughts flashed through his mind: the Alps, and they appeared on the screen above. Taj Mahal. New York City. Each time, the screen pictured it, and the ship seemed to turn.

Parrish and McClellan. What had happened to them? The screen showed nothing. Harry tried again: What happened if you fell out? The screen showed something—not really a man, but humanoid—falling through the doors and being gently lowered to the ground below. The ship still whipped around, and the ground he could see through the doors whirled, but Harry felt no motion at all. He tried to stand and was slammed back down into the chair with horrible force, and he almost passed out.

Where to go? The ship could take him anywhere . . . the Moon, the planets . . . a picture of an airless world pitted with craters formed on the screen. Mars! She'd take him to Mars! First man there . . .

Harry choked for breath. Anoxia. The word swam somewhere in his mind, but he didn't care. His ship! It could do anything! Harry Logan was the most powerful man in the world! They'd have to listen to him now. . . .

The screens faded, everything was getting gray, but Harry didn't care. It was wonderful up here, and Harry Logan was master of the world. He could make them . . . he could . . .

The Pentagon. The enormous building formed on the screen as Harry thought of it. That was the place to go. Take the ship to the Pentagon and make the United States listen to Harry Logan. All the world's problems were so simple once you saw them right. And those companies who'd fired him, they'd be sorry. But Harry Logan wouldn't use his ship for revenge. He'd bring peace and happiness to the world. Pentagon, that's the ticket. Right into the little courtyard in the middle of the hollow Pentagon, right there in the five-sided funny farm, Harry Logan would set up his throne. . . .

He didn't know how long it took but he was there. Thickset windows pierced dirty granite walls all around him. The ship rested on trampled grass. Logan grinned and tried to stand up again. It was all right. The ship waited obediently. Harry went to the hatchway and took the logs out. He needed sleep, and he didn't want anyone messing with his ship while he got it. The inner log came out easily, but the ship had tried to close the outer door and the log was jammed in good. Harry had to climb out to get a grip on it. He tugged hard, and the log came away and fell on top of him.

Harry lay on the grass and looked up at his ship. He smiled, thought the door closed, took a deep breath—and passed out.

He was in a windowless room and bright lights glared in his eyes. He'd never had such a horrible hangover in his life. God, that was a bad one, he'd dreamed about flying saucers and . . . Harry sat bolt upright.

"Now, now," a soft voice told him. Strong hands pushed him down with a rustle of starched linen.

When he tried to turn his head, a strange thing happened. His head turned but his brain didn't. Then the brain would snap around with a horrible shock and an audible twang. His eyes wouldn't focus, but there were blurs in the room, a flurry of activity, bright lights, noise. Horrors upon horrors.

"Do you speak English?" someone kept demanding. What the hell did they think he spoke? When he didn't answer, they said other weird things. "*Parlez-vous Francaise? Sprechen Sie Deutsch*?" And growls that Harry wouldn't have believed a human throat could utter. Had the saucer taken him to its home planet? It wasn't a dream, there *had* been a saucer. . . .

"*Hing-song yin kuo* . . ." "Sir, he doesn't respond to . . ." "If you'd get out of the way, Professor . . ." Everyone spoke at once.

"Damn it, say something!" an authoritative voice demanded.

"Hello," Harry replied. He hadn't thought anything could be so loud. Was that horrible noise just Harry Logan trying to talk? "Where am I?"

"You're in the emergency detention—uh, in a guest room in the Pentagon. Do you know what the Pentagon is?" the voice asked him. It seemed to be trying to be friendly and didn't know how. A polite crocodile voice.

Any damn fool knows what the Pentagon is, Harry thought. It hurt too much to answer. Instead, he groaned.

"He seems hurt," another voice said quietly. "Not knowing . . . I mean, General, if it weren't for that *thing* out there I'd say he was a normal human with no detectable injury, but . . ."

"Hell, he's *got* to talk. Fast," the general barked. "You. Sir. Where are you from?"

"Tujunga," Harry tried to say. It didn't come out very well.

"Where's that?"

"Sounds Spanish . . ." "I never heard of any such place . . ."

"*Habla usted Español—*"

One brittle-dry loud lecture hall voice cut through the renewed babble. "Perhaps it means 'Earth' in his language. Most peoples have . . ."

"Crap." The general got shocked silence. "You can spare me the goddam lectures. And since he seems to understand English, we won't need all you goddam civilians. Sergeant, clear this room."

"Yes, sir." There was more commotion, but Harry wasn't interested. Didn't they understand? He needed to die.

"Do you want anything?" the general asked.

Harry opened one eye with an effort. He saw a blue uniform, three stars on the shoulders. Behind the Air Force lieutenant general were two air police with automatic rifles. A doctor in a white coat twisted his hands together. There was no one else in the room, which was bigger than Harry had thought it would be.

"Water," Harry croaked. The doctor moved around and came back with a plastic glass and a drinking straw. Harry gulped it gratefully. "Aspirin. And a double shot of brandy."

The general looked at him closely. "Aspirin? Brandy?" There was a gleam of triumph on the craggy face. "As I thought. There's your goddam alien, doctor. An ordinary Earthman with a hangover."

"A hangover and a flying saucer in the Pentagon courtyard," the doctor reminded him. "Really, General Bannister, it would be better to leave him alone for a while. There might be something really wrong with him."

"Yeah, there might. But we haven't got long. I haven't, anyway." He got a crafty look. "Doc, get him in shape and send him to me as quick as you can. I've got to talk to him before the Navy finds him."

"Yes, sir." There was more activity, and Harry was left in the room with the doctor. He gulped aspirin gratefully and asked again for brandy, but nobody brought any.

The hospital gown flapped. The sandal-slippers kept falling off his feet. Harry had never felt more undignified in his life as the air policemen ushered him into the office.

The room overlooked the Pentagon courtyard. Harry's saucer was out there, its unlikely shape gleaming dully, light patterns rippling over the hull. Swarms of uniforms bustled around it, cheered on by more uniforms with gold and silver braid on their hats.

General Bannister sat behind a battered mahogany desk that looked like something out of the twenties. Actually it was out of the twenties, since this wasn't a general's office. The guards pushed Harry into an oak and leather swivel chair.

"All right," Bannister said. "Let's make this quick. Tell me about *that.*" He jerked a thumb over his shoulder but refused to turn to look.

"Why are there guards pulling me around? What have I done?" Harry asked. "And where are my *clothes* . . . ?"

"Cut the crap," Bannister said. "You were found unconscious in the Pentagon courtyard in the dead of night. You and *that.* Now where'd you come from, and no shit about Mars. Jayzeus, man, you've got the whole government out of its mind. You bring *that*"—the general still carefully avoided looking out the window—"into Washington without being detected and set it down in the Pentagon courtyard! You've got some explaining to do, son."

"Yeah." Oh Christ, what do I say? Why *did* I come here? "Where do I start?"

"With who you are and where *it* came from."

"My name's Harry, and I don't know where it came from."

"But you can operate it." It wasn't a question. "How?"

"I don't know that either. I don't remember." He thought about it. The machine had done what he thought at it—he tried. He sent out a picture of the ship lifting from the ground. Nothing happened.

Bannister inspected his fingernails as he fought for self-control. "What do you want, Harry?" he asked reasonably. The pleasant tone obviously cost him.

Good question, Harry thought. What did he want? The hangover to go away. Peace and quiet. Money. Hey. . . .

The door burst open. A Navy admiral and a hard-eyed civilian stamped in, followed by so many people they couldn't all fit in the room. There were loud voices in the corridor.

"All right, Bannister, we found you," the admiral growled. "Tried to hide him, didn't you? Just because you were working late last night doesn't mean you own that ship!"

"It flies," Bannister protested. "That makes it Air Force."

"The Navy flies too," the admiral said.

"You have both missed the point," the civilian interrupted. He had a voice like a corpse, flat, atonal, and he spoke so softly that you'd think you couldn't hear him, but he was heard. When he spoke, everyone in the room was silent. "That object is obviously of foreign make. Therefore it belongs to us. Not to the services."

"Crap!" General Bannister exploded. "Horse puckey!" shouted the admiral. Both faced the civilian with determined looks. "What makes you think it's foreign?" Bannister demanded.

"It employs technology well beyond that of any known science. We cannot open the doors. We cannot chip away any of the hull for analysis, or understand the monopole effect it exhibits. Thus I conclude it was not constructed on Earth, and it is therefore foreign." There was no triumph in the voice; it merely stated facts, coldly, with precision.

"Yeah, I thought of that," Bannister growled. "That makes it outer space. And *that*'s Air Force."

"Navy too," the admiral said.

"What about NASA?" an Air Force captain asked.

Bannister and the admiral both swiveled toward the junior man. "Get him out of here!" the general yelled. "Fuck off!" the admiral added.

"Outer space is nevertheless foreign," the corpse voice said. "Thus I will have to ask you gentlemen to leave the room, or to release this man to me. Come along, sir," he told Harry.

"I'll be damned," Bannister growled. "Sergeant, block that door!"

"Get my Marines!" the admiral snapped.

Harry tried to shrink down into the seat. What had he got himself into? The military people were bad enough, but that civilian—CIA?—terrified him. Harry could imagine being taken into a windowless room and staying there until he had a long beard. Did the CIA operate that way? Logan didn't know, but that man looked like *he* did.

"Stop it!" Harry yelled. Everyone turned to face him. Even the civilian. "I don't belong to any of you! Neither does my ship! It's mine, and I'll decide who I talk to about it." He willed the ship to come to life but nothing happened. Nothing, and he *needed* it. . . .

Did he have to be in the seat? No, the doors had closed last night. . . .

"Stick with us, Harry. We'll take care of you," General Bannister said soothingly. The admiral moved into place with him, a solid show of military strength. The civilian stared at them coldly.

"Sure," said Harry. "I'm with you, General. You asked me what I want. I want some coffee. A pot of coffee and a bottle of brandy." Harry held his aching head in both hands. "A *big* bottle of brandy, you understand."

"Get the coffee." "Brandy?" "He's nuts." "A wino." "So he's a drunk, what's that?" They all talked at once.

"Will you get me what I asked for?" Harry looked at Bannister.

"Brandy?"

"Yes." Harry tried to look like a drunk in need of a shot. It wasn't hard. He *was* a drunk in need of a shot.

"And you'll tell me how . . .?"

"No brandy, no talkee."

Bannister nodded. "Sergeant, get that man what he wants. And move."

"But sir, in the Pentagon . . ."

"Goddammit, the Secretary of the Navy keeps brandy," the admiral said. "Chief, get up there and scrounge me some."

A minute later a Marine came in with a bottle of Courvoisier. The admiral muttered, "Now we have to wait for the goddam coffee."

Harry felt great. He couldn't remember a time when he'd felt better. He drained the last of his fourth cup and looked at the assembly of people, uniformed and civilian. The coffee had brought him fully awake, and there was a warm feeling inside him. The office was still jammed, and although somebody had quieted those out in the corridor Logan knew they were still there. No way out.

"Very well, sir," the cold-eyed civilian said. "You've had your drink. Now perhaps you'll be good enough to give us some explanations?"

"Sure. Just take me to the ship."

The civilian laughed politely. It wasn't a pleasant sound. "Surely you're not so drunk as that. In any event I assure you we aren't."

"Yeah." Harry stood with an effort. It was harder to walk to the window than he'd thought it would be. Shouldn't have had the last one, he thought. But I feel so damn good! Just who do these jokers think they are?

The window was closed and it wasn't obvious how to open it. Maybe it didn't open at all. Harry gulped hard, stood back from the window, and called his ship.

There was a crash and the saucer protruded several feet into the office. Two burly Marines, rifles at ready, leaped in front of their admiral with a do-or-die look. An air policeman ran screaming out into the corridor. General Bannister put his hand on his pistol.

Harry had time to see that the wreckage of the wall had not come plummeting down, but fell, *slowly,* to the floor. The saucer waited for him.

It was faced the wrong way. He couldn't see the airlock at all. And while the Marines menaced the ship with their rifles, the civilian sighed, took out a pair of handcuffs, and shouldered his way toward Harry.

Time to go, Harry decided. But how? There was only one way. He leaped at the ship, fell onto the flat part astern, and thought it away from the Pentagon. There was a sudden rush, and Harry was a thousand feet above a toy city of Washington. He looked down, gulped hard, gulped again, but it did no good. He lost the contents of his stomach. Adrenalin flowed. To his horror, Harry was getting cold sober!

BALTIMORE SUN:

FREAK ROBBERY OF
LIQUOR STORE
MANIAC BATTERS DOWN
WALLS TO STEAL BOOZE!

VANCOUVER SUN:

RCMP IN CONFUSION
DAWSON TIMBER HEIR
DEMANDS ACTION
AMERICAN ENGINEER
ACCUSED OF SAUCER
THEFT

Dawson: Wealthy timber heir David McClellan insisted he will take his case to Ottawa if the Royal Canadian Mounted Police will not give him satisfaction. McClellan, exhausted from a trek through the northern bush country, could not be reached for comment, but it is reliably reported that he has asked the Mounties to track down and recover a stolen flying saucer.

TOPEKA STAR:

POLICE HOLD
ROBBERY SUSPECT
REPEAT OF BALTIMORE
LIQUOR STORE BURGLARY
SUSPECT HELD—PLOT
SUSPECTED

Topeka, Kansas: Police are holding George Herndon, liquor store manager, who was found with the contents of the store's cash register in a park near Radcliffe's Flask and Bottle. Herndon, 29, was employed as the chief clerk and manager in the store, and was found dead drunk two blocks from the wrecked building. Herndon told police a wild story of a flying saucer which battered down the rear wall of the store, and explained that he had rescued the night's receipts from the invading saucer.

A prize ten-liter flask of Napoleon brandy was also taken and has not been recovered. Store owners say the rare brandy is almost two hundred years old.

LOS ANGELES TIMES:

BEL AIR MILLIONAIRE
ESCAPES DEATH
ONE-IN-A-MILLION
ACCIDENT

Los Angeles: Millionaire playboy Larry Van Cott was nearly killed today when an empty ten-liter brandy bottle fell onto his patio from a great height. Van Cott was in the swimming pool only a yard from the point of impact, and was cut by glass flying from the over-sized bottle which totally shattered. FAA officials are investigating.

"Harry Logan, stop messing around with that junk and Get A Job! And no more of these mysterious trips either! You came home drunk!"

"Yes, dear." Couldn't she leave him alone? Ever? She had the thousand, wasn't that enough?

He hadn't dared tell her what really happened. He'd been barely sober enough to hide the saucer out in the arroyo. He'd been so clever, hiding his liquor in the ship where Ruth couldn't find it. . . .

And now the ship wouldn't open the doors for him! "You took all my money. Give me five bucks, please, Ruth. Please."

"No! You'd just walk down to the liquor store! I know you, Harry Logan!" She stomped off.

Harry held his aching head. The liquor store was five miles away. The ship only worked when he was drunk. And he didn't have any money. . . .

There was a sound of crunching gravel. A car was coming up the long drive from the highway. Harry looked out to see Air Force blue and froze. Good Lord, they'd traced him!

I give up, Harry thought. He went outside as the car drove up. General Bannister climbed out of the back seat of the sedan. There were two majors with him, silver wings gleaming on their chests. Each of them held a bottle of Christian Brothers brandy, and the general was staggering. . . .

# THERE WILL BE WAR, VOLUME I: PREFACE

by Jerry Pournelle

## Editor's Introduction

In 1980 Ace Books publisher, Tom Doherty, left Ace to form his own company, Tor Books. He took with him Jim Baen, who became his senior editor of science fiction. With Jim Baen's encouragement, Jerry and I had edited two volumes of *Endless Frontier* anthologies, about near-Earth space colonies, for Ace Books and they had sold very well. At the time, Jerry was an officer in the L-5 Society and very active in promoting his life-long concern about getting mankind into space.

Rather than repeat his efforts at Ace, Jim encouraged Jerry to do a new anthology series—on future warfare. At Ace Books, Jim had gotten Reginald Bretnor to do a series of books on future war and conflict, entitled *The Future At War*. Ace had published three volumes and they had done surprisingly well, considering the antiwar sentiment of the post-Vietnam era. Since Jerry had a sizeable following for his John Christian Falkenberg stories, Jim thought having Jerry and I edit a new science-fiction war series was a capital idea.

I remember when Jerry, after a long phone call from Jim Baen, came down to my office on the first floor. He had a bemused look on his face. "John, I just got off the phone with Jim and he wants us to do a new anthology series on warfare."

I nodded. "Great idea."

Jerry nodded back. "But get this, Jim wants to call it 'There Will Be War!'" Then he laughed. "That ought to bring the Wrath of God upon us from every peacenik in the country!"

I agreed, replying, "Isn't that the point!"

He agreed, rubbing his hands together. "This should be fun!"

We did have a lot of fun with the series and even introduced some new writers. *The There Will Be War* series ran for nine volumes and a few years ago was brought back into print with a new tenth volume. The Wikipedia entry "Military Science Fiction" states: "The series of anthologies with the group title *There Will Be War* edited by Pournelle and John F. Carr (nine volumes from 1983 through 1990) helped keep the category active, and encouraged new writers to add to it."

As a protest, Harry Harrison—a died-in-the-wool socialist who had a love/hate relationship with Jerry—edited a volume entitled *There Won't Be War*. I remember when he called Jerry to inform him that his new series would be as successful as *There Will Be War*, which was then up to eight books. There weren't any sequels to *There Won't Be War* and that was the last we heard from Good Ol' Harry. . . .

What convinced me to include Jerry's preface to Volume I of *There Will be War* was Larry King's note to me—after I told him I would be editing a new anthology on Jerry—in which he said:

When I read this [preface], it convinced me that Pournelle was right and Heinlein was wrong about war. Of course, Pournelle deeply admired Heinlein, and might not have wanted to set himself against his mentor! But Heinlein, who never actually saw combat, believed that if one side is fighting for a noble cause, they will probably win.

Pournelle, in my opinion, was more realistic: No matter how much a soldier loves his wife, his family, and his country, when there are bullets flying above his head, he might forget about them. But he won't forget about his comrades who are standing next to him. So while ideals and home are important, if you want your army to win wars, you have to build an *esprit de corps* so strong that each soldier is willing to risk his life for the man next to him. And that's why a mercenary army whose leaders treat the men well can defeat a badly run army that's fighting for some ideal—as often happens in Pournelle's tales.

❂❂❂

**EVERYONE DESIRES PEACE;** but there have been few generations free of war. Paradoxically, the few eras of peace were times when men of war had high influence. The Pax Romana was enforced by Caesar's Legions. The Pax Britannica was enforced by the Royal Navy and His Majesty's Forces. The era of (comparative) peace since 1945 has been marked by deployment of the most powerful weapons in history.

The Swiss Republic has long enjoyed peace; but ruthlessly enforces universal manhood conscription and military training.

Historically, peace has only been bought by men of war. We may, in future, be able to change that. It may be, as some say, we have no choice. It may be that peace can and must be bought with some coin other than the blood of good soldiers; but there is no evidence to show that the day of jubilee has come.

In war, Clausewitz says, everything is simple, but the simplest things are difficult. Indeed, the simple truths of war are difficult to understand. The study of war is a study in contradictions. Men of war must, to be successful, be willing to risk death. An army not willing to die is an army that wins few victories. But why will they risk their lives?

It is fashionable to say there are as many reasons as there are soldiers, but in fact that is not so. There are not so very many reasons why soldiers will stand and face the enemy. Sometimes the reasons are very simple, and easily understood.

When you enter West Point, you find that the Army doesn't care a hang about the first verses of "The Star-Spangled Banner." It's the last verse you must learn. It goes:

O thus be it ever when freemen shall stand
Between their lov'd home and the war's desolation!

Blest with vict'ry and peace, may the heav'n rescued land
Praise the Power that hath made and preserv'd us a nation!
Then conquer we must, when our cause it is just,
And this be our motto: "In God is our trust,"
And the star-spangled banner in triumph shall wave
O'er the land of the free and the home of the brave.

To stand between one's home and war's desolation is an ancient and glorious military tradition, and certainly one reason why men fight.

There are others. When the Black Company marched during the German Peasant Wars of 1525, they sang:

When Adam delved and Eve span,
Kyrie Eleison
Who then was the gentlemen?
Kyrie Eleison
Lower pikes, onward go!
Set the red rooster on the cloister roof!

To set the red rooster on a thatch roof is to set fire to it; the Black Company and other peasant units were so thoroughly successful at destroying religious establishments that Martin Luther turned to the princes of Germany, bidding them to burn and slay and kill. Yet the Black Company was certain that it did the Lord's work in liberating the lower classes from domination by the nobility.

Not all warriors have the excuses of the Black Company. There was once recorded a remarkable conversation between Genghis Khan and one of his soldiers. The Ka Khan asked a guard officer what, in all this world, could bring greatest happiness.

"The open steppe, a clear day, and a swift horse," said the officer. "And a falcon at your wrist to start up the hares."

"Not so," replied the Khan. "To crush your enemy, to possess his wife as he watches, to see your enemies fall at your feet. To take their horses and goods and hear the lamentations of their women. That is best."

Mephistopheles tempts Faust: "Is it not pleasant, to be a king, and ride in blood to Samarkand?"

Some soldiers fight for money. Scottish troops have often fought for pay; in the words of the song, "Not for country, not for king, but for my Mary Jane," which is to say, for enough to buy a crofter's hut and support a wife and family. Yet surely no one dies for a standard of living? Why, then have some paid soldiers been feared and admired, while others, equally well trained, have been merely despised?

There are also the legions of the damned, who have often been responsible for deeds thought glorious; men who marched into battles for nothing more than the honor of the regiment. The best known of these is the French Foreign Legion, whose marching song, stirring as its music might be, glorified nothing more glamorous than blood sausages.

It is no easy thing to determine why men fight. For those who live in free lands, it may be enough to rejoice: Until now, at least, we have always found enough defenders, even if we have not appreciated them.

History shows another strong trend: When soldiers have succeeded in eliminating war, or at least in keeping the battles far from home, small in scope, and confined largely to soldiers; when, in other words, they have done what one might have thought they were supposed to do; it is then when their masters generally despise them.

This too is an established tradition, old when Kipling wrote of it:

*Yes, makin' mock o' uniforms that guard you while you sleep,*
*Is cheaper than them uniforms, an' they're starvation cheap;*
*An' hustlin' drunken soldiers when they're goin' large a bit*
*Is five times better business than paradin' in full kit.*

*Then it's Tommy this, an' Tommy that, an' "Tommy, 'ow's yer soul?"*
*But it's "Thin red line of 'eroes" when the drums begin to roll,*
*The drums begin to roll, my boys, the drums begin to roll,*
*O it's "Thin red line of 'eroes" when the drums begin to roll.*

It may be that in this century of Grace the drums will not roll. It may be that we have seen the last of war.

It may be that we will not; that it will not be long before we in the United States, like the Israelis and the Afghanis, must again turn to warriors for protection; for that is the oldest tradition of all.

*While it's Tommy this, an' Tommy that, an' "Tommy fall be'ind,"*
*But it's "Please to walk in front, sir," when there's trouble in the wind . . .*

# CONSORT

## by Jerry Pournelle

## Editor's Introduction

In the early 1970s Jerry grew increasingly disenchanted with NASA; the space agency had pretty much dropped the ball after the Apollo program and lost its focus. It's easy to forget that the space race began in the 1950s with Sputnik, when the US and Soviet Union were each launching competing satellites for world attention and economic/technological dominance. With the Saturn rocket and the Apollo program, which put a man on the Moon in 1969, the US won the space race; afterward the space program quickly ran out of steam.

Jerry quickly began to realize that it was growing more and more unlikely that a government program would put mankind permanently into space. Thus, he envisioned that it would be up to wealthy industrialists to put man into space. He came up with two different individuals, the first was Jeremy Lewis, the old curmudgeon who runs Nuclear General with his special assistant, Bill Adams. When US government and political opposition to nuclear reactors forced Lewis into building his reactors outside the US, in places like Africa and Tonga with little government regulation, Lewis begins to focus on space development.

The other industrialist is wealthy Laurie Jo Hansen, who is determined to foil the antagonistic government forces, which have grown increasingly powerful—under US president Greg Tolland, an ardent socialist—and open space for mankind. She engages Aeneas

MacKenzie, an old lover and ex-attorney general, to help her gain her dream and leave Earth.

The sad reality is that it took almost fifty years for the world to catch up with Jerry's ideas of private space exploration and travel. Now, we have several competing multibillionaires and visionaries competing for the near-Earth satellite market and journeys to the Moon and Mars as well as a possible lunar base. According to Wikipedia: " . . .as of June 2013 and in the United States alone, ten billionaires have made 'serious investments in private spaceflight activities' at six companies, including Stratolaunch Systems, Planetary Resources, Blue Origin, Virgin Galactic, SpaceX and Bigelow Aerospace. The ten investors are Paul Allen, Larry Page, Eric E. Schmidt, Ram Shriram, Charles Simony, Ross Perot Jr., Jeff Bezos, Richard Branson, Elon Musk and Robert Bigelow."

According to *Time Magazine*, Jeff Bezos, founder of Amazon and 2018's richest man, " . . .pours one billion dollars a year into his space-exploration venture Blue Origin, aiming to create the next generation of reusable rockets and further propel his legacy." Internet mogul Elon Musk is behind SpaceX, Space Exploration Technologies, which was founded with the idea of revolutionizing space technology, and "with the ultimate goal of enabling people to live on other planets."

Instead of flashy launches and over-hyped missions, we are now seeing steady progress toward the ultimate goal of using reusable spacecraft to establish a permanent presence in space for mankind. Within another decade, we should see the kind of space activities and presence that Pournelle prophesized some fifty years ago in his stories.

❂ ❂ ❂

**THE SENATOR LOOKED UP** from the bureau with its chipped paint and cracked mirror to the expensive woman seated on the sagging bed. My God, he thought. What if one of my constituents could see me now? Or the press people got wind of this? He opened the leather attaché case and turned knobs on the console inside. Green lights winked reassuringly. He took a deep breath and turned to the girl.

"Laurie Jo, would it surprise you to know I don't give a damn whether the President is a crook or not?" the senator asked.

"Then why are you here?" Her voice was soft, with a note of confidence, almost triumphant.

Senator Hayden shook his head. This is a hell of a thing. The Senate majority leader meets with the richest woman in the whole goddamn world, and the only way we can trust each other is to come to a place like this. She picks the highway and I pick the motel. Both of us have scramblers goin', and we're still not sure nobody's makin' a tape. Hell of a thing. "Because you might be able to *prove* President Tolland's a crook. Maybe make a lot of people believe it," Hayden said.

"I can."

"Yeah." She sounds so damned confident, and if what she sent me's a good sample of what she's got, she can do it, all right. "That's what scares me, Laurie Jo. The country can't take it again."

He drew in a lungful of air. It smelled faintly of gin. Hayden exhaled heavily and sank into the room's only chair. One of the springs was loose, and it jabbed him. "Christ Almighty!" he exploded.

"First Watergate. No sooner'n we get over that, and we're in a depression. Inflation. Oil crisis. The Equity Trust business. One damn thing after another. And when the party gets together with a real reform wing and wins the election, Tolland's own solicitor general finds the Equity people right next to the President! So half the White House staff goes, and we get past that somehow and people still got something to believe in, and you're tellin' me you can prove the President was in on all of it. Laurie Jo, you just can't do that to the country!"

She spread her skirts across her knees and wished she'd taken the chair. She never liked sitting without a backrest. The interview was distasteful, and she wished there was another way, but she didn't know one. We're so nearly out of all this, she thought. So very near.

"DING."

It was a sound in her mind, but not one the senator could hear. He was saying something about public confidence. She half listened to him, while she thought, "I WAS NOT TO BE DISTURBED."

"MISTER MC CARTNEY SAYS IT IS VERY IMPORTANT.

SIGNOR ANTONELLI IS CONCERNED ABOUT HIS NEXT SHIPMENT."

"WILL IT BE ON TIME?" she thought.

"ONLY HALF. HIS BIOLOGICALS WILL BE TWO DAYS LATE," the computer link told her. The system was a luxury she sometimes regretted: not the cost, because a million dollars was very little to her; but although the implanted transceiver link gave her access to all of her holdings and allowed her to control the empire she owned, it gave her no peace.

"TELL MC CARTNEY TO STALL. I WILL CALL ANTONELLI IN TWO HOURS," she thought.

"MISTER MC CARTNEY SAYS ANTONELLI WILL NOT WAIT."

"TELL MC CARTNEY TO DORK HIMSELF."

"ACKNOWLEDGED."

"AND LEAVE ME ALONE."

"OUT."

And that takes care of that, she thought. The computer was programmed to take her insulting commands and translate them into something more polite; it wouldn't do to annoy one of her most important executives. If he needed to be disciplined, she'd do it face to face.

The senator had stopped talking and was looking at her.

"I can prove it, Barry. All of it. But I don't want to."

Senator Hayden felt very old. "We're almost out of the slump," he said. He wasn't speaking directly to Laurie Jo any longer, and he didn't look at her. "Got the biggest R&D budget in twenty years. Unemployment's down a point. People are beginning to have some confidence again." There was peeling wallpaper in one corner of the room. Senator Hayden balled his hands into fists and the nails dug into his palms.

When he had control of himself, he met her eyes and was startled again at how blue they were. Dark red hair, oval face, blue eyes, expensive clothes; she's damn near every man's dream of a woman, and she's got me. I never made a dishonest deal in my life, but God help me, she's got me.

I have to deal, but— "Has MacKenzie seen your stuff? Does he know?"

Laurie Jo nodded. "Aeneas didn't want to believe it. Your media friends aren't the only ones who want to think Greg Tolland's an honest man. But he's got no choice now. He has to believe it."

"Then we can't deal," Hayden said. "What the hell are you wasting my time for? MacKenzie won't deal. He'll kamikaze." And do I admire him or hate him for that?

There's something inhuman about a man who thinks he's justice personified. The last guy who got tagged as "The Incorruptible" was that Robespierre character, and his own cronies cut his head off when they couldn't take him any longer.

"I'll take care of Aeneas," Laurie Jo said.

"How?"

"You'll have to trust me."

"I've already trusted you. I'm here, aren't I?" But he shook his head sadly. "Maybe I know more'n you think. I know MacKenzie connected up with you after he left the White House. God knows you're enough woman to turn any man around, but you don't know him, Laurie Jo, you don't know him at all if you think—"

"I have known Aeneas MacKenzie for almost twenty years," she said. "And I've been in love with him since the first day I met him. The two years we lived together were the happiest either of us ever had."

"Sure," Barry Hayden said. "Sure. You knew him back in the old days before Greg Tolland was anything much. So did I. I told you, maybe I know more'n you think. But goddam it, you didn't see him for ten, twelve years—"

"Sixteen years," she said. "And we had only a few weeks after that." Glorious weeks, but Greg Tolland couldn't leave us alone. He had to spoil even that damn him! I have more than one reason to hate Greg Tolland— "Why don't you listen instead of talking all the time? I can handle Aeneas. You want political peace and quiet for a few years, and I can give them to you."

I don't listen because I'm afraid of what I'll hear, the senator thought. Because I never wanted this day to come, and I knew it would when I went into politics, but I managed for this long, and it got to lookin' like it never would come and now I'm in a cheap motel room about to be told the price of whatever honor I've got left. God help us, she's got all the cards. If anybody can shut MacKenzie up—

The room still smelled of cheap gin, and the senator tasted bile at the back of his throat. "Okay, Laurie Jo, what do I have to do?"

Aeneas MacKenzie switched off the newscast and stared vacantly at the blank screen. There had been nothing about President Greg Tolland, and it disturbed him.

His office was a small cubicle off the main corridor. It was large enough for a desk as well as the viewscreen and console that not only gave him instant access to every file and data bank on *Heimdall* station, but also a link with the master Hansen data banks on Earth below. He disliked microfilm and readout screens and would greatly have preferred to work with printed reports and documents, but that wasn't possible. Every kilogram of mass was important when it had to go into orbit.

There was never enough mass at *Heimdall.* Energy was no problem; through the viewport he could see solar cells plastered over every surface, and further away was the power station, a large mirror reflecting onto a boiler and turbine. Everything could be recycled except reaction mass: but whenever the scooters went out to collect supply pods boosted up from Earth that mass was lost forever. The recent survey team sent to the Moon had cost hideously, leaving the station short of fuel for its own operations.

He worked steadily on the production schedules, balancing the station's inadequate manpower reserves to fill the most critical orders without taking anyone off the *Valkyrie* project. It was an impossible task, and he felt a sense of pride in his partial success. It was a strange job for the former solicitor general of the United States, but he believed his legal training helped; and he was able to get the crew to work harder than they had thought they could.

Get *Valkyrie* finished, Laurie Jo had said. It must be done as quickly as possible, no matter what it does to the production schedules. She'd said that, but she couldn't have meant it; Aeneas knew what would happen if *Heimdall* didn't continue sending down space-manufactured products. *Heimdall* was a valuable installation, now that there were no risks left in building it, and Laurie Jo's partners were ruthless; if she defaulted on deliveries, they'd take it away from her.

Eventually the assignments were done. By taking a construction shift himself (he estimated his value as sixty-five percent as productive as a trained rigger, double what it had been when he first tried the work) he could put another man on completing the new biological production compartment. The schedule would work, but there was no slack in it.

When he was done, he left the small compartment and strode through the corridor outside. He was careful to close and dog the airtight entryway into his office, as he was careful about everything he did. As he walked, his eyes automatically scanned the shining metallic cloth of *Heimdall*'s inner walls, but he was no more aware of that than he was of the low spin gravity and Coriolis effect.

The corridor curved upward in front of and behind him. When he reached the doorway to the Chief Engineer's office, it stood open in defiance of regulations. Aeneas nodded wryly and ignored it. Kittridge Penrose made the regulations in the first place, and Aeneas only enforced them. Presumably Penrose knew what he was doing. If he doesn't, Aeneas thought, we're all in trouble.

Penrose was in the office, as Aeneas knew he would be; one of his prerogatives was to know where everyone was. The engineer was at his desk. A complex diagram filled the screen to his left, and Penrose was carefully drawing lines with a light pen. He looked up as Aeneas came into the office. "What's up, boss?"

"I don't know." Aeneas peered at the screen. Penrose noticed the puzzled look and touched buttons on the console below the picture. The diagram changed, not blinking out to be replaced, but rearranging itself until it showed an isometric view which Aeneas recognized instantly.

"Right on schedule," Penrose said. "Just playing about with some possible improvements. There she is, *Valkyrie,* all ready to go."

"Except for the engines."

Penrose shrugged. "You can't have everything. Nothing new from Miss Hansen about getting that little item taken care of?"

"Not yet."

"Heh. She'll manage it." Penrose went back to his game with the light pen. "I used to think my part of this was the real work," the engineer said. He sketched in another line. "But it isn't. I just design the stuff. It's you people who get it built."

"Thanks." And it's true enough: Laurie Jo put together the syndicate to finance this whole station.

"Sure. Meant that, you know," Penrose said. "You've done about as well as Captain Shorey. Didn't think you'd be much as commander here, but I was wrong."

Now that, Aeneas thought, is high praise indeed. And I suppose it's even true. I do fill a needed function here. Something I didn't do when I was down there with Laurie Jo. Down there I was a Prince Consort, and nothing else. True enough I came here because I was the only one she could trust to take control, but I've been more than just her agent.

"Sit down, boss," Penrose said. "Have a drink. You look like you're in need of one."

"Thanks, I'll pass the drink." He took the other chair and watched as Penrose worked. I could never do that, he thought, but there aren't a lot of jobs up here that I can't do now. . . .

The newscast haunted him. Laurie Jo had the whole story, all the evidence needed to bring Greg Tolland down. We can prove the President of the United States is a criminal. Why hasn't she done it? Why?

I don't even dare call and ask her. We can't know someone isn't listening in. We can't trust codes, we can't even trust our own computer banks, and how have things come to this for the United States?

"Got a couple of new reports from the Lunatics," Penrose said. "Had a chance to go over them?"

"No. That's what I came to talk to you about." The console would have given him instant communications with Penrose or anyone else aboard *Heimdall,* but Aeneas always preferred to go to his people rather than speak to them as an impersonal voice.

"Pretty good strike," Penrose said. "Another deposit of hydrides and quite a lot of mica. No question about it, we've got everything we need."

Aeneas nodded. It was curious: Hydrogen is by orders of magnitude the most common element in the universe, but it had been hard to find on the Moon. There were oxides, and given the plentiful energy available in space that meant plenty of oxygen to breathe, but hydrogen was rare.

Now the Lunar Survey Team sent up from *Heimdall* had found hydrogen locked into various minerals. It was available, and the colony was possible—if they could get there. The survey team's fuel requirements had eaten up a lot of the mass boosted up to *Heimdall*, and without more efficient Earth orbit to lunar orbit transport it would take a long time to make a colony self-sustaining.

"We've either got to bring the survey party home or send another supply capsule," Penrose was saying. "Which is it?"

"Like to hold off that decision as long as we can." And please don't ask why. I don't know why. Just that Laurie Jo says do it this way.

Penrose frowned. "If you'll authorize some monkey motion, we can do the preliminaries for going either way. That'll hold off the decision another couple of weeks. No more than that, though."

"All right. Do it that way."

"What's eating you, Aeneas?"

"Nothing. I've been up here too long."

"Sure." Kit Penrose didn't say that he'd been aboard *Heimdall* nearly two years longer than MacKenzie's eighteen months, but he didn't have to. Of course, Penrose thought, I've had my girl here with me; and MacKenzie's seen his precisely twice since he's been here, a couple of weekends and back she went to look after the money. Wonder what it's like to sleep with the big boss? What a silly thing to wonder about.

The diagram faded and another view came on the screen. "There she is," Penrose said. "Lovely, isn't she?"

*Valkyrie* may have been lovely to an engineer, but she was hardly a work of art. There was no symmetry to the ship. Since she would never land, she had neither top nor bottom, only fore and aft. "All we need is the NERVA, and we're all set," Penrose said. "No reason why the whole Moon colony staff can't go out a week after we have the engines."

"Yes."

"Christ, how can you be so cold about it? Moon base. Plenty of mass. Metals to work with. Who knows, maybe even radioactives. We can cut loose from those bastards down there!" He waved at the viewport where Earth filled the sky before the station slowly turned again to show the sequined black velvet of space. "And we've very nearly done it."

"Very nearly." But we haven't done it, and I don't see how we can, he thought.

"What we need are those military aerospace-planes," Penrose said. His voice became more serious. "I expect they'll be coming round for visits whether we invite them or not, you know."

"Yes. Well, we got on with their chaps all right—"

"Sure," Penrose said. "Sure. Visiting astronauts and all that lot. Proud to show them around. Even so, I can't say I'm happy they can get up here whenever they like. . . ."

"Nor I." Aeneas opened a hinged panel beside the desk and took out a coffee cup. He filled it from a spigot near Penrose's hand. "Cannon shot," he said.

"I beg your pardon?"

"In the old days, national law reached out to sea as far as cannonballs could be fired from shore. Three miles, more or less. It became the legal boundary of a nation's sovereignty. There used to be a lot of talk about international law in space, and the rest of it, but it will probably be settled by something like cannon shot again. When the national governments can get up here easily, they'll assert control."

"Like to be gone when that happens," Penrose said. "Can't say I want more regulations and red tape and committees. Had enough of that lot."

"So have we all." Aeneas drank the coffee. "So have we all."

Penrose laughed. "That's a strange thing to say, considering that you were one of the prime movers of the People's Alliance."

"Maybe I've learned something from the experience." Aeneas stared moodily into his coffee cup. I wasn't wrong, he thought. But I wasn't right either. There's got to be more than comfort and security, and we didn't think of that, because the Cause was all the adventure *we* needed. I wonder how long it will take them to tame space? Forms to fill out, regulations always enforced, not because of safety but because they're regulations. . . .

Penrose looked at the digital readouts above his drafting console: Greenwich time, and Mountain Daylight time. "Big shipment coming up next pass over Baja. I'd best be getting ready for it."

"Yes." Aeneas listened without paying much attention as Penrose told him what the big lasers in southern Baja would send up this time. It didn't really concern him yet, and when he needed to know more, the information would be available through his desk console.

As the engineer talked, Aeneas remembered what it had been like to watch the launches: the field covered with lasers, their mirrors all focusing onto the one large mirror beneath the tramway. The squat shapes of the capsules on the tramway, each waiting to be brought over the launching mirror and thrust upward by the stabbing light, looking as if they were lifted by a fantastically swift-growing tree rising out of the desert; the thrumming note of the pulsed beam singing in hot desert air.

It had been the most magnificent sight he had ever seen, and Laurie Jo had built it all. Now she was ready to move onward, but her partners were not. They were content to own *Heimdall* and sell its products, raking in billions from the miracles that could be wrought in space.

Biologicals of every conceivable kind. Crystals of an ultimate purity grown in mass production and infected with precisely the right contaminants, all grown in mass production. *Heimdall* had revolutionized more than one industry. Already there were hand calculators with thousands of words of memory space, all made from the chips grown in orbit. Deserts bloomed as the production crews sent down membranes that would pass fresh water and keep salt back; they too could be made cheaply only in zero gravity conditions.

Why take high risks on a Moon base when there was so much more potential to exploit in orbital production? The investors could prove that more money was to be made through expanding *Heimdall* than through sending *Valkyrie* exploring. They remembered that they would never have invested in space production at all if Laurie Jo hadn't bullied them into it, and that had been enough to give her some freedom of action; but they could not see profits in the Moon for many years to come.

And they're right, Aeneas thought. Laurie Jo doesn't plan for the next phase to make profits, not for a long time.

She wants the stars for herself. And what do I want? Lord God, I miss her. But I'm *needed* here. I have work to do, and I'd better get at it.

The airline reception lounge was no longer crowded. A few minutes before, it had been filled with Secret Service men and Hansen Security agents. Now there was only one of each in the room with Laurie Jo. They stayed at opposite ends of the big room, and they eyed each other like hostile dogs.

"Relax, Miguel," Laurie Jo said. "Between us there are enough Security people to protect an army. The President will be safe enough—"

"*Si, Doña* Laura." The elderly man's eyes never left the long-haired younger man at the other end of the room. "I am willing to believe *he* is safe enough."

"For heaven's sake, I'm meeting the President of the United States!"

"*Si, Doña* Laura. *Don* Aeneas has told me of this man who has become President here. I do not care for this."

"Jesus." The Secret Service man curled his lip in contempt. "How did you do it?" he demanded.

"How did I do what, Mr. Coleman?" she asked.

"Turn MacKenzie against the President! Fifteen years he was with the Chief. Fifteen years with the People's Alliance. Now you've got him telling tales about the Chief to your peasant friend there—"

"Miguel is not a peasant."

"Ah, *Doña* Laura, but I am. Go on, *señor*. Tell us of this strange thing you do not understand." There was amusement in the old vaquero's eyes.

"Skip it. It just doesn't make sense, that's all."

"Perhaps my *patrona* bribed *Don* Aeneas," Miguel said.

"That will do," Laurie Jo said. Miguel nodded and was silent.

"Bullshit," Coleman said. "Nobody ever got to MacKenzie. Nobody has *his* price. Not in money, anyway."

He looked at Laurie Jo in disbelief. He didn't think her unattractive, but he couldn't believe she was enough woman to drive a man insane.

"You're rather young to know Aeneas that well," Laurie Jo said.

"I joined the People's Alliance before the campaign." There was pride in the agent's voice. "Stood guard watches over the Chief. Helped in the office. MacKenzie was with us every day. He's not hard to know, not like some party types."

"INFORMATION," Laurie Jo thought. "COLEMAN FIRST NAME UNKNOWN, SECRET SERVICE AGENT. RECENTLY APPOINTED. SUMMARY."

"COLEMAN, THEODORE RAYMOND. AGE 25. PAID STAFF, PEOPLE'S ALLIANCE UNTIL INAUGURATION OF PRESIDENT GREGORY TOLLAND. APPOINTED TO SECRET SERVICE BY ORDERS OF PRESIDENT TO TAKE EFFECT INAUGURAL DAY. EDUCATION—"

"SUFFICIENT." Laurie Jo nodded to herself. Coleman hadn't been like the career Secret Service men. There were a lot of young people like Coleman in the undercover services lately, party loyalists who had known Greg before the election. Personally loyal bodyguards have been the mark of tyrants for three thousand years, she thought. But some of the really great leaders have had them as well. Can any President do without them? Can I? Not here. But I won't need guards on the Moon. I won't—

"DING."

"WHAT NOW?"

"THERE IS A GENERAL STRIKE PLANNED IN BOLIVIA. TWO HANSEN AGENTS HAVE INFILTRATED THE UNION. THEY HAVE FOUND OUT THE DATE OF THE STRIKE, AND WERE DISCOVERED WHEN TRANSMITTING THEIR INFORMATION. SUPERINTENDENT HARLOW WISHES TO TAKE IMMEDIATE ACTION TO RESCUE THEM.

"WILL YOU APPROVE?"

"GIVE HARLOW FULL AUTHORIZATION TO TAKE WHATEVER ACTION HE THINKS REQUIRED. REPORT WHEN HIS PLANS ARE COMPLETE BUT BEFORE EXECUTION."

"ACKNOWLEDGED."

Another damned problem, she thought. Harlow was a good man, but he thought in pretty drastic terms. What will that do to our other holdings in Bolivia? One thing, it will hurt my partners worse than it will hurt me. I'll have to think about this. Later, now I've got something more important.

The door opened to admit another Secret Service man. "Chief's on the way," he said.

"DO NOT CALL ME FOR ANY PURPOSE," she thought.

"ACKNOWLEDGED."

It was almost comical. The Secret Service men wouldn't leave until Miguel had gone, and Miguel wouldn't leave his *patrona* alone with the Secret Service men. Finally they all backed out together, and

Laurie Jo was alone for a moment. Then President Greg Tolland came in.

He's still President, she thought. No matter that I've known him twenty years and fought him for half that time. There's an aura that goes with the office, and Greg wears it well. "Good afternoon, Mister President."

"Senator Hayden says I should talk with you," Tolland said.

"Aren't you even going to say hello?" She thought he looked very old; yet she knew he was only a few years older than herself, one of the youngest men ever to be elected to the office.

"What should I say, Laurie Jo? That I wish you well? I do, but you wouldn't believe that. That I'd like to be friends? Would you believe me if I said that? I do wish we could be friends, but I hate everything you stand for."

"Well said, sir!" She applauded. "But there's no audience here." And you only hate that the fortune I inherited wasn't used to help your political ambitions, not that I have it. You always were more comfortable with wealthy people than Aeneas was.

He grinned wryly. It was a famous grin, and Laurie Jo could remember when Congressman Tolland had practiced it with Aeneas and herself as his only audience. It seemed so very long ago, back in the days when her life was simple and she hadn't known who her father was, or that one day she would inherit his wealth.

"Mind if I sit down?"

She shrugged. "Why ask? But please do."

He took one of the expensively covered lounge chairs and waited until she'd done the same. "I ask because this is your place."

True enough. I own the airline. But it's hardly my home and this is hardly a social visit. "Can I get you anything? Your agents have sampled everything at the bar—"

"I'll have a bourbon, then. They shouldn't have done that. Here, I'll get—"

"It's all right. I know where everything is." She poured drinks for both of them. "Your young men don't trust me. One of them even accused me of seducing Aeneas away from you."

"Didn't you."

She handed him the drink. "Oh good God, Greg. You don't have to be careful what you say to me. Nothing I could tape could make things worse than I can make them right now. And I give you my word, nobody's listening."

His eyes narrowed. For a moment he resembled a trapped animal.

"Believe that, Greg. There's no way out," she said. "With what I already had and what Aeneas knows—"

"I'll never know how I put up with that fanatic S.O.B. for so long."

"That's beneath you, Greg. You wouldn't be President if Aeneas hadn't helped you."

"Not true."

It is true, but why go on? And yet— "Why have you turned so hard against him? Because he wouldn't sell out and you did?"

"Maybe I had no choice, Laurie Jo. Maybe I'd got so far out on so many limbs that I couldn't retreat, and when I came crashing down the Alliance would come down with me. Maybe I thought it was better that we win however we had to than go on leading a noble lost cause. This isn't what we came here to talk about. Senator Hayden says you've got a proposition for me."

"Yes." And how Barry Hayden hates all of this. Another victim of patriotism. Another? Am I including Greg Tolland in that category? And what difference does it make? "It's simple enough, Greg. I can see that you'll be allowed to finish your term without any problems from me. Or from Aeneas. I can have the Hansen papers and network stop their campaigns against you. I won't switch to your support."

"Wouldn't want it. That would look too fishy. What's your price for all this?"

"You weren't always this direct."

"What the hell do you want, Laurie Jo? You've got the President of the United States asking you for a favor. You want me to crawl too?"

"No. All right, the first price is your total retirement from politics when your term is over. You don't make that promise to me. You'll give it to Barry Hayden."

"Maybe. I'll think about it. What do you want for yourself?"

"I want a big payload delivered to *Heimdall.*"

"What the hell?"

"You've got those big military aerospace planes. I want something carried to orbit."

"I'll think about it."

"You'll do it."

"I don't know." He stared into his glass. "If it means this much to you, it's important. I'd guess it's tied in with that lunar survey party, right? Your Moon colony plans?"

She didn't answer.

"That's got to be it." He drained the cocktail and began laughing. "You can't throw me out because you'd never get anyone else to agree to this! It's pretty funny, Laurie Jo. You and Mister Clean. You *need* me! More than just this once, too, I expect— What is it you want delivered?"

"Just a big payload."

Tolland laughed again. "I can find out, you know. I've still got a few people inside your operation."

"I suppose you do. All right, I've got a working NERVA engine for *Valkyrie.* It's too big for the laser launching system. We could send it up in pieces, but it would take a long time to get it assembled and checked out." And I don't have a long time. I'm running out of time. . . .

"So you want me to hand over the Moon to a private company. That's what it amounts to, isn't it? The People's Alliance was formed to break up irresponsible power like yours, and you want me to hand you the Moon."

"That's my price, Greg. You won't like the alternative."

"Yeah. It's still pretty funny. A couple more years and you won't have a goddam monopoly on manned space stations. So you want me to help you get away."

"Something like that. We see things differently."

"You know you're doomed, don't you? Laurie Jo, it's over. You sit there in your big office and decide things for the whole world. Who asked you to? It's time the people had a say over their lives. You think I'm ambitious. Maybe. But for all of it, everything I've done has been in the right direction. At least I'm not building up a personal empire that's as anachronistic as a dinosaur!"

"Spare me the political speeches, Greg." God, he means it. Or he thinks he does. He can justify anything he does because he's the agent for the people, but what does it mean in the real world? Just how much comfort is it to know it's all for the good of the people when you're caught in the machinery? "I won't argue with you. I've got something you need, and I'm willing to sell."

"And you get the Moon as a private fief."

"If you want to think of it that way, go ahead. But if you want to be President three months from now, you'll do as I ask."

"And why should I think you'll keep your bargain?"

"When have I ever broken my promises?" Laurie Jo asked.

"Don't know. Tell you what, get MacKenzie to promise. That way I'll be sure you mean it."

"I'll do better than that. Aeneas and I are both going to the Moon. We can hardly interfere with you from there."

"You are crazy, aren't you?" Tolland's face showed wonder but not doubt. "You know you're going to lose a lot. You can't manage your empire from the Moon."

"I know." And how long could I hold out to begin with? And for what? "Greg, you just don't understand that power's no use, money's no use, unless it's for something that counts."

"And getting to the Moon is that big?" He shook his head in disbelief. "You're crazy."

"So are a lot of us, then. I've gotten volunteers for every opening. Pretty good people, too—as you should know."

"Yeah. I know." Tolland got up and wandered around the big room until he came to the bar. He filled his glass with ice cubes and water, then added a tiny splash of whiskey. "You've got some of my best people away from me. You can pay them more—"

"I can, but I don't have to. You still don't understand, do you? It's not my money, and it's not my control over the Moon colony that counts. What's important is this will be one place that you don't control."

"Hah. I hadn't thought I was that unpopular with the engineers."

"I don't mean you personally," Laurie Jo said. "Your image control people have done well. But, Greg, can't you understand that some of us want out of your system?"

"Aeneas too?"

"Yes." More than any of us, because he knows better than any of us what it's going to be like—

"I should have known he'd go to you after I threw him out."

"There wasn't anywhere else he could go. Mister President, this isn't getting us anywhere. You'll never understand us, so why try? Just send up that payload and you'll be rid of us. You may even be lucky. We'll lose people in the lunar colony. Maybe we'll all be killed."

"And you're willing to chance that—"

"I told you, you won't understand us. Don't try. Just send up my payload."

"I'll think about it," Tolland said. "But your other conditions are off. No promises. No political deals." The President stood and went to the door. He turned defiantly. "You get the Moon. That ought to be enough."

He felt dizzy and it was hard to breathe in the high gravity of Earth. When he poured a drink, he almost spilled it, because he was unconsciously allowing for the displacement usual in *Heimdall*'s centrifugal gravity. Now he sat weakly in the large chair.

The Atlantic Ocean lay outside his window, and he watched the moving lights of ships. The room lights came on suddenly, startling him.

"What—*Miguel!*" Laurie Jo shouted. Then she laughed foolishly. "*No esta nada. Deseo solamente estar, por favor.*" She came into the room as Miguel closed the door behind her. "Hello, Aeneas. I might have known. No one else could get in here without someone telling me—"

He stood with an effort. "Didn't mean to startle you." He stood uncomfortably, wishing for her, cursing himself for not telling her he was coming. But I wanted to shock you, he thought.

"You didn't really. I think Greg has called off his dogs. I'm safe enough. But—you're not!"

"I'll take my chances."

"Why are we standing here like this?" she asked. She moved toward him. He stood rigidly for a moment, but then stepped across the tiny space that separated them, and they were together again.

For how long? he thought. How long do we have this time? But then it didn't matter anymore.

"Laurie Jo—"

"Not yet." She poured coffee for both of them and yawned. Her outstretched arms waved toward the blue waters far below their terrace. "Let's have a few minutes more."

They sat in silence. She tried to watch the Atlantic, but the silence stretched on. "All right, darling. What is it?"

"There's been nothing on the newscasts about Greg. And then I got a signal. Prepare *Valkyrie* at once. The engines will be up, intact."

"And you wondered if there was a connection?" she asked.

"I knew there was a connection."

There was no emotion in his voice, and that frightened her. "I've bought us the stars, Aeneas. The engines will go up in a week. Tested, ready for installation. And you've done the rest, you and Kit. We can go to the Moon, with all the equipment for the colony—"

"Yes. And Greg Tolland stays on."

She wanted to shout: What is that to you? But she couldn't. "It was his price. The only one he'd take."

"It's too high."

She drew the thin silk robe around herself. Despite the bright sun she felt suddenly cold. "I've already agreed. I've given Greg my word."

"But I haven't. And you didn't tell me you were doing this."

"How could I? You wouldn't have agreed!"

"Precisely—"

"I can't lie to you, Aeneas." And now what do I lose? You? Everything I've worked for? Both? "The deal hasn't been made. Greg wants your word too."

"And if I don't give it?"

"Then he won't send up the engines. You're close enough to know what happens then. I'm at the edge of losing control of *Heimdall* to my partners. This is my only chance."

But it didn't have to be, he thought. You're in trouble because you insisted on speeding up the schedule, no matter what that cost, and it cost a lot. Technicians pulled off production work for *Valkyrie*. The Lunatic expedition. "You've put me in a hell of a fix, Laurie Jo."

"Damn you! Aeneas MacKenzie, damn you anyway!"

He tried to speak, but the rush of words stopped him as she shouted in anger. "Who appointed you guardian of the people? You and your damned honor! You're ready to throw away everything, and for what? For revenge on Greg Tolland!"

"But that's not true! I don't want revenge."

"Then what do you want, Aeneas?"

"I wanted out, Laurie Jo. It was you who insisted that I direct your agents in the investigation. I was finished with all that. I was willing to leave well enough alone, until we found—" Until it was clear that Greg Tolland had known everything. Until it was clear that he wasn't an honest man betrayed, that he was corrupt to the core, and had been for years. Until I couldn't help knowing that I'd spent most of my life electing— "You intended this all along, didn't you?" His voice was gentle and very sad.

Her anger was gone. It was impossible to keep it when he failed to respond. "Yes," she said. "It was the only way."

"The only way—"

"For us." She wouldn't meet his eyes. "What was I supposed to do, Aeneas? What kind of life do we have here? It takes every minute I have to keep Hansen Enterprises going. Greg Tolland has already tried to have you killed. You were safe enough in *Heimdall*, but what good was that? With you there and me here? And I couldn't keep the station if I lived there." And we've got so little time. We lost so many years, and there are so few left.

They were silent for a moment. Gulls cried in the wind, and overhead a jet thundered.

"And now I've done it," she said. "We can go to the Moon. I can arrange more supplies. *Valkyrie* doesn't cost so much to operate, and we'll have nearly everything we need to build the colony anyway. We can do it, Aeneas. We can found the first lunar colony, and be free of all this."

"But only if I agree—"

"Yes."

"Laurie Jo, would you give up the Moon venture for me?"

"Don't ask me to. Would you give up your vendetta against Greg for the Moon?"

He stood and came around the table. She seemed helpless and vulnerable, and he put his hands on her shoulders. She looked up in surprise: his face was quite calm now.

"No," he said. "But I'll do as you ask. Not for the Moon, Laurie Jo. For you."

She stood and embraced him, but as they clung to each other she couldn't help thinking, thank God, he's not incorruptible after all. He's not more than human.

She felt almost sad.

Two delta shapes, one above the other; below both was the enormous bulk of the expendable fuel tank which powered the ramjet of the atmospheric booster. The big ships sat atop a thick, solid rocket that would boost them to ram speed.

All that, Laurie Jo thought. All that, merely to get into orbit. And before the spaceplanes and shuttles, there were the disintegrating totem poles. No wonder space was an unattractive gamble until I built my lasers. The lasers had not been a gamble for her. A great part of the investment was in the power plants, and they made huge profits. The price she paid for *Heimdall* and *Valkyrie* hadn't been in money.

There were other costs, though, she thought. Officials bribed to expedite construction permits. Endless meetings to hold together a syndicate of international bankers. Deals with people who needed their money laundered. It would have been so easy to be part of the idle rich. Instead of parties I went to meetings, and I've yet to live with a man I love except for those few weeks we had.

And now I'm almost forty years old, and I have no children. But we will have! The doctors tell me I have a few years left, and we'll make the most of them.

They were taken up the elevator into the upper ship. It was huge, a squat triangle that could carry forty thousand kilos in one payload, and do it without the thirty-g stresses of the laser system. They entered by the crew access door, but she could see her technicians making a final examination of the nuclear engine in the cargo compartment.

She was placed in the acceleration couch by an Air Force officer. Aeneas was across a narrow passageway, and there were no other passengers. The young A.F. captain had a worried frown, as if he couldn't understand why this mission had suddenly been ordered, and why two strange civilians were going with a cargo for *Heimdall*.

You wouldn't want to know, my young friend, Laurie Jo thought. You wouldn't want to know at all.

Motors whined as the big clamshell doors of the cargo compartment were closed down. The A.F. officer went forward into the crew compartment. Lights flashed on the instrument board mounted in the forward part of the passenger bay, but Laurie Jo didn't understand what they meant.

"DING."

"MY GOD, WHAT NOW?"

"SIGNOR ANTONELLI HAS JUST NOW HEARD THAT YOU ARE GOING UP TO HEIMDALL. HE IS VERY DISTURBED."

I'll just bet he is, Laurie Jo thought. She glanced across the aisle at Aeneas. He was watching the display. "TELL SIGNOR ANTONELLI TO GO PLAY WITH HIMSELF."

"I HAVE NO TRANSLATION ROUTINE FOR THAT EXPRESSION."

"I DON'T WANT IT TRANSLATED. TELL HIM TO GO PLAY WITH HIMSELF."

There was a long pause. Something rumbled in the ship, then there were clanking noises as the gantries were drawn away.

"MISTER MC CARTNEY IS VERY DISTURBED ABOUT YOUR LAST MESSAGE AND ASKS THAT YOU RECONSIDER."

"TELL MC CARTNEY TO GO PLAY WITH HIMSELF TOO. CANCEL THAT. ASK MISTER MC CARTNEY TO SPEAK WITH SIGNOR ANTONELLI. I AM TAKING A VACATION. MC CARTNEY IS IN CHARGE. HE WILL HAVE TO MANAGE AS BEST HE CAN."

"ACKNOWLEDGED."

"Hear this. Liftoff in thirty seconds. Twenty-nine. Twenty-eight. Twenty seven. . . ."

The count reached zero, and there was nothing for an eternity. Then the ship lifted, pushing her into the couch. After a few moments there was nothing, another agonizing moment before the ramjets caught. Even inside the compartment they could hear the roaring thunder before that, too, began to fade. The ship lifted, leveled, and banked to go on course for the trajectory that would take it into an orbit matching *Heimdall*'s.

"GET MC CARTNEY ON THE LINE."

There was silence.

Out of range, she thought. She smiled and turned to Aeneas. "We did it," she said.

"Yes."

"You don't sound every excited."

He turned and smiled, and his hand reached out for hers, but they were too far apart. The ship angled steeply upward, and the roar of the ramjets grew louder again, then there was more weight as the rockets cut in. Seconds later the orbital vehicle separated from the carrier.

Laurie Jo looked through the thick viewport. The islands below were laid out like a map, their outlines obscured by cotton clouds far below them. The carrier ship banked off steeply and began its descent as the orbiter continued to climb.

Done, she thought. But she looked again at Aeneas, and he was staring back toward the United States and the world they had left behind.

"They don't need us, Aeneas," she said carefully.

"No. They don't need me at all."

She smiled softly. "But I need you. I always will."

# FIRST PATROL

## by Jerry Pournelle

### Editor's Introduction

I have no information regarding the history of this short story, other than this is its first publication. Jerry used his Wade Curtis pseudonym on the "First Patrol" manuscript, so it was most likely one of the stories he planned to send to John W. Campbell at *Analog*. After Campbell's death, Kay Tarrant—his placeholder—did not buy any more stories, leaving Jerry cut off from his primary market. One of the reasons Campbell was so successful was he not only paid top dollar, but he paid on acceptance. A real blessing to new writers and those living on the knife edge, like many science-fiction writers. And Campbell was a quick reader, often giving a yea or nay within a day or two, especially to his favored authors, like Heinlein, Anderson, Piper and Pournelle.

All the other SF magazines of the time, *The Magazine of Fantasy & Science Fiction*, *Galaxy Science Fiction* and *Amazing Stories* paid lower rates and some of them took six months or more before a writer learned if he'd sold a story or it was rejected. If it was bought, the author typically didn't get paid until publication—if ever. In addition, at the time this story was written (approximately 1971), Jerry was now concentrating on his new collaboration with Larry Niven, *The Mote in God's Eye*, which was quickly followed by *Inferno*. Thus, it was that Jerry turned away from writing SF short stories and novellas to writing novels and his *Galaxy* science fact columns.

"First Patrol" does have the distinction of being the only short story to ever take place in the First Empire of Man. Unlike the CoDominium period of his future history, Jerry never wrote many Empire stories, and most of those were novels, *King David's Space Ship*, *The Mote in God's Eye* and *The Gripping Hand*. It's unfortunate since the imperial period has a fascinating history, one we as readers want to learn more about.

This story takes place in the New Caledonia System during the dark years following the collapse of the First Empire. The system is discovered by Jasper Murcheson, a relative of Emperor Alexander IV, during his exploration of the Trans-Coalsack region. There he discovers a red super giant star (the closest such star to Earth), which will later be known as "Murcheson's Eye." Important mines are located on several lifeless moons, requiring a sizable fleet to protect them from Outie raids and the terraforming of two planets, New Scotland and New Ireland, in the New Caledonia System. In less than a century, a naval base is established on New Scotland and both worlds are settled by imperial colonists.

⁂

**A COLD WIND BLEW** across the quadrangle, and Francis ruthlessly suppressed a shiver, hoping that no one saw the tiny movement. As little as he had moved, his neck was again sawed by the stiff collar of his dress tunic, taking his mind for the moment from his stiff fingers in their white thin klatan gloves. His Excellent Highness droned on and on about the war.

Francis did not resent the presence of His Most Excellent Highness, Imperial Viceroy for New Scotland and the New Caledonian System, Patrician of the Empire, Knight Commander of the Order of Comets and Sunburst, and only the Holy Father knew how many more titles and honors. It never occurred to him that he could resent him. The war had left New Scotland few resources other than her men, and boys were taught to take their Imperialism seriously. As the last visible link with Empire, His Most Excellent Highness was, despite his rather bulging stomach and popping eyes, the most important symbol on the planet. What he represented was the only thing that made life worth living to the remnants of the old

Navy base workers—or rather their descendants, as the last real links with the Empire had vanished with the Fleet almost two centuries before.

There wasn't anything amusing about what he was saying, either, but Mr. Midshipman Francis Kane wished mightily that the speech would be over and he could find out what ship he'd been posted to. That would be far more interesting than the usual patriotic fare.

No such luck, he thought. The military situation of New Scotland was so desperate that the viceroy was losing no chances to inspire the audience with Imperial zeal, and graduation with its attendant speeches was a most important ceremony in the life of a midshipman. Perhaps it was a little more important to the parents and officials of the Imperial Government than it was to the boys, but then seventeen-year-olds couldn't be expected to take such things as seriously as they ought to. His Excellent Highness spoke on:

"You young men who graduate here today, like those in the other academies, are truly the hope of New Scotland. Perhaps one of you will be the means by which we reestablish contact with the Emperor. Or perhaps, and it is more than perhaps, it is a certainty, one of you will be so fortunate as to engage the enemy bent on making a new assault on the Yards. When that time comes, you may feel alone, but remember that the Empire is with you." His Highness paused to consult his notecard, then continued.

"Out among the planets—dare I say out among the stars?—many of you will find death. The Admiralty records show that as many as half the midshipmen of a class have failed to come back from their first patrols during years when the enemy assaults have been heavy. But you must understand, the Empire has already claimed your life as it has claimed mine. Some die with honor, a credit to their classmates and shipmates. Some die wretchedly, cowards, remembered only by their families, and then only with shame. But there are none of those in this class. There are none aboard our ships."

There was a fly crawling up the back of Mr. Midshipman McLaughlin's neck. Freddy McLaughlin was Frank Kane's roommate and best friend at the Academy, and if there had been some way to do something about the fly, Frank would have done it. Without moving, though, he couldn't think of a thing short of spitting at it, and he thought Freddy would rather have the fly. The sight of the insect set Frank thinking about a lecture his biology teacher had given.

"All life on New Scotland and New Ireland is imported," the old man had said, limping back and forth in the narrow space between the laboratory bench and the blackboard. Professor Captain Beecher, ISN, Ret., had preferred to conduct his classes in a laboratory theater, even the ones that never got laboratory demonstrations. Since he held the Imperial Sunburst with clusters, the Academy was inclined to humor his requests.

"The first settlements in the New Caledonian System were bases to service the scientific expedition to study Murcheson's Eye, the only red supergiant star within human-explored space. To most of the Empire, the Eye is hidden behind the Coal Sack. Our system is on the same side of the Coal Sack as the Eye, and only thirty-five light-years away. The scientists established a station in orbit around our gas giant Dagda to observe the big red mess. Then the Empire got interested in the mines on Mider. The little installations on the moons were just too small and too cold, and there's nothing inhabitable out that far. They needed a base for repairs, and after the barbarian raids started, they needed a sizable fleet to protect the mines. The scientists had to give up, but by then the mines were important. There's nothing inhabitable closer than New Scotland, so they partially terraformed us and put the base here. While they were at it they terraformed New Ireland, intending to put in a full colony. . . ." Beecher's voice had trailed off, and the class remembered he had originally been from New Ireland. The gray old man stood proudly erect as he faced his class. "And by God they did a good job. They set up a whole ecology.

"Do you have any idea how complex a thing like that can be? How each interrelated each species is with others, everything dependent on something else? How many insects needed to dispose of the carcasses, and birds to catch the insects? It was an incredibly complex job, ecological planning. But the Imperial Colony Service had faced it many times. They had five standard ecological packages, each adapted to a particular set of conditions. So that's how we got ours, chosen to suit the bare rock and no-life conditions of the young worlds in the system. The next time you get unhappy with an insect or one of the other life forms here, just remember they all have a purpose."

They might all have a purpose, Francis Kane thought, but he was sure Freddy would be glad to trade all the flies in on something that didn't land on you during parade. Up on the stand, His Excellent Highness was just finishing:

"And so, midshipmen of the Empire, I am pleased to welcome a new class of seniors to the service of the Emperor. May you serve honorably and well, and make the next class envious." His Highness stepped back, a swirl of crimson cape and starched white blouse, standing stiffly on the reviewing stand as the band struck up the Imperial Anthem.

The speech may have been predictable, but its every word was true. The new officers of the Navy stood between the enemy and the end of a way of life, centuries of dedication to an idea which might never be realizable, but which stood for the kind of liberty men enjoyed in the interior provinces. And there were so few cadets in his class. There seemed to be fewer every year as the war took its toll of the young men when they stopped the enemy, and the people at home when they could not.

As the music died away, Mr. Midshipman Kane sniffed hard and batted his eyelids to clear away the tears that always seemed to form when the anthem was played. He hoped no one noticed, and never realized that fully half the brigade was hoping the same thing.

"COMPANIES, ATTENSHUN!" the cadet commander called. From his post as commander of Company B, Mr. Midshipman Kane prepared to march his men.

"OFFICERS DRAW—SABERS." With practiced motions, the archaic weapons were snicked from their scabbards and brought to the salute. No one had ever explained why a young man about to embark as an officer of a spaceship needed a saber, but it seemed right in his hand as he turned to face his troops.

"PASS IN REVIEW!" The piper major raised his baton, and the piper squealed as the brigade of midshipman marched past the reviewing stand, each company saluting their commandant, then bowing to His Most Excellent Highness as representative of His Imperial Majesty himself.

***

The list was posted in the quadrangle of the ancient brick Academy. When the brigade was dismissed, Kane ran past the fortified Marine Barracks and the Fortress which generated the Langston Field to protect the naval installations of the capital and only city of New Scotland, racing his other classmates to the bulletin boards. Bonnets flew from young heads to be retrieved by lowerclassmen for their betters, as seniors demonstrated that for all the dignity of a first classman, the nature of boys had not changed since the Academy was built. Francis Kane was among the first to reach the list, but before he could find his name he was surrounded by a yelling pack of others, the taller ones inexplicably thrusting their way to the front to obscure the view of the flimsy papers. It was several minutes before he managed to worm his head between two other boys.

This time he found his name almost at once. Kane, Francis X. Brand of Service: General Line Officer. Duty Station: *INS Reliance*. He pulled away from the pack and strode to the middle of the quadrangle, his polished boots scuffed because Mr. Midshipman Altando had stepped on the toe of each, but scuffed or not, Kane did not believe they touched the hard cobblestones of the yard.

*Reliance*, he thought. A battle cruiser, one of the fastest fighting ships in the Navy. Not as powerful as the precious great battleships, or the half-legendary starcruising dreadnoughts the Emperor's forces had somewhere in the galaxy, but fast, equipped for long patrol duties and able to fight almost anything the enemy would try to sneak past. She'd been in for repairs at the base on the inner moon, and Francis hoped she'd leave orbit soon with him aboard. He knew it was likely, and felt guilt as he realized his mother would want him to have a full leave at home with her. Father would be proud, though. They knew he would be posted to watch-keeping duties, his grades assured that, but to go in *Reliance* as his first ship was beyond what he'd hoped for.

Kane saw Altando approaching, a smile on his fact, obviously bursting to tell him of his new post. "What'd you make, Frank?" his classmate boomed, but instead of waiting for an answer he shouted, "I got Marines. On *MacArthur*. It's New Ireland and the war after leave, I'm sure of it."

Kane let him gloat for a few moments, then recalling his ruined boots said, "I didn't get much. General line in *Reliance*." He stayed just long enough to watch the look of envy come into Altando's face before he went back to his room.

Freddy McLaughlin was there ahead of him, his longer legs and six month advantage having given him the opportunity to get to the bulletin board before Kane. As Frank came into the spartan quarters, his roommate was already packing his gear.

"You made engineering, of course," Francis said. McLaughlin nodded, and Francis added, "I got *Reliance*. Did you make it, too?"

"Yes!" Freddy shouted. "Engineering in *Reliance*. Maybe we'll share a cabin in her. Just like old times."

"Oh, come on, Freddy. You can be so dumb for someone so smart. *Reliance* is a cruiser, there won't be any cabins for middies. The gun room, that's our quarters." Kane had hoped for a cruiser, and spent the previous week reviewing what he could find of her in the library. There wasn't much. The Academy was supposed to teach the boys the general principles of Navy life, but was a liberal college education otherwise. There was no secret information in the library, and very little given to midshipmen. Time enough for that when they were sworn to the service and aboard their ships, or off to the specialty schools. Frank thought for a moment, then asked, "Why do they call it the gun room anyway? There aren't any guns in it."

Freddy smiled. "There used to be ship's arms kept in the midshipmen's quarters so that the middies could guard the officers against mutiny." He went back to packing.

Well, Francis thought, I'm no better off than I was before. When he thought of it, he never was, asking Freddy something like that. His roommate always had an answer, but Francis was never sure the answer was right, and there was no way of checking it. One day, he thought, one day I'm going to catch McLaughlin on something I know that he's made up. . . .

But Freddy's explanation made sense. There had never been a mutiny in the Imperial Navy, at least not in the New Scotland station. Everyone on New Scotland was descended from the survivors of the original Yards on the planet, and was a dedicated Imperialist. Well, nearly everybody. There was the Peace Party, it called itself, which wanted to scrap the Imperial symbols and make peace with the Secessionist enemy, saying that all the rebels ever wanted was for everyone to live in what they called a democratic way. But the Party was small, and surely it could never make any converts in the Navy. But hadn't Freddy mentioned some kind of trouble with New Ireland conscripts? That was the Army, of course, but . . .

"Better get packing," Freddy said. "Swearing in and official orders in half an hour. You don't want to have to come back here, do you?"

Francis turned to his locker and dragged out his space bags, stuffing all the issue equipment and some of the personal items inside. By tradition, anything he couldn't carry to his new post belonged to the seniors who would occupy the room next, and as Frank hadn't managed to send a lot of his books and pictures home the week before, he was leaving a treasure trove. Well, so much the better for the new men, he thought, but he winced at the money he'd spent on some of those items. His parents could ill afford the little extra they'd sent him during his four years, and it was too bad so much of it was forfeit. Well, maybe the new men would need it more than he did; all the officer families seemed a little poorer each year.

His homecoming two hours later was spoiled by his orders. *Reliance* was due for a patrol within the week, and instead of the twenty days his mother had expected, Kane would be home for only two. He looked around the big house, symbol of the Kanes's membership in the old families of the capital but impossible to keep up on their present income, and hoped his younger brother would be successful in business. It wasn't likely that Francis Kane would restore the family fortunes.

The interview with his father went well. Although he had been unable to come to the graduation ceremonies, Commander Alphon Kane, ISN, Ret., had got his uniform on, with Cecil standing stiffly behind the wheelchair, waiting in the entrance hall for Francis's return. Frank saluted formally; it was the first time he had seen his father in uniform for years, and it seemed right to do it somehow. The commander returned the salute just as formally, then grinned and held his arms out to embrace his son.

"What ship, boy, what ship?" he asked impatiently.

"How do you know I wasn't posted to a school, father?" Francis asked.

"Bah. You're not an intellectual. You'll be a fighting sailor like your father and my father. School indeed. The General Staff's not for the Kanes."

"*Reliance*."

"Ah, ha. I knew it, I knew it. Almost as good as *Dundee*, better for a first tour, a man ought to learn about the big ships before he takes his proper post." His father smiled, remembering his last command in *Dundee*, a light patrol and scouting craft, shortly after the war between New Scotland and New Ireland had reignited following decades of relative peace. The original *Dundee* had been destroyed in the blast of fire that cost the elder Kane his legs and his health, but there was a new one incorporating steel and engines space-salvaged from the original. The new *Dundee* was one of the last ships they had managed to build on New Scotland.

Raiders had penetrated the fleet and damaged the Yards again, and it would be some time before new ships could be completed. If the Emperor sent his forces back to New Caledonia, and the great dreadnoughts came back in a burst of fire, they would cross the star lanes to the other component of their binary system and put paid to the rebels. Until then, the fleet had to prevent another raid on the Yards.

"Boy, you're going on patrol aren't you? Soon. They can't keep *Reliance* in orbit here. They timed her refit to come with graduation and she'll be off soon. When, lad?"

And when Francis told him and mother came in and heard, he wished he were leaving that evening. He hated himself for the thought, but his mother's tears upset him, and her criticism of the service for not giving a boy any more time at home than *that* was almost more than he could stand.

"His ship's needed, Mother," Commander Kane said quietly. "And if the patrols can't stop reinforcements getting to New Ireland, we're going to lose that planet. This is a critical point in the war, Mother, and they can't keep a battle cruiser in home space just to let a boy take his leave."

But his mother never realized that Francis had no life but the Navy. She hadn't known it years ago when Frank first realized that to be father's oldest son was to have a destiny.

⁂

Inactivity on the long flights from home orbit to the patrol regions out beyond Mider and Dagda was a source of constant trouble for the older officers and the crew, but Francis Kane found that a new midshipman had no time to himself whatsoever. He stood one watch in three, and was expected to complete his formal studies, learn everything there was to know about the ship, understand the strategy of the war and the tactics of space engagements, learn to use the equipment for going outside, and learn to pilot the ship's boats in his offwatch time. He found that between formal meals and compulsory studies, he never wanted to do anything when left to himself but sleep.

There was no time for talk with Freddy, and as to the elaborate hobbies which the lieutenants and permanent warrant officers engaged in, Frank did not have enough time to learn what they were doing except for seeing the final products of those who engaged in handicrafts. The older midshipmen left the new middies to themselves for the trip out, although it was understood they would reclaim their traditional privileges over men not yet in a firefight when they reached the patrol stations.

Francis was shown through the ship, all of her two hundred meter spherical shape. The Langston Field, which absorbed energy of all kinds as an exponential function of its kinetic energy, was explained to him although no one really understood the basic principles by which it operated. With the other new middies, Kane found himself handed over to the engineering officer for instruction.

"The Field's a tricky thing, lads," the gray-bearded engineering commander told them. Mister MacReedy spoke with a thick accent common among men raised in the back country of New Scotland. "You could put your hand through it slow like, but the faster something's moving in it, the more it grabs you—you might say. So a fusion bomb set off right outside the ship won't hurt a thing barring we get shook up by light pressure tossing us about a bit. But torpedoes, now, they can come in slow like and get through the Field, go off against the midway armor where only half the Field's left. Bit of that goes a long way, if they can hit us."

Fontaine, a new midshipman Kane had known only casually in the Academy, asked, "How much energy can a Langston Field absorb?"

"Enough lad, enough. But there's a limit. Problem is you can't use the energy that comes into the Field without expending energy generated by the ship's engines to control it. So when the enemy pumps us up with beams and bombs, it costs us to dissipate that excess. Have to radiate if off, and the problem is to keep the Field from radiating to the inside as well as outside. In a battle, the ships glow from the excess, you can tell from the color how close the Field is to collapsing. Here, take a look at it now."

They saw a dull black in the screens.

"Sir, why is the Field on now if it costs us energy to maintain it?" Fontaine asked.

"We use it as part of the ship's drive process, lad. But we've got her up stronger than we need for that because this is part of the patrol. Not likely to find a raider in close, but we might, and even a small ship could knock us out with torpedoes if we didn't have the Langston Field up. Collapse us in the first burst."

The phrase sounded ominous to the midshipmen. Kane knew from his father what a Field collapse would do: vaporize everything inside the ship. Before that happened, though, there were usually local failures, partial penetrations of the Field by photon beams or projectiles. That had happened to the *Dundee*, beamed through in four places during a multiship battle which had moved on before the enemy could utterly destroy the little escort vessel.

MacReedy took the midshipmen out of the Field control room to the main engine station, where Francis saw Freddy McLaughlin sitting self-importantly at a console. On the panel above Freddy was painted a model of the fusion drive process, gauges and lights at each component symbol. The engine room computer as well as the ship's main computer normally monitored the drive system, but Navy regulations insisted that human officers also man each station. Freddy McLaughlin took his duties seriously, waving absently at Francis, then returning to his watch. The engine room was interesting, but the whole time he was there, Francis kept thinking of the fate of *Dundee*, trying to imagine life in a wheelchair. He also tried to imagine a universe without Francis Kane, but was unable to do so.

Frank submitted to the engine room tour and the rest of his instruction, but his main interest lay in learning to pilot the ship's auxiliary craft. At first, they got no practice at all, only dull theory classes. The ship was accelerating so fast that bringing the needle-shaped longboats up to *Reliance* and getting them docked was a tricky task even for the ship's computers. There was too much chance of accidents.

But when the acceleration was slowed, Captain Duncan insisted that the watch-keeping middies get instruction on boat handling, so Kane found himself sitting in the second pilot's chair of the longboat for three days running. At first, it was as much fun as he had expected, but then it became a nightmare. The main computer on board the longboat was fully capable of flying the ship under general orders. All it needed was to be told what its human operators wanted and it would compute the velocities necessary, controlling the engines itself for such delicate maneuvers as docking and matching velocities with *Reliance.* But Lieutenant Preston, the longboat pilot, wouldn't let Kane use the computer after the first time out. Francis found himself forced to maneuver the ship to some arbitrarily chosen point in space relative to *Reliance*, his performance always monitored on the boat's computer and always unacceptable. Then Preston would carefully and deliberately point out Francis's failings, lingering over each aspect of his total inadequacy as a pilot and an officer.

Kane was glad enough to leave his education in handling the longboats when the ship resumed acceleration, but he found that even this did not save him. Once a week he was required to practice bringing the craft alongside *Reliance* while the cruiser's velocities were constantly changing. First the computer would do it, then Frank had to try it manually. When the sessions were over, he looked forward to other tasks, only to find them equally as difficult. Life as a midshipman seemed to be one impossible job after another.

His new problem was the first lieutenant, Mr. Blackpool. Not only did the officer have the general responsibility for midshipman instruction, but Francis had drawn Blackpool's watch, so he was under the eye of his superior and instructor most of the day. He thought life could hold no greater misery, as nothing he ever did seemed to be good enough for the unemotional Blackpool. Once, Francis spilled a full cup of coffee on the first lieutenant, and stood in terror, expecting the man to explode. Instead, Mr. Blackpool calmly and unexcitedly discussed Kane, midshipmen in general, the deterioration of the Navy and the probable fate of an Empire defended by officers not even competent to carry coffee in low gravity.

Kane's station as midshipman of the watch was on the bridge, where he sat at a console much like the one Freddy McLaughlin manned in the engine room. An enormous panel, partially duplicating the main control station of the officer of the watch, gave the status of every important system on the ship. A much smaller group of keys and dials allowed inputs to the ship's computer, or, by switching the emergency control, to the drive engines. In addition, a complex of circuits allowed both the midshipman and the officer of the watch to communicate with the crew stations. Francis learned that the computer actually flew the ship, continuously displaying alternate actions for the crew to accept, and choosing from the top one on the list if there was no response.

"*Reliance* can handle herself pretty well without us," Blackpool told him one day as he stood behind Frank's acceleration chair to drink his coffee. "But there's always battle damage, and then we earn our keep. Or some of us do. That's why you've got to learn to do everything the computer does, although you won't be as fast or as accurate as it is. Don't forget, Kane, the brain can't think of any tactics somebody hasn't already programmed into it, and there come up situations that aren't in the book. What's the fuel status, mister?"

Frank searched over the complex of dials frantically before finding the display which told him how many tons of hydrogen were in the ship's tanks, and how long they could maintain present acceleration with the fuel. Before he could answer, Blackpool said, "Too long, mister. I want you to write it out every half hour on your next watch. Then you'll know how to find it when I want it."

"Aye, aye, sir," Kane responded. He had found that there were only about ten useful remarks in a midshipman's vocabulary, and that was the one most often used. He wondered why the Academy had bothered with courses on writing and speaking. A soft tone sounded.

"By your leave, sir," Kane said, using another tenth of the midshipman's vocabulary, "It's time to take the star sights."

"Get to it." Blackpool returned to his console. "I have her, mister."

Francis manipulated the controls to bring a view of the New

Caledonia sun, officially named Murcheson A but universally called Cal, onto his screen. Then he brought other stars into the field, checked their appearance against a book of star charts, and moved a dial to bring a ring of light around one of them. Finally he pressed an input key. As far as the ship was concerned the course calculations were made within an instant, the computer measuring the angle to the selected star pattern and comparing the results with precalculated figures for the selected course and destination. No warning lights came on, so they were on course. Kane glanced at the correction board and found that the deviation from predicted position was well within the expected error of measurement, noted it on his log and signed the entry.

But although *Reliance* was finished with the calculations, Kane still had his own busy work to do. Using the sextant he obtained a reading which stopped the tiny clock built into the instrument itself, and took out the tables for the laborious calculations required to get a line of position for *Reliance*. By the time he obtained it, the ship had covered a great distance and his calculations were useless for navigation, but Blackpool accepted them with a grunt, noted the time it had taken to prepare them, and fed his results into the ship's computer. The brain only took moments to compare Francis's results with the position of the ship at the time he had taken the sight. Blackpool wrote the error at the bottom of the page before returning it to the midshipman with his initials.

"Better, Mister Kane. Bloody awful, but better. Paste this in your book and make your plot."

This was another onerous and unnecessary duty. The computer kept a running position fix at all times, requiring only that human operators check from time to time to see that it was tracking the right stars, but Blackpool unreasonably demanded that the midshipman of the watch keep a paper chart of the position of the ship relative to all known objects in the Caledonian System. They were allowed to use the computer to find most of the planets, but sometimes they would find that Blackpool had blocked their console from receiving current information, and there was nothing for it but to compute the various positions. Kane had barely finished the plot and brought the watch log up to date when his duty ended for the day. He stumbled down to the gunroom and further studies.

Francis had just wearily finished trying to memorize the location and effectiveness of each of the ship's gun installations, and turned to other tasks when Freddy McLaughlin came off watch, delayed as usual by some crisis or another MacReedy had found to keep his midshipman busy. Freddy climbed into the upper bunk above Francis and collapsed exhausted. A few moments later first one boot, then the other, floated strangely down to the deck in the partial gravity.

Frank had been alone in the after gunroom, the other midshipmen being either on watch or assembled along the long table in the forward gunroom adjacent to their sleeping quarters. Francis had long since found that he was unable to study at the table with the others, and Mister MacReedy was giving him only two more days to understand the basic physics of the fusion generators which drove the ship. He was absorbed in the engine flow diagram and transfer equations when Freddy stirred above him.

"Where are we?" Freddy asked sleepily from above as Francis struggled with the first tensor describing the conversion of hydrogen to energy.

"Crossing the orbit of New Ireland tomorrow," Francis answered absently.

"New Ireland's inside the orbit of New Scotland and we're going to Dagda. Don't be ridiculous," Freddy said, by now almost asleep.

"You've let being on watch after watch fog your brain," Francis retorted. "I never expect the engineers to know anything, but what did you do in basic astronomy, sleep?" When he heard no answer, he went on. "Look, New Ireland's the second planet, New Scotland's third, and then there's Fomar. Then there's a big gap, and you've got Mider and Dagda in the same orbit. But Dagda's nearly the other side of Cal from where New Scotland is right now, so we have to fly inside the orbit of New Ireland to reach it. We're already passed through the orbit of Conchobar, and that's the *first* planet. He wasn't anywhere near at the time, but we'll go close to New Ireland. Don't be a plantean."

"Uh, yeah, I see it," the sleepy voice replied. Freddy was, Francis knew, able to visualize almost anything he set his mind to. A working model of the Cal system, complete with the multiple moons of New Scotland and Dagda, wouldn't be beyond him if he decided to mentally construct one. But Freddy could be so stupid!

Francis tried to study, but his friend wanted to talk. Frank was starved for conversation himself. Anything was better than the ten-phrase vocabulary he used on the bridge, even the horrible coming session with MacReedy when he had to confess that he didn't yet understand the engines. He put the books aside and they discussed life in the Academy, and how the Navy was so much different from what they had expected.

"I didn't think it was going to be just a lot of busy work," Francis said. "Half of what I do the computers have already done, and the other half they could do better than me. I don't mind the study and the real duty, but most of it isn't real at all . . . and Freddy, I never seem to do anything right. How could I when the work's designed to be done by machines I can't use?"

"You've noticed," McLaughlin said. "Mr. MacReedy seems to think an engineering midshipman exists to run errands for the big brain. Monitor the output of the engines, check the strength of the Field, calculate predicted velocities at various energy trade-off levels, and the computer has already done every bit of it. It's enough to drive me insane on top of everything else. The Hell with the Navy."

Frank could never have brought himself to say it, but he had second thoughts about the Navy himself. Since it had been his whole life, and his father's before him, he felt a terrible sense of loss and an inability to understand what he would do now. But until this patrol was finished there wasn't anything to do but try to keep out of Blackpool's way, get through each day as best he could.

"Why do you think they do it, Freddy?" he asked.

"They had to do it, and by all the saints we will too," McLaughlin replied. "It takes a certain type of low-grade mentality to be a Naval officer nowadays. They lost so many of their capabilities during the war and the raids that there's not a lot left. The good ones get killed off, the rest run the Navy." The boy's voice trailed off.

Francis went back to his page of physics, wishing for some of Freddy's selective stupidity. McLaughlin didn't always have much common sense, but he knew everything there was about engines and power. Or it seemed to Kane that he did, although Mr. MacReedy had other ideas. Someday they'd show them, Frank thought. Only now, since he wasn't cut out for the Navy after all? What would he do?

"Frank," McLaughlin asked suddenly, "can you call me to the bridge next time you have watch? I'd like to see New Ireland. Do you think we'll stop there?"

"I'll call you, but we won't stop. The rebels have protected bases down there, and there are running gun battles between them and the gunships the Navy towed into orbit to support the Marines. The cruiser wouldn't stand a chance near New Ireland. And I heard the skipper tell Mr. Blackpool there may be supply ships trying to come in to reinforce the rebels, or even cruisers and stuff to help their ground stations fight our gunships. The line from the rebels' Alderson Jump point to New Ireland goes along our course, and we're supposed to look out for them. The skipper said it was awful important that they not get anything through right now because we could lose the whole planet to them, and once they got bases established there with real ground fortresses around them we'd never get them out. Then New Scotland would be in trouble, or we might have to blast New Ireland so bad just to survive you could never colonize the planet."

He looked at the pages of figures which danced teasingly across the paper and threw them down. "Freddy, we could be in action in thirty hours."

"This close to home? If they can get in this far, they could raid the Yards again. Mary and Joseph, old MacReedy's kept me so busy crawling through the inside of the engines when I'm not on watch I don't even know where we are, and you say we go on alert now?"

"Not full alert, but the watch starts earning its pay from here on," he said with the smug assurance of a seventeen-year-old who knows more than an eighteen-year-old. He thought for a second more and said, "Freddie, what if we captured a rebel starship? Got a real stellar drive in good condition. We could go find the Emperor and bring back the fleet."

"Sure, and klatans start flying. Let me get some sleep." Freddy turned heavily in his bunk, and Francis tried to go back to his studies.

He couldn't concentrate. He kept seeing the ceremony in which the viceroy awarded metals to everybody in *Reliance*, and then his imagination ran on, until somehow it was *his* starship, he had captured it and he was commander, and they went to find the

Emperor. "Your Imperial Majesty, New Scotland remains loyal. I have come in the name of Your Majesty's loyal viceroy to ask for a fleet to crush the rebels and return all the stars of the Trans-Coalsack Sector to the Empire . . . only for God's sake, Your Majesty, hurry, because I don't think we can hold out for another hundred years. . . ."

But the Emperor would send dreadnoughts, and Francis would see the Imperial capital Sparta, and even Earth itself, and walk along the streets where heroes walked thousands of years ago. Earth had to be all right, it just had to be. The last contact with Sparta and Earth had been nearly two hundred years ago, when almost every starship in this frontier edge of the Empire had been called home for defense of the capital. And shortly after that, the planet which circled Cal's distant binary, Murcheson B, had revolted; these rebels had destroyed New Scotland's few remaining interstellar ships, attacked the Yards on New Scotland, and destroyed most of the cities. The little fleet of planetary cruisers had fought back against the rebel forces. The history books showed that the loyalists of New Scotland had lost the war, yet somehow the raids had stopped.

They had learned later that another group of rebels from further away had attacked Murcheson B and sacked the planet, destroying much of its fleet, giving the survivors on New Scotland a chance to rebuild the Yards and construct more planetary ships. But they couldn't replicate the Alderson Drive which allowed ships to travel through hyperspace from star to star. The only men who had known how were dead in the raids, and the last components of the star drives were a heap of slag, and the war went on and on, with no prospect of an end, while the rebels got a little stronger every generation.

A week past the orbit of New Ireland, Captain Duncan ordered the ship's engines shut down. They coasted along, but despite their velocity there was no sensation of motion on the ship. Star positions changed so slowly that only the instruments could measure the difference. The ship was now in a weightless condition, with little for the men to do, and Francis found his first experience at command when he was appointed exercise master on alternate days. He was also expected to inspect the men to see that they wore their exercise harnesses at all times. Crewmen had a tendency to take them off and glory in no weight, but this produced calcification of their blood vessels. The tension harness substituted for gravity, making it an effort to bend arms and legs, or even to expand the chest to breathe.

After a week of running around passing out demerits to crewmen old enough to be his father, Francis found himself posted to a new duty station as copilot of the longboat. The ship's boats would accelerate away from *Reliance* to stations enormous distances away, then correct their velocity to match the cruiser, floating thousands of kilometers ahead of her and off to the side until the Langston Field which protected the auxiliary craft decayed and they had to return to *Reliance* to have it regenerated.

Field generators were heavy and bulky, and could not be carried on craft as small as the longboats which also had rocket engines to allow them to land on planetary surfaces while *Reliance* floated in orbit. The big warships almost never went planetside.

They would stay aboard *Reliance* only a few hours, which were usually made painful for Francis because Blackpool took that opportunity to inspect his progress in his studies. Then, the Field regenerated, the longboat would set out again to widen the net *Reliance* was spreading through space in its desperate search for supply ships or raiders.

After the second trip, Preston gave the pilot task to Francis, and would sit in the command chair with his head rolled back, half asleep, or read one of the innumerable romances he carried with him. Even on patrol duty, Francis found that he was required to do most of the piloting by hand, and criticized whenever he was not as good as the computer in getting on station.

Time passed slowly on the patrols, even for a beginning midshipman. The tours were made more difficult by the tiny space aboard the longboats, and the lack of watchkeeping officers. Someone had to be on the bridge and awake at all times, and that turned out to be Frank. There was little to do but study and wait. The ship's detectors were far more sensitive than any human and would warn them of approaching intruders. At first, Francis had been excited, waiting for the detectors to sound their alarm, waiting to flash the message back to *Reliance* and close with the enemy, but after weeks of inactivity, it was impossible to believe they would ever see anything. Time dragged on.

They were approaching the orbit of Dagda, and had been through three periods of deceleration. It would soon be time to match velocities with the great gas giant and take on more hydrogen for the ship's reactors before taking up patrol stations again. Preston had finished his supply of romances, and devoted part of his time to inspecting Francis's work on astrophysics. He was friendly enough, at times, but had the typical Navy attitude that nothing a midshipman did was quite good enough. Just when Frank would feel that the older man was becoming more reasonable, he would find some of the busywork that Kane hated, plotting positions or making calculations which the computers had already made.

Frank served as second officer on the longboat, inspecting the crew and reporting infractions of the rules to Preston. Crew quarters were aft of the control station, and Frank went there only for his morning tours. He learned the names of the men, and some of their vices, but they were competently led by Chief Soames, a gray-bearded veteran of thirty years' service who took advantage of the privileges of rank to grow a fine set of muttonchop whiskers that were the envy of *Reliance*. The Navy discouraged unnecessary contact between officers and men, so Kane knew little of the man other than his obvious competence.

They were ending the last tour on scouting patrol before going to Dagda. Francis measured the strength of the Field and reported, "First measurable decrease, Mr. Preston." The Field would decay with increasing speed until it was renewed by *Reliance*.

"Sound acceleration warning," Preston said. "Take her home, Mr. Kane, and report in."

"Aye, aye, sir." Francis touched keys to turn the ship around her long axis, glancing at the computed intercept point for standard acceleration. The computer would have taken the entire maneuver if told to do so, but Preston insisted that Francis display his piloting abilities. For once Naval policy relieved the boredom of patrol duty, and Kane was glad of the chance, although he suspected he would be in trouble for sloppy work by the time they arrived. He had turned the ship and prepared to start engines when the gong sounded.

"Photon beams at forty thousand kilometers," the petty officer of the watch said from his station below. The computer confirmed the sighting. There was a pause as the ship's radars swept the area, searching for the ship which had flashed its engines where no ship should be. "Definitely a ship," the petty officer announced. "Size data complete."

"I've got the helm," Preston snapped. "Notify *Reliance* and sound general quarters."

"Aye, aye, sir," Francis answered. The warning horn sounded through the longboat as Francis broadcast the alert to the cruiser. At the same time, all information on the intruder in the longboat's computer was flashed to the main computer on *Reliance*.

In moments, there was an answer from Lieutenant Blackpool. "There's nothing scheduled for out here. Close with her for inspection."

"Aye, aye, sir," Francis said. Preston gave the problem to the computer and the acceleration alarm sounded, then the longboat's engines responded. Kane felt the drag of three gravities, four, more, and the pressurized compartments of his battle armor fought to keep his circulatory system from collapsing. He watched the screens through a red haze, every movement an effort.

The main screen showed a brilliant beam of light which suddenly appeared in the black of space. "They're trying to run off," Preston said grimly. "It's rebels all right. Neuts might try to sneak past, but they wouldn't run."

"What is it, sir?" Kane gasped.

"Supply ship for New Ireland, most likely." Preston paused for breath. "They were trying to go off at a tangent to our inspection pattern and come around from the back side. Might be a raider, it's fast."

Francis thought they might be falling behind already. Certainly *Reliance* was drawing away from them, going off to port.

The chase went on for hours. *Reliance* drew steadily away from her boat. "Be a near thing," Preston muttered. The longboat's computer had determined that the crew could not survive the extended acceleration and cut back to two gravities. On board *Reliance*, all the men would be in full high-g tanks, but the longboats did not carry such elaborate equipment. Preston scanned the gauges and said, "Not much fuel left, and the Field down to three-quarter strength. Pass the word to *Reliance*."

The answer was brief. "Continue pursuit." The longboat was expendable, and would not intercept until long after the cruiser was engaged with the enemy. Captain Duncan had no time to spare picking up its boats. If the enemy was an enemy raider, it might yet get through the patrols, despite the warning now sent to all the Navy bases in the system. Stopping it was worth a longboat.

It was a strange chase. Aside from monitoring the computer outputs, Preston and Kane had nothing to do, yet it was impossible to relax in the high acceleration and higher tension of the pursuit. Francis sat at his station, trying to follow Preston's orders and sleep, but was too excited to do more than close his eyes. He managed to drift off in fits and starts, but would suddenly come awake, to peer at the situation plot before trying once again to relax.

The hours went by, and Francis finally managed to fall into a doze, not sleeping soundly but at least unaware of what was going on around him until he was suddenly awakened by the action stations alarm. *Reliance* had engaged the enemy, and the longboat was catching up rapidly.

"It's a commerce raider," Preston grunted. "Well armed."

He watched as the enemy ship returned fire. The screens on both ships began to take on a dark dull red color.

"They're both shunting power to the Field and guns, not much left for the engines," Preston said. "We'll catch them soon enough now." As they drew closer, the lieutenant stared at the screens intently. "By the saints, midshipman, we've got something near a battleship out there. Better armor than *Reliance*, and a lot of firepower. Pray it hadn't had a chance to take on fuel after coming through the transition point, or we could lose this one."

The rebel ships usually came in pairs, a warship and a merchantman with hydrogen, but they generally didn't travel exactly together.

The space ahead of them was brightly lighted as photon beams from the two ships played against each other. *Reliance* was about to overhaul the enemy, using her superior speed to maneuver into a better fighting position. The longboat now had work to do, establishing the enemy's position and relaying it back to the parent cruiser. Preston took the boat off to starboard, away from the side engaged by *Reliance*.

"Duncan's blind now," Preston said. "Every sensor that could bear on the enemy will be cooked as fast as it extends outside the Field, but the enemy can't see *Reliance* either." He programmed instruction to the longboat computer. "We'll get in closer and slip a torpedo into her. That'll give them something to worry about."

His attack plan called for maximum acceleration toward the enemy before torpedo launch. The acceleration warning sounded, then another gong rang out.

"Second vessel astern," Soames reported. "Lancer from everything I can get. Must have come in after the chase started."

"Oh, Lord," Preston sighed. A lancer was the smallest armed vessel, but still much larger and better armed than a longboat. "He's seen us for sure."

As he spoke the computer flashed a series of alternate maneuvers and predicted outcomes on the screen, automatically taking evasive action when no orders were given.

The computer showed that the longboat had no chance of closing with the enemy rocket battleship before the lancer destroyed the longboat. After that, with the lancer to spot *Reliance* for the enemy and make torpedo runs, the cruiser had less than fifty percent chance of winning the battle.

"If he gets through, it could mean the end of New Scotland," Preston said. "We've got to damage him so the fleet can find him and finish him off." He touched the communicator controls and hailed the cruiser. "Lancer approaching," Preston said. "Your orders, sir?"

There was a pause of several seconds, far longer than the delay caused by the distance between the ships, before the answer came back. "Engage the lancer."

"Aye, aye," Preston snapped. He glanced at the alternatives on the screen in front of him and unhesitatingly pressed a key. He had selected the attack most likely to destroy the lancer without regard to the survival of the longboat. Unless the lancer simply ran away, the longboat had no chance of escaping undamaged and very little of remaining in space after the engagement.

"Prepare for battle damage," Preston called through the ship. "God bless the Navy."

"All secure below," Soames answered. "Torpedoes ready."

The longboat accelerated, curving in a great arc toward the

lancer. Their attack called for an approach well into range of the enemy's guns before launching a spread of torpedoes which might penetrate and destroy the enemy ship. The gravity increase was enough to partially black Kane out, but there was no need for human pilots to be conscious. They were fully committed.

"Know any prayers, Midshipman?" Preston asked.

"Yes, sir."

"Say a few. Say one for me while you're at it."

"Aye, aye, sir."

Through a red haze, Kane watched the main battle on the screens. *Reliance* was alongside the raider, and the Fields on both ships glowed bright red, radiating energy at a furious rate into the interstellar dark, each ship attempting to overload the screens of the other. The reaction from the guns of the combatants drove them apart, and the drive engines would then be used to force them closer again. Torpedoes shot out from each ship, exploding near the other, or vanishing in a fiery wave as secondary armament was directed at them for a moment before returning to the main target.

Then the situation was dominated by the approaching battle between the smaller ships. Kane was fascinated by the approach of the lancer, now firing photon bombs of its own at the longboat. Like the enemy battleship, it had obviously had no time to refuel and the lancer's captain was trying to conserve energy for the main battle. Probably for the same reason only one torpedo was launched from it and it was easily intercepted by the longboat's guns, which, small as they were against a protected ship with a Field, were more than enough to melt unprotected objects in seconds.

The enemy played still more energy across the longboat and the temperature inside the little ship rose steadily. From time to time a blast of cooled air, circulated through the liquid hydrogen fuel, was injected into the crewmen's suite, bringing welcome relief from the heat.

They bore in closer, and the lancer turned away, intent on joining battle with *Reliance*, but the longboat would not be ignored. Its Field glowing cherry red, reaching the critical point, it slammed on toward the enemy.

Then the ship shuddered under Kane.

"Torpedoes away!" Soames shouted.

A crash sounded through the bridge, and Kane's earpiece went dead. The screens in front of him were dark; he was isolated, alone.

Francis struggled with the webbing of his battle harness. The emergency lights came on, and he could see around the control room.

Lieutenant Preston's helmet was missing and from the trunk of his headless body dark blood welled out, dripping down across his suit, forming little blobs as the longboat ceased to accelerate. The panels in front of the pilot's seat were fused, a half-meter hole burned completely through the central position. A beam had penetrated the weakened Field.

Francis sat staring in horror at the dead man, then slowly repeated the prayer the lieutenant had asked for. He fumbled with the keys on the panel in front of him, realizing that he must do something, but unable to think.

The screens in front of him were completely dark and the ship was not under power.

He forced himself to remember emergency instructions and turned on the intercom system. There was a crackling in his earpiece. "Soames here, sir," he heard.

"Report damage below!" Francis shouted, his voice cracking.

"Main engines and torpedo room intact, sir. We're hulled in three places. No response from the main computer at this station."

"There's no one here," Francis said. He looked over the damage to the control room and saw that the panels above his own station were undamaged. He pressed the keys to give control of the ship to the second pilot's station with its smaller auxiliary computer, then examined the screens.

The lancer was gone. One or more of the longboat's torpedoes had penetrated its Field, or perhaps several had exploded against it, overwhelming the lancer's Field momentarily and bringing on collapse.

Francis spent only a moment examining the situation before turning to the communicators, but then his attention was caught by the main battle. The *Reliance* and the pocket battleship were still engaged, their screens glowing furiously now. If there were any difference in color of the two ships' protective Langston Fields, Francis could not tell it.

He shouted into the communicator, changing channels, finally switching to another transmitter. After what seemed like ages, there was a reply. "*Reliance* here. What is your situation?"

"Heavy damage sustained," Francis said, trying to ape the calm of the *Reliance* talker. "Lieutenant Preston's dead, Midshipman Kane commanding."

It might have been his imagination, but Francis thought he heard a shouted "Damnation!" in the background, possibly Captain Duncan's reaction to learning that a middie was in charge of his only auxiliary vessel within range of the battle. There was a pause, then the talker said, "We have no reports from you on the position of the enemy. Provide position reports immediately."

"I'll tr—uh—aye, aye, sir." Kane had no idea how to restore the reporting system and thought of the various things that might be wrong with it. Perhaps it would be necessary to take manual sightings. Then he had an idea.

"Soames," he called.

"Aye, sir," the imperturbable voice answered.

"Provide reports to *Reliance* on the position of the enemy."

"Aye, aye, sir."

Francis turned back to the status board, estimating the capabilities of the longboat. In a few minutes, the communications lights glowed indicating that information was passing to the cruiser. Then the earpiece buzzed.

"Impossible to provide accurate information from this distance, sir," Soames told him.

"I'll take her closer, Soames. Prepare for acceleration."

"Aye, aye, sir."

Nervously, he jockeyed the ship toward the enemy, staying out of range of beam weapons and hoping that his ship was still capable of reacting to an enemy torpedo attack. As the eyes of *Reliance*, he would be valuable enough to shoot several at. Then it occurred to him that if the enemy couldn't see *Reliance*, he couldn't see the longboat either; he brought his ship out beyond the cruiser to face the blind side of the pocket battleship. The secondary computer was not capable of giving Francis attack plans, and he held position, watching the battle. It seemed to him that the enemy glowed just a little brighter than the cruiser now, and its guns put out beams perhaps a little weaker than before.

"Torpedoes readied, sir," Soames reported. "Three launchers functional."

"Thank you, Soames." Francis called *Reliance* again.

"Engage the enemy as you think best, Mister Kane," Blackpool told him. "If you can steer to her unengaged side and launch torpedoes, do so. We now have a high probability of winning this battle, but any distraction to the enemy or diversion of his firepower would be useful. Use your judgment, mister, it's what you're paid for."

"Aye, aye, sir." Kane manually activated the ship's engines to bring the longboat astern of the enemy ship. He had heard that no small boat skipper ever wanted to return from a space battle with torpedoes aboard and, although he was afraid, an icy interior calm had settled over him, giving him complete control over himself. At least he hoped so, although there was a twitch to his legs he couldn't understand.

As he approached the enemy, a beam washed over his ship, destroying the sensors. He allowed the computer to erect others, and noted that the pocket battleship did not fire again. As the enemy's Langston Field overloaded, her captain shunted more and more energy from his drive and guns to Field maintenance, cutting down what he could do to *Reliance* and leaving very little energy at all for long-range shots at the longboat.

But the less the pocket battleship could fire at *Reliance*, the more power Captain Duncan could spare for the cruiser's guns. Single ship duels often ended in this kind of progressive spiral effect until one ship was destroyed.

As Francis closed with the enemy ship, brilliant flashes appeared in several places on the enemy's hull, indicating local weakening of the ship's Field and consequent penetration to the structure below, much as had happened to the longboat. *Reliance* was firing torpedoes now, and Francis added his spread to the attack. He saw two of his torpedoes intercepted, then the third detonated somewhere near the battleship's stern. He ordered the tubes reloaded and cautiously maneuvered his ship to a position opposite *Reliance*. He was determined to make the next attack at full acceleration.

While he waited for Soames to report the tubes loaded, he heard the distress hailing signal in disbelief. He selected a key to accept the call.

A frantic voice sounded in his headset.

"We surrender! In the name of God, cease firing!"

Frank keyed the call into his own transmitter so that it would be received on *Reliance*, then realized he was in the enemy's shadow and could not be head by the cruiser. He changed his position, and asked the enemy, "Why do you not surrender to my captain?"

"We have tried," the heavily accented voice said. "Your ship does not hear us. It has no sensors bearing on us." The voice sounded young to Francis, too young to be the commander of a rebel battleship. "And if we cease fire, what will happen to us?" the rebel asked.

"He's got a point," Kane heard Blackpool say on the other communicator. "If we can put all our energy into the guns for even a few moments, we can collapse his Field. But he's got enough functional weapons to damage us badly or destroy us if we give him any time to spare, so we can't stop firing on him either. Surrender is difficult after battle is joined and with both ships nearly overloaded."

"What do I do, sir?" Francis asked.

"We'd like him intact, mister. Try to arrange it."

"Aye, aye, sir."

Francis called the enemy ship. "You must decrease your rate of fire or we will destroy you. We cannot accept your surrender until you are not capable of harming our destroyer."

"We have taken hits," the rebel said. "Damage is extensive. The bridge is destroyed. I will attempt to comply with your instructions but my communication is not working properly."

Moments later there was a noticeable decrease in enemy firing at the cruiser.

"We accept their surrender," Blackpool told Francis. "But we want to be sure he's disabled. Go aboard, mister. If you can't do that, we'll have to blow them out of space."

"Aye, aye, sir. I can maneuver alongside."

"You'll do it from the dark side, Mr. Kane. Stay in his shadow or you'll be destroyed by *Reliance*. We have to keep fire on him to be sure that he doesn't recover."

"Uh, aye, aye, sir." Francis examined the controls of the longboat, wondering if he could accomplish the delicate maneuver.

"One more instruction, mister," Blackpool told him. "Get your torpedoes alongside him as soon as you get there, and have the crew stand by to detonate them if the enemy tries anything. Some of these rebels have been fanatics about taking us with them instead of surrendering."

"Aye, aye, sir." Of course, torpedoes detonated alongside the enemy would take the longboat too, but a midshipman's useful phrases did not include any explaining that to Blackpool.

Kane called his chief petty officer. "Mister Soames, please launch a message reflector. We'll be going into the shadow of the enemy ship and you'll need contact with *Reliance*. Once we're alongside, stand by to detonate our torpedoes if the rebel fires on the cruiser."

"Aye, aye, sir. Good luck, Mr. Kane."

"Thank you." Francis waited for the message reflector, discovering he was half paralyzed with terror. I'll be damned if I'm going to be like this, he told himself. The chief down below had to sit there waiting for orders to blow himself out of space. All Kane had to do was go aboard the enemy. There wasn't much to it, he'd crossed space before. And down there was an enemy starship, a surrendering starship . . . his thoughts went back to the reverie he had enjoyed about finding the Emperor. It could happen now, he thought. Why wasn't Blackpool more excited about the prospect?

"Message unit deployed, sir," Soames reported.

"Thank you. Acceleration warning, Chief."

"Aye, sir."

Frank touched the keys, giving a brief acceleration to the longboat, then cut the engines to let his boat coast up to the rebel. It wouldn't do to get there with too much velocity. Another touch moved him completely into the shadow of the enemy. Without the computer, he found he had to correct continuously for drift out of the shadow. He watched the enemy ship grow closer and closer, its field glowing bright red. It couldn't hold out much longer, even under the reduced fire laying on it from *Reliance*.

As the longboat approached, the general radiation from the enemy was high enough to cause problems for the longboat, but there wasn't much he could do about it.

He was sure the enemy was a starship. They had located it near the Alderson point where a ship from Murcheson B would appear—

the endpoint of the hyperspace path between the enemy star and Cal. For reasons Imperial engineers did not understand, ships in hyperspace had to travel an exact line between stars not very widely separated, and the entry and exit points were difficult to locate, and never deep in a star's gravity well. The theory of the hyperspace drive had been lost, along with all of the men who could build one, in the great raid on the Yards almost two centuries ago.

But that had to be a starship, and they would soon be aboard it. Then the loyalists could learn how to build the drives and go for help. His thoughts were interrupted by the need for another course correction and he took the opportunity to reduce his forward velocity again. Without the computer he was afraid of having too much velocity when he got close to the rebel.

The three-dimensional picture of the relationship of the two ships swam teasingly through his head, but it would not stay still long enough to be useful. He had to deal with the piloting task as a purely intellectual problem. He was surprised at what he could do when there was no other choice—that seemed to be the whole story of his Navy life. Its men could do more than anyone would ever have asked for.

Now he was quite close, and touched the keys for the final deceleration. His little ship brought up alongside the enemy pocket battleship with almost no leeway, and he shot a tiny magnetic cleat against the enemy, trailing its tether through the enemy field to rest against the rebel's hull. Below, Soames and the crew were pushing a torpedo in through the enemy Field, with a jury-rigged detonating wire passing through the Field to the longboat. Now there was little the enemy could do to escape.

Francis called *Reliance*. "I'm alongside. I don't see any open hatches, but I just anchored."

"He's ceased firing at us," Blackpool announced. "Send him a hailing signal and see what happens."

"Aye, aye, sir." Francis knew the enemy was still dangerous. If it had a few moments to dissipate the overload of energy poured into its Field, it would be able to fire a blast at the *Reliance* that could severely damage the cruiser, penetrating at least one point. The rebel wouldn't survive the renewed engagement, but neither would the longboat.

Not that there was nothing to do but wait for the enemy to open a hatch. They seemed to be taking their time, and the longboat was overheating badly.

"You have that connected to a deadman switch, Chief?" Francis asked.

"Yes, sir. If we're out of action, the torpedo goes off."

"Very good, Chief." So that problem was covered. The longboat's field was now almost as bright as the rebel's. Francis had a mental picture of a debate going on aboard the enemy ship, one faction arguing for a final effort to damage the enemy, the other for surrender, but he could put no faces to the shadowy rebels. He wondered about the officer who had called to surrender; he had seemed terribly young, certainly not old enough to command a starship. What if he were not authorized to surrender? But, of course, he had managed to silence the pocket battleship's guns.

The prospect of going through the enemy's Field was frightening as well. It glowed angrily. In a few more minutes it would be too late for anything, he thought, but then he saw the dark opening in the red of the enemy's hull. Marker flags were erected around it so that Francis would be sure to see the hatch. He slipped outside the longboat and aimed himself at the opening, accelerating with the reaction unit on his battle armor.

He almost missed the hatch in his haste to get through the Field, feeling the slowing effect of it before he broke through to crash against the wall of the airlock. The outer hatch sealed—the cycling took ten seconds by his watch—but almost three hours subjective time before the inner hatch opened.

"Well done, Kane," Mister Blackpool was saying. Francis, still wearing his battle armor with splotches of Lieutenant Preston's blood dried into little cakes, stood on the bridge of the *Reliance*, casually holding himself from floating about the control room, but whether his levity was due to zero gravity or pride he couldn't tell. Captain Duncan was at the main control station, and looked around.

"Satisfactory, mister," the skipper said. As far as Kane could remember, these were the first words he had ever heard the captain address him individually. Fontaine, midshipman of the watch, swiveled around momentarily to glance at Francis, then turned to his station.

Blackpool turned to the communicator, ordering off a crew to deal with the rebel ship to see that she was spaceworthy enough for a trip to Etain, Mider's moon where the Empire maintained a fortress and emergency repair station. Kane started to leave, then when Blackpool was finished, asked, "Uh, sir, was there a stellar drive aboard her?"

"There had been one, mister. It was like the other ships we've captured. Fused, with the personnel who knew anything about it. The ship was surrendered by a junior lieutenant. All the staff officers and engine room crew were cooked." Blackpool turned back to his station, then added, "It's always like that, you know. They're determined to see we don't get a star drive. They want to see us coming if we try to carry the war to their homeland."

"Yes, sir." Francis thought of the dream he'd had, of going to find the Emperor, and almost cried. He thought too of his decision to leave the Navy, and Preston's unhesitating selection of the attack which killed him. Joseph and Mary, they couldn't keep the drive forever. One day we'll get a ship intact, he thought. If we have to take a fleet across to their planet and take it away from them right there.

"Are you still here, Midshipman?" Duncan asked. "Blackpool, haven't you got anything better for your brats to do than stand around the bridge?"

"Mister MacReedy needs you, Kane," Blackpool snapped. "And when he's finished I want to see you about the last stellar plot you turned in. I've seen better work from second classmen. On your way, mister."

"Aye, aye, sir." Mister Kane was back to the ten useful remarks which made up a midshipman's vocabulary in the service of His Majesty. As he launched himself through the hatch to the main corridor, he couldn't resist giving Mister Fontaine an enormous wink.

# RETROSPECTIVE

## by Larry Niven

Jerry stalked me. He's spoken about it often. He was considering pursuit of a career in writing. A collaborator would be convenient. He looked around for a writer of proven skill who wasn't finding the success Jerry thought he could give him. He chose me. I think it would have been Poul Anderson if he'd lived closer to Studio City.

Sunday afternoon at the first Bouchercon, he suggested collaborating. "I'll make you rich and famous."

"I'm already rich."

"I'll get rich, you get famous." We made two rules. One of us must have a veto, and that was me. One of us should rewrite from scratch once we had a draft, to smooth out discrepancies in style; and that was him.

One evening and late night in my living room, running on coffee and brandy, we worked to merge Jerry's CoDominium universe with an alien I'd dreamed up for a novelette. Our friend Dan Alderson had worked up an interstellar transport system that would allow Jerry to write as if future space travel could be treated like Napoleonic era naval battles. I'd realized that—based on Dan's transport system—I could put an alien star system, undiscovered, right in the middle of Jerry's all human Empire of Man. My orphaned alien became the Motie Engineer.

That night we carved out the frame of a novel, and a million years of history of the Mote Prime natives, and a dozen subspecies of the original asymmetric alien. I've never had a night more creative, before or since.

We talked about the novel, not yet called *The Mote in God's Eye*, with friends while we wrote it. The Los Angeles Science Fiction Society grew tired of it; we were taking too long. The LASFS voted us "Best Unwritten Novel" two years running.

Upon publication, Jerry set forth to publicize the book. I wasn't involved much: too shy. Jerry went on an endless succession of autographings and talk shows. I heard about it later. His/our agent Lurton Blassingame told him, "You'd be surprised how many insomniacs read!" so he put up with the late hours. One night he had to keep interrupting a host until he could tell him that *The Mote in God's Eye* wasn't a religious tract, but a space opera.

Jerry got me into hiking because he had four sons coming into Boy Scout age, and he needed an assistant Scoutmaster. We sailed together because he had built a boat. I'm a lazy guy; I owe my health partly to Jerry getting me to exercise.

The landscape of Dante's *Inferno* had been playing in my head since college. I made Jerry write a sequel with me, depending on the extensive religious knowledge he kept displaying whether I asked or not. Most of what we've written took two or three years; we wrote *Inferno* in four months. Unpleasant territory. We wanted out.

We went back because after a couple of decades Jerry had more to say. *Inferno* was mostly mine, but *Escape From Hell* was mostly Jerry's.

Jerry carved out a career by testing computers and computer systems. He wrote "Chaos Manor" for *Byte Magazine*. He put together an ideal computer writing system with one Tony Peitsch, and when they had it perfected, I bought a copy from Tony. I bought two, one for Marilyn, my wife the computer programmer, and also for spare parts. I switched over from typewriters in the middle of *Ringworld Engineers*, around 1980.

We used to drink and plot stories. After Jerry gave up drinking, on the advice of every friend and relative he had, we used to hike and plot stories. Hiking works better. It brings blood to the brain. We'd walk and plot and carve out ways to save the world, and Jerry would record. He had a blog to fill too.

Robert Gleason had been part of my career since long before I noticed. Now he made a suggestion to Jerry: "It's time to write a novel about an invasion of Earth in present time."

When Jerry told me this I laughed. "I hope you broke it gently that that's been done." Missing the point entirely. Bob was very familiar with the science fiction world. What he meant was that it hadn't been done *well.*

When we got into it I realized that H. G. Wells's Martians would be in zoos within twenty-four hours if they tried that today.

Interstellar invaders are another matter. The trick is to design invaders who can lose. Crossing interstellar space with intent to conquer implies immense power. We rapidly saw that giant meteoroid impacts would be their basic weapon. . . .

When we turned in an outline for *Footfall*, Bob Gleason's reaction was, "Forget the aliens. Do the asteroid impact."

I made it a comet, for the visuals.

Jerry called me one evening, late in writing *Lucifer*'s *Hammer*. "I'm trying to show how awful things have gotten after the comet impact. My problem is, all of my characters have gotten used to it. They're not seeing the horror. Think about it."

I thought of something. I wrote a little. I called Jerry back at two in the morning. "They're surrounded by corpses. How would they react to the corpse of a kangaroo?"

*Hammer* held the record, for a little while, for the most money paid for paperback rights in science fiction. Jerry used to say, "Money will get you through times of no awards better than awards will get you through times of no money." Then the Los Angeles WorldCon gave him a chocolate Hugo Award.

After we turned *Hammer* in, Bob Gleason saw to it that bookstores had an emergency number in case they sold out. Copies could be replenished immediately. The book's success is largely due to Bob's efforts. Then he wanted the invasion novel too; and of course he got it.

Forty years after *Lucifer*'s *Hammer* reached the stores, *Nature Magazine* published a retrospective. We were surprised and delighted. It began, "You never forget the surfer."

What Jerry used to tell people was, "I work like Hell getting every crazy thing rational, and then everything anyone remembers is Niven's." Jerry did write more of the words in most of our books together, and he did more of the planning. He would come up with a framework such as Todos Santos, a city-sized building one-fifth mile high by two miles square, for *Oath of Fealty*; and I put a diving board on the roof.

What *I* used to say was, "Going into a collaboration, you should each count on doing eighty percent of the work. Communicating eats up effort. You're expecting to make a more successful book by getting another mind involved."

In our middle years we and our wives attended several AAAS gatherings to listen to the latest news in science. I've a vivid memory of a heated hotel pool in Canada that was built half inside, half outside, with a rubber gasket to dive under. A few minutes outside and Jerry noticed ice in my hair. His too. We got out for a very short snowball fight before jumping back in.

Another memory: dinner at a Mexican restaurant that (we discovered) no taxi would come to. The Pournelles begged a ride home from an employee, but Marilyn and I were stuck. Jerry had to get a taxi at the hotel and bring it to us. "You owe me," he said. "I had my pants off."

We attended science fiction conventions too. MidAmeriCon in Kansas City was memorable. Heinleins as Guests of Honor. A twelve-pound lobster for a shared midnight snack in our room, courtesy of Russell Seitz, silverware courtesy of the Heinleins. Russell carrying cognac for pouring, throughout the con. We were both up for multiple Hugo Awards. I won the one I had to take away from Jerry's "He Fell Into a Dark Hole," and then (in a maze of twisty passages backstage, running) I dropped and broke it.

We were at Dragon Con, Jerry's first, a week before his death. He sat on several panels and had a wonderful time. Alex took care of holding civilization together during the con.

In September of 1980, Jerry said to me, "Ronald Reagan is going to win the election. His science advisor was my best student at Pepperdine. We can have the ear of the President if we have anything to say. Let's gather some brains for a weekend's symposium at your house to carve out a space program for the United States. It's Congress's job, but they're not doing it."

I said, "I'll ask my wife."

It was the hardest work I've ever done. I'm not sure how Marilyn managed her end. Jerry gave her credit for "The Treaty of Tarzana" in which several groups agreed to stop dissing each other's missile-killing devices in public. They were arguing it out, hungry and swamped in the smells of her cooking, when one asked Jerry when dinner was due. He said, "When you've come to an agreement."

Jerry was in charge, giving us our orders in the living room, then breaking us into groups for special tasks. He'd invited industrialists, rocket scientists and engineers, NASA folk (off duty), a lawyer . . . the science fiction writers were crucial. We could interpret among the various disciplines.

Vivid memory: Friday afternoon, session to determine how to get private industry into space. After a time Art Dula the lawyer volunteered to write up our findings. Come night, after dinner, Jerry told me to rewrite it. I discovered he meant "Now."

The party was just starting, among the brightest people I knew. I could hear the festivities downstairs. I was upstairs rewriting Art's lawyerese, with Art Dula at my shoulder so I could ask him what things meant. I got it into English, though it never quite sings, and then wanted Jerry to read it right away. No, too busy.

But he kept my title. "How to Save Civilization and Make a Little Money." The legal changes we suggested did get passed, though it took nine years.

All told there were six gatherings of the Citizens Advisory Committee for a National Space Policy. In every case Jerry did weeks of work rewriting and assembling what we produced. Some of our wording got into Ronald Reagan's speeches on the Strategic Defense Initiative, Star Wars if you're a Democrat. What I've heard since is that the Soviet rocket scientists all thought it was bullshit. The Soviet politicians couldn't make themselves doubt that we could carry out our promise/threat. We'd beaten them to the Moon! Gorbachev jumped through hoops to get SDI cancelled. Ultimately, too many hoops.

You don't believe we can put up a shield to stop most incoming missiles? In that case—the Soviet Union was driven bankrupt by a science fiction story written at Larry Niven's house. Jerry Pournelle was our spearhead.

Jerry didn't write much short fiction. The three works in this book are it for our collaborations.

We took a crack at writing a story as good as "To Bring Home the Steel," an asteroid mining story. "Spirals" was the result, and you may judge it as you like.

"Reflex" was Jerry's opening for *The Mote in God's Eye*. I tried to write a better opening. We showed that first draft to Lurton Blassingame and Robert Heinlein, and both said, "Chop off the first hundred pages." We did that, but we wrote the results into something more. My opening we expanded into "Building the Mote in God's Eye."

Four of us were hiking the hill behind Jerry's house when we started talking about *Lucifer*'s *Hammer*. I said, "They all want us to save the surfer. I know just how to do it. I've always known." Evie King and Steve and Jerry said, "Write it!" So I tried—and realized that I didn't want the surfer saved. I wrote "Story Night at the Stronghold" as a ghost story.

Getting Steven Barnes involved in our collaboration was immense fun. Jerry was a born and trained teacher. He loved lecturing Steve, and so did I, not just on writing but on every subject under the sun. Steve loves learning, and he loves lecturing too. Steve would bring us a first draft, and we'd tear it apart and put it back together. We wrote two novels and a novelette in the *Legacy of Heorot* universe.

Jerry had a tumor in his brain that had to be burned out with radiation. Recovering from the radiation damage cost him energy. He and I tried to write a novel that would have used all of his skills and little of mine. Not a good way to get him back in the game. We had to return the advance. But a second sequel to the Heorot series would be easier work, and would keep him involved.

Jerry and Steven and I were finishing the third novel when Jerry died. Steven and I had his notes to finish the ending.

*Starborn and Godsons* is currently in limbo.

—Larry Niven
Tarzana, July 3, 2018

# SPIRALS

## by Larry Niven & Jerry Pournelle

### Editor's Introduction

"Spirals" appeared in the April/June 1979 issue of *Destinies*, a new paperback magazine launched by Jim Baen during his tenure at Ace Books. This turned out to be one of the pair's most unusual collaborative efforts. First, it was the first short story they wrote together. And, second, it was written especially at the behest of Jim Baen, at the time when everything they wrote was at the top of the bestsellers list, a period when major publishers and editors were begging for novels from them. As a favor, Jim Baen asked Jerry to write a novella with Larry for his *Destinies*. Early sales of the new magazine weren't all that spectacular, and Jim figured having a new Niven and Pournelle collaboration inside would really help launch his new paperback magazine. Despite being the senior editor of Ace Books, Jim enjoyed publishing magazines and had the clout to make it happen. (Jim would later revive *Destinies* at Baen Books, renaming it *New Destinies*.) Not surprisingly, Jerry would once again have a science column in his new magazine, named appropriately, "New Beginnings."

Jerry's agent at the time, as I recall, wasn't happy about it. They were working on *Oath of Fealty* at the time and Kirby would have much preferred for them to stay on course. Jerry always had more fun knocking out his science columns than writing stories and novels; the success of his *Byte Magazine* computer column pretty much ended his fiction writing with a few exceptions. However,

Jerry never forgot that Jim had helped him on his way with his "Step Farther Out" columns for *Galaxy Magazine* and the two of them always had a great time throwing ideas back and forth concerning Jerry's latest science piece.

**THERE ARE ALWAYS PEOPLE** who want to revise history. No hero is so great that someone won't take a shot at him. Not even Jack Halfey.

Yes, I knew Jack Halfey. You may not remember my name. But in the main airlock of Industrial Station One there's an inscribed block of industrial diamond, and my name is sixth down: Cornelius L. Riggs, Metallurgist. And you might have seen my face at the funeral.

You *must* remember the funeral. All across the solar system work stopped while Jack Halfey took his final trek into the sun. He wanted it that way, and no spacer was going to refuse Jack Halfey's last request, no matter how expensive it might be. Even the downers got in the act. They didn't help pay the cost, but they spent hundreds of millions on sending reporters and cameras to the Moon.

That funeral damned near killed me. The kids who took me to the Moon weren't supposed to let the ship take more than half a gravity. My bones are over a hundred years old, and they're fragile. For that young squirt of a pilot the landing may have been smooth, but she hit a full g for a second there, and I thought my time had come.

I had to go, of course. The records say I was Jack's best friend, the man who'd saved his life, and being one of the last survivors of the Great Trek makes me somebody special. Nothing would do but that I push the button to send Jack on his "final spiral into the sun," to quote a downer reporter.

I still see Tri-V programs about ships "spiraling" into the sun. You'd think seventy years and more after the Great Trek the schools would teach kids something about space.

When I staggered outside in lunar gravity—lighter than the twenty percent gravity we keep in the *Skylark*, just enough to feel the difference—the reporters were all over me. Why, they demanded, did Jack want to go into the sun? Cremation and scattering of ashes is good enough for most spacers. It was good enough for Jack's wife. Some send their ashes back to Earth; some are scattered into the solar wind, to be flung throughout the universe; some prefer to go back into the soil of a colony sphere. But why the sun?

I've wondered myself. I never was good at reading Jack's mind. The question that nearly drove me crazy, and did drive me to murder, was: Why did Jack Halfey make the Great Trek in the first place?

I finally did learn the answer to that one. Be patient.

Probably there will never be another funeral like Jack's. The Big Push is only a third finished, and it's still two hundred miles of the biggest linear accelerator ever built, an electronic-powered railway crawling across the Earthside face of the Moon. One day we'll use it to launch starships. We'll fire when the Moon is full, to add the Earth's and Moon's orbital velocities to the speed of the starship, and to give the downers a thrill. But we launched Jack when the Moon was new, with precisely enough velocity to cancel the Earth's orbital speed of eighteen miles per second. It would have cost less to send him into interstellar space.

Jack didn't drop in any spiral. The Earth went on and the coffin stayed behind, then it started to fall into the Sun. It fell ninety-three million miles just like a falling safe, except for that peculiar wiggle when he really got into the sun's magnetic field. Moonbase is going to do it again with a probe. They want to know more about that wiggle.

The pilot was a lot more careful getting me home, and now I'm back aboard the *Skylark*, in a room near the axis where the heart patients stay; and on my desk is this pile of garbage from a history professor at Harvard who has absolutely proved that we would have had space industries and space colonies without Jack Halfey. There are no indispensable men.

In the words of a famous American president: Bullshit! We've made all the downers so rich that they can't remember what it was like back then.

And it was grim. If we hadn't got space industries established before 2020 we'd never have been able to afford them at all. Things were that thin. By 2020 A.D. there wouldn't have been any resources to invest. They'd have all gone into keeping eleven billion downers alive (barely!) and anybody who proposed "throwing money into outer space" would have been lynched.

God knows it was that way when Jack Halfey started.

I first met Jack Halfey at UCLA. He was a grad student in architecture, having got his engineering physics degree from Cal Tech. He'd also been involved in a number of construction jobs—among them Hale Observatory's big orbital telescope while he was still an undergrad at Cal Tech—and he was already famous. Everyone knows he was brilliant, and they're right, but he had another secret weapon: He worked his arse off. He had to. Insomnia. Jack couldn't sleep more than a couple of hours a night, and to get even that much sleep he had to get laid first.

I know about this because when I met Jack he was living with my sister. Ruthie told me that they'd go to bed, and Jack would sleep a couple of hours, and up he'd be, back at work, because once he woke up there was no point in lying in bed.

On nights when they couldn't make out he never went to bed at all, and he was pure hell to live with the next day.

She also told me he was one mercenary son of a bitch. That doesn't square with the public image of Jack Halfey, savior of mankind, but it happens to be true, and he never made much of a secret of it. He wanted to get rich fast. His ambition was to lie around Rio de Janeiro's beaches and sample the local wines and women; and he had his life all mapped out so that he'd be able to retire before he was forty.

I knew him for a couple of months, then he left UCLA to be a department head in the construction of the big Tucson arcology. There was a tearful scene with Ruthie: She didn't fit into Jack's image for the future, and he wasn't very gentle about how he told her he was leaving. He stormed out of her apartment carrying his suitcase while Ruthie and I shouted curses at him, and that was that.

I never expected to see him again.

When I graduated there was this problem: I was a metallurgist, and there were a lot of us. Metallurgists had been in big demand when I started UCLA, so naturally everybody studied metallurgy and materials science; by the time I graduated it was damned tough getting a job.

The depression didn't help much either. I graduated right in the middle of it. Runaway inflation, research chopped to the bone, environmentalists and Only One Earthers and Friends of Man and the Earth and other such yo-yo's on the rise; in those days there was a new energy crisis every couple of years, and when I got my sheepskin we were in the middle of, I think, number six. Industry was laying off, not hiring.

There was one job I knew of. A notice on the UCLA careers board. "Metallurgist wanted. High pay, long hours, high risk. Guaranteed wealthy in ten years if you live through it."

That doesn't sound very attractive just now, but in those days it looked better. Better than welfare, anyway, especially since the welfare offices were having trouble meeting their staff payrolls, so there wasn't a lot left over to hand out to their clients.

So, I sent in an application and found myself one of about a hundred who'd got past the paperwork screening. The interview was on campus with a standard personnel officer type who seemed more interested in my sports record than my abilities as a metallurgist. He also liked my employment history: I'd done summer jobs in heavy steel construction. He wouldn't tell me what the job was for.

"Not secret work," he said. "But we'd as soon not let it out to anyone we're not seriously interested in." He smiled and stood up, indicating the interview was over. "We'll let you know."

A couple of days later I got a call at the fraternity house. They wanted me at the Wilshire headquarters of United Space Industries.

I checked around the house but didn't get any new information. USI had contracts for a good bit of space work, including the lunar mines. Maybe that's it, I thought. I could hope, anyway.

When I got to USI the receptionist led me into a comfortable room and asked me to sit down in a big Eames chair. The chair faced an enormous TV screen (flat: Tri-V wasn't common in those days. Maybe it was before Tri-V at all; it's been a long time, and I don't remember). She typed something on an input console, and we waited a few minutes, and the screen came to life.

It showed an old man floating in midair.

The background looked like a spacecraft, which wasn't surprising. I recognized Admiral Robert McLeve. He had to be eighty or more, but he didn't look it.

"Good morning," he said.

The receptionist left. "Good morning," I told the screen. There was a faint red light on a lens by the screen, and I assumed he could see me as well as I could see him. "I'd kind of hoped for the Moon. I didn't expect the O'Neill colony," I added.

It took a while before he reacted, confirming my guess: a second and a half each way for the message, and the way he was floating meant zero gravity. I couldn't think of anything but the Construction Shack (that's what they called it then) that fit the description.

"This is where we are," McLeve said. "The duty tour is five years. High pay, and you save it all. Not much to spend money on out here. Unless you drink. Good liquor costs like transplant rights on your kidneys. So does bad liquor, because you still have to lift it."

"Savings don't mean much," I said.

"True." McLeve grimaced at the thought. Inflation was running better than twenty percent. The politicians said they would have it whipped Real Soon Now, but nobody believed them. "We've got arrangements to have three quarters of your money banked in Swiss francs. If you go back early, you lose that part of your pay. We need somebody in your field, part time on the Moon, part time up here in the Shack. From your record I think you'd do. Still want the job?"

I wanted it all right. I was never a nut on the space industries bit—I was never a nut on anything—but it sounded like good work. Exciting, a chance to see something of the solar system (well, of near-Earth space and the Moon; nobody had gone further than that) as well as to save a lot of money. And with that job on my record I'd be in demand when I came home.

As to why me, it was obvious when I thought about it. There were lots of good metallurgists, but not many had been finalists in the Olympic gymnastics team trials. I hadn't won a place on the team, but I'd sure proved I knew how to handle myself. Add to that the heavy construction work experience and I was a natural. I sweated out the job appointment, but it came through, and pretty soon I was at Canaveral, strapping myself into a shuttle seat, and having second and third thoughts about the whole thing.

There were five of us. We lifted out from the Cape in the shuttle, then transferred in Earth orbit to a tug that wasn't a lot bigger than the old Apollo capsules had been. The trip was three days, and crowded. The others were going to Moonbase. They refueled my tug in lunar orbit and sent me off alone to the Construction Shack. The ship was guided from the Shack, and it was scary as hell because there wasn't anything to do but wonder if they knew what they were doing. It took as long to get from the Moon to the Shack as it had to get to the Moon from Earth, which isn't surprising because it's the same distance: the Shack was in one of the stable libration points that make an equilateral triangle with the Earth and the Moon. Anything put there will stay there forever.

The only viewport was a small thing in the forward end of the tug. Naturally we came in ass-backward so I didn't see much.

Today we call it the *Skylark*, and what you see as you approach is a sphere half a kilometer across. It rotates every two minutes, and there's all kinds of junk moored to the axis of rotation. Mirrors, the laser and power targets, the long thin spine of the mass driver, the ring of agricultural pods, the big telescope; a confusion of equipment.

It wasn't that way when I first saw it. The sphere was nearly all there was, except for a spiderweb framework to hold the solar power panels. The frame was bigger than the sphere, but it didn't look very substantial. At first sight the Shack was a pebbled sphere, a golf ball stuck in a spider's web.

McLeve met me at the airlock. He was long of limb, and startlingly thin, and his face and neck were a maze of wrinkles. But his back was straight, and when he smiled the wrinkles all aligned themselves. Laugh lines.

Before I left Earth I read up on his history: Annapolis, engineer with the space program (didn't make astronaut because of his eyes); retired with a bad heart; wrote a lot of science fiction. I'd read most of his novels in high school, and I suppose half the people in the space program were pulled in by his stories.

When his wife died he had another heart attack. The Old Boys network came to the rescue. His classmates wangled an assignment in space for him. He hadn't been to Earth for seven years, and low gravity was all that kept him alive. He didn't even dare go to the Moon. A reporter with a flair for mythological phraseology called him "The Old Man of Space." It was certain that he'd never go home again, but if he missed Earth he didn't show it.

"Welcome aboard." He sounded glad to see me. "What do they call you?" he asked.

A good question. Cornelius might sound a dignified name to a Roman, but it makes for ribald comments in the USA. "Corky," I told him. I shrugged, which was a mistake: We were at the center of the sphere, and there wasn't any gravity at all. I drifted free from the grabhandle I'd been clinging to and drifted around the airlock.

After a moment of panic it turned out to be fun. There hadn't been room for any violent maneuvers in the tug, but the airlock was built to get tugs and rocket motors inside for repairs; it was big, nine meters across, and I could twirl around in the zero gravity. I flapped my arms and found I could swim.

McLeve was watching with a critical air. He must have liked what he saw because he grinned slightly. "Come on," he said. He turned in the air and drifted without apparent motion—it looked like levitation. "I'll show you around." He led the way out of the airlock into the sphere itself.

We were at the center of rotation. All around, above and below, were fields of dirt, some plowed, some planted with grass and grains.

There were wings attached to hooks at the entrance. McLeve took down a set and began strapping them on. Black bat wings. They made him look like a fallen angel, Milton's style. He handed me another pair. "Like to fly?" he asked.

I returned the grin. "Why not?" I hadn't the remotest idea of what I was doing, but if I could swim in the air with my hands, I ought to be able to handle wings in no gravity. He helped me strap in, and when I had them he gave some quick instructions.

"Main thing is to stay high," he said. "The further down the higher the gravity, and the tougher it is to control these things." He launched himself into space, gliding across the center of the sphere. After a moment I followed him.

I was a tiny chick in a vast eggshell. The landscape was wrapped around me: fields and houses, and layout yards of construction gear, and machinery, and vats of algae, and three huge windows opening on blackness. Every direction was down, millions of light-years down when a window caught my attention. For a moment that was terrifying. But McLeve held himself in place with tiny motions of his wings, and his eyes were on me. I swallowed my fear and looked.

There were few roads. Mostly the colonists flew with their wings, flew like birds, and if they didn't need roads, they didn't need squared-off patterns for the buildings either. The "houses" looked like they'd been dropped at random among the green fields. They were fragile partitions of sheet metal (wood was far more costly than sheet steel here), and they could not have borne their own weight on Earth, let alone stand up to a stiff breeze. They didn't have to. They existed for privacy alone.

I wondered about the weather. Along the axis of the sphere I could see scores of white puffballs. Clouds? I gathered my courage and flapped my way over to the white patch. It was a flock of hens. Their feet were drawn up, their heads were tucked under their wings, and they roosted on nothing.

"They like it in zero gravity," McLeve said. "Only thing is, when you're below them you have to watch out."

He pointed. A blob of chicken splat had left the flock and moved away from us. It fell in a spiral pattern. Of course the splat was actually going in a straight line—we were the ones who were rotating, and that made the falling stuff look as if it were spiraling to the ground below.

"Automatic fertilizer machine," I said.

McLeve nodded.

"I wonder you don't keep them caged," I said.

"Some people like their sky dotted with fleecy white hens."

"Oh. Where is everybody?" I asked.

"Most are outside working," McLeve said. "You'll meet them at dinner."

We stayed at the axis, drifting with the air currents, literally floating on air. I knew already why people who came here wanted to stay. I'd never experienced anything like it, soaring like a bird. It wasn't even like a sail plane: You wore the wings and you flew with them, you didn't sit in a cockpit and move controls around.

There were lights along part of the axis. The mirrors would take over their job when they were installed; for the moment the lights ran off solar power cells plastered over the outside of the sphere. At the far end of the sphere was an enormous cloud of dust. We didn't get close to it. I pointed and looked a question.

"Rock grinder," McLeve said. "Making soil. We spread it over the northern end." He laughed at my frown. "North is the end toward the sun. We get our rocks from the Moon. It's our radiation shielding. Works just as well if we break it up and spread it around, and that way we can grow crops in it. Later on we'll get the agricultural compartments built, but there's always five times as much work as we have people to do it with."

They'd done pretty well already. There was grass, and millet and wheat for the chickens, and salad greens and other vegetable crops. Streams ran through the fields down to a ring-shaped pond at the equator. There was also a lot of bare soil that had just been put in place and hadn't been planted. The Shack wasn't anywhere near finished.

"How thick is that soil?" I asked.

"Not thick enough. I was coming to that. If you hear the flare warnings, get to my house. North pole."

I thought that one over. The only way to ward yourself from a solar flare is to put a lot of mass between you and the sun. On Earth that mass is a hundred miles of air. On the Moon they burrow ten meters into the regolith. The Shack had only the rock we could get from the Moon, and Moonbase had problems of its own. When they had the manpower and spare energy they'd throw more rock our way, and we'd plaster it across the outer shell of the Shack, or grind it up and put it inside; but for now there wasn't enough, and come flare time McLeve was host to an involuntary lawn party.

But what the hell, I thought. It's beautiful. Streams rushing in spirals from pole to equator. Green fields and houses, skies dotted with fleecy white hens; and I was flying as man flies in dreams.

I decided it was going to be fun, but there was one possible hitch.

"There are only ten women aboard," I said.

McLeve nodded gravely.

"And nine of them are married."

He nodded again. "Up to now we've mostly needed muscle. Heavy construction experience and muscle. The next big crew shipment's in six months, and the company's trying like hell to recruit women to balance things off. Think you can hold out that long?"

"Guess I have to."

"Sure. I'm old Navy. We didn't have women aboard ships and we lived through it."

I was thinking that I'd like to meet the one unmarried woman aboard. Also that she must be awfully popular. McLeve must have read my thoughts, because he waved me toward a big structure perched on a ledge partway down from the north pole. "You're doing all right on the flying. Take it easy and let's go over there."

We soared down, and I began to feel a definite "up" and "down"; before that any direction I wanted it to be was "up." We landed in front of the building.

"Combination mess hall and administration offices," McLeve said. "Ten percent level."

It took a moment before I realized what he meant. Ten percent level—ten percent of Earth's gravity.

"It's as heavy as I care to go," McLeve said. "Any lighter makes it hard to eat. The labs are scattered around the ring at the same level."

He helped me off with my wings and we went inside. There were several people, all men, scurrying about purposefully. They didn't stop to meet me.

They weren't wearing much, and I soon found that was the custom in the Shack; why wear clothes inside? There wasn't any weather. It was always warm and dry and comfortable. You mostly needed clothes for pockets.

At the end of the corridor was a room that hummed; inside there was a bank of computer screens, all active. In front of them sat a homely girl.

"Miss Hoffman," McLeve said. "Our new metallurgist, Corky Riggs."

"Hi." She looked at me for a moment, then back at the computer console. She was mumbling something to herself as her fingers flew over the keys.

"Dot Hoffman is our resident genius," McLeve said. "Anything from stores and inventories to orbit control, if a computer can figure it out she can make the brains work the problem."

She looked up with a smile. "We give necessity the praise of virtue," she said.

McLeve looked thoughtful. "Cicero?"

"Quintilian." She turned back to her console again.

"See you at dinner," McLeve said. He led me out.

"Miss Hoffman," I said.

He nodded.

"I suppose she wears baggy britches and blue wool stockings and that shirt because it's cool in the computer room," I said.

"No, she always dresses that way."

"Oh."

"Only six months, Riggs," the admiral said. "Well, maybe a year. You'll survive."

I was thinking I'd damned well have to.

I fell in love during dinner.

The chief engineer was named Ty Plauger, a long, lean chap with startling blue eyes. The chief ecologist was his wife, Jill. They had been married about a year before they came up, and they'd been aboard the Shack for three, ever since it started up. Neither was a lot older than me, maybe thirty then.

At my present age the concept of love at first sight seems both trite and incredible, but it was true enough. I suppose I could have named you reasons then, but I don't feel them now. Take this instead:

There were ten women aboard out of ninety total. Nine were married, and the tenth was Dot Hoffman. My first impression of her was more than correct. Dot never would be married. Not only was she homely, but she thought she was homelier still. She was terrified of physical contact with men, and the blue wool stockings and blouse buttoned to the neck were the least of her defenses.

If I had to be in love—and at that age, maybe I did—I could choose among nine married women. Jill was certainly the prettiest of the lot. Pug nose, brown hair chopped off short, green eyes, and a compact muscular shape, very much the shape of a woman. She liked to talk, and I liked to listen.

She and Ty had stars in their eyes. Their talk was full of what space would do for mankind.

Jill was an ex-Fromate; she'd been an officer in the Friends of Man and the Earth. But while the Fromates down below were running around sabotaging industries and arcologies and nuclear plants and anything else they didn't like, Jill went to space. Her heart bled no less than any for the baby fur seals and the three-spined stickleback and all the fish killed by mine tailings, but she'd thought of something to do about it all.

"We'll put all the dirty industries into space," she told me. "Throw the pollution into the solar wind and let it go out to the cometary halo. The Fromates think they can talk everyone into letting Kansas go back to buffalo grass—"

"You can't *make* people want to be poor," Ty put in.

"Right! If we want to clean up the Earth and save the wild things, we'll have to give people a way to get rich without harming the environment. This is it! Someday we'll send down enough power from space that we can tear down the dams and put the snail darter back where he came from."

And more. Jill tended to do most of the talking. I wondered about Ty. He always seemed to have the words that would set her off again.

And one day, when we were clustered around McLeve's house with, for a few restful hours, nothing to do, and Jill was well out of earshot flying around and among the chickens in her wonderfully graceful wingstyle, Ty said to me, "I don't *care* if we turn the Earth into a park. I like space. I like flying, and I like free fall, and the look of stars with no air to cloud them. But don't tell Jill."

I learned fast. With Ty in charge of engineering, McLeve as chief administrator, and Dot Hoffman's computers to simulate the construction and point up problems before they arose, the project went well. We didn't get enough mass from the Moon, so that my smelter was always short of raw materials, and Congress didn't give us enough money. There weren't enough flights from down below and we were short of personnel and goods from Earth. But we got along.

Two hundred and forty thousand miles below us, everything was going to hell.

First, the senior senator from Wisconsin lived long enough to inherit a powerful committee chairmanship, and he'd been against the space industries from the start. Instead of money we got "Golden

Fleece" awards. Funds already appropriated for flights we'd counted on got sliced, and our future budgets were completely in doubt.

Next, the administration tried to bail itself out of the tax revolt by running the printing presses. What money we could get appropriated wasn't worth half as much by the time we got it.

Moonbase felt the pinch and cut down even more on the rock they flung out our way.

Ty's answer was to work harder: get as much of the Shack finished as we could, so that we could start sending down power.

"Get it done," he told us nightly. "Get a *lot* of it finished. Get so much done that even those idiots will see that we're worth it. So much that it'll cost them less to supply us than to bring us home."

He worked himself harder than anyone else, and Jill was right out there with him. The first task was to get the mirrors operating.

We blew them all at once over a couple months. They came in the shuttle that should have brought our additional crew; it wasn't much of a choice, and we'd have to put off balancing out the sex ratio for another six months.

The mirrors were packages of fabric as thin as the cellophane on a package of cigarettes. We inflated them into great spheres, sprayed foam plastic on the outside for struts, and sprayed silver vapor inside where it would precipitate in a thin layer all over. Then we cut them apart to get spherical mirrors, and sliced a couple of those into wedges to mount behind the windows in the floor of the Shack.

They reflected sunlight in for additional crops. Jill had her crew out planting more wheat to cut down on the supplies we'd need from Earth.

Another of the mirrors was my concern. A hemisphere a quarter of a kilometer across can focus a lot of sunlight onto a small point. Put a rock at that point and it melts, fast. When we got that set up we were all frantically busy smelting iron for construction out of the rocks. Moonbase shipped up when they could. When Moonbase couldn't fling us anything we dismounted rock we'd placed for shielding, smelted it, and plastered the slag back onto the sphere.

Days got longer and longer. There's no day or night aboard the Shack anyway, of course: open the mirrors and you have sunlight, close them and you don't. Still, habit dies hard, and we kept track of time by days and weeks; but our work schedules bore no relation to them. Sometimes we worked the clock around, quitting only when forced to by sheer exhaustion.

We got a shipment from Moonbase, and in the middle of the refining process the mounting struts in the big smelter mirror got out of alignment. Naturally Ty was out to work on it.

He was inspecting the system by flying around with a reaction pistol. The rule was that no one worked without a safety line; a man who drifted away from the Shack might or might not be rescued, and the rescue itself would cost time and manpower we didn't have.

Ty's line kept pulling him up short of where he wanted to go. He gave the free end to Jill and told her to pay out a lot of slack. Then he made a jump from the mirror frame. He must have thought he'd use the reaction pistol to shove him off at an angle so that he'd cross over the bowl of the mirror to the other side.

The pistol ran out of gas. That left Ty floating straight toward the focus of the mirror.

He shouted into his helmet radio, and Jill frantically hauled in slack, trying to get a purchase on him. I made a quick calculation and knew I would never reach him in time; if I tried I'd likely end up in the focus myself. Instead I took a dive across his back path. If I could grab his safety line, the jerk as I pulled up short, ought to keep him out of the hottest area, and my reaction pistol would take us back to the edge.

I got the line all right, but it was slack. It had burned through. Ty went right through the hot point. When we recovered his body, metal parts on his suit had melted.

We scattered his ashes inside the sphere. McLeve's Navy prayer book opened the burial service with the words "We brought nothing into this world, and it is certain that we shall take nothing out." Afterward I wondered how subtle McLeve had been in his choice of that passage.

We had built this world ourselves, with Ty leading us. We had brought *everything* into this world, even down to Ty's final gift to us; the ashes which would grow grass in a place no human had ever thought to reach until now.

For the next month we did without him; and it was as if we had lost half our men. McLeve was a good engineer if a better administrator, but he couldn't go into the high gravity areas, and he couldn't do active construction work. Still, it wasn't engineering talent we lacked. It was Ty's drive.

Jill and Dot and McLeve tried to make up for that. They were more committed to the project than ever.

Two hundred and forty thousand miles down, they were looking for a construction boss. They'd find one, we were sure. We were the best, and we were paid like the best. There was never a problem with salaries. Salaries were negligible next to the other costs of building the Shack. But the personnel shuttles were delayed, and delayed again, and we were running out of necessities, and the US economy was slipping again.

We got the mirrors arrayed. Jill went heavily into agriculture, and the lunar soil bloomed, seeded with earthworms and bacteria from earthly soil. We smelted more of the rocky crust around the Shack and put it back as slag. We had plans for the metal we extracted, starting with a lab for growing metal whiskers. There was already a whisker lab in near-Earth orbit, but its output was tiny. The Shack might survive if we could show even the beginnings of a profit-making enterprise.

Jill had another plan: mass production of expensive biologicals, enzymes and various starting organics for ethical drugs.

We had lots of plans. What we didn't have was enough people to do it all. You can only work so many twenty-hour days. We began to make mistakes. Some were costly.

My error didn't cost the Shack. Only myself. I like to think it was due to fatigue and nothing more.

I made a try at comforting the grieving widow, after a decent wait of three weeks. When Ty was alive everyone flirted with Jill. She pretended not to notice. You'd have to be crude as well as rude before she'd react.

This time it was different. I may not have been very subtle, but I wasn't crude; and she told me instantly to get the hell out of her cabin and leave her alone.

I went back to my refinery mirror and brooded.

Ninety years later I know better. Ninety years is too damned late. If I'd noticed nothing else, I should have known that nearly eighty unmarried men aboard would all be willing to comfort the grieving widow, and half of them were only too willing to use the subtle approach: "You're all that keeps us working so hard."

I wonder who tried before I did? It hardly matters; when my turn came, Jill's reaction was automatic. Slap him down before it's too late for him to back away. And when she slapped me down, I stayed slapped, more hurt than mad, but less than willing to try again.

I hadn't stopped being in love with her. So I worked at being her friend again. It wasn't easy. Jill was cold inside. When she talked to people it was about business, never herself. Her dedication to the Shack, and to all it stood for in her mind, was hardening, ossifying. And she spent a lot of time with Dot Hoffman and Admiral McLeve.

But the word came: another shuttle. Again there were no women. The senator from Wisconsin had found out how expensive it would be to get us home. Add fifty women and it would be half again as expensive. So no new personnel.

Still they couldn't stop the company from sending up a new chief engineer, and we heard the shuttle was on its way, with a load of seeds, liquid hydrogen, vitamin pills, and Jack Halfey.

I couldn't believe it. Jack just wasn't the type.

To begin with, while the salary you could save in five years amounted to a good sum, enough to let you start a business and still have some income left, it wasn't *wealth*. You couldn't live the rest of your life in Rio on it; and I was pretty sure Jack's goals hadn't changed.

But there he was, the new boss. From the first day he arrived things started humming. It was the old Jack, brilliant, always at work, and always insisting everyone try to keep up with him although no one ever could. He worked our arses off. In two months he had us caught up on the time we lost after Ty was killed.

Things looked good. They looked damned good. With the mirrors mounted we could operate on sunlight, with spare power for other uses. Life from soil imported from Earth spread throughout the soil imported from the Moon; and earthly plants were in love with the chemicals in lunar soil. We planted strawberries, corn and beans together; we planted squashes and melons in low-gravity areas and watched them grow into jungles of thin vines covered with fruit.

The smelter worked overtime, and we had more than enough metals for the whisker lab and biological vats, if only a shuttle would bring us the pumps and electronics we needed; and if necessary we'd make pumps in the machine shops, and Jack had Dot working out the details of setting up integrated-circuit manufacture.

But the better things looked in space, the worse they looked on Earth.

One of the ways we were going to make space colonies pay for themselves was through electricity. We put out big arrays of solar cells, monstrous spiderwebs a kilometer long by half that wide, so large that they needed small engines dotted all over them just to keep them oriented properly toward the sun.

We made the solar cells ourselves; one of the reasons they needed me was to get out the rare metals from the lunar regolith and save them for the solar-cell factory. And it was working; we had the structure and we were making the cells. Soon enough we'd have enormous power, megawatts of power, enough to beam it down to Earth where it could pay back some of the costs of building the system. The orbiting power stations cost a fortune to put up, but not much to maintain; they would be like dams, big front-end costs but then nearly free power forever.

We were sure that would save us. How could the United States turn down free electricity?

It looked good until the Fromates blew up the desert antenna that we would have been beaming the power down to, and the lawyers got their reconstruction tied into legal knots that would probably take five years to untangle.

The senator from Wisconsin continued his crusade. This time we got *three* Golden Fleece awards. Down on Earth the company nominated him for membership in the Flat Earth Society. He gleefully accepted and cut our budget again.

We also had problems on board. Jack had started mean; it was obvious he had never wanted to come here in the first place. Now he turned mean as a rattlesnake. He worked us. If we could get the whisker lab finished ahead of time, at lower cost than planned, then maybe we could save the station yet; so he pushed and pushed again; and one day he pushed too hard.

It wasn't a mutiny. It wasn't even a strike. We all did a day's work; but suddenly, without as far as I know any discussion among us, nobody would put in overtime. Ten hours a day, yes; ten hours and one minute, no.

Jill pleaded. The admiral got coldly formal. Dot cried. Jack screamed.

We cut work to nine and a half hours.

And then it all changed. One day Jack Halfey was smiling a lot. He turned polite. He was getting his two or three hours sleep a night.

Dot described him. "Like Mrs. Fezziwig," she said. "'One vast substantial smile.' I hope she's happy. I wonder why she did it? To save the Shack. . . ." She was trying to keep her voice cheerful, but her look was bitter. Dot wasn't I; just terrified. I suppose that to her the only reason a woman would move in with a man would be to save some noble cause like the Shack.

As to Jill, she didn't change much. The Shack was the first step in the conquest of the universe, and it was by God going to be finished and self-sufficient. Partly it was a memorial to Ty, I think; but she really believed in what she was doing, and it was infectious.

I could see how Jack could convince her that he shared her goal. To a great extent he did, although it was pure selfishness; his considerable reputation was riding on this project. But Jack never did anything halfheartedly. He drove himself at whatever he was doing.

What I couldn't understand was why he was here at all. He must have *known* how thin the chances were of completing the Shack before he left Earth.

I had to know before it drove me nuts.

Jack didn't drink much. When he did it was often a disaster, because he was the world's cheapest drunk. So one night I plied him.

Night is generally relative, of course, but this one was real: the Earth got between us and the sun. Since we were in the same orbit as the Moon, but sixty degrees ahead, that happened to us exactly as often as there are eclipses of the Moon on Earth; a rare occasion, one worth celebrating.

Of course we'd put in a day's work first, so the party didn't last long; we were all too beat. Still it was a start, and when the formalities broke up and Jill went off to look at the air system, I grabbed Jack and got him over to my quarters. We both collapsed in exhaustion.

I had brought a yeast culture with me from Canaveral. McLeve had warned me that liquor cost like diamonds up here; and a way to make my own alcohol seemed a good investment. And it was. By now I had vacuum-distilled vodka made from fermented fruit bars and a mash of strawberries from the farm—they weren't missed; the farm covered a quarter of the inner surface now. My concoction tasted better than it sounds, and it wasn't hard to talk Jack into a drink, then another.

Presently he was trying to sing the verses to "The Green Hills of Earth." A mellower man you never saw. I seized my chance.

"So you love the green hills of Earth so much, what are you doing here? Change your mind about Rio?"

Jack shook his head; the vibration ran down his arm and sloshed his drink. "Nope . . ." Outside a hen cackled, and Jack collapsed in laughter. "Let me rest my eyes on the fleecy skies . . ."

Grimly I stuck to the subject. "I thought you were all set with that Tucson arcology."

"Oh, I was. I was indeed. It was *a beautiful* setup. Lots of pay, and—" He stopped abruptly.

"And other opportunities?" I was beginning to see the light.

"Welllll . . . yes. But you have to see it the way I did. First, it was a great opportunity to make a name for myself. A city in a building! Residential and business and industry all in the same place, one building to house a quarter . . . of a million . . . people. And it would have been beautiful, Corky. The plans were magnificent! I was in love with it. Then I got into it, and I saw what was really going on.

"Corky, everyone was stealing that place blind! The first week I went to the chief engineer to report shortages in deliveries and he just looked at me. 'Stick to your own work, Halfey,' says he. Chief engineer, the architects, construction bosses, even the catering crew—every one of them was knocking down twenty-five, fifty percent! They were selling the cement right off the boxcars and substituting sand. There wasn't enough cement in that concrete to hold up the walls."

"So you took your share."

"Don't get holy on me! Dammit, look at it my way. I was willing to play square, but they wouldn't let me. The place was going to fall down. The weight of the first fifty thousand people would have done it. What I could do was make sure nobody got inside before it happened." Jack Halfey chortled. "I'm a public benefactor, I am. I sold off the reinforcing rods. The inspectors couldn't possibly ignore that."

"Nothing else?" I asked.

"Well, those rods were metal-whisker compote. Almost as strong as diamond, and almost as expensive. I didn't need anything else. But I made sure they'd never open that place to the public. Then I stashed my ill-gotten gains and went underground and waited for something to happen."

"I never heard much about it. Of course, I wouldn't, up here."

"Not many down there heard either. Hush hush while the FBI looked into it. The best buy I ever made in my life was a subscription to the *Wall Street Journal.* Just a paragraph about how the Racket Squad was investigating Mafia involvement in the Tucson arcology. That's when things fell into place."

I swung around to refill his glass, carefully. We use great big glasses, and never fill them more than half full. Otherwise they slosh all over the place in the low gravity. I had another myself. It was pretty good vodka, and if I felt it, Jack must be pickled blue. "You mean the building fell in?"

"No, no. I realized why there was so *much* graft." Jack sounded aggrieved. "There was supposed to be graft. I wasn't supposed to get in on it."

"Aha."

"Aha you know it. I finished reading that article on a plane to Canaveral. The FBI couldn't follow me to Rio, but the Mafia sure could. I'd heard there was a new opening for chief engineer for the Construction Shack, and all of a sudden the post looked very, very good."

He chuckled. "Also, I hear that things are tightening up in the USA. Big crackdown on organized crime. Computer-assisted. Income tax boys and Racket Squad working together. It shouldn't be long before all the chiefs who want my arse are in jail. Then I can go back, cash my stash, and head for Rio."

"Switzerland?"

"Oh, no. Nothing so simple as that. I thought of something else. Say, I better get back to my bunk." He staggered out before I could stop him. Fortunately it was walking distance from my place to his; if he'd had to fly, he'd probably have ended up roosting with the chickens.

"Bloody hell," says I to myself.

Should I add that I had no intention of robbing Jack? I was just curious: what inflation-proof investment had he thought up? But I didn't find out for a long time. . . .

A month later the dollar collapsed. Inflation had been a fact of life for so long that it was the goal of every union and civil service organizer to get inflation written into their contracts, thereby increasing inflation. The government printed money faster to compensate: more inflation. One of those vicious spirals. Almost suddenly, the dollar was down the drain.

There followed a full-scale taxpayer revolt.

The administration got the message: they were spending too much money. Aha! Clearly that had to stop. The first things to go were all the projects that wouldn't pay off during the current President's term of office. Long-term research was chopped out of existence! Welfare, on the other hand, was increased, and a comprehensive National Health Plan was put into effect, even though they had to pay the doctors and hospitals in promissory notes.

The senator from Wisconsin didn't even bother giving us his customary Golden Fleece Award. Why insult the walking dead?

We met in our usual place, a cage-work not far from the north pole. Admiral McLeve was in the center, in zero gravity. The rest of us perched about the cage-work, looking like a scene from Hitchcock's *The Birds.*

Dot had a different picture, from Aristophanes. "Somewhere, what with all these clouds and all this air, there must be a rare name, somewhere. . . . How do you like Cloud-Cuckoo-Land?"

Putting on wings does things to people. Halfey had dyed his wings scarlet, marked with yellow triangles enclosing an H. Dot wore the plumage of an eagle, and I hadn't believed it the first time

I saw it; it was an incredibly detailed, beautiful job. McLeve's were the wings of a bat, and I tell you he looked frightening, as evil as Dracula himself. Leon Briscoe, the chemist, had painted mathematical formulae all over his, in exquisite medieval calligraphy. Jill and Ty had worn the plumage of male and female Least Terns, and she still wore hers. There were no two sets of wings alike in that flock. We were ninety birds of ninety species, all gathered as if the ancient roles of predator and prey had been set aside for a larger cause. Cloud-Cuckoo-Land.

A glum Cloud-Cuckoo-Land.

"It's over," McLeve said. "We've been given three months to phase out and go home. Us, Moonbase, the whole space operation. They'll try to keep some of the near-Earth operations going awhile longer, but we're to shut down."

Nobody said anything at first. We'd been expecting it, those of us who'd had time to follow news from Earth. Now it was here, and nobody was ready. I thought about it: back to high gravity again. Painful.

And Jill. Her dream was being shot down. Ty died for nothing. Then I remembered McLeve. He wasn't going anywhere. Any gravity at all was a death sentence.

And I hated Jack Halfey for the grin he was hiding. There had been a long piece in the latest newscast around the roundup of the Mafia lords; grand juries working overtime, and the District of Columbia jail filled, no bail to be granted. It was safe for Jack down there, and now he could go home early.

"They can't do this to us!" Jill wailed. A leftover Fromate reflex, I guess. "We'll—" Go on strike? Bomb something? She looked around at our faces and when I followed that look I stopped with Dot Hoffman. The potato face was withered in anguish, the potato eyes were crying. What was there for Dot on Earth?

"What a downer," she said.

I almost laughed out loud, the old word was so inadequate. Then McLeve spoke in rage. "Downers. Yes. Nine billion downers sitting on their fat arses while their children's futures slides into the muck. Downers is what they are."

Now you know. McLeve the wordsmith invented the word, on that day.

My own feelings were mixed. Would the money stashed in Swiss francs be paid if we left early, even though we had to leave? Probably, and it was not a small amount; but how long would it last? There was no job waiting for me . . . but certainly I had the reputation I'd set out for. I shouldn't have much trouble getting a job.

But I like to finish what I start. The Shack was *that* close to being self-sufficient. We had the solar power grids working. We even had the ion engines mounted all over the grid to keep it stable. We didn't have the microwave system to beam the power back to Earth, but it wouldn't be that expensive to put in . . . except that Earth had no antennae to receive the power. They hadn't even started reconstruction. The permit hearings were tied up in lawsuits.

No. The Shack was dead. And if our dollars were worthless, there were things that weren't. Skilled labor *couldn't* be worthless. I would get my francs, and some of my dollar salary had been put into gold. I wouldn't be broke. And—the clincher—there were women on Earth.

McLeve let us talk a while. When the babble died down and he found a quiet lull, he said, very carefully, "Of course, we have a chance to keep the station going."

Everyone talked at once. Jill's voice came through loudest. "How?"

"The Shack was designed to be a self-sufficient environment," McLeve said. "It's not quite that yet, but what do we need?"

"Air," someone shouted.

"Water," cried another.

I said, "Shielding. It would help to have enough mass to get us through a big solar flare. If they're shutting down Moonbase we'll never have it."

Jill's voice carried like a microphone. "Rocks? Is that all we need? Ice and rocks? We'd have both in the asteroid belt." It was a put-up job. She and McLeve must have rehearsed it.

I laughed. "The Belt is two hundred million miles away. We don't have ships that will go that far, let alone cargo . . . ships . . ." And then I saw what they had in mind.

"Only one ship," McLeve said. "The Shack itself. We can move it out into the Belt."

"How long?" Dot demanded. Hope momentarily made her beautiful.

"Three years," McLeve said. He looked thoughtful. "Well, not quite that long."

"We can't live three years," I shouted. I turned to Jill, trusting idiot that I was then. "The air system can't keep us alive that long, can it? Not enough chemicals—"

"But we can do it!" she shouted. "It won't be easy, but the farm is growing now. We have enough plants to make up for the lack of chemical air purification. We can recycle everything. We've got the raw sunlight of space. Even out in the asteroids that will be enough. We can do it."

"Can't hurt to make a few plans," McLeve said.

It couldn't help either, thought I; but I couldn't say it, not to Dot and Jill.

II

These four were the final architects of The Plan: Admiral McLeve, Jill Plauger, Dot Hoffman, and Jack Halfey.

At first the most important was Dot. Moving something as large as the Shack, with inadequate engines, a house in space never designed as a ship; that was bad enough. Moving it farther than any manned ship, no matter the design, should have been impossible.

But behind that potato face was a brain tuned to mathematics. She could solve any abstract problem. She knew how to ask questions; and her rapport with computers was a thing to envy.

Personal problems stopped her cold. Because McLeve was one of the few men she could see as harmless, she could open up to him. He had told me sometime before we lost Ty, "Dot tried sex once and didn't like it." I think he regretted saying even that much. Secrets were sacred to him. But for whatever reason, Dot couldn't relate to people; and that left all her energy for work.

Dot didn't talk to women either, through fear or envy or some other reason I never knew. But she did talk to Jill. They were fanatical in the same way. It wasn't hard to understand Dot's enthusiasm for The Plan.

McLeve had no choices at all. Without the Shack he was a dead man.

Jack was in the Big Four because he was needed. Without his skills there would be no chance at all. So he was dragged into it, and we watched it happen.

The day McLeve suggested going to the asteroids, Jack Halfey was thoroughly amused, and showed his mirth to all. For the next week he was not amused by anything whatever. He was a walking temper tantrum. So was Jill. I expect he tried to convince her that with sufficient wealth, exile on Earth could be tolerable. Now he wasn't sleeping, and we all suffered.

Of course our miseries, including Jack's, were only temporary. We were all going home. All of us.

Thus we followed the downer news closely, and thus was there a long line at the communications room. Everyone was trying to find an Earthside job. It hardly mattered. There was plenty of power for communications. It doesn't take much juice to close down a colony.

We had no paper, so the news was flashed onto a TV for the edification of those waiting to use the transmitter. I was waiting for word from Inco: they had jobs at their new smelter in Guatemala. Not the world's best location, but I was told it was a tropical paradise, and the quetzal was worth at least as much as the dollar.

I don't know who Jack was expecting to hear from. He looked like a man with a permanent hangover, except that he wasn't so cheerful.

The news, for a change, wasn't all bad. Something for everyone. The United States had issued a new currency, called "marks" (it turns out there were marks in the US during revolutionary times); they were backed by miniscule amounts of gold.

Not everyone was poor. Technology proceeded apace. Texas Instruments announced a new pocket computer, a million bits of memory and fully programmable, for twice what a calculator cost. Firestone Diamonds—which had been manufacturing flawless blue-white diamonds in a laboratory for the past year, and which actually was owned by a man named Firestone—had apparently swamped the engagement ring market, and was now making chandeliers. A diamond chandelier would cost half a year's salary, of course, but that was expected to go down.

The "alleged Mafia chieftains" now held without bail awaiting trial numbered in the thousands. I was surprised: I hadn't thought it would go that far. When the dollar went worthless, apparently Mafia bribe money went worthless too. Maybe I'm too cynical. Maybe there was an epidemic of righteous wrath in government.

Evidently someone thought so, because a bond issue was approved in California, and people were beginning to pay their taxes again.

Something for everyone. I thought the Mafia item would cheer Jack up, but he was sitting there staring at the screen as if he hadn't seen a thing and didn't give a damn anyway. My call was announced and I went in to talk to Inco. When I came out Jack had left, not even waiting for his own call. Lack of sleep can do terrible things to a man.

I wasn't surprised when Jack had a long talk with McLeve, nor when Jill moved back in with him. Jack would promise anything, and Jill would believe anything favorable to her mad scheme.

The next day Jack's smile was back, and if I thought it was a bit cynical, what could I do? Tell Jill? She wouldn't have believed me anyway.

They unveiled The Plan a week later. I was invited to McLeve's house to hear all about it.

Jack was there spouting enthusiasm. "Two problems," he told us. "First, keeping us alive during the trip. That's more Jill's department, but what's the problem? The Shack was designed to last centuries. Second problem is getting out there. We've got that figured out."

I said, "The hell you do. This isn't a spaceship, it's just a habitat. Even if you had a, a big rocket motor to mount on the axis, you wouldn't have fuel for it, and if you did, the Shack would break up under the thrust." I hated him for what he was doing to Jill, and I wondered why McLeve wasn't aware of it. Maybe he was. The admiral never let anyone know what he thought.

"So we don't mount a big rocket motor," Jack said. "What we've got is just what we need: a lot of little motors on the solar panels. We use those and everything else we have. Scooters and tugs, the spare panel engines, and, last but not least, the Moon. We're going to use the Moon for a gravity sling."

He had it all diagrammed out in four colors. "We shove the Shack toward the Moon. If we aim just right, we'll skim close to the lunar surface with everything firing. We'll leave the Moon with that velocity plus the Moon's orbital velocity, and out we go."

"How close?"

He looked to Dot. She pursed her lips. "We'll clear the peaks by two kilometers."

"That's close."

"More than a mile," Jack said. "The closer we come the faster we leave."

"But you just don't have the thrust!"

"Almost enough," Jack said. "Now look. We keep the panel thrusters on full blast. That gives us about a quarter percent of a gravity, not *nearly* enough to break up the Shack, Corky. And we use the mirrors." He poked buttons and another diagram swam onto McLeve's drafting table. "See."

It showed the Shack with the window mirrors opened all the way for maximum surface area. My smelter mirror was hung out forward. Other mirrors had been added. "Sails! Light pressure adds more thrust. Not a lot, but enough to justify carrying their mass. We can get to the Belt."

"You're crazy," I informed them.

"Probably," McLeve muttered. "But from my viewpoint it looks good."

"Sure. You're dead anyway, no offense intended. We're playing a game here, and it's getting us nowhere."

"I'm going." Jill's voice was very low and very convincing. It stirred the hair on my neck.

"Me too," Dot added. She glared at me, the enemy.

I made one more try. They'd had more time to think about it than I did, but the thrust figures were right there, scrawled in an upper corner of the diagram. "Now pay attention. You can't possibly use the attitude jets on the solar panels for that long. They work by squirting dust through a magnetic field, throwing it backward so the reaction pushes you forward. Okay, you've got free solar power, and you can get the acceleration. But where can you possibly get enough dust?" I saw Jack's guilty grin, and finished, "Holy shit!"

Jack nodded happily.

"Why not?" Jill asked. "We won't need solar flare shielding around Ceres. On the way we can keep what we do have between us and the Sun, while we grind up the surplus."

They meant it. They were going to make dust out of the radiation shields and use that.

In theory it would work. The panel engines didn't care what was put through them; they merely charged the stuff up with electricity gathered from the solar cells and let the static change provide the push. A rocket is nothing more than a way to squirt mass overboard; any mass will do. The faster you can throw mass away, the better your rocket.

At its simplest a rocket could be a man sitting in a bucket throwing rocks out behind him. Since a man can't throw very fast that wouldn't be a very good rocket, but it would work.

But you have to have rocks, and they were planning on using just about all of ours.

It was a one-way mission. They'd have to find an asteroid, and fast, when they got to the Belt; by the time they arrived they'd be grinding up structure, literally taking the Shack apart, and all that would have to be replaced.

It would have to be a special rock, one that had lots of metal, and also had ice. This wasn't impossible, but it wasn't any sure thing either. We knew from Pioneer probes that some of the asteroids had strata of water ice, and various organics as well; but we couldn't tell which ones. We knew one more thing from the later probes, and The Plan was geared to take advantage of that.

The *Skylark*—newly named by McLeve, and I've never known why he called it that—would head for Ceres. There were at least three small-hill-sized objects orbiting that biggest of the asteroids.

A big solar flare while they were out that far would probably kill the lot of them. Oh, they had a safety hole designed: a small area of the Shack to huddle inside, crowded together like sardines, and if the flare didn't last too long they'd be all right—

Except that it would kill many of the plants needed for the air supply.

I didn't think the air recycling system would last any three years either, but Jill insisted it was all right. It didn't matter. I wasn't going, and neither was Jack; it was just something to keep Jill happy until the shuttle came.

There was more to The Plan. All the nonessential personnel would go to Moonbase, where there was a better chance. Solar flares weren't dangerous to them. Moonbase was buried under twenty feet of lunar rock and dust. They had lots of mass. There's oxygen chemically bound in lunar rock; and if you have enough power and some hydrogen you can bake it out. They had power: big solar mirrors, not as big as ours, but big. They had rocks. The hydrogen recycles if it's air you want. If you want water, the hydrogen has to stay in the water.

We figured they could hang on for five years.

Our problem was different. If Moonbase put all its effort into survival, they wouldn't have the resources to keep sending us rocks and metal and hydrogen. Hydrogen is the most abundant element in the universe; but it's rare on the Moon. Without hydrogen you don't have water. Without water you don't have life.

I had to admit things were close. We were down to a shuttle load a month from Earth; but we needed those. They brought hydrogen, vitamins, high-protein foods. We could grow crops; but that took water, and our recycling systems were nowhere near one hundred percent efficient.

Now the hydrogen shipments had stopped. At a cost of fifty million dollars a flight before the dollar collapsed, the USA would soon stop sending us ships!

Another thing about those ships. They had stopped bringing us replacement crew long ago. Jack was the last. Now they were taking people home. If they stopped coming, we'd be marooned.

A few more years and we could be self-sufficient. A few more years and we could have colonists, people who never intended to go home. They were aboard now, some of them. Jill and Ty, before Ty was killed. Dot Hoffman was permanent. So was McLeve, of course. Of the seventy-five still aboard—we'd lost a few to the shuttles—twenty-five or so, including all the married couples, thought of themselves as colonists.

The rest of us wanted to go home.

Canaveral gave us fifty days to wind up our affairs. The shuttles would come up empty but for the pilots, with a kind of sardine-can-with-seats fitted in the hold.

I could understand why McLeve kept working on The Plan. Earth would kill him. And Jill: Ty's death had no meaning if the Shack wasn't finished. Dot? Sure. She was valuable, here.

But would you believe that I worked myself stupid mounting mirrors and solar panel motors? It wasn't just for something to do before the shuttle arrived, either: I had a nightmare living in my mind.

McLeve was counting on about twenty crew: the Big Four, and six of the eight married couples, and up to half a dozen additional men, all held by their faith in The Plan.

The history books have one thing right. The Plan was Jack Halfey's. Sure, Jill and McLeve and Dot worked on it, but without him it couldn't be brought off. Half of The Plan was no more than a series of contingency operations, half-finished schemes that relied on Halfey's ingenuity to work. McLeve and Halfey were the only people aboard who really knew the Shack—knew all its parts and vulnerabilities, what might go wrong and how to fix it; and McLeve couldn't do much physical work. He wouldn't be outside working when something buckled under the stress.

And there would be stress. A hundredth of a gravity doesn't sound heavy, but much of our solar panel area and all our mirrors were flimsy as tissue paper.

Without Halfey it wouldn't, couldn't work. When Halfey announced that he was going home on that final shuttle, the rest would quit too. They'd beg the downers for one more shuttle, and they'd get it, of course, and they'd hold the Shack until it came.

But McLeve couldn't quit, and Dot wouldn't, and I just couldn't be sure about Jill. If Halfey told her he wasn't really going, would she see reason? The son of a bitch was trading her life for a couple of hours sleep. When *Skylark* broke from orbit, would she be aboard? She and Dot and the Admiral, all alone in that vast landscaped bubble with a growing horde of chickens, going out to the asteroids to die. The life support system might last a long time with only three humans to support: they might live for years.

So I worked. When they finally died, it wouldn't be because Cornelius Riggs bobbled a weld.

The first shuttle came and picked up all nonessential personnel. They'd land at Moonbase, which was the final staging area for taking everyone home. If The Plan went off as McLeve expected, many of them would be staying on the Moon, but they didn't have to decide that yet.

I was classed as essential, though I'd made my intentions clear. The Plan needed me: not so much on the trip out, but when they reached the Belt. They'd have to do a lot of mining and refining, assuming they could find the right rock to mine and refine.

I let them talk me into waiting for the last shuttle. I wouldn't have stayed if I hadn't known Halfey's intentions, and I confess to a squirmy feeling in my guts when I watched that shuttle go off without me.

The next one would be for keeps.

When you have a moral dilemma, get drunk. It's not the world's best rule, but it is an old one: the Persians used the technique in classical times. I tried it.

Presently I found myself at McLeve's home. He was alone. I invited myself in.

"Murdering bastard," I said.

"How?"

"Jill. That crazy plan won't work. Halfey isn't even going. You know it and I know it. He's putting Jill on so she won't cut him off. And without him there's not even a prayer."

"Your second part's true," McLeve said. "But not the first. Halfey is going."

"Why would he?"

McLeve smirked. "He's going."

"What happens if he doesn't?" I demanded. "What then?"

"I stay." McLeve said. "I'd rather die here than in a ship."

"Alone?"

He nodded. "Without Halfey it is a mad scheme. I wouldn't sacrifice the others for my heart condition. But Halfey isn't leaving, Corky. He's with us all the way. I wish you'd give it a try too. We need you."

"Not me."

***

How was Halfey convincing them? Not Jill: she wanted to believe in him. But McLeve, and Dot—Dot had to know. She had to calculate the shuttle flight plan, and for that she had to know the masses, and the total payload mass for that shuttle had to equal all the personnel except McLeve but including the others.

Something didn't make any sense.

I waited until I saw eagle wings and blue wool stockings fly away from the administration area, and went into her computer room. It took a while to bring up the system, but the files directory was self-explanatory. I tried to find the shuttle flight plan, but I couldn't. What I got, through sheer fumbling, was the updated flight plan for the *Skylark*.

Even with my hangover I could see what she'd done: It was figured for thirty-one people, plus a mass that had to be the shuttle. *Skylark* would be carrying a captain's gig. . . .

The shuttle was coming in five days.

Halfey had to know that shuttle wouldn't be taking anyone back. If he wasn't doing anything about it, there was only one conclusion. He was going to the Belt.

A mad scheme. It doomed all of us. Jill, myself, Halfey, myself—

But if Halfey didn't go, no one would. We'd all go home in that shuttle. Jill would be saved. So would I.

There was only one conclusion to that. I had to kill Jack Halfey.

How? I couldn't just shoot him. There wasn't anything to shoot him with. I thought of ways. Put a projectile into a reaction pistol. But what then? Space murder would delight the lawyers, and I might even get off; but I'd lose Jill forever, and without Halfey . . .

Gimmick his suit. He went outside regularly. Accidents happen. Ty wasn't the only one whose ashes we'd scattered into the soil of the colony.

Stethoscope and wrench: stethoscope to listen outside the walls of Halfey's bed chamber, a thoroughly frustrating and demeaning experience; but presently I knew they'd both be asleep for an hour or more.

It took ten minutes to disassemble Jack's hose connector and substitute a new one I'd made up. My replacement looked just like the old one, but it wouldn't hold much pressure. Defective part. Metal fatigue. I'd be the one they'd have examine the connector if there was any inquiry at all. And I had no obvious motive for killing Jack; just the opposite, except for Jill and McLeve I was regarded as Jack's only friend.

Once that was done I had only to wait.

The shuttle arrived empty. Halfey went outside, all right, but in a sealed cherry picker; he wasn't exposed to vacuum for more than a few moments, and apparently I'd made my substitute just strong enough to hold.

They docked the shuttle, but not in the usual place, and they braced it in. It was time for a mutiny. I wasn't the only one being shanghaied on this trip. I went looking for Halfey. First, though, I'd need a reaction pistol. And a projectile. A ballpoint pen ought to do nicely. Any court in the world would call it self-defense.

"I'm a public benefactor, I am," I muttered to myself.

Jill's quarters were near the store room. When I came out with the pistol, she saw me. "Hi," she said.

"Hi." I started to go on.

"You never talk to me anymore."

"Let's say I got your message."

"That was a long time ago. I was upset. So were you. It's different now. . . ."

"Different. Sure." I was bitter and I sounded it. "Different. You've got that lying bastard Halfey to console you, that's how it's different." That hurt her, and I was glad of it.

"We need him, Corky. We all need him, and we always did. We wouldn't have got much done without him."

"True enough—"

"And he was driving all of you nuts, wasn't he? Until I—helped him sleep."

"I thought you were in love with him."

She looked sad. "I like him, but no, I'm not in love with him." She was standing in the doorway of her quarters. "This isn't going to work, is it? The Plan. Not enough of you will come. We can't do it, can we?"

"No." Might as well tell her the truth. "It never would have worked, and it won't work now even if all of us aboard come along. Margin's too thin, Jill. I wish it would, but no."

"I suppose you're right. But I'm going to try anyway."

"You'll kill yourself."

She shrugged. "Why not? What's left anyway?" She went back into her room.

I followed. "You've got a lot to live for. Think of the baby fur seals you could save. And there's always me."

"You?"

"I've been in love with you since the first time I saw you."

She shook her head sadly. "Poor Corky. And I treated you just like all the others, back then when— I wish you'd stay with us."

"I wish you'd come back to Earth with me. Or even Moonbase. We might make a go of Moonbase. Hang on until things change down there. New administration. Maybe they'll want a space program, and Moonbase would be a good start. I'll stay at Moonbase if you'll come."

"Will you?" She looked puzzled, and scared, and I wanted to take and hold her. "Let's talk about it. Want a drink?"

"No, thank you."

"I do." She poured herself something. "Sure you won't join me?"

"All right."

She handed me something cold, full of shaved ice. It tasted like Tang. We began to talk, about life on Earth—or even on Moonbase. She mixed us more drinks, Tang powder and water from a pitcher and vodka and shaved ice. Presently I felt good. Damned good.

One thing led to another, and I was holding her, kissing her, whispering to her—

She broke free and went over to close and lock her door. As she came back toward me she was unbuttoning the top of her blouse.

And I passed out.

When I woke I didn't know. Now, ninety years later, I still don't. For ninety years it has driven me nuts, and now I'll never know.

All that's certain is that I woke half dressed, alone in her bed, and her clothes were scattered on the deck. I had a thundering hangover and an urgent thirst. I drank from the water pitcher on her table—

It wasn't water. It must have been my own 100 proof vodka. Next to it was a jar of Tang and a bowl that had held shaved ice—and a bottle holding more vodka. She'd been feeding me vodka and Tang and shaved ice.

No wonder I had a hangover worthy of being bronzed as a record.

I went outside. There was something wrong.

The streams weren't running correctly. They stood at an angle. At first I thought it was me. Then they sloshed.

The Shack was under acceleration.

There were a dozen others screaming for blood outside the operations building. One was a stranger—the shuttle pilot. The door was locked, and Halfey was talking through a loudspeaker.

"Too late," he was saying. "We don't have enough thrust to get back to the L-4 point. We're headed for the Belt, and you might as well get used to the idea. We're going."

There was a cheer. Not everyone hated the idea. Eventually those who did understood: Halfey had drained the shuttle fuel and stored it somewhere. No escape that way.

No other shuttles in lunar orbit. Nothing closer than Canaveral, which was days away even if there were anything ready to launch. Nothing was going to match orbits with us.

We were headed for the Moon, and we'd whip around it and go for the Belt, and that was as inevitable as the tides.

When we understood all that they unlocked the doors.

An hour later the alarms sounded. "Outside. Suit up. Emergency outside!" McLeve's voice announced.

Those already in their suits went for the airlocks. I began halfheartedly putting on mine, in no hurry. I was sure I'd never get my swollen, pulsing head inside the helmet.

Jack Halfey dashed past, suited and ready. He dove for the airlock.

Halfey. The indispensable man. With a defective connector for an air intake.

I fumbled with the fasteners. One of the construction people was nearby and I got his help. He couldn't understand my frantic haste.

"Bastards kidnapped us," he muttered. "Let them do the frigging work. Not me."

I didn't want to argue with him, I just wanted him to hurry.

A strut had given way, and a section of the solar panel was off center. It had to be straightened, and we couldn't turn off the thrust while we did it. True, our total thrust was tiny, a quarter of a percent of a gravity, hardly enough to notice, but we needed it all.

Because otherwise we'd go out toward the Belt but we wouldn't get there, and by the time the Shack—*Skylark*, now—returned inevitably to Earth orbit there'd be no one alive aboard her.

I noticed all the work, but I didn't help. Someone cursed me, but I went on, looking for Halfey.

I saw him. I dove for him, neglecting safety lines, forgetting everything. I had to get to him before that connector went.

His suit blew open across the middle. As if the fabric had been weakened with, say, acid. Jack screamed and tried to hold himself together.

He had no safety line either. When he let go he came loose from the spiderweb. *Skylark* pulled away from him, slowly, two and a half centimeters per second per second; slow but inexorable.

I lit where he'd been, turned, and dove for him. I got him and used my reaction pistol to drive us toward the airlock.

I left it on too long. We were headed fast for the airlock entrance, too fast, we'd hit too hard. I tumbled about to get Jack across my back so that I'd be between him and the impact. I'd probably break a leg, but without Halfey I might as well have a broken neck and get it over with.

Leon Briscoe, our chemist, had the same idea. He got under us and braced, reaction pistol flaring behind us. We hit in a *ménage a trois,* with me as Lucky Pierre.

Leon cracked an ankle. I ignored him as I threw Halfey into the airlock and slammed it shut, hit the recycle switch. Air hissed in.

Jack had a nosebleed, and his cough sounded bad; but he was breathing. He'd been in vacuum about forty seconds. Fortunately the decompression hadn't been totally explosive. The intake line to his suit had fractured a half second before the fabric blew. . . .

The Moon grew in the scopes. Grew and kept growing, until it wasn't a sphere but a circle, and still it grew. There were mountains dead ahead.

"How close?" I demanded.

Dot had her eyes glued to a radar scope. "Not too close. About a kilometer."

"A *kilometer!*" One thousand meters. "You said two, before."

"So I forgot the shuttle pilot." She continued to stare at the scope, then her fingers bashed at the console keyboard. "Make that eight hundred meters," she said absently.

I was past saying anything. I watched the Moon grow and grow. Terror banished the last of my hangover; amazing what adrenalin in massive doses can do.

Jill looked worse than I did. And I didn't know. Were we lovers?

"Thirty seconds to periastron," Dot said.

"How close?" McLeve asked.

"Five hundred meters. Make that four-fifty."

"Good," McLeve muttered. "Closer the better."

He was right; the nearer we came to the Moon, the more slingshot velocity we'd pick up, and the faster we'd get to the Belt.

"Periastron," Dot announced. "Closest approach, four twenty-three and a fraction." She looked up in satisfaction. Potato eyes smiled. "We're on our way."

## III

On Earth we were heroes. We'd captured the downers' imaginations. Intrepid explorers. Before we were out of range we got a number of offers for book rights, should we happen to survive.

There were even noises about hydrogen shipments to the Moon. Of course there was nothing they could do for us. There weren't any ships designed for a three-year trek.

Certainly *Skylark* wasn't. But we were trying it.

There were solar flares. We all huddled around McLeve's house, with as much of our livestock as we could catch stuffed into his bedroom. It took weeks to clean it out properly afterward. We had to re-seed blighted areas and weed out mutated plants after each flare. More of our recycled air was coming from the algae tanks now.

In a time of the quiet sun we swarmed outside and moved all of the mirrors. The sun was too far away now, and the grass was turning brown, until we doubled the sunlight flooding through the windows.

But it seemed we'd reach Ceres. Already our telescopes showed five boulders in orbit around that largest of the asteroids. We'd look at them all, but we wanted the smallest one we could find: the least daunting challenge. If it didn't have ice somewhere in its makeup, the next one would, or the next.

And then we'd all be working like sled dogs, for our lives.

I was circling round the outside of *Skylark*, not working, just observing: looking for points with some structural strength, places where I could put stress when the real work began. Win or lose, with or without a cargo, we would have to get home a lot faster than we came. The life support system wouldn't hold up forever. Something would give out. Vitamins, water, something in the soil or the algae tanks. Something.

Our idea was to build a mass driver, a miniature of the machine that had been throwing rocks at us from the Moon. If we found copper in that rock ahead—a pinpoint to the naked eye now, near the tiny battered disk of Ceres—we could make the kilometers of copper wire we'd need. If not, iron would do. We had power from the sun, and dust from the rocks around Ceres, and we'd send that dust down the mass driver at rocket-exhaust speeds. Home in ten months if we found copper.

I went back inside.

The air had an odd smell when I took off my helmet. We were used to it; we never noticed now unless we'd been breathing tanked air. I made a mental note: mention it to Jill. It was getting stronger.

I had only the helmet off when Jean and Kathy Gaynor came to drag me out. I was clumsy in my pressure suit, and they thought that was hilarious. They danced me around and around, pulled me out into the grass, and began undressing me with the help of a dozen others.

It looked like I'd missed half of a great party. What the hell, Ceres was still a week away. They took my pressure suit off and scattered the components, and I didn't fight. I was dizzy and had the giggles. They kept going. Presently I was stark naked and grabbing for Kathy, who took to the air before I realized she had wings. I came down in a stream and surfaced still giggling.

Jack and Jill were on their backs in the grass, watching the fleecy white hens and turning occasionally to avoid chicken splat. I liked seeing Jill so relaxed for once. She waved, and I bounced over and somersaulted onto my back next to them.

A pair of winged people were way up near the axis, flapping among the chickens, scaring them into panic. It was like looking into Heaven, as you find it painted on the ceilings of some of the European churches. I couldn't tell who they were.

"Wealth comes in spirals too," Jill was saying in a dreamy voice. I don't think she'd noticed I wasn't wearing clothes. "We'll build bigger ships with the metal we bring home. Next trip we'll bring back the whole asteroid. One day the downers will be getting all their metal from us. And their whisker compotes, and drugs, and magnets, and, and free-fall alloys. Dare I say it? We'll own the world!"

I said, "Yeah." There were puffball chickens drifting down the sky, as if they'd forgotten how to fly.

"There won't be anything we can't do. Corky, can you see a mass driver wrapped all around the Moon? For launching starships. The ships will go round and round. We'll put the mag—mag, net, ic levitation plates overhead, to hold the ships down after they're going too fast to stay down."

Halfey said, "What about a hotel on Titan? Excursions into Saturn's rings. No downers allowed."

"We'll spend our second honeymoon there," said Jill.

"Yeah," I said, before I caught myself.

Halfey laughed like hell. "No, no, I want to build it!"

I was feeling drunk and I hadn't had a drink. Contact high, they call it. I watched those two at the axis as they came together in a tangle of wings, clung together. Objects floated around them, and presently began to spiral outward, fluttering and tumbling. I recognized a pair of man's pants.

It made me feel as horny as hell. Two hundred million miles away there was a planet with three billion adult women. Out of that number there must be millions who'd take an astronaut hero to their beds. Especially after I published my bestselling memoirs. I'd never be able to have them all, but it was certainly worth a try. All I had to do was go home.

Hah. And Thomas Wolfe thought *he* couldn't go home again!

A shoe smacked into a nearby roof, and the whole house *bonged.* We laughed hysterically. Something else hit almost beside my head: A hen lay on her back in the wheat, stunned and puzzled. The spiral of clothing was dropping away from what now seemed a single creature with four wings. A skinny blue snake wriggled out of the sky and touched down. I held it up, a tangle of blue wool. "My God!" I cried. "It's Dot!"

Jill rolled over and stared. Jack was kicking his heels in the grass, helpless with laughter. I shook my head; I was still dizzy. "What *have* you all been drinking? Not that Tang mixture again!"

Jill said, "Drinking?"

"Sure, the whole colony's drunk as lords," I said. "Hey . . . black wings . . . is that McLeve up there?"

Jill leapt to her feet. "Oh my God," she screamed. "The air!"

Jack bounded up and grabbed her arm. "What's happened?"

She tried to pull away. "Let me go! It's the air system. It's putting out alcohols. Not just ethanol, either. We're all drunk and hypoxic. Let me go!"

"One moment." Jack was fighting it and losing. In a moment he'd collapse in silliness again. "You knew it was going to happen," he said. His voice was full of accusation.

"Yes," Jill shouted. "Now will you let me go?"

"How did you know?"

"I knew before we started," Jill said. "Recycling isn't efficient enough. We need fresh water. Tons of fresh water."

"If there's no ice on that rock ahead—"

"Then we probably won't get to another rock," Jill said. "*Now* will you let me go work on the system?"

"Get out of here, you bitch," Jack yelled. He pushed her away and fell on his face.

It was scary. But there was also the alcohol. Fear and anger and ethanol and higher ketones and God knows what else fought it out in my brain. Fear lost.

"She's kept it going with Kleenex and bubble gum," I shouted. "And you believed her. When she told you it'd last three years. You believed." I whooped at the joke.

"Oh, shut up," Jack shouted.

"We've had it, right?" I asked. "So tell me something. Why did you do it? I was *sure* you were putting Jill on. I *know* you intended to go with the shuttle. So why?"

"Chandeliers," Jack said.

"Chandeliers?"

"You were there. Firestone Gems will sell you flawless blue-whites. A chandelier of them for the price of half a year's salary."

"And—"

"What the fuck do you think I did with my stash?" Jack screamed.

Stash. His ill-gotten gains from the Mafia. Stashed as blue-white diamonds.

Funny. Fun-nee. So why wasn't I laughing?

Because the bastard had kidnapped me, that's why. When he found his stash was worthless and he wasn't rich, and he'd probably face a jail term he couldn't bribe his way out of, he'd run as far away as a man could go. And taken me with him.

I crawled over to my doorway. My suit lay there in a sprawl. I fumbled through it to the equipment belt.

"What are you doing?" Halfey yelled.

"You'll see." I found the reaction pistol. I went through my pockets, carefully, until I found a ballpoint pen.

"Hey! No!" Jack yelled.

"I'm a public benefactor, I am," I told him. I took aim and fired. He tumbled backward.

There are always people who want to revise history. No hero is so great that someone won't take a shot at him. Not even Jack Halfey.

Fortunately I missed.

# DISCOVERY

## by Jerry Pournelle

### Editor's Introduction

The War World shared-world series was the brainchild of Jim Baen, when he was the newly minted publisher of Baen Books. Here's how it came about:

When Ace Books offered Jim the position of senior editor in 1977, Baen left *Galaxy Magazine*. One of his first acts as Ace senior editor was to approach Jerry about editing some anthologies for Ace Books. Jerry at that time was very involved with the L-5 Society, and told Jim he wanted to do an anthology on near-space and L-5 colonies; thus, the Endless Frontier series was born. It was my first big editorial project with Jerry and it came together quite quickly. Jim was so pleased with the success of *Endless Frontier* that he quickly asked us to do another. Meanwhile, with Jerry's encouragement, Baen sought out the H. Beam Piper estate and purchased it for Ace Books—one of the biggest publishing coups in the SF field's history.

Before the Piper anthologies could be published, Baen jumped ship again in 1980—this time to his former boss's new line, Tor Books. He was made vice-president under Tom Doherty and was put in charge of the Tor science-fiction line. One of his first moves at Tor was to contact Jerry about a new anthology series: "This time, I want a military-themed anthology series from you."

Jerry thought it sounded like a great idea, but quickly cooled off when he heard the title Jim offered, "There Will Be War." Jim convinced Jerry that this was a title—despite the antiwar sentiments popular in the early 1980s—that would sell books. Jerry shrugged and said, "You're the marketing genius. We'll do it."

The There Will Be War series was very successful for Tor Books, and went on for nine volumes and into the 1990s. It was so successful that when Baen left Tor three years later (with Tom Doherty's blessing) to found Baen Books he was most unhappy to leave it behind.

As the new publisher of Baen Books, one of Jim's first phone calls was to Jerry. He wanted another war-themed anthology from us, only this time he wanted it set in a war-based shared-world anthology. Jim was the editor who created the idea of fantasy and SF theme-world anthologies with Robert Lynn Asprin's *Thieves World* in 1978 while at Ace Books. The Thieves World series was a great success, spawning a dozen anthologies (in its first incarnation) and a number of spin-off novels. It was followed by George R.R. Martin with Wild Cards, a shared-world series about superheroes—which was way ahead of its time—and Janet Morris's Heroes in Hell, as well as several others.

I remember Jerry coming down the staircase from his second floor Great Hall, shaking his head. "Well, John, that was Baen on the phone."

I nodded; nothing new, they often spent hours on the phone together.

"Jim wants a new war anthology from us."

I rubbed my hands together. "This sounds like fun! An update on There Will Be War series?"

"No. This one's going to be a shared-world anthology, taking place on a planet in the CoDominium. We need a name: Any ideas?"

I scratched my head and put my thinking hat on: then it came to me—"War World," I said. "No one in the field has ever used it."

"I like it. Let me call Baen back and see what he thinks."

Jerry came back down to my office about an hour later. "I talked it over with Jim, and he likes it, too. We were talking and decided to make this War World a moon of a Jovian planet, one with a really harsh environment—hellish even."

"Okay," I said. "Then, let's call it Haven."

He laughed. We talked about who were going to be the first

settlers and came up with a religious sect based on Earth, the Harmonies.

"John, you work up a planetary history and I'll design the star system and its planets." I spent a couple of months working out a history of Haven, while Jerry, with Poul Anderson's help, got involved with the orbital mechanics and suddenly—War World came to life.

Later that week Jerry dropped a bombshell: "You've been working with me for a long time. I'm not in a position tax-wise to set up a pension, instead when you leave: I will give you ownership of War World. You'll be able to write and commission other writers to create new stories in my CoDominium/Empire of Man future history."

I was speechless. I had never heard of any writer, in this field or any other, who had willingly given blanket permission to another writer to write new stories and nonfiction in his universe. I knew Jerry was generous: I'd been there when he helped set up the SFWA Medical Fund with Robert Silverberg and knew of several other down and out authors he had helped. Still, it was quite a shock, a pleasant one—I might add.

Before the first book was published, *War World: The Burning Eye*, we got a lot of help. Roland Green, who was co-authoring books in Jerry's Janissaries series, helped with the War World background—especially planetary ecology. Steven Shervais became our continuity editor and provided valuable feedback on the physical constraints of the Byers' Star System, Cat's Eye and Haven itself.

We contacted a number of our favorite authors to write stories for the first War World anthology. Jerry collared Poul Anderson and Mike Resnick and convinced them to write stories, while I roped in Harry Turtledove, a friend and neighbor, and got Steve Stirling involved. There were a number of requests for a comprehensive author's guide to explain all the oddities and peculiarities of the Byers System, the Jovian planet Cat's Eye and its moon, Haven—more a loophole for life than a hospitable environment. The authors wanted detailed information about Haven's astronomy, geography, day/night cycle, seasons, geology, biology, history, flora and fauna, inhabitants, etc., so a War World authors' concordance of some four hundred pages was created.

Don Hawthorne, who was working at Chaos Manor as our editorial assistant, offered his assistance and, on his own, ended up writing the pivotal story, "The Coming of the Eye," on the Saurons. I am certain that the series would never have been as successful as it was without Don's ideas and stories. A number of prominent authors, John Dalmas, Harry Turtledove, Mike Resnick, David Drake, Poul Anderson, S.M. Stirling and a few newcomers wrote stories for the first four War World anthologies. The books sold very well; the Baen edition of *War World: The Burning Eye* went into four printings—almost unheard of for an original anthology. The series even spawned two War World novels, *Blood Feud* and *Blood Vengeance* by Harry Turtledove, S.M. Stirling with Judith Tarr and Susan Schwartz, and a companion volume, *CoDominium: Revolt on War World* which told the story of the early days of Haven while under CoDominium rule.

Unfortunately, when Jerry went into semiretirement in the mid-1990s and decided to stop doing any more anthologies, the War World series came to a halt. When I left, he transferred ownership to me as promised. The following note—written in response to a fan wanting to know why I was editing new War World volumes—was posted on Jerry's online "Chaos Manor in Perspective" on November 18, 2008, which answered his question: "John Carr has permission to write in the War World, and to commission stories in it. Indeed, one reason I created the War World was to give John Carr something as a reward for long faithful, service. Jerry Pournelle."

In 2007, I decided to revive War World under the Pequod Press imprint. This time I decided to redo War World properly: that is, put the stories in chronological order with lots of new yarns and novels. The first of these new works was the novel *War World: The Battle of Sauron*, by me and Don Hawthorne. The new novel revitalized the series and got an excellent review by Tom Easton in *Analog Science Fiction and Fact*. Sales were good and in November of 2010 Pequod released the first of a series of new War World anthologies, *War World: Discovery*.

Tom Easton had this to say about the new anthology in his review column in the March 2011 issue of *Analog*:

⌘⌘⌘

About twenty-years ago, Jerry Pournelle and John F. Carr brought about a shared-world series called War World. The five anthologies and two novels of the original series featured stories by a raft of authors, including Poul Anderson, Larry Niven, Mike Resnick, Susan Schwartz, S. M. Stirling, Harry Turtledove and William F. Wu. The stories were as diverse as their authors, ranging from pure military strategy to humor to surprisingly tender fables. The last volume, the novel *Blood Vengeance*, appeared in 1994, and the fun was over.

At least until 2007, when John F. Carr brought War World back in *War World: The Battle of Sauron*. Apparently, his intent is to bring the entire corpus of War World stories back into print, supplemented with a substantial number of new stories, portraying the saga in chronological order (the original volumes jumped around haphazardly through history). *War World: Discovery* is the first volume in this grand reissue.

The War World is Haven, a just-habitable moon of a gas giant called Cat's Eye. In the future, Haven will become a battleground between humans and the Saurons, a genetically enhanced master race bent on universal domination. In the beginning, however, Haven was a peaceful colony that soon became a prison planet, a dumping ground for malcontents and undesirables of all types. When criminal gangs take over the place and start causing trouble, the Imperial Marines are sent to bring peace to a planet everyone considers a hell-hole.

Of the fourteen stories in this volume, five appeared previously; the other nine are brand-new. Work by ten authors is included . . . if you're a fan of War World and want to see how it all began, it's worth it.

Since that review was written, Pequod Press has brought out three more new War World CoDominium-era anthologies and three more novels, including the recently released novel *War World: Falkenberg's Regiment*. All are available in both hardcover versions and as e-books. The next new anthology *War World: The Fall of the CoDominium* will appear within the next year or two.

The Pournelle story you are about to read is the tale of the original survey ship and its crew and the problems they encountered both while surveying Haven, and then later trying to sell their discovery.

⁂

*2032 A.D., Deep Space*

***CDSS RANGER*** was not a happy ship. It wasn't that there was anything wrong with her. *Ranger* wasn't new, far from it—she'd been one of the first exploratory ships built after the discovery of the Alderson Drive made star flight possible—but she was well maintained. Captain Jed Byers saw to that. No, Allan Wu thought, that wasn't the problem. It wasn't even the food. That was getting pretty monotonous after ten months in space, but Allan had been brought up on rice and whatever could be found to cook with it. He didn't need variety, he simply wanted enough to eat, and *Ranger* provided that, even if the rest of the crew made jokes about Purina Monkey Chow.

It wasn't the ship. It wasn't even the crew, not really. The problem was that they weren't accomplishing anything. No one was going to get rich on *Ranger*'s discoveries, least of all Allan Wu, and Allan needed the money.

It was Captain Byers's fault. Byers was fine at running a ship, but he didn't know beans about negotiating with the Bofors Company and the CoDominium. None of the systems he'd been given the right to explore had inhabitable planets. That was to be expected, habitable planets were rare, but the systems hadn't anything else either. One did have an asteroid belt with plenty of carbon, and even water ice—but no inhabitable planets, and no gas giant in the whole system. No place for merchantmen to get cheap hydrogen fuel. Belters could live without planets, but they couldn't live without *some* trade with Earth. Byers could file claims, but Bofors wasn't going to pay any bonuses for that find.

Probably not for the one coming up, either. Allan frowned and stared at the computer screen. It didn't tell him anything he didn't already know. A G2 star four light-years away and some twenty parsecs, over sixty light-years from Earth. Not that the distance mattered so much. There were two star systems nearby that could be reached by two Alderson Jumps. Not this one. "It's a bear to get to, and there's nothing when you get there."

"You can't know that," Linda said. "We know there are planets—"

"At least one planet," Allan agreed. "Maybe more. Pity the bloody telescope fritzed, we'd know more about that planet. I think it's a big one."

"A gas giant and a Belt," Linda mused. "And a habitable planet, green, about—what? Point seven AU out—?"

"That would do it," Allan said. "Riches in plenty. But it's a pipe dream."

"We still have to go look," Linda said. "And maybe we'll get lucky." She grinned, and Allan caught his breath as he always did when she smiled. He wondered if he'd ever get over that, and hoped he wouldn't.

"Read the contract lately?" she asked.

"Which one? Mine, yours, or ours?"

"Ours." She patted her stomach. "Just in time, too. Mother will be pleased. . . ."

"HEAR THIS. PREPARE FOR ALDERSON JUMP."

"SECURE FOR ALDERSON JUMP."

Linda shuddered and began strapping herself into the seat in front of her console.

"I saw that," Allan said. "Still worried about Jumps?"

"Well, some. Aren't you?"

He nodded slowly. No one had any information on the effects of the Alderson Drive on pregnant women or their unborn children. "Damn, I wish we weren't going on with—"

"Don't be silly," Linda said. "Two more Jumps can't matter."

"Sure," he said, but he didn't believe it. Alderson Jumps had unpredictably unpleasant effects on healthy adults. They couldn't be good for fetuses. Allan didn't care about their child, or at least could convince himself that he didn't, but the thought of something happening to Linda turned him to jelly.

"ALDERSON JUMP PLOTTED. INITIATING COUNTDOWN."

Allan checked his straps, then looked to make sure Linda's were properly fastened. All correct.

"STATION CHECK. BIOLOGICAL SECTION REPORT READY FOR JUMP."

"BIOLOGY READY AYE, AYE."

"Biology," Allan snorted.

"Sounds nicer than waste disposal."

"ENGINEERING REPORT READY FOR JUMP."

"ENGINEERING READY AYE, AYE."

"SCIENCE SECTION REPORT READY FOR JUMP."

Allan touched a switch, and his computer screen went blank. He glanced at the status lights on his console. "SCIENCE READY AYE, AYE," he reported.

"QUARTERMASTER SECTION REPORT READY FOR JUMP."

The station check continued. Then the speakers said, "ALDERSON JUMP IN ONE MINUTE. ONE MINUTE AND COUNTING."

"Science section," Allan said. There was contempt in his voice. "If I was a real scientist, I'd be investigating things. Why does the Alderson Jump rack people up?"

"Nobody knows that—"

"Exactly. I should be finding out—"

"STAND BY FOR JUMP."

There was a moment of silence, and the universe exploded around them.

Allan hung limply from the straps. He felt drool run down his chin, but for the moment he was too sick to care. His thoughts spun wildly.

For a moment—

For a moment he had known everything. He was sure of it. During that moment, when he, and Linda, and *CDSS Ranger* had ceased to exist in the normal universe, he had known, known with utter certainty, how planets formed, how the universe began, why the Alderson Drive worked. Now he couldn't remember any of it, only that he'd once known.

It was a common experience. Probably half the people who had made Jumps had felt it at least once. It was also an odd experience, because no experiment ever devised had measured the time a Jump took. To the best anyone could measure, it took literally no time at all. Yet during that zero interval, humans had thoughts and dreams while computers went mad, so that it was routine to shut down all computers except the ones needed for the Jump, and to have those on timers set to cut power as soon as the Jump was made.

"Linda?" he croaked.

"I'm fine."

She didn't sound fine. But at first it was hard to care about her or anything else, and after he began to recover from Jump Lag he had work to do. He started the power-up sequences on his computers.

"All right, damn it, so what do we do now?" Captain Byers demanded. He reached into a sideboard and took out a bulb of scotch whiskey, popped the top, and squeezed a shot into his mouth.

"I'm looking," Allan protested. "Look, it takes time. First I have to establish the plane of the ecliptic. That means I have to find more than two planets, or wait long enough for one to move."

"Yeah, I understand that," Byers said. "I don't suppose it will hurt your search if I mosey on over to the gas giant?"

"Not a bit," Allan said. "I was going to suggest that. It looks interesting. Hey—"

"Yeah?"

"Moons," Allan said. "The giant's got some. Ten anyway. They'll be in the ecliptic plane."

"Well, hell, of course they'll be in the ecliptic," Byers said. He looked critically at Allan, then shook his head.

"Sir?" Allan asked.

"I keep forgetting," Jed Byers said. "Not your fault. Mine."

"Captain, I don't understand at all," Allan Wu pleaded.

Jed Byers shrugged and reached into the cabinet. "Have a beer?"

"Well, thank you, sir—"

"By way of apology," Byers said. "Look, you can't help it if they deliberately crippled your education."

Allan frowned. "Captain, I—"

"You've got a PhD, from Cornell, and you're a licensed scientist," Byers said. "That what you were going to say?"

"Well—"

"And it don't mean beans," Byers said. "Not your fault. Look, nobody knows anything nowadays. It's all in the computers, so there's no point in knowing anything, right?"

"Well—it's not worthwhile memorizing facts," Allan said. "It's easier to learn where to find them—"

"Where to find them. In the computer. Ever think the computers might be wrong?"

"Sir?"

Jed Byers sighed. "Look, maybe I've had too much to drink." He eyed Allan carefully. "No recorders. Maybe you got one built into your teeth—the hell with it. Look, Dr. Wu, there was a time when 'scientist' meant somebody who knew something, who thought for himself—"

"Yes, sir," Allan said. "I know, and I don't measure up. I know that; I was just telling Linda. They don't let us do real research—"

"Maybe it's worse than that," Byers said. "Think on it, laddie. The CoDominium Treaty is supposed to stop the arms race, right? So if the CoDominium powers abide by it, everybody else has to, or one of the little guys might get ahead of the CoDominium. Only one problem. Any scientific discovery is likely to have military value. Better to stop it all. So tell me, if you were in CoDominium Intelligence, how would you stop scientific discovery?"

"Well—"

"Get control of everybody's research budget, every country and every company, not just the US and the Sov world, all of them, Swiss and Swedes and the other neutrals. Put your people on the editorial boards of all the journals. Take over the faculty and administration of the big universities. Elementary stuff. But how can you stop people from thinking? And putting what they think into computer networks?"

Byers laughed bitterly. "When I was a kid—Wu, do you know how old I am?"

"No, sir—"

"Older than God. I've heard you say it," Byers said. "Oh, yeah, *Ranger*'s wired up pretty good. And I know her. I took her out on her first run—"

"Sir? But that was—"

"A long time ago. Yep. Making me old enough to remember when 'scientist' meant something, which is the point. When I was a kid, we used to think the computer networks would end censorship forever. How can you censor on-line communications? Hah. You don't. What you do is corrupt them." Byers swigged hard at the bulb of scotch. "Think about it. Control research, control publications, and feed false data into the system. Know what Planck's Constant is? No? Look it up in your machine. Maybe you get the right answer. Maybe you don't."

"Sir—" Allan was interrupted by three chirps from his comcard.

"PLANET DETECTED, POINT SIX THREE AU FROM PRIMARY."

"Hey, a good distance," Allan reported. "Maybe we're lucky after all. Sir, if you'll excuse me—"

"Excuse hell! Doctor Wu, go find out if we're rich, and be quick about it!"

Five minutes later Allan knew the worst. The planet was barren. So was the only other one in the Habitable Zone. There couldn't be any life in the system.

"That's the story," Geoffrey Wu said. He signaled to the waiter for another platter of pot stickers. "A new planetary system, with a gas giant. No Belt, though."

"I suppose that's why I'm buying the dinner," Bill Garrick said. "Pity. But how'd you end up coming to an expensive school like this?"

Jeff grinned and fished in the pocket of his tunic, found a pink slip of paper, and laid it on the table. "No Belt, but there was something else."

Garrick looked at the check and whistled.

"Peanuts," Mary Hassimpton snorted.

"Yeah, well maybe to you, Miss Imperial Banks, but not to Dad," Jeff said.

"Lighten up, Mary," Garrick said. He drained his Chinese beer and lit a pipe of *borloi.*

"You're still grinning," Elayne van Stapleton said.

"And you've got money. Tell us about it."

"Now who's turn to lighten up?" Mary demanded.

"Aw, let Elayne be," Bill Garrick said. "Somebody's got to study. Why not her? So, Jeff, where did the money come from?"

Jeff grinned even wider. "Well, none of the real planets were of any use, but they found a good planet after all. It's a moon of the gas giant."

"Oh, for heaven's sake," Mary said.

"Yeah, I heard about that," Garrick said, "Haven, right?"

"Right. Not what Captain Byers named it, but it's official now that the Holy Joes bought it."

"So. Your old man did all right after all." Garrick took the check and held it out for Jeff. "So you pay for the Peking Duck."

"Well, all right," Jeff said. "But I can tell you, nobody got rich—not real rich—from selling out to Garner Castell."

# THE SCIENCE AND TECHNOLOGY OF JERRY POURNELLE'S CoDOMINIUM/EMPIRE OF MAN UNIVERSE

by Doug McElwain

## Editor's Introduction

Doug McElwain is the science and technology continuity editor for the War World series. Since Jerry's passing, no one knows more about the science of Jerry's CoDominium/Empire of Man universe than Doug. I'm also very pleased to include him among the writers of the War World books. He even tackled the very difficult job of writing the story behind the development of the Alderson Field—something Jerry's future history had long needed.

* * *

**IN MOST SCIENCE FICTION** it's easy to separate out the whiz-bang technology from the world an author creates. An author's ideas can be innovative and exciting but usually they can be moved to a range of backgrounds with little thought. Jerry Pournelle's CoDominium/Empire of Man universe is different. The technology and the events of his future history are closely tied together. In Pournelle's universe technology, while providing capabilities we don't have today, does not provide unlimited degrees of freedom. It is uncommon in science fiction for technology and culture to be thought through with an eye for detail. And certainly not over a thousand-year period and numerous books. Pournelle does this.

There are cycles in Pournelle's future history. Four main periods and two interregnums form his historical tapestry. The four periods are: the CoDominium (1990–2103), the Empire of Man aka First Empire (2250–2640), the Second Empire of Man (2903–3041), and the Empire of Man and Motie (3042–). Interregnums separate the first two major historical periods. As in our world technologies change over time. They are invented, honed and improved, and sometimes replaced just as we would experience.

Four science-fiction technologies run deep through the entire length of Pournelle's universe and determine the cultures and civilizations that develop. While knowledge and technologies can be lost over time in the CoDominium/Empire of Man universe, the Imperial Libraries are the important glue that keeps most knowledge and technologies available in all but the first period. They give continuity over long spans of time.

The four technologies are: the Alderson Drive, the Langston Field, fusion power (propulsion and power generation), and genetic engineering. Of these the last two are within our grasp today, albeit not in the near term. Both the Alderson Drive for interstellar Jumps and the Langston Field that protects anything inside of it from electromagnetic phenomenon are the real science fiction in Pournelle's universe. Having said that, both were created for him by the late Dan Alderson at JPL and are logically consistent yet still assume that all the physical laws we know today apply. This latter point provides constraints on what can and can't be done and therefore the outcome of tales told. As an example, spaceships can't Jump from anywhere to anywhere. Instead they have to move to particular places in a star system and that takes time. And even then they can't go just anywhere. More on this later.

In Pournelle's universe a series of treaties in 1990 between the United States and the Soviet Union create the CoDominium, an organization that brought an uneasy peace to mankind. Before the treaties could take full effect fusion power, genetic engineering and the Alderson Drive were invented. Going forward the

CoDominium Treaties limited weapons research and development. This was intended to prevent either the United States or the Soviet Union from gaining an advantage over the other. However, it turned out that almost any technology could be weaponized. Over time the research restrictions became more and more severe. Eventually all new science and technology innovation ceased. Earth's libraries were corrupted by the CoDominium intelligence services and all scientific research was closely monitored. Some out-system worlds conduct secret research but the CoDominium dealt harshly with transgressors. This is the background for the science and technology of Pournelle's universe. Now we'll look in more detail at some of the most significant science and technology in that tapestry.

**Alderson Drive**

In the CoDominium/Empire of Man universe there are two drives needed to travel between the stars. We'll discuss the Alderson Drive here and come back to the fusion drive later. As mentioned in Pournelle's future history, both are invented early in the CoDominium period. The Alderson Drive allows spaceships to travel from star system to star system instantaneously. However, there are limitations on what the Drive can do. And these limitations mean that spaceships cannot sneak up on a planet and attack it. This is critical for the formation of interstellar organizations.

Here are some of the characteristics of the Alderson Drive. Alderson points (aka Jump points) are found outside the habitable zone in solar systems. For instance, a G2 star like the sun has Alderson points between 2.2 and 30 AU (astronomical units) from Sol. This is the distance from the sun to the inner edge of the asteroid belt and Neptune, respectively. This means that spaceships do not travel through interstellar space in our universe though they do Jump through interstellar space from star system to star system in hyperspace. This, in turn, means that spaceships must travel through normal space to reach an Alderson point, the place where you can make a Jump to another star system. Fusion drives or a variation of them serve to propel spaceships through normal space to, from and between these points. The normal space distances are still immense and, as a result, take a lot of time (weeks or months) to cross (remember the physics we know still applies).

A single-star system with Alderson points can have anywhere from one to six of them. Multiple-star systems may (but usually don't) have more than six Alderson points. The number of additional Jump points in this case would still be small. Because systems with no Alderson points are not visited, and systems with only one point are dead ends, the average number of Alderson points in any system in the network is likely higher than three.

Each Alderson point connects to one Alderson point in another star system and only one. These connections are called tramlines. Tramlines always connect to that same point in that same star system. If you draw a line between the two stars the tramline would be on that line.

The lengths of Jump distances vary. In the published literature Jumps of anywhere from 1/3 to 35 light-years have been described. It is possible, in rare cases, for Jumps to be longer. However, most Jumps are between 5 and 15 light-years in length.

To get from one star system with a habitable planet to another star system with a habitable planet in most cases requires multiple Jumps (i.e., a series of Jumps). Possibly a lot of Jumps. There is a tradeoff between making a lot of little Jumps between low mass stars and one Jump to a bigger star. As a simple example, it is faster to make seven 5 light-year Jumps through M-class star systems than one 35 light-year Jump to an F-class star. This is because the average normal space transit distance through the M-class stars to reach their Alderson points adds up to less than the normal space distance through an F-type star system.

Alderson points are fixed locations in space. That is, they remain a fixed distance from their star and do not move relative to the background stars. Planets move in orbits around their sun. Alderson points do not. Therefore, the distance between planets and Alderson points continually change in single-star systems but in a repetitive manner except if the point is directly above the star system's planetary plane. Alderson points can shift some under certain circumstances but they do not move far. There is a major exception to this rule. Multiple-star systems may have Alderson points that are in fixed locations in space or they may have Alderson points that shift position some as the stars in the system orbit each other (or there may be some combination of fixed and shifting). Also, if one of the stars has a variable energy output the location of the Alderson points can shift.

Jumps take no measurable time. The travel is through the continuum universe (aka hyperspace). So, the Alderson Drive can be used to cross light-years instantaneously. But once you arrive at an Alderson point, interplanetary distances must be crossed using normal space drives (e.g., fusion drives) to either get to the next Alderson point, to a planet in that system or to a refueling station. And this travel takes time. Depending on spaceship velocity, fuel levels and system geometries it can take a long time (weeks or months). This is fundamental in determining what kind of interstellar political entities can form (i.e., the CoDominium, empires, etc.). The reason for this is that if a spaceship could materialize right next to a habitable planet then an interstellar organization like an empire couldn't protect it from raiders. There would be no reason for a planet to join an empire.

## Langston Field

The Langston Field (aka the Field) is a force field in the shape of a sphere, egg or more generally an ellipsoid. Its function is to absorb, store and release electromagnetic energy in a controlled manner. Electromagnetic energy includes photons, the kinetic energy of particles (both the random kinetic energy of heat and nonrandom kinetic energy) as well as magnetic and electrostatic fields. It is able to absorb energy from both real and virtual photons (hence its ability to absorb kinetic energy). It releases its stored energy as black-body radiation.

The Field's black-body radiation (frequency/color) depends on its temperature. In turn, the temperature depends on the amount of energy it has absorbed and is releasing and the Field's surface area. At room temperature or below, the Field would appear black because the energy it absorbed would be released as infrared radiation (which we cannot see). As the temperature increases the frequency of the light (color) moves up from infrared, to red and then through the visible spectrum toward blue-white. If the Field's temperature then decreases through the net release of energy, the color moves back down the visible spectrum toward infrared. The color green does not show up much in a black body spectrum and would rarely be seen. The Field has the appearance of a large balloon (as indicated above that doesn't necessarily mean spherical). Around a city at room temperature, where half of the Field extends underground, it would appear like the top half of a buried black balloon. Around a spaceship, again at room temperature or below, it would appear to be a large black balloon.

The Langston Field is analogous to a black hole but solely for electromagnetic phenomena. Think of it as an electromagnetic event horizon or optical singularity. The Field's black-body radiation is similar to Hawking radiation. Real and virtual particles associated with the other four forces (i.e., strong force, weak force, gravity and Alderson force) in the CoDominium/Empire of Man universe are not affected by the Field. Although the Field's energy release can be controlled the Field can still be damaged or destroyed. The integrity of the Field can be temporarily damaged (called a burn through) by a very quick and high level of localized energy input (like a big nuke). As a result a burst of energy can penetrate into the ship. The Field can experience a catastrophic failure (called an overload or collapse) if too much energy is pumped into it in too short a period of time, energy that it doesn't have time to safely release. When the Field collapses, all the energy of the Field is released at once both inward and outward; everything inside vaporizes and damage is caused to anything nearby on the outside. Like a heat flash from a nuke, but much larger.

The Langston Field is used in the First and Second Empire periods of the CoDominium/Empire of Man. It was discovered through a series of unlikely accidents to men in very different scientific fields. Pournelle wrote that the natural shape of a Field is a solid. If the Field absorbs real and virtual photons then the Field must generate an effect similar to the Casimir effect (the suppression of some virtual photon wavelengths between two plates.). Any virtual wavelengths inside the volume of space surrounded by the Field that are longer than the Field would be absorbed by the Field. This in turn would cause a small differential in the zero-point energy between the vacuum within the Field and the vacuum in the external universe. This would cause the Field to collapse inward (like two plates being pulled together) and would explain Pournelle's statement.

The Field is used primarily for protection and spaceship propulsion. In terms of protection there are two effects. First and most important, the Field absorbs incoming energy. Second, as it releases that energy it creates a wall of heat or firewall. The more energy the Field releases (and therefore the closer to blue-white its color) the more intense the radiation and the better protection it is against low-speed material objects penetrating the Field.

The Field must conform to the physics laws of conservation of energy and conservation of momentum. It can absorb and store electromagnetic energy, but not momentum. Rather momentum from a laser, a nuke, particle beams, railguns or collisions is spread out to the Field as a whole, but simultaneously that momentum is transferred to the Field generator and ultimately to the ship or planet where it is mounted. This means that in a spaceship battle, there will be a lot of shaking. Not so much for a city. Therefore, the bigger the ship (in terms of mass) the better it will be able to absorb all the shaking.

The Langston Field has size limits: an ellipsoid 30 meters along its longest axis is the smallest, 10,000 meters along its longest axis the largest. By 3000 A.D., after nine hundred years of development and manufacturing, the Empire's Langston Field generators are as well designed and foolproof as they can be, absent battle damage. The Langston generators and accumulators are not found everywhere. They are controlled (licensed in the Second Empire period and likely in earlier periods) and expensive. They are modular in design so they can be removed or re-installed from a spaceship without it going into a shipyard's dry-dock facilities.

### Fusion Drive

As mentioned previously the Alderson points where spaceships can Jump across interstellar space instantaneously are far from Earth.

With stars like Sol they lie between 2.2 and 30 AU from the sun. Given these distances powerful propulsion systems are needed to produce enough acceleration for a long enough period of time for a spaceship to travel to and from an Alderson points in a reasonable amount of time. Therefore, without fusion drives interstellar organizations, if they form, will take longer to develop and planets would have more local autonomy. Based on the amount of mass of the fuel converted to energy a fusion drive produces ten times the power of a fission drive. This means that fusion drives allow spaceships to travel faster and therefore further than a fission drive. Ion or chemical propulsion systems are even less energetic.

**Photon Drive**

During the CoDominium period it seems fusion drives are used to propel spaceships. Sometime during the First Empire period a new kind of reaction drive is invented. Fusion drives on warships are directed into their Langston Field which then creates an extremely efficient high-intensity beam of light in the shape of a cone that is used for propulsion. For the Field to work as described, energy must be emitted perpendicular to its surface and then naturally spreads out due to the inverse square law. The cone shape is a result of the Field being an ellipsoid with the beam coming from a small, curved section of it combined with this inverse square law spreading. This photon drive is utilized for propulsion by the Second Empire warships too. Therefore, only spaceships having a Langston Field can utilize this light-pressure propulsion system: all other spaceships still use fusion drives directly for thrust. The drive cannot be used as a long-range weapon because of beam spreading but it would be unhealthy for another ship without a Langston Field to pass through it especially if it were a close passage.

Note that fusion drives release photons and energetic plasma into the Field. The Field absorbs the photons (energy and momentum) and the kinetic energy from the plasma (momentum). From the stories, it is clear that the Field can be controlled to release the photons directionally or uniformly in all directions. As noted above, if directionally, the Field releases the absorbed photons in one direction to propel the spaceship. The photons released must contain the momentum from both the original photons and from the plasma. Because of the requirement for the conservation of momentum, this means that the frequency (energy level) of the Field-released photons must be of a much higher frequency than those originally released by the fusion reaction.

## Genetic Engineering

Genetic engineering plays at least two major roles in the future history series. First, genetic engineering technology developed early in the CoDominium period allowed Earth plants and animals to be modified to thrive on alien planets. Therefore, these genetic engineering techniques allowed mankind to colonize planets that already had some indigenous life forms. In the case of Sparta this genetic engineering allowed very rapid terraforming of the land surface of that planet. Note, the First Empire developed additional terraforming technologies beyond these. Their technologies allowed lifeless planets with suitable atmospheres, gravity and temperatures to be terraformed.

The second major role genetic engineering played was in the creation of both the Sauron supermen and Sauron cyborgs. This led directly to the Secession Wars which devastated the First Empire interstellar civilization. This led to several centuries of dark ages until the Second Empire of Man rose from the ashes of the First.

Technologies that artificially allow gene insertion similar to CRISPR gene editing allow the creation of superhuman genomes. Cloning allows their duplication. Both would presumably be needed for the artificial creation of a master race and both are here today, although not for humans. Yet.

Other technologies are being researched today. Prosthetic limbs are improving as are robotic exoskeletons that increase the strength a single person can wield. A neural control interface directly connecting computers to the brain is being researched and progress (albeit slow) is being made there too. Both, while not mentioned specifically by Pournelle, are implied in the creation of the Sauron cyborgs.

**Final Thoughts**

It's also important to mention some technologies that are not in Pournelle's future history. There is no faster-than-light radio communications nor are there any gravity generators although artificial gravity on spaceships is provided by spinning a ship or a portion of one to create centrifugal force. Again, for storywriters this constrains what they can have their characters do but it also puts in place a rational and consistent world that readers can immerse themselves in.

I've only scratched the surface of the technologies in Pournelle's future history here. There are holographic communications devices (Tri-V), direct conversion of heat to electricity, cold sleep, regeneration stimulators, Nemourlon body armor, sonic stunners and much, much more. These are things which, while they don't exist yet, are not prohibited by current science and may yet come to pass. One of the inventions that Pournelle did predict has come about and that is the wireless pocket computer (i.e., the smartphone). Jerry Pournelle may have passed, but his imagination and science-fiction legacy live on.

# REFLEX

## by Larry Niven & Jerry Pournelle

### Editor's Introduction

"Reflex" was the original opening of "Motelight," the working title of *The Mote in God's Eye*. The name was changed after Jerry sent the final draft of "Motelight" to Robert Heinlein. Mr. Heinlein did a line-by-line edit of much of the entire manuscript, which ran well over three hundred single-spaced pages. Jerry and Larry wisely took it for the compliment that it was and made almost all of the changes that Mr. Heinlein suggested: cutting some sixty thousand words, including "dropping the opening battle scene," and changing the title.

Jerry was quite proud of Mr. Heinlein's edit and often promised to publish it as a help to new authors. Unfortunately, that never happened; however, *The Virginia Edition: A Sample of the Series*, featuring selections from the forty-six volume *Complete Works of Robert A. Heinlein*, contains the original letter in its entirety.

Still, Jerry always regretted having to cut that original battle and years later included it in *There Will Be War, Volume I*. He had this to say in the introduction: "It was quite a good battle; the problem was that the battle wasn't really relevant to the main themes of the book, and the book was more than long enough already. . . . Scenes chopped from a novel don't usually make a story, but among the scenes we cut was that introductory battle, which was a complete story all by itself. The novel assumes that the battle happened as originally presented."

*Any damn fool can die for his country.*
—General George S. Patton

***3017 A.D.***

**THE UNION REPUBLIC WAR CRUISER** *Defiant* lay nearly motionless in space a half billion kilometers from Beta Hortensi. She turned slowly about her long axis.

Stars flowed endlessly upward with the spin of the ship, as if *Defiant* were falling through the universe. Captain Herb Colvin saw them as a battle map, infinitely dangerous. *Defiant* hung above him in the viewport, its enormous mass ready to fall on him and crush him, but after years in space he hardly noticed.

Hastily constructed and thrown into space, armed as an interstellar cruiser, but without the bulky Alderson Effect engines which could send her between the stars, *Defiant* had been assigned to guard the approaches to New Chicago from raids by the Empire. The Republic's main fleet was on the other side of Beta Hortensi, awaiting an attack they were sure would come from that quarter. The path *Defiant* guarded sprang from a red dwarf star four-tenths of a light-year distant. The tramline had never been plotted. Few within New Chicago's government believed the Empire had the capability to find it, and fewer thought they would try.

Colvin strode across his cabin to the polished steel cupboard. A tall man, nearly two meters in height, he was thin and wiry, with an aristocratic nose that many Imperial lords would have envied. A shock of sandy hair never stayed combed, but he refused to cover it with a uniform cap unless he had to. A fringe of beard was beginning to take shape on his chin. Colvin had been clean-shaven when *Defiant* began its patrol twenty-four weeks ago. He had grown a beard, decided he didn't like it and shaved it off, started another. Now he was glad he hadn't taken the annual depilation treatments. Growing a beard was one of the few amusements available to men on a long and dreary blockade.

He opened the cupboard, detached a glass and bottle from their clamps, and took them back to his desk. Colvin poured expertly despite a Coriolis effect that could send carelessly poured liquids sloshing to the carpets. He set the glass down and turned toward the viewport.

There was nothing to see out there, of course, even the heart of it all, New Chicago—Union! In keeping with the patriotic spirit of the Committee of Public Safety, New Chicago was now called Union. Captain Herb Colvin had trouble remembering that, and Political Officer Gerry took enormous pleasure in correcting him every damned time. Union was the point of it all, the boredom and endless low-level threat; but Union was invisible from here. The sun blocked it even from telescopes. Even the red dwarf, so close that it had robbed Beta Hortensi of its cometary halo, showed only as a dim red spark. The first sign of attack would be on the bridge screens long before his eyes could find the black-on-black point that might be an Imperial warship.

For six months *Defiant* had waited, and the question had likewise sat waiting in the back of Colvin's head.

Was the Empire coming?

The Secession War that ended the first Empire of Man had split into a thousand little wars, and those had died into battles. Throughout human space there were planets with no civilization, and many more with too little to support space travel.

Even Sparta had been hurt. She had lost her fleets, but the dying ships had defended the capital; and when Sparta began to recover, she recovered fast.

Across human space men had discovered the secrets of interstellar travel. The technology of the Langston Field was stored away in a score of Imperial libraries; and this was important because the Field was discovered through a series of improbable accidents to men in widely separated specialties. It would not have been developed again.

With Langston Field and Alderson Drive, the Second Empire rose from the ashes of the First. Every man in the new government knew that weakness in the First Empire had led to war—and that war must not happen again. This time all humanity must be united. There must be no worlds outside the Imperium, and none within it to challenge the power of Emperor and Senate. Mankind would have peace if worlds must die to bring it about.

The oath was sworn, and when other worlds built merchantmen, Sparta rebuilt the Fleet and sent it to space. Under the fanatical young men and women humanity would be united by force. The Empire spread around Crucis and once again reached behind the Coal Sack, persuading, cajoling, conquering and destroying where needed.

New Chicago had been one of the first worlds reunited with the Empire of Man. The revolt must have come as a stunning surprise. Now Captain Herb Colvin of the United Republic waited on blockade patrol for the Empire's retaliation. He knew it would come, and could only hope *Defiant* would be ready.

He sat in the enormous leather chair behind his desk, swirling his drink and letting his gaze alternate between his wife's picture and the viewport. The chair was a memento from the liberation of the Governor General's palace on New Chicago. (On Union!) It was made of imported leathers, worth a fortune, if he could find the right buyer. The Committee of Public Safety had realized its value.

Colvin looked from Grace's picture to a pinkish star drifting upward past the viewport, and thought of the Empire's warships. Would they come through here, when they came? Surely they were coming.

In principal *Defiant* was a better ship than she'd been when she left New Chicago. The engineers had automated all the routine space-keeping tasks, and no United Republic spacer needed to do a job that a robot could perform. Like all of New Chicago's ships, and like few of the Imperial Navy's, *Defiant* was as automated as a merchantman.

Colvin wondered. Merchantmen do not fight battles. A merchant captain need not worry about random holes punched through his hull. He can ignore the risk that any given piece of equipment will be smashed at any instant. He will never have only minutes to keep his ship fighting or see her destroyed in an instant of blinding heat.

No robot could cope with the complexity of decisions damage control could generate, and if there were such a robot it might easily be destroyed in battle. Colvin had been a merchant captain and had seen no reason to object to the Republic's naval policies but now that he had experience in warship command he understood why the Imperials automated as little as possible and kept the crew working routine tasks: washing down corridors and changing air filters, scrubbing pots and inspecting the hull. Imperial crews might grumble about the work, but they were never idle. After six months, *Defiant* was a better ship, but . . . she had lifted out from . . . Union with a crew of mission-oriented warriors. What were they now?

Colvin leaned back in his comfortable chair and looked around his cabin. It was too comfortable. Even the captain—especially the captain!—had little to do but putter with his personal surroundings, and Colvin had done all he could think of.

It was worse for the crew. They fought, distilled liquor in hidden places, gambled for stakes they couldn't afford, and were bored. It showed in their discipline. There wasn't any punishment duty either, nothing like cleaning heads or scrubbing pots, the duties an Imperial skipper might assign his crewmen. Aboard *Defiant* it would be make-work, and everyone would know it.

He was thinking about another drink when an alarm trilled.

"Captain here," Colvin said.

The face on the viewscreen was flushed. "A ship, sir," the communications officer said. "Can't tell the size yet, but definitely a ship from the red star."

Colvin's tongue dried up in an instant. He'd been right all along, through all those months of waiting, and the flavor of being right was not pleasant. "Right. Sound battle stations. We'll intercept." He paused a moment as Lieutenant Susack motioned to other crew on the bridge. Alarms sounded through the *Defiant*. "Make a signal to the fleet, Lieutenant."

"Aye, aye, sir."

Horns were blaring through the ship as Colvin left his cabin. Crewmen dove along the steel corridors, past grotesque shapes in combat armor. The ship was already losing her spin and orienting herself to give chase to the intruder. Gravity was peculiar and shifting. Colvin crawled along the handholds like a monkey.

The crew were waiting. "Captain's on the bridge," the duty NCO announced. Others helped him into armor and dogged down his helmet. He had only just strapped himself into his command seat when the ship's speakers sounded.

"ALL SECURE FOR ACCELERATION, STAND BY FOR ACCELERATION."

"Intercept," Colvin ordered. The computer recognized his voice and obeyed. The joltmeter swung hard over and acceleration crushed him to his chair. The joltmeter swung back to zero, leaving a steady three gravities.

The bridge was crowded. Colvin's comfortable acceleration couch dominated the spacious compartment. In front of him three helmsmen sat at inactive controls, ready to steer the ship if her main battle computer failed. They were flanked by two watch officers. Behind him were runners and talkers, ready to do the captain's will when he had orders for them.

There was one other.

Beside him was a man who wasn't precisely under Colvin's command. *Defiant* belonged to Captain Colvin. So did the crew—but he shared that territory with Political Officer Gerry. The political officer's presence implied distrust in Colvin's loyalty to the Republic. Gerry had denied this, and so had the Committee of Public Safety; but they hadn't convinced Herb Colvin.

"Are we prepared to engage the enemy, Captain?" Gerry asked. His thin and usually smiling features were distorted by acceleration.

"Yes. We are doing so now," Colvin said. What the hell else could they be doing? But of course Gerry was asking for the recorders.

"What is the enemy ship?"

"The hyperspace wake's just coming into detection range now, Mister Gerry." Colvin studied the screens. Instead of space with the enemy ship black and invisible against the stars, they showed a series of curves and figures, probability estimates, tables whose entries changed even as he watched. "I believe it's a cruiser, same class as ours," Colvin said.

"Even match?"

"Not exactly," Colvin replied. "He'll be carrying interstellar engines. That'll take up room we use for hydrogen. He'll have more mass for his engines to move, and we'll have more fuel. He won't have a lot better armament than we do, either." He studied the probability curves and nodded. "Yeah, that looks about right. What they call a 'Planet Class' cruiser."

"How soon before we fight?" Gerry gasped. The acceleration made each word an effort.

"Few minutes to an hour. He's just getting under way after coming out of hyperdrive. Too damn bad he's so far away, we'd have him right if we were a little closer."

"Why weren't we?" Gerry demanded.

"Because the tramline hasn't been plotted," Colvin said. And I'm speaking for the record. Better get it right and get the sarcasm out of my voice. "I requested survey equipment, but none was available. We were therefore required to plot the Alderson entry point using optics alone. I would be much surprised if anyone could have made a better estimate using our equipment."

"I see," Gerry said. With an effort he touched the switch that gave him a general intercom circuit. "Spacers of the Republic, your comrades salute you! Freedom!"

"Freedom!" came the response. Colvin didn't think that more than half the crew had spoken, but it was difficult to tell.

"You all know the importance of this battle," Gerry said. "We defend the back door of the Republic, and we are alone. Many believed we need not be here, that the Imperials would never find this path to our homes. That ship shows the wisdom of the government."

Had to get that in, didn't you? Colvin chuckled to himself. Gerry expected to run for office, if he lived through the coming battles.

"The Imperials will never make us slaves! Our cause is just, for we seek only the freedom to be left alone. The Empire will not permit this. They wish to rule the entire universe, forever. Spacers, we fight for liberty!"

Colvin looked across the bridge to the watch officer and lifted an eyebrow. He got a shrug for an answer. Herb nodded. It was hard to tell the effects of a speech. Gerry was said to be good at speaking. He'd talked his way into a junior membership on the Committee of Public Safety that governed the Republic.

A tiny buzz sounded in Colvin's ear. The executive officer's station was aft, in an auxiliary control room, where he could take over if something happened to the main bridge.

By Republic orders Gerry was to hear everything said by and to the captain during combat, but Gerry didn't know much about ships. Commander Gregory Halleck, Colvin's exec, had modified the intercom system. Now his voice came through, the flat nasal twang of New Chicago's outback. "Skipper, why don't he shut up and let us fight?"

"Speech was recorded, Greg," Colvin said.

"Ah, he'll play it for the city workers," Halleck said. "Tell me, skipper, just what chance have we got?"

"In this battle, pretty good."

"Yeah. Wish I was so sure about the war."

"Scared, Greg?"

"A little. How can we win?"

"We can't *beat* the Empire," Colvin said. "Not if they bring their whole fleet in here. But if we can win a couple of battles, the Empire'll have to pull back. They can't strip all their ships out of other areas. Too many enemies. Time is on our side, if we can buy some."

"Yeah, way I see it, too. Guess it's worth it. Back to work."

It had to be worth it, Colvin thought. It just didn't make sense to put the whole human race under one government.

Someday they'd get a really bad Emperor. Or three Emperors all claiming the throne at once. Better to put a stop to this now, rather than leave the problem to their grandchildren.

The phones buzzed again. "Better take a good look, skipper," Halleck said. "I think we got problems."

The screens flashed as new information flowed. Colvin touched other buttons in his chair arm. Lieutenant Susack's face swam onto one screen. "Make a signal to the fleet," Colvin said. "That thing's bigger than we thought. This could be one hell of a battle."

"Aye, aye," Susack said. "But we can handle it."

"Sure," Colvin said. He stared at the updated information and frowned.

"What is out there, Captain?" Gerry asked. "Is there reason for concern?"

"There could be," Colvin said. "Mister Gerry, that is an Imperial battle cruiser. 'General' class, I'd say." As he told the political officer, Colvin felt a cold pit in his guts.

"And what does that mean?"

"It's one of their best," Colvin said. "About as fast as we are. More armor, more weapons, more fuel. We've got a fight on our hands."

***

"Launch observation boats. Prepare to engage," Colvin ordered. Although he couldn't see it, the Imperial ship was probably dong the same things. Observation boats didn't carry much for weapons, but their observations could be invaluable when the engagement began.

"You don't sound confident," Gerry said.

Colvin checked his intercom switches. No one could hear him but Gerry. "I'm not," he said. "Look, however you cut it, if there's an advantage that ship's got it. Their crew's had a chance to recover from their hyperspace trip, too." If we'd had the right equipment—No use thinking about that.

"What if it gets past us?"

"Enough ships might knock it out, especially if we can damage it, but there's no single ship in our fleet that can fight that thing one-on-one and expect to win."

"Including us."

"Including us. I didn't know there was a battle cruiser anywhere in the Trans-Coalsack region."

"Interesting implication," Gerry said.

"Yeah, they've brought one of their best ships. Not only that, they took the trouble to find a back way. Two new Alderson tramlines. From the red dwarf to us, and a way into the red dwarf."

"Seems they're determined." Gerry paused a moment. "The Committee was constructing planetary defenses when we lifted out."

"They may need them. Excuse me . . ." Colvin cut the circuit and concentrated on his battle screens.

The master computer flashed a series of maneuver strategies, each with the odds for success if adopted. The probabilities were only a computer's judgment, however. Over there in the Imperial ship was an experienced human captain who'd do his best to thwart those odds while Colvin did the same. Game theory and computers rarely consider all the possibilities a human brain can conceive.

The computer recommended full retreat and sacrifice of the observation boats—and at that only gave an even chance for *Defiant*. Colvin studied the board. "ENGAGE CLOSELY," he said.

The computer wiped the other alternatives and flashed a series of new choices. Colvin chose again. Again and again this happened until the ship's brain knew exactly what her human master wanted, but long before the dialogue was completed the ship accelerated to action, spewing torpedoes from her ports to send H-bombs on random evasion courses toward the enemy. Tiny lasers reached out toward enemy torpedoes, filling space with softly glowing threads of bright color.

*Defiant* leaped toward her enemy, her photon cannons pouring out energy to wash over the Imperial ship. "Keep it up, keep it up," Colvin chanted to himself. If the enemy could be blinded, her antennas destroyed so that her crew couldn't see through her Langston Field to locate *Defiant*, the battle would be over.

Halleck's outback twang came through the earphones. "Looking good, boss."

"Yeah." The very savagery of unexpected attack by a smaller vessel had taken the enemy by surprise. Just maybe—

A blaze of white struck *Defiant* to send her screens up into orange, tottering toward yellow for an instant. In that second, *Defiant* was as blind as the enemy, every sensor outside the Field vaporized. Her boats were still there, though, sending data on the enemy's position, still guiding torpedoes.

"Bridge, this is damage control."

"Yeah, Greg."

"Hulled in the main memory bank area. I'm getting replacement elements in, but you better go to secondary computer for a while."

"Already done."

"Good. Got a couple other problems, but I can handle them."

"Have at it." Screens were coming back on line. More sensor clusters were being poked through the Langston Field on stalks. Colvin touched buttons in his chair arm. "Communications. Get number three boat in closer."

"Acknowledged."

The Imperial ship took evasive action. She would cut acceleration for a moment, turn slightly, then accelerate again, while constantly changing the drive power. "He's got an iron crew," he muttered to Halleck. "They must be getting the guts shook out of them."

Another blast rocked *Defiant.* A torpedo had penetrated her defensive fire to explode somewhere near the hull. The Langston Field, opaque to radiant energy, was able to absorb and redistribute the energy evenly throughout the Field, but at a cost. There had been an overload at the place nearest the bomb: energy flaring inward.

The Langston Field was a spaceship's true hull. Its skin was only metal, designed to hold pressure. Breech it and—

"Hulled again aft of number two torpedo room," Halleck reported. "Spare parts, and the messroom brain. We'll eat basic protocarb for a while."

"If we eat at all." Why the hell weren't they getting more hits on the enemy? He could see the Imperial ship on his screens, in the view from number two boat. Her Field glowed orange, wavering to yellow, and there were two deep purple spots, probably burnthroughs. No way to tell what lay under those areas. Colvin hoped it was something vital.

His own Field was yellow tinged with green. Pastel lines jumped between the two ships. After this was over, there would be time to remember just how *pretty* a space battle was. The screens flared, and his odds for success dropped again, but he couldn't trust the computer anyway. He'd lost number three boat, and number one had ceased reporting.

The enemy ship flared again as *Defiant* scored a hit, then another. The Imperial's screens turned yellow, then green; as they cooled back toward red another hit sent them through green to blue. "Torps!" Colvin shouted, but the master computer had already done it. A stream of tiny shapes flashed toward the blinded enemy.

"Pour it on!" Colvin screamed. "Everything we've got!" If they could keep the enemy blind, keep him from finding *Defiant* while they poured energy into his Field, they could keep his screen hot enough until torpedoes could get through. "Pour it on!"

The Imperial ship was almost beyond the blue, creeping toward violet. "By God we may have him!" Colvin shouted.

The enemy maneuvered again, but the bright rays of *Defiant*'s lasers followed, pinning the glowing ship against the star background. Then the screens went blank.

Colvin frantically pounded buttons. Nothing happened. *Defiant* was blind. "Eyes! How'd he hit us?"

"Don't know," Susack's voice was edged with fear. "Skipper, we've got problems with the detectors. I sent a party out but they haven't reported—"

Halleck came on. "Imperial boat got close and hit us with torps."

Blind. Colvin watched his screen color indicators. Bright orange and yellow, with a green tint already visible. Acceleration warnings hooted through the ship as Colvin ordered random evasive action. The enemy would be blind too. Now it was a question of who could see first. "Get me some eyes," he said. He was surprised at how calm his voice was.

"Working on it," Halleck said. "I've got minimal sight back here. Maybe I can locate him."

"Take over gun direction," Colvin said. "What's with the computer?"

"I'm not getting damage reports from that area," Halleck said. "I have men out trying to restore internal communications and another party's putting out antennas—only nobody really wants to go out to the hull edge and work, you know."

"Wants!" Colvin controlled blind rage. Who cared what the crew wanted? His ship was in danger!

Acceleration and jolt warnings sounded continuously as *Defiant* continued evasive maneuvers. Jolt, acceleration, stop, turn, jolt—

"He's hitting us again." Susack sounded scared.

"Greg?" Colvin demanded.

"I'm losing him. Take over, skipper."

*Defiant* writhed like a beetle on a pin as the deadly fire followed her through maneuvers. The damage reports came as a deadly litany. "Partial collapse, after auxiliary engine room destroyed. Hulled in three places in number five tankage area, hydrogen leaking to space. Hulled in the after recreation room."

The screens were electric blue when the computer cut the drives. *Defiant* was dead in space. She was moving at more than a hundred kilometers a second, but she couldn't accelerate.

"See anything yet?" Colvin asked.

"In a second," Halleck replied. "There. Wups. Antenna didn't last half a second. He's yellow. Out there on our port quarter and pouring it on. Want me to swing the main drive in that direction? We might hit him with that."

Colvin examined his screens. "No. we can't spare the power." He watched a moment more, then swept his hand across a line of buttons.

All through *Defiant* nonessential systems died. It took power to maintain the Langston Field, and the more energy the Field had to contain the more internal power was needed to keep the Field from radiating inward. Local overloads produced burnthroughs, partial collapses sending energetic photons to punch holes through the hull. The Field moved toward full collapse, and when that happened, the energies it contained would vaporize *Defiant*. Total defeat in space is a clean death.

The screens were indigo and *Defiant* couldn't spare power to fire her guns or use her engines. Every erg was needed simply to survive.

"We'll have to surrender," Colvin said. "Get the message out."

"I forbid it!"

For a moment, Colvin had forgotten the political officer.

"I forbid it!" Gerry shouted again. "Captain, you are relieved of command. Commander Halleck, engage the enemy! We cannot allow him to penetrate our homeland!"

"Can't do that, sir," Halleck said carefully. The recorded conversation made the executive officer a traitor, as Colvin was the instant he'd given the surrender order.

"Engage the enemy, Captain." Gerry spoke quietly. "Look at me, Colvin."

Herb Colvin turned to see a pistol in Gerry's hand. It wasn't a sonic gun, not even a chemical dart weapon as used by prison guards. Combat armor would stop those. This was a slugthrower—no. A small rocket launcher, but it looked like a slugthrower. Just the weapon to take to space.

"Surrender the ship," Colvin repeated. He motioned with one hand. Gerry looked around, too late. As the quartermaster pinned his arms to his side. A captain's bridge runner launched himself across the cabin to seize the pistol.

"I'll have you shot for this!" Gerry shouted. "You've betrayed everything. Our homes, our families—"

"I'd as soon be shot as surrender," Colvin said. "Besides, the Imperials will probably do it for both of us. Treason, you know. Still, I've a right to save the crew."

Gerry said nothing.

"We're dead, mister. The only reason they haven't finished us off is we're so bloody helpless the Imperial commander's held off firing the last wave of torpedoes to give us a chance to quit. He can finish us off any time."

"You might damage him. Take him with us, or make it easier for the fleet to deal with him—"

"If I could, I'd do that. I already launched all our torpedoes. They either got through or they didn't. Either way, they didn't kill him since he's still pouring it on us. He has all the time in the world—look, damn it! We can't shoot at him, we don't have power for the engines, and look at the screens! Violet! Don't you understand, you blithering fool, there's no place for it to go! A little more, a miscalculation by the Imperial, some little failure here, and that Field collapses."

Gerry stared in rage. "Maybe you're right."

"I know I'm right. Any progress, Susack?"

"Message went out," the communications officer said. "And they haven't finished us."

"Right." There was nothing else to say.

A ship in *Defiant*'s situation, her screens overloaded, bombarded by torpedoes and fired on by an enemy she cannot locate, is utterly helpless; but she has been damaged hardly at all. Given time she can radiate the screen energies to space. She can erect antennas to find her enemy. When the screens cool, she can move and she can shoot. Even when she has been damaged by partial collapses, her enemy cannot know that.

Thus, surrender is difficult and requires a specific ritual. Like all of mankind's surrender reflex, no unambiguous species-wide signal to save him from death after defeat is inevitable. Of the higher animals, man is alone in this.

Stags do not fight to the death. When one is beaten, he submits, and the other allows him to leave the field. The three-spined stickleback, a fish of the carp family, fights for its mates but recognizes the surrender of its enemies. Siamese fighting fish will not pursue an enemy after he ceases to spread his gills.

But man has evolved as a weapon-using animal. Unlike other animals, man's evolution is intimately bound with weapons and tools; and weapons can kill farther than man can reach. Weapons in the hand of a defeated enemy are still dangerous; indeed, the Scottish *skean dhu* is said to be carried in the stocking so that it may be reached as its owner kneels in supplication. . . .

*Defiant* erected a simple antenna suitable only for radio signals. Any other form of sensor would have been a hostile act and would earn instant destruction. The Imperial captain observed and sent instructions.

Meanwhile, torpedoes were being maneuvered alongside *Defiant.* Colvin couldn't see them. He knew they must be in place when the next signal came through. The Imperial ship was sending an officer to take command.

Something massive thumped against the hull. A port had already been opened for the Imperial. He entered carrying a bulky object: a bomb.

"Midshipman Horst Staley, Imperial Battle Cruiser *MacArthur,*" the officer announced as he was conducted to the bridge. Colvin could see blue eyes and blond hair, a young face frozen into a mask of calm because its owner did not trust himself to show any expression at all. "I am to take command of this ship, sir."

Captain Colvin nodded. "I give her to you. You'll want this," he added, handing the boy the microphone. "Thanks for coming."

"Yes, sir." Staley gulped noticeably, then stood at attention as if his captain could see him. "Midshipman Staley reporting, sir. I am on the bridge and the enemy has surrendered." He listened for a few seconds, then turned to Colvin. "I am to ask you to leave me alone on the bridge, except for yourself, sir. And to tell you that if anyone else comes on the bridge before our Marines have secured this ship, I will detonate the bomb I carry. Will you comply?"

Colvin nodded again. "Take Mister Gerry out, quartermaster. You others can go, too. Clear the bridge."

The quartermaster led Gerry toward the door. Suddenly the political officer broke free and sprang at Staley. He wrapped the midshipman's arms against his body and shouted, "Quick, grab the bomb! Move! Captain, fight for your ship, I've got him!"

Staley struggled with the political officer. His hand groped for the trigger, but he couldn't reach it. The mike had also been ripped from his hands. He shouted at the dead microphone.

Colvin gently took the bomb from Horst's imprisoned hands.

"You won't need this, son," he said. "Quartermaster, you can take your prisoner off this bridge." His smile was fixed, frozen in place, in sharp contrast to the midshipman's shocked rage and Gerry's look of triumph.

The spacers reached out and Horst Staley tried to escape, but there was no place to go as he floated free in space. Suddenly he realized that the spacers had seized his attacker, and Gerry was screaming.

"We've surrendered, Mister Staley," Colvin said carefully. "Now we'll leave you in command here. You can have your bomb, but you won't be needing it."

# KENYONS TO THE KEEP

by Jerry Pournelle

## Editor's Introduction

There's a good story behind how this yarn got published. Anthologies are typically poor sellers and publishers usually only authorize them to placate an important author, who wants to do one for prestige, or to court someone who's publishing at another house. A few editors, like Isaac Asimov and Martin Greenberg, have actually made money on them. Most are loss leaders. However, ours did very well, with many of our anthologies going into multiple printings.

The There Will Be War books were making real money for Tor Books: They contained a good mix of fiction to Jerry's factual essays and no one else was publishing much military science fiction. The first three volumes all contained stories Jerry wrote: in Volume I, "His Truth Goes Marching On," Volume II, "Manual of Operations," Volume III, "Silent Leges," but by Volume IV we were running out of material—the story cupboard was empty. Jerry added a nonwar story, "He Fell Into A Dark Hole," to Volume V, but Jerry was no longer writing new short fiction. "Spirals," which he wrote with Larry, was one of his last short pieces.

Tor left us alone for the next few books, but for some reason—maybe sales were dropping? (as a rule, publishers rarely inform authors of book sales, unless they have to pay royalties)—Tor suddenly wanted another Pournelle story. I was the Keeper of the Archives, so Jerry came to me, asking if I knew of anything in the files that could easily be turned into a short story. I remembered "Renaissance"—a post-apocalypse novel that Jerry had started in the early 1970s. The US—or at least the west coast, where the story took place—had been atom-bombed and the survivors—even hundreds of years after the war—were barely hanging on. The setting was late Renaissance with armored men-at-arms and flintlock rifles. The file contained four chapters, lists of characters and a lot of background information. No plot outline.

I read over the introductory chapters and decided they would make a good short story; the ending was a downer, but then, the title of the book was: *There Will Be War: After Armageddon.* I showed it to Jerry and he read the chapters I'd picked out. He asked me to put the chapters into machine-readable format and *voila*—it was done and published.

After that, Jerry and I discussed turning "Renaissance" into a collaborative novel, with a better title; but it never went any farther than talk. I still believe "Kenyons to the Keep" contains the seed of a good novel. I'll let you judge that for yourself.

**I**

**THE LEGENDS SAID MAN** had once walked on the Moon.

Ross Kenyon didn't believe it, but the Moon rising full and blood red over Griffith Castle seemed close enough to touch. He knew that the Sierra tribesmen flew. They soared like the great condors. Ross had heard of other aircraft that could lift themselves from the ground, although he had never seen one. If men could fly, surely they could go to the Moon. Perhaps when it was only rising, not so high above and far away.

The sun had fallen into the Pacific, but dusky twilight hung across the great battlements of Kenyon Keep. Out ahead, directly in front of Ross, torches and campfires dotted the San Fernando Valley. They stretched north, then ended abruptly. Ross could not see the ruins that marked the northern boundary of Kenyon land, but he had seen them often enough to know where each stood.

For three hundred years the northern San Fernando and the Newhall Valley beyond had been battlefields in an endless multisided war. The Highland and Sierra clans of the mountains, the Oxnard outreaches of Santa Barbara, desert nomads, Ecofreak and Greenpeace, all contended with the divided forces of the Civilized Lands of the South, and none could hold the Valleys. The Kenyons had pushed farther than most, but even they had been driven back. From the day of his birth Ross had been at war.

Ross hated it. The Kenyons held the northern keep of Civilization, and always they tried to push forward, to take and hold the San Fernando and Newhall Valleys. Ross Kenyon was seventeen; when he was ten his father had laid Kenyon boundary stones westward past Topanga. When Ross became El Señor Kenyon it would be his turn, and in his lifetime he might take five more miles. Five more miles for a lifetime probably cut short. It did not seem a fair exchange.

The Valleys were good land; but were they worth endless war? Ross imagined them in the darkness. Valleys covered with ruins, except where the nomad tribes had leveled them. If those lands were cleared they could be held with a new keep at the top of the Newhall Pass, a lesser keep to guard the Big Tujunga canyon; two strong places, and the Valleys could be held. Ross had designs for the keeps, and there would be plenty of stone for building. The Valleys were covered with stone.

Fallen buildings, ash heaps, flat stone in slabs, white stone roads, black stone, all remains of what the Ancients had built. How? Ross had never understood how the Ancients could waste such good land, covering it with stone and trees that bore no fruit. If the Ancients could waste the best land for miles, then perhaps the old legends were true. Only the fabulously powerful could conjure food from a valley of stone.

The Moon rose steadily and now there were blue witchlights on Mount Wilson to the east. Sorcerers lived there on the mountain towering high above the Dead Lands. They had built a great stone place, larger and stronger than Kenyon Keep, stronger even than the Mayor's Palace in Los Angeles. The sorcerers had neither lands nor religion nor army, but their fortress had stood for five hundred years, since before the Burning and the Plagues—or so they said, and who could dispute it? They lived in uneasy peace with the Sierra and the Highlands who held the Angeles Mountains. They had little enough contact, demanding nothing from the lowlands, but farmers often took them tribute, and sometimes received gifts, or heard the Oracle tell them of the weather to come, and the proper time for planting. The sorcerers lived well.

Yet they were only men. They could not fly, not even as well as the Sierra. They knew things that others did not; sometimes of events that happened far away, or the coming rains long before anyone in the City or the Hills or the Valley could see any cloud; but they were only men. They could be killed, and had been, when the tribesmen penetrated into the valley and the Civilized Lands beyond . . . and the tribesmen were coming again.

They knew much, these witchmen, but they seldom spoke to anyone not their own. Sometimes their stewards, led by officers with strange titles—Grad and Postdoc—came to the lowlands to trade. Sometimes they bought women: young girls, orphans of good family, whose ancestry was known. "Not slaves," the Postdoc had told Ross's father. "Never slaves. The girls will marry." Flintridge Kenyon had made the Postdoc swear.

Ross Kenyon's private reverie was interrupted by the galloping of hooves. He watched as three horsemen rode fast up the winding road from the Valley to the ramparts of the Keep. Kenyon touched the thick walls with reverence. Ten feet thick, built of stone quarried from the ruins below, they circled the brow of the hill, enclosed a large horseshoe-shaped ridge. The central courts were large, more than ample to hold the Kenyons and their retainers and their flocks. There were enormous cisterns, kept always full from rainfall and water carried from the Los Angeles River below. There were the long cannon, with a range of over three miles, and the smaller guns which could shoot grape and canister. The fortress had been started by other families, driven out so long ago their names were forgotten; but since Ross Kenyon's great-great-grandfather had taken the hill and strengthened the walls, it had killed every army that marched against it. Highlander, Ekofreak, Sierra, Santa Paula, Berdoo, Greenpeace, Apace, the Mayor of Los Angeles himself; all had tried, and still the Kenyons held. Three horsemen were no danger.

Ross heard the shouted challenge from the gates, and the response; the creaking gates, just shout for sundown, now opened again; and hooves clattered on the cobblestones of the outer courtyard. Now there were other sounds: running men climbing the great stone stairways to the high rampart tower where Ross stood. Five men at least. Two carried torches.

The flickering light showed two of the Kenyon household guard, dull reflections from the links of their mail armor, crimson sash of the officer of the watch. He was not much older than Ross: John Stephenson, a cousin. When they were younger John had been a good friend. Now the difference between the heir and a relative came between them. Ross recognized Wenceslas, *vaquero jefe* of the Kenyon herds and another in the blue and gold Kenyon livery. The fifth man wore dark robes with no flash or ornament.

"Don Ross," Wenceslas shouted. He spoke rapidly in the San Diego patois, part Spanish, part Mexican, part ancient English and part nothing ever heard before the Burning. The Kenyon family had never spoken anything but Anglic until Ross's father had in his youth gone on a diplomatic mission to the Alcalde of Escondido and returned with the daughter of the house. The Alcalde had insisted that his daughter should go to the North in a way fitting to her ancestry, and sent fifty vaqueros and their families as her dowry. Now the Kenyon house was bilingual. Ross could not remember a time when he did not speak both Anglic and Sandiegan.

"A message from your father," Wenceslas was saying. "A message from Don Flintridge. Padre Gutierrez has brought it, *hijo de mi patron*."

Ross interrupted the rapid flow of words. "And what is so urgent that you have brought Padre Gutierrez to me before offering him the hospitality of Kenyon Keep?" he demanded. "You have brought him with the dust of the road on his feet and in his throat."

"It is urgent, Don Ross," Gutierrez said. The voice was younger than the man. Gutierrez seemed withered, bent with age, although some of his weariness would be from the ten-mile ride from the Abbey San Francisco de Chatsworth to Kenyon Keep. He had never seen Gutierrez without robe and cowl, not even in the heat of the day, and often wondered if the clothing concealed deformities. There were monsters in the world, and some of them grew to be men, and the Church was a natural refuge for them. Celibacy kept them from breeding more monsters. . . . Ross became aware that Gutierrez was silent.

"Prepare rooms and dinner for the Padre," Ross ordered. "And ask my uncle and my mother to join me in the Library." He said the word proudly. There were only a few great families who collected books, and the Kenyon collection was magnificent, almost five hundred volumes.

Ross waved dismissal to his retainers. John Stephenson hung back for a moment, eager to hear the news, but he caught the displeasure in Ross's eye and went with the others. Ross regretted sending him away. John was a loyal officer, not eager to grasp more than should come to him, and probably could be trusted with any news; but it was too late. Stephenson had turned angrily away.

A vaquero put his torch into a niche on the rampart, where it added its smoke to the soot of countless torches that had burned there before. The high ramparts were a place of meditation for five generations of Kenyons. When all had left, Ross said, "My father is well?"

"Don Flintridge lives," Padre Gutierrez said.

Ross kept his face impassive. "That is good news, but you would not come to tell me only that."

"He is badly injured. An arrow in the chest, and he fell from his horse. He is now in the Great Keep at Ramona. The Alcalde is with him."

"I will go immediately."

"You cannot, Don Ross. You could not enter. The Mexicali forces, with many mercenaries have the Keep under siege. It was while cutting his way in to aid his father-in-law that Don Flintridge was wounded."

Padre Gutierrez did not say that Ross would be unable to take a tenth of the forces that his father had led south. He didn't have to. Kenyon Keep was stripped of its professional soldiers. Flintridge Kenyon took his family obligations seriously, and had ridden immediately to the Alcalde's aid; if his household guards had a difficult time entering Ramona Keep, the vaqueros and other mobile troops available to Ross would have no chance at all.

"The Abbot has ordered perpetual prayer for Don Flintridge," Gutierrez said.

Ross kept his face in shadow, careful to show no emotion in his eyes. "You're a Kenyon!" his father had thundered. Countless times:

when Ross had fallen from his horse, when his brother had died, when the *mamacita* of his infancy lay with blackened tongue and the bursting pustules of plague; when the tribesman's arrow had pierced his shoulder; and when a favorite pony had broken a foreleg and Ross himself had to take the loaded musket to the stable. . . . "You're a Kenyon. We command, and command shows no fears."

But his father was hurt, besieged more than a hundred miles to the south. In these times men lived and died quickly, and Flintridge had lived more than his share of years; but Ross was only seventeen. His feeling for his father was a mixture, love and duty and fear and respect; and always there was the knowledge that when Flint Kenyon was laid with his fathers in the vault below Kenyon Chapter, Ross would be Señor Kenyon, Master of Encino, responsible for a thousand families. . . .

"There is worse news, Don Ross."

"What can be worse?"

"The tribes are gathering in the Mojave. Yesterday they held a Great Council at the Palmdale Stone Field. Chiefs of the Sierra were there. Among them the Mahons of Solamint. The Sierra Chiefs returned safely to their mountains."

And that said it all, Ross thought. If the Mojave tribesmen sat at Council with the mountain clansmen and the clansmen went home alive . . . then the way from the Mojave into the Newhall and San Fernando Valleys was no longer closed to the tribesmen. "How do you know this?"

Gutierrez shrugged. "The Church has her miracles."

Ross nodded. On Mount Wilson they called it sorcery. The Church said miracles. Master Yorumma, Ross's tutor, called it "science" and said that certain Ancient devices had survived. Some of the books in the Kenyon Library said the same thing, but there was no point in discussing it. Who would listen? Certainly not Gutierrez; the Church had not since time out of mind let anyone who knew the secret of the farspeakers go outside heavily defended walls.

However they did it, everyone knew that some of the monasteries and episcopal palaces—but not all of them—learned of distant events long before messengers could ride with the news. But although the Church *could* know, the message might not be true. His Most Holy Excellency Don Jaime O'Riley Cardinal San Diego,

Archbishop of Western Noramerica and secular prince of San Diego, had his own political plans. Abbey San Fernando de Chatsworth was strong allied with the Kenyons and wouldn't deliberately lie, but the message was no more reliable than those who had sent it.

But to what purpose? Ross wondered. "Does the Mayor know?"

Gutierrez shrugged again. "Not from us. My instructions were to inform you. I have done so."

And to the devil with the Protestant Mayor and his Council and people, Ross thought. The padre's attitude was natural. More than one Mayor of Los Angeles had led armies against the Abbey before Ross's mother brought it under Kenyon protection, and the Church in the City proper had been despoiled, reduced to a tiny diplomatic mission existing within the Mayor's place, not even granted its own quarters.

"But you have no objections if I tell His Honor?" Ross asked.

"I repeat my instructions, Don Ross. Dom Julian sent me to inform Don Ross Kenyon. I have done so. And now, if I may, I will accept the hospitality you have offered."

"Yes. Certainly. Thank you, Padre. I will show you to the dining hall. If you wish anything else, you only have to ask." Automatically he led Padre Gutierrez to the lesser hall, not the Great Hall; for although the Church was always welcome, and Padre Gutierrez had ridden hard to carry his message to Kenyon station, there were, after all, proprieties to be observed and Gutierrez was only a priest—and probably a hunchback at that.

II

The Library was a hard room, as hard as the men who had held Kenyon Keep for generations. It was stone, with an oak council table; the books which stood behind locked glass doors could not soften the effect of massive granite and splintered concrete blocks. Even the tapestries and hangings, with their battle scenes, looked hard.

Doña Estrella Almoravez Kenyon had borne nine children and buried four of them. There were deep lines in her face, lines that all the expensive creams and ointments Flintridge Kenyon bought couldn't erase. She had grown thin with age, so that she seemed very tiny in the enormous chair at the end of the great council table, inside her dark blue gown and black shawl with silver trim. Her eyes peered brightly from the lace folds. She waited expectantly for Ross to speak.

"Father is alive," he said. "But—"

"How badly?" Ross's mother asked.

"There was no word. An arrow, and a fall from his horse. And now he is besieged in the Great Keep at Ramona, with Grandfather. Dom Julian has ordered perpetual prayer."

She sat very still for a moment, then held up her arms, and Ross ran to her. He knelt beside her and she drew his head to her chest. He blinked back tears, then sniffed loudly.

"We must both be brave," his mother said. "But the walls will not fall if we cry, a little, before you uncle comes. . . ." She held him and whispered in the border language of her childhood, and then they were both quiet for a while. "And now you take your place at the head of the Council," she said. "You must not shame your father."

"We can't hold them," Jeremiah Weigley, Colonel of Cavalry in the service of the City of Los Angeles, drained his wine glass and stared moodily into it. "Most of the City army has gone east, to Berdoo. We've sent riders, but it will be three days before much of our strength gets here. We all know what the raiders could do in that time."

They all nodded. Everyone at the council table had seen the results of nomad raids. Women taken into slavery, if they survived. Men thrown into the blazing wreckage of their houses, or dismembered alive, buried under the works of man. . . .

Ross traced the route to Berdoo with a finger. Hand-drawn, his chart was a copy of a copy; the original lay in a keg in the donjon of Kenyon Keep. The scribe who had copied the ancient road map had worked well. He had left off a hundred roads that time had ground into dust, and added new symbols. The map showed a peculiar patchwork of lands dotted with fields and irrigation ditches and ranchos; great stoneyard areas, the ruins of Ancient cities; and the great highways that stitched across the land like seams on a garment made from scraps of cloth. The highway to Berdoo was broken in many places. "Why did the Mayor take the City troops to Berdoo?" Ross demanded.

Before Weigley could answer, a smooth voice interrupted. "A hurried call for help, Don Ross." Councilman Letterman's voice was reassuring. A politician who kept his seat by favor of the Mayor, not because he had the support of any powerful family. "There were reports of a tribal invasion through Cajon Pass. Better to stop them at Cajon then to allow them into civilized lands. And there wasn't time to call a Council meeting."

Ross said nothing, but he looked down the table and saw his own anger reflected in the face of his uncle, Colonel Amos Yaegher. The Kenyons owned two seats on the City Council, and it was one point of dispute that Mayor Dortmund more and more acted without the Council's advice. He hadn't called a meeting in six months. One day there would be trouble over that, but City politics could wait. There was a more immediate danger.

"They'll be here tomorrow. Day after at the latest." Amos Yaegher's voice fit the hard room. It was a voice that could be heard in the thick of battle. Ross thought sometimes that Yaegher could bring down the high rafters with their banners and trophies if he shouted; he seemed to shake the walls when he spoke.

Yaegher didn't need a map. He had it memorized. Certainly he had risen to his post as colonel of the Kenyon forces through influence; he had married Flintridge Kenyon's only sister. Even so, he was respected as a fighting man, a soldier who spoke bluntly and shared rations with his troops; the men would follow him. "They'll be here, and what do we have to stop them?"

"Household troops," Weigley said. "City Council guardsmen. Bits and pieces. Not a proper regiment in the lot. We will call up the militia, but you've got the best troops here."

"The hell we have!"

"Amos," Estella's voice was soft, almost inaudible, but it brought silence to the room and a blush to Amos Yaegher's face. She was the daughter of the House of Escondido, and two hundred years of command was in her manner. She did not need to raise her voice to be obeyed in her own house.

"Your pardon, Doña Estrella. Colonel, you know that most of the Kenyon troops are south. There are plenty of other households in the city that can stand in the way of the tribesmen—"

"We are sending for them," Weigley said.

"The City has enemies," Councilman Letterman added. "You face barbarians on this frontier. The southern families must keep guard against Civilized armies—"

"Bah." Amon Yaegher didn't try to hide his contempt. "They fight mercenary troops. Pitched battles, and nobody killed—unless they fall off their horses! Big men in big armor riding in circles all day, and when it's over a few dozen prisoners are ransomed, and you call it war! If you want the problems of the south taken care of, send *us*. We'll show them war."

"Which is what Don Flintridge has gone south to do now," Letterman said. "And meanwhile, the southern landholders must stand guard. We will send for them, Colonel Yaegher, but it will take time to summon the City Militia—and, as you have said, the tribesman will be here tomorrow."

"Amos, we are masters of Encino," Ross's mother said.

"Aye." Amon Yaegher's booming voice fell low—a soldier's trick, to speak so low that everyone had to listen carefully. "The last time the tribes gained free access to the Valley we took the field," Amos said. "We blunted them. Ross wouldn't remember."

Not remember? I was only six years old, Ross thought, but you do not forget a day such as that. . . .

"We went out to meet them," Yaegher said. "The first Ross Kenyon, young Ross's grandfather. He was Master then. The tribes came into the Valley and we met them at that big stone field in the east Valley. I'll never forget that. Ruins everywhere around, and those long stone strips on the ground. The plainsmen's horses don't like it. Shod horses are always better on stone.

"We beat them, damned well we beat them, but a regiment rode north out of Kenyon Keep that morn, and we brought a corporal's guard back. I say we don't do that again. I say we pull into the Keep, and hold Laurel Canyon; let the Mayor's troops hold the Cahuenga Pass."

"But the Master of Encino guards all the passes from the Valley," Ross's mother said. "And there are settlements north of Cahuenga."

"Not ours."

"Civilized people," Councilman Letterman said.

"It's your job," Colonel Weigley said. "You hold the keep here as officers of the City."

"No!" Amon Yaegher's voice thundered to the captured banners hung high above the table. "The Kenyons are Masters of Encino because we hold Kenyon Keep! We took our lands and we hold them. We owe no lands to the City."

"Pride." Colonel Weigley stared into the fire. "Pride. The Ancients were here no more than two hundred years, no more than that, and they built Civilization across all of Noramerica. In five hundred years since the Burning, we have not been able to reunite Los Angeles. And we won't for a thousand, because of pride. Amon, I am no soldier. Like you. Can you hold your forces in the Keep and look out on slaughter? And do nothing?"

"If I have to. What is it you're asking for?"

"March with us. With what I have of the City Guard. Stop the tribesmen north of the Los Angeles River, before they can reach City lands and houses—and people."

"And if we lose? Who holds the Keep?"

"Your guns will hold," Weigley said. "Councilman Letterman. You are in charge for the Mayor. Will you send gunpowder for Kenyon Keep?"

Letterman looked distressed. "I don't have the authority—"

"Then by God, we won't march," Amon Yaegher said. "We'll not risk the Keep—"

"The Mayor would have my head," Letterman added. "That powder costs— The cost is unbelievable. And we have so little."

The room fell silent. Not completely silent, though, Ross noted. Outside were the sounds of frantic activity. Vaqueros driving the stock into the Keep. Outlying detachments of Kenyon retainers and landholders riding in. The armed ranchers assembling at the walls, as they had done at Kenyon summons for a hundred years and more.

"We're ranchers and farmers," Ross said quietly. "You're asking us to fight your battles for you, but you won't pay the costs. If we had our own powder mills—" He fell silent at the look of alarm Letterman showed. The Mayor didn't want the Kenyons getting into industry. Los Angeles and her Guilds had an effective monopoly on ironworks, with the rich mines opened in what had been refuse heaps for the Ancients; but even more precious was the monopoly on gunpowder. It was through the powder supplies that the Mayor kept even a loose hold on the great families who owed allegiance to Los Angeles.

"I'll do it," Letterman said. "Twenty— All right. Thirty tons. By noon tomorrow."

"And if you do not ride with us, you will have much blood on your soul, Don Ross," Colonel Weigley said. "You've seen what the tribesmen do. They kill for sport, worse, for religion, and they do not let their victims die easily. Your pardon, Doña Estella, but these things must be said."

"We will consider." Ross got up from the table and went to a crimson cord at the wall. He pulled it, and two officers came into the room. "Please entertain Councilman Letterman and Colonel Weigley," Ross ordered.

Once again the room fell quiet except for the sounds that came in from the outside. A bell tolled: the timekeeper guildsman was striking the twenty-third hour. Ross imagined the crippled old man and his crippled apprentices, turning sand glasses and filling water clocks.

"We have defended the northern borders of civilization for a hundred years, Amon," Estella Kenyon said.

"Yes, Estella, and while we held off the barbarians the mayors have played politics," he said. "Instead of building more keeps as he ought to do, our current Lord Mayor pulls down the ones we have. Tears down keeps so that no bossman can resist him. The Mayor would rather the tribesmen burn out half the City than give up one ounce of power. 'Unification' Lord Mayor Dortmund calls it, I can think of better words. And Weigley has the infernal gall to accuse *us* of pride!"

"But we do have pride," Estella Kenyon said. "It is our conceit that since the Kenyons have been Masters of Encino, no tribesmen have passed without war to the death. We have never taken bribes to look the other way while they ride into the City. We are the outpost of Civilization."

"So Ross's grandfather said," Amos thundered. "I carried him off the Field of Stone myself. I lashed him onto his horse and watched him bleed to death while we rode for the Keep. That's pride and honor for you."

"Do you think I'm anxious to send my only remaining son into battle?" she demanded. "Ross, you must decide. Your father left you master here. I do not think he would wish you to forget the duty of this House. Duty to God and to Civilization."

## III

Trumpets sounded in the dawn light. Trumpets and drums, the bandsmen of Kenyon Keep, sending men to battle; and as always there were the women, silent on the walls and along the winding road down into the Valley. They had said their farewells, and now there was nothing more than silent prayer.

The Kenyon troops rode proudly, but there were not many of them. A hundred in armor, half of them regulars and the others armed landholders. Another three hundred with leather jackets and helmets, muskets and sabers. The vaqueros with their short horn-backed bows waited below, falling in with the other cavalry as they rode past. There were also infantrymen, none of them regular soldiers. The Kenyons crossed the river on the great stone bridge, a relic of Ancient days. The other bridges across the Los Angeles River had been torn down to make the line more easily defended.

The City troops waited on the other side. They fell in with the Kenyons.

"Look sharp there," Sergeant Major Highbee growled. "Show the City bastards what real troopers look like. Number five, Loris, get that lance higher! Line up the banner!"

"He doesn't look retired," Ross said. He nodded toward Highbee.

"A good man," Colonel Yaegher said. "But it's still a fool's errand. One we'll regret."

"You don't have to come," Ross replied.

"Nephew, I'll forget you said that," Amos Yaegher said. He didn't say that Ross could stay behind. When the regular guardsmen rose out they might be led by any of their officers, but when the Kenyons summoned the vaqueros and relatives and friends and tenants they were always led by a Kenyon.

"I'm sorry, Uncle," Ross said. He got a curt nod in answer. I'm scared, Ross thought. Does everyone feel this way? They can't. They wouldn't be going.

But you are, he told himself.

The troops nearest him were a personal guard. Five vaqueros, led by Guillermo, oldest son of the *vaquero jefe*. Guillermo was nearly thirty, and had been in danger most of his life. The vaqueros held the northern reaches of the Kenyon lands and were often sent into the desert as scouts. Behind Guillermo was Sergeant Keller, another old regular guard, long past the time when he should be retired to the walls, and the five regulars who rode with him were not much younger—except for Harry Benton, trumpeter, barely twelve years old.

Tension showed in their faces, and in the easy remarks they made to each other. They felt something, too. *Premonition*? Ross wondered. The Old Woman at the Keep had no Sight, or at least none that she admitted to. That was an evil omen, to be kept secret, but soldiers find these things out.

A wave from Yaegher sent Wenceslas and thirty vaqueros galloping ahead, fanning out as scouts. The desert tribes had been known to send in advance parties in the night, but the vaqueros were as good at *ambuscado* as the tribesmen.

The rest of the Civilized force, Kenyons and the City Guard, rode straight up the San Fernando Valley. At times there were many stone ranch houses, homes of hardy families who dared live in the Valley because they had faith in the Kenyons—and, Ross admitted to himself, in the hostility of the mountain clansmen who usually kept the passes into the Mojave sealed.

Usually, but not always. The mountain clans were not allies of Civilization, but they did live in uneasy truce with the City dwellers. They stayed to their mountains, and the City stayed to the plains, and the tribes stayed in their high desert—until, suddenly, the tribes would make common cause and burst into the hills, and the clan chiefs would let them through the passes rather than endure the raids themselves.

Every effort to cooperate with the clan chiefs or their war lords ended in disaster and distrust. The Highlanders did not have the feral hatred of Civilization that drove the desert tribes, but they had no love for its cities and politics.

The ranchlands ended abruptly. Beyond were the ruins: twisted hulks of Ancient buildings, crumbling bridges over nothing at all, vast fields covered in black stone, flat and level and useless. No one could protect this land. The Highlanders came down to salvage the ruins, and the war parties of nomads burst through the passes—but that was not why the land was never reclaimed. The Kenyons would never allow anyone else to fortify the north Valley—and the Mayor wanted no expansion of Kenyon lands and power. For a generation and more that stalemate had kept the ruins intact, with no one to profit from it.

The ruins ended a mile after they began. Beyond them was a strange area cleared by Ekofreak and Greenpeace tribesmen in the years when they held the north Valley. The land was broken by mounds and hills, and the remains of underground dwellings the tribesmen built themselves. There were no other signs of human activity.

It was the tribal religion to remove Man's defilements from their Mother Earth, and they did the work well. They broke up walls, removed the remains of burned buildings, pried up the stones from roads and heaped them into mounds which they covered with earth and sod. They planted trees and vines, creating artificial laurel thickets and cane patches. No one knew what they would do if they ever held the entire basin. Their ecologists and lesser leaders did not disclose their plans.

The Kenyon forces rode on, northward, hoofs pounding. Ross held his head high. He wanted to run, to go back to the keep, but he sat proudly and rode north.

Ross Kenyon wasn't a warrior by nature. His father had been, and his grandfather as well. The Kenyons had always been warriors, although there had been something else as well, a strain of builder and administrator, and, sometimes, even a dreamer. Rumor had it that three generations before a Kenyon had gone to the fortress atop Mount Wilson, sent his servant back with the message that he was well, and was never heard from again. But mostly the Kenyons made war.

Perhaps it was Doña Estella's influence, but Ross could admire the deeds of his ancestors without wanting to duplicate them. Fighting and killing, eternal war and battle held no glory for him. They were necessary, and he would do what had to be done, but he took no joy in it. Let the others sing war songs, Ross would rather read books. Few books had survived the Burning, of course, but there was one on building and another on agriculture, copies of copies, with words he did not understand, but he worked at them patiently anyway. He learned the skills of a warrior because he had to; but he studied what little was known about raising crops and breeding cattle because those were skills he wanted.

But they were no use now, as he rode north through the Valley, into fields that his family had coveted for generations, and the hot California sun beat down on helmet and armor.

They halted at noon, with the sun high overhead. The Valley was clear, the morning haze all burned away. Up ahead was a small cloud of dust—the scouts returning—but their message was already known.

The tribesmen were coming over the San Fernando Pass. They threw up no betraying dust cloud, because they stayed on the splendid roads the Ancients had thrown through the Pass. Their vanguard was in sight, then over and down into the Valley; behind them was an endless column of light cavalry.

"Mount up," Yaegher called. It would be an hour before the battle. No more.

Condors and vultures wheeled high above the Valley. Do they know? Ross wondered. They should. When men ride in large numbers, there is always food for vultures.

And for vultures of another kind. High up on the hills ringing the Valley was another warrior host—the Sierra tribesmen. Ross looked for the telltale triangles in the sky, the flying men of the Sierra, but there were none there. Not yet. But up above, on Mendenhall Peak, on the ridges to the east, there were flashes of bright color: Sierra clansmen. On foot, as always. They seldom rode. They did not hold the Angeles Mountains, and all the highlands north to the High Sierra itself, with horses. Cavalry for the valleys, mules for the highlands, both for the desert. And other creatures, camels, in the Mojave. They hadn't brought camels with them on this raid, at least Ross hadn't seen any.

Weigley and Yaegher clustered around him. "With your permission, Nephew," Yaegher said, "here's the battle plan. Kenyon regiment will take the right wing and press forward. The City forces will cover our left flank and hold back a few hundred yards. When there's enough of the tribal force committed, we'll roll down toward the City troops with the vaqueros to cover our right. We'll blood them, and fall back toward the River. That might be enough."

It might be. The tribesmen were a superstitious lot. They believed in their luck. Medicine, some tribes called it. Luck. Fortune. Ross didn't know much about the nomads. No one did. They never met Civilized people in peace. All that Ross knew came through the Highlanders, who sometimes made truce with the City, and sometimes made truce with the Mojave tribes.

But everyone knew the tribes didn't take defeat well. Inflict losses on them early, and their chiefs—what did they call them? Ecologists—their ecologists might take an early defeat as a sign of disfavor from whatever gods the tribes worshipped, and then the whole horde would run back to their desert and cast their spells. . . .

But the Old Woman had no vision, no Sight, and it all came down to the decision of a seventeen-year-old boy who had never before in his life seen two thousand enemies gathered together.

Yaegher was colonel—but a Kenyon commanded. Always.

"What else might we do?" Ross asked.

"Nephew, we could hit and run. Fall back toward the River line. But somewhere we have to make a stand, and better up ahead where the ground's clear than here among the ruins. Open ground favors heavy cavalry. . . ." Yaegher's voice trailed off. This was no classroom, and no time to teach Ross something the boy had learned years before. "At your orders, Nephew."

Weigley was listening silently. Ross looked into the City colonel's eyes, trying to understand what he saw there. Something. Fear? But it seemed to be more, and Weigley wouldn't meet his gaze. Do we trust this man? Ross wanted to ask, but it was too late; he couldn't ask that while Weigley listened. That would certainly make him an enemy.

And the plan made sense. Part of the City force was infantry. Crossbowmen, good at defense. They could hold the north edge of the ruins. With cover like that to shoot from they could hurt the tribes, while the Kenyon cavalry rolled through them, breaking them—

And whatever we do, we must do it *now*, Ross thought. He looked up at the wheeling vultures, looking for a sign—but there was none. "Forward, Uncle, command the regiment."

"Sir."

"Where do you want me, Uncle?"

"With the vaqueros on the right wing, Nephew. You understand them better than me. Better than any of us." And, Yaegher didn't add but could have, they are only loyal to your mother, and thus to you; not to the Kenyon name, but to Estrella Trujillo Kenyon, infant of the House of the Alcalde de Escondido. "It won't be the safest place in the battle. You'll have to move fast, to cover our right when we wheel west and south. God go with you."

"And with you, Uncle." Ross waved to his guards and cantered off to join the returning vaquero scouts. The dust of the valley stuck in his throat, and he felt the knot of fear tearing at his stomach. At least it will be over, he thought. Soon. One way or another.

## IV

The battle was a screaming confusion of dust and trumpet calls, the bark of musketry and the clatter of horses. It was the smell of blood, the moans of dying men, lamed horses thrashing in the dirt. It was half-naked men charging with spear and bow, to be met by armored riders with lance and musket and saber. It was men firing their muskets and holstering them to draw their thirsty sabers because there'd never be enough time to reload. And through it all it was trumpets and the smell of blood.

It was John Stephenson, only two years older than Ross, leading an insane charge into the thick of screaming savages, lance shattered and then saber flashing until his horse went down, and still Ross's cousin fought, screaming his defiance and rallying the shattered remains of the score of men he'd led. It was Hyman Silverberg, tenant on Stephenson land, swinging a great axe and rushing to his young officer's defense. It was heads severed by Silverberg's axe until an arrow grew between his shoulder blades and the giant yeoman went to his knees with a puzzled expression in his eyes, dying without knowing he was dead.

It was Ross Kenyon leading his vaqueros to aid his cousin. It was a blond man with long hair and a painted shield charging Ross, and Ross spurring his stallion forward, lance cocked as he'd been taught in a hundred mock battles, and the lance piercing the leather shield and ramming home in the nomad's throat, and the man's weight hanging horribly on the lance, bright blood spurting, and the lance coming free but too late, and Guillermo coming from nowhere to fling a javelin and rescue his master.

It was Ross coming to his cousin's aid and seeing the white ropes of intestines trailing in the dust, and the bright blood, and John Stephenson screaming for his mother before falling to the ground with a dozen hostiles in leather breeches rushing to count coup before he died, and the trumpets sounding again, commanding the vaqueros forward and to the left to aid the faltering right wing of the Kenyon forces, leaving Ross no time to recover his cousin's body. It was Guillermo, at a nod from Ross, throwing one more dart, straight and true into Stephenson's heart, then Ross and his guard with sabers cutting through a new wave of tribesmen to answer the trumpet's imperious call.

It was two hours of madness, and it was disaster.

"Retreat," the trumpets sang. "Kenyons to the Keep!" Ross had never heard that call sounded except for practice. "Kenyons to the Keep!"

"But who?" Ross demanded. "Who?"

He reined in, gathered his guardsmen around him. They were a small island of calm for a moment. Dust lay thick across the Valley. Ross stared south at the hills in wonder. There, above the battlements of Kenyon Keep, flew the Red Ball. It was the most urgent summons known. *The Keep was in danger!* Yet—they were miles from the Keep, and the tribesmen had not broken through, could not have broken through.

"Retreat," sang the trumpets. "Kenyons to the Keep!"

"Who?" Ross demanded again. Guillermo and Keeler gave him only blank stares. "Ride, then. To the Keep."

The horses were exhausted. The left-wheeling maneuver had carried Ross and his vaqueros far to the west, beyond the old highway and far toward the Santa Susanna hills. The horses could never gallop all the way to the Keep.

As they rode, the Red Ball fell, and then, incredibly, the blue and gold Kenyon banner wavered, and fluttered down from the high battlements—a lifetime away across the Valley. There was an eternity of time, then another banner climbed in triumph to stand out proudly in the wind above Kenyon Keep.

"Green and gold," Keeler growled. "Green and gold."

"The Mayor!" Ross screamed. "But—"

"Treason!" someone else cried.

There was no time to say more. Another knot of nomads, white men, brown men, black men, all on the small unshod horses of the desert; screaming men with bloodlust in their voices. They charged, and Ross's tiny command was surrounded, their horses too exhausted to fight on, but they fought. Keeler was down, his left arm severed by an axe blow meant for Ross, and then trumpeter Benton who wouldn't live to see his thirteenth birthday.

He woke in darkness. There were sounds of activity around him. He lay with his eyes half open, not daring to move, not even to test whether his hands were bound. Captured! He had only one thought, to gather his strength and find a weapon, to die fighting before the tribesmen could give him to their gods.

But slowly the voices around him began to make sense. Anglic and Sandiegan. Not the gutturals of the Mojave dialects.

"Don Ross. Don Ross."

No tribesman would call him by that name. Ross opened his eyes.

Darkness, with flickering firelight. Rough homespun wool cowl hovering above him. The crinkled face of Padre Gutierrez, and from somewhere nearby Guillermo endlessly repeating his name.

"You awake?" Gutierrez asked.

His head swam in confusion. Ross struggled to move. His hands were not bound. He was free. "Where—" he croaked.

"You are in the Abbey." Ross heard without comprehension. A hand lifted his head, another put a cup to his lips. Cool water trickled into his mouth. He swallowed eagerly.

"More—"

"In a moment."

Slowly the memories came back. The Red Ball. And— "The Keep! To the Keep!" he shouted.

"No. It is too late." The voice held both sadness and finality. It had come from beyond Padre Gutierrez, and it took moments for Ross to recognize it. Dom Julian, Abbot. "The Keep is in the hands of the Lord Mayor."

Ross tried to speak again, but the cup was put to his lips. The taste was bitter. Herbs of some kind, steeped in water and wine. The oddly bitter taste was pleasant. Ross drank, and again felt the world reeling, and sank back into darkness.

It was daylight when he woke again. Padre Gutierrez still sat beside him.

Ross struggled to sit up. He was in a small room, no more than a cell. Bright sunlight streamed in though a narrow window. Again the memories came, and the Padre saw terror in his eyes.

"How?" Ross asked.

"After you have eaten. You have much to do before dark. Come. I'll help you walk."

The monks cleaned him and fed him, but they would not answer his questions. He was given new clothing: rough wool clothing, no fine fabrics, and none of it with the Kenyon colors. Still they would not talk to him. Finally, he was led into the Abbot's study.

Dom Julian sat at a large desk. He motioned Ross to a chair nearby. "You have eaten?"

"Yes, Dom Julian."

"And you look well."

"I am all right."

"A miracle. I have seen the dent the war hammer put in your helmet."

"What happened, Dom Julian?" Ross demanded. "How—"

The Abbot's lips were tightly pressed together. "I scarcely know how to begin. The Mayor holds Kenyon Keep—"

"I saw the banner hoisted. It was nearly the last thing I ever saw. For that I thank God, that my last sight was not—"

The Abbot held up his hand. "Be careful, my son. God has spared you for some great purpose. You should be dead. The Mayor has placed an enormous price on your head."

"He wouldn't dare!"

"He has dared. Your retainers are scattered or dead, Don Ross."

"Mother. What has—"

There was pain in the Abbot's eyes. He looked away, then back at Ross. "Dead also," he said bluntly. "The Mayor's troops despoiled her chapel. She died defending the altar. Defending the Faith."

It was too much. His home lost, his mother dead— "You're a

Kenyon! Command shows no fears!" his father's voice rang in his head. Ross sat tight-lipped, his hands clinched into fists, the mails digging into his palms. He spoke carefully. "That is war. The Alcalde—"

"Your grandfather is in no position to send aid," Dom Julian said. "Escondido is under siege. This is no ordinary rising. Guillermo brought in arrows and other signs. At least five tribes, a dozen septs here, and as many more have risen in the south."

"But they were also raiding San Berdoo—"

The Abbot shook his head slowly. "No. That is what Mayor Dortmund said. But he did not ride to Berdoo. He kept his troops much closer, and when you rode out into the Valley they stormed the Keep. There is more. The tribesmen plundered Kenyon lands freely. Then they turned and went back. They are camped at the head of the Valley now."

"And they never raided the City at all," Ross said wonderingly. "Was it planned all along? The Lord Mayor and the tribesmen together—"

"We think so," Dom Julian said.

"But why? Why would the tribesmen aid the Mayor?"

"Perhaps they are less in fear of Kenyon Keep held by the Mayor than by Kenyons," Dom Julian said. "I would be. The advantages to Dortmund are obvious, and he is too proud to believe the tribes might deceive him." The Abbot looked uncomfortable. "What will you do now?"

"I don't know."

"If you ask for sanctuary, we will give it. I want that understood," Dom Julian said.

"But you don't want me to ask."

"Frankly, with you here we might not be able to hold the Abbey. I do not think the Lord Mayor will storm this place soon. It has held too often, and the Highlanders around us would not care to see the Mayor in possession here. It would be a dangerous game for the Mayor, one he will not play unless he has a powerful motive. You would be such a motive."

Ross said nothing.

"So long as you are alive, you are witness to his treachery," Dom Julian said. "I do not know what stories Dortmund will tell. He will need powerful lies to justify himself. Other Masters and bossmen will not be pleased to hear that Kenyon Keep has fallen into the Mayor's hands. But with no one to deny his tales . . ."

"He will expect me to go to Escondido," Ross said.

"Yes. You may be certain that he will be watching the roads."

"I can't stay here and I can't go to Escondido. Where?"

"I point out that you will be safer if I do not know," Dom Julian said. "More: if I do not know, you cannot suspect the Church of aiding the Mayor if—"

"If he finds me, I won't be able to suspect anything," Ross finished.

"Even so, I would not care to have my name among your dying curses," Dom Julian said.

"Your miracles," Ross said. "Can you get word to Escondido? I need instructions from my father."

Before Dom Julian spoke, Ross knew the final horror to come. Don Flintridge was dead, and the remains of his guard besieged in Escondido. Ross was El Señor Kenyon, the last of Kenyons, but he was not Master of Encino. He was utterly alone.

But a Kenyon. Now and forever.

# HE FELL INTO A DARK HOLE

## by Jerry Pournelle

## Editor's Introduction

Jerry was fascinated by black holes and was one of the first authors to write an SF story about them. As he put it:

My first black hole story appeared way back when, before all the hoopla in the popular press, and I wrote several columns about them in my *Galaxy Magazine* column, "A Step Farther Out." I can't say I have a patent on black holes, but by gollies I did manage to get into print about them before Isaac Asimov, and considering the number of books he writes each week that's an accomplishment.

For all their new popularity, black holes remain a theory. No one has ever seen one—indeed, by definition no one will ever see one—and all we know has been deduced from various mathematical theories. The primary concept of a black hole—an object near which gravity is so strong that nothing, not even light, can escape, thus making the object invisible—can be and was deduced from Newton; but the real theoretical work came only after Einstein.

Although they're studied by high-powered mathematics and have their origin in some of the most complicated ideas ever spawned by humanity, black holes are rather simple things. You can easily imagine them through "thought experiments," which is just as well, because we can't actually do the experiments. This story is the reason I am editor of this book. Some years ago my friend and partner Larry Niven published a story called "Neutron Star" which made use of what was then a new concept, neutron stars. He won a Hugo with the story, and also introduced the idea into science fiction.

I couldn't be absolutely first with black holes. There had been a few stories about holes already published although I hadn't seen them. (Writers have very little time to read fiction.) Still, I would be among the first, and with any luck I'd be able to do for black holes what Larry Niven had done for neutron stars.

I set the story in my world of the CoDominium, which takes us from a few years hence into the far future. A number of my other stories—the best known being *The Mercenary* and *The Mote in God's Eye* (with Larry Niven)—make use of this future history. The series assumes that the United States and the Soviet Union end the cold war by joining in an uneasy alliance. Their respective governments find it far better that there be only two Great Powers, even as rivals, than for there to be a number of independent power centers. As a part of this alliance structure they create the CoDominium Space Navy. They also try to control all scientific research, since new developments might threaten the CoDominium's supremacy.

As a result there is little basic or theoretical research, and nearly everyone has forgotten about black holes, until . . .

❖ ❖ ❖

**CDSN CAPTAIN BARTHOLOMEW RAMSEY** watched his men check out, each man leaving the oval entry port under the satanic gaze of the master-at-arms. After nearly two years in space the men deserved something more exciting than twenty hours dirtside at Ceres Base, but they were eager for even that much. CDSS *Daniel Webster* got all the long patrols and dirty outsystem jobs in the Navy because her captain didn't protest. Now, when these men got to Luna Base and Navy Town, Lord help the local girls. . . .

Well, they'd be all right here, Ramsey thought. The really expensive pleasures were reserved for Belt prospectors and the crews of Westinghouse mining ships. Bart glanced at the screens displaying ships docked at Ceres. None of the big ore-processing ships were in Thorstown. Things should be pretty quiet. Nothing Base Marines couldn't handle, even if *Daniel Webster*'s crew hadn't been on a good drunk for twenty months. Ramsey turned away from the entry port to go back to his cabin.

It was difficult to walk in the low gravity of Ceres. Very inconvenient place, he thought. But of course low gravity was a main reason for putting a Navy yard there. That and the asteroid mines. . . .

He walked carefully through gray steel bulkheads to the central corridor. Just outside the bridge entrance he met Dave Trevor, the first lieutenant.

"Not going ashore?" Ramsey asked.

"No, sir." Trevor's boyish grin was infectious. Ramsey had once described it as the best crew morale booster in the Navy. And at age twenty-four Dave Trevor had been in space eleven years, as ship's boy, midshipman, and officer. He would know every pub in the Solar System and a lot outside. . . . "Never cared much for the girls on Ceres," he said. "Too businesslike."

Captain Ramsey nodded sagely. With Trevor's looks he wouldn't have to shell out money for an evening's fun anywhere near civilization. Ceres was another matter. "I'd appreciate it if you'd make a call on the provost's office, Mister Trevor. We might need a friend there by morning."

The lieutenant grinned again. "Aye, aye, Captain."

Bart nodded and climbed down the ladder to his cabin. Trevor's merry whistling followed him until he closed the door. Once Ramsey was inside he punched a four-digit code on the intercom console.

"Surgeon's office, Surgeon's Mate Hartley, sir."

"Captain here. Make sure we have access to a good dental repair unit in the morning, Hartley. Even if we have to use Base facilities."

"Aye, aye, sir."

Ramsey switched the unit off and permitted himself a thin smile. The regeneration stimulators aboard *Daniel Webster* worked but there was something wrong with the coding information in the dental unit. It produced buck teeth, not enormous but quite noticeable, and when his men were out drinking and some dirtpounder made a few funny remarks . . .

The smile faded as Ramsey sat carefully in the regulation chair. He glanced around the sterile cabin. There were none of the comforts other captains provided themselves. Screens, charts, built-in cabinets and tables, his desk, everything needed to run his ship, but no photographs and solidos, no paintings and rugs. Just Ramsey and his ship, his wife with the masculine name. He took a glass of whisky from the arm of the chair. It was Scotch and the taste of burnt malt was very strong. Bart tossed it off and replaced it to be refilled. The intercom buzzed.

"Captain here."

"Bridge, sir. Call from Base Commandant Torrin."

"Put him on."

"Aye, aye, sir." The watch midshipman's face vanished and Rap Torrin's broad features filled the screen. The rear admiral looked at the bare cabin, grimaced, then smiled at Ramsey.

"I'm going to pull rank on you, Bart," Torrin said. "Expect that courtesy call in an hour. You can plan on having dinner with me, too."

Ramsey forced a smile. "Very good, sir. My pleasure. In an hour, then."

"Right." The screen went blank and Ramsey cursed. He drank the second whisky and cursed again, this time at himself.

What's wrong with you? he thought. Rap Torrin is as good a friend as you have in the Navy. Shipmate way back in *Ajax* under Sergei Lermontov. Now Rap has a star, well, that was expected. And Lermontov is Vice Admiral Commanding, the number two man in the whole CoDominium Space Navy.

And so what? I could have had stars. As many as I wanted. I'm that good, or I was. And with Martin Grant's influence in the Grand Senate and Martin's brother John in charge of United States security, Senator Martin Grant's son-in-law could have had any post no matter how good. . . .

Ramsey took another whisky from the chair and looked at it for a long time. He'd once had his star, polished and waiting, nothing but formalities to go, while Rap and Sergei grinned at his good luck. Sergei Lermontov had just made junior vice admiral then. Five years ago.

Five years. Five years ago Barbara Jean Ramsey and their son Harold were due back from Meiji. Superstitiously, Bart had waited for them before accepting his promotion. When he took it he'd have to leave *Daniel Webster* for something dirtside and wait until a spacing admiral was needed. That wouldn't have been long. The Danube situation was heating up back then. Ramsey could have commanded the first punitive expedition, but it had gone out under an admiral who botched the job. Barbara Jean had never come home from Meiji.

Her ship had taken a new direct route along an Alderson path just discovered. It never came out into normal space. A scoutcraft was sent to search for the liner, and Senator Grant had enough influence to send a frigate after that. Both vanished, and there weren't any more ships to send. Bartholomew Ramsey stayed a captain. He couldn't leave his ship because he couldn't face the empty house in Luna Base compound.

He sighed, then laughed cynically at himself. Time to get dressed. Rap wanted to show off his star, and it would be cruel to keep him waiting.

The reunion was neither more nor less than he'd expected, but Admiral Torrin cut short the time in his office. "Got to get you home, Bart. Surprise for you there. Come along, man, come along."

Bart followed woodenly. Something really wrong with me, he thought. Man doesn't go on like this for five years. I'm all right aboard Old Danny Boy. It's only when I leave my ship, now why should that be? But a man can marry a ship, even a slim steel whiskey bottle four hundred meters long and sixty across; he wouldn't be the first captain married to a cruiser.

Most of Ceres Base was underground, and Bart was lost in the endless rock corridors. Finally they reached a guarded area. They returned the Marines' salutes and went through to broader hallways lined with carpets. There were battle paintings on the walls. Some reached back to wet navy days and every CD base, in-system or out, had them. There were scenes from all the great navies of the world. Russian, Soviet, US, British, Japanese . . . there weren't any of Togo at Tshushima, though. Or Pearl Harbor. Or Bengal Bay.

Rap kept up his hearty chatter until they got inside his apartment. The admiral's quarters were what Bart had visualized before he entered, richly furnished, filled with the gifts and mementos that a successful independent command captain could collect on a dozen worlds after more than twenty years in service. Shells and stuffed exotic fauna, a cabinet made of the delicately veined snake-wood of Tanith, a table of priceless Spartan roseteak. There was a house on Luna Base that had been furnished like this. . . .

Bart caught sight of the man who entered the room and snapped to attention in surprise. Automatically he saluted.

Vice Admiral Lermontov returned the salute. The admiral was a tall, slim man who wore rimless spectacles which made his gray eyes look large and round as they bored through his subordinates. Men who served under Lermontov either loved him or hated him. Now his thin features distorted in genuine pleasure. "Bartholomew, I am sorry to surprise you like this."

Lermontov inspected Ramsey critically. The smile faded slightly. "You have not taken proper care of yourself, my friend. Not enough exercise."

"I can still beat you. Arm wrestling, anything you name—uh, sir."

Lermontov's smile broadened again. "That is better. But you need not call me 'sir.' You would say 'sir' only to Vice Admiral Lermontov, and it is quite obvious that the Vice Admiral Commanding cannot possibly be on Ceres. So, since you have not seen me. . . ."

"I see," Ramsey said.

Lermontov nodded. "It is rather important. You will know why in a few moments. Rap, can you bring us something to drink?"

Torrin nodded and fussed with drinks from the snake-wood cabinet. The ringing tone of a crystal glass was very loud in the quiet apartment. Ramsey was vaguely amused as he took a seat at the roseteak table in the center of the lush room. A rear admiral waiting on a captain, and no enlisted spacers to serve the Vice Admiral Commanding, who, after all, wasn't really there in the first place—the whisky was from Inveraray and was very good.

"You have been in space nearly two years," Lermontov said. "You have not seen your father-in-law in that time?"

"More like three since Martin and I really talked about anything," Ramsey said. "We—we remind each other too much of Barbara Jean and Harold."

The pain in Ramsey's face was reflected as a pale shadow in Lermontov's eyes. "But you knew he had become chairman of the appropriations committee."

"Yes."

"The Navy's friend, Grand Senator Grant. Without him these last years would have been disaster for us all. For the Navy, and for Earth as well if those politicians could only see it." Lermontov cut himself off with an angry snap. The big eyes matching his steel-gray hair focused on Bart. "The new appropriations are worse," the admiral growled. "While you have been away, everything has become worse. Millington, Harmon, Bertram, they all squeeze President Lipscomb's Unity Party in your country, and Kaslov gains influence every day in mine. I think it will not be long before one or the other of the CoDominium sponsors withdraws from the treaties, Bart. And after that, war."

"War." Ramsey said it slowly, not believing. After a hundred and fifty years of uneasy peace between the United States and the Soviets, war again, and with the weapons they had. . . .

"Any spark might set it off," Lermontov was saying. "We must be ready to step in. The fleet must be strong, strong enough to cope with the national forces and do whatever we must do."

Ramsey felt as if the admiral had struck him. War? Fleet intervention? "What about the Commanding Admiral? The Grand Senate?"

Lermontov shrugged. "You know who are the good men, who are not. But so long as the fleet is strong, something perhaps can be done to save Earth from the idiocy of the politicians. Not that the masses are better, screaming for a war they can never understand." Lermontov drank quietly, obviously searching for words, before he turned back to Ramsey. "I have to tell you something painful, my friend. Your father-in-law is missing."

"Missing—where? I told Martin to be careful, that Millington's Liberation Army people. . . ."

"No. Not on Earth. Out-system. Senator Grant went to Meiji to visit relatives there. . . ."

"Yes." Ramsey felt the memory like a knife in his vitals. "His nephew, Barbara Jean's cousin, an officer in the Diplomatic Corps on Meiji. Grew up in the senator's home. Barbara Jean was visiting him when . . ."

"Yes." Lermontov leaned closer to Ramsey so that he could touch his shoulder for a moment. Then he took his hand away. "I do not remind you of these things because I am cruel, my friend. I must know—would the senator have tried to find his daughter? After all these years?"

Bart nodded. "She was his only child. As Harold was mine. If I thought there was any chance I'd look myself. You think he tried it?"

"We do." Lermontov signaled Torrin to bring him another drink. "Senator Grant went to Meiji with the visit to his relatives as cover. With the Japanese representation question to come up soon, and the budget after that, Meiji is important. The Navy provided a frigate for transportation. It took the usual route through Colby and around, and was supposed to return the same way. But we have confirmed reports that Senator Grant's ship went instead to the jumpoff point for the direct route."

"What captain in his right mind would let him get away with that?"

"His name was Commander John Grant, Jr. The senator's nephew."

"Oh." Bart nodded again, exaggerating the gesture as he realized the full situation. "Yeah. Johnny would do it if the old man asked. So you came all the way out here for my opinion, Sergei? I can give it quick. Senator Grant was looking for Barbara Jean. So you can write him off and whatever other plans you've got for the goddam Navy you can write off too. Learn to live without him, Sergei. The goddam jinx has another good ship and another good man. Now if you'll excuse me I want to get back to my ship and get drunk."

Captain Ramsey strode angrily toward the door. Before he reached it the Vice Admiral's voice crackled through the room. "Captain, you are not excused."

"Sir." Ramsey whirled automatically. "Very well, sir. Your orders?"

"My orders are for you to sit down and finish your drink, Captain." There was a long silence as they faced each other. Finally Ramsey sat at the expensive table.

"Do you think so badly of me, Bart, that you believe I would come all the way out here, meet you secretly, for as little as this?"

Bart looked up in surprise. Emotions welled up inside him, emotions he hadn't felt in years, and he fought desperately to force them back. No, God, don't let me hope again. Not that agony. Not hope. . . . But Lermontov was still speaking.

"I will let Professor Stirner explain it to you, since I am not sure any of us understand him. But he has a theory, Bart. He believes that the senator may be alive, and that there may be a chance to bring him home before the Senate knows he is missing. For years the Navy has preserved the peace, now a strong fleet is needed more than ever. We have no choice, Bart. If there is any chance at all, we must take it."

Professor Hermann Stirner was a short Viennese with thinning red hair, improbable red freckles, and a neat round belly. Ramsey thought him about fifty, but the man's age was indeterminate. It was unlikely that he was younger, but with regeneration therapy he could be half that again. Rap Torrin brought the professor in through a back entrance.

"Dr. Stirner is an intelligence adviser to the fleet," Lermontov said. "He is not a physicist."

"No, no physicist," Stirner agreed quickly. "Who would want to live under the restrictions of a licensed physicist? CoDominium intelligence officers watching every move, suppressing most of your discoveries. . . ." He spoke intently giving the impression of great emotion no matter what he said. "And most physicists I have met are not seeing beyond the end of their long noses. Me, I worry mostly about politics, Captain. But when the Navy loses ships, I want to know what happened to them. I have a theory about those ships, for years."

Ramsey gripped the arms of his chair until his knuckles were white, but his voice was deadly calm. "Why didn't you bring up your theory before now?"

Stirner eyed him critically. Then he shrugged. "As I said, I am no physicist. Who would listen to me? But now, with the senator gone . . ."

"We need your father-in-law badly," Lermontov interrupted. "I do not really believe Professor Stirner's theories, but the fleet needs Senator Grant so desperately we will try anything. Let Dr. Stirner explain."

"Ja. You are a bright young CoDominium Navy captain, I am going to tell you things you know already, maybe. But I do not myself understand everything I should know, so you let me explain my own way, ja?" Stirner paced briskly for a moment, then sat restlessly at the table. He gave no chance to answer his question, but spoke rapidly, so that he gave the impression of interrupting himself.

"You got five forces in this universe we know about, ja? Only one of them maybe really isn't in this universe, we do not quibble about that, let the cosmologists worry. Now we look at two of those forces, we can forget the atomics and electromagnetics. Gravity and the Alderson force, these we look at. Now you think about the universe as flat like this table, eh?" He swept a pudgy hand across the roseteak surface. "And wherever you got a star, you got a hill that rises slowly, gets all the time steeper until you get near the star when it's so steep you got a cliff. And you think of your ships like roller coasters. You get up on the hill, aim where you want to go, and pop on the hyperspace drivers. Bang, you are in a universe where the Alderson effect acts like gravity. You are rolling downhill, across the table, and up the side of the next hill, not using up much potential energy, so you are ready to go again somewhere else if you can get lined up right, okay?"

Ramsey frowned. "It's not quite what we learned as middies—you've got ships repelled from a star rather than—"

"Ja, ja, plenty of quibbles we can make if we want to. Now, Captain, how is it you get out of hyperspace when you want to?"

"We don't," Ramsey said. "When we get close enough to a gravity source, the ship comes out into normal space whether we want it to or not."

Stirner nodded. "Ja. And you use your photon drivers to run around in normal space where the stars are like wells, not hills, at least thinking about gravities. Now, suppose you try to shoot past one star to another, all in one Jump?"

"It doesn't work," Ramsey said. "You'd get caught in the gravity field of the in-between star. Besides, the Alderson paths don't cross each other. They're generated by stellar nuclear activities, and you can only travel along lines of equal flux. In practice that means almost line of sight, with range limits, but they aren't really straight lines. . . ."

"Ja. Okay. That's what I think is happening to them. I think there is a star between A-7820 and 82 Eridani, which is the improbable name Meiji's sun is stuck with."

"Now wait a minute," Admiral Torrin protested. "There can't be a star there, Professor. There's no question of missing it, not with our observations. Man, do you think the Navy didn't look for it? A liner and an explorer class frigate vanished on that route. We looked, first thing we thought of."

"Suppose there is a star there but you are not seeing it?"

"How could that be?" Torrin asked.

"A black hole, Admiral. Ja," Stirner continued triumphantly. "I think Senator Grant fell into a black hole."

Ramsey looked puzzled. "I seem to remember something about black holes, but I don't remember what."

"Theoretical concept," Stirner said. "Hundred, hundred and fifty years ago, before the CoDominium Treaty puts a stop to so much scientific research. Lots of people talk about black holes then, but nobody ever finds any, so now there's no appropriations for licensed physicists to work on them.

"But way back we have a man named Schwarzschild, Viennese chap, he thinks of them." Stirner puffed with evident pride. "Then another chap, Oppenheimer, and some more, all make the calculations. A black hole is like a neutron star that goes all the way. Collapsed down so far, a whole star collapsed to maybe two, three kilometers diameter. Gravity is so tough nothing gets out. Not light; not anything gets out of the gravity well. Infinite red shift. Some ways a black hole isn't even theoretically inside this universe."

The others looked incredulous and Stirner laughed. "You think that is strange? There was even talk once about whole galaxies, a hundred billion stars, whole thing collapsed to smaller than the orbit of Venus. They wouldn't be in the universe for real either."

"Then how would black holes interact with—oh," Rap Torrin said, "gravity. It still has that."

Stirner's round face bobbed in agreement. "Ja, ja, which is how we know there is no black galaxy out there. Would be too much gravity, but there is plenty room for a star. Now one thing I do not understand though, why the survey ship gets through, others do not. Maybe gravity changes for one of those things, ja?"

"No, look, the Alderson path really isn't a line of sight, it can shift slightly—maybe just enough!" Torrin spoke rapidly. "If the geometry were just right, then sometimes the hole wouldn't be in the way."

"Okay," Stirner said. "I leave that up to you Navy boys. But you see what happens, the ship is taking sights or whatever you do when you are making a Jump, the captain pushes the button, and maybe you come out in normal space near this black hole. Nothing to see anywhere around you. And no way to get back home."

"Of course." Ramsey stood, twisted his fingers excitedly. "The Alderson effect is generated by nuclear reactions. And the dark holes—"

"Either got none of those, or the Alderson force stuffs is caught inside the black hole like light and everything else. So you are coming home in normal space or you don't come home at all."

"Which is light-years. You'd never make it." Ramsey found himself near the bar. Absently he poured a drink. "But in that case—the ships can sustain themselves a long time on their fuel!"

"Yes." Lermontov said it carefully. "It is at least possible that Senator Grant is alive. If his frigate dropped into normal space at a sufficient distance from the black hole so that it did not vanish down."

"Not only Martin," Bart Ramsey said wonderingly. His heart pounded. "Barbara Jean. And Harold. They were on a Norden Lines luxury cruiser, only half the passenger berths taken. There should have been enough supplies and hydrogen to keep them going five years, Sergei. More than enough!"

Vice Admiral Lermontov nodded slowly. "That is why we thought you should go. But you realize that. . . ."

"I haven't dared hope. I've wanted to die for five years, Sergei. Found that out about myself, had to be careful. Not fair to my crew to be so reckless. I'll go after Martin and—I'll go. But what does that do for us? If I do find them, I'll be as trapped as they are."

"Maybe. Maybe not." Stirner snorted. "Why you think we came out here, just to shake up a captain and maybe lose the Navy a cruiser? What made me think about this black hole business, I am questioning a transportee. Sentence to the labor market on Tanith, the charge is unauthorized scientific research. I look into all those crazies, might be something the Navy can use, ja? This one was fooling around with gravity waves, theories about black holes. Hard to see how the Navy could use it. I was for letting them take this one to Tanith when I start to think, we are losing those ships coming from Meiji, and click! So I pulled the prisoner off the colony ship."

"And he says he can get us home from a dark hole in blank space?" Ramsey asked. He tried to suppress the wave of excitement that began in his bowels and crept upward until he could hardly speak. Not hope! Hope was an agony, something to be dreaded. It was much easier to live with resignation. . . .

"Ja. Only is not a him. Is a her. Not very attractive her. She *says* she can do this." Stirner paused significantly.

"Miss Ward hates the CoDominium, Bart," Lermontov said carefully. "With what she thinks is good reason. She won't tell us how she plans to get the ship home."

"By God, she'll tell me!" Why can't anything be simple? To know Barbara Jean is dead, or to know what mountain to climb to save her. "If I can't think of something we can borrow a State Security man from the—"

"No." Lermontov's voice was a flat refusal. "Leave aside the ethics of the situation, we need this girl's creative energies. You can get that with brainscrubs."

"Maybe." And maybe I'll try it anyway if nothing else works. Barbara Jean, Barbara Jean . . . "Where is this uncooperative scientist?"

"On Ceres." Vice Admiral Lermontov stretched a long arm toward the bar and poured for everyone. Stirner swished his brandy appreciatively in a crystal snifter. "Understand something, Bart," the admiral said. "Miss Ward may not know a thing. She may hate us enough to destroy a CD ship even at the cost of her life. You're gambling on a theory we don't know exists and could be wrong even if she has one."

"So I'm gambling. My God, Sergei, do you know what I've been through these last years? It isn't normal for a man to brood like I do, you think I don't know that? That I don't know you whisper about it when I'm not around? Now you say there's a chance but it might cost my life. *You're* gambling a cruiser you can't spare, my ship is worth more to the Navy than I am."

Lermontov ignored Ramsey's evaluation, and Bart wished it had been challenged. But it was probably true, although the old Bart Ramsey was something else again, a man headed for the job Sergei held now.

"I am gambling a ship because if we do not get Martin Grant back in time for the appropriations hearings, I will lose more than a ship. We might lose half the fleet."

"Ja, ja," Stirner sighed. He shook his round head sadly, slowly, a big gesture. "It is not usual that one man may be so important, I do not believe in the indispensable-man theory myself. Yet, without

Senator Grant I do not see how we are getting the ships in time or even keeping what we have, and without those ships . . . but maybe it is too late anyway, maybe even with the Senator we cannot get the ships, or with the ships we can still do nothing when a planet full of people are determined to kill themselves."

"That's as it may be," Lermontov said. "But for now we need Senator Grant. I'll have the prisoner aboard *Daniel Webster* in four hours, Bart. You'll want to fill the tanks. Trim the crew down to minimum also. We must try this, but I do not really give very good odds on your coming home."

"STAND BY FOR JUMPOFF. Jump stations, man your Jump stations." The unemotional voice of the officer of the watch monotoned through steel corridors, showing no more excitement than he would have used to announce an off-watch solido show. It took years to train that voice into Navy officers, but it made them easier to understand in battle. "Man your jump stations."

Bart Ramsey looked up from his screens as First Lieutenant Trevor ushered Marie Ward onto the bridge. She was a round, dumpy woman, her skin a faint red color. Shoulder-length hair fell almost straight down to frame her face, but dark brown wisps poked out at improbable angles despite combings and hair ribbons. Her hands were big, as powerful as a man's, and the nails, chewed to the quick, were colorless. When he met her Ramsey had estimated her age in the midthirties and was surprised to learn she was only twenty-six.

"You may take the assistant helmsman's acceleration chair," Ramsey told her. He forced a smile. "We're about to make the Jump to Meiji." In his lonely ship. She'd been stripped down, empty stations all through her.

"Thank you, Captain." Marie sat and allowed Trevor to strap her in. The routine for jumpoff went on. As he listened to the reports, Ramsey realized Marie Ward was humming.

"What is that?" he asked. "Catchy tune."

"Sorry. It's an old nursery thing. 'The bear went over the mountain, the bear went over the mountain, the bear went over the mountain, to see what he could see.'"

"Oh. Well, we haven't seen anything yet."

"'The other side of the mountain, was all that he could see.' But it's the third verse that's interesting. 'He fell into a dark hole, and covered himself over with charcoal—'"

"Warning, warning, take your posts for jumpoff."

Ramsey examined his screens. His chair was surrounded by them. "All right, Trevor, make your search."

"Aye, aye, sir."

Lieutenant Trevor would be busy for a while. He had been assigned the job of looking after Marie Ward, but for the moment Ramsey would have to be polite to her. "You haven't told us much about what we're going to see on the other side of that mountain. Why?"

"Captain, if you knew everything I did, you wouldn't need to take me along," she said. "I wish they'd hurry up. I *don't* like star jumps."

"It won't be long now—" Just what do you say to a convict genius? The whole trip out she'd been in everybody's hair, seldom talking about anything but physics. She'd asked the ship's officers about the drive, astrogation, instruments, the guns, nearly everything. Sometimes she was humorous, but more often scathingly sarcastic. And she wouldn't say a word about black holes, except to smile knowingly. More and more Ramsey wished he'd borrowed a KGB man from the Soviets. . . .

"WARNING, WARNING. Jumpoff in one minute," the watch officer announced. Alarm bells sounded through the ship.

"Lined up, Captain," Trevor said. "For all I can tell, we're going straight through to 82 Eridani. If there's anything out there, I can't see it."

"Humph," Marie Ward snorted. "Why should you?"

"Yes, but if the Alderson path's intact, the hole won't have any effect on us," Trevor protested. "And to the best we can measure, that path is there."

"No, no," Marie insisted. "You don't measure the Alderson path at all! You only measure the force, Lieutenant. Then your computer deduces the existence of the path from the stellar geometry. I'd have thought they'd teach you that much anyway. And that you could remember it."

"FINAL WARNING. Ten seconds to jump." A series of chimes, descending in pitch. Marie grimaced. Her mannish hands clutched the chair arms as she braced herself. At the tenth tone everything blurred for an instant that stretched to a million years.

There is no way to record the time a Jump takes. The best chronological instruments record nothing whatever. Ships vanish into the state of nonbeing conveniently called "hyperspace" and reappear somewhere else. Yet it always *seems* to take forever, and while it happens everything in the universe is wrong, *wrong*, WRONG. . . .

Ramsey shook his head. The screens around his command seat remained blurred. "Jump completed. Check ship," he ordered. Crewmen moved fuzzily to obey despite the protests of tortured nerves. Electronic equipment, computers, nearly everything complex suffers from Jump induced transients although there is no known permanent effect.

"Captain, we're nowhere near Meiji!" the astrogator exclaimed. "I don't know where we are. . . ."

"Stand by to make orbit," Ramsey ordered.

"Around what?" Lieutenant Trevor asked. "There's no star out there, Captain. There's nothing!"

"Then we'll orbit nothing." Ramsey turned to Marie Ward. "Well, we've found the damn thing. You got any suggestions about locating it? I'd as soon not fall into it."

"Why not?" she asked. Ramsey was about to smile politely when he realized she was speaking seriously. "According to some theories, a black hole is a time/space gate. You could go into it and come out—somewhere else. In another century. Or another universe."

"Is that why the hell you brought us out here? To kill yourself testing some theory about black holes and space/time?"

"I am here because the CoDominium Marines put me aboard," she said. Her voice was carefully controlled. "And I have no desire to test any theory. Yet." She turned to Lieutenant Trevor. "Dave, is it really true? There's no star out there at all?"

"It's true enough."

She smiled. A broad, face-cracking smile that, with the thousand-meter stare in her eyes, made her look strangely happy. Insanely happy, in fact. "My god, it worked! There really is a black hole."

"Which we haven't found yet," Trevor reminded her.

"Oh. Yes. Let's see—it should have started as about five stellar masses in size. That's my favorite theory, anyway. When it began to collapse it would have radiated over eighty percent of its mass away. X rays, mostly. Lots of them. And if it had planets, they might still be here. . . . Anyway, it should be about as massive as Sol. There won't be any radiation coming out. X rays, light, nothing can climb out of that gravity well . . . just think of it, infinite red shift! It really happens!"

"Infinite red shift," Ramsey repeated carefully. "Yes, ma'am. Now, just how do we find this source of tired light?"

"It isn't tired light! That's a very obsolete theory. Next I suppose you'll tell me you think photons slow down when they lose energy."

"No, I—"

"Because they don't. They wouldn't *be* photons if they *could* slow down. They just lose energy until they vanish."

"Fine, but *how do we find it*?"

"It can't reach out and grab you, Captain," she said. The grin wasn't as wide as before, but still she smiled softly to herself. It made her look much better, although the mocking tones didn't help Ramsey's appreciation. "It's just a star, Captain. A very small star, very dense, as heavy as most other stars, but it doesn't have any more gravity than Sol. You could get quite close and still pull away—"

"If we knew which direction was away."

"Yes. Hm-m-m. It will bend light rays, but you'd have to be pretty close to see any effect at all from that. . . ."

"Astrogation!" Ramsey ordered crisply. "How do we find a star we can't see?"

"We're about dead in space relative to whatever stopped us," the astrogator told him. "We can wait until we accelerate toward it and get a vector from observation of other stars. That will take a while. Or we can see if it's left any planets, but with nothing to illuminate them they'll be hard to find—"

"Yeah. Do the best you can, mister." Marie Ward was still looking happily at the screens. They showed absolutely nothing. Ramsey punched another button in the arm of his command chair.

"Comm room, sir."

"Eyes, there are ships out there somewhere." God, I hope there are. Or one ship. "Find them and get me communications."

"Aye, aye, sir. I'll use the distress frequencies. They might be monitoring those."

"Right. And Eyes, see if your bright electronics and physics boys can think of a way to detect gravity. So far as I can make out that's the only effect that black hole has on the real universe."

"On *our* real universe. Imagine a universe in which there are particles with nonzero rest masses able to move faster than light. Where you get rid of energy to go faster. Sentient beings in that universe would think of it as real. It might even be where our ships go when they make an Alderson jump. And the black holes could be gates to get you there."

"Yes, Miss Ward," Ramsey said carefully. Two enlisted spacers on the other side of the bridge grinned knowingly at each other and waited for the explosion. They'd been waiting ever since Marie Ward came aboard, and it ought to be pretty interesting. But Ramsey's voice became even softer and more controlled. "Meanwhile, have you any useful suggestions on what we should do now?"

"Find the hole, of course. Your astrogator seems quite competent. His approach is very reasonable. Yes, quite competent. For a Navy man."

Carefully, his hands moving very slowly, Captain Bartholomew Ramsey unstrapped himself from his command chair and launched himself across the bridge to the exit port. "Take the con, Mister Trevor," he said. And left.

For fifty hours *Daniel Webster* searched for the other ships. Then, with no warning at all, Ramsey was caught in the grip of a giant vise.

For long seconds he felt as if titanic hands were squeezing him. They relaxed, ending the agony for a brief moment. And tried to pull him apart. The screens blurred, and he heard the sound of rending metal as the hands alternately crushed, then pulled.

Somehow the watch officer sounded General Quarters. Klaxons blared through the ship as she struggled with her invisible enemy. Ramsey screamed, as much in rage and frustration as pain, hardly knowing he had made a sound. He had to take control of his ship before she died, but there were no orders to give. This was no attack by an enemy, but what, what?

The battle-damage screen flared red. Ramsey was barely able to see as it showed a whole section of the ship's outer corridors evacuated to space. How many men were in there? Most wouldn't be in armor. My God! *Daniel Webster* too? My wife and now my ship?

Slowly it faded away. Ramsey pulled himself erect. Around him on the bridge the watch crew slumped at their stations. The klaxons continued, adding their confusion, until Ramsey shut them off.

"What—what was it?" Lieutenant Trevor gasped. His usually handsome features were contorted with remembered pain, and he looked afraid.

"All stations report damage," Ramsey ordered. "I don't know what it was, Lieutenant."

"I do!" Marie Ward gasped excitedly. Her eyes darted about in wonder. "I know! Gravity waves from the black hole! A tensor field! And these were tensor, not scalar—"

"Gravity waves?" Ramsey asked stupidly. "But gravity waves are weak things, only barely detectable."

Marie Ward snorted. "In your experience, Captain. And in mine. But according to one twentieth-century theory—they had lots of theories then, when intellectuals were free, Captain—according to one theory if a black hole is rotating and a mass enters the Schwarzschild Limit, part of the mass will be converted to gravity waves. They can escape from the hole and affect objects outside it. So can Alderson forces, I think. But they didn't know about the Alderson force then. . . ."

"But—is that going to happen again?" Ramsey demanded. Battle-damage reports appeared on his screens. "We can't live through much of that."

"I really don't know how often it will happen," Marie answered. She chewed nervously on her right thumbnail. "I do know one thing. We have a chance to get home again."

"Home?" Ramsey took a deep breath. That depended on what had been done to Danny Boy. A runner brought him another report. Much of the ship's internal communications were out, but the chief engineer was working with a damage-control party. Another screen came on, and Ramsey heard the bridge speaker squawk.

"Repairable damage to normal space drive in main engine room," the toneless voice said. "Alderson Drive appears unaffected.

"Gunnery reports damage to laser lenses in number one battery. No estimate of time to repair."

Big rigid objects had broken. Ramsey later calculated the actual displacement at less than a millimeter/meter; not very much, but enough to damage the ship and kill half a dozen crewmen unable to get into battle armor. Explosive decompression wasn't a pretty death, but it was quick.

With all her damage, *Daniel Webster* was only hurt. She could sail, his ship wasn't dead. Not yet. Ramsey gave orders to the damage-control parties. When he was sure they were doing everything they could he turned back to the dumpy girl in the assistant helmsman's seat.

"How do we get home?"

She had been scribbling on a pad of paper, but her pencil got away from her when she tried to set it down without using the clips set into the arm of the seat. Now she stared absently at her notes, a thin smile on her lips. "I'm sorry, Captain. What did you say?"

"I asked, how do we get home?"

"Oh." She tried to look serious but only succeeded in appearing sly. "I was hasty in saying that. I don't know."

"Sure. Don't you want to get home?"

"Of course, Captain. I'd just love to get back on a colony ship. I understand Tanith has such a wonderful climate."

"Come off it. The Navy doesn't forget people who've helped us. You aren't going to Tanith." He took a deep breath. "We have a rescue mission, Miss Ward. Some of those people have been out here for five years." Five years of that? Nobody could live through five years of that. O God, where is she? Crushed, torn apart, again and again, her body drifting out there in black space without even a star? Rest eternal grant them, O Lord, and let light perpetual shine upon them. . . .

"How do we get home?"

"I told you, I don't know."

But you do. And come to think of it, so do I. "Miss Ward, you implied that if we knew when a mass would enter the black hole, we could use the resulting Alderson forces to get us out of here."

"I'll be damned." She looked at Ramsey as if seeing him for the first time. "The man can actually—yes, of course." She smiled faintly. "I *thought* so before we left Ceres. Theory said that would work. . . ."

"But we'd have to know the timing rather precisely, wouldn't we?"

"Yes. Depending on the size of the mass. The larger it is, the longer the effect would last. I think. Maybe not, though."

Ramsey nodded to himself. There was only one possible mass whose entry into the hole they could predict. "Trevor."

"Sir?"

"One way you might amuse yourself is in thinking of ways to make a ship impact a solar mass not much more than two kilometers in diameter; a star you can't see and whose location you can't know precisely."

"Aye, aye, skipper." Dave Trevor frowned. He didn't often do that and it distorted his features. "Impact, Captain? But unless you were making corrections all the way in, you'd probably miss—as it is, the ship would pick up so much velocity that it's more likely to whip right around—"

"Exactly, Lieutenant. But it's the only way home."

One hundred and eight hours after breakout Chief Yeoman Karabian located the other ships. *Daniel Webster*'s call was answered by the first frigate sent out to find the Norton liner:

> DANIEL WEBSTER THIS IS HENRY HUDSON BREAK BREAK WE ARE IN ORBIT ELEVEN ASTRONOMICAL UNITS FROM WHATEVER THAT THING DOWN THERE IS STOP WE WILL SEND A CW SIGNAL TO GIVE YOU A BEARING STOP.
>
> THE NORTON LINER LORELEI AND CDSN CONSTELLATION ARE WITH US STOP YOUR SIGNAL INDICATES THAT YOU ARE LESS THAN ONE AU FROM THE DARK STAR STOP YOU ARE IN EXTREME DANGER REPEAT EXTREME DANGER STOP ADVISE YOU MOVE AWAY FROM DARK STAR IMMEDIATELY STOP THERE ARE STRONG GRAVITY FLUXES NEAR THE DARK STAR STOP THEY CAN TEAR YOU APART STOP ONE SCOUTSHIP ALREADY DESTROYED BY GRAVITY WAVES STOP REPEAT ADVISE YOU MOVE AWAY FROM DARK

STAR IMMEDIATELY AND HOME ON OUR CW SIGNAL STOP.

REQUEST FOLLOWING INFORMATION COLON WHO IS MASTER ABOARD DANIEL WEBSTER INTERROGATIVE BREAK BREAK MESSAGE ENDS.

Ramsey read the message on his central display screen, then punched the intercom buttons. "Chief, get this out:"

HENRY HUDSON THIS IS DANIEL WEBSTER BREAK BREAK CAPTAIN BARTHOLOMEW RAMSEY COMMANDING STOP WE WILL HOME ON YOUR BEACON STOP HAVE EXPERIENCED GRAVITY STORM ALREADY STOP SHIP DAMAGED BUT SPACEWORTHY STOP.

IS SENATOR MARTIN GRANT ABOARD CONSTELLATION INTERROGATIVE IS MRS RAMSEY THERE INTERROGATIVE BREAK BREAK MESSAGE ENDS.

The hundred-and-sixty-minute round trip for message and reply would be a lifetime.

"Trevor, get us moving when you've got that beacon," Ramsey ordered. "Pity he couldn't tell us about the gravity waves before we found out the hard way."

"Yeah." Pity indeed. But communications did all they could. Space is just too big for omni signals, and we had maser damage to boot. Had to send in narrow cones, lucky we made contact this soon even sweeping messages. And no ecliptic here either. Or none we know of.

"Communications here," Ramsey's speaker announced.

"Yes, Eyes."

"We're getting that homing signal. Shouldn't be any problem."

"Good." Ramsey studied the figures that flowed across his screen. "Take the con, Mister Trevor. And call me when there's an answer from *Henry Hudson*. I'll wait in my patrol cabin." And a damn long wait that's going to be. Barbara Jean, Barbara Jean, are you out there?

The hundred and sixty minutes went past. Then another hour, and another. It was nearly six hours before there was a message from the derelicts; and it was in code the Navy used for eyes of commanding officers only.

Captain Ramsey sat in his bare room and stared at the message flimsy. In spite of the block letters from the coding printer his eyes wouldn't focus on the words.

DANIEL WEBSTER THIS IS HENRY HUDSON BREAK BREAK FOLLOWING IS PERSONAL MESSAGE FOR CAPTAIN BARTHOLOMEW RAMSEY FROM GRAND SENATOR MARTIN GRANT BREAK BREAK PERSONAL MESSAGE BEGINS

BART WE ARE HERE AND ALIVE STOP THE SCOUTSHIP WAS LOST TO GRAVITY WAVES STOP THE LINER LORELEI THE FRIGATE HENRY HUDSON AND THE FRIGATE CONSTELLATION ARE DAMAGED STOP LORELEI IN SPACEWORTHY CONDITION WITH MOST OF CREW SURVIVING DUE TO HEROIC EFFORTS OF MASTER OF HENRY HUDSON STOP

BOTH BARBARA JEAN AND HAROLD ARE WELL STOP REGRET TO INFORM YOU THAT BARBARA JEAN MARRIED COMMANDER JAMES HARRIMAN OF HENRY HUDSON THREE YEARS AGO STOP BREAK BREAK END PERSONAL MESSAGE BREAK BREAK MESSAGE ENDS.

Ramsey automatically reached for a drink, then angrily tossed the glass against the bare steel wall. It wouldn't be fair to the crew. Or to his ship. And *Daniel Webster* was still the only wife he had.

The intercom buzzed. "Bridge, Captain."

"Go ahead, Trevor."

"Two hundred eighty plus hours to rendezvous. Captain. We're on course."

"Thank you." Damn long hours those are going to be. How could she—but that's simple. For all Barbara Jean could know she and the boy were trapped out here forever. I can bet there were plenty of suicides on those ships. And the boy would be growing up without a father.

Not that I was so much of one. Half the time I was out on patrol anyway. But I was home when he caught pneumonia from going with us to Ogden Base. Harold just had to play in that snow. . . .

He smiled in remembrance. They'd built a snowman together. But Harold wasn't used to Earth gravity, and that more than the cold weakened him. The boy never did put in enough time in the centrifuge on Luna Base. Navy kids grew up on the Moon because the Navy was safe only among its own. . . .

Ramsey made a wry face. Hundreds of Navy kids crowding into the big centrifuge . . . they were hard to control, and Barbara Jean like most mothers hated to take her turn minding them. She needed a hairdo. Or had to go shopping. Or something. . . .

She should have remarried. Of course she should. He pictured Barbara Jean with another man. What did she say to him when they made love? Did she use the same words? Like our first time, when we—oh, damn.

He fought against the black mood. Harriman. James Harriman. Fleet spatball champ seven years ago. A good man. Tough. Younger than Barbara Jean. Harriman used to be a real comer before he vanished. Never married and the girls at Luna Base forever trying to get—never married until now.

Stop it! Would you rather she was dead? The thought crept through unwanted. If you would, you'll goddammit not admit it, you swine. Not now and not ever.

She's alive! Bart Ramsey, you remember that and forget the rest of it. Barbara Jean is alive!

Savagely he punched the intercom buttons.

"Bridge. Aye, aye, Captain."

"We on course, mister?"

"Yes, sir."

"Damage-control parties working?"

"Yes, sir." Trevor's voice was puzzled. He was a good first lieutenant, and it wasn't like Ramsey to ride him.

"Excellent." Ramsey slapped the off button, waited a moment, and reached for another whiskey. This time he drank it. And waited.

There was little communication as *Daniel Webster* accelerated, turned over, and slowed again to approach the derelicts. Messages took energy, and they'd need it all. To get out, or to survive if Marie Ward proved wrong with her theories. Someday there'd be a better theory. Lermontov might come up with something, and even now old Stirner would be examining ancient records at Stanford and Harvard. If Ward was wrong, they still had to survive. . . .

"Getting them on visual now," the comm officer reported. The unemotional voice broke. "Good God, Captain!"

Ramsey stared at the screens. The derelicts were worse than he could have imagined. *Lorelei* was battered, although she seemed intact, but the other ships seemed bent. The frigate *Constellation* was a wreck, with gaping holes in her hull structure. *Henry Hudson* was crumpled, almost unrecognizable. The survivors must all be on the Norton liner.

Ramsey watched in horror as the images grew on the screens. Five years, with all hope going, gone. Harriman must be one hell of a man to keep anyone alive through that.

When they were alongside Navy routine carried Ramsey through hours that were lifetimes. Like one long continuous Jump. Everything wrong.

Spacers took *Daniel Webster*'s cutter across to *Lorelei* and docked. After another eternity she lifted away with passengers. CDSN officers, one of the merchant service survivors from *Lorelei*—and the others. Senator Grant. Johnny Grant. Commander Harriman. Barbara Jean, Harold—and Jeanette Harriman, age three.

"I'll be in my cabin, Trevor."

"Yes, sir."

"And get some spin on the ship as soon as that boat's fast aboard."

"Aye, aye, sir."

Ramsey waited. Who would come? It was his ship, he could send for anyone he liked. Instead he waited. Let Barbara Jean make up her own mind. Would she come? And would Harriman be with her?

Five years. Too long, he's had her for five years. But we had ten years together before that. Damned if I don't feel like a middie on his first prom.

He was almost able to laugh at that.

The door opened and she came in. There was no one with her, but he heard voices in the corridor outside. She stood nervously at the bulkhead, staring around the bare cabin, at the empty desk and blank steel walls.

Her hair's gone. The lovely black hair that she never cut, whacked off short and tangled—God, you're beautiful. Why can't I say that? Why can't I say anything?

She wore shapeless coveralls, once white, but now grimy, and her hands showed ground-in dirt and grease. They'd had to conserve water, and there was little soap. Five years is a long time to maintain a closed ecology.

"No pictures, Bart? Not even one of me?"

"I—I thought you were dead." He stood, and in the small cabin they were very close. "There wasn't anybody else to keep a picture of."

Her tightly kept smile faded. "I—I would have waited, Bart. But we were dead. I don't even know why we tried to stay alive. Jim drove everybody, he kept us going, and then—he needed help."

Ramsey nodded, it was going to be all right. Wasn't it? He moved closer and put his hands on her shoulders, pulling her to him. She responded woodenly, then broke away. "Give me—give me a little time to get used to it, Bart."

He backed away from her. "Yeah. The rest of you can come in now," he called.

"Bart, I didn't mean—"

"It's all right, Barbara Jean. We'll work it out." Somehow.

The boy came in first. He was very hesitant. Harold didn't look so very different. He still had a round face, a bit too plump. But he was *big*. And he was leading a little girl, a girl with dark hair and big round eyes, her mother's eyes.

Harold stood for a long moment. "Sir—ah," he began formally, but then he let go of the girl and rushed to his father. "Daddy! I knew you'd come get us, I told them you'd come!" He was tall enough that his head reached Bart's shoulder, and his arms went all the way around him.

Finally he broke away. "Dad, this is my little sister." He said it defiantly, searchingly, watching his father's face. Finally he smiled. "She's a nuisance sometimes, but she grows on you."

"I'm sure she does," Ramsey said. It was very still in the bare cabin. Ramsey wanted to say something else, but he had trouble with his voice.

*Daniel Webster*'s wardroom was crowded. There was barely room at the long steel table for all the surviving astrogation officers to sit with Ramsey, Senator Grant, and Marie Ward. They waited tensely.

The senator was thinner than Ramsey had ever seen him despite the short time he'd been marooned. *Constellation* had been hit hard by a gravity storm—it was easier to think of them that way, although the term was a little silly. Now the senator's hands rested lightly on the wardroom table, the tips of the fingers just interlocked, motionless. Like everyone else Senator Grant watched Commander Harriman.

Harriman paced nervously. He had grown a neatly trimmed beard, brown, with both silver and red hairs woven through it. His uniform had been patched a dozen times, but it was still the uniform of the service, and Harriman wore it proudly. There was no doubt of who had been in command.

"The only ship spaceworthy is *Lorelei*," Harriman reported. "*Henry Hudson* was gutted to keep *Lorelei* livable, and Johnny Grant's *Constellation* took it hard in the gravity storms before we could get him out far enough from that thing."

Senator Grant sighed loudly. "I hope never to have to live through anything like that again. Even out this far you can feel the gravity waves, although it's not dangerous. But in close, before we knew where to go . . ."

"But *Lorelei* can space?" Ramsey asked. Harriman nodded. "Then *Lorelei* it'll have to be. Miss Ward, explain what it takes to get home again."

"Well, I'm not sure, Captain. I think we should wait."

"We can't wait. I realize you want to stay out here and look at the black hole until doomsday, but these people want to go home. Not to mention my orders from Lermontov."

Reluctantly she explained her theory, protesting all the while that they really ought to make a better study. "And the timing will have to be perfect," she finished. "The ship must be at the jumpoff point and turn on the drive at just the right time."

"Throw a big mass down the hole," Harriman said. "Well, there's only the one mass to throw. *Lorelei.*" He stopped pacing for a moment and looked thoughtful. "And that means somebody has to ride her in."

"Gentlemen?" Ramsey looked around the table. One by one the astrogation officers nodded mutely. Trevor, seeing his captain's face, paused for a long second before he also nodded agreement.

"There's no way to be sure of a hit if we send her in on automatic," Trevor said. "We can't locate the thing close enough from out here. We can't send *Lorelei* on remote, either. The time lag's too long."

"Couldn't you build some kind of homing device?" Senator Grant asked. His voice was carefully controlled, and it compelled attention. In the Grand Senate, Martin Grant's speeches were worth listening to, although senators usually voted from politics anyway.

"What would you home on?" Marie asked caustically. "There's nothing to detect. In close enough you should see bending light rays, but I'm not sure. I'm just not sure of anything, but I know we couldn't build a homing device."

"Could we wait for a gravity storm and fly out on that?" Trevor asked. "If we were ready for it, we could make the Jump. . . ."

"Nonsense," Harriman snapped. "Give me credit for a little sense, Lieutenant. We tried that. I didn't know what we were up against, but I figured those were gravity waves after they'd nearly wrecked my ships. Where there's gravity there may be Alderson forces. But you can't predict the damn gravity storms. We get one every thousand hours, sometimes close together, sometimes a long time apart, but about a thousand-hour average. How can you be in a position for a Jump when you don't know it's coming? And the damn gravity waves do things to the drives."

"Every thousand hours!" Marie demanded excitedly. "But that's impossible! What could cause that—so much matter! Commander Harriman, have you observed asteroids in this system?"

"Yeah. There's a whole beehive of them, all in close to the dark star. Thousands and thousands of them, it looks like. But they're *really* close, it's a swarm in a thick plane, a ring about ten kilometers thick. It's hard to observe anything, though. They move so fast, and if you get in close the gravity storms kill you. From out here we don't see much."

"A ring—are they large bodies?" Marie asked. Her eyes shone.

Harriman shrugged. "We've bounced radar off them and we deduce they're anywhere from a few millimeters to maybe a full kilometer in diameter, but it's hard to tell. There's nothing stable about the system, either."

Marie chewed both thumbnails. "There wouldn't be," she said. She began so softly that it was difficult to hear her. "There wouldn't be if chunks keep falling into the hole. Ha! We won't be able to use the asteroids to give a position on the black hole. Even if you had better observations, the hole is rotating. There must be enormous gravitational anomalies."

Harriman shrugged again, this time helplessly. "You understand, all we ever really observed was some bending light and a fuzzy occupation of stars. We deduced there was a dark star, but there was nothing in our data banks about them. Even if we'd known what a black hole was, I don't know how much good it would have done. I burned out the last of the Alderson Drives three years ago trying to ride out. We were never in the right position. . . . I was going to patch up *Constellation* and have another stab at it."

Just like that, Ramsey thought. Just go out and patch up that wreck of a ship. How many people would even try, much less be sure they could . . . so three years ago they'd lost their last hope of getting out of there. And after that, Barbara Jean had . . .

"Did you ever try throwing something down the hole yourself?" Trevor asked.

"No. Until today we had no idea what we were up against. I still don't, but I'll take your word for it." Harriman drew in a deep breath and stopped pacing. "I'll take *Lorelei* down."

Bart looked past Harriman to a painting on the wardroom bulkhead. Trevor had liked it and hung it there long ago. John Paul Jones strode across the blazing decks of his flagship. Tattered banners blew through sagging rigging, blood ran in the scuppers, but Jones held his old cutlass aloft.

Well, why not? Somebody's got to do it, why not Harriman? But—but what will Barbara Jean think?

"I want to go too." Marie Ward spoke softly, but everyone turned to look at her. "I'll come with you, Commander Harriman."

"Don't be ridiculous," Harriman snapped.

"Ridiculous? What's ridiculous about it? This is an irreplaceable opportunity. We can't leave the only chance we'll ever have to study black holes to an amateur. There is certainly nothing ridiculous about a trained observer going." Her voice softened. "Besides, you'll be too busy with the ship to take decent observations."

"Miss Ward." Harriman compelled attention although it was difficult to say exactly why. Even though Ramsey was senior officer present, Harriman seemed to dominate the meeting. "Miss Ward, we practically rebuilt *Lorelei* over the past five years. I doubt if anyone else could handle her, so I've got to go. But just why do you want to?"

"Oh—" The arrogant tone left her voice. "Because this is my one chance to do something important. Just what am I? I'm not pretty." She paused, as if she hoped someone would disagree, but there was only silence.

"And no one ever took me seriously as an intellectual. I've no accomplishments at all. No publications. Nothing. But as the only person ever to study a black hole, I'll be recognized!"

"You've missed a point." Ramsey spoke quickly before anyone else could jump in. His voice was sympathetic and concerned. "We take you seriously. Admiral Lermontov took you so seriously he sent this cruiser out here. And you're our only expert on black holes. If Commander Harriman's attempt fails or for any other reason we don't get out of this system on this try, you'll have to think of something else for us."

"But—"

Harriman clucked his tongue impatiently. "Will *Lorelei* be mass enough, Miss Ward?"

"I don't know," she answered softly, but when they all stared at her she pouted defensively. "Well, I don't! How could I! There should be more than enough energy but I don't *know!*" Her voice rose higher. "If you people hadn't suppressed everything we'd have more information. But I've had to work all by myself, and I—"

Dave Trevor put his hand gently on her arm. "It'll be all right. You haven't been wrong yet."

"Haven't I?"

Senator Grant cleared his throat. "This isn't getting us anywhere at all. We have only one ship capable of sailing down to that hole and only one theory of how to get away from here. We'll just have to try it."

There was a long silence before Bart spoke. "You sure you want to do this, Commander?" Ramsey cursed himself for the relief he felt, knowing what Harriman's answer would be.

"I'll do it, Captain. Who else could? Let's get started."

Ramsey nodded. "If 'twere done, 'twere best done quickly . . ."—what was that from? Shakespeare? "Mister Trevor, take an engineering crew over to *Lorelei* and start making her ready. Get all the ship's logs too."

"Logs!" Marie smiled excitedly. "Dave, I want to see those as soon as possible."

As Trevor nodded agreement, Ramsey waved dismissal to the officers. "Commander Harriman, if you'd stay just a moment . . ."

The wardroom emptied. There was a burst of chatter as the others left. Their talk was too spirited, betraying their relief. *They* didn't have to take *Lorelei* into a black hole. Ramsey and Harriman sat for what seemed like a long time.

"Is there something I can say?" Ramsey asked.

"No. I'd fight you for her if there wasn't a way home. But if there's any chance at all—you'll take care of Jeanette, of course." Harriman looked at the battered mug on the table, then reached for the coffee pot. After years in space he didn't notice the strange angle the liquid made as it flowed into the cup under spin gravity. "That's fine coffee, Captain. We ran out, must be three, four years ago. You get to miss coffee after a while."

"Yeah." What the Hell can I say to him? Do I thank him for not making me order him to take that ship in? He really is the only one who could do it, and we both knew that. Unwanted, the image of Barbara Jean in this man's arms came to him. Ramsey grimaced savagely. "Look, Harriman; there's got to be some way we can—"

"There isn't and we both know it, Sir. Even if there were, what good would it do? We can't both go back with her."

And I'm glad it's me who's going home, Ramsey thought. Hah. The first time in five years I've cared about staying alive. But will she ever really be mine again?

Was that all that was wrong with me?

"Your inertial navigation gear working all right?" Harriman asked. "Got an intact telescope?"

"Eh? Yeah, sure."

"You shouldn't have too much trouble finding the jumpoff point, then."

"I don't expect any." Marie Ward's ridiculous song came back to him. "He fell into a dark hole, and covered himself over with charcoal, he went back over the mountain—" But Harriman wouldn't be going back over the mountain. Or would he? What was a black hole, anyway? Could it really be a time tunnel?

Harriman poured more coffee. "I better get over to *Lorelei* myself. Can you spare a pound of coffee?"

"Sure."

Harriman stood. He drained the mug. "Don't see much point in coming back to *Daniel Webster* in that case. Your people can plot me a course and send it aboard *Lorelei*." He flexed his fingers as if seeing them for the first time, then brushed imaginary lint from his patched uniform. "Yeah. I'll go with the cutter. Now."

"Now? But don't you want to—"

"No, I think not. What would I say?" Harriman very carefully put the coffee mug into the table rack. "Tell her I loved her, will you? And be sure to send that coffee over. Funny the things you can get to miss in five years."

DANIEL WEBSTER THIS IS LORELEI BREAK BREAK TELL TREVOR HIS COURSE WAS FINE STOP I APPEAR TO BE ONE HALF MILLION KILOMETERS FROM THE BLACK HOLE WITH NO OBSERVABLE ORBITAL VELOCITY STOP WILL PROCEED AT POINT 1G FROM HERE STOP STILL CANNOT SEE THAT BEEHIVE AT ALL STOP NOTHING TO OBSERVE IN BEST CALCULATED POSITION OF BLACK HOLE STOP TELL MARIE WARD SHE IS NOT MISSING A THING STOP BREAK BREAK MESSAGE ENDS.

Barbara Jean and her father sat in Captain Ramsey's cabin. Despite the luxury of a shower she didn't feel clean. She read the message flimsy her father handed her.

"I ought to say something to him, hadn't I? Shouldn't I? Dad, I can't just let him die like this."

"Leave him alone, kitten," Senator Grant told her. "He's got enough to do, working that half-dead ship by himself. And he has to work fast. One of those gravity storms while he's this close and—" Grant shuddered involuntarily.

"But—God, I've made a mess of things, haven't I?"

"How? Would you rather it was Bart taking that ship in there?"

"No. No, no, no! But I still—wasn't there any other way, Daddy? Did somebody *really* have to do it?"

"As far as I can tell, Barbara Jean. I was there when Jim volunteered. Bart tried to talk him out of it, you know."

She didn't say anything.

"You're right, of course," Grant sighed. "He didn't try very hard. There wasn't any point in it anyway. Commander Harriman was the obvious man to do it. You didn't enter the decision at all."

"I wish I could believe that."

"Yes. So does your husband. But it's still true. Are you coming down to the bridge? I don't think it's a good idea but you can."

"No. You go on, though. I have to take care of Jeanette. Bill Hartley has her in the sick bay. Daddy, what am I going to do?"

"You're going to go home with your husband and be an admiral's lady. For a while, anyway. And when there aren't any admirals because there isn't any fleet, God knows what you'll do. Make the best of it like all the rest of us, I guess."

The bridge was a blur of activity as they waited for *Lorelei* to approach the black hole. As the minutes ticked off, tension grew. A gravity storm just now would wipe out their only chance.

Finally Ramsey spoke. "You can get the spin off the ship, Mister Trevor. Put the crew to Jump stations."

"Aye, aye, sir."

"Can we talk to Harriman still?" Senator Grant asked.

Ramsey's eyes flicked to the screens, past the predicted time of impact to the others, taking in every detail. "No." He continued to look at the data pouring across the screens. Their position had to be right. Everything had to be right, they'd get only the one chance at best. . . . "Not to get an answer. You could get a message to *Lorelei* but before we'd hear a reply it'll be all over."

Grant looked relieved. "I guess not, then."

"Damnedest thing." Harriman's voice was loud over the bridge speaker. "Star was occulted by the hole. Made a bright ring in space.

Real bright. Just hanging there, never saw anything like it."

"Nobody else ever will," Marie Ward said quietly. "Or will they? Can the Navy send more ships out here to study it? Oh, I wish I could *see!*"

They waited forever until Harriman spoke again. "Got a good position fix," they heard. "Looks good, Ramsey, damn good."

"Stand by for jumpoff," Bart ordered. Alarm bells rang through *Daniel Webster*.

"Another bright ring. Must be getting close."

"What's happening to his voice?" Senator Grant demanded.

"Time differential," Marie Ward answered. "His ship is accelerating to a significant fraction of light velocity. Time is slowing down for him relative to us."

"Looks good for Jump here, skipper," Trevor announced.

"Right." Bart inspected his screens again. The predicted time to impact ticked off inexorably, but it was only a prediction. Without a more exact location of the hole it couldn't be perfect. As Ramsey watched, the ship's computers updated the prediction from Harriman's signals.

Ramsey fingered the keys on his console. The Alderson Drive generators could be kept on for less than a minute in normal space, but if they weren't on when *Lorelei* hit . . . he pressed the key. *Daniel Webster* shuddered as the ship's fusion engines went to full power, consuming hydrogen and thorium catalyst at a prodigal rate, pouring out energy into the drive where it—vanished.

Into hyperspace, if that was a real place. Or on the other side of the Lepton Barrier. Maybe to where you went when you fell through a black hole if there was anything to that theory. Marie Ward had been fascinated by it and had seen nothing to make her give it up.

Wherever the energy went, it left the measurable universe. But not all of it. The efficiency wasn't that good. The drive generators screamed. . . .

"There's another bright ring. Quite a sight. Best damn view in the universe." The time distortion was quite noticeable now. Time to impact loomed big on Ramsey's screens, seconds to go.

Marie Ward hummed her nursery rhyme. Unwanted, the words rang through Ramsey's head. "He fell into a dark hole—" The time to impact clicked off to zero. Nothing happened.

"Ramsey, you lucky bastard," the speaker said. "Did you know she kept your damned picture the whole time? The whole bloody time, Ramsey. Tell her—"

The bridge blurred. There was a twisted, intolerable, eternal instant of agony. And confusion. Ramsey shook his head. The screens remained blurred.

"We—we're in the 82 Eridani system, skipper!" Trevor shouted. "We—hot damn, we made it!"

Ramsey cut him off. "Jump completed. Check ship."

"It worked," Marie Ward said. Her voice was low, quiet, almost dazed. "It really worked." She grinned at Dave Trevor, who grinned back. "Dave, it worked! There are black holes, and they do bend light, and they can generate Alderson forces, and I'm the first person to ever study one! Oh!" Her face fell.

"What's wrong?" Trevor asked quickly.

"I can't publish." She pouted. That was what had got her in trouble in the first place. The CoDominium couldn't keep people from thinking. *Die Gedanken, Sie sind frei*. But CDI could ruthlessly suppress books and letters and arrest everyone who tried to tell others about their unlicensed speculations.

"I can arrange something," Senator Grant told her. "After all, you're *the* expert on black holes. We'll see that you get a chance to study them for the fleet." He sighed and tapped the arm of his acceleration chair, then whacked it hard with his open palm. "I don't know. Maybe the CoDominium Treaty wasn't such a good idea. We got peace, but—you know, all we ever wanted to do was keep national forces from getting new weapons. Just suppress military technology. But that turned out to be nearly everything. And did we really get peace?"

"We'll need a course, Mister Trevor," Ramsey growled. "This is still a Navy ship. I want the fastest route home."

Home. Sol System, and the house in Luna Base compound. It's still there. And I'll leave you, *Daniel Webster*, but I'll miss you, old girl, old boy, whatever you are. I'll miss you, but I can leave you.

Or can I? Barbara Jean, are you mine now? Some of you will always belong to Jim Harriman. Five goddam years that man kept his crew and passengers alive, five years when there wasn't a shred of hope they'd get home again. She'll never forget him.

And that's unworthy, Bart Ramsey. Neither one of us ought to forget him.

"But I still wonder," Marie Ward said. Her voice was very low and quiet, plaintive in tone. "I don't suppose I'll ever know."

"Know what?" Ramsey asked. It wasn't hard to be polite to her now.

"It's the song." She hummed her nursery rhyme. "What did he really see on the other side of the mountain?"

# THE SECRET OF BLACK SHIP ISLAND

**by Larry Niven, Jerry Pournelle and Steven Barnes**

## Editor's Introduction

I've always thought that *Legacy of Heorot* was one of Jerry and Larry's best books, in many ways almost as good as *Lucifer's Hammer* and *The Mote In God's Eye*. This was also the first book where they brought in a third party, in this case Steven Barnes who I suspect did a lot of the legwork.

For me personally, it's a special treat because of one of the main characters: Cadmann Weyland is Jerry down to a T. Cadmann is not the first time Jerry wrote himself as a character in one of his books; Preston Sanders in *Oath of Fealty* shares a lot of Jerry's opinions and character, and—as Alex Pournelle reminded me—Colonel Nathan MacKinnie from *King David's Spaceship* is a younger version of Jerry.

For those of you who haven't read *Legacy of Heorot* and its sequels, the story concerns a group of Earth's best, both physically and mentally, who volunteer to travel a hundred-year journey in a generation ship, sponsored by National Geographic, to a new planet circling Tau Ceti. The expedition is successful, but when they arrive and are reanimated many of them find that their brains have suffered damage from ice forming while under meta-sleep—"ice on the brain" they call it. For some it's just a few forgotten memories, others are reduced to imbecility.

❁❁❁

**UNBEKNOWNST TO ME,** Jerry had a personal insight into their problem. One day after lunch, I remember him pensively walking through my office on his way upstairs. "Anything wrong?" I asked.

He shook his head. "I've been working on the new Grendel book with Larry, and it got me to thinking."

Jerry rarely confided personal information to me, or anyone else to my knowledge, but he'd piqued my curiosity, so I asked, "What about?"

"Ice on the brain." He went on to explain he was writing about the memory problems the Avalon colonists were facing after emerging from meta-sleep and how their brains were clouded by ice. He ended with: "It reminds me of my own memory problems."

That was a shock; as far as I knew, from talking with him and hearing him recite long poems from memory and complete passages from classic military and history tomes, I thought Jerry's recall was far superior to almost anyone I'd ever known. In fact, I'd only known one other person—John D. Sutherland, my medieval history prof, who'd also had an eidetic memory. Dr. Sutherland could recite from memory long passages of Medieval Latin taken from obscure Church writings he'd read while studying in different monasteries in Italy. Then, on a dime, he could translate them and quote them in English. It was an impressive feat, which I observed a number of times.

I knew Jerry's educational history: he'd grown up in rural Tennessee and spent his first seven or eight years in a one-room schoolhouse. Bored to death, he started reading the entire *Encyclopedia Britannica* to keep from going mad. Later, he'd been sent to the Christian Brothers High School in Memphis—after an experiment with homemade TNT went awry—where he found a home for his gifts. On more than one occasion, he mentioned how they'd changed his life and opened many doors. He generously donated funds to them on a monthly basis for most of the time I worked with him.

After his service in the Korean War, Jerry used his GI Bill benefits to attend the University of Nebraska—later transferring to the University of Washington in Seattle. Perfect recall would explain his numerous educational degrees and achievements in multiple subjects: systems engineering, psychology, political science, etc.

"Memory problems!" I said in surprise.

Jerry nodded. "Up until my late twenties, I had perfect recall of everything I'd ever read. It's not uncommon for people with perfect memories to lose them late in childhood or a decade later."

News to me.

He shook his head. "What they don't tell you is how frustrating it is to not be able to recall information that used to at your fingertips! Writing this book just brings it all back."

Jerry not only had a Ph.D. in psychology, but I knew that for a short time he had a small counseling practice. Jerry had no patience for your garden-variety neurotic. Instead, Jerry counseled bright adolescents who were bored in school—like he had been—and were acting out and headed for trouble. Jerry had this to say in a September 29, 2016, post on his Chaos Manor site:

"I once had a psychology practice in association with a leading pediatrician; I only took cases of bright children who were not doing well in school. I tended to teach them self-discipline, and give them interesting things to do and read, and was successful in those cases. It was a lucrative but time-consuming practice and I gave it up."

When I read the galleys to *Legacy of Heorot*—Jerry always had me proofread his book galleys, so I got to read them long before they were published, another perk of my job—I quickly realized that the character, Cadmann Weyland, was not only Jerry's creation, but heavily modeled after him.

## CHAPTER ONE: THE STARBORN

In the constellation Cetus, so distant that Earthlight requires almost twelve years to make the voyage, burns a medium-sized star named Tau Ceti. Three-quarters the mass of Sol, it is a stable and nurturing orb, providing light and warmth to its seven children. Of the seven major planets surrounding the star, Tau Ceti IV is the only one known to support life in all its splendor and infinite variety.

Tau Ceti IV attracted children of Earth. Evidence of this is to be found in the starship *Geographic*, now orbiting Tau Ceti IV, its depleted deuterium snowball fuel-sack shrunken to little more than a husk. The meta-sleepers who once occupied it for more than a century during its journey at ten percent of lightspeed have long since descended to the planet's surface. The embryonic animals frozen in storage for their use have almost all descended as well. Fewer than ten percent still remain.

Life remains aboard *Geographic*, but it is no longer biological life. The supercomputer known as Cassandra still lives, communicating with her children below whenever needed, although their smaller computational units satisfy all but the most complex requirements.

The human beings who traveled here from Earth have had critical needs indeed. Some of their brains have been clouded by ice crystals from imperfect meta-sleep, damaging their minds in ways both subtle and profound.

Still, they conquered this planet, or strove to until the world fought back, doing all in its power to wipe them from its face. When humans became part of the ecological cycle, they disrupted that of a local life form. Pseudo-reptilian creatures they called grendels rose against them in vast numbers, fueled by terrible hunger and buoyed by speed and ferocity beyond human experience.

Humans survived that too, and to the degree possible for such frail and flawed creatures, gained wisdom.

They bore and raised their children, both through their bodies and by decanting embryos, whose plasticity weathered the rigors of frozen sleep far better than had the adults who cared for them. And in this new world, terrible but partially tamed, those children grew.

Wisely, humans decided not to attempt immediate domination of the entire planet, confining the first generation's encampment and exploration to the island they called Avalon, founding the colony named Camelot. Camelot was inland, near Avalon's northern tip. On Avalon's western coast, along a strip of beach between jungle-covered mountains and the eternal rolling surf, some of their children, the Starborn, gathered to create their own society, not in rejection of their parents but in acceptance of the inevitable fact that this was *their* planet. That in time they would inherit it, and that that inheritance was accompanied by the responsibility to find their own peace with the ways and rhythms of this new world.

And they called this colony Surf's Up. And it was good.

Night had shadowed the bamboo huts and scattered fire pits comprising Surf's Up. Even at a distance, wafting music and laughter warmed the ear. The children of Avalon were the very best Earth's cultures and genetics had to offer: strong, intelligent, almost fearless, blessed with everything a twenty-second century technology could offer, even when simplified to make such an extreme, one-way pilgrimage.

While the days required labor, and all shared in the duties of life, the nights were for revelry, and adventure, and love. In a place where there was no disease, and every child was welcomed, civilization coexisted with animal appetites so strong and basic that their expression was all but mandatory. The children, dozens of them, openly touched and caressed, but also sang and danced, argued and debated, explored and mapped their world, and dreamed of the time when their parents would give them leave to leave this womb and travel across the sea to the main continent, that mankind might continue its march of colonization and conquest.

The waves rolled black against the shore, as they had since long before the men of Earth had dreamed of visiting Tau Ceti IV, or any planet, or indeed had even known that other worlds existed at all. Black, but silver-crested by the light of twin moons, the waves beckoned the children, who were engaging in an ancient and rowdy earthly sport known as Night Surfing: paddling out onto the calm water, belly to board, lighting torches and then awaiting the swell. Rising to their feet with firebrands in hand and then riding those boards in toward the shore. Their torches added depth and shadow to the rolling waves, another small way of declaring mastery of the elements.

Five surfers rode the waves just north of the main protected, artificial cove directly abutting their little clutch of huts. On the beach, their friends cheered them on with equal enthusiasm whether an aspirant rode those waves all the way to the shallows, or was pitched off halfway down the tube.

Happy children, alien skies.

Three surfers had made one hell of a run, balanced on their foamed plastic boards, poised to perfection while balancing a torch in one hand with the other arm spread as much for visual effect as balance.

Leading the way was a fifteen-year-old boy named Aaron Tragon. He was perfect in limb and aspect, golden curls plastered to his forehead, a leader as much by charisma as by surfing or any other sport or skill. Two others challenged him for lead and elegance of form. Close behind him, but not too close, was Willow Wozniac, a tomboy just now exploding into glorious young womanhood. Behind her rode Archie Drell, who could easily have been mistaken for a younger, shorter version of Aaron.

The crowd gathered on the sand applauded as the three of them finished their ride. Archie lost his balance and spilled over into the surf. Willow and Aaron completed the game unscathed, their torches still burning bright.

Aaron whooped as if he had just won a world championship—and perhaps he had, as there was no one on Avalon skilled enough to challenge him. He whipped his lean muscular arm up and out and the torch arched up into the air, peaked, fell down into the ocean with an inaudible hiss and *pop*.

"What a ride!" he howled, collecting hugs from the girls, backslaps from the guys, and a wet salty kiss from Willow as she splashed ashore. After kissing, they planted their boards tail-first in the sand.

The boards themselves were constructed of brightly painted, almost indestructible foamed plastic. Aaron's resembled a phoenix with tongues of red flame, blue talons, and white wings. The underside of Willow's board resembled a smiling dolphin, one of the creatures that had accompanied humanity from Earth, although as yet the aquatic mammals had not been allowed out of the artificial bay.

This was not cruelty, or the urge to control. It was simple common sense. There were deadly creatures upon the land, and while those had been mastered at great cost, there were others in the oceans larger even than the land beasts. A whale-sized predator called the goliath was the central reason dolphins had yet to be released: It would be no kindness at all to set loose the gentle mammals into such a hostile world, at least until better understood, and perhaps until there was enough of a pod for them to support each other in battle.

The bottom of the third board was more . . . unusual. More arresting. It portrayed a creature with a body similar to an alligator or a Komodo dragon, with oversized jaws and a stubby spiked tail. While stylized, it was not depicted with the phoenix's bright palette. Muted grays and browns, reminiscent of the more realistic colors composing Willow's dolphin. There was something about the jaws, and the eyes, and the shape of the claws . . . though they never lost their smiles, the eyes of each of the kids was drawn, in turn, to this image, more than the others, as if by conditioned reflex.

Aaron looked at the bottom of the board . . . and then the top. The same image graced both. He chuckled, and tapped directly on one black, staring eye. "And that, Archie, is cheating. Told you as much before you did it, and still think so."

"What do you mean?" Archie feigned innocence.

"Take your eyes off the wave and you're asking for trouble. You know damned well that we've been programmed from the cradle to flinch at that silhouette. You know your opponents will glance at your board when they should be paying attention to their own. If I hadn't been ahead of you on the wave, I'd have gotten rag-dolled like Rocket."

The half-Samoan behemoth called Rocket looked more like a stereotypical surfer than anyone on the beach. He agreed, nodding soberly . . . which was somewhat paradoxical, because at the moment the term *sober* described him not in the least. "Truth," he said. "I was doing great, saw the grendel and almost dogged Willow out. Down I went."

Archie wagged his head sadly, and drained a pod of beer. "Excuses, excuses."

The night was warm, even by Avalonian standards. The music of handmade instruments and untutored human voices filled the air. A glowing volleyball bounced back and forth across a net, to lusty cheers and jeers from players and onlookers. A lazy, sensual haze had settled across the encampment. Forty kids, in perfect mental and physical health, savoring life. Tomorrow would be work, but not too much: Things were too perfectly balanced on Avalon. Every one of them was capable of running most of the basic apparatus providing food, and shelter, and other amenities. In a colony this small, skills redundancy was critical. And that, in combination with automated equipment, meant that little of the work was compulsory.

Before Earth's Koisan culture disappeared in the middle of the twenty-first century, anthropologists estimated that a Kalahari hunter-gatherer worked between three and five hours a day gathering enough food and materiel to provide for himself and his family, one of the lowest lifework ratios of any known human society. On Avalon, that number was three to four hours a day, giving citizens more free time to devote to art, learning, and exploration than any group in history. Excellence and daring had its rewards.

Archie, Aaron and Willow plopped down on the sand. Aaron and Willow sat close to each other, thighs brushing, the heat between them arcing like sparks. Archie took another drink and looked down the beach to where some of the younger kids, barely out of Grendel Scouts, played volleyball under the jolly supervision of Archie's brother Marshall. In that group was a girl who could have been Willow's sister. While Starborn, Jennifer was not a crèche kid, what was often tastelessly referred to as a Bottle Baby.

But whether delivered by natural childbirth or the result of incubators and artificial wombs, Avalonians were classic K-strategists, nurturing every child as if it were the only one in existence. In their opinions, the Earth they'd abandoned had become a hive of R-strategists, as if children were no more precious than a bucket of minnows or pollywogs, to be abandoned to their own devices, and survival of the fittest.

Jen was the child of the current mayor of Avalon, Carlos Ortega (the position rotated from year to year), and a botanist named Sheree Porter. Jennifer was also twelve years old. And that meant that she was unofficially off limits. There were few hard and fast rules on Avalon when it came to sex—other than a lethal prohibition against rape that had been enforced a single time.

And that once was enough. Hangings were not a pleasant sight, especially when preceded by castration. Archie had been eight, and the memory plagued his dreams still.

But although any woman who had achieved her menses was technically fair game, the social prohibitions against such activities before the age of fifteen were powerful. Older brothers and sisters had been known to administer severe beatings under the guise of "practice" in the community challenge circle. Judo *randori* was bruising enough between friends. Archie had no interest in nerve strangles and dislocations.

But little Jennifer would grow quickly, and there had already been stolen kisses, a sweetness more than a tease but less than a promise. Archie was fifteen, and still a virgin, and probably would not be for long. . . .

On the other hand, the poet in Archie's soul wondered if some things were not best savored when fully ripened. And if that particular body gift might not be one of them. Certainly there was precedent. . . .

"Now that," Aaron said, interrupting the flow of Archie's thoughts, "was a ride."

"Mmm?" Willow asked, leaning back on her elbows, her lovely face painted silver by the moons. *That* was what he wanted—the special bond Aaron and Willow had found. They were almost certainly headed for bonding in a few years. No hurry. All the time in the world.

Archie loved his brother Marshall, the First among crèche children. First decanted, the oldest of them, if not necessarily the best. But Aaron was the prince, and as such had the privilege of courting the princess. Archie liked that idea.

"Now that I'm looking at it," Willow said, "we're too close to the reef. That would be no fun at all." The surfing zone was north of the artificial bay, and gifted with tasty waves. The artificial bay had a central gate or "keyhole" which could be swung aside to allow passage of human beings, animals or even waves, creating ankle-snappers good for tyros, but of no challenge to anyone with experience and two good legs.

Further north there were tastier waves. Just around the curve of the sand. But that was also a place of dangerous reefs. It had been blackballed, and that just made it more delicious, of course.

During the night the party had slowly drifted further north, closer and closer to the forbidden zone. Eventually, someone would pretend to "finally" notice, and they would pull back south. Until then, though . . .

"You," Aaron said, "are what they used to call 'chicken.'"

She smiled at him. Archie thought he'd die for a smile like that. "And what do they call it now?"

"Willow."

She punched Aaron's muscular shoulder and might have followed up by wrestling him to the ground, but Marshall's voice interrupted. "Catch a beer!" he called, and both Aaron and Willow turned in time to snatch pods from the air.

Marshall waved and broke into some kind of impromptu running game with Rocket and another husky friend, but Archie knew that the interruption smacked of desperation: from his toes to his scraggly goatee Marshall was in love with Willow, and everyone knew it.

And Willow belonged to Aaron.

Want a woman like Willow? Simple. Be the Big Kahuna. Be a guy like Aaron. Some math didn't require Cassandra.

"I'm just sayin'," Aaron said, sipping.

"Saying what?"

"That the waves are better up thar."

Willow clucked with disapproval. Damn it, she was only a year older, but that look nailed him every time. "We are not supposed to surf past the marker." She gestured toward a cairn of rocks on the beach about a hundred meters north. Nothing natural, a demarcation line placed by Cadmann Weyland, Avalon's unofficial leader. Mayors came and went, but Cadmann commanded more respect than any three other citizens combined.

Once upon a very ugly time the colony had rejected his advice. Then the Grendel Wars had proven him horribly right, and since that time every word he uttered was studied like scripture.

He and Aaron had a special bond, father to stepson, perhaps. Just another reason that Archie wanted to be Just Like Aaron when he grew up.

Aaron drained his pouch and tossed the skin over his shoulder. That was all right: He was on pickup detail tomorrow.

Archie decided to say it before Aaron could. "Come on, man. Who's gonna stop us? I was watching those old surf movies, and they tamed some seriously gnarly bone-breakers."

Willow's eyebrow shot up. "Gnarly?"

Aaron chuckled. "He's been watching old Gidget vids. Sally Field? Spider-Man's Aunt May? Practice, huh?"

"Just a little."

Willow was not amused. Or . . . maybe she was, and just

concealing it skillfully. "Aaron, I swear. You go past the rocks, and I'm not going with you."

Aaron spent perhaps twenty seconds considering. The moons were bright, the air warm, and a lazy haze of fatigue had settled around the camp. One of these next runs would be the last. Already, new waves were calling to new surfers, and those new surfers were tumbling merrily off their boards. A few hours ago their fail rate might have been alarming. Now . . . it was merely the cause for much bleary amusement.

"What about one run?" Aaron said.

"No," Willow said, but her voice was not quite as certain.

"One." Aaron managed to curl up to his knees.

"Just one?"

He nodded, and pushed himself further up, and buckled a bit before catching his balance.

Willow saw that buckle, and her resolve instantly firmed. "No, Aaron. It's just not smart. Even when we're at our best, it's not safe. Fall off your board at the wrong time, get caught in the wrong tidal pattern . . . we're decent, but we're not *real* surfers, if you know what I mean."

Now he was irritated. "No, I really don't."

"I mean the culture thing. We don't have old surfers sharing their experiences on old beaches. . . ."

"Hey, Old Carlos used to surf. Some others, too."

"Not the same thing," she said. "We don't invite them out here. They wouldn't know these waters, anyway. We're making this up as we go along."

"You, Willow, are just a Willow," Archie said, and stuck his tongue out at her.

She remained unamused. "I'm not going," she said.

"That may be true, but you'll be here when we get back," Aaron said.

"Kinda cocky, aren't you?" She didn't add *Marshall is right over there*, but the threat hovered right behind that cheery smile.

"It's not bragging if it's true."

"Yes," Willow said. "It is."

He leaned down into her face until their lips were just an inch apart. She didn't move. He leaned closer, and finally when they were separated by no more than a whisper, she puckered, then pulled her head back.

"Be right back."

With a low, powerful *brrrrring* sound, one of the little skeeter autogyros buzzed over the trees, out of the mountains, heading just south of them.

"Whoa," Archie said. "Visitors."

The skeletal dragonflies had a range of two hundred and fifty miles, or an hour of flight, on a single charge of their hydrogen cells. The lone autogyro landed between the beach party and the huts, flurrying sand as it did. From all directions, they ran to greet the pilot, a tall strong lad two inches shorter than Aaron, but broader across the shoulders. Takashi Toru, only a decent surfer but probably the best rock-climber among them.

"And we come bearing gifts!" Takashi said, arms raised high. "We have offerings from the Plantation: genuine coffee beer, first crop of the year! Yeah!"

The kids descended like locusts, raiding the cargo rack beneath the skeeter, carrying away the treasure within. Willow slapped him fondly on the cheek. "How'd you get your hands on this?"

He did his best to make his grin mysterious. "I have many talents."

The beer, fortified with a variety of coffee that existed only in the mountains above Avalon, possessed the fascinating capacity to simultaneously relax and stimulate. There followed an orgy of consumption, and celebration that the party would extend to dawn and beyond.

Aaron looked with increasing interest at the cairn of rocks marking the farthest extent of surfing territory. He took a swig, an energetic glow expanding through his limbs. He was, in simple terms, starting to feel rather foggy.

"I remember," said Archie beside him, "reading that on Earth, they had laws about when you could start drinking."

"Yep." Aaron took another swig. "Different places had different laws." There were few laws on a world where everyone knew everyone else . . . although there were certainly rules and principles. Anyone who provided alcohol or other intoxicants to someone incapable of handling the effects risked a shunning. Or a thumping. Or both.

"Yeah, well . . . screw Earth." They toasted.

"They pretty much did that," Aaron said.

Aaron looked out at the water. Beautiful. But it was inarguable that the waves were a little stronger, a little higher and more vibrant just a few feet further down the beach. . . .

"Those waves look awfully tasty," Archie said.

Aaron took another drink, and it seemed to Archie that his resolve was starting to weaken. Success was within his grasp.

"The little moon is high," Aaron said at last. "The waves are high, and I think that we are both in an adventurous mood. What say we take our boards over, maybe a few more adventurous spirits . . . and we *carpe* the living *diem* out of it."

"Hell, yeah."

Aaron made it successfully to his feet this time. "People! I propose a glorious act of civil disobedience. It is our bounded duty to push every limit proposed by our beloved but ice-brained elders. All that remains of grendels is *this*!" He slapped his hand against the dragon guarding the underside of Archie's surfboard.

"And *that*!"

He pointed south. Eight stakes marked out a rough rectangle around the main cluster of huts. Most held torches, but two bore heads that looked like huge, toothy newts, their plastic eyes reflecting the firelight.

"I say," Aaron screamed, "that we take back the night!"

Fifty tired but enthusiastic cheers buoyed their spirits. They tromped down the sand *en masse*, clearing the cairn and reaching the stretch of beach between the artificial bay and the maze of reefs—beautiful for snorkeling, but dangerous for surfing. It was all right. They could stay clear of the reefs with ease.

When he looked around, Willow was close behind, carrying her board and wearing an amused expression. "All right, all right," she said. "No big deal. I'm just along for the ride."

When they reached the new spot, some began blearily paddling out, others plopped down on the beach, the rush provided by the coffee beer balancing with the alcohol and fatigue to create a state very near to walking sleep.

Willow peered out across the silvered water. Just visible in the moonlight, barely high enough above the horizon to be distinguished from the ocean itself, rose a crescent of land.

"Black Ship Island," she said. "If grendels swam the oceans, the goliaths would eat them like hors d'oeuvres."

"Now, you're thinking," Aaron said. "Let's do this!"

Five of them charged out into the ocean, paddled out, awaiting the rising wave.

The night was calm, although in the distance, ripples promised healthy waves to come. Aaron lay back on the board, staring up at the dual moons. He smiled, at peace with his world. This was not a common feeling for him. Ever since he could remember, a restlessness ate at his gut like a worm, drove him to explore the outer and inner worlds. People often told him he was special. *Different.* He tended to scoff at this. If he had a capacity that made him unusual, it was this drive, this hunger, and the ability to focus upon a goal until it became a reality.

"Wave coming!" Willow said. Aaron's eyes snapped open.

"Well, all right!" Archie said.

They paddled to get ahead of it, put their boards in proper position, and as the wave lifted them, they pushed up to standing and rode it in.

Expert surfers, perfect form. The ride was long and sweet, and left them exhilarated.

Even Willow was impressed. Her touchy nerves dissolved in adrenaline as she slid into the beach. "Wow!"

Archie was next ashore. "Get those torches burning," he howled. "Now *this* is what I call night surfin'!"

All up and down the beach, the kids lit their torches and embraced the night, paddling out into the water and back and out and back. . . .

## CHAPTER TWO: DARKNESS THEIR DOMAIN

Something was down there, in the water. *Two* somethings. Three. More. They coiled together, in a dance almost as old as the rhythm of the waves rolling above them.

They had been drawn by magnetic maps inscribed upon their genes. Night was their time, darkness their domain. And this was the season when the eggs held within the bodies of the females were receptive to the seed of the males. When they mated their sperm passed the permeable membranes of those eggs, which shortly afterward thickened and stiffened in response.

This was their time, and always had been.

But for the creatures who danced in the dark, there was something different about this evening. There were lights above, lights which had never ever been there before, in the countless seasons that they had lived and loved in the oceans off Avalon.

Changes in temperature they knew, but always within a given range. Predators they knew, but were programmed by genetics and experience to deal with such marauders effectively.

But strange lights? This was . . . new. In all their experience, in the experience of all their ancestors, nothing like this had ever occurred before. And something so new, so unique, called for investigation.

Not all of them, of course. Most, male and female, grew sleepy after mating, and sank toward the ocean floor to rest and allow their bodies to make the changes that reproduced their kind. But one was curious, and instead of sinking deep, rose high.

Dawn was no more than an hour away, and the revelry was winding down, even with the stimulant. In solitary weaving steps or by cozy pairs, most made their way to beds and cots and hammocks, and the arms of sleep or exhausted carnal fumblings.

Even Aaron, Archie and Willow had reached the end of their reserves, at last. Well, almost there. Enough remained in the tank that one last run seemed possible.

"Last run?" Aaron said. "How 'bout a little further north? I'm seeing some bigger breakers over there."

Willow, although she'd been losing such arguments all day, found enough grit to shake her head. "Little close to the reef for my taste. I really think that's what they're more worried about, comes right down to it."

"Ah." Aaron momentarily cast about in search for one last pod of coffee beer. He didn't want to be more awake, really. Nor did he wish to be more intoxicated. It was pretty much an urge to stay right at his current state of buzz, and the certain knowledge that that delicate point was surely slipping away from him. "Just that ol' debbil grendel, eh? You know, I wonder sometimes."

"Wonder what?" Willow asked. All three were staring toward the eastern horizon. The first blush was beginning to appear, even if the shadows were still deep enough to swallow detail.

"If the Earthers told us everything. I mean, was it really that bad? We had guns. Explosives. Skeeters. They were just freakin' *animals*, you know?" It was not the first time he'd expressed the opinion. Aaron had seen the holos. Heard the lectures. Studied the specs and like all Starborn had undergone the rigorous reflex programming designed to create an unconscious, instantaneous and lethal response to anything grendel-shaped and moving fast. But still, a part of him remained unconvinced.

"*Fast* animals," Willow said.

Before they could descend into *that* mire once again, Archie grabbed his board. Daylight was just breaking, the eastern mountain range flushing pink. The first touch of sunlight on the ocean was sublime, the waters clear as a newborn's conscience. One last run . . .

"I'm fast," he said. "Come on. Let's do this."

"I'm running. Right to sleep." She cocked a hip at Aaron. "Come on. If you catch me now I might have enough energy to make it worthwhile."

"*Buck buck buck-kaw!*" Aaron crowed at her, and followed Archie into the water. Willow shrugged and trudged back down the beach, heading south to her hut.

"Don't try the door," she said back over her shoulder.

He didn't seem to hear her. She watched them paddling out, toward the darkness. She had a sudden and confusing urge to join them. Or to beg Aaron and Archie not to go. The sense that somehow he was slipping away from her.

"Stay away from the reef!" she yelled, irritated at the stridence in her own voice.

"Yes, Mommy!" they called back.

She laughed. Well, maybe she didn't want another surf run. But she could certainly wait here for them. It shouldn't take long, she reasoned. This shouldn't really take long at all.

Aaron and Archie drifted on the rippling water, waiting for a wave worth the run.

"You ever wonder?" Archie asked.

"Wonder what?" A lazy reply. Aaron lay on his belly, paddling at the water with his palm. *Splish, splash.* He looked almost as if he wanted to just go to sleep, right there. Surfers had done that on Earth, of course. And drifted out into the open ocean.

"What it would be like to go up against a grendel," Archie said.

"I dream about it. . . ." Aaron began, then suddenly his voice and body language sharpened. "Whoops! Here we go!"

Archie whipped his head around. The water rolled and swelled toward them. A beauty. A worthy end to a very full night's entertainment. Just this one, and then twelve hours of sleep, and they'd be ready for more adventure. Wash, rinse, repeat.

The creature was closer to the surface now. There was enough light to make out the shapes above her, and she found it impossible to turn away. The fertilized eggs in her womb had stirred normally dormant emotions to life. It was this time in her cycle, a time when she cared more about the welfare of prospective young than the normal rhythm of hunting, sleeping, and finally mating. Soon after they were born that urge would change, and she would watch passively as the males hunted her young.

But some would survive that culling, the fastest and strongest. And those she would protect from the males, offering sex to convert their hunger to lust. And the males would be gentle, and begin to nurture the survivors, even as the new fertilized eggs ripened within her. In time, she would extrude an egg sack, which would birth a thousand young. . . .

And the cycle would begin anew.

Something dangled over the sides of a flat thing, thrashing the water with a clumsy rhythm, almost like a crippled animal. Weak. No threat.

But as the light grew brighter, there was something else. The shape above her was both alien and familiar. A flat image with swollen jaw and stubby, spiked tale. She had never actually *seen* such a creature, but her kind possessed a genetic memory, and it was making her blood churn. Closer she came. And then closer still.

As the wave rose, the two boys battled their buzz down to a dull roar, rising to the challenge of the water beneath them.

Archie was, this time, the first to find his footing. He almost lost it, then spread his arms, happy that he wasn't carrying a torch. "Unreal, dude!" he yelled at Aaron, ahead of him and fighting his own battle.

Aaron managed to look back over his shoulder. "Just hold tight, little brother—"

It was advice easier to hear than to follow. Archie had been surfing and drinking much of the night, and even his young, strong body had finally had enough. His board tipped over, and he fell into the water.

He laughed as he hit, but then the laughter froze in his throat.

*Something.* Something he had never seen before was in the water with him. A brief glimpse of darkness, deeper than the night, and something reaching for him. A mouth rimmed with tentacles, and jagged with teeth. . . .

"Aaron!" Aaron heard Archie's call, and thought at first it was just another call to *look at me! Look at me!* from the kid. But there was something in it, something that made him whip his head around. Between the arching wave and the rising sun, in a moment frozen between shadow and dawn, he saw something that would stay with him until the light faded from his eyes.

Archie was clawing for his board, splashing as the wave rose around him. And something *had* him. As if a walrus had swallowed a squid headfirst. Grabbing Archie. Pulling his friend down. Aaron had a brief, intense impression of Archie's eyes starting from his face, swollen and rolling white, mouth wide and screaming then filling with foam as the wave crested and he was just . . . gone.

Aaron lost his balance, hit the water and then thrashed away, aware that the board that had so recently carried him would crash down upon him if he was in the wrong space. The foamed plastic was far lighter than the wooden boards that had once been standard fare, not the same skull-crackers that had maimed so many generations of earthly surfers. Still, they were heavy enough to stun.

The board slammed down to his left. He instantly eeled about in the water, swimming against the curling wave with great strong strokes, heading back to the place where he had last seen his friend.

The wave smashed him under, with barely a chance to grab a

mouthful of air before being sucked under in a terrible rip. He remembered to swim parallel to the beach to find his way out of it, rather than trying to swim directly out of the tidal grasp. He tumbled and swam and tumbled, and by the time he broke surface again, sucking air, the wave was ahead of him, thundering upon the beach.

He tried to swim back toward where he'd last seen Archie, but the second wave hit. Hard, like a board along the side of his head, and again he barely had time to gasp for breath before being hammered under once again.

Aaron's head slammed against the bottom, and he lost part of his desperate mouthful, swallowing water. Thoughts of Archie left his mind as the survival instinct in all its pitiless power took control of his mind. He remembered little more until he was crouching on his knees in the shallows vomiting water and trying to suck in enough air to gather his wits.

Willow had seen some of it. Not all, but enough to cleanse the fog from her mind. Mark had appeared behind her. From where she did not know, such tunnel vision had possessed her. "What happened?"

"Bad," she said, coming to her feet. "Bad wipe out. Come on."

She scanned the beach, and finally saw Aaron where he knelt gagging in the sand, one hand to his head. Willow broke into a run, was at his side in moments. "What happened? Where's Archie?"

"He was right next to me." Aaron gasped. "Behind me. Something grabbed him."

That brought her up short. "*Something*? What are you talking—"

Her thought never had the chance to be fully formed. From down the beach, another scream.

"Archie!" It was Rocket, calling out into the early morning shadows.

And within a few seconds, his voice was joined by another. "Archie!" The sun was half-born now, and there was light enough to make out faces, but whoever had screamed was facing away, and she couldn't make them out. Others were running up from the huts. Perhaps some had been sleeping in the sand. She didn't know.

Within minutes, the beach swarmed with Starborn, Naturals and crèche kids, taking boats out onto the waves, paddling out on surfboards. Mark's skeeter buzzed back and forth along the beach regularly and ventured out into the ocean, casting its dragonfly shadow upon the rolling waves.

Aaron's emotions whiplashed him, contracting all thought to a narrow tunnel. It had been his original suggestion to surf further north, nearer to the reef. If something had happened, if this wasn't a gigantic and splendid prank, then it was impossible not to conclude that Aaron Tragon was responsible for the strangest and most terrible occurrence of any of their young lives.

What had . . . ? Why had . . . ? What did it mean . . . ?

"Over here!" someone called, and waved from thirty meters further north, Aaron ran, heels kicking up sand and dust, praying that this was some kind of sick prank, that Archie would be found hiding and giggling, the biggest *gotcha* in the history of Avalon. Please, please . . .

A circle of kids stood and knelt around whatever they had found, blocking it from view. There, he pushed his way into the center of the circle, dreading, hoping, fearing. . . .

Not Archie. Neither giggling nor drowned, ravaged and dead.

They circled his surf board. Its caricatured grendel on bottom and top had been savaged by the reef. The kids stared at it, and then looked up at Aaron.

He knelt, running his fingers along the board's waxed surface, dipping fingers into the holes. Not tooth marks. Clearly, the board had been dragged over the reef, the remains of creatures resembling earthly coral, as dangerous as their lookalikes off Australia, Hawaii, or any other surfer's paradise.

He couldn't hear. Light registered on his eyes, but although he could resolve images, nothing seemed to make sense. It was very much as if until this moment, he had not fully registered the horror which now cascaded upon him like an avalanche. He could hear his own breathing, feel his own heartbeat, see his hands if he held them out in front of him, but nothing made sense.

Archie was here, somewhere. Hiding. Laughing.

He *had* to be.

Aaron cupped his hands around his mouth and screamed. "Archie!" Willow appeared, pale in the morning light. Her face looked tauter, older than it had just hours before. And the awareness of that change, of what he had lost in her esteem if nothing else, was in a strange way, the cruelest blow of all.

The sun had rested a moment at zenith, and begun its slow decline to the horizon. By now the kids looked shell-shocked, exhausted. Skeeters buzzed up and down the shoreline, out to the ocean and back.

Willow fought to keep despair from swallowing her entirely. In one single, terrible night, all her dreams and hopes for life had changed. Everything she thought she knew had dissolved like mist in the morning sun.

Perhaps . . . perhaps this is just growing up, she thought. Perhaps this is just a peek behind the mask. She had been no different from the others, had assumed that she and Aaron would be together, find their way to love, marriage, raising children, and perhaps leading Camelot. That certainly seemed the assumption made by everyone, at every turn, whether spoken aloud or not. Seeing Aaron stripped so bare, so vulnerable, sitting on the sand while Evelyn Niles, a small woman with a narrow, intense face examined him.

Willow wanted to reach out to him. Wanted to support him, but he seemed . . . prickly now. As if he might bite if she approached too closely. Or perhaps fragile where just hours before he had seemed invulnerable.

Was it possible to be both? Simultaneously? If she embraced him, nurtured him, was she doing more harm than good? And if she gave him space, was she doing it for his benefit, or hers?

A full search was in operation now, with the full resources of Avalon. A half-dozen skeeters buzzed above, heading a mile north and a mile south and a mile out to sea. *Geographic*'s sensors had been brought to bear, deep-scanning the oceans, although they knew there was little hope of differentiating between the . . . the body of their friend and brother, and any of the thousand uncategorized sea denizens lurking off their shores.

At this point, everyone knew that they were merely going through the motions.

A seventh skeeter buzzed in from the mountains and landed. A tall, graying man exited, one of the largest and certainly most imposing men on Avalon.

Cadmann Weyland.

In an odd way, she wasn't certain whether she was relieved, or dreaded the moment when Colonel Weyland gave vent to his opinions. *I tried. I tried to stop it. But then I went right along and surfed.*

*Oh, God. Nowhere to hide.*

Cadmann strode up to Aaron, his rectangular, weathered face unreadable. "Are you all right?"

"Yeah," Aaron said, so softly that she might have imagined the syllable. Perhaps he had merely hunched his shoulders in response.

"Let's go over this again," Cadmann said. "What did you see?"

Aaron sighed, and repeated the same story Willow had heard a dozen times now. "We were riding the wave. I was ahead of Archie, and I heard him yell something about . . . seeing something."

Cadmann's eyes tightened. "Something like . . . what?"

"He didn't have time to say. I looked back, and he was on his knees on the board. Something had grabbed his ankles. His waist."

"Something?"

Aaron nodded. "Teeth. Acres of teeth. I couldn't see it clearly, but it looked a little like . . . I don't know. Never seen anything like it."

One of the other adults, an engineer named Reese, spoke up. "A grendel?"

Cadmann frowned at him. "A salt-water grendel?"

"Hell," Reese said. "We can't be sure we know its life cycle. Anything is possible. Salmon are both fresh and salt water. . . ."

Cadmann shook his head. "You know, every time something goes wrong, we say 'grendel.' We've got grendels on the brain. They probably aren't even the most dangerous things on this planet."

"What?"

Cadmann grunted. "What is the likelihood that human beings land here on a big island, and within a year encounter the most dangerous creature an entire planet has to offer? But because it almost destroyed us, every boogey man has speed."

"It wasn't a grendel," Aaron said. "It wasn't a god damned grendel. I don't know. . . ."

Although primarily a biologist, Dr. Evelyn Niles was one of eight members of *Geographic*'s crew qualified as a physician, and one of four whose capacity, so far as anyone could determine, was unaffected by ice. She had examined Aaron's head on first arriving from Camelot, bandaged a bad gash, and played light and motion games to check for concussion. She clucked and spoke sympathetically. "You took a pretty bad bump there."

"Dinged by my own board," he said, shaking his head, and then belatedly seemed to grasp what they were saying. "Hey, stop it. Maybe I got concussed, maybe not. But I know what I saw. *I know.*"

Cadmann, Niles and Willow all exchanged expressions.

"I saw what I saw," he said. "I know what I know."

"Of course you do," Niles said.

"Something came out of the water, and grabbed him."

"The surfboard had marks," Cadmann said. "Reef marks. You were near the reef. You were exhausted, intoxicated, and in the forbidden zone. Can you blame us?"

Aaron stared at them, each of them in turn, shame and anger warring in his eyes. The longest look was exchanged with Cadmann.

When he broke his gaze away, he made a sound that might have been a sob. It might.

Aaron rose unsteadily to his feet. "All right. I see how it is," he said. The emotion that had been, so briefly, revealed in his eyes disappeared, like the doors of a furnace slamming shut. He looked up. Fewer skeeters overhead now. The search was winding down. They were tired, and discouraged. . . .

And as far as they were concerned, they already knew what had happened.

"All right then. That's the way it is. I won't stop. I won't stop looking, ever, until I find him."

He began to jog clumsily north up the beach. "Archie!" He broke into a run. "Archie!"

Willow looked down at her hands. One part of her wanted to run after him, help him, be with him.

The other wanted to be as far away from Aaron Tragon as she could possibly get.

And God help her, she wasn't certain which part of her was more right.

## CHAPTER THREE: AVALON

*ONE YEAR LATER*

At the northern tip of the island of Camelot, north of the vast expanse of Isenstein Glacier and west of the Miskatonic River, lies the colony of Avalon. Avalon is a collection of artificial ponds, home of the spaceport serving their sole surviving Orion vehicle, their only road back to orbit.

They will never return to Earth. If this is not their home, they have no home.

The colony had been rebuilt since the agony of the Grendel Wars. A dozen huts, dining hall and administration buildings, machine shops and pens for chickens, sheep, horses and cattle. Their border fences sported additional thermal sensors now, inevitably tuned to grendel physiology and attack patterns.

The people of Avalon had never lost a bit of wariness, but also carried themselves as warriors who have survived their first test of combat: loss of illusion, the establishment of new identities, a bit of concern that even these new, stronger ego walls might be broached.

It is said that only sixty thousand years ago, humanity on Earth came perilously close to extinction. We know, deep in our genes, that once upon a time we were almost undone. From the perspective of evolutionary psychology, our urge to reproduce and prevent this from ever happening again originates in this time. The gods and sages who told us that women should stay in their homes and bear young, and that men should go out into the world and expose themselves to enemy warriors, natural calamities and vicious beasts, to use anything and everything in our environments as we see fit, were little more than this drive to survive, inscribed on our genes and memes.

Some say that we almost destroyed the planet attempting to satisfy this fear. Depending on one's perspective, we either awakened or were brainwashed into thinking we needed to limit ourselves. We socially engineered such changes, or else they happened naturally with the emancipation of women, the coming of the industrial revolution, improved birth control, democracy, and education . . . we either naturally limited ourselves, or nature herself designed and defined our limits.

An argument impossible to resolve. What was true was that here, ten light-years away from Earth, there was no longer a need for population control. In fact, following the Grendel Wars, an empty womb was something very close to an insult to the species. There were no infertile females on Avalon, and despite the neurological reality of ice, their genetics were as close to perfect as could be arranged. The result had been something close to a reproductive free-for-all, and the streets of Camelot swarmed with the resulting children.

At the moment, the busiest building in the encampment was the town hall. Used for dances, lectures, debates and the occasional group cinema or game, at the moment it hosted a town hall meeting, the primary sides of the discussion separated by the sharpest age-gap in human history. There were Starborn, none older than seventeen. And Earthborn, none younger than forty. And nothing in-between.

The sides of the discussion were arrayed along two different tables. Cadmann Weyland, his friend Carlos Martinez, Dr. Evelyn Niles, and Louisa Goodman were on the Earthborn side.

Willow, Marshall, and Takashi Toru were the primary representatives for the Starborn.

They'd been talking nonstop for an hour now.

Louisa Goodman was Avalon's current mayor, a tall, willowy woman with dark red hair and a schoolmarm's manner. She had been an executive at a multinational communications firm, but had given that up for a chance at a new world. "We have been apprised of plans for the annual Grendel Scouts 'Hell Night' outing, a cooperative between Surf's Up and the main colony. All in favor?" She looked around, out at the forty citizens who witnessed the meeting from their rows of folding chairs.

With barely a pause, the room replied: "Aye."

"Opposed?"

Silence in reply.

Dr. Evelyn Niles raised her hand. "I have no opposition, but a cautionary note. I propose that one adult—"

Even before he could finish, the kids groaned in protest.

"Come on, Evelyn!" Marshall protested, twisting his wispy goatee with his fingers, a clear sign of irritation. "This is our game. We can handle it, and you know that."

Niles held her palms up in a placating gesture. "One adult be present on Black Ship Island during conduction of the Grendel Scout Overnight. Preferably with medical training, in case of emergency. Of course, a skeeter will be standing by on the mainland."

Cadmann, who had said little during the talk, nodded. "I agree. There is no need for excess risk." He drummed his fingers on the table in front of him. "Cassandra?"

The children of Camelot had many names from many cultures. By mutual but noncompulsory agreement, no one named their child "Cass" or "Cassandra" because simply speaking those three syllables triggered the link to the main computer up on *Geographic*.

"*Yes, Cadmann*?"

"Map please. Surf's Up Bay and Black Ship."

"*Of course.*" The map appeared. The island of Camelot, as well as the colony of Avalon appeared. The image shifted rapidly east to the subcolony called Surf's Up, including the artificial bay, and beyond that, the crescent called Black Ship Island.

"*Sufficient*?" Cassandra asked in her eternally cool voice.

"Yes, thank you," Cadmann replied. "The way I see it, with the plan proposed, there are really only two points of danger."

Marshall sniffed. "And what are those?"

"Well . . . The bay is safe. We made it safe, and most of the shoreline would have been safe, if no one had tried surfing near the reef. Once you leave the bay, there are two miles of ocean to cover. We know everything that breeds there, and most of what uses it as a hunting ground. The goliaths hunt there. They breach the surface but have never attacked a boat or a swimmer. You'll be using the big inflatables, and everyone will have life vests and tracers, and the skeeters on standby, but I figure that there, those two miles before you reach the island, we might see some trouble."

Talk ricocheted the room, but there was no hard disagreement.

"And what's the other point?" Willow asked.

Cadmann laughed, but there was little humor in it. "Just . . . the unknown. We've been to Black Ship dozens of times. The oil refinery runs itself, but it's been fine every time we visit. Then again everything *always* seems fine . . . until it's not. So we need to be aware. Prepare for the unknown. Isn't that what we really want to teach the Grendel Scouts?"

Willow proceeded as if she thought he was setting a snare. "Yes, but you don't trust us to do this?"

"Yes," Cadmann said. "I do. I just don't think there's anything wrong with putting in a little extra help. In case."

The kids considered that, and as the words passed the first hurdle of common sense conferred among themselves in whisper-tones for a minute, and then came back up for air.

"All right. Agreed," Willow said, combing her lustrous hair from her forehead with her fingers. "One adult."

Louisa nodded, looked around the room seeking any complaint, and then banged her gavel on the podium. "Then approval is granted. The chit for all supplies will be issued."

"Strike one!" The umpire screamed, and the spectators jeered derisively. Willow watched Carlos Martinez, the colony's premier sculptor and lothario, grit his teeth and stamp his feet on the plate, squinting against the morning sun as he faced the pitcher, a tall, skinny mop-top named Horace.

She'd heard that once, a lifetime ago and ten light-years away, he had been a damned good ball player. That may have been true, but something about the pitcher just seemed to give him fits, and the crowd cheered as he swung and missed a second time, and then struck out, handing his bat off with a few heartfelt phrases in Spanish that needed no translation.

The next batter was Takashi Toru, whose rock-climber physique didn't translate into batting success. Takashi barely managed a base hit on the third swing, sliding in only a half second before a gangly black girl named Kola Andewala hurled the softball in for the second baseman.

It was just a casual pick-up game on the diamond back behind the mess hall and the supply depot, so everyone was cheering for everyone. Willow applauded along with the rest of them, but caught the pitcher's eye and motioned him over: There was business to conduct.

He gestured to the relief pitcher and trotted over to her, all smiles and sweaty hug. "Willow!" he said. "You see me? I did good!"

The supply depot had once been one of two dormitories, both

decommissioned as almost all members of the colony had their own dwellings. Occasionally a remodeling or fumigation or breakup motivated a citizen to seek public housing, but a single dorm now sufficed for that.

Marshall was waiting for her at the supply shed's broad, open window. A few Grendel Scout–aged kids hovered around as well, fascinated. They understood that something was going on even if they didn't know exactly what. They hovered around the older kids, as youngsters always had and probably always would.

A chunky blond youngster named Buddy bugged Willow as she walked to the front of the line, and the pitcher slipped through a side door. "Watcha got, Willow?" he asked, pointing a chubby forefinger at the slate clutched to her chest.

She grinned and hid her slate, on which the requisition was printed in scanpaper type. "Now, now, no peeking. Haven't you ever heard of surprises?"

Marshall was less kind. "All kinds of good things," he said. "Grendel guts, pterodon poop . . . yummy campfire fare."

"Yuck!"

"You bet, yuck!" Marshall agreed. "Now fly away, little birds, we have business. Trust me . . . you'll see us tomorrow."

The erstwhile pitcher, now counter attendant, was a slender man with unkempt hair and now a slightly vague expression, as if his emotions and intellect were just slightly out of synch. His name was Horace Fuentes, known generally as "Uncle Horace." Horace had ice on his mind: he was one of the colony's direst examples. Once upon a time, he had been . . . well, a different man.

Now, Horace could barely be trusted to disperse shovels and flares and such goods from a public facility, where in actuality all citizens were pretty much trusted to fetch their own merchandise goods. That trust, and a mean softball pitch, were all that remained of one of Cuba's greatest mathematicians.

The supply depot job was make-work, pure and simple.

Make-work or not, Horace took his job very seriously. He was methodical, if just a little slow. Checked every tag twice. He seemed constantly on the edge of frustration, counting repeatedly to be certain he had it right. He looked up, and saw the kids looking at him. And trying not to stare.

"I'm sorry. Everything takes me longer now. Just something you get used to."

Marshall felt embarrassed for Uncle Horace, more embarrassed than Horace himself. "Damned ice." Then more gently, as countless colonists had said to others over the course of almost two decades, perhaps the single most common phrase in the colony: "It's not your fault."

His eyes flickered, as if refocusing. "Hey!" he said. "Did you know that before 1995, the eastern part of Kiribati was a whole day and two hours behind the western part of the country where its capital is located?"

The non sequitur took Willow aback for a moment. "Why?"

"International Date Line split the country," he said, blinking. "Did you know my name means 'Hour'?"

"No, Horace," she said, although she had heard this at least a dozen times before.

"And where is Kiribati?" Marshall asked. Willow wanted to elbow him.

Horace blinked again, and his eyes shifted back and forth as he searched for the information, and came up blank. He shrugged, and combed his hair with his fingers. "Don't remember."

"*It's not your fault.*" Horace was sweet, and very limited . . . and perfect.

Marshall and Willow exchanged an embarrassed look. Then Marshall pulled at his goatee, his eyes shifted sideways. "Horace," Marshall said. "Horace . . . I'd like to ask you for a favor. . . ."

"No!" Louisa Goodman slammed her little fist down on the desk, her face dark with fury and frustration. "No! You know damned well that the intent—"

The rest of her words hung in the air, unspoken. Her eyes had gone from Willow to Marshall and back again without fixing on Horace. His head hung down and he wrung his hands together in misery. Suddenly, Louisa realized what her tirade was doing to this good and simple man.

*Damnation.*

She was furious with herself, and furious at the ease with which Willow and Marshall had checkmated her. "No offense, Horace, but you know that your . . . that ice . . . you know."

"I know," Horace said.

"Damn it," Louisa whispered. "You have no right to put me in this position."

Marshall batted the ball right back to her. "But you have the right to object when we obey the law that *you* insisted we conform to."

"Yes, I do!" she yelled. "I have the responsibility to—"

"What?" Marshall said. "Demand we return the supplies?"

Louisa came very close to saying the first thing that came to mind, realizing at the last second that she needed to take control of this, while there was still time. "I'm not interested in going to war with you, Marshall. We could just withhold permission from the Grendel Scouts."

Cadmann had been leaning against the office wall, observing the entire exchange. "Louisa," he said. "May I speak with you, alone?"

She glared at him, but nodded.

Cadmann turned to the kids. "A moment, please."

The kids filed out of the office, and Cadmann closed the door.

They both exhaled at the same time. "Well," Louisa said. "Here's another fine mess."

"Oh, yes," Cadmann said. "That was Marshall. We should have known he'd find the loophole. We didn't think about it because we don't *like* thinking about it."

Silence hung in the air for a moment. "So . . . what do we do?"

"Well . . ." he said. "Whatever we do, it can't be about this one trip. It has to be about everything that happens as those kids get older and . . . well, aren't kids any more. Do we want them parsing every agreement, finding loopholes? Do we want a rebellion on our hands, one we can't possibly win?"

"Crap," Louisa said, feeling pinned.

"Yeah. Crap indeed. Listen. Things will either go well out there. . . ."

"Your lips to God's ear."

"Or not. If something goes wrong, they'll either cope with it, call us in and we'll cope with it, or . . . not."

The third person in the room was Evelyn Niles. "Sister . . . ?" Louisa began.

Niles raised her hand, smiled. "Please. It's just Evelyn. I was a Dominican, but that was another life. If I hadn't renounced the habit I couldn't have come on this trip." She'd given that speech a thousand times, and probably would a thousand more.

Cadmann considered that answer. "You renounced it before you were a candidate, didn't you . . . ? Or to get married . . . ? I was never really sure. . . ."

Niles smiled again. It was a polite and pretty smile, but it answered nothing. There were some questions she'd never seen fit to answer. "Let's just say that at some point, it seemed to me I could do more good to the world by a more direct contact with its mysteries. We cannot be protected by doctrine. And our children cannot be protected by the hopes, dreams, and fears of their parents. No matter how much we love them."

"Still," Louisa said, "whether you want it or not, you represent a certain voice, and I can't quite get Catholicism out of my head. Still hoping to find answers."

"I have some excellent questions for you," Niles said. "No answers, though."

"I'll take a good question."

Niles nodded. "All right. When and where is the best time to let our children make mistakes?"

A moment's pause, and then the answer. "When their victories will teach them right, and their mistakes will cause pain . . . but not destruction."

"A good answer. So we stand by."

"Are they making a mistake? We know what's on Black Ship. What about the stretch of ocean they'll have to cross?"

Niles considered. "Two miles. We can track goliaths, and there've been two in the vicinity, but they aren't known to have ever attacked a boat. We chummed the waters three times last years, and no predators larger than jellysharks took the bait. That's a foot long at worst, and seemed to be carrion eaters. There's a kind of active seaweed. You wouldn't want to fall into a mass of it, but again it seems more interested in carrion."

"What about seasonal?"

She nodded. "That's a damned good question. We've been on this planet almost twenty years, and couldn't possibly have mapped everything. We can know everything that lurks in the waters year-round, but if they only come in one season . . . or only return every six years, well, we don't know."

"Best guess?"

"Looking at the vegetation, figuring the amount of animal biomass that could live on that, and then the number of predators that could be living on those . . . the life cycle seems pretty stable," Niles said. "I don't see any really scary things coming in, slaughtering wholesale. None of our models allow for anything like that. I think we're pretty safe."

Niles was as good as it got. Cadmann felt the whole room give a silent, collective sigh of relief. "I think traveling two miles in rafts to a well-mapped island is probably safer than rock climbing. And we know that Uncle Horace is damned good at basic first aid, and CPR, and neural stim. He proved that. He saved your life, Louisa, during the Grendel Wars."

"All right . . ." Louisa said, perhaps wondering where this was going.

"And if that is your choice, I'd be happy to pray to St. Pancras, patron saint of children."

Louisa looked at Cadmann, who shrugged. "Not my turn in the barrel. You're on rotation."

"Crap crappity crap. All right . . . let them in," Louisa said. "But at times like these, I really, really hope there's someone listening when I pray."

"Amen," Cadmann said, without a trace of irony. "I think that's something most of us hope for."

"What?" Niles asked.

"That there is something out there. God or Buddha or the Great Pumpkin."

"I don't care if it's the Golden Golliwog. When it comes to our kids, I'll take all the help I can get."

## CHAPTER FOUR: GASTRIC SPECIAL

The shadows narrowed as morning crept toward noon. Skeeter Gamma was a good old girl, with over a half-million air-miles creaking her metal bones. As far as Cadmann was concerned, that just meant she'd gotten her bugs out.

He skimmed across the treetops, heading for a mountain south of the colony. It was a beautiful, alien view. Horsemane trees, twenty meters of ramrod straight oval shaped paper-white trunks, with a fringe of dark green running like a stallion's mane down the leeward side mixed with terrestrial coconut palms. At the top of each horsemane tree was a network of branches supporting nests of odd crab-like creatures. Grendels ate anything that moved, and the arthropods never descended to the ground, which long puzzled the colony biologists until they realized that the mountain-dwelling pterodons could land in the nests. A complex symbiosis resulted, with the pterodons somehow conveying genetic material from one treetop to another, providing genetic diversity sufficient to preserve the species.

There were also groves of terrestrial coconut palms and citrus trees in complex checkerboard patterns. More patches of what amounted to impenetrable jungle. Grendels had simplified the animal ecology of the island, but there was plenty of plant life to puzzle the agronomists.

Light momentarily brightened as the cloud cover parted. The windshield polarized. He shielded his eyes a bit, checked his inertial position display, then visually oriented, heading toward a cleft crowded with trees and heavy with moss.

He loved piloting skeeters, but never regretted an opportunity to touch down safely, either.

He fanned dust across a broad, flat triangular landing zone chopped and burned into the underbrush. A few people watched, curious, pausing as they carried sacks to or from one of the three huts surrounding the pad. There were other huts, set further back, and if one looked carefully there were still more up in the forested area.

Cadmann exited the autogyro, shaking the hands of a short, broad sunburnt guy wearing wraparounds. "How are things, Jeter?"

"Pretty straight forward. We got a little too much rain, and the roots are a little mushy. We're on our third course of antifungals. We'll cope. What brings you?"

"I'm here to see Aaron."

Jeter lifted his sunglasses. "Ah! Mickey will walk you up." He stuck two fingers in his mouth and let loose with a piercing whistle.

"Up?" Cadmann asked.

Jeter pointed up into the mountains protecting the clearing. "Pterodon nests."

"What in the hell? Oh." He looked as if he wanted to slap his forehead. "Gastric Special."

Jeter grinned. "One finds delicacies where one can."

He whistled again and made a come-hither to a jug-eared kid who, if his given name hadn't been Michael, might well have been nicknamed Mickey anyway. Just for the big ears.

"Cadmann?"

"Hey, Mickey. Walk me up?"

"Can do will do," the kid said, and threw in a snappy salute for good measure.

"Sounds good." Cadmann pulled a backpack out of the skeeter and shouldered it.

They headed up a shoulder-wide path burned and chopped in the underbrush. Cadmann named a dozen species silently, then gave up. It would be generations before even a fraction of Avalon's wildlife and flora were categorized. A plaintive *skaw* jerked his head up, and the familiar silhouette of a bald eagle winged past overhead.

Cadmann couldn't stop himself from smiling. "They seem to be doing well."

"I heard you Earthers weren't sure."

"We weren't sure about a lot of things. But eventually, we just had to try." Eventually, you just have to let them go.

They climbed for three hours, until the day began to cool, the territory increasingly steep.

The clearing just ahead had been cleared by machete and defoliant. It sheltered a single tent, and a low, crackling campfire in a circle of rocks. No one seemed to be present.

"Aaron?" Mickey called. "Company."

After a moment's pause, the tent flap opened, and Aaron climbed out. His hair was long and chopped square. The months had stripped fat from his body, so that to Cadmann he seemed unhealthily lean, wiry more than muscular. His eyes were narrow and suspicious.

"Cadmann," he said, too many emotions in that single word for Cadmann to tease out his mood.

"Aaron."

The boy ran his fingers through his hair. "What brings you all the way up here?"

"Trade," Cadmann said. "Carlos said you commissioned this." He pulled a satchel out of his backpack and opened it, producing two knives with grendel-bone handles.

Aaron emerged from his suspicious trance, eyes delighted. "Wow!"

"Yeah," Cadmann said. "Wow. You offer to trade some Gastric?"

Aaron plopped down on a folding camp stool, motioned Cadmann toward a second. Aaron twirled the knives with liquid wrists, slicing patterns in the air. Then suddenly he seemed to remember Cadmann had spoken. "Yeah, yeah. Got it right here." He went into the tent, emerged a few minutes later with two pounds of beans.

"That . . ." Cadmann marveled, "is a bloody fortune."

"Worth it," Aaron said. "A good knife is . . ." He was playing with the blade, rotating it, and then suddenly, he remembered who he was talking to. His eyes narrowed. "Why did you bring these up? Why not Carlos?"

Cadmann stretched. "Wanted to get out, up to the mountains. Felt like a hike. Wanted to talk."

Aaron snorted doubt.

"Mickey?" Cadmann said.

"Yeah?" Mickey asked.

"I can handle this now. Want to do some collecting?" In other words, *leave us alone for a while.*

"Sure." Mickey dusted his shoes off and retreated politely. Aaron and Cadmann faced each other across the fire. For the first time, Cadmann noticed Aaron's hands were trembling. Looked like the boy was drinking too much of his own product.

For a few moments the only sounds were the crackle of the fire and the distant *skaw* of the pterodons. Then Cadmann spoke. "We know that some of you kids feel like you don't belong to anyone."

"Ah," Aaron said. "That little no mother, no father thingie?"

"The whole crèche thing could have been . . . should have been handled a little better. I don't know what they were thinking." Cadmann spoke the clear truth. As theory, the idea of frozen embryos made sense. As always, practice was . . . quite another thing.

"Spare parts. Need a population bump? Just thaw out a few kidsicles."

Cadmann winced. "We always tried to make you feel as if you belonged to all of us."

Aaron smiled. "Which is the same as belonging to none of you."

"I tried to stand up for you, Aaron. You know that's true. No one sentenced you to pick coffee beans out of pterodon shit. This was your choice."

That seemed to set Aaron back a bit. "Was it? Did I have an option?"

"There are always options."

Aaron's answering laugh was cruel. "You saw their faces. So a bottle baby kills a Starborn—"

"You are Starborn. And you didn't kill anyone."

"Tell it to Marshall. You know damned well what I mean. There's a difference."

"Aaron . . . at some point in everyone's life you have to stop caring about what other people think, and stand on your own for a while. They'll come back."

Aaron fisted his hands, and ground them into his thighs. "Maybe I don't want them to."

"Is that true?"

"Yes."

Cadmann waited a moment before speaking the words in his mind. "And Willow?"

"What about her?"

"Right," Cadmann said. "Like you don't know what I mean. Listen, Aaron. I'm going to say something to you that I probably shouldn't."

A pause.

Aaron stepped into the gap. "Have some coffee."

Cadmann winced. He'd actually never tried the stuff. No matter what anyone said, the thought of eating something that had been through another creature's digestive system was just repulsive. "Ah, no thank you. . . ."

Aaron read his mind, but had no mercy. "Didn't anyone ever tell you it's impolite to refuse hospitality?"

Cadmann paused, chewing it over, realizing he had no real choice. "Fair enough. Please."

Aaron chuckled. He liked to win. From a pot on the campfire he poured a stream of black liquid. "Powdered milk? Honey?"

"Honey, please."

Aaron handed him a small pot. "Here you go. You know, I've always thought that when you really want to experience something, you should try it without seasonings or flavors first."

"I've always thought that, too."

They both laughed. Cadmann mixed in some honey, and then sipped.

"Well?"

"My," Cadmann said. "That's tasty." He took another sip or two, and then set it down.

"That's actually very good."

"Wait," Aaron said.

"For what?"

Aaron smiled with pride. "Not like the other Gastrics, is it? It's in the roasting. Passing through the pterodon digestive system balances some of the alkaline in the caffeine, but I roast using nettlebark."

"I'd think that was too harsh."

"Only to touch. The smoke turns out to be a flavor enhancer. I think I have a little industry here. Also adds pseudo polyphenols as free radical scavengers. Caffeine acts to sensitize your body to norepinephrine, and *speed* traces break down in your body to provide precursives. More like cocaine than traditional caffeine, but milder and kinder. A nice smooth lift, then lets you down gently."

Cadmann sputtered. "Pseudo-*what*?"

Aaron's lips turned up, just a bit, in the ghost of a *gotcha.*

Cadmann sipped again, enjoying the java. Not bad at all.

"So this isn't just exile?"

"Started that way. Now . . . I've found something I'm good at."

"You're good at a lot of things, Aaron. That's part of what I wanted to say."

"What?"

Cadmann took another sip. He didn't feel buzzed, but the day had just gotten . . . clearer. Oh, this stuff was dangerous. "The thing that I really shouldn't say. Mmm. Can I buy a pound of this?"

Aaron almost giggled. For a moment, he looked about seven years old again, still the lean athletic little ball of energy that had dogged his shadow endlessly, wanting to beat him up one moment and curl in his lap the next. The boy Cadmann had taught to fish, who Carlos had taught to carve and hit a ball. "We can work out a trade. If I like what you have to say."

"I think you will. All right. Aaron. I think you're going to inherit this colony."

Aaron rolled his eyes. "That again. We've been down this road before."

"Not like this you haven't. I didn't say 'the Starborn' or 'the Crèche Kids.' I said *you.* Aaron Tragon."

Aaron stared, doing his version of a slow burn. "What are you talking about?"

"Aaron. I know a leader when I see one. Part of what the Army trained me to do. You're smarter, stronger, than any other kid on this planet."

Another snort. But there was something in Aaron's eyes in that moment, Cadmann saw it. He wanted to believe. "What about what happened at Surf's Up? Did that seem level-headed to you? Everyone thinks I hallucinated a monster."

"I don't know what happened there. I know I believe that *you* believe it. On Avalon, what we call monsters a native would call an animal. I also know you took a nasty bump. That can make the best of us see things. Scramble memories."

"Yeah," Aaron said. "Right."

"Let me put it another way, Aaron . . . I know what happened. Not for an instant should you think I don't. But despite that, I still sit here, telling you that you're the best of the bunch."

Was that another smile? "Yeah, well . . . what am I supposed to do with that? Be a leader without followers?"

"I know your mind and body. I don't know your heart. That's up to you."

Aaron took another sip. His hands were shaking again. "You got that right."

"There's one thing I suspect was in your heart, though. Willow."

Aaron glared at him. "I don't know what you're talking about."

"Let's not start lying to each other, shall we?"

"That," Aaron said, "that would be a unique situation."

"Between us? On Avalon?"

"In human history."

"Well," Cadmann replied. "Let's make history, then. Cards on the table. Since you've been gone, how many times has Willow been to see you?"

Aaron turned away a bit, concealing his expression. "Twice. I wouldn't see her."

"Right. So . . . now she's hanging with Marshall."

An ugly laugh. "That figures."

"Maybe I'm not totally happy with that."

A curious look. "Why not?"

"Competition is a healthy thing. Whether in the animal kingdom . . . sports teams . . . or colonies." A pause. "Ever wonder about the competition that made grendels?"

"Yeah," Aaron said. "Yeah, I've thought about it."

Cadmann sipped. His eyes widened.

"Different from Earth coffee?" Aaron said. Definitely a smile.

"Let's put it this way. If you could export it to Earth, you'd get rich."

Coffee with both caffeine and speed. Nothing like it. Cadmann could almost see the commercials now. Grendel King–brand coffee, with animated quasi-lizards as fast as race cars zipping around or tap-dancing in a line. No one on Earth had ever had to deal with one, or could imagine what it was like to face a predator that could turn on a supercharger. Put a grendel in your cup!

The next sip tasted sour. Too many bad memories. What the hell, he'd get over it. Everyone else seemed to have.

"Something in the soil?"

"Think so. I'd bet there are other things on this planet that have speed. They compete with each other, and you can see what we get. So Willow and you."

"What about us?"

"We might have been wrong. Everybody might have been wrong. But we all thought it was going to be you and Willow. That was the safe money."

"Council might have had something to say about that."

Cadmann nodded. "There's politics, and then there is leadership. Then something happened, and you dropped out of the running. And Marshall got the sympathy vote."

"Because of Archie?"

Cadmann nodded.

Aaron snorted with disgust. "So . . ." he said. "What now?"

"What now?" Cadmann asked. "Well—life goes on out at Surf's Up. Everybody's learning and growing, and in a few days, it's time for another Grendel Scout overnight."

Aaron smiled wistfully. "How are the kids?"

"You miss them? You were pretty good with them, you know."

Aaron paused again, as if counting something in his head. "What's the play?"

"Black Ship Island," Cadmann replied.

"Good spot," Aaron said. "We did some good things out there. Scary, and safe."

"My thought exactly. Caves, beach, woods . . . pretty damned good place for survival training."

"Orienteering, team building, foraging . . . any of the pumping stations up for grabs?"

"Off limits. Some of the botanical groves might be incorporated into the games. There'll be reflex conditioning." The world record for a human being in the 100 meters was 7.97 seconds. A cheetah, the fastest earthly animal, could achieve a top speed of 30 meters per second, which would equal 100 meter time of 3.33 seconds. A grendel on speed could cover 100 meters in 2.3 seconds. With a grendel coming at you, there was simply no time for conscious thought, only a conditioned response.

"I remember. Those were good times."

"I'm sure they were. Probably better than my best scout jamboree in Kentucky. Willow and Marshall are heading things up. They have a few surprises set for the kids."

Aaron sighed, aware that Cadmann had set the hook. "What do you want from me?"

Cadmann leaned in. "For you to decide what you want. If you want Willow, and you were expecting her to come up here over and over again until she wore you down . . . it's not going to happen. She's got feelings too. Upset Marshall's apple cart a bit, throw him off balance . . . it might not be too late."

Aaron chuffed. "Throw him off balance. Things like that start fights."

Cadmann shrugged. "If he starts it, you can finish it."

"That what you think?"

Cadmann stood up. As he did, he felt a twinge in his right knee. Sucked getting old. "It's what I know. Hey, listen. What the hell. Maybe I'm wrong about everything. But had to put in my two cents. What you do with it is up to you." He cupped his hands around his mouth. "Mike! I'm leaving now."

He extended his hand, and Aaron shook it. "For what it's worth, thanks."

The boy was almost as tall as Cadmann, but still a beanpole. One day he would be as broad, and perhaps as strong. That day hadn't quite arrived. "One more thing . . . Willow always asks about you. Every time she comes in."

Then, bearing just a trace of a smile, Cadmann waved to Mike, who was coming down the hill. Together, they headed back down, leaving Aaron scanning his surroundings. He sipped, considering.

## CHAPTER FIVE: SURF'S UP

The waters off Surf's Up were tranquil and dark. Outside the lagoon, they were actually quite calm, only occasionally choppy.

The goliath broke the surface, rolling like a sea serpent, and then dove back down. Those who had given it a Biblical name considered it to be about three times the size of an orca, if shaped more like an eel. It smelled something in the water. Seminal fluid, the mating season for an ancient enemy. It would have to be careful, but this would be a good feeding time. It dove down deep, and saw something much smaller than itself, three times as long as it was thick. This, the flexible tail and worm-rimmed snout triggered a response stronger than conscious thought. It went for the kill. Its enemy was heavy with freshly fertilized eggs.

This was the perfect time for the kill: Its enemy was slow, and if it survived this season, would lay those eggs and they would increase the number of enemy.

It was a cow, surrounded by her young, none more than a single year old. The goliath struck from below, from the shadows and darkness, jaws snapping once but that once was enough, tearing through flesh and shearing bone, inflicting damage so massive that the cow barely had time to register pain before she was dead.

The young scattered, frantic. The goliath slowed, chewing, grinding the cow's flesh into shreds, savoring.

Then . . . for the first time in its life, the goliath felt pain, as if its underside had been ripped open by a reef. It had been attacked by a bull only a fraction of its own size. Belly ripped open, the creature rolled, tearing the bull free, biting and killing it.

But even as it did, a second bull struck. And then a virgin cow. And another bull. At first the predator, the leviathan became the prey as the creatures grabbed at it, as their mandibles dug in and began to inject digestive fluid.

Now, at last, it knew pain. It forgot its hunger, seeking only to escape. But there was no escape, as the smell of its blood seeped into the water, attracting more and more of its enemies.

It fought its way to the surface. If a human had witnessed its agonies, it might have looked somewhat like a flattened shark swarmed by lampreys. Then it rolled, as the digestive juices broke down the membranes around its heart and lungs, and it shuddered, dying.

The body floated there, slowly becoming oddly . . . shapeless. And then rolled. And sank out of the moonlight, leaving behind only a fading crimson slick.

Dawn came to the clustered huts near the edge of the lagoon. There was something both casual and clever about their design and placement.

In the largest, neatest hut, Willow shared space with Marshall. She awakened first, and rubbed at her teeth with a peppermint floss stick. She looked back at Marshall as he slept. He was perfect, of course, but she could not be faulted for momentarily thinking of someone else as she plopped down next to him.

She kissed his shoulder, and he moaned drowsily. "Wakey, wakey, eggs and bakey."

"Hey, there," he said, and tried to drag her down to the mattress.

"Hey there. No, we don't have time for that. We're expecting visitors, and there's work to do."

Marshall crinkled his nose in pretense of anger. "Aww."

She tousled his hair, getting him awake. He tried to wrestle her down onto the bed again, but she slipped away. "There'll be time for that tonight, after we put the Scouts to bed."

Finally, he sighed and relented. "Be right with you."

Willow smiled. "No rest for the wicked," she said, and headed out.

She squinted as the morning light struck her eyes. The cluster of huts and the rolling waves were her first taste of the new day. Like most of the Starborn, she had researched Earth, the lost homeland. And of all places on Earth, Avalon reminded her most of Polynesia, especially Fiji, but with its own, strange flora. Not strange to her, of course: this was home.

Some of the others were starting to rouse themselves, and they waved to her across the sand. Five of them would be in control of this adventure.

First was Marshall, just awakening himself. A majority of Avalonians considered him Aaron's replacement, the kid most likely to inherit the colony. They were all polymaths, but Marshall's combination of skills and presence gave him a special edge.

She, Willow, of course. She was the alpha female, without a doubt, and the best biologist among the Starborn.

Skeeter pilot Takashi Toru was a rock climber, an engineering specialist with a soft spot for children.

Kola Andewala's Nigerian genes made her as dark as coal and the tallest woman among the Starborn. She actually had a younger clone named Nnedi. Sometimes they behaved like sisters, and at other times like mother and daughter.

An oddly matched group.

Takashi bent and stretched and rotated every joint of his body in sequence. His invariable morning rock-climber routine made him flexible as a pipe cleaner. "Morning, Willow. Good day for Hell Night!"

"Well, get out there," she called back. "We can't have the kids seeing our surprise, now can we?"

Takashi yelled at a tall gangly guy wrestling a tarped package into a motorized rubber raft. "Porter!"

"Ahoy the beach!" Porter called. "All is well. Give me a hand?"

"Let me get my bag." Takashi turned. "Willow, when are the kids coming?"

"We have about twenty minutes," she replied.

She looked east toward the mountains separating the coast from the inland. Other Starborn were wandering over from their huts. Kola kissed Willow on both cheeks, and nodded to Takashi.

"What weather can we expect?" Takashi asked.

"Higher winds and tides by noon." Kola replied.

"By noon," Willow said, "we'll be on the beach."

"Marching inland, I'd think," Marshall said behind her, blinking as he emerged into the light.

Kola chuckled. "Sleepy head. Wear you out again?"

"Hah hah. Not this side of the grave."

Porter ran to pudgy, despite a strong work ethic and a talent for rock climbing. "We sure we don't want to skeeter the kids over to Black Ship?"

Willow grinned. "Where's the fun in that?"

The teens began checking the five boats. These were large, motorized inflatable rafts, a simple, sturdy design. They carefully checked, cleaned, bundled, and prepared, bickering good-naturedly as they did. Despite their play, the work was quite efficient. There was no wasted motion at all.

"Screwdriver," Porter said. He raised his hand, and Kola threw without looking, and he snatched it out of the air almost as blithely. Made an adjustment in the engine.

A burring roar slowly grew louder as three skeeters zipped over the mountains in unison, an elephant-sized cargo container suspended between them with cables.

Marshall shaded his eyes. "And . . . here they come!"

The skeeters landed on the beach, whipping up the sand. Three pilots exited: Louisa, Dr. Niles, and Carlos Martinez.

"Morning," Carlos said. His hair was graying a bit, but he was still the dashing figure he'd been while cutting a swath through the colony's single women two decades ago.

The cargo container opened, and within were twenty kids, aged eight to twelve. The first out were the team leaders, bright-eyed scrappy kids named Kelly, Percy, Thor, and Nnedi, Kola Andewala's younger sister.

"Kola!" Nnedi cried. A little black girl, her hair in cornrows and braids, ran to Kola. She looked like a miniature of the older girl, which was high praise indeed.

Nnedi looked in her sister's eyes. "Are you going to keep me safe?"

"No, little darling. I'm going to teach you how to keep yourself safe."

"Oh, okay, I guess that'll have to do," Nnedi said.

"It's all there is."

Porter clucked. "You are such a cynic."

She stuck her tongue out, and hugged Nnedi fiercely.

Carlos caught her attention. "So you're taking the Runners out. Everything checked?"

"Everything except the last thing," Willow said.

"Which is?"

"Don't know yet. But there's always a last thing. Kids!"

The Grendel Scouts gathered around, and look up at Willow with adoring, slightly frightened and hopeful eyes.

"Grendel Scouts! Form into clans!"

They formed four lines of five, four each behind Kelly, Percy, Thor, and Nnedi. They were precise, very focused. Desperate for approval, and filled with expectation.

"Not bad," Willow said.

"Not bad?" Kola asked. "This is the best we can do? The cream of Earth? The fruit of the superfolk? We'll see." She strode with the presence and power of a lioness. When she passed her clone, little Nnedi, she secretly winked an eye . . . and Nnedi hid her answering smile.

"We have three rules, and three rules only!" Porter said.

"One, You will do what you are told, at all times, and without question. Anyone. Any of you who feel you can't do this. . . ."

"Step forward *now!*" Takashi said. "Go home! Go back to your safe, warm beds."

Predictably, not a single Scout stepped forward.

"Good," Marshall said.

"Good!" Takashi agreed. "Rule two! Tell the truth. No matter how hard it is. No matter how shameful it is. The only way you will survive, any of you, is if you know you can trust what your brothers and sisters say. If you know what their strengths and weaknesses are. *Really* are. Not their hallucinations, hopes, and dreams."

"You don't have to be the strongest, or the smartest—" Willow said.

One of Nnedi's teammates, a chunky straw-haired munchkin named Buddy, chirped up. "They can't be. *I* am."

The kids laughed, and some of it was actually amusement rather than unease.

"Are you?" Kola leaned close. "Are you now, little man? Well. We'll see." She straightened, a seventeen-year-old Amazon glaring down at a twelve-year-old boy. Their eyes locked, until he flinched and broke contact, just a hint of fear on his face, as well as anger that she did this to him. She grinned, satisfied. "Three! Pay attention. It isn't what you don't know that will kill you. It's what you think you know that ain't so. There is only one cure for lies. Only one cure for ignorance. PAY ATTENTION."

"Can you do that?" Willow asked.

A couple of the kids nodded.

Takashi raised his voice louder. "Do what you are told! Tell the truth! Pay attention! These rules will keep you and your brothers and sisters alive. Can you do it?"

The same few kids nodded.

Willow frowned at the meek response. "What kind of weak-ass little kittens . . . Can you do it? Let's hear those voices!"

"Yes." More of them, this time.

"*Looouder! What are the rules*!"

"*Do what you're told! Tell the truth! Pay attention*!"

"Well, all right!" One at a time he went down the rows, naming them. "Kelly: Blue Team, Nnedi: Red Team, Percy: Green Team, Thor: Yellow."

"The game starts now!" Kola said. "Grab your gear, get to the boats, and let's get going. Let's hear it one more time. Are you sprouts ready?"

"Yeah!" the kids said.

"Let 'em hear it on Black Ship Island!" Marshall yelled.

"*Yeah*!!"

And a mile away across the water, their young, strong voices were heard. Floating up and down on the waves ahead of them was an orange inflatable motorized raft. In it was one of the three pairs of twins among the colonists. Starborn Evan and Heather, as well as Uncle Horace.

Evan cupped his hand to his ear. "Wait. Did you hear something? Something calling?"

Heather paused, then shrugged. "Wind through the waves, maybe. Your ears can play tricks. . . ."

They paused in their paddling. Distantly, from across the water, came a sound: "*Yeah*!"

"Sounds like kids," Uncle Horace said.

Again, distantly, "*Yeah*!"

"Probably getting ready to shove off," Heather said.

"We can overthink this stuff," Evan said. "Come on. Steer away from the rocks."

They guided the inflatable through the clashing waves and onto the beach. The twins worked well together, and Uncle Horace took orders with enthusiasm.

"And here we go!" he chortled.

A dark bulky bundle filled the prow of the raft, large and heavy enough to require both Heather and Horace to wrestle it ashore.

Evan lifted a sealed, waterproof olive backpack from the raft's floor. He checked the seals carefully.

Heather laughed. "Your flash-bangs are fine, Evan."

"Can't be too careful."

Horace stumbled as a low wave slapped against his knees, and almost dropped his end of the package.

"Hey! Don't let her get wet," Evan said.

"She won't mind," Heather said.

Uncle Horace frowned. "'She' . . . ? Oh, you're joking!"

Heather and Evan glanced at each other. "Yes, Horace. We're joking." The expression they shared was part pity, and part *there but for the grace of God* relief.

"Let's get the boat up. Don't want to leave tracks," Uncle Horace said, and the Twins looked at each other and nodded mildly surprised agreement.

"Don't worry," Heather said. "They'll be coming in east of us."

She hopped down into the water. Heather was athletic, brilliant, observant. Together they unloaded seven bundles of gear. Resting after the exertion, Heather took time to point out a spot where the water swirled within a circle of rocks.

"Anything risky here?"

"On Earth those tidal pools would be filled with anemones and hermit crabs. Maybe lobsters. Nothing too active or dangerous."

"Assuming similar developmental paths," Evan said. "That remains to be seen. What would that be? Genetic xenobiology? We could get a dozen doctorates writing papers about this place."

"Tell you what," Heather said. "After this is over, we come back, collect some samples. Fair?"

"Fair. Come on. . . ."

Together, they carried the boat up, and then deflated the cells, and hid it in the bushes.

Heather looked up. Black Ship had steep cliffs, dense jungle. She thought it looked a lot like the original Willis O'Brien glass paintings of Skull Island for the 1933 *King Kong*: misty, romantic, mysterious.

"You think they'll suspect anyone is watching them?"

"Not the slightest," Evan said. "They'll look at those cliffs, and get spooked. Then they'll remember they're supposed to be brave, and put the spooking down to nerves and soldier on like good little scouts."

Heather grinned. "They are going to piss their pants, aren't they?"

"Only if we do our jobs right."

"That's right. Let's get in place."

They continued dragging the package up the beach. Heather stopped, and looked up at the cliffs, frowning for a moment. Then she shrugged and continued on.

## CHAPTER SIX: OPEN WATER

The cove's artificial crescent had been constructed over three years by dropping rocks from skeeters. After a sufficient base had been built, earthly coral was then implanted and protected until it had taken root. What would happen when Earth's colony creatures finally competed with Avalon's was anyone's guess.

But the crescent was not unbroken. Precisely centered was a motorized gate ten feet across called the "keyhole." Through this swinging gap boats and eventually dolphins would pass in and out, the domesticated released into the wild. The smiling cetaceans might not survive long, but even measuring the duration of that survival, and the manner of their dying, might be valuable.

"Hold on!" Willow said. "The water's going to get choppy."

Buddy perked up. "'Cause we aren't protected once we leave the bay."

"That's right," Marshall yelled from the boat just behind Red Team's. "Two miles to Black Ship. Everybody's life vest in place. Everybody check their buddy's vest. You do *not* have permission to drown on my watch!" The kids checked their vests, checked each other.

Nnedi's closest buddy on Red Team was a gap-toothed blond kid named Cole. Although they were very young, a mischievous spark already burned between them.

"Are you ready for this?" Cole asked.

"Born ready," Nnedi said. Then giggled.

Marshall took a deep breath. "Everyone ready? Then here we go! Practice paddling. Everyone together. . . ."

The boats paddled around in the breakwater, the kids practicing working in unison.

"Stroke! Stroke!" Willow cried.

Takashi's rafts pulled up next to them. He watched, approving. "Looks like practice has paid off. Shall we try the gate?"

"Absolutely!" Willow yelled across the water. "Absolutely! But keep a hand on the engine in case you need a boost."

"You got it!" Takashi yelled back.

They headed through the breakwater "gate" and into the open ocean, four boats in a caravan.

"Time the waves," Willow said. "We don't want to be thrown back against the rocks."

"That would put definitely put a crimp in the day," Marshall said. "Now! Stroke!"

The kids paddled like crazy, oars splashing in happy synchrony in the calm troughs between waves.

"Paddle like your life depended on it! We have about fifty seconds to get twenty feet from the rocks, before the next wave hits." Fighting to keep from laughing with pride, Willow put as much sincerity into her voice as she could.

The next wave swelled in. Marshall kept one hand on the red lever that doubled as throttle and rudder as the swell lifted them. The slightest hint that the kids were losing control and he would gun the engine.

"Whoa!!"

They were riding the waves and loving it, like kids on a whitewater raft. They paddled like crazy. The raft spun.

"Right side!" Willow called. "Stop. Left side, put some back in it!"

The wave hit them, water spraying. They turned the raft around, and headed out. They stopped at least five feet from the break, and then continued on.

"*Yea*!!!" The kids screamed.

"All right," Marshall said. "We're out fifty feet and then waiting."

They putted out a little deeper into the ocean, and then circled back around, looking back to see how the other boats were doing. One at a time, the other rafts made it through the keyhole into the open ocean.

Thor, the cocky Yellow-Team leader in Kola's raft, was happy as a clam. "Let's do this! Last on the beach is a crippled grendel!"

The kids stroked in unison, the waves rocking and shaking them. They giggled and paddled as the morning sun grew stronger.

"Northwest a hair," Marshall said. "And . . . there it is!"

Mist and glare-shrouded, Black Ship Island emerged from the morning fog like a mythic fairyland.

The kids stared. Black Ship wasn't as easy to see from Surf's Up. Something about the sight gave them pause for a moment. Then Nnedi put her paddle back in the water, breaking everyone's trance. Tommy followed, and then the kids were all paddling.

"Stroke! Stroke!" Willow called. She had one hand on the engine. In an emergency, technology would take over.

"Off starb'rd." Takashi shaded his eyes with the flat of his hand. "What's that?"

Something floated in the water to their right. The waves were thick with something vaguely resembling transparent prawns. They swarmed in the water near . . . whatever it was.

Willow frowned. "What in the hell is *that*?"

"Don't know," Kola said. "Not sure if I want to. The jellysharks are out in force. They're scavengers. That means that whatever is dead is meat, and that's enough for me." Jellysharks were palm-sized, mostly scavengers, with a sting about as toxic as a honeybee's: uncomfortable but not lethal.

"Something big, and dead," Marshall said. "I think it was a behemoth. It's not stinking yet, so it happened recently."

They carefully guided around the dead . . . something.

"I wonder what killed it," Willow muttered as they passed.

"Old age, I hope," Takashi said. "Can't wait to get out of the water." The dead behemoth was curiously flattened out. Little jellied things nibbling around the edges, building to a frenzy.

The kids continued to paddle, a few of them looking back at the dead giant.

"Keep your mind on your job!" Takashi said. "Keep paddling."

"What do you think that was?" Nnedi asked.

"Don't know. But 'was' is the operative word. Eyes will be worn forward."

And they continued onward, traveling through a thinning blood slick. Thor trailed his fingers down into the water, got a little of the blood on them, rubbed them together.

"Oily," he said. And one of the other kids put her hand down to test.

Kola went ballistic. "Get your hands out of the water!"

"Sorry," she said, and withdrew her fingers, shaking them dry.

"Idiot," Nnedi muttered.

"Hey. Said I'm sorry."

The island was closer now. Waves crashed against rocks with impressive violence, causing spectacular but relatively mild whirlpools.

"Come about now," Marshall said. "The symplegades coming up!"

"What?" Percy asked over on Takashi's raft.

"Someone's been neglecting their classics," Willow said sweetly. "The clashing rocks that almost ate the Argonauts. Rafts have flipped."

"Was anyone hurt?" Yellow Team–leader Thor asked.

Marshall's look was pitying. "Someone is always hurt."

"What?" Nnedi asked.

"Didn't you know that? It's the only way we can get you to take anything seriously. To watch one of your own go down."

"Drown?"

"You probably wouldn't have time to drown. Don't worry: We've got plenty of spares."

"Look alive!" Kola called.

There was chaos as the rafts navigated between the whirlpools, spinning and then righting themselves. The elder Starborn winked at each other. The kids were safe enough, but damned if they'd admit that aloud! Then, just as they cleared the whirlpools—one of the kids went over the side of the raft. Nnedi.

"Help!" she screamed.

"Circle back around!" Kola said.

Nnedi's eyes were open underwater, and she caught a glimpse of pale shadows drifting toward her. Jellysharks. She winced as something stung her bare leg. The current pulled at her, sucking her under, but her orange life vest buoyed her back up.

Kola brought her raft around, reached out with an oar. Nnedi reached out for it, almost grabbed it, but the current spun the raft, tearing the oar from her hand. "I'm going in!" Kola yelled.

Before Kola could dive, Marshall called "I've got it!" and was over the side in a flash. He cleft the water smoothly, and a few powerful side-strokes brought him to Nnedi's side.

They maneuvered the rafts around to provide support without crashing into the struggling pair, keeping their eyes peeled for predators.

"I've got you!" Marshall called.

Her eyes were wide and frightened. "Ow! Something bit me!"

"Hang onto me!" Marshall said.

She linked her arms around his neck, and Marshall struck out for Blue Team's raft. They were at the lip of the whirlpool, and Kelly and his teammates grabbed her and hauled her up.

Nnedi heaved for breath in the bottom of the boat.

Nnedi loved an audience. "My leg. . . ." she moaned, as if in the last act of *Camille*.

Marshall flicked out his knife, and then a pocket torch, heating the tip. The triangular point quickly started to glow. He took a piece of flat metal and put it next to the jellyshark—which looked a lot like a translucent sand dollar—and touched the glowing point to the opposite side. The jellyshark crept away from the heat, leaving a pentagonal marking on Nnedi's skin. It crept onto the metal shingle.

"It burns," Nnedi moaned.

"Nasty things, but not much poison," Marshall said, eyeing the little beast and then tossing it over the side. "Mostly scavengers. Just enough venom to discourage bigger things from eating them. We'll take care of it when we hit the beach."

Nnedi gritted her teeth and returned to her oar.

"You all right?" Red Team's Jelli Gleason called over from their raft.

Nnedi glared. "Never better. You wanna try it?"

"Maybe later."

When all four boats had made it through the whirlpool, they headed in toward the beach. And then landed. Willow breathed a sigh of relief. If the tides had caught them just wrong they might have been swept north. Not a disaster, but that would have put them in sight of several oil storage tanks, used by the automated pumping stations. As much as they could, they wanted the illusion of a mythic, untamed wilderness to last as long as possible. "All right all right all right! Out of the boats, onto the beach, anchor the boats. If they drift off, we are *not* going home. Anyone who wants to spend the next year eating Black Ship berries just think I'm kidding. The rest of you, hop to it!"

The kids scrambled out of the boats, and worked together rapidly to beach and then anchor them.

"How far up does the tide come?" Percy, Green-Team leader asked.

"Darned good question. See these rocks?" Takashi said.

"Yes."

"Well, at high tide you won't," he said. "Get the rafts up higher, and lash them down. Get your gear out, and then take ten. We've got hiking to do!"

The kids followed the directions, looking back at the mountains, up at the cliffs . . . a slightly awe-filled silence, no one making jokes. Looking at Nnedi, who limped a bit.

"Farley . . . can you carry this?" Nnedi moaned. "My leg's a little . . ." She was playing up the limp.

"Sure. Sure. Red Team! Right?"

"Right."

From the limp, one'd think her foot had been torn off by a grendel. Poor Nnedi. Then Kola caught her eye, asking a silent "So?"

Nnedi grinned. She'd gotten someone to carry her gear. Kola shook her head in reluctant admiration. Nnedi stuck her tongue out.

The kids moved up-beach and collapsed for their break.

"All right, Nnedi," Willow said. "Let's see that leg."

Then suddenly Willow thought she glimpsed a flash of light, up in the rocks. She turned to look, but saw nothing. Oh well, she didn't want to draw the kids' attention there. . . .

High up among the cliffs, someone was indeed watching Willow as she cared for Nnedi. Watched Marshall come and kneel beside her, one proprietary hand on her shoulder. A tight, hard smile curled Aaron's lips. "Tonight's the night," he said. He crawled back from the edge of the cliff and disappeared into the woods, humming to himself. He'd forgotten just how much fun Hell Night really was.

## CHAPTER SEVEN: BLACK SHIP ISLAND

Once on the beach and out of the boats, the kids took deep relieved breaths, and began to unpack their gear.

"Nnedi?" Kola asked. "Take my pack, would you?" She had to ask a second time, so taken was Nnedi with the jungle setting.

Nnedi's eyes were bright. "This place is . . ."

"What?" Her older sister asked.

"Kinda spooky?"

Marshall laughed. "Just wait."

Willow raised her hand. "We'll have five minutes' rest, then I want everyone on the move."

She sidled over to Marshall.

"Think the Twins have everything in shape?" he asked.

"I hope so. This is going to be great!"

The Grendel Scout ages ranged from eight to twelve. The

"leaders" were thirteen to fifteen. After their rest, they wound up a trail along the side of a cliff until high above the ocean. Vines had begun to overgrow the paths, and the Teen Leaders wielded their machetes liberally. Tripping and falling could not be tolerated.

One of the kids slipped, and grendel-quick, Marshall grabbed his wrist and pulled him to safety. They were taking no chances with these precious kids. Finally they were up and over the edge of a cliff, and in a broad, flat area. Their campground.

"This is the space," Takashi said. "All right: Kelly? Blue Team over there. Nnedi? Red Team to the north. Percy? Green Team south. Thor? Yellow Team East. Let's get moving!"

Willow decided to make a game of it. "Let's see who gets their campsite up first? Losers do fifty push-ups. A little competition starting . . . now!" The kids scrambled, putting up air-filled tents as the older kids supervised sternly.

As the Scouts got their camp set up, their leaders got the fire pits running, and started cooking lunch. They unloaded masses of packaged brown-bag sandwiches, hot chocolate, and cake for desert.

Green Team won, and the others groaned but cranked out their push-ups without undue complaint. Fair was fair, and their turns would come.

After the exertion ended, the kids flopped over and panted. Takashi gave them about a minute's rest, then cracked the whip in a commanding voice. "Teams will eat together. I would suggest you assign cleanup duties quickly."

Still sweating, Roderick crawled over to Nnedi. "I am officially starved," he said.

"Not sure Red Team is supposed to talk to the Greens, but they did get up their tent fast," Nnedi said.

"What's our tactic?" Jelli asked.

Nnedi grinned. "When Red Team gets our first clue, I think we need to beat their pants off. That's our tactic." The kids high-fived each other, and looked over at their rivals, grinning and waving.

Buddy had a plan. "I'll handle the compass, we'll all work the riddles. Fair?"

"Fair," Roderick said.

"Five minutes' rest," Willow said. "And then the game resumes!"

"Think there's anything really dangerous here?" Roderick asked.

Buddy laughed. "No . . . but that won't stop them from trying to make us think there is." The kids laughed, but there was an uneasiness. Nnedi asked the question they were all thinking. "Why can't there be anything dangerous?"

"Come on," Buddy mocked. "They wouldn't take any chances."

"Not deliberately, no. But they can make mistakes. Our parents made mistakes."

"They're not your parents."

The other kids look at each other. *Oooooh!* "Something you want to say?" Nnedi's voice was ice cold.

Buddy shrugged. "Bottle babies . . . just sayin'."

Nnedi stood up. "You want to try for team captain?"

He showed teeth. "Maybe I do. Maybe I think you only got it because of your sister."

Jelli Gleason whooped with glee. "Challenge circle!"

Nnedi glared at the smaller girl. "This may not be the time."

"Right," Buddy said. "Right. And it never will be."

Now Roderick joined in. "Challenge circle!"

The other kids in the Yellow, Blue, and Green groups became aware of the noise, and they gathered around, like kids had since the invention of schoolyards. The Teen Leaders glanced at each other.

Marshall's brow wrinkled. "We need to stop this."

Kola put out her arm, with a reptilian smile. "Let them go."

Willow glanced from Marshall to Kola and then back to Nnedi. "Well . . . all righty then. Family rules. No biting, no gouging."

Nnedi rolled up her pants legs. "How about balls?"

Buddy's eyes widened. "What?" He glanced down, hands twitching toward coverage.

"You know. Balls. You've heard of them."

"No!"

"You challenged me," she said sweetly. "I make the rules." Buddy suddenly looked a little less certain. She shrugged. "All right. No balls. Not that you have any I could find without a microscope."

Buddy yelled and ran at her, grabbing. She ducked under his arms, elbowing him in the gut as she did. He *woofed* and spun and she punched him right in the nose. He backed up, and she kicked him in the gut. He grabbed her leg as she did, and stepped in and swept her standing leg. She went down. He jumped on her, and she kicked him in the belly as he came down. The kids *ooohed* and *ahhed* and she scrambled up, then managed a jab and a decent cross before he grabbed her and dumped her again.

He was grinning now, and slapped her, hard. Her eyes watered. "Bottle baby." He lunged in, but she was faking. The little girl spun and nailed him right in the solar plexus with her heel. He stopped, eyes bugging out, gasping for breath without finding it.

He dropped to his knees, face pursed in an "O," sucking air.

Kola rushed to Buddy, pressed him onto his back, started massaging his stomach. "Breathe, big guy. Breathe." Buddy finally started sucking air, his eyes watering, and sat up.

"Stings a little, don't it?" Nnedi laughed, but there was concern in her eyes.

He nodded, gasped, "Good one," and extended his hand. She took it and pulled him up.

"Well?" Kola asked.

"I guess she's team leader," he said, and everybody cheered.

"All right," Marshall said. "Have we gotten that out of our systems? Anybody else? No?"

The kids shook their heads.

"I think we're good," Roderick said.

"Good. Then . . . we have four envelopes, one for each team. You will take your envelopes and head in the corresponding directions. Now, a warning: your paths will eventually converge. At that point you *will* obey standard Grendel Scout rules of engagement. Shoving and pulling allowed. If there is water, safety rules apply. No striking, and everyone is responsible for everyone's safety. Is that understood?"

The kids nodded. "All right then," Takashi said. "Play hard!"

The team leaders were handed envelopes. Nnedi, still breathing a little hard, got hers, and her team retired to the Red corner.

"Open it up!" Jelli squeaked impatiently, and Nnedi tore it open.

"*The pirates landed long ago,*
*Our ancient legends tell us so.*
*So travel north instead of south,*
*And look within the Dragon's mouth.*"

Nnedi looked up. "What's this?"

"What does that mean?"

"It means we go north," Nnedi said. She looked up at Willow, who was tagging along with them.

Willow smiled and held up her palms. "Don't ask me. I'm strictly neutral."

Willow and the kids headed north. The kids were searching every shrub and rock. For anything.

"What are we looking for?" Buddy asked. "I'm ready to go!"

"I'm not sure," Nnedi said. "I'll make a guess. The first clue won't be too far off. We don't know this territory. If we have to go too far to find our first clue, we might get off true."

She looked back at Willow. "Let's go!" she yelled, and they headed off through the brush.

## CHAPTER EIGHT: PUZZLE TIME

About four hundred feet to the east, Marshall and his Blue Team were reading another poem aloud.

"*Smooth and strong and white as milk,*
*You'll find your goal a road of silk.*
*Though not a native form, they say,*
*Their roots will help you find your way.*"

Their leader, a little redheaded ball of energy named Kelly, brother of Red Team's resident pessimist Roderick, made a face. "'Road of silk'? What are we looking for?"

"Cloth, maybe?" the kid beside him said. "What was the road of silk?"

They were chopping their way through an overgrown foot path. The local vegetation was heavy but not unpleasant. They paused. Within a cluster of fleshy pitcher plant–type leaves writhed what looked like a knot of hairy spider legs. Spider-legs was struggling slowly, the torpor increasing even as they watched, as if fatiguing or losing hope.

Kelly squealed. "Oh! Poor thing."

"Behold," Marshall sighed. "The wonder of nature."

"What is it doing?"

"Lunch," a redheaded girl said, and got jostled.

"There's nothing we can do, kids, not really," Marshall said.

"Why?" the redhead asked.

"Everything has to eat," Marshall said. "And we're on a mission, kids. No time, really."

The kids looked at each other.

Then Kelly turned. "I'm taking a vote. Who sides with the plant?"

"Come on . . ." Marshall said.

The kid stood his ground. "Let's do this." Kelly and his teammates drew their little machetes and began to hack at the plant. The hairy cluster suddenly took heart and increased its struggles. The plant stopped trying to eat it, and the legs wrenched themselves away. It swung up into a tree and chittered at them. A few broken sucker-fronds still adhered to its skin.

"Hmmm," Marshall said.

"You're welcome!" Kelly said.

The thing chittered at them. The kids grinned at it and continued on their way.

The thing tore away the suckers, exposing little patches of red where fur had been torn. It cursed in hairy-leg language at the plant, which seemed almost to be sulking and nursing its damaged vines. The tree spider followed the kids.

"Uh-oh," Kelly said. "Don't look now. We've got company."

Marshall grinned. "You save a life, you own a life."

Kelly looked back. Spider-legs was following them, all right, swinging from branch to branch like a monkey with no torso.

"Back to business," the redhead said. "'Road of silk.' Heck, we could walk right past something and not know what it is."

"Maybe," Marshall said. "Maybe not. We worked hard to be sure that the clues were fair."

Kelly suddenly stopped. "Wait a minute. What's this?" In the middle of a group of reddish flowers was a row of green bushes, all approximately the same size and rough shape. Clearly . . . cultivated. Marshall said nothing, merely watching. "Marshall? Is this something we should pay attention to?"

Marshall said nothing. The kids clustered. The bushes had not only been planted, but labeled.

"Look at the label," Kelly said. "It says White Russian Mulberry—*Morus alba var. tatarica.*"

His teammates began to chatter:

"Well, it doesn't belong here."

"What is it doing here?"

"Isn't that . . . a mulberry plant?"

"Isn't . . . don't silkworms eat mulberry leaves?" The kids looked at each other, and suddenly slapped hands. "Booyah! Road of silk!"

They swarmed around. They were getting into it now.

"What now?" Kelly asked. "'White Russian'? Does that mean something?"

Marshall sighed. "I've read about a drink called a White Russian."

"What's it made from?"

"Vodka, coffee liqueur, cream. Like that. Sounds yummy."

"Coffee?" another Blue Teamer asked.

Kelly perked up. "Don't pterodons help make coffee? There are nests up on the volcano."

The kids look up at the misted mountain above them. "We gotta climb all the way up *there*?"

The redhead raised her hand. "Wait. Let's read the poem again."

There was a squealing sound behind them. Spider-legs was watching them. They assumed: no eyes were visible. For that matter, no head, either.

"Spider baby seems to like that idea," Kelly said. "'*Smooth and strong and white as milk, tah-dum tah-dum . . . their roots will help you find your way.*'"

"Their roots. *Roots.*" The redhead lit up like a little light bulb. They dropped to their hands and knees. No one had noticed before, but there were ribbons: white, red, blue, and green, pointing out into the cardinal directions. They sighed with relief. They were chattering now, so swiftly it was hard to tell who was saying what.

"Well, that helps . . . but do we dig? Or what?"

"Look. Only . . . four of the trees have the ribbons. . . ."

"Do the colors mean something?"

"White as milk. Silk. White Russian. I think white means something."

"All right . . ." Kelly said, cutting through the chatter. "If we draw a line between the trunks and the colored ribbons . . ."

"Then the lines would all intersect . . ."

"About right . . . *here*!!"

And there was indeed a patch of ground that looked recently disturbed. With almost supernatural intensity, they dug it up, and found a glass tube. Kelly cracked it open, and pulled out another scroll. "Tah-daaah!"

"What does it say?"

"Wait a minute, wait a minute . . ." Kelly said.

Spider-legs was hovering close behind him. Kelly turned and glared, and it backed up.

"Do you mind?" Kelly cleared his throat. "Ahem:

"*Where sky and rock and surf all meet,*
*You'll find a source of liquid heat.*
*It's there you'll test your skills, my friend,*
*So hurry to the Southern end.*"

The redhead frowned. "Southern end?"

"Of the island. Let's go!"

Marshall tried to hide his approval, and failed miserably. The kids were good!

Far overhead, *Geographic*'s empty corridors hummed. No humans rested in cryosleep, not even embryos. A few animals remained, but that was all.

The computer screens rotated with images from across Avalon, across Tau Ceti IV. One of the screens suddenly cleared and flashed: "Relay Active."

The web of its communication reached down through the clouds to Avalon, and Camelot. In the communications hutch, Cadmann Weyland and Zack Moskowitz watched the screens, sipping freshly brewed cups of Gastric Special.

"What have we got?" Cadmann asked.

"Well . . . everything seems fine. No problems. They've split into four groups, as usual. They're orienteering."

"Skeeters standing by?"

Mary Anne squeezed him fondly. "Absolutely. Cadmann . . . we can follow them above ground. What about when they go down into the caves?"

"Deep scan can track them," Zack said, "but we won't know what's going on. They'll be on their own."

"Like we were," Cadmann said.

"It's different," Zack replied.

Cadmann shook his massive head. "When it comes right down to it . . . no, it's not."

On the island, Red group had discovered a bamboo and plastic mock-up of a pterodon, a note concealed within its beaked mouth.

Nnedi unfolded the paper and read as her teammates gathered around.

"*The opposite of cold is heat,*
*The opposite of plant is meat.*
*So find the place these ideas mesh,*
*And fight the fiend that feeds on flesh.*"

"Now that," little Jelli said, "is a sucky poem."

Nnedi squinted. "We need to find a hot plant? 'The ideas mesh'? Combine?"

"Maybe," Roderick said. "Doesn't make much sense. On the other hand, the trail is marked, if we don't get off the trail, we'll find what we're looking for."

Jelli wasn't sure. "A hot plant."

"I'm hungry," Buddy said.

They trooped past. Heather was hiding in the bushes, and Willow lagged behind to speak to her. "Is Uncle Horace in place?"

"Everything should be set," Heather said. "How is everything going?"

"Kids are sharp," Willow said. "Where are the other teams?"

"Right about where we want," Heather said. "We're running them around and wearing them out. Let me check." She touched her communicator. "Are you there? What's going on?"

"*Yellow Team is playing a reflex game,*" Kola replied. "*Thermal goggles and shooting darts at a grendel mock-up. We're doing well, but . . .*" She dropped her voice a little lower. "*Slow Red group down by about ten minutes, though. We don't want a bottleneck here.*"

"Roger." Willow spanked her hands together. "Break time!" she said, and sprinted ahead to rejoin her charges.

Heather chuckled, and began a stealthy movement through the brush, keeping track without being seen. She paused, suddenly certain that she heard something passing behind her. She scanned the jungle without seeing anything, and after a while shrugged and continued on.

Red Team had thoroughly enjoyed its unexpected break, using the time to rest, compare theories about the clues and pick burrs out of their socks.

Willow glanced at her watch. "All right, break time over."

Roderick groaned. "Oh, my legs. No more hills, please."

"Well," Willow said. "A little more, then downhill, and it's a run. Everybody up!"

The kids got up, toed the line. . . .

"On your mark . . . get set . . . the first to the next goal shoots for the team!"

"That's me!" Jelli squealed.

"Hell with that!" Nnedi said.

"Go!"

And the kids were off! They ran like crazy, up the hill, a jostling mob of blurring skinny legs and knobby elbows.

A hot springs bubbled at the end of their run. Tear-drop shaped, and shadowed by a plant that looked more like a twisted mushroom than a true tree, its roots twisting pale forearm-thick fleshy things disappearing into the steaming water. Preceded by a drum roll of thundering feet, the kids powered around the curving dirt trail and came huffing and puffing up to the spring.

"Hot plants!" Nnedi said. "Here we go."

"I was first," Roderick said.

Uncle Horace grinned. "And the winner is . . ." He stopped, frowning. "What was your name again?"

The kid opened his mouth in protest.

Horace howled laughter. "Roderick! Your name is Roderick. I know that."

With relief, Willow realized he was just playing with them, had a little sense of humor about his own terrible situation. And everyone laughed, not all the laughter comfortable.

"All right!" Willow said. "Now, all of you know what a grendel's greatest advantage is?"

"Speed!" Buddy said.

"That's right. An oxygenating secretion like a turbocharger, dumped into the blood stream that allows it to function in an excited anaerobic state, an extended sprinting capacity," Willow chimed in.

"But that same ability generates serious heat, and we've been able to gain advantage in two ways: programming our reflexes from the cradle, and infrared lenses."

"The infrared lenses take advantage of the heat profile, the fact that grendels run hot." Willow continued. "And the fact that when they're too hot, they need water to cool off. Most of their kills are near water, and if they aren't near water, they are less likely to go on speed."

Roderick, the little speedball, donned goggles. In them, the heat of the hot spring glared like a glance at the sun . . . but then settled back down. The contrast was terrible: either the hot spring glared, with a pitch-black background, or the reverse.

Uncle Horace handed Roderick a paint ball gun.

"Cadmann Weyland, our greatest warrior, was best friends with a man named Ernst," Willow said. "Once, the two of them sat in a hunting blind, waiting to kill a creature they did not understand."

She bounced the mental ball back to the others. "Ernst died because Cadmann didn't understand what they were up against. You do. Grendels are so fast that you'll only have a moment to see it. You are next to your best friend, who is helpless. If you shoot a half second too late, the grendel will *kill* him. If you shoot too soon, the grendel will know you're there, and might escape . . . and come back later. And kill *you*."

Willow got close, right into Roderick's freckled face. "Can you do it, Roddy?"

The boy nodded, sweat dripping down his face.

"You'll have something Cadmann didn't have, Roddy."

"What's that?"

"More than one chance," she said. "Get in the blind."

They'd set up a nest of thorn bushes, with a little place for Roddy to lie, concealed, looking at the hot spring. He slid down into it. Uncomfortable. The glare was blindingly strong. Roddy flinched away.

Willow sidled up closer to Uncle Horace. "We've got lenses. We can compensate for the heat, y'know."

Uncle Horace grinned. "Where's the fun in that?"

"We are bastards," she said.

"Speak for yourself."

"What?" Willow said, peering at him. Was that a touch of snark? A bottle-baby reference? She was never totally certain how aware Uncle Horace was of what he said. He was smiling at her blandly.

Finally she gave up and turned to Roderick. "Are you ready?"

"I'm ready."

"Then . . . begin!" Uncle Horace had a rope connected to the mock-up. He shook it a little. Roderick jumped, and fired . . . at nothing.

"Damn!" he yelled. Then settled himself back down. "Calm down," he said.

"Calm down, Roddy!" Nnedi said. "Take your time."

"Shhhh," Willow said.

"Can you see it, Roddy?" Uncle Horace asked. "What can you see? Calm yourself. One shot. Just one . . ." The thorn blind shook again, but this time Roddy didn't respond. He wiped sweat from his face. There was something . . . something in the water. Barely made it out. The thorn bush shook again.

"The bush shaking is a distraction," Roddy whispered. "That's the goat. Grendel's in the water. Grendel's hot. Water's hot. Won't be much difference in the skin temperature. Just a second . . ."

The brush rattled again. Then . . . the water exploded as Uncle Horace pulled the other rope, and a mock grendel exploded up out of the water. Then . . . it dangled like a piñata. Roderick crawled out from the thorn blind.

"Roddy?" Horace asked. "You quit?"

Roderick grinned. "Take a closer look."

They examined the grendel, and saw two darts side by side in the mock-grendel's hide.

"Whoa," Uncle Horace said.

The other kids gathered around cheering. . . .

## CHAPTER NINE: THE MAZE

The night stars witnessed a celebration, and Nnedi giving little Roddy the biggest kiss he'd ever had, as the kids counted up to "ten" and cheered. By the time she was done with him, his eyes were fairly bugging out, and he resembled a happy coronary victim.

"And the winner is!" Buddy said.

"All right," Marshall yelled above the chaos. "We're not done! We're not done! We have a lot more tomorrow, so I'd suggest that you enjoy the food, we have plenty of everything, and get plenty of rest."

"Screw rest," Jelli screamed. "*Par-tay*!"

Nnedi wasn't so certain. "Rest might be a good idea. I wouldn't trust them if I were you. Tricks up the sleeve, and sleeves worn long."

Buddy toasted her. "Got that right."

"On the other hand," the little girl said and flipped her braids, "we ended the day in second place, right behind Red Team. I think we can make up points tomorrow."

The central campfire hadn't been fed in the last half hour, and had begun the process of dying to ashes. "Have you finished prep?" Evan asked.

"Not quite," Heather answered. "I was waiting until everything settles down. Then we can go down, get things set up, and roust the little bastards."

"Sounds like a plan." Willow and Marshall were cuddling, as were Kola and Evan. Nothing inappropriate in front of the kids, but lots of whispering and smoky gazes. Willow was a little distracted when he tried to smooch. "What's wrong?" he asked.

"I don't know. Everything's going well, but . . . something always goes wrong. I'm just waiting to see what it is."

"True enough," Takashi said. "Once it's gone wrong, you can deal with it."

Willow raised her glass. "Toast."

"To what?" Marshall asked.

"To dealing with it. Whatever 'it' is."

***

The ball of legs had been lingering around the edge of the camp, crawling in the branches, shifting side to side and watching. If it had eyes. It was hard to tell.

"Hey! There you are! Heard about you from Kelly," Nnedi said.

It looked at them, shifting side to side, and not coming closer.

"Here." She rolled over a piece of hot dog. The thing circled it, then extruded a nozzle and fastened on the bun. Then on the hot dog sausage, and recoiled, tossing it away. It went back to the bun. Spider-legs probed with one of the hairy appendages, which suddenly fountained a greenish fluid upon it. With alarming speed the bun collapsed, dissolving into soggy chunks. Spider-legs slurped in the resulting brown glop with gusto.

"That," Buddy groaned, "is just gross."

"Aw, it's cute," Nnedi said.

"Cute and gross," Buddy said.

"Sort of like you. Maybe he wants to come with us?"

The kids tossed scraps to the little creature, which was obviously in heaven, vibrating with evident pleasure.

The kids began to settle down. They were singing songs around the campfire.

*"My name is Yon Yonson*
*I come from Wisconsin*
*I work in the lumberyard there.*
*All the people I meet*
*As I walk down the street,*
*They say, hello, I say hello, they say what's your name?*
*My name is Yon Yonson*
*I come from Wisconsin I work in the lumberyard there . . ."*

* * *

This went on for quite a while, then died down, and another song took its place.

*"From this valley they say you are going*
*We will miss your bright eyes and sweet smile*
*For they say you are taking the sunshine*
*That has brightened our path for a while . . ."*

Horace sang for a while, then he seemed to lose focus, and went to sit closer to the fire, near Willow and Marshall.

"Did you know," he said. "The first sundial was called a gnomon. Just a stick in the ground to tell time."

They said nothing in response, and he went on. "The Romans made the first sundial in 164 B.C." He smiled. "Did you know the name Horace means hour?"

"Yes, Horace," Willow said. "We know."

"*Come and sit by my side if you love me*
*Do not hasten to bid me adieu*
*But remember the Red River Valley*
*And the cowboy who loved you so true* . . ."

Horace's eyes cleared, and for a moment, he knew, too. "How many times have I told you that?" he asked.

"Horace . . ." she said, suddenly deeply embarrassed for him. "It's all right."

"Probably can't count that high," he laughed. And she almost believed it. "Used to be able to. Used to know about numbers. Used to be good for something besides baby-sitting. Or throwing a knuckleball."

He was staring into the fire. Too close, perhaps, because the smoke seemed to be irritating his eyes. "We had a few suicides after the Grendel Wars, you know. We don't talk about it. Ice depression. Feeling useless. I never let it get to me. Held on. I love watching the kids grow."

"Horace . . ."

"You guys can take care of the little ones now. I don't know why I'm still here. You like me. Like old Horace. But you don't need me."

Willow stretched out her hand, and gripped his arm.

"It's all right," he said. "I'm not the kind who needs to be needed. Wanted is enough." His smile was wistful. "It kind of has to be." He brightened. "Did you know that a 'jiffy' is actually a unit of time?"

Marshall nodded. "One one-hundredth of a second," he said.

Horace smiled. "Yes."

"Did you know that your name means 'hour'?" Marshall said.

Willow held her breath.

Horace laughed. "Never heard that," he said. "It's good to know."

Sparks spiraled up toward the twin moons. The kids had moved on to another song:

"*Down in the valley, valley so low*
*Hang your head over, hear the wind blow*
*Hear the wind blow, love, hear the wind blow;*
*Hang your head over, hear the wind blow.*
*Roses love sunshine, violets love dew,*
*Angels in Heaven know I love you,*
*Know I love you, love, know I love you,*
*Angels in Heaven know I love you . . .*"

Horace and Willow and Marshall watched them sing, nodding along.

It was a good night.

The hot dogs and hamburgers had been devoured. Songs had been sung, and games of charades played. Things were starting to wind down.

Willow hunched around the counselor's fire, assembling her co-conspirators. "They'll be settling down in fifteen minutes. Asleep in an hour. Give them another hour to slide into REM."

"Then Hell Night?" Kola asked, eyes wide with glee.

They grinned at each other.

"Better get going," Kola said.

A few minutes later, Takashi broke the revelry. "All right!" he called. "Lights out in ten! Everybody bus your plates and get ready for bed." Nnedi and the spider-monkey thing seemed to be bonding pretty well. It was creeping close, and actually let her touch it once as it sucked up its dinner. Its fur was both soft and prickly.

"Bedtime," she said. "Wanna come with?"

"That's not safe," Roderick said. "You might wake up with Daddy Long Legs eating your face."

She reached out for it again, and this time it scooted back away from her.

"Guess it doesn't matter."

Nnedi didn't let her disappointment show. "She's smart. Doesn't make friends too quickly."

"She?"

"Well, I didn't see, you know, a thingie."

"Maybe all those hairy legs are 'thingies.'"

"You're a thingie," she said sweetly.

"Well," Roderick said, "if she's still around tomorrow, you never know. We could just throw a net over her, take her back home. . . ."

"No!" Nnedi said. "Well . . . maybe. Tomorrow. We'll see."

She blew it a kiss. "G'night."

The creature chittered back to her, and climbed back up into its tree, watching. Perhaps.

Later that night, Heather and Evan slipped away, both humping waterproof rucksacks. Uncle Horace joined them at the cliff, and together they climbed down a winding path until, a third of the way down, they found a shoulder-high hole and crouched to enter.

Spider-legs had crept along behind them, watching and following.

They'd made two previous trips to Black Ship in the past week, and much of the equipment was already set up, including lamps and set dressing.

Here at the top level of the cave the oil-pumping equipment was in plain sight, and was disguised with nets and screens. The lamps cast yellowish shadows across the lava-bubble walls.

"All right," Evan said. "We've got an hour."

They turned up lights, the caves slowly coming into fuller relief. Huge and beautiful. The air was dank and warm, and the cave walls, floors and ceilings twisted with pale mushroom-like fungal spires and knobs, almost enough to produce the illusion of stalactites and stalagmites.

"Put the mock-up there," Evan said. "What do we think about the lighting?"

"We can use the gel lamps I think."

"Yes," Heather agreed.

Back up top, Takashi, Kola, Willow and Marshall were conferring around a popping campfire. "So here's the map," Takashi said.

One of the kids wandered over near them. "Hey!" Takashi said, pretending anger. "Back over to the fire."

"Damn kids," Kola grunted.

"As I was saying," Takashi said, tracing the ovals and lines with a slender finger. "Roughly speaking, we have four levels: the entrance, Upper Maze, Lower Maze, and the Cathedral, which is basically sea level. They interlock and overlap a bit. Now . . . have we laid out rules of engagement?"

Willow nodded. "A little water wrasslin' is all right. Submarines. But we have to keep them in a group, and have referees."

"Look," Takashi said. "There's nothing we can do about rock walls. All the kids are good swimmers, but heads can get knocked."

"*Will* get knocked," Willow said. "A little risk is all right. So is a little competition. But we have to be careful, and quick on the whistle if things get out of hand."

"Right," Marshall said. "So . . . The routes are weighted for difficulty. So are the clues. We're being as fair as we can be."

"Fairer than this damned planet, that's for sure. Winners get gold badges, bragging rights, and no chores for a week. Everybody gets to celebrate. I don't know how much better we can make it."

"Not much. So the only choice is: when do we go. Everything in place?"

"Evan's in place," Kola said. "He'll make his way down to Cathedral, checking the routes and placing clues and props as he goes. He's got his flash-bangs ready for the climax in the Cathedral. Should be spectacular. Then they'll swim out to the ocean, and Hell Night is over!"

"So are we ready to go?"

"Put 'em down, and then wake 'em up," Willow said. She looked over at Jelli, who waved at her sleepily, and Willow waved back sweetly. Jelli yawned and climbed into her tent. "Aww. Sweet little things. They die."

"Sounds like a plan," Takashi said.

The others left.

Aaron was creeping from shadow to shadow in the forest surrounding the campfire. There was no actual penalty for being discovered, but he still took pleasure in making a game of it. Willow's tent glowed with artificial light, but the girl herself was still sitting near the fire. Marshall hovered around her, his straggly goatee line like a bit of chocolate on his chin.

"Hey, we have a little time," Marshall said.

"Later," Willow said. "It's going to be a long night." She slapped his hand away. "I said *later*."

"Oh," Marshall said, disappointed. "Oh, all right."

Willow entered her tent, and a minute later, the light went out.

It felt as if she'd barely closed her eyes before hearing a "pop" against the side of her tent. *Pop-pop*. The same noise, again. *What the . . . ?*

Willow crawled out of her sleeping bag and stuck her head out of the tent. A pebble hit her cheek. "Ow!" What?

Then she blinked hard. By the light of the twin moons, she saw a balled up piece of paper, just two feet away. It was a note wrapped around a pebble. She picked it up. *Meet me at midnight, Wedgie Wall. A.*

"Well I'll be damned. . . ." she whispered.

The cave was dark and appropriately creepy. The ceiling was twenty feet high, smooth and rounded like the frozen bubble it was, remnant of volcanic activity on Black Ship an eon before.

A week of work had wrought miracles. The oil-pumping apparatus was safely stowed or concealed, and the first set of obstacles had already been erected. "This is good," Uncle Horace said. "Be good for the kids."

"They'll think it's fun a year from now," Evan said. "But we're hoping for a few screams and curses tonight."

"Let them sleep just long enough for the adrenaline to wear off, not long enough to get rest. They'll be sore and pissed."

Evan chuckled. "Shall we sally forth?"

They slipped into the warm water, wading toward a partially submerged pathway. Spider-legs followed them, crawling along the ceiling.

Then . . . suddenly . . . it stopped. Backed up a few inches, then began to shiver as if caught in extreme cold. It backed up out of the tunnel, and shivered on the bank of the pool. Hopped from mushroom to mushroom, chittering at the darkness.

They exited the tunnel and climbed down a fall of rocks to the

Lower Maze cave systems, with lower ceilings and a few rain-water rivulets grooving the floors. Water on Black Ship percolated up through the pools, flowed back down through the caves, and pooled from rain water. During the torrential seasonal rains water ran through the caves freely, and in dry seasons the miniature lakes dried up. Enough water flowed now to create constant trickles, miniature waterfalls, and swollen lakes both simultaneously below ground and above sea level.

Evan played his lantern light across the walls until it revealed a brown sack about the size and shape of a pineapple. Or a large human skull, which is what it reminded him of. The shadowy planes reminded him of eye sockets more than the ridges of a tropical fruit. It was webbed against the wall at shoulder height. "What in the world is this?"

"Never seen it before," Heather said.

"Looks like some kind of egg sack."

Heather shrugged. "Make any guesses about the mommy?"

"Amphibious?"

"How could you tell?"

"Just a guess. From proximity to the water. Hatchlings could easily fall in and not make their way to land."

"Why not lay your eggs in the water, then?" Horace asked.

"Predators, perhaps?" Heather said. "Maybe genetic rivals eat them if the mommies aren't careful." She approached more closely, but was careful not to touch. The surface was leathery. There was something . . . her teeth felt like they were vibrating when she came closer, as if there were a high-pitched sound she could hear with her bones but not her ears.

"If Mommy put it up here she's got reach. Some skills. Strength."

Evan whistled. "Never seen anything quite like it. A little like a spider sack."

"Then this stuff might be analogous to silk," Heather said. "A new building material. We should take a sample back."

Evan nodded: The thought appealed to him. "If it's anything near as strong . . ." He stretched out his hand.

"No. Let's not. You might leave a scent. Sometimes mommies don't bond to babies carrying human scent. Don't want to screw with a life cycle we don't understand."

"True. Already been down that road. No joy there."

***

"Evan," Heather said. "We have six more lamps. Would you take them into the Cathedral, leave them there for the team?"

"What is going to happen, Heather?"

"Well . . . in a few hours the kids will come down into the tunnel. We'll spin yarns about treasure and such. Get some of the brave ones to get in the water, go through the passage into the Cathedral. There's a bit of a maze here, and they'll have to follow the directions to get out."

"The teams will play against each other?"

"That's the plan," Heather said. "I'm going down to the other end. Set up the last puzzle."

"I love it," Evan said. "Okay. Gimme a hug."

Horace reached out.

Evan slapped his arm away playfully. "Not you, Horace."

"Oh," he said, and pretended to pout as the Twins embraced.

"And . . . see you later! You know, Heather . . . I'm never really sure how aware he really is."

Evan dove into the water, the bag of homemade pyrotechnic flash-bangs trailing behind him.

## CHAPTER TEN: DEATH IN THE CATHEDRAL

The passage was narrow, and a little scary as Evan breaststroked through the darkness, his fingers brushing the sides. A flash of panic tickled him before he popped up into an air bubble. Plenty of room. Someone could actually hide in there, if they wanted. He placed a lamp, and lighted it, showing the way to air.

Diving back down, he swam on.

He came up in another bubble, paused and cocked his head sideways. Was that a sound? Something echoing in the dark and wet? A hollow, splashing sound? He paused. No sound, but he felt the water pulse as if something was moving within it. Not a tide . . . there would certainly be no tides in these cave pools. But something had moved . . . hadn't it?

After a minute he was convinced he'd been mistaken, and continued on.

Evan swam on to the next bubble. He was setting up the lamp, head above the water level, a light on his head.

Suddenly, he felt something, a stinging pain. His eyes widened. He was yanked down below the surface, swallowing water. He came back up, eyes wide and frightened.

"What the hell?" He thrashed, righting himself. "Help! Help!" He seemed to grasp the uselessness of his screams, and climbed up onto the shelf of rock. He examined his leg. The flesh was sliced beneath the torn fabric, swelling even as he examined. He probed at it, frightened. He looked down into the water. . . . The surface of the water exploded with thick, ropy tentacles. He squirmed away, eyes wide, the light from his headlamp giving indistinct images of something swarming up out of the water. He smashed at one of the tentacles with a rock, and it pulled back.

The water was clear, and empty. He was breathing hard now. "Think. Think. The Cathedral. Got to get down to the Cathedral. Maybe out to the ocean."

He clutched at his knife, hand trembling. "All right, you bastard. I don't know what you are, but I've got something for your ass right here."

The water was choppy, and then calm. He made a torch from his lamp, and shone it around. Nothing. Evan clutched his ten-inch blade, and gathered his courage.

"All right. All right. Let's do this." He dove into the water. With the light of his headlamp filtering through the murk, he looked left and right. Nothing. Came back up to the surface. Looked around. Nothing. Began to swim along the corridor.

The water erupted at him again. He slashed, cutting through a tentacle, and the water clouded with blood. He came up at a small air bubble, gasped for breath, before being pulled down again. He slashed with the knife, fighting for his life, and finally broke away and crawled up over a rock lip and began to slide down a long smooth tube, tumbling and screaming. When the tube disappeared, he fell about five feet and smashed into the water.

Floundering and spitting, he managed to right himself. Evan had managed to hang onto his lamp as well as the waterproof sack tied to his foot. He splashed the strong yellow-white beam up and down and around. He was in a vast chamber filled by an underground lake.

The lake's surface was studded with fungus spires, and mushrooms grew out of the walls as well. Over his head, perhaps at the level of the Lower Maze, was a suspension bridge perhaps twenty feet above the surface of the lake.

Evan thrashed his way to the shore and collapsed. His leg was lacerated, the flesh puffy and melting along painful-looking wounds.

"Damn it!" He looked up at the top of the ceiling, and saw a little light coming down. Tried to stand and walk, limping.

A rock pile. He looked at the rock. He unsealed the waterproof rucksack and extracted a flare, popping it to life and filling his end of the lava bubble into pale reddish relief.

All the way opposite him, he could make out the entrance to another lava tube, probably the one leading out to the ocean. If he could swim that far, he might be safe. But the water . . . the idea of entering that black liquid again, for any reason at all . . . good *lord*.

Above and behind him, opposite the ocean approach, the wall opened with multiple smaller lava tubes, testaments of a time in the distant past when molten rock had burrowed through solid stone. Four tubes that he could see. Despite the pain he could almost imagine that time, in Black Ship's recent geologic past . . . but ages ago in human terms.

Was there anyone on the other side of the tubes? For just an instant, he was almost overwhelmed by the sheer beauty of the setting. "Hello?" The call echoed through the chamber. He limped closer to the rock waterfall. "Hello!! Can anyone hear me?"

He sat on a low, toadstool-shaped fungal spire.

"All right," he said to himself. "Calm down. You can wait. They'll come." Suddenly, something occurred to him. "They'll bring the kids. Oh, god, the Grendel Scouts. Help! Can anyone hear me?"

A sound from behind him. He turned, and saw the water boiling.

He backed away, new fear boiling his veins.

Something came out of the water, knocking over the lamp. For just an instant, he glimpsed something man-sized and slug-shaped, mouth framed with snakelike protrusions.

Evan screamed as a shadowy shape heaved itself up, and grabbed his leg. He slashed with a knife against a rubbery tentacle. The thing groaned. Another *something* was coming up out of the water, and

Evan crawled toward the "waterfall." He tried to climb, and managed to get part of the way up, then something grabbed his ankle, and pulled him back down.

Evan's fingers gripped the rock desperately. Tentacles gripped. Spikes extruded, and injected his leg.

Evan screamed, eyes rolling up as fire filled his veins. He lost his grip on the rock.

More of the shadowy shapes crawled up out of the water, surrounding his body. He twitched a bit, as their tentacles gripped him, and spikes pierced him, but there were no more screams.

## CHAPTER ELEVEN: THE TREASURE OF CAPTAIN SQUID

"Have you seen my brother?" Heather asked.

Marshall shook his head. "Thought I did, while back. Hot dog?" He offered her a sausage in a bun.

"Love one," Heather said, and rolled over onto her back. "What a great night. That sky. Think that right now, there's someone on Earth looking up at the same stars?"

"Some of the same stars," Marshall said. "Some different ones. Different constellations. There," he pointed. "Ernst, the hunter."

Their meeting place was a wide spot in the seaward path, punctuated by a seven-foot wooden panel held erect by cross braces. Willow tried to radiate anger as she strode forward, but as she saw Aaron leaning cross-armed against the barricade, she felt her frown melting. "What are *you* doing here?"

"I came to see you, Willow," Aaron said. "Remember this place?"

She nodded. "That was our treasure hunt on our Hell Night, three years ago. The Wedgie Wall." The memory triggered a giggle. "Really hurt getting over this." She slapped her hand against the wooden panel.

Aaron smiled. "I grabbed your belt and helped you over, but that was one of those unkind cuts."

Despite her anger, she laughed, then settled back down. "Why? Why are you here? Why now?"

"Thought maybe you could use some help."

She watched his face. “Is that it? Really? After all this time, that’s all you have to say to me?”

“What am I supposed to say?”

“Nothing,” she said. “Nothing. Maybe nothing at all.” The silence stretched painfully. “I’m with Marshall now.”

He hunched his shoulders. In the moonlight they seemed thinner, and he seemed smaller than he had a year before. “I screwed up, Willow. I just came apart after Archie died.”

“A lot of us did,” Willow said. “We put it behind us.”

“I was there. I saw it. That makes a difference.”

“It’s always different when it’s about you, Aaron. You’re not the only one who bleeds.”

He gestured vaguely. A plea. “Willow . . . I’m back.”

She shook her head. “It’s too late.”

“Only if you say it is.”

“I’m saying it. It’s too late.” He reached for her hand. As if to take some of the sting from her words, she reached out to cup his cheek with her palm. “Aaron. It’s good to see you. We’re in the middle of something now.”

A wan smile. “Hell Night? How are the kids doing?”

“Handled the clashing rocks great. And the orienteering . . .” Her face clouded with sudden suspicion.

“What?” Aaron said, all innocence.

“You’ve been *watching*, haven’t you?”

He nodded. “Monitoring.”

“I don’t like games, Aaron,” she said. “Or self-pity. We don’t have time for that. We have a planet to explore and conquer, and any time spent navel-gazing is going to get someone else killed.”

“*Else*? So . . . you blame me, too?”

She shook her head, backtracking. “I didn’t mean it that way.”

“All right, Willow.”

“We could use an extra hand, Aaron. With the kids.”

“Doing what?”

“Right now, lot of it boils down to babysitting. We have our roles lined up. It would be a way back in.”

He half turned away. “I . . . I don’t know. I know I’m a part of this. Not much choice—it’s the only home I’ve got. But I came out here for you. Cadmann said . . .”

"You talked to Cadmann?"

"Doesn't everyone? He's sort of the universal connector. He said you might need me out here. He said you needed me. Was he wrong?"

"Maybe. Maybe he was."

Aaron seemed deflated. Defeated. "All right. Okay. Well, good luck with everything."

He turned and left her.

"Aaron!" she called after him.

He paused, as if deciding whether or not to turn back . . . then disappeared into the brush.

On the way back into camp, Willow ran into Kola, who immediately noted her distressed state.

"Thought you were napping," Kola said.

"Couldn't sleep," Willow said. "What time is it?"

Kola's smile was evil. "About *that* time."

The other Teen Leaders gathered out of sight of the cluster of kiddy tents. They donned tacky pirate gear: hats, eyepatches, tailed coats. Willow, Kola, Marshall, Takashi. The camp was quiet, and then as if they had timed it with a stopwatch, commenced their screaming in unison. "Get up! Get up! Dream time's over! Game time is here!"

One of the kids groggily appeared at the mouth of the tent, disbelieving. "I thought we were done until tomorrow!"

Marshall sneered piratically. "It is tomorrow! Up up up! It is now half past midnight, and most officially 'tomorrow.' Move your narrow little butts!"

They crawled out of their bunks, rubbing their eyes, groaning and cursing with impressive creativity. Half dead. Willow giggled to herself: Their timing had been impeccable. The kids hunched in exhausted rows, sleepy, shivering, and more than a little worried. "What is all of this about?" Jelli asked.

Willow swung her bamboo sword. "We'll tell you what this is about. It's about pirate gold!"

A bit of awareness filtered through Jelli's fog. "Pirate . . . what?" Intrigued in spite of herself. Then she scratched at her left ear. "Do you hear that?"

"What?" Takashi asked.

"It's like . . . a little whine. Like a little bug or something. Can't you hear it?"

"No, and you need to stay on the ball," Willow said.

"Get ready for anything!" Takashi said. "Anything goes, but you are responsible for each other's safety. Match up, people! Your team is your tribe! First team to get three members to the final stage wins! Winner gets thirty points, and highest total wins. No chores for a week! So those of you who are worried that your team is behind . . . this is your chance."

"Any of you can win," Kola said. "*Any team can still win*, do you understand?"

The kids nodded, shivering but engaged. The leaders gathered the kids around the fire.

"Arrr, now, then, me hearties," Marshall mugged. "Listen as I tell the tale of Captain Squid." He squinted one-eyed until they stopped giggling.

"Human beings were not the first to travel between the stars, nor will they be the last. And where there are pilgrims, traders, and travelers, there will be pirates."

Kola appeared beside him, wearing a scarf tilting across half her face like an eyepatch. "Arrr! And where there are pirates, there be treasure, mateys!" She ran back and forth, mugging ferociously.

"What your parents didn't tell you," Takashi said, "is that the grendels were not alone here! That they waged a terrible war and that there are dangers untold, that you will have to face. Pirates. Traders."

"Aargh . . ." Kola said. "Ye haven't been told everything, no, ye haven't. And thar be treasure in the earth, little mateys."

"So that be the challenge," Takashi said. "The gold and jewels of Captain Squid lie deep in the caverns beneath your feet. You will seek it."

"Teams will stick together," Kola said. "Each team will have their monitor. And now the time for talk is over. Are you ready?"

"Yes!" the kids screamed.

"Then . . . on your feet, ya lubbers!"

The kids clambered up, and toed the mark.

"No more clues," Willow said. "No more puzzles. From now on its team against team, until three of your team makes it all the way to the end. Are you ready?"

"Yes!"

Marshall grinned. "Then on your mark . . . get set . . . GO!"

And in their T-shirts, treaded sandals and cut-off jeans the kids sprinted down the path. The leaders hustled them around the curves, past torch-lit curves and then . . . to the wide wooden barrier everyone called the Wedgie Wall. The kids scrambled over, helping each other and grabbing each other to help them up, discreetly knocking a few members of another team down into a mud pit. Jelli struggled to jump high enough to grab the edge, and then lacked the upper body strength to pull herself over. Buddy leaned down to give her a hand, grabbing the belt on her jeans and yanking. She shrieked with pain and surprise as the Wedgie Wall earned its name yet again . . . but made it over the top.

Squeals and howls as they climbed nets, sprinted, ran along logs and then down along the cliff trail, where they pretended not to notice the rope safety rails that had been erected in the night. And then . . . they were into the caves.

Beneath the blistered ceiling, Kola and Heather were guiding the kids one way or another.

"Where are we going?" Nnedi asked.

"Over here!" Heather said.

Uncle Horace motioned from the other side. "Or over here! Make your choice!"

"Swimmers here!" Heather said.

Some of the kids took the time to doff their shoes before they plunged into the warm water, heated by the springs, which bubble-steamed up through the pools. The kids splashed along, picking their way through the lamplit caves.

Heather leaned to Willow. "I guess Evan's in the Cathedral. I haven't been able to raise him."

"Let me try," Willow replied, and switched on her communicator. "Evan? Evan . . .?"

No response. They waited. Still nothing. Willow and Heather shrugged. "Interference, I'd guess. Maybe he just got into the beer. Come on . . . can't let the tots have all the fun!"

For hours now, Camelot's communications center had been relatively quiet, and now that silence had deepened.

Zack Moskowitz blinked, staring at the screens. Various high angles on Black Ship Island, various magnifications on the camp site. Except for the cooling campfire, there was only one teen-sized heat signature remaining. "Welp," he said, smacking his hands together, "That's that. They've moved underground now. We can see some moving signatures through the rock, but that's about it. I'd reckon we won't get anything else until morning."

Mary Anne looked at them questioningly. "Maybe we should go to bed?"

"Maybe," Cadmann said. "I'm not sleepy."

"Sweetheart, you have to let them go. It's not even what's best. It's the only option." Mary Anne slipped her arms around his neck, and kissed him.

Finally he sighed. "All right. Take me to bed, you vixen. And you'd better have plans to keep my mind off the Overnight."

"I think I can manage something." She kissed him lightly.

"All right. G'night, Zack."

They left. Zack sat in front of the console, staring, then rubbed his chin, and yawned.

"Oh, to hell with it."

He grabbed his jacket, and headed out. The camp was quiet. It was easy to remember when all of this had been empty, when they had first descended on pillars of fire to conquer a new world, when every day had been an adrenalized adventure.

Now . . . the animal pens were dark, the fences hummed with protective electrical power. Nothing dangerous lurked in the shadows. All seemed right with the world. And yet. . . .

Zack pulled his jacket collar up around his neck. Must be getting old, he thought. The night was warm, but still, he felt a chill. . . .

The light splashed back from the bubble-pocked walls, as if they still glowed with heat from eons past. The kids were splashing, running knee high through pools of water, fatigue forgotten as they heard their voices and footsteps echoing back to them from the ceilings. They pushed, jostled, and tripped, rough with each other. The referees kept the brutality to a minimum, but closed an eye to anything short of murder. No autopsy, no foul.

"You!" Kola called. "Thor! That's one warning for unnecessary roughness. One more and you're out! Remember that you need three team members reaching the end to win!"

The little wheat-haired aggressor released a handful of his opponent's hair. "Sorry!" Yellow Team's leader said.

The kids split into two different routes, different caves.

"Yo ho ho!" Takashi called. "This way, mateys!"

None of them paid much attention to another pineapple-sized egg sack, this one against the wall, out of the torchlight.

The kids were having the time of their lives. But from time to time one of them flinched, looking around as if worried something was in the water with them.

"Did you see something?" Nnedi asked.

"Like what?" Buddy asked.

"I'm not sure," Nnedi asked. "Something in the water."

"Yeah. *We're* in the water. Come on!" And they scrambled over a fall of rocks, and down a sloping tunnel heading into the next chamber.

## CHAPTER TWELVE: LOWER MAZE

The kids jumped over and down, howling with glee. They scrambled over the few feet of rock that separated the pool from the lip of the next drop. A glowing green arrow pointed the way down, and they didn't hesitate.

Down and down, tumbling, laughing . . . SPLASH! They were splashing in the pool for five minutes before little Nnedi saw the mock grendel set up.

It should have been atop a waist-high cairn of rocks, flanked by dim lanterns, grinning hungrily. Instead it looked like an oversized chew toy that had been thrown to a pack of dogs, split-seamed and scattered.

Willow splashed up out of the pool. "Whoa. This . . . is strange. Who did this? Red Team?"

Kola was hopping mad. "Not cool. This isn't cool at all. Who would do something like this?"

Willow's face clouded with anger. "I know someone who might do something like this. *Aaron*!"

"What?" Takashi asked.

"He's here. On the island."

Even Marshall seemed doubtful. "Screwing with Hell Night?" Then suddenly growing angry. "*Really*?" He said it as if accusing someone of apostasy.

"Who else. *Aaron*!" she screamed. Her voice echoed through the entire cave. They all quieted, listening for a response. Nothing.

"That's strange," Nnedi said.

"What is?" Marshall asked.

"That whining sound. Can't you hear it?"

They paused, and then the older kids shook their heads. "Nope. Nothing. Come on."

Jelli punched Nnedi's shoulder lightly.

"Hey," she said. "I hear it."

Up atop the bluff, the dull night wind stirred the tent flaps. Despite having been soaked, the firepit still hissed and steamed a bit, but that was the only sound and movement other than Aaron Tragon's footsteps.

He had walked the abandoned square, dejected, toeing at the remnants of the fun other people had. He looked around as if wondering if anyone was watching, and then climbed into Willow's tent.

He had to stoop inside, then go to his knees. At this moment, he wasn't certain what he wanted, what he intended, knew only that he needed to be close to her, or to someone. A year's loneliness burst upon him like a breaking wave, and he crawled into her sleeping bag. Her perfume, the smell of the lilac soap with which she washed her hair, spilled out of it as if the scent had been waiting for him, trying to pull him back into old and painful memories.

He felt utterly lonely and miserable. How had life gone so badly, so swiftly. Had it been so long ago that he'd felt atop the entire world? That he'd needed no lecture from Cadmann to know that Avalon was his to lose?

"*Aaron . . .*"

Faint. Indistinct. Aaron came back out of the tent for a moment, looking this way and that. Cool breezes. Twin moons among pale scrambled clouds.

Nothing. Nothing anywhere for Aaron Tragon. He was just a

fertilized egg that had been shipped halfway across the universe to populate an alien world, like one of the frozen dogs. Or frozen bits of corn seed. Irrelevant as an individual, just another part of the master plan. Heck, if he didn't work out, they'd just thaw out another. And another.

Whether he laughed or cried, lived or died, Aaron Tragon meant nothing. And perhaps, he never had. He crawled back in, laid on her sleeping bag, and closed his eyes.

In the caverns of the Lower Maze, the organizers of Hell Night were dealing with the bitter realization that their planned surprise had been trashed.

"Arrr!" Marshall said, improvising swiftly. "The pirates left a guardian for their treasure. The nastiest beast they could find! And see what happened to it!"

The kids *ooohed* and *ahhed.*

Kola played along. "Thar be nastier things than grendels in these waters, mateys. . . ."

The kids giggled.

"Nice save," Willow whispered.

"Thank you, thank you very much," Kola said.

"Down to sea level!" Willow said.

The kids headed down the tunnel, and the leaders plodded after them, suddenly more fatigued and uncertain than their charges.

Curled in Willow's tent, Aaron roused himself from a brief and unsatisfying sleep, and wiped his face. His hands came away wet. Damn. He'd been crying.

He crawled out, and gazed up at the night sky. "If you're watching, *Geographic* . . . Cadmann . . . screw you. Just . . . screw all of you."

He took his backpack, and headed out of the camp. He saw something flit around the edge of the camp. That spider-legged thing that had followed Kelly, then been adopted by Nnedi. "What are you doing up here? I thought you'd found friends?"

It hissed at him from its invisible mouth, then crawled up to the top of a tree. A couple of other leg-clusters hissed at each other, then down at Aaron. Almost . . . as if it was trying to tell Aaron something. Then they hissed at each other, and disappeared.

"Yeah, well . . . well screw you too."

The boy made his way down the side of the cliff, twin moons dancing on the waves below. "Tide coming in," he said to no one in particular.

He went down to his boat. It was hidden behind bushes. He pulled it out, looked back at the vine-shrouded cliffs. Something almost caught his eye. *Something . . .*

What was it? Perhaps just a memory of thinking he'd heard his name . . . ?

It was just the night, and the pain. Aaron shook his head, started the engine, and headed out.

Down in the tunnels and caverns that composed the Lower Maze, Heather, Uncle Horace, and Takashi supervised the other kids. The second mock grendel lay in shreds. This second act of vandalism drained whatever slight amount of fun remained in the proceeds. Despite careful deep slow breathing, Heather was getting nervous. "What in the *hell* happened here?"

"We'd better check in with the others," Takashi said, and switched on his communicator. "Hello. Willow, are you there?"

The reception was shoddy, but adequate. "We're here. What say?"

"We have an issue here?" Takashi said. "Our mock-up was torn to pieces."

"Crap!" Willow said.

"You know anything about this?"

A sigh. Hesitation, confusion, and then an inescapable conclusion. "It was Aaron. He's on the island, and he's pissed off. Improvise around it, and meet us in the Cathedral. We'll sort this out later."

"Evan better be on his job," Heather said. "Last chance to scare them."

"Oh, I think he'll scare 'em," Takashi said, and looked around nervously. "Your brother is a very scary fellow."

Heather turned off her comm link. "Everybody swim hard, then take a whack!"

The kids jumped into the narrow body of still water, churned it into foam with their skinny arms and legs, and then jumped out, picked up a padded sword and whacked a grinning, dangling grendel piñata.

A sugared rainbow of cellophaned twists spilled to the ground. The kids grabbed and munched and dove back into the water, swept along through the current. One of the kids dunked another, and whatever small amount of order they had been able to maintain dissolved into an orgy of thrashing water-war.

"Percy!" Takashi said. "One demerit! Keep it safe!"

"Whoa!!" Heather, Willow, and Takashi went over the lip, from the narrow pool into the deeper wider lake at sea level. They hit the water. This was the most beautiful chamber that they had seen yet. Spectacular, a bubble so huge that in the puny light of their lamps they could hardly detect the curve in the walls. "Wow," Roderick said. "This is just . . ."

"Where are all the, you know, stalagtits?"

Nnedi glared at him. "That's stalac*tites*."

"Seen pictures. Sure look like titties—"

*Whack*!

Nnedi slapped him, so fast and hard that his eyes crossed.

Willow swiftly interjected herself, separating the combatants. As they sputtered, she lectured to disrupt Roderick's thoughts of revenge.

"These aren't limestone caves," Willow said. "They weren't formed by water erosion, and so you don't get the kind of limestone drip buildup over centuries that creates those structures. This was a lava cave, formed by bubbles in molten rock."

"Wow."

Willow splashed up onto the land, and the kids were coming out. "Ah . . . we were supposed to have a surprise about now," she said to Takashi. "Weren't we?"

"Damn it!" Heather yelled. "Evan! Where are you?"

"I don't know," Horace said. "He was supposed to be here. Look." They climbed up on the rock. A fourth exceedingly detailed, four-foot mock-grendel crouched in position.

"Well," Heather said. "This is a fine mess. Where is he?"

Uncle Horace was paddling in a circle. "When was the last time you saw him?"

"Evan!" Heather called out. "If you're playing some kind of game, I swear. . . ."

"Aaron," Willow whispered.

"Aaron and Evan, together?"

"They were friends once. I'll bet they still are, secretly. Trying to turn Hell Night into their private haunted house."

Heather gritted her teeth. "I'm going to skin them, and roll them in salt." They looked at each other.

"Listen! Everybody!" Heather said. "We have a little mystery. A bit of a problem. We're going to combine teams. Green and Blue, go with Marshall."

"What's going on?" Marshall said.

Heather hesitated. "We seem to have misplaced Evan." Her smile was tight and poisonous.

"What the hell is happening around here?" Marshall said.

"That's what I want to find out," Heather replied. "We have some side chambers to search, and I suggest we search them quietly. This is no time to a panic."

"And if we can't find him?"

Heather's smile flickered. "Time to panic."

"All things considered," Willow said. "Panic is starting to sound like a viable option."

"All right," Marshall said. "Blue and Green Teams, with me and Takashi. Willow? You take Red and Yellow?"

"Will do. Okay, kids. It looks like we've got some sick game of hide and seek going on."

Takashi followed her lead. "Evan is hiding, and we're seeking. Sound cool?"

"What if we can't find him?" Nnedi asked.

"Then . . . I think we head back up top, and call in the troops."

Kola nodded. They checked their flashlights and made sure that each Teen Leader and team leader had one, and that their communicators worked as well as they were going to, here in the caves.

Takashi didn't like the clarity on their communicators. "These aren't much good down here. Are you sure we shouldn't call them in now?"

No one needed ask who "them" was. "Right," Marshall said. "And prove they were right, that we couldn't handle things. This is probably a very bad joke."

"One of the all-time worst," Willow agreed. "All right. Let's give it an hour, meet back in Upper Maze."

"Time?" Kola asked.

"Two twenty-five," Willow said.

"All right," Takashi said. "Meet back here at three thirty? We'll take most of the kids with us, up closer to the surface. You take White group, but also Kola and . . . Uncle Horace, just to be careful."

"Three thirty it is," Kola said. "And everyone?"

"Yeah?"

"Be careful. Something's going on here, and I don't much like it."

"Evan!" Willow called. The name shattered on the far wall, washing back to them in echoed fragments.

They splashed through the tunnels. Rarely more than ankle deep here, the water was no longer fun. It was just wet, and clammy, despite the steam rising from various hot springs. They arrived at a branch, two tunnels haring off in a Y-split from the main channel. "What's down there?" Roderick asked, gesturing to the right.

"Another drop off, leading to the Cathedral," Kola said. "Pretty steep. There's a bridge across it. No real way down from here. Walls are too slick."

"But Evan certainly could have gotten to sea level through one of the other tunnels."

"We should at least take a look," Kola said.

They sloshed along through the darkness, playing their flashlights carefully until the floor vanished totally into black. They'd reached the edge of a drop-off. The fungal growths were clustered, as if strengthened by the heat and the damp. It was tough as bamboo, and in fact the rope bridge had been intertwined and anchored in the twisted shoots.

Willow tested it with one careful foot. Thirty feet below her was sea level, and an underground lake bubbling with steam and punctuated with a few twisting fungal spires. The bridge led across to some of the oil-pumping equipment: They could hear it humming from where they were. But they'd been cautioned against using the bridge. The pumping station was served from sea level these days, not down from the top of the mesa, and the bridge was not maintained properly. Some of the rocks and foundational fungus seemed a little unstable. "I don't like this," Willow said.

"Listen," Kola said. "One of us can creep out there. If anything happens, it's just a dunk in the lake."

"The others can go for help."

"Worst-case scenario is we swim out to the ocean."

"Sounds like a plan."

"I'm little," Nnedi said. "I can go out and there's less chance something will go wrong."

Willow and Kola exchanged an expression. Shook heads: "No."

"I'll do this." Kola edged out onto the bridge. It was a triangle balanced on its apex, with big healthy knots for footfalls. It groaned a bit, but held her. She looked down.

The lake beneath them was built like a lollypop, and the lava-tube exit to the sea was the stick.

At the top of the candy circle was a crescent of rocky beach, and although she couldn't quite see from this angle, it looked to her as if a backpack or rucksack lay abandoned a few feet from the water.

"Evan!" Kola called. "Evan!" She looked down, and could see where the water flowed into the pool below.

"Can you see anything?"

Kola frowned. "I can't . . . wait!" Through the mist, she could barely see something. The shape of a waterproof rucksack on the rocks below.

"I think so," Kola said.

"Is it Evan?"

"Some of his stuff . . . Evan! Evan!" Willow edged further out on the bridge. She shined her lamp down, but the Cathedral was vast enough to swallow the light. "I'm not sure. Too many shadows. It's possible." She looked back. "How long would it take to back up and find our way to the tubes leading down to Cathedral?"

"Maybe fifteen minutes."

Buddy had edged out behind her. "I think I see a foot or something. Evan!"

Dammit, that was just a shadow he pointed at. No, it might have been a foot, or a human leg, there in the depths of a shadow her lamp couldn't pierce.

Several more kids edged out on the bridge.

"Evan!" Nnedi called, growing alarmed. "Evan!" They were all edging out on the bridge now, shouting and pointing.

"Evan! Are you all right?" Buddy yelled down.

Willow motioned them back, suddenly aware that they were all on the bridge. "Kids, get back, it's—"

The fungus anchored to the rock had been growing for at least a century, fed by minerals and nourished by the damp and warmth, leaching minerals to construct itself cell by cell with infinite patience long before human beings ever landed on Tau Ceti IV, colonized Camelot, or named Black Ship Island. When the engineers tested its strength and found it admirable, and considered its bonding to the rock superior to driven pitons, they anchored their ropes and metal struts to it to construct a bridge spanning the Cathedral, splitting the distance between the steaming lake and the arching ceiling. And for over a decade that bridge had served, until an auxiliary pump station was built down on the beach, and men tended to come up from sea level rather than down and across from the mesa. The bridge, which had supported countless feet over the years, fell into disuse.

And disrepair. The fungus was just as strong as the engineers had thought, but the rope itself had begun to rot in the warmth and damp . . . and when seven children and one adult stood on it, the strands began to split and unravel.

The first clue was just a lurch, followed by a wan POP as woven fibers released their strain. The teens and their kids froze, suddenly forgetting the question of whether a shadowed lump might belong to their friend, and remembering that they were thirty feet in the air, suspended on a decade-old rope bridge.

"Nnedi," Willow whispered. "There's a rock shelf above you. Try to take some of your weight off the fungus bridge. . . ." She did, but then the wall crumbled a bit. The kids were terrified.

"I—" *Crack*! The bridge tilted as one of the rope strands surrendered to the pressure, placing a sudden and giant strain on the remaining two strands. The one at the bottom was secure, but the rope at the top, tied into a mass of twisting fungal vines, suddenly ripped free. They plunged thirty feet down toward the water. Uncle Horace grabbed onto one of the ropes as it unraveled, and when he jarred to a stop *that* ripped out of the wall of the cave as well, showering them with vines, rope, metal slats, chunks of fungus, and rocks.

All things considered, they were lucky nobody died then.

Two teenagers, five kids. One adult. They came up, sputtering but relatively unscathed. Buddy came up spitting water. "Whoa! That was fun! Let's do that again!"

Willow dog-paddled furiously. "Everyone all right?"

They struck out for land, and pulled themselves out. Horace asked, "What is this place?" There were a number of skull-shaped egg sacks attached to the lava-smooth walls.

"What are those?" Jelli stretched out her fingers, almost touched, then pulled her hand back. "And . . . that whining sound. Can't you hear it? It's louder, now?"

"I don't hear anything," Kola said. "And I don't know what this is. Never seen it before."

"This wasn't part of the game," Willow said.

They looked at each other and then back up at the broken fungal shelf.

"They'll need to lower ropes," Willow said.

Uncle Horace shook his head. "Need to wait for everyone to come back to the meeting place. When we don't show up, they'll look for us."

"Evan. *Evan*!" Kola screamed. She splashed across the rock, seeking her lover. Rounded the rock, slowly, partially eager, and partially afraid of what she was going to see.

"Evan?" Kola said.

But Evan was not there . . . just the waterproof rucks.

Willow pulled out her communicator. "Hello? Marshall? Marshall, can you hear me?" There was no reply.

"Anything?" Kola asked.

"No," Willow replied. She gathered herself, trying to remain calm. "All right, kids, stay high up on the rocks."

Uncle Horace seemed unclear on the concept. "Why?"

"I think we stumbled into the egg chamber of some kind of amphibious creature."

"Do you think something happened to Evan?"

"Remember the goliath?" Kola asked. "Something killed it."

"Yes. The goliath," Willow said. "But anything big enough to kill a goliath would never fit in the Cathedral."

"Maybe it wasn't an it. Maybe it was a *them.*"

The kids' unease was shading into panic.

"Evan. Evan," Kola called, but it was increasingly clear she expected no answer.

"Kola. I need you here. With me, now."

"Okay. All right," Kola said.

"We have to get a message to the others."

Kola shook her head. "How do we do that?"

"I don't know. Either the communicator's broken . . ."

"Maybe wet," Horace asked.

"That shouldn't stop it." She pointed up at the lava-blistered ceiling. "I think it's the rock. Too much of it."

"They're all in the caves," Horace said.

Suddenly the water rippled. *Something* was coming. "Kids!" Willow yelled. "Kids! Get back!"

"Ahh!" Horace screamed. A thick gray ropelike appendage stretched up out of the steaming water, snaking Uncle Horace's ankle. He screamed, tried to stand, and was dragged back across the rocks.

Nnedi grabbed a rock and smashed it down on the tentacle. For a moment something appeared out of the water. It was shaped like a giant banana slug, its mouth rimmed with tentacles. Hideous. Then it rolled and disappeared back beneath the surface of the water.

"What was that thing?" Roderick screamed.

"I don't know!" Uncle Horace bellowed. "I don't know! It's burning me!"

"Tear off the pant leg," Willow said. "Let's look at that wound."

Uncle Horace screamed, "Ahhh!" Then settled down. "What was that thing. It looked like . . . like . . . Cthulhu."

"What?" Willow asked.

"H.P. Lovecraft," Horace said. "Horror stories. Miskatonic."

"Right, Horace. Cthulhu. Can you walk on that?"

"Willow?" Jelli said. "We've barely got room here."

"We'll be safe," Kola said.

"Kola . . . Something put those egg sacks up on the walls."

"All right. . . . so?"

"So . . . if it was the cthulhus, then . . . then they came out of the water to do it."

Now they regarded the water's calm surface with both suspicion and growing horror. "I'm not sure it matters," Kola said quietly. "I'm not sure it matters. But the tide is coming in."

Willow snatched up her communicator again. "Hello? Hello? Can anyone hear me?"

## CHAPTER THIRTEEN: HELL NIGHT

Under Marshall's and Hiroshi's watchful eyes, the combined Green and Blue Teams were still searching the Upper Maze, in a system east of the main cave. Heather's communicator crackled, and he snatched it to his ear. "Hello? Hello? I didn't get that."

Just static.

"What is it?" Percy asked.

"Shhh," Marshall said.

"I thought I got a ping," Heather said. "Spoken to Kola or Willow?"

"No," Marshall said, "but the communicators suck in here. We've got a half hour before we're supposed to meet back up top."

Heather clucked. "I don't know. Something doesn't feel right. Would they mess up a Hell Night?"

"The question," Marshall said, "The question is whether they'd think it was messing them up."

Willow was fighting panic. "Hello? Can anyone hear me?"

"Anything?" Kola asked.

"No. Nothing at all." Then . . . the communicator crackled.

It was Aaron's voice, filtered through static. "Hell . . . is that . . . Willow?"

Relief flooded her veins, like ice quenching fire. "Aaron? Where are you? We're in trouble. We're in the main bubble at the end of the lava tube. The Cathedral."

"Did he hear you?" Horace said.

"I don't know," Willow replied.

"What do we do?" Nnedi asked.

"Well," Willow said. "We can wait here for a while, but the tide is going to eat this ground. We'll have to retreat into one of the higher tubes, hope to find a way out."

"Was that Aaron?" Nnedi asked.

"Yes," Willow said. "I think it was."

Nnedi set her jaw. "Aaron will come."

"He's been gone a long time," Roderick said.

"He'll come. Come on. Let's move up higher."

Aaron, a mile out from the island, wrinkled his brow. Their communication was barely coming through. "Hello? Lava tube?"

He could see the lava tube leading into the island. The moonlight was clear.

"*We . . . can . . . Evan . . .*"

"What about Evan? Hello?" he looked with disgust at the device in his hand.

"*Hel . . . you can . . .*"

He glared again. "What are you up to, Willow? All right. All right." He turned his boat around, and aimed the engine. Some kind of a damned joke. Right. Good old Aaron, about to play the fool. Serve him right for trusting.

"Lava tube. Cathedral. All right. Let's see about this."

It took him ten minutes to reach the seaward opening of the island's largest lava tube, gaping like a leviathan's black maw. He shined his flashlight into the shadows. "*Yoo-hoo* . . . I sure hope you're not messing with me. I am in no mood. . . ."

He ran the engine at low and entered the tube, immediately swallowed by shadows. His flashlight painted the fused walls. Aaron tilted the lamp down into the water. The beams penetrated shallowly. His skin crawled, and he wasn't certain exactly why.

*Something* passed beneath him, a shadow that was gone almost as soon as it could be seen.

"What the hell is that?" He looked back at the mouth of the lava tube, and fought a swift urge to make for the open sea.

Aaron's eyes widened. He quieted the engine, peering down through the water. Brought his face closer . . . closer . . . He saw a shape that reminded him of the thing he'd seen a year ago. Tentacles burst up out of the water, writhing for him. Aaron pulled back, grendel-quick reflexes just saving him.

"Son of a bitch!" He gunned his engine, and the little boat rocketed down the lava tube. He barely kept it from ramming into a wall, but had to back it up. When he did, tentacles grabbed the sides of the boat, yanking the back section down.

Aaron headed toward the stern, about to whack at it with a machete, and their combined weights almost flipped the boat. He moved back toward the front, to balance the weight, watching the thing trying to clamber aboard the boat from the rear.

The boat slid out of the lava tube, entering the main chamber. He watched with widening, horrified eyes as a nightmare of tentacles and slick swollen flesh hunched up awkwardly from the water. Now he could see Willow and the others on the "shore" waving at him.

"Aaron!"

The raft ploughed into one of the fungal towers, throwing Aaron into the air. He splashed down into the water. It was warm, and under other circumstances would have seemed kind of pleasant.

"Aaron!" Willow screamed. "Get out!" He looked back, and saw the creature flop back into the water and head toward him—

"Swim!" Kola screamed. "Swim!"

Aaron cut through the water with champion speed, but nothing compared to the speed with which the creature came after him. Aaron's legs went like propellers, ploughing through the water to the hoped-for safety of a fungal spire. He scrambled up as the creature hit the spire, swarming up, tentacles lashing.

Aaron climbed. The creature pursued. There wasn't much room to hide.

WHAM!

Uncle Horace hurled a chunk of rock right in its eye. It screamed, whipped around, and was hit by another rock. The kids hurled chunks of rock and *whack whack whack* . . . Aaron had climbed to safety. The cthulhu disappeared back beneath the surface.

Aaron panted, holding onto the top of the spire. The water below him calmed. He looked up at Willow, fifteen feet away across the water. "I uh . . . I guess you believe me now, right?" She broke contact, her face filled with regret and shame.

"Better late than never?" Kola offered.

Strained laughter. Nnedi laughed, and then started to cry. Roderick said, "Actually, the timing sucks."

"Good arm there, Uncle Horace." Aaron said.

"Thanks, Aaron! I'm the best pitcher on Avalon."

"The best for ten light-years, I'd reckon."

Willow broke up the laughter with a serious question. "What are we going to do?"

Aaron caught his breath. "First is to figure out a way to get from here to there without, you know . . . getting eaten and stuff." This was followed by another forced laugh, but the mirth swiftly soured. He looked over into the shadows. Saw the rucksack, but no Evan. "Is that . . . ?"

Kola nodded. "Evan's. We don't know where he is."

"What happened?"

"I don't know. He just disappeared." She trembled, then bit her lip and seemed to regain control.

"What in the hell *are* those things?"

"We don't know," Willow said, kneading Kola's shoulder. "But there's got to be more than just one of them. If we assume they created the egg sacks, and one egg sack per cthulhu—"

"What?"

"Cthulhu. You know," Willow said. "The Miskatonic River, Yog-Sothoth, Nyarlathotep, the Goat with a Thousand Young. . . ."

"Oh, yeah, that crew. Well, let's suspend the literary allusions, please. How the hell do I get down from here?"

"And even if you did . . . what do we do?"

"Willow . . . remember our overnight? We took the Yellow Brick Road. The lava tubes are like a maze. We found another way back up. I think we could find it again."

Kola sighed. "But first we have to get you over here."

Aaron looked around.

Uncle Horace considered. "We could make lots of noise over here. Far over here. Then you could slip into the water and sneak over."

Aaron seemed simultaneously impressed and skeptical. "I don't know . . ."

"We can give it a try, Aaron!" Willow called.

"Well . . . okay."

The kids and Uncle Horace went to the far side and started yelling.

Willow had an idea. "Take off your pants, Uncle Horace. Kola."

"What?"

"I want to beat on the water, but we can't get too close the edge. Those things may not like coming up, but they sure as hell *can*."

"That's not fair," Aaron said. "I tried to get Kola's pants off for months, and here you went and did it in a couple of seconds."

Kola glared at him. The teens and Horace took off their pants, while Roderick and Buddy gaped and whistled.

"Ooh!"

"Shut up!" Kola said.

They knotted the pants together. Uncle Horace said: "Let me do that. Make it longer."

It was truly a bizarre scene, the three half-naked kids stood six feet back from the water's edge . . . and then whipped the pants, thrashing the water.

At first nothing. Then the surface of the water rippled, and the cthulhu headed toward them . . . Aaron slipped down off the fungal spire to slip into the water, and almost as soon as he did a second tentacled knot appeared, snapping at him. No one's fool, he climbed back up. "What the hell! There's more than one of these things."

"It's worse than that," Willow said.

"And how exactly does it get worse?"

"Ah . . . they didn't both go for the bait. One of them stayed behind to watch you."

Aaron groaned. "Oh that's just great."

"They're smart," Kola said. "They cooperate."

One of the kids started crying. "What are we going to do?"

"Whatever it is," Kola said, "it had better be fast. The tide's coming in."

Aaron thought for a while. "You need to go on without me. Can you find the Yellow Brick Road again, Willow?"

She shook her head. "Yellow Brick . . ."

"The sulfur traces made the tube yellowish, remember?"

Her eyes suddenly widened. "Yes!"

Aaron focused on the rock crescent sheltering his friends, and then back at his own spire. "Well, it's too bad we don't have another ten pairs of pants, we could run a line and I might be able to shimmy across, out of the water."

A long pause, and then Nnedi's reedy little voice broke the silence. "What about the bridge?"

"What?"

"The bridge was made of rope," she said, and pointed.

They all stared. Aaron shook his head. "From the mouths of babes," he said.

"Look out!" Kola screamed. One of the cthulhus begins to rise up again. Another shower of lava chunks drove it back down.

Aaron was shaking by now. "I'm really, really not kidding. I need to get down from here."

"How do we get it?" Kola asked.

The rope bridge was floating out of reach of the shore. But only about ten feet from Aaron's spire. He stared, and then blinked.

"Horace!" he called. "Can you throw me the pants?"

Horace looked at it. "Maybe. Make ball, and throw like a discus?"

"Or a shot put. You can do it."

"But can you catch it?"

"I caught that pop fly ball two years ago. I can damned well do this. Let's try."

Horace balled the pants up, bit his lip, wound up, spun around and threw.

Aaron leaned way out, and just barely managed to grab it. The cave reverberated with their cheers.

Aaron came down as low as he could, and made a careful judgment and threw the ball of pants, holding onto one end of the line, and **splash!**

Missed. Then pulled it up, looking at the water, and threw again. **Splash!** Hit the bridge. Nothing. Slowly, he reeled it in. It was almost within reach. Looked at it . . . and Aaron made a decision. Untied one of the sets of pants, balled it, and threw it into the water. A cthulhu instantly grabbed the pants, as Aaron reeled up the fragments of the bridge. Pulled it out of the water as the pants went down.

He wiped sweat from his forehead, relieved. "Whoa."

"Whose pants were those?" Kola asked.

"I'll give you mine," Aaron said.

"Won't fit my butt," she said.

"Don't think I hadn't noticed."

Aaron untied the bridge rope, unraveled it. Tied one end of it to the spire. "All right," Aaron said. "I'm going to have to throw this across, as far as I can. I don't know if I can."

"You're strong enough," Horace said.

"I don't have any room to wind up. Can't make a running start."

A pause. Then, "We need more pants."

⁂

Aaron had tied the rope to a wooden slat salvaged from the rope bridge. He hurled it—and it fell five feet short.

On the shore, Buddy and Roderick were now in their underwear, knotting their pants into a rope. They threw it. Snagged the wood—

A cthulhu came up out of the water, and Uncle Horace threw glassy chunks of lava rock until it retreated.

"Damn, that was close," Kola said. "We've got it."

"Get as high as you can," Aaron said. "Anchor it."

The kids climbed up on a rock jumble. "Come on, everybody hold it . . ."

The kids and teens piled on, and pulled until the makeshift rope was as taut as they could get it.

Aaron tried to smile. "If there's anyone over there who hates my guts, this would be the time to tell me."

"Don't you like surprises?" Jelli said sweetly.

"Not really. No. Here goes." Aaron heaved himself up and began to shimmy across. The water below him was quiet. Then, blink-fast a cthulhu lunged up, lashing at him. It missed, but he lost his handhold, almost fell in. Dangled, then got himself back together. The kids slid around a bit, losing some of their position, and Aaron fell a little closer to the water . . . then hiked his feet up and shimmied the rest of the way.

"Damn," he said, hopping down. "I don't want to try *that* again."

Willow wrapped her arms around his neck, and kissed him soundly. "Don't you ever, ever scare me like that again."

"I'll do my best," he said.

## CHAPTER FOURTEEN: YELLOW BRICK ROAD

"Now," Willow said. "What the hell is the way out of here?"

"I'd say back the way I came . . . except I think we'd need a boat."

"There's your boat."

"Yeah. And . . . Uncle Horace? Good throw."

Horace looked down bashfully. "You're welcome, Aaron. Can you get us out of here?"

"Yeah. Let's get my boat first."

Horace looked doubtful. "But it's ruined."

"That's true," he said, "But . . . the engine still has fuel." They edged around the bank of the underground lake.

When they reached the wrecked boat, Aaron worked with the fuel tank.

"Here," Aaron said. "The fuel mix is pretty much synthetic speed. Could come in useful."

"We have Evan's bag of flash-bangs," Willow said.

"That might be useful. Low-yield explosive plus a good oxygenator might be useful. You never know. Here, Uncle Horace? Carry?"

Horace grinned. "I'll carry, Aaron. I'll take good care of them."

"I know you will," Aaron said. They helped Horace slip his arms through the shoulder straps.

"Now what?"

"We head up. And hopefully . . . out. They've got to be looking for us."

They climbed up and entered one of the lava tubes. Aaron was confused now. He looked first at one, and then the other. "Yellow Brick Road."

"Which one?" Willow asked.

Aaron looked back at the rock spire, changing angles until something in his head went *click.*

"Here. Come on. I think that this was the one."

"You think?" Kola asked.

"If you've got a better idea, I'm open."

Uncle Horace looked back. "Tide coming in. We should move."

The waters swarmed with cthulhus now. They came briefly up onto the land, slid back down into the oily water. They followed the humans a bit . . . then back down into the water.

"Come on!" Willow said.

The kids looked back at the path they'd taken, the murky water aswarm with cthulhus. Water lapped at the tubes.

"We've got problems," Aaron said.

After a long, confusing and frightening struggle up the deeply shadowed caves, Blue Red and Green Teams had finally made it back up to the main camp.

"What are you going to do, Hiroshi?" one of the kids asked.

"We're calling the mainland. This is a search and rescue, and I don't care who knows it." He used the camp radio. "Black Ship Island calling Camelot. Please. Come in Camelot. . . ."

Camelot's communications room was empty. When the message came in, no one was there.

Zack Moskowitz was deep asleep, dreaming of new constellations swirling in the stars when the message was relayed.

Cassandra's voice was as patient as always. "Zack. Wake up, please. You are receiving a priority message from Black Ship Island."

Zack was groggy, but came to rather quickly. "Cass? What is it."

Hiroshi's voice. "Zack? I don't know how to say this, but . . . we've lost track of some of our campers."

"*Lost*? What the hell?"

"Well, they're probably in the lower levels. But you know that we'd rather be safe than sorry. Would you please send over a search team?"

"Absolutely," Zack said. "Cassandra?"

Hiroshi's image faded. "Yes, Zack?"

"Put a standard rescue team on alert, get them over to Black Ship."

"Emergency, Zack?"

"Everything on this damned planet is an emergency."

Cadmann's eyes opened before he knew where he was, only aware of a soft warmth curled against his back. Mary Ann. Each wife had a separate bedroom, but last night had been Mary Ann's. Why had he awakened? A flashing orange light pulsed against the ceiling. Emergency message alarm. He rolled over to look at the foot of the bed. A hologram window expanded with a flashing red message: *Hikers missing on Black Ship Island. Request assistance.*

"What?" He groaned. "Ohhh . . ."

He swung up out of bed. Sylvia appeared at the doorway.

"What's wrong?" Mary Anne asked.

"We have an emergency. At least I think it is."

"Do you have to go?" Sylvia asked.

He groaned, wishing he could be talked out of it. Dammit, he'd had enough emergencies for one lifetime.

"Don't want to, but I'd hate myself if I didn't."

"Then I'm coming too," Sylvia said.

"Should I come, Cadmann?" Mary Ann asked. In her voice and face was the belief that she already knew the answer. No. I'm damaged. Ice on my mind. I'm . . . only good for this.

"Not this time," Cadmann said, and kissed her as gently as he could.

He rolled off the bed and opened his closet. On a vertical rack on the left side was the modified shotgun they called the grendel gun, firing an elephant-gun-sized slug, as well as a variety of shock and explosive rounds. It had been a long time . . . but he knew that other closets were opening even now. No one would respond to an emergency without their most lethal equipment.

Damn. He'd hoped all this was behind them.

He was dressed in minutes, grendel gun slung over his shoulder and emergency medical backpack in place. Cadmann ran out to his air pad, where a skeeter was coming in, piloted by Carlos.

"Amigo, if this is a stunt. . . ."

"Rumps will be worn *glowing.*"

"You hold, I'll paddle. Standard kit?"

"Grendel guns all around. Explosive rounds." They nodded at each other, mirroring ugly thoughts.

"You never know." As they lifted off and headed west, they were looking down over the colony, and saw three more skeeters lifting off. Heading west, toward the saw-toothed mountains and beyond.

On the mesa atop Black Ship Island, the kids had been herded into huddled groups. The teens were counting the kids.

"Is everyone here?" Takashi asked.

"Everyone," Marshall said. He saw something near Willow's tent, bent and picked it up. After a moment's read he said, "Takashi—look over here."

*WILLOW. MEET ME AT MIDNIGHT, WEDGIE WALL. A.*

"What is this?" Takashi asked.

"A note to Willow from Aaron. Aaron was here."

"You can tell that from the initial?"

"No. From the term 'Wedgie Wall.' That's what he called the first barrier."

"What are you saying?"

"I'm saying Aaron was here, and now people are missing."

"I don't believe this."

"Willow is missing, Takashi."

As it slid over the cool air above the mountains, Cadmann's skeeter hit the warm air rising up from the ocean and bounced. He was behind Evelyn Niles and ahead of Sylvia just two minutes from Surf's Up now.

"What in the hell is going on out there?" Carlos said.

"I don't know," Cadmann said. "And I'm not going to speculate. Yet."

A few minutes later, the skeeters were landing atop Black Ship Island. The teens and kids gathered around.

"Anything change?" Carlos asked.

"No," Marshall said. "No. We have no sign of anyone. They were supposed to meet us in Upper Maze, and never made it."

"Lost?"

Takashi and Marshall exchanged a quick expression. Then Takashi nodded. "You know how easy that can be."

"Well," Cadmann said. "We can fix that."

But then after a moment, he reluctantly said, "No sign of . . . anything . . . ?"

"No grendels, if that's what you mean," Takashi said. "No. But Cadmann . . . we think Aaron's down there. Is that possible?"

"Yeah. It's possible. All right! Upgrade communications gear. We're going to do standard sweeps. Starting top-down, and bottom-up. Mark the tubes with glo-sticks, and stay in contact. We'll find everything in there, and bring them out."

"Want me at ground level? Take the sea route through the Cathedral and up?" Carlos asked.

"Absolutely. Take an inflatable with the skeeter, set it up, and go in through the lava tube. That should do it."

"We'll find them," Carlos said, then motioned to a couple of the others: "Come with me!"

"All right," Cadmann said. "Keep guards with the kids, the rest of us . . . let's get to work." And they entered the labyrinth.

Aaron, Willow, Uncle Horace, Kola, and the five kids were moving through those tubes, which were shadowy and slick. The water was rising enough that it ran in through the cracks.

"Those things can come out of the water," Willow said, "but I don't think they like it."

"Why do they hang their egg sacks up?" Aaron said.

"I don't know. Maybe the females do it to keep the males from killing the young. Competitors."

Aaron managed a wan smile.

"You know how men are," Kola said.

Roderick stiffened. "I hear something."

"What?"

"It's like a little whine," he said. "Insects, maybe. Can't you hear it?"

"No. Can you, Horace?"

Horace shook his head. "Nothing."

"You're just hearing that now?" Jelli scoffed. "Been giving me a headache for the last hour."

They climbed through into another chamber, and played their torches around the shadows. Fungal clusters, chunks of lava rock . . . and odd, pineapple-sized egg sacks clustered ominously along the walls.

"Jesus Christ," Aaron said.

"I'm . . . not sure we should be here," Willow said.

"Was this stuff here before, the last time you were in?" Kola asked, examining the egg sacks more closely.

"No," Aaron said. "Not at all. This . . . is new."

Sounds now. Distant, vaguely aquatic. Coming closer.

"Want to wait for a second opinion?" Kola asked.

"Hell no," Aaron said. "Kids, keep going."

Even before the dust and sand settled, Carlos and his people had scrambled from the skeeter, unloading the inflatable and medical equipment, climbing gear . . . and fat-barreled, lethal grendel guns, one for each of them.

"Let's get it going," he said. "Sweep the beach, make sure no one has already exited. Set up a camp, so that we're working bottom-up while Cadmann works top-down. Any other tubes exit to the ocean?"

Sylvia shook her head. "No."

"Let's get to work," Carlos said, "and get that boat inflated."

Cadmann and the others had moved down from the mesa top, along the cliff path with the safety ropes, and into the top level of the caves. He splashed his lights around the cave, as did the others behind him. "Willow!"

Just ahead of him, Evelyn Niles called, "Uncle Horace!"

The tunnels were empty and seemed more . . . threatening now.

No answer. "I don't suppose there's a patron saint of lost children?"

She sighed. "No. But St. Clotilde protects *adopted* children. That ought to be close enough."

The kids scrambled through the tubes. Aaron and Willow in the lead, Uncle Horace and Kola in the rear. Water was starting to slosh into the tunnels.

"Aaron!" Horace said.

"What?"

"Something back there!"

Darkness defeated the lamps. Things were humping through the shadows, just beyond the edge of sight. From time to time they caught a brief torch-lit glimpse of slug shapes, humping in the darkness.

The kids were exhausted. A punishing day and adrenal night had emptied them. One at a time they clambered through a narrow spot in the tunnel, Uncle Horace bringing up the rear.

They made it another fifty meters down the tunnel, but then Roderick collapsed against the wall, his feet ankle deep in warm water. "I'm wiped out," he said. "I have to rest."

"We can't," Willow said. "Just a little further on." She looked at Aaron. *Is that right? Just a little further?*

"We need to buy some time," he said.

"Got an idea?" Willow asked.

It seemed as if they all stopped breathing. Stared at him, expecting a miracle.

"Better than that," Aaron said. "I have a plan." He stopped. "Horace! Fuel Pod! Willow—the flash-bangs." He unscrewed and mixed. Hurrying.

"There's something back there, Aaron," Horace said.

"I just need a minute. Buy me a minute. Use the torches."

Horace's lips pressed together tightly, the muscles bunching at the corner of his jaw. He seemed torn, but then finally said, "Give me the torches. We got a rise here. They won't be able to cross easy. I can hold them long enough."

"Are you sure?"

"How long do you want me to hold them?" Horace asked, trembling.

Aaron looked back at the kids, crouching in the darkness, staring with huge fearful eyes. "As long as you can."

They shook hands.

Horace took his position in the pinch. Aaron moved them along, into another chamber. He took the fuel and the fireworks. "Here," Aaron said. "Open this."

They twisted it open.

"How long does he have to hold?" Kola asked.

Aaron stared at her until she dropped her eyes.

The powder from the fireworks and the oxidizing motor fuel were combined. The fireworks tubes refilled, with scratch fuses Evan had scavenged from flares. Four of the deadly little weapons. "All right," Aaron said. "I'm going back."

"Take care, Aaron," Willow said. And kissed him. "I'm so sorry."

"Me, too."

Kola hugged him. "Come back. Bring Horace back." And he headed back up the tunnel.

Aaron splashed his way back up the tunnel, his flashlight flaring against the lava tube's glazed walls. He almost stumbled across Horace, who crouched at the darkness, just at the pinched spot where the tunnel crimped. "Anything yet?"

"I can hear," Horace said. "Something's out there."

Aaron nodded. "They're coming. We have to give our people a chance to get away. We can do that much."

Uncle Horace nodded. "Are you afraid?"

"No," Aaron said.

Horace smiled. "I like lying, too. Lies are good, sometime."

Something was moving up the tunnel. They couldn't see it yet.

"Did you know that Mongolia used to have three different time zones."

"How many does it have now?"

"Just one."

The water was warm, but Horace was shivering. Aaron realized he was, as well. If the children get away . . . he thought. As long as the kids get away, it will all be all right.

"I know what you're thinking," Horace said. "You're thinking that it would be all right if you died here."

"What makes you think that?"

"Because I've been thinking about that ever since I woke up. Ever since I found out that my head didn't work right anymore."

"About where you'd die?"

"And how. This would be all right," he said, and ran his fingers through his unruly hair.

He noted the sack at Aaron's side. "What do you have there?"

"We made some bombs. I think they'll work all right, but we have to give the others more time to get down the tunnel. Then throw them and run like hell."

"Like we've got a base hit," Horace said.

They chuckled a bit, and then the laughter settled back down. "Do you think they'd remember me, Aaron? Would anyone remember Uncle Horace?"

"I'll remember," Aaron said.

Horace grinned. "But you're stuck here with me."

Aaron opened his mouth to speak, but before a sound emerged, the shadows beyond the pinched tube exploded into violent life.

A walrus-sized cthulhu lunged up, cilia writhing, skin glistening like wet leather. Aaron smashed his machete down on the tentacle and it made a whistling sound, like a whale clearing its blowhole.

His flashlight was ripped from his hands, and spun down into the water. Horace hacked at the tentacles as the cthulhu tried to squeeze its bulk through. Aaron hacked, and a tentacle wreathed his arm, pulling him in toward a gaping, beaked maw.

He saw what Archie, poor Archie must have seen in his own final moments, and Aaron froze. The tentacle yanked, and he felt little toothed ridges chewing at him, pulling at him. His right arm, so that in the dim and dying light his face was closer and closer to the mouth every moment.

A high-pitched wet whistling sound, and something sticky splattered against his face. Blood.

Cthulhu blood. Uncle Horace, wielding his machete with the same strength of arm that he had used on the softball diamond.

Horace had time to howl in triumph, to hack again at the bulk of a looming cthulhu, when a second rose up, wrapping its tentacles around his throat. Aaron hacked, but flesh was already gone from Horace's throat, and a diagonal strip across the left eye. Aaron gripped at the tentacles, his fingers ripped by the sharp ridges.

"Aaron!" Horace screamed. "The bombs! Save yourself!" He made no more than a gargling sound, but Aaron could hear it too clearly, and refused to obey.

Horace thrashed out, kicking Aaron in the gut, driving him back. The cthulhu was pulling. Another had joined it, gripping Horace's chest, pulling him partially off his feet and up over the low wall. "*Aaronnn*!"

Blood ran down Aaron's forehead from the gashed scalp, and the fear coursed through him like fire. Horace's single remaining eye was huge, loomed as large as all the world, imploring.

With a curse, Aaron flung the bag to Horace, and then turned and ran. He thought, he hoped, that the last thing he saw as Horace's hands fumbled into the bag was a fierce and deadly smile curling Horace's torn lips, where moments before there had been only pain.

He ran, trying not to hear the screams behind him, the tearing sounds, almost happy when the world around him turned to light and the air to fire, and he was lifted and flung along the tunnel as if by an enormous hand. There was pressure, but was no sound, because sound is in the mind, not in the disturbance of the air.

He knew that, because insanely, he was thinking of this as he pushed his mouth out of the water, the phrase *If a tree falls in the forest and Horace is not there to hear it, does it make a sound . . . ?*

And his answer. No. It makes no sound at all.

The Grendel Scouts and their minders were not supposed to be in the tunnel called the Yellow Brick Road, not since gas pockets had been discovered. They most especially were not supposed to light torches there. Or set off explosives, of any kind. There was enough gas in the tunnel to magnify the power of the explosives and weaken the walls. The same pools of petroleum that furnished the colony with chemicals and energy filled the walls with pockets of gas.

Evan would never have been allowed to set off his flash-bangs, even in the safest parts of the caverns. But if he had, there probably would have been no disastrous result. But here, the walls ruptured and a fireball hot enough to melt sheet metal rolled through the narrow tunnels, searingly hot and blindingly bright.

Carlos and his people were coming into the tube, paddling along in their boat. "What was *that*?"

The ignited gas pocket created a chain reaction of collapsing tunnels and caves, flames rushing along the oily surfaces, and finally into the lava tube. The ceiling gave way.

"Back!" Carlos screamed. "Back! Back! Jesus Christ!" Gas pockets exploded, the walls gave way, and Carlos's people dived over the side of the boat as a fireball rushed down the passage—

Carlos watched from underwater as the fireball passed overhead. Underwater, they swam back toward the entrance. Rock falling. They surfaced, and then dived back down again and again. As they reached the end of endurance the survivors emerged on the beach, shaken, burned, stunned. The communicator chimed.

"Carlos? Are you all right?" Cadmann's voice.

"Some kind of explosion," Carlos said. "We've got a collapsed tunnel. I'm guessing that they may have collapsed all through the mountain."

"Any idea what happened?"

"None," Carlos said. "We'd better get more people over here, though. This is a mess."

Up top, transport was arriving, ferrying children out and equipment in. The sun was dawning.

"What have we got?" Zack asked.

Hiroshi answered. "We have five missing teens, a dozen missing kids. Collapsed tunnels, and a fire."

"Jesus Christ. We'll need to repurpose Cassandra's deep scans, see what we can pick up. The fires would be eating up oxygen if those pockets are cut off."

Hiroshi shook his head. "After we get those kids out . . . it could take a year to put these fires out, get things back under control."

Evelyn Niles regarded him with disdain. "I think we have a little more urgent concern right now."

"I wasn't trying to say . . ."

"Save it," Zack said. "We have work to do. Explosion or not, we have to assume that people are alive, but need our help. No other assumption makes any sense at all at a time like this."

## CHAPTER FIFTEEN: AFTERMATH

Blinking and coughing, the kids emerged from the nightmare rubble of a partially collapsed lava tube.

Nnedi shook her head. "What happened?"

"Gas pockets," Kola said. "The explosion set off a methane reaction."

"Holy shit."

"Watch the language."

"You're not my mother," Nnedi said. "We're going to die down here. If I'm ever going to start cursing, I think now's the time."

Kola opened her mouth, then closed it again. "Can't argue with that," she said, and ruffled Nnedi's braids. They hugged.

Willow collared Aaron. "What happened to Horace?"

Aaron shook his head instead of answering.

He changed the subject. "Everyone all right? All right?"

"I want to go home," Roderick said.

"We'll get home," Willow said. "Right now, we have to keep going."

"Can't you hear that?" Jelli said.

"Hear what?"

Buddy shuddered. "It's like a whine. I've been hearing it since we first came in here. First came into the mountain."

"I don't hear it at all," Aaron said.

Another sound took over. Rising water. "We need to get back. Into the shadows," Willow said.

They moved into the shadows, getting the kids out of there, as the water rippled . . . and several cthulhus appeared, crouching at the water's edge.

Aaron stared. "What . . . ?"

"Shh," Willow said.

"I think I hear it too," Kola said.

The egg sacks begin to vibrate. . . . The sacks began to hatch. Out of each swarmed dozens of banana-slug sized cthulhus, tiny mouth-tentacles writhing blindly. The adults were making sounds too, and the cthulhu babies headed toward them, into the water.

"What's going on?" Kola said.

"Hatching. The sounds . . . I think they might be talking to each other, saying it's time to hatch. Communication between the eggs. They didn't hatch until the adults were here . . . maybe to protect them. Coordinating birth times, patterns, I don't know. Maybe none of them are safe unless they're all born at the same time."

A wave of cthulhu larvae were crawling across the wet floor toward them. The adults moved painfully onto the land. There was a gentleness as they herded the babies into the water. Some of the babies seemed reluctant to enter the water. The "mommies" were a thousand times their size, but still seemed somehow tender, doting. They made grunting sounds, pulsed like the whines, but at a far lower pitch.

And every time they grunted, a flock of cthulhu spawn crawled blindly toward them. They were being herded.

"Oh my God. No human being has ever seen this before."

"We don't know how long they're going to be doing this," Aaron said. "We have to get to the other side of the cave."

"Let's be quiet and careful," Willow said.

They shepherded the kids across a narrow strip of rock, toward another lava tube. With a little luck, they had a damned good chance of making it out alive.

Kola sloshed through knee-deep warm water. She was carrying the sack with the rest of the fireworks. When she stumbled, one of the shoulder straps slipped sideways, disgorging some of the contents. Aaron and Willow were so busy concentrating on the way ahead that they didn't see two of the tubes slip into the water. The speed-based oxidizer hit the water and spread. . . .

When the smell reached the cthulhus, genetic tripwires older than thought reacted with deadly speed, squealing and protecting the young, while males headed for the human children.

"Move!"

He hustled the kids, Willow and Kola into the next chamber as the tunnel behind them shook with another massive explosion.

Cracks ran along the ceiling. Chunks of cave ceiling tumbled, and they ran, screaming. A chunk of rock the size of a child's head glanced against the back of Willow's skull. She groaned and sagged to her knees. Aaron pulled her upright, and hauled her along to the next chamber.

Cadmann and his searchers were close, but above them, in the section known as the Upper Maze. A helpless world away.

He stopped his constant forward motion and held out a flattened hand, demanding stillness and silence. "Did you hear that?"

Evelyn Niles flinched. "What?"

Another, distant cry. "Help . . . !"

"Hello!" Cadmann yelled. "Can you hear me?"

There was no answer.

"Listen. What's under *us*?"

"The map says Lower Maze. Then the Cathedral, which is sea level. The fire is in the east section of the Cathedral and Lower Maze, and it's spreading. We've got fire-suppressing foam in there, but we can't pump it in blind. Anything that kills fire can kill kids. But that means the fire can spread faster than we can reach them."

Cadmann glared. "We have two teams. One is spreading the fire foam. But if we can drill through here without setting off a methane pocket, we can reach them."

"Can't use laser drills," Evelyn Niles said. "Can't use explosives."

"No. Our hands are almost tied. But we can use any cold drill tech. Get it over from the equipment sheds. NOW!"

The air was thick and increasingly acrid. In the patchy light the kids looked pale and terrified.

"Aaron," Willow said. "Do you know where we are?"

"Sort of halfway between the Cathedral level and Lower Maze. If this is the right tunnel, it should curve up. We should be able to find our way up to Lower Maze, maybe find our way out." He tried to sound optimistic. "Turn around," he said. "Let me look at you."

Blood seeped from a patch at the back of her head. When he turned her around, her eyes seemed too large, too reflective in the darkness. "I think I understand a little better what we're dealing with, Aaron."

"What?"

"It's all about grendels."

"Isn't everything?" One of her eyes wasn't tracking right. He cradled her head in his arms, terrified.

"How is it about grendels?"

"Remember the surfboard? Archie's surfboard had an image of a grendel on the underside."

"It did?" Nnedi asked.

"Yes, I remember."

"And I think maybe Evan was setting up a mock grendel when he was attacked. They've started associating us with their genetic enemy. That's not good."

"Oh, shit."

"Yeah, oh shit," Kola said. "Think anyone heard us in here?"

"I don't know. Smell that? Oil. The fire could spread into here. It's possible. It could hit methane pockets. What would I do if I were a cthulhu? Go after the grendels? Get their young out to the ocean?"

"Might be possible to do both," Kola said.

"Let's just hope someone's looking for us," Aaron said. "We may have gone as far as we can."

Additional cargo skeeters had arrived atop the mesa, and were busy evacuating the children and bringing in additional equipment.

Gas pockets made it too hazardous to use laser drills. What the engineers needed were pneumatics and other power equipment, capable of piercing a wall or a floor without generating heat or sparks.

Cadmann had supervised an emergency breach into the Lower Maze. The normal access tunnels were now choked with smoke. Rescue workers would certainly fight their way through with rebreather gear, but there was another hope: that Willow and her charges might have found a breathable pocket to hole up in, perhaps an air bubble sealed by water. And there they might hope for rescue.

They had to meet their children halfway, or risk losing them totally.

Beset by drills and sledge hammers, the floor collapsed. Flashlights gazed down into a dusty darkness. Nothing except a whiff of oily smoke smell.

"Ropes," Cadmann said. Pitons were set, ropes attached, and he climbed down to the next level. Flames flickered in methane pockets.

"If the map is right," Cadmann said, "we could have gotten a sound trace from here. If we can drill a hole through the ceiling, we can drop down on them if they're cornered. I'm thinking that Aaron might be trying to get them out through the same tunnels we used for his Grendel Scouts initiation. There were lots of sulfur stains. I think they called them the Yellow Brick Road."

"That would make sense," Evelyn Niles said, dropping down beside him, the light atop her yellow hard hat like a cyclops eye gazing through the fog.

"Let's go." He paused. "Do you have a saint for this?"

"St. Barbara. Patron Saint of Miners."

"I'll take him."

"The air's getting bad," Roderick said.

"Here," Aaron said, handing him a rag torn from his shirt. "Wrap this around your nose."

They had gone up and down, and sideways through branching tunnels. This chamber was no more than ten paces in diameter, with a narrow aperture on one side, and a drop-off to the ocean on the other. Aaron peered over the edge, shining his flashlight down.

Some kind of freak tidal whirlpool, where the water swept in from the tide, met a sinkhole of some kind, about eight feet below them. He wouldn't want to dive down there, but thought that if he was lucky, and strong, he might be able to fight his way free. There would be a tunnel, and maybe a hundred yards out to the ocean. He might be able to make it.

None of the others could. But if he made it, it might be possible to bring back help. If anyone was looking for them.

The air was foul with smoke, and Willow coughed. She seemed to be slowing down, dizzy, having problems standing. She lay in Aaron's arms, hugging him weakly, unable to pull herself to her feet.

The kids huddled together against a side of the cave, watching both openings as if unable to decide what kind of disaster might spring upon them next, and from what direction.

"Let's see," Roderick said. "Maybe a comet will hit the planet too, just to round things out."

There was a faint squealing sound. Now low and loud enough for all to hear.

"What the hell is that?" Kola said.

"Something's coming." Aaron said.

Willow, hurt and groggy, was still fierce. "Get back! Get back."

The rock wall fell away, and they backed away to the rear of the chamber. Cthulhus and their young came pouring through. Aaron faced them with the torches. The kids on one side. Cthulhus and their young on the other.

Aaron blanched. "Oh shit, shit!" The smoke was getting closer.

"Aaron! They're running from the fire."

"What? Through us?" Kola asked.

"We must be between them and a way out."

For once, Aaron seemed confused. "What do we do?"

"We have to let them pass, Aaron. We have to show them we're not their enemies. Either we all live, or we all die." Unsteadily, she motioned to them, held the torch back. The cthulhus, hissing and snarling, looked at her for a long moment. And begin to edge around her, out over the edge and into the ocean.

The adults hissed and whistled at them, but the humans remained backed against the far wall, lamps and torches held high, trying to remain out of the way.

One of the young lost its way, humping blindly toward the humans instead of over the edge.

One of the adults, a scarred old thing with a broken tentacle, hissed, but hesitated to approach the humans, watching but clearly wary of their machetes and fire.

Then . . . Willow took the machete from Aaron's hands. Very gently, using the flat edge of her machete, with the last of her strength, she crouched and guided the pup back toward the edge as the adult watched. The pup slipped over the edge and tumbled down into the water.

The scarred adult paused a moment, and then followed.

Nnedi looked at Willow and then Kola and the others, eyes wide. "Wow. Just . . . wow."

She came a little closer to the edge of the drop-off, gazing down. "What just happened . . . ?" she asked. Then another explosion rocked the chamber. Little Nnedi lost her balance, and fell. The whirlpool loomed below, but the girl managed to grab onto a rock just at the last minute, and prevented the rest of the lethal plunge.

Nnedi shrieked in fear, stretching up, unable to reach the edge. Aaron laid down on his belly and stretched his arm down for her, their hands separated by almost a foot. He couldn't reach her. He had to, but couldn't.

She fell, and the water took her, swirled her around. The girl fought and screamed, went down, came up vomiting water, and then down again—

And then it seemed she almost had wings, propelled out of the water so powerfully that her hands were able to grip the rock again, and Aaron was able to grab her wrist.

The scarred cthulhu popped up in the swirling water below her. Watched them with glassy black eyes for a moment. . . .

And then disappeared.

They helped Nnedi up. The kids were all huddling. Willow had collapsed into Aaron's arms. The fire was closer.

"Aaron," Willow said. "I'm so sorry about everything."

"Stay with me." He said that, but despite the miracle they had just witnessed, wasn't certain it would matter. The air was half smoke now. They could feel hot air from the fires approaching, eating the oxygen as it came.

Then . . . distant voices just above them, through cracks in the ceiling. "Hello!!"

"We're here! Down here."

"Aaron," Willow whispered as the kids cheered. She had collapsed bonelessly into Aaron's arms.

"Willow?" Her hands, so weak just moments before, clutched at him like talons.

"Listen to me!" Her voice was a ragged whisper. "If they don't know about the cthulhus, don't tell them."

"Why?"

"They're smart. Smart. But our parents are so afraid. All they'll see is the threat. They'll hunt them. Kill them. We have one enemy on this world. The cthulhus thought we were trying to hurt their children. Maybe . . . maybe we just found an ally . . . if we have time to know them. Please. If I don't make it. . . ."

"You will," Aaron said.

"If I don't. Please."

She looked at the kids. Kola looked at Nnedi. "It saved me," Nnedi sobbed.

The ceiling broke open and ropes flagged down. Cadmann shimmied down, and motioned for ropes and rebreathers to be lowered behind him.

"Are you all right?" Cadmann asked.

"Willow needs help. We have all the kids."

"Evan? And Uncle Horace?"

"Horace is dead," Kola said. "We never saw Evan."

## CHAPTER SIXTEEN: ENDINGS

Willow was lifted away in a medical cocoon suspended between two skeeters.

"What happened down there?" Marshall asked.

The kids and teens were spent, exhausted, smeared by smoke and scratched by rocks. No one spoke.

Kola squeezed Nnedi's hand. "She saved us."

Cadmann looked at them, not quite believing.

The sun was rising along the eastern horizon, bronzing the jagged mountains.

The kids, parents, most of the colony gathered around the medical facility. Dr. Niles emerged, shook her head, and the kids huddled and cried around Aaron. Marshall was on the outside of this, more alone with his grief.

Virtually the entire colony had gathered in the town hall. Aaron and Kola were there, central to the matter at hand.

"Not all the questions have been answered, Aaron," Zack said.

"We are not entirely satisfied about the events on Black Ship Island."

"We were lost," Aaron said. "We used fire to light our way, and explosives to try to breach a wall. Things went wrong, terribly wrong. No one is sorrier than I am."

"Willow was able to talk, for a little while . . ." Cadmann said, the memory painful. "That was the story that Willow gave, and it is not entirely satisfying."

"Uncle Horace was a hero. We don't know what happened to Evan." That, at least, was the truth.

Heather glared at him, certain that there was more to the story. "Is that all you have to say?"

"If you think there is more, please go to Black Ship Island. Investigate. And tell us all. I'm confused myself."

"It might take years to put out the fires."

"We can wait," Aaron said without blinking. "None of us are going anywhere."

There was talk. The children were interviewed separately and together. And in the end . . . the Earthborn were forced to accept the story they had been offered, no matter how unsatisfying it was.

Outside the chamber, Cadmann pulled Aaron aside. "Is that all you have to say?"

"That's all there is to say."

"All right, Aaron. I'm sorry."

"Me, too."

Aaron walked away. For a moment Cadmann's hand rose, as if to grab him by the shoulder. Pull him back. Talk to him. Then the moment was gone.

And moments like that never come back.

The teens were sitting around at Surf's Up.

"All right, Aaron. I need to know. What happened to my brother?"

"I'll tell you everything I know. What Willow knew. And when you know, you'll have to make a decision."

"What decision is that?"

He looked out at the bay. Black smoke drifted up.

"Whether or not to keep the secret of Black Ship Island."

⁂

A public funeral ceremony was held at the main colony, each of them mourning in their own way. Many speeches were given, remembrances of Evan and Uncle Horace, and tears were shed. Then their possessions were distributed among the community. There were no bones to bury.

The Starborn remained at Camelot much of the day, but by night had returned to Surf's Up. A few of them, who knew the truth, attended a very private ceremony at which Aaron presided.

They sat in circle around a campfire, by the edge of the waves, as the sun disappeared below the horizon.

"I was with Horace at the end," he said. "And he died so that I could . . . so that we could live. And all he asked was to be remembered." He pulled a piece of paper out of his pocket, and unfolded it with shaking fingers. "I found something I thought he'd like. Something that would be easy for us to remember. He was always telling us his name meant hour. Well, another form of it, Horatio, meant something else. At least it does to me. I'm hoping after I read this, it will to you too. It's a poem by Thomas Babington Macaulay: about a village threatened by invaders, and only one way to save it: that someone hold off the invaders long enough to destroy the bridge."

Aaron wiped his eyes. "And . . . whoever stays behind is going to die. That's just the way it is. And it goes:

*Then out spake brave Horatius,*
*The Captain of the Gate:*
*"To every man upon this earth*
*Death cometh soon or late.*
*And how can man die better*
*Than facing fearful odds,*
*For the ashes of his fathers,*
*And the temples of his gods."*

Aaron paused. "Or for the children he loved. He loved us. He . . ." Aaron paused, searching for the right words. "If back on Earth, he'd known what was going to happen to him, that he would lose part of himself, but that he would save so many of us, I think he would have come anyway."

He lifted a pod of beer. “To Horace,” he said. And looked up into the stars. “See that bright one? Almost blue? And draw a line down, and you have a head, and a hip, and maybe a foot. See that?”

Kola nodded. They all did.

“Horace, the Pitcher,” he said.

“Horace, the Pitcher,” they repeated, and one and all, they drank in toast.

## AFTERWARD

The cthulhus were swimming in a pod, old, young, and the infants. As they had for countless thousands of years. There was something different about their world now, but they were spreading the word.

*There are Others.*
*They are Strange.*
*But they are not Enemy.*

And for now . . . that was enough.

# REMEMBERING A MASTER OF EXCELLENCE

by Steven Barnes

"*Master one thing, master ten thousand things.*"
—Musashi Miyamoto

"*Once you know how to master one thing,*
*you know how to master anything else.*"
—Jerry Pournelle

Look up "polymath" in *Webster*'s, and in a better world I'd expect to see a picture of Dr. Jerry Pournelle. He was as close to an archetypical Heinlein hero as I've ever been honored to know: bestselling author, essayist on a dozen subjects, computer and technology expert, military officer, space scientist, psychologist, historian, husband and father. That's a load, and I'm leaving a lot out.

What you had here was an extraordinary mind, organized and honed to an edge, with vast amounts of information correlated for ready access. He had a structured, carefully designed internal library, a data tree originally organized by Jesuit brothers, but later refined through endless hours of study and a boundless hunger to be and do and know.

I still remember the first time I met Jerry. I'd heard that he and Larry Niven held court at the LASFS clubhouse on Thursday nights, and went there looking for Larry. Jerry was surrounded by a circle of fans, this tall, bluff figure debating a half-dozen different subjects at once, and generally winning. Intimidating as hell, but also fascinating. I felt I had encountered a higher order of mind, arguably the smartest guy I'd ever observed at close range.

He loved to mentor and advise, and I suspect watched to see who would take and run with that advice. If you did, you were worth his time, and he might then throw you another bone and see how you did with THAT. A natural teacher. The first advice he gave to me, as a young writer, was to buy and read Dwight V. Swain's *Techniques of the Selling Writer*. A fabulous piece of advice, as Swain broke writing down into tiny, manageable units and then built them back up again to a functional whole: all you need add was honest emotion and human empathy. I'd still suggest that book to anyone starting the path.

Countless other pieces of advice followed over the years, not all of them appropriate for a printed medium. Ahem. But all of it valuable, and none more than the words "*Once you master one subject, you know how to master anything else.*"

That philosophy, and the implications behind it, were in my opinion the secret to his wide-ranging expertise. Let's leave out the obvious quality: *genius*. Jerry was simply superbly intelligent. It was like watching my own mind with a rocket strapped on. You have to start with that. But assuming a person starts with at least an average mind, what might one learn from his life and behaviors that would be useful? Here is a partial list of what I'd noticed over the years.

1. Be constantly learning and studying. Books and magazines in every room some new, some well-thumbed. Jerry had a commitment to learning about everything that was worth learning about, and came as close as anyone I've known to just that.
2. Constantly discuss and test your ideas and perspectives by contrasting them to the thoughts of the smartest people you can find. I still remember one party at Jerry's house, filled with experts in at least ten different disciplines, watching Jerry flit from conversation to conversation, making intelligent, measured, riveting comments at each. Mind-blowing mental agility.
3. Connect your world view to your core views of the universe and humanity. Jerry had strongly considered views on those two most important questions: *What are human beings, and what is*

*the world they experience*? I didn't always agree with his positions, but they were ALWAYS well considered.

4. Develop a crushing work ethic. Jerry could write a book in a week, at the rate of about 10,000 words a day. And had. Several times.
5. Don't let people waste your time. Jerry suffered fools less gladly than almost anyone I'd ever met. But he was also quick to help people he considered worth his time and energy.
6. Become a real, no-B.S. expert in at least one arena. Jerry had two doctorates, and I think it reasonable to extract from this that he knew how to focus his mind and heart to burn through all resistance, and touch a space of excellence. And as both he and the Greatest Swordsman in the World suggested, once you have found the place inside yourself capable of such excellence, all you need do is apply the same energy and concentration, over time, to anything else, use the same strategies of commitment and persistence and modeling other excellent minds . . . and you will leap ahead of the generalists who never really shine at anything.

There is more, of course. Much more. But those are the things that I remember most clearly. Frustrating, challenging, inspiring, and ultimately just a hell of a good friend, he was exactly the kind of person *Reader's Digest* lauds in every issue: an Unforgettable Character, in the very best sense of the terms.

# THE LAST SHOT
## by Jerry Pournelle

### Editor's Introduction

There's an interesting backstory to "The Last Shot." Jerry, like most of the SF fraternity, wanted to be included in Harlan Ellison's genera-busting anthology, "Dangerous Visions." The first two volumes, *Dangerous Visions* and *Again, Dangerous Visions*, were the defining works of science-fiction's "New Wave." The books won awards for their authors and heavily influenced the next several generations of SF writers, especially those who identified themselves as New Wave or literary SF authors.

Now, Jerry was never part of the New Wave; in fact, many fans saw him, with his allegiance to John W. Campbell, as a throwback to the Neanderthal days of SF. A badge Jerry wore with honor, since he most identified with Campbellian writers, such as Robert A. Heinlein, H. Beam Piper, Poul Anderson and Gordon R. Dickson. And he wrote with the same direct and deceptively "simple" style. As Jerry always said to me, if you want to influence other writers, write them letters rather than dabble in stylistic effects.

A few years after I went to work for him, I asked Jerry why he'd stopped writing stories in the Nuclear General series. Pocket Books had just published *High Justice* and it was one of my Pournelle favorites.

Jerry gave me a wry smile and said, "Ask Harlan Ellison."

"What! Why?" I asked in confusion.

"A few years ago, I thought it would be a real coup to have a story in Harlan's *The Last Dangerous Visions*. In fact, Harlan asked me for a story. I came up with a doozy, but then I didn't think it would take this long for it to appear. In fact, it ended the Nuclear General series since I can't write any more stories until this story is published."

I asked what made the story so "dangerous."

He laughed. "Nuclear energy! In today's climate, this story will have the ecology and Sierra Club minions screaming from the rooftops."

Unfortunately—because I'd like to read it myself—*The Last Dangerous Visions* was never completed, despite Harlan's many promises that it would be out "Any Day Now." Over the decades it became science fiction's most talked about and desired unpublished book. And, the more fans pressured Ellison to finish it, the more defensive he got about it.

Wikipedia has this to say about *The Last Dangerous Visions:*

It was originally announced for publication in 1973, but other work demanded Ellison's attention and the anthology has not seen print to date. He has come under criticism for his treatment of some writers who submitted their stories to him, whom some estimate to number nearly 150 (and many of whom have died in the ensuing more than four decades since the anthology was first announced). In 1993 Ellison threatened to sue New England Science Fiction Association (NESFA) for publishing "Himself in Anachron," a short story written by Cordwainer Smith and sold to Ellison for the book by his widow, but later reached an amicable settlement. British SF author Christopher Priest critiqued Ellison's editorial practices in a widely disseminated article titled "The Book on the Edge of Forever." Priest documented a half-dozen instances in which Ellison promised *The Last Dangerous Visions* would appear within a year of the statement, but did not fulfill those promises. Ellison has a record of fulfilling obligations in other instances, including to writers whose stories he solicited, and has expressed outrage at other editors who have displayed poor practices.

I asked Jerry why he didn't just pull the story since it was obvious, even in 1978, that Harlan was not going to put the book out for a long time—if ever.

Jerry grinned. "I promised Harlan I wouldn't publish it anywhere else until either one of us were dead. We both got a good laugh out of that." Jerry was as good as his word.

Well, sadly, now they are both gone. So, here for the first time in print is Jerry's defining Nuclear General story, "The Last Shot."

❂ ❂ ❂

**THE WHITE HOUSE FELT SHABBY.** It was a curious feeling, and Bill Adams couldn't see anything to justify the emotion. The carpets were new. Everything was freshly painted and gleaming. If there was a slouch in the guards' posture, it was just at the threshold of perception. Yet, without saying anything definite, Adams was reminded of decayed greatness.

They walked through the long corridor from the heliport entrance. As they neared the President's office, the steel engravings on the corridor walls changed to oil paintings, each with a bronze lamp above it to bring out the brilliant colors in the super-realistic scenes. There was *Eagle* on the Moon, Earth behind gleaming in white clouds and blue flashing seas, so lovely that it put a catch in his throat. And here were American soldiers marching in perfect ordered ranks, each man's bayonetted musket held just so, the drums beating the final charge while British gunners and officers face good Whig buff-and-blue uniforms and exclaimed, "Those are regulars, but God!"

Maybe that's it, Bill Adams thought. The White House looks all right, but now we're a nation of lizards baking in the sun while an ice age creeps down on us. But there was greatness once.

They stopped for only a moment in the office at the end of the corridor. A darkly tanned girl sat at the big desk in the center of the anteroom. She smiled to show perfect white teeth. "The President will see you immediately, Mr. Adams." She smiled again and put a little extra in it for this tall man with pale blue eyes and a worried expression. She thought he might be fifty years old at least, but he looked good, slim and hard, and—what? she asked herself. Determined. That's it. There aren't too many like that here. She wondered if Adams were a soldier in civilian clothes.

Bill and his escort went into the Oval Office. Seeing the President was a physical shock. My God, he's aged, Adams thought. The man at the enormous American meadow oak desk looked up to smile briefly before turning his attention back to papers laid out on the varnished surface. Adams waited as his escort fidgeted beside him.

It was still an important room. Not what it used to be, Adams thought, but the power's still here. If only somebody would use it.

"That will be all, Carruthers. How are you, Bill?" The President got up from his desk and came around it to a big brown leather chair. He indicated a short couch at right angles to the chair and waved Bill to it. "Sit down. Coffee? Brandy? Anything you'd like?"

"Nothing, thank you, Mister President." They waited until the office was empty. And just how private is it? Adams thought. Just how many people are listening and watching? The President's people. Congressional spies? The Coal Trust? Union spies? Hell, maybe even the Soviets. Probably all of them and the CIA to boot, none of them aware of the others, or maybe all aware of each other . . . they know, and we know they know, but do they know that we know?

The President launched into more pleasantries, but Adams's normally handsome face was set into a grim look that stopped him. The older man sighed. The aura of *that office* filled the room, but the President wasn't one of the great ones who'd sat there, and he knew it. The thought sometimes filled him with sadness. "All right, Bill. I'm sorry. There's nothing I can do for you."

"Nothing you can do for us," Bill said. "Before I even make my pitch, you can say there's nothing?"

"That's right. Bill, you think I don't know what you're going to say?"

"Why not let me try anyway? Just for drill."

The President shrugged. The gesture said it all.

"Yeah. But all the same, Mister President, when that Moratorium goes into effect and shuts down our fission plants, the United States is going to have blackouts. Power rationing. Even before the blackouts, you'll have layoffs. More people on the dole in case you don't have enough already. And the industries that'll hurt the worst are the high-technology producers, your only foreign trade income. Just how goddam long do you think you can keep this country running on paper money and inflation? When you stop the energy producers, you stop production of *everything*."

"I know that."

"Oh, hell, of course you do." Adams momentarily pressed his lips together in a tight, mirthless smile. "I'm prepared to show you there's no reason for the Moratorium. I have films on the precautions we've taken to insure total public safety. Five Nobel Prize winners, the whole American Society of Nuclear Engineers. . . ."

"I believe you, Bill. I don't think there's a chance in hell that Nuclear General is going to kill anyone. But Congress passed the Moratorium Act, and I've got to go along with it. Incidentally, I'm not going to sign it."

"You won't sign it, but you won't veto it, either. It's a law anyway, that wipes out whatever chance this country ever had of catching up with the Japanese and Soviets. Or Europe. There aren't enough votes to pass it over your veto, you know."

The President gave him a thin smile. American politics was one thing he knew better than anyone alive. "How's the weather in Santa Barbara?"

"I don't get there enough to know." The strain showed heavily in Bill Adams's voice. "I've been here in Washington trying to kill this damned Moratorium. Doing *your* work, Mister President, trying to keep this country from making the biggest mistake in her life—look, it was a close vote. Close enough to justify a veto on something this important."

The President shook his head. "I don't see it that way. I've seen the campaign the Coal Trust is ready to put on. The Moratorium has the Unions, a segment of business, the eco-freaks, and all the universities in the country behind it."

"Universities? You mean those damned relics like Harvard, not the real universities. Westinghouse isn't for it. GE's not. I leave out Nuclear General. . . ."

"The people still think of Harvard and Berkeley as 'real universities,' Bill. Look, if I veto the Moratorium, the Coal Trust is going after the defense budget. They can win. And if I lose *that*, what's left to lose? In this job you learn to set priorities, and I've set mine. I've got to have that defense appropriation."

"Sure." It was sinking in now, down deep where Adams felt things. For weeks he'd known intellectually that he was going to lose, but it hadn't reached his emotional centers. He slumped back onto the couch, drained. "Yeah. Defense, welfare—getting elected again, that's even more—"

"No." The President's voice matched his face, hard, contemptuous. "I'd thought better of you than that. If all I wanted was another term, do you think I'd have fought for the *defense* appropriation? Do you think that got me voters? Don't hand me guff I don't deserve, Mr. Adams. I don't have to take it from you or anybody you represent."

Adams shrugged. "Mr. Lewis isn't likely to be pleased. He'll have me field candidates for all the three party primaries. There are more corporations than Nuclear General involved in this, too." It was a dirty game, bringing the political and economic power of the big corporations against the President, but it was a game Adams understood.

The President stretched a long arm toward the oak desk. He lifted a sheaf of papers from it and riffled through them before passing it across to Adams. "All these will be in the camp against me. Have I left any out?"

"Hmm." Despite what it meant, Adams felt a wave of admiration. The President was thorough. "I see you have Reynolds Aluminum with us three months after the Moratorium takes effect. I think we estimated six. Otherwise you haven't missed much. Think you can fight this combine?"

"I may not have to." The President was very serious. "The Moratorium won't go into effect for years. Before it does, anything can happen. You can't build your combine until there's a real power shortage, and the Moratorium crowd has their act together *right now*. Bill, did you ever hear the story of the condemned man who told the king he could teach a horse to sing hymns in just one year? When the other prisoners said he was crazy, the thief said: 'But anything could happen in a year. The king might die. I might die. Or what the hell, the horse might learn to sing hymns.' That was one of Henry VIII's stories. It fits here, too. Time is always worth something in politics, Bill."

"But whether the Moratorium goes into effect or not, it's halted new fission plants! You'll need those new plants, the ones we can't build until the country wakes up, and when they let us build them, it's going to be too damn late!"

"Maybe." The President stood. "But the public and Congress won't see any effect from the Moratorium for a long time. . . . I've got to have that time, Bill. The Moratorium Act is going to become law and you'd better be ready for it. Now, if you'll excuse me. . . ."

Wind rushed through Courtney's long blonde hair. It was a delicious feeling to drive in the Santa Barbara sunshine with the top down on Bill Adams's Oldsmobile Electric. The dancing wind was warm, baking out the chill that long weeks in Washington had settled into her bones. It was so pleasant she wore a new spring outfit with a short skirt, leaving the long ugly trousers for the moths.

They drove up to a gate and Bill got out to open it. She could just see white stucco and red tile in the thick pine woods high above them. The big white mission-style house sprawled across a lot of the hill, although most of it was invisible from the road. Behind them the city of Santa Barbara was spread out like a map, more white stucco and red tile roofs, a city that had retained its individuality here on the California coast. Most hadn't. As the car climbed higher on the ridge Courtney saw blue water and flashing white waves, gleaming sands of beach, and out to the horizon were islands. Somewhere out there, too, there would be enormous Antarctic icebergs towed in by Nuclear General to furnish water for a thirsty Los Angeles.

"Shouldn't there be guards?" Courtney asked.

"There are. I wouldn't care to get in here without permission. Not only is there a transponder in my car, but I've made some recognition signals to show I'm not being held prisoner. . . ."

"Really?"

"Yeah. Little like a dime novel, isn't it?" They pulled up in front of the house itself. Adams leaped out, and Courtney followed her boss up wide stone steps into the mansion. Her heels clicked hollowly on tile floors, echoing through big room with very little furniture. Everything seemed old. There were carvings on the cornices around the ceilings and the high exposed overhead beams were hand painted.

"Where is everyone?" Courtney asked.

"Mr. Lewis doesn't keep a large staff."

Courtney looked around unashamedly. It was said that a big

magazine had unsuccessfully offered a hundred thousand dollars for a picture story about Jeremy Lewis and his lair.

The library was as big as Courtney's whole apartment down in Santa Barbara. The walls were covered with books, rare first editions, leather-bound volumes cracked with age, a shelf of cheap paperback mysteries, modern works with bright jackets. The fire place was large enough to roast an ox. A log blazed cheerfully in a smaller fireplace inside the big one. In front of the stone hearth was a table fully seven feet square and two thick, a massive slab sawn from a single tree. Except for the giant redwoods there probably wasn't a tree left on Earth that could yield a piece of wood like that.

"Conquistador period," Adams said. "A lot of stuff here is. Mr. Lewis likes it."

A double door at the end of the room slid noiselessly open. A wiry man in hard gray work clothes totally inappropriate to the room's splendor pushed in a bright steel wheelchair. There was a sunporch behind the doors and the light streaming into the dark library blinded her until they were closed.

Courtney couldn't help staring. She'd worked for Nuclear General for years, but this was her first chance to see the boss. Most employees never had a glimpse of El Supremo.

He was old. She'd known that, of course, but she hadn't known how it would show. Jeremy Lewis had the shrunken appearance of the very aged, but he wasn't small. He'd been over six feet tall when he could walk. Now, well over seventy, confined to that chair for twenty years, his hair was mostly gone and what was left wispy white. She'd never seen anyone who looked more alive than this old, withered, crippled man. . . .

"Good morning, sir," Adams said carefully.

"Morning Bill. Courtney." He eyed her carefully, and Courtney almost blushed. Automatically she smoothed her skirt.

"Very nice," Mr. Lewis said. He spoke carefully as if it hurt his throat to talk. "I like that white linen outfit. Should have brought her around before, Bill. Bring her more often. Okay, tell me about it."

"What's there to say?" Adams asked. "I blew it, Mr. Lewis. I thought I could defeat the Moratorium and I couldn't." His tone was a confession of failure that couldn't be forgiven.

No! Courtney thought. Don't talk like that! If you couldn't do it, it couldn't be done.

"Want a drink?" Lewis said.

"Bit early for me," Adams replied.

"Yeah. Allan, get me a Bloody Mary. And a cigar. Get a pot of coffee for Bill, and Courtney here drinks tea. Don't you, girl?"

"Why—yes, thank you."

The attendant sucked his teeth and didn't move.

"Oh hell, get 'em," Lewis demanded. "You can tell the goddam doctors later. I've just lost a billion dollars, don't you think I deserve a drink?"

"Okay." Allan winked at Courtney. He was younger than Mr. Lewis, how much younger she couldn't tell, but he was certainly sixty. Yet his muscles were hard, and there was a look of strength and vitality to him. She would have noticed it before if the shrunken man in the wheelchair hadn't so dominated the room. Allan screwed his face into what might have been a close-mouthed grin, and jerked his head toward the door.

"I can help him," Bill Adams said. He followed Allan from the room. When they were gone Jeremy Lewis laughed. It was a sudden, hearty sound, and it startled Courtney.

"Gone to find out what mood the boss is in," Lewis chuckled. His voice was suddenly strong. Courtney's eyes saw the thin arms and even thinner legs under a gay colored Indian blanket, but there was no impact to these. There was only vitality. "He's taking this pretty hard, isn't he, Courtney?" Lewis asked.

"Sir? Yes, sir. He is really. I've never seen him so upset. He thinks he's failed you. And it isn't true, nobody could have done more than—"

"Dah. Stop it." His eyes were light green, another contrast, unexpected; somehow they ought to be dark. She stood in silence while Mr. Lewis looked her over. "You think I need a pep talk about Bill Adams. I always knew that damn Moratorium was going to pass. Waste of time fighting it. When a country's determined to commit suicide it's going to do it. Sit down, I don't like looking up at people."

"Yes, sir." Courtney found a chair on the other side of a massive pine table. It wasn't as big as the coffee table, but it was enormous, made up of planks fully a foot thick.

"Bring the chair around where I can see you," Jeremy Lewis said.

"I'm not so old I can't enjoy looking at a girl's legs. One of the few things they can't take away from one. Where the hell are they with my drink? And a cigar. I want a cigar."

The others came back soon after. Allan handed Mr. Lewis a cigar encased in an aluminum cylinder. It was opened with almost sensual pleasure, the cedar shaving taken out and sniffed appreciatively before the cigar itself was unwrapped and carefully warmed in the flame of a wooden match. He took several puffs in silence. Then, abruptly, "Okay, Bill. We got a Moratorium. No new fission plants for ten years. Phase out of the existing system starting five years from now. What do we do about it?"

Bill Adams shrugged. "Buy stock in the Coal Trust, I guess. The country's going to need electricity, and the price will go up plenty. We can still make a profit."

"You don't sound too happy." Jeremy Lewis puffed his cigar again, then turned almost reverently to his drink. He didn't look like a man who'd just lost a billion dollars.

"Well, no sir. Even with their liquefaction process, coal is fifty years behind current technology. It pollutes no matter what you do to it. Not to mention the $CO^2$, there's going to be oxides of nitrogen—but mainly, it took millions of years to form that coal. We'll set a match to all of it within our lifetimes. They're going to be taking ten million tons a day out of strip mines."

Lewis snorted. "Never knew you were an ecology bug. Is there enough profit in coal to make it worthwhile?"

"The Coal Trust has it pretty well sewed up. I've got people on contingency plans, should I send for them?"

"No." The old man chuckled. When he raised his drink he had to move very slowly, as if he weren't completely in control of his arm, and a little of the red tomato juice spilled down across his jaw. Courtney wanted to wipe it away, but she didn't. Jeremy Lewis set the glass down again. "I've done a little work while you were in Washington, Bill. Tell me, if we can't use fission and we don't like coal, what's left?"

Now that's obvious, Courtney thought. She was surprised to see that Bill was thinking hard about the question.

"Fusion, sir? Last I heard that was thirty years away. Have we got a breakthrough in the labs?"

The man in the wheelchair sighed. "Wish we did. No, I don't see any practical solution to using fusion. But there has been a breakthrough in solar cell technology." He said it slyly, like a rich uncle revealing a pony for a birthday present. "Increase in conversion efficiency by a factor of thousands."

Bill took his slide rule from his pocket. He still called it a slide rule although he'd long since given up his circular slipstick for the tiny Hewlett-Packard computer. It hummed, a tiny warbling note indicating that it was in microwave communication with a larger computer somewhere. Of course, Courtney thought. Mr. Lewis must have an antenna hooked into the company's primary data banks right here in this room, and Bill is working on that.

Finally Adams looked up. "Still no cheap way to store power for night operations. What do you have in mind? Pumped storage? We'll never get that past the eco-freaks. I'm not even sure I want to. Besides, there's the land question, hundreds of square miles for screens, and even Arizona desert is going to cost us too much. I don't think it will work." But he said it carefully. Bill Adams was treating it as silly.

"We don't need storage if the solar screens are out in space," Lewis said. "Put 'em where there isn't any night. Synchronous orbit and beam the power down by microwave. We use the technique to get power from island to island in the Tonga right now."

"Yes, sir," Adams frowned in puzzlement. "But space? We've had no real space program since Congress cancelled the shuttles."

"The shuttles still exist, don't they?" Lewis demanded. "We can buy them."

"Well, yes, sir," Adams said. "North American Rockwell would be glad to unload their space labs for anything they could get—for that matter, we've picked up some of their best engineers, but they haven't come up with anything practical that I've seen."

There was total silence in the room. This is idiocy, Courtney thought. The cost of a pound in orbit was—what? She took out her pocket computer and pressed in her identity code. As she'd thought, the tiny screen flashed acknowledgment from the Nuclear General central computer banks. She punched for the code ID of space operations, costing, and let the file titles roll across the face of the gadget until she caught the one she wanted, then punched for expansion. Cost per pound, synchronous orbit, $120 by shuttle, $550 by direct rocket. She looked up but the room was still silent.

"Pretty expensive, eh?" Lewis said. He seemed to be enjoying himself. "But think what we get. Happens that crystals for the new solar screens can't be grown in quantity without zero gravity and high vacuum. We'll have that in space." Lewis lifted his drink and sipped luxuriantly.

The old man's lost his mind, Courtney thought. She looked back from Lewis to Bill Adams. Bill didn't think Lewis was insane. He was listening attentively, waiting for Lewis to spring his surprise. Strange how she knew what Bill was thinking. Or was it? She'd been with him ten years, now, and they were closer than most married couples she knew.

Adams fiddled with his slide rule, but he wasn't setting up problems. Finally, he said, "Nuclear General is as big as there is, Mr. Lewis, but not even the US Government could finance space factories."

"But it needs to be done," Lewis answered. There was more fire in his eyes now. "Get the hell off this overcrowded stinking ball. I thought the kids would do it once, but they're both too interested in saving the world to do any hard work. It's still up to us old crocks."

Lewis's attendant made a strangled sound that might have been laughter. Adams looked at him in annoyance, then smiled.

"That's better," Jeremy Lewis said. "You look better, too. Hell yes, I've got an idea. There's a way we can get ten million pounds in synchronous orbit for about a hundred million bucks. The ground receivers and land fees cost fifty million more, but that comes later. Space hardware is ninety million. Two hundred and forty million dollars, Bill. A lot of money, but here's the good part: We get eight thousand megawatts of power out of the setup, as well as the space labs."

"But—" Adams thought furiously. "A regular fission plant would cost us over three hundred bucks a kilowatt. You're saying we can go to space, build a plant that has no fuel costs whatever to run, and do it for about what we'd pay for a conventional reactor. If that's true, why didn't we do it before."

"We didn't have to do it before. And we're not in space yet, Bill. There are some problems, and we haven't bought the switchyards yet. The package comes to maybe three forty a kilo, more than ten percent higher than we usually pay, but the boys tell me it's competitive with coal given the price of money right now—and it gets power for the United States during the pinch."

Allan laughed, only this time the attendant had a hearty laugh, strong for a man of sixty. "Patriotism? You're patriotic as long as it doesn't cost you anything, but—"

"Crap." Mr. Lewis threw his attendant a black look, but if it registered Allan didn't show it. "Giving the economy a boost makes sense, that's all. When'd you get interested in saving me money? Go get that engineer friend of yours. Make yourself useful instead of standing around absorbing my money."

Allan shrugged and left. "Not true, you know," Mr. Lewis said, as Allan went out the door. "He's got plenty of money of his own. Doesn't need mine. He invested in Nuclear General thirty years ago. . . ."

"This is Ferguson, Jimmy Ferguson," Allan announced. He led in a tall, gangling young man in his twenties. Ferguson tripped on the edge of the carpet coming in, recovered quickly as if he were used to stumbling. He stood nervously in the middle of the room.

"Sit down for God's sake," Lewis told him. "You know Bill Adams, my special assistant? He won't let me make him president of the company."

Now, he might get a day off if he were president, Courtney thought. Presidents keep long hours but Bill never rested. He could fire the company president, for that matter, but routine administration was too simple for Bill. As Lewis's assistant, Bill looked over the whole empire, and it had cost him any personal life he might ever have had.

"You've got something hot, Ferguson?" Bill Adams asked.

The younger man nodded vigorously. "If what you want is a cheap way to get pounds in orbit, I've got it. Ever hear of Project Orion?"

"No." Adams sounded puzzled. He took out his slide rule and punched at keys while Ferguson talked.

"Nothing in the company files . . . under that name," Ferguson said. "Try Fergiedream 222." Ferguson grinned. He had a very wide mouth that looked even bigger on his thin face.

"Just what is Orion?"

"Bang bang," Ferguson said gleefully. He seemed to be enjoying himself. "You take a great big ship and you set off fusion bombs behind it. Cawhambo! Up you go, and I mean fast. Uses up tritium like nothing you ever saw. Get you Delta-v. Cheap."

There was total silence in the room. Jeremy Lewis carefully lifted his drink. When he put it down, only the ice cubes were left. Bill Adams's slide rule hummed.

"Hee—hoo!" Everyone stared at Allan. "I can just see old Bill Adams trying to get permission from the AEC to lift off a hundred atom bombs! Some of them atmospheric at that!" Lewis's companion chuckled loudly, his face a twisted grin. "Let's do it!"

"This thing will really work?" Bill asked carefully.

"Damn right!" Allan said. "Fergie, you just tell 'em the way you told me."

Ferguson cleared his throat and launched in. "I don't have all the details—it isn't my idea, you know. There was a Department of Defense study under the code name Orion, way back—fifties? Sixties? Somewhere in there. It's still classified. But I talked to some people who were on the project, and it *would* work. Actually, the technology is simple."

"Simple." Bill Adams was staring at his slide rule. "You call it simple to build something that can take the shock of an atom bomb going off right under it? J. Comrade Christ, that's the silliest thing I've ever heard of."

"Yeah!" Allan was shouting in glee. "That's what's so wonderful about it. Nobody'll ever believe it even if they find out what you're going to do! Come on, Fergie, tell 'em."

The gangling engineer responded eagerly. "The base plate's simple enough, Mr. Adams. The shock absorbers get kind of hairy"—he was interrupted by Allan's gleeful snort—"but they're not new technology, either. The only really difficult problems are the second detonation—that's got to be timed just right or the whole thing will fall back down before it can get moving fast enough to give a margin of error—and coupling the explosions to the ship after it's out in space. In the atmosphere coupling is simple enough, and I think I've got a technique for doing the coupling after you're outside the atmosphere too. . . ." He ran down finally.

"You really are serious, aren't you?" Adams asked. He wasn't incredulous now, and Courtney looked around quickly to see why.

Jeremy Lewis was thoughtfully chewing the end of his cigar, staring at Ferguson, his mouth working in deep concentration.

"There is no way we can launch that thing in the United States," Adams said. He looked sourly at the model of *Prometheus* on the big pine table in Jeremy Lewis's big library. It didn't look like much, simply a large cylinder with a domed top resting on a thick metal plate.

When the cylinder was lifted to reveal the inner workings there was a complex arrangement of springs and hydraulic shock absorbers connecting the base plate to the rest of the ship, and another network of tubes leading out to the point just below the base itself.

"What is all this gup, anyway?" Adams asked. "You've been doing things to this model."

Ferguson shrugged. "The tubes are for feeding the bombs out. Each weapon has to go off at the right place or we won't go in a straight line. The shock-absorbing junk ought to be obvious."

"Yeah. Obviously. Look, Fergie, will this thing *work*? It still seems like the silliest idea I ever heard of."

"Why wouldn't it work?" the gangling engineer asked. "There's plenty of energy in an atomic bomb. The only problem is to couple it to the ship so it gives propulsion, and I've worked that out. You won't guess how."

"I'm sure I won't." Adams tried to seem uninterested, but the engineer said nothing. "Okay, how?"

"Let's wait for Mr. Lewis. Courtney and Allan are bringing him now."

Adams stared at the model until they arrived. Even if there weren't any real technical problems that couldn't be solved by engineering and a lot of money, the project seemed hopeless.

Allan wheeled Lewis in. He and Courtney looked very serious.

"Hi boss," Adams said. "Ferguson was going to explain this thing."

Lewis nodded stiffly. Adams glanced up at Allan standing impassively behind the wheelchair and got a slow headshake. The boss wasn't feeling well today, and it wasn't just temper or Allan would be riding him. . . . Will the old man last long enough to see this out? Adams wondered. Both of Lewis's sons were dead, one in the futile defense of Turkey and the other on the disastrous Mars Expedition, which had ended space exploration. Lewis's grandson was still in high school, and if Lewis died now, Bill Adams would be executor of everything he owned. It scared him. Without the old man to backstop him. . . .

"Styrofoam!" Ferguson said loudly. The others stared at him. "Sure, we use Styrofoam to couple the bombs to the ship. It's light enough. Should work fine. That's what the tubes here are for." He pointed to his model.

"Hah!?" Allan cackled. "The last hopes of the human race, powered by bombs and Styrofoam! Why not?"

"It won't matter much anyway," Adams said. "I can't get any permit to launch that thing in the United States. There's a treaty, if nothing else."

"Never thought we could," Lewis muttered. "You didn't either. So we go to the Namib Desert station."

"No, sir," Adams said. "We don't own that complex outright. Neither the Bayer Kartel or I.G. Farbenwerke will let us use it to compete with them. Bayer worked out the coal liquefaction process."

"So where?" Lewis demanded testily.

"I don't know yet," Adams admitted. "The only major outfits who didn't sign the Test Ban Treaty are the French and the Chinese. Neither one's going to be very interested in helping us. So we've got to go somewhere so small they didn't bother to sign the damn treaty."

"Ta'avu?" Courtney asked. "Be nice to go to the Tongas again. Mr. Lewis, you never went there, and you ought to."

"Not there either," Adams said. "The king isn't going to get every big power in the world down on him even for us. I don't blame him. Asking him would cost good will, and for what?" Adams sat dejectedly. "I can't think of anything else, Mr. Lewis."

"Crap." Lewis tried to say something else, but it was lost in a coughing fit. Courtney brought him a glass of water.

"You better get some rest, Jer," Allan said. There was none of the usual banter in his voice.

The coughing subsided. "Crap, I said! Bill, you don't believe in this project, do you? You don't think it will work."

"Sir, I'm trying as hard—"

"No. You don't believe in it. Bill, I *order* you to believe in it. I mean *really* believe. This may be the most important thing we've ever done, you and I."

"It will ruin the company, Mr. Lewis," Adams said carefully.

"Why? Ferguson, just how damn much radiation pollution are you going to cause with this thing?"

Ferguson pulled charts from his briefcase. "I've checked it five times, Mr. Lewis—Bill was able to get some data from the Atomic Energy Commission, I don't know how. . . ."

"I bribed an official to give us TOP SECRET information, that's how," Adams said angrily. "If you're going to talk about a conspiracy, you might as well be in on it all the way."

"Uh—" Ferguson gulped, then recovered his enthusiasm. "Mr. Lewis, I showed it to you. There's almost no pollution. We use laser-triggered fusion bombs, so there's no plutonium primary to scatter anything really bad. On the first two detonations the fireball touches water—good Lord, it's *under* water—so there's some secondary stuff, but it's all short half-life and there just isn't that much. Fifty miles downwind you'd be safe in a bathing suit."

"Safe isn't the question," Adams said. "I saw your figures, too. The fall-out is detectible worldwide!"

"Detectible isn't dangerous!" Ferguson yelled. "Look, the average citizen's exposed to more radiation drinking a can of beer than from *Prometheus*!"

"All right," Lewis said. "So you've got one requirement. Fifty miles of uninhabited area downwind. You launch from water so there's another. What else?"

"Well, we need a lot of tritium," Ferguson said.

"That's no problem," Courtney told him. "If we got every station setting up to collect it. There will be more than enough before you can complete *Prometheus*."

"Yeah," Adams agreed. "Engineering won't stop old Bang-Bang. The problem is, no matter what I do the United States government will use this as an excuse to take over Nuclear General. All over the world countries are going to do the same thing! When this is finished, the only thing we'll have left will be Ta'avu, and even there the king's going to be hopping mad."

"But why?" Ferguson said. "It isn't dangerous. . . ."

"Neither are our fission power plants," Adams said. His voice fell to a low steady note, very patient. "The fact remains that as badly as the United States needs electric power, Congress passed the Moratorium. When *Prometheus* goes up, the news media are going to have a little orgy about irresponsible business endangering the human race—we'll be lucky we aren't lynched, much less be able to hold on to the company."

"Yeah." Lewis looked sourly around his library. "Allan, take Ferguson out of here, will you? Thanks." He waited until the engineer had left the room. "Okay. Bill, I want you to liquidate the company."

"Sir?"

Courtney held her breath.

"Sell us out! Turn it into gold in Swiss banks. They can't seize that before the Throne of God."

Bill Adams was very quiet. He'd spent his life working for Jeremy Lewis and Nuclear General. He believed in both of them.

Jeremy Lewis studied his chief assistant. He knew what Adams was thinking. After twenty years of close association, Lewis could read every emotion on his prime minister's face—although Adams could still beat him at poker, sometimes. "Bill, you don't think I know what I'm doing."

"It's just—we spent twenty years building Nuclear General, and . . ."

"And I'm throwing it away on some quixotic scheme, eh? Thought you knew me better than that. Bill, Van Cott and I put this company together by sinking every dime we could borrow in fast breeders. We knew damn well it was going to pay off. Okay. We build Nuclear General on fission power—but if this space deal goes, what's left for fission? Hell, no matter what we do, the company's not going anywhere. Nobody is. The freeloaders are having their inning all over the world. Nobody's looking for anything but a free meal. There is a danger that one of the plants will cause a real disaster—"

"We've got the best safety engineers in the world!" Bill protested. "There are plenty of people with ambition left."

"Save it for the media, Bill. Something *could* happen. Sabotage, maybe. War. I agree the chances are pretty low, and the worst that could happen wouldn't be as bad as not having the power in the first place, but the environmentalists have a point and we both know it." Lewis was more relaxed now, and some of the vitality that had so impressed Courtney came back to him. "Yeah, and how many control anything more than a hill of beans? It won't be long before we're both unemployed, and we both know it. Out in space there aren't any naysayers! Space, Bill, real space laboratories not hoisted up for a few weeks, but a real station in space. . . .

"If this goes, Bill, what's to stop you from sending colonies out to other planets? We'll still know how to build fission plants, and we'll have the power screens—"

"But we won't have the company!"

"Balls. Come *on*, Bill. *Believe* in this! You know better'n to sell all the divisions. We want to keep the best men out of what we do sell. There's not another man in the world who could handle a deal this big, but you can. . . ."

"Yes, sir."

"No enthusiasm. Bill what do you want the company for?"

"It—the company's bigger than either one of us, Mr. Lewis."

It sure has been, Courtney thought sadly. She kept hoping Bill would—

"Not with the Moratorium unless we get space power!"

"I—" Adam's didn't know what to say. It was true enough. "You'll lose a lot of money. I can't liquidate anything that big for its present value."

"So what? It was your money, anyway."

"Mine?—your grandson—"

"My grandson is well fixed for life, but since my boys died you've always been slated to get the company. So now it's Interplanet instead of Nuclear General. Come on, boy! The human race has to bust off Earth one of these days, why not us to do the busting?"

Adams looked at the ugly hemispheric model. "Will that really work?"

Courtney moved closer to Bill Adams, trying to help him somehow. Jeremy Lewis and Nuclear General, together they were Bill's life since she'd known him, and now—"Bill, it will work," she said. And I'm sorry it will. I thought with this trouble, I might get some of you to myself.

Bill looked from Lewis to Courtney. The Old Man was never wrong, and Courtney knew technology better than any man in the company. She was no engineer, she was something more—she could understand engineers.

Nuclear General—Mr. Lewis was right. There was more for mankind than just old Earth. Interplanet! It sounded right. "Yes, sir."

Lewis grinned. The fires behind his eyes still burned brightly. "One more thing. Marry that girl."

"Sir?"

"I said, MARRY THAT GIRL. You two've been in love for ten years but you kept yourself so goddam busy you never noticed. It may be up to us old crocks to save the race, but how in hell are you going to keep this dynasty going without heirs. MY DYNASTY."

Adams stared in amazement.

"You never figured it out? You're my son, Bill. My wife was alive when you were born, I couldn't acknowledge you. When you were growing up, Van Cott and I had everything we owned tied up. I couldn't do much for you but arrange those scholarships—and give you a job."

"I see. I thought I'd earned my position with the company."

"Goddam right you did. You never saw my other kids around here, did you?" Lewis glared until Bill's face softened. "Right. Now you look better. Hell, I wouldn't tell you if it wasn't important. I'm not going to live out this project. Van Cott never had any kids. My grandson's been brought up by his mother." Lewis grimaced. "Not like you, Courtney. You'll give me a grandson who can take Interplanet to the stars!"

Lewis slumped back in his chair, exhausted, but his eyes sparked and flashed still. "Now get out of here and get married. I'll give you a week for honeymooning. You can spend it looking for places to launch that goddam thing."

For a moment Courtney didn't know where she was. There was the steady thrum of engines, and she lay alone on a big bed in a tiny cabin with plastic walls. Sparkling blue seas flashed below.

*Cerberus.* Nuclear General's enormous atomic-powered seaplane. Its propellers could keep it in the air for weeks. She'd met Bill aboard the *Cerberus* almost ten years ago. She smiled lazily and looked at the new rings, then suddenly sat upright. Now, where was Bill?

She dressed hurriedly and went out into the plane's big main lounge. Bill was sitting at the conference table with Mike King, who'd been his assistant before Courtney got the job. They were looking through the *Prometheus* Project Book.

"Be no problem, Mr. Adams," Michael was saying. "We can supply all you need—good morning, Mrs. Adams." Mike grinned self-consciously.

"Good morning, Mike." Courtney was icily polite. "Bill, just what are you doing?"

"Uh—" Adams looked up guiltily, and Mike tried to hide a grin. It was the first time he'd ever heard Adams at a loss for words. "I was just asking Mike about protein concentrates for *Prometheus*," Bill said. "You were asleep, and—"

"Um-huh." She sat at the table. "I told you I'd taken care of the food supplies. Mike, I'm sorry you can't join us for breakfast. Oh—you'll find something interesting in the last fifty pages of this." She handed him the project book. "Ask the steward in on your way out, will you?"

Mike smiled. "Sure, Courtney." He took the thick loose-leaf book and left quickly.

They landed outside the lagoon at Ta'avu Station late in the afternoon. Most of the Tongan technicians were waiting at the biological lock, and their long outrigger canoes were festooned with flags and pennants. There were even five members of the Royal Band in one canoe. Courtney had been stationed at Ta'avu for four years before she met Bill Adams, and although she'd been there only a few times since, they remembered her.

"Twenty whales, Courtney," Danual shouted. "Five pregnant." The burly Tongan boatman looked at Courtney's rings and turned away, embarrassed for a moment. "You will stay a long time?"

"No," she sighed. They climbed down from the huge airplane to Danual's boat. "Only three days. Bill, you remember Danual don't you?"

"Sure." Bill looked across the fifteen-mile-wide lagoon. It seemed hardly changed from the last time he'd seen it, but it was a profitable sea farm now. Nuclear General piped nutrient rich water up from the stygian depths, warmed it as it cooled the Ta'avu breeder reactors, and then dumped it into the lagoon where it supported a fantastic variety of sea life. Trained dolphins patrolled the farm, keeping out predators and assisting the Tongan sea people. Two dolphins splashed up to stand on their tails near the canoe as Bill climbed aboard and Danual set the outrigger sail to catch the trade wind.

It's a nice place for a honeymoon, Bill thought. Ta'avu in the Tonga Islands, very romantic. We built it because we needed a place for really fast breeders, but now we get more than forty million a year profit from protein production. Ta'avu alone can supply all the concentrates we'll need for *Prometheus*—he turned suddenly as Courtney grabbed the project book from his hand. Before he could say anything she pitched it out into the lagoon.

"Courtney, there's not another copy of that nearer than Santa Barbara!"

She smiled. "I know."

Well, I had him to myself for four whole days, Courtney Adams thought. That's a long time with a man like Bill.

They'd sailed on the lagoon, picnicked on the fringing reef under slanting palm trees, and laid there in the sudden darkness as the sun set without twilight. She'd taught him to skin dive in the clear water, and to hunt tentacled two-foot-long anemones spread on the sand at low tide. And always there were whales, half the Earth's population of the largest creatures that ever lived. With the help of the dolphins and the Tongan Navy they kept most of the herd outside the lagoon, but pregnant females stayed inside the atoll.

Courtney signed, then went to find her husband. Bill was seated in the lanai above the squat concrete structures anchored into the reef. Dolphins danced for attention in the bright sunlit water, but Adams wasn't watching them. He smiled as she came in.

"This what you want?" she asked. He eagerly seized the pocket computer and activated it, then shut it off. "Honey, I'm sorry—"

"Go on," she said. She gave him a reassuring smile. Keeping Bill Adams away from his work would be like caging a lion.

He punched in codes and studied the computer for a while, then stood and kissed her. "Thanks. I do love you—"

"I know."

He shook his head worriedly. "Just don't forget that, will you? I'm going to have a lot of balls in the air pretty soon—you don't sell out a four-billion-dollar company every week."

"Is that what's bothering you?"

"No. I can handle that. I've already got my dummy corporation set to buy the pieces we need. The real problem's the same as always, where do we build and where do we launch?"

One of the dolphins splashed them in her determination to get attention, and Bill laughed for a moment, but then his brows knotted again. "We've got to build in secret, Courtney. If word gets out, they'll stop the launch. Now, I can take a few men from a lot of different places, pay them bonuses for a year's work on a secret project—but where do we put it so they can't talk?"

"What about here?" she asked.

"I can't launch anywhere near here. It takes deep, calm water with a long uninhabited stretch downwind."

"You'll tow it out, won't you?"

"No. That's what I was just checking. Empty, we can tow the shell anywhere, but when it's full up and ready to launch we'll have fifty thousand tons—big as the *Queen Mary*. It floats, of course, but there's no seakeeping ability. Not stable except in calm water."

"Oh."

"Oh is right. Worse, how do we service the thing once it's up? Men can't live in null gravity more than a few months. Even with the shuttles we may run out of money before we've got any power to sell. By the time the media are through, there won't be many governments who'll let us have launch sites."

"Poo. You'll think of something."

"Maybe. First I've got to think of a place to set off a hundred atom bombs. Know of any governments who want *that* in their backyard?"

"You pregnant yet?" Jeremy Lewis demanded.

"Mr. Lewis! I—"

"Courtney, if you were about to say it's none of my business, don't. Of course, it's my business. Are you?"

"No."

"Good. Wait a year. Bill, where are you going to launch those things?"

"Things?" Bill asked quickly.

"Yeah." Jeremy Lewis gave Adams a smug look. "Got to thinking about the servicing problem. You're right, we run out of money before we can get enough coming in—if the damn government would let us finish in the first place. They'll take us over whether it works or not. You were right, Bill—a government could build a power satellite. So could a private company with some government help. But the government won't do that, and before long there won't be any private corporations."

"I see." Bill pulled up a heavy oak and leather chair and sat at the big pine table. "So just what do you have in mind for Interplanet?"

Lewis grinned. "Good. Now you're thinking positive. Ferguson, tell him what you've designed now."

Ferguson dramatically lifted the cover from another model on the table. It didn't look much different from Prometheus, and he waited impatiently for Adams to react. Finally, he said, "It's a Moon base. A permanent Moon base!"

"I see," Adams said quietly. "A permanent Moon base. Wonderful. Nobody's ever stayed on the Moon more than a couple of weeks, and you design a permanent base. Why not?"

"But it will work! We can put six million pounds on the Moon with each *Diana*. We send up two. Sixty thousand tons of power equipment, machine ships, scientific instruments—"

"And air," Bill said quickly. "You did think of air, didn't you?"

"We make our own air. Out of water."

"And what the hell do you make the water out of? Sweat?"

"We mine water on the Moon," Ferguson said triumphantly. "We *know* we can do that. Some of the lunar rocks are seven percent water bonded in carbonaceous chrondrites. Even the worst areas, the maria, are one percent water! All it takes to get it out is power, and we'll have solar screens for electricity, parabolic mirrors for really high temperatures—" Ferguson glared at Adams, waiting. There was a long silence.

"You know, he's right," Courtney said. "There's empirical data from the old lunar program. And theory says there may be real ice in the permafrost zone."

"I suppose you've figured out what to do when it's dark out," Bill said.

"Certainly," Ferguson snapped. "We take a fission power plant along. With turbines and everything it doesn't come to more than five thousand tons. Then there are heat engines. We can store heat in lunar rock. We can reclaim the air, too. We liquefy it—plenty of cold—then fractionate, break up carbon dioxide and water vapor, and there we are. Between recycling and rock mining we've got plenty of air. This thing's going to be *big*, and it isn't a completely closed system so—"

"Okay," Adams protested. "I believe you. But what are you supposed to *sell*? If we don't have a power satellite in orbit, just what are we doing it for?"

"But you don't *understand*," Ferguson protested. "We can do *anything* on the Moon. Clean rooms. Crystallography. Pure metals—really pure, not what we call pure down here! Vacuum, cold, it's all free. . . ."

"Yeah, I see that, but what do we *sell*?" Bill repeated.

"You don't have to sell it, Bill," Jeremy Lewis answered. "Not at first. You'll be too damn busy just staying alive. One of these days you'll be able to sell microcomputers and things like that, but until then all you'll have is knowledge, and the freedom to use it."

"It won't be long," Ferguson insisted. "It's easier to send stuff down than up—"

"Now just hold it," Adams said. "We're supposed to put a self-sustaining colony on the Moon, hoping that one day it'll pay for itself. The US government couldn't do it, but we're going to. I don't think that sounds right."

"The US government quit just when they could do it," Courtney said quietly. "You said that yourself, Bill. That they built the house and didn't put the roof on."

"Tell me where I'm wrong?" Ferguson asked. "We can put twelve million pounds on the Moon. With five hundred people, that's better than twenty thousand pounds per colonist—a lot more than you put in an Antarctic station, or one of your iceberg ships. We get metals and water and power from the Moon itself. We know plants can grow in zero gravity and artificial light, so they sure as hell will grow on the Moon. We take vitamin pills, protein concentrates and eggs we can grow fish from. We'll stay alive, and all around us there's going to be the greatest cryogenic and vacuum laboratory anybody ever dreamed of. I don't know what we'll discover but if you can't find something to sell out of that we ought to change jobs!"

"Well, maybe not quite that," Lewis said slowly. "But he's got quite a point, Bill. Interplanet may be the last private company in the solar system."

"What, five hundred people?" Adams said breathlessly. "Five hundred people on a one-way ride—"

"*Mayflower* didn't have more," Jeremy Lewis said grimly. "And they didn't have a nuclear power plant. Only problem is, now you've got two of the bastards to find launching places for . . ."

"I got that one figured out," Adams said. "But you realize that no matter what happens, there won't be anything left of the company. Atom bombs scare the hell out of people."

"Fine," Lewis said. "I want you to go along as manager anyway. Did you say you know where you're going to launch?"

"Yeah, I know." It was Bill Adam's turn to grin slyly. Lewis was right, of course. There weren't going to be any private companies—not for long. At least, not big ones. What is there for me down here? A job as a G5-18? "Courtney, want to go to the Moon with me?"

"I thought you'd never ask."

George Harrington brought his check home directly from the welfare office. By now the neighbors knew he was home during working hours, so it didn't matter. For the first few weeks after he lost his job he'd gone to the library, or fishing, or anywhere to protect the secret, but there was no point now. Besides, he'd run into three other men from his suburb doing the same thing.

"Nothing?" she asked.

"No. Who wants a retreaded astronaut who never got to space in the first place? It isn't like I was famous. . . ."

"You were doing fine with Westinghouse. You're a good engineer," Judy protested.

"Maybe. Doesn't matter, they had to cut back too. Let's face it, kid, we're on the dole and we'll stay that way." The government had jobs for some people. Planting trees. I've got nothing against trees, but where is anybody doing anything exciting? Isn't *anybody* going anywhere?

"There's a letter for you," she said. His wife handed him a large envelope. There was no return address, but his name was written in a feminine hand on the cover, and it had come special delivery.

"Some kind of magazine advertisement," he said. He started to throw it away, but he had nothing better to do, so he opened it.

The letterhead indicated a firm of "employment specialists" he'd never heard of, and the letter was obviously human typed. George read eagerly, hardly daring to hope.

*Dear Mr. Harrington. We represent a large firm which is offering permanent employment to a select group. We must state immediately, however, that the position which you might be able to fill requires that you and your family emigrate from the United States and resettle on company property at a remote location for a considerable length of time. Salary and other benefits are exceedingly generous and lifetime employment is guaranteed. If you would be interested in working on an exciting project and feel that contributing to important new research would compensate for living in complete isolation from everyone except for your coworkers and their families, please reply collect by telephone at your earliest convenience.*

Harrington read it again, then handed it to Judy.

"What do you think it is?" she asked. "Complete isolation? What company—"

"Oh, come on," George said. "It's the US government, of course. Some super-secret deal." He looked at his wife, then started to throw the letter away.

"Aren't you going to answer it?"

"What for? You don't want to live in some isolated hole. . . ."

"George, there was a time when I thought you'd be isolated for years going to Mars—don't you think I'd rather be isolated with you than see you drinking yourself to death on welfare?"

A month later, George Harrington didn't know any more than he did the first day.

He'd been told he was on the payroll of a Canadian mining firm, flown to what seemed to be an old army camp with his wife and their twelve-year-old son, and once there he was put through more tests than the astronaut office ever thought of.

They lived in a geodesic dome. Young Walter attended school taught by the families of other applicants—they'd given Judy a teaching job—and the entire group was the strangest collection of people he'd ever met. There were miners, metallurgists, scientists, sailors, agronomists and astronauts—and nobody knew any more than George.

There was a constant stream of people in and out of the camp. Some applicants didn't last a week. The "oldest hands" had been there two weeks longer than George, so that he soon became an old hand himself. When they finished testing him they began on his wife and son. George protested, but one of the personnel officers carefully explained that since they'd all have to live together in extremely close quarters for a number of years, it was important that they be compatible.

Speculation in the camp eventually settled on some kind of undersea experimental base as the most likely project, but no one could understand the secrecy.

Harrington was conducted down the long hall of the administration building to what he hoped was his final interview. The office was plain and bare like all the others, but the tall gray-blue-eyed man seated at the metal desk had an air of importance. George guessed his age as fifty, and the woman with him as maybe thirty. She was very pretty with long blonde hair and a heart-shaped face.

"Sit down, Mr. Harrington. My name is Bill Adams and I'll be manager of this project."

"Yes, sir," George said.

"I'm going to ask you a lot of embarrassing questions, George," Adams said. "If you survive that, I'll ask if you want to work with us."

"I presume you'll tell me what this is all about first."

"That's just what I won't do. If we decide we can get along, you and your family will go to the project directly from here. We have cover stories for you to give your friends and relatives back in the States—and you won't see them, or communicate with anyone outside the project, for two years."

"What happens if I quit?" George asked.

"After today, you can't quit," Bill Adams told him seriously. "Everyone who signs on stays with the project for two years. If you want to go home, leave now."

"The personnel people said this was a lifetime job for an engineer who wanted adventure," Harrington said quietly. "Ask away, Mr. Adams."

*Cerberus* dipped low over the Pacific and landed in the lee of the iceberg. When Harrington and his family left the plane they saw a monstrous tower of ice looming two hundred feet above them; it stretched for two miles in both directions. A chill wind blew across the sea, but the water was calm as they walked onto a floating pier strutting out to the plane.

The top of the iceberg was warm in the afternoon sunshine. It had been coated with Styrofoam insulation, as were most of the bergs towed north through the Humboldt current from the Antarctic to Los Angeles. This, however, was honeycombed with caves and tunnels, all insulated, and had two jagged humps near the stern. Nearly two thousand men worked on *Diana One* and *Diana Two* under their Styrofoam camouflage. Adams had built a floating city. It would last only eighteen months, but they didn't need it longer than that.

The colonists lay on acceleration couches as *Diana Two* gently lifted and fell to the Pacific swells. Overhead television screens showed *Diana One* floating ten miles away. Suddenly a column of water seemed to push *Diana* upward. The ungainly craft rose swiftly, separating from the water, but a black column of rolling steam followed it higher and higher. *Diana* climbed, her ascent slowing at each second, until she seemed to hang motionless four hundred feet above the sea.

A brilliant pinpoint of light flashed beneath the surface, and another ugly black column of steam began to form within the first stalk. It kicked the cylindrical spacecraft upward again, and the unearthly silence in *Diana Two* was broken by a loud cheer. Everyone began talking at once.

"We can't take this, we can't," a male voice shouted. "Let me out of here!"

"Shut up!" someone else commanded. "It's going, it's going. Go you beautiful bird, go. . . ."

This time the bright light flashed in the air a thousand feet below the ship. It overloaded the television's ability to produce it, but everyone could imagine a light brighter than the sun. A clock ticked away seconds in the upper corner of the screen.

"He's made it," Courtney said. She wished she could reach Bill's hand, but the straps were too tight for that. She turned to her left, away from Bill. "He's going to be all right, Judy."

"I—God, I—"

"It's all right," Courtney said. "It won't be long before we hear from him." The seconds ticked off until the shock wave of the first bomb reached them. It was surprisingly gentle, and Courtney relaxed momentarily. She'd done the calculations a thousand times: four kilotons at ten miles was such a negligible pressure that it only appeared as a three mile an hour wind. Calculations were wonderful, but like everyone else she'd been brought up in horror of atomic bombs. . . .

*Diana One* was out of sight, although they could still see periodic bright flashes somewhere above the atmosphere. Then they felt a slight jolt as the tugs took up the slack in their tow cables and began moving *Diana Two* into position. The TV image blurred, then became bright with the ancient face of Jeremy Lewis.

"There's not much I can say," Lewis began. "I wish I was aboard, but I haven't got much time left. I wish we could wait to see *Diana One* land on the Moon before you start off, but that's not possible either. We've only got a few minutes before somebody tries to put a stop to this project.

"I will say this to all of you, those aboard *Diana Two* and those who couldn't go, you're—" Lewis stopped for a moment, listening to something. "We've heard from Captain Harrington. *Diana One* is on course and every thing's working."

"Thank you, God," Judy Harrington said softly. She began to cry.

"We're getting about fifteen percent better efficiency than we figured," Lewis continued. "The coupling system works fine. *Diana One* at four hundred miles range had forty percent of the velocity needed."

"Bill, I love you," Courtney said quietly.

"Worried?"

"Yes. I'm scared stiff."

"You're scared. I guess I ought to be then. I always left the technical details to you."

"I wish you could hold me."

"Something we forgot. Should have had Ferguson design an acceleration couch for two." Mr. Lewis was talking about the great adventure in space, but Bill wasn't listening. First time I never cared what the boss said, he thought. There was some babble from the colonists, but most were quiet. The ones most likely to panic had been sedated by the medical staff before *Diana Two* was launched from her perch on the iceberg.

Damndest thing, Bill thought. Fantastic. I have to be out of my mind to be lying here waiting for a goddam atom bomb to go off a thousand feet below me.

The couch rose suddenly, shoving him hard down against it. "MY GOD!" someone screamed. There had been no warning at all.

The pressure took a long time to ease. It was actually no more than a second, but that second seemed to stretch out indefinitely. Normal weight returned as *Diana Two* coasted upward.

The second jolt was much harder, crushing him into the couch. Red blobs swam in front of his eyes. Once again time stretched, then a moment of calm. Hang on and wait, he thought. Think about something else. O' Lord who has safely brought us to the beginning of this day protect us in the same with Thy mighty power—

The third jolt lasted much longer. Each successive bomb had a larger yield, until the sixth was one hundred kilotons taking four full seconds before all its energy had been released.

"I love you," he said. "You okay, kid?"

"Sure," Courtney answered. "It's really not anything like what I thought. Figures don't mean much when it's going to happen to you. I knew with all that much energy we didn't have to take very high g loads, but—"

"Four g's is a lot!" Judy cried out. "Jesus, when will it be over? Let it be over, please let it be over. Why didn't I let them give me something?"

After a long time, Bill and Courtney heard a voice in their earphones. "This is on the Old Man's private circuit," Allan said. "He's not dead, but close to it. I don't know how he held out this long. We had a heart transplant arranged, but he passed up his chances so he could watch you go. They're going to try to keep him alive until we can find another donor. Bill, all Hell's breaking out here. The government's figured out what you did and they want blood. I'm getting Mr. Lewis off some place where they won't find him. I never thought it was much of his business, and it sure as hell isn't mine but—have a lot of kids, will you?"

Allan's voice faded out as the screens above them came alive with the image of the Moon, still a quarter of a million miles away. They wouldn't see it grow for hours, but they watched very closely anyway.

# STORY NIGHT AT THE STRONGHOLD

### by Larry Niven & Jerry Pournelle

## Editor's Introduction

I missed this one, as I suspect most of you did, when it was published in the June 2, 2016, issue of *Analog Science Fiction*. It's a return to *Lucifer*'s *Hammer* and tells the story of some of the survivors. It was written to answer the question of "What Became of the Surfer?"

**EVERYBODY ATE EARLY** in those post-comet days.

Monte had exercised himself to a frazzle, riding the fanribbon all morning. At a dinner that was mainly rice, they'd offered him raw homemade whiskey, and he couldn't resist one drink. He was already thinking of that stretch of thick rug they'd offered as a bed. But these farmers weren't going to let him sleep, were they? They had him talking and talking.

In fading twilight, somebody turned on the lights.

The stronghold's big gray common room turned to gold. Captain Monte Martini stopped in midsentence. Several voices among the thirty-odd said, "Ooh!"

Lights.

Randall in a chair near the desk, grinned and announced, "Give my children the lightning!" Harvey Randall still sounded like a commentator/interviewer. His resonant voice easily interrupted anyone. "Monte, you were saying?"

Monte looked around. He'd missed most of the names, but Randall and his wife Maureen seemed to be in charge of story night. Monte had caught another famous name. Muscular, long-headed guy. Tim Hamner was the one who had found the comet that had smacked the Earth over a year ago. That was his wife, Eileen, who'd brought him the whiskey, neat. Not as smooth as they made back home, but—

Monte said, "Yeah. They've got two jet planes going again at Colorado Springs. You say you saw one last spring. But Gildings couldn't find a place to land. We do things simpler down at Hoover. The vehicle I use is just me, a chair, a box or whatever for cargo, a tank for gasoline, a great big fan, and that ribbon of parachute that does the lifting. It's wonderfully safe. Whatever goes wrong, you've already bailed out! It's wonderfully cheap, too, compared to a helicopter. Farmers are using them to spray our fields. We can make one for you if you've got anything to trade. But we already have, uh, lightning."

"Good for you. Boulder Dam survived? And we've got the atomic plant. Where were you when the Hammer hit?"

"We mostly call it Hoover Dam. On duty. I was in charge of a security detail at the dam."

"Did you take a hit?" A lanky guy nobody had introduced. He seemed to be popular, though. "We had a dam, but we had to blow it up."

"You had to blow up your own dam?"

"Cannibals were coming," the guy said as if that explained it all. It did, too, at least as far as this crowd was concerned.

"Cannibals we didn't have. Elvis impersonators."

That got a laugh. "It's funny now, but a lot of Vegas people came out to the dam looking for a place to hide. They seemed to think we could feed them. Hell, it was tough enough feeding my troops, until the Air Force cadets got down there and the Cheyenne Mountain people took over."

"How'd that work?" Harvey asked.

"Pretty well, once things got settled. First winter was bad until the population—well, thinned out." Monte took another sip of the whiskey.

"Cadets. How were things in Colorado Springs?" That was Tim Hamner. "I had relatives there. May still have. Penelope Joyce Wilson?"

"I wouldn't know. I don't get up there much, but that's where the government is, so it's doing pretty well."

"Good. What do they govern?"

Monte laughed. "They claim to be the United States. We don't argue with them, but we have the dam. They don't." Monte swallowed the last drop of whiskey, then set the glass on a table. "I take it you all were already here?"

The laughter that erupted was flavored with hysteria. Randall said, "Some of us were. Senator Jellison set up the Stronghold where he already had a ranch. But me and a lot of others had to fight our way here."

A big man named Christopher said, "Even if we were here, we still had to fight off the cannibal army. Save the nuke plant. Grow enough to eat. Jennifer here is visiting from the Shire. It's weird, but those hippies were growing rice before it got wet, and maybe that saved us till spring. Harry the Mailman here has stories to match anything you've got. And Rick here was in orbit when that thing hit."

"We saw it all," the lone black man said. "Mostly it hit the northern hemisphere. From space it looked like someone was poking lit cigars through the back of a map."

Monte asked, "Cannibal army?"

"They're pretty near gone now. Survivors are working our crops," Randall said. "But we weren't all there in safety, Captain Martini. Helena?"

A big woman said, "We were caught out there in rain and the floods. It's a wonder we survived long enough to get to the atomic plant. But we saw an SUV driving over the water, and that was a tale too."

There was laughter, and Eileen Hamner said, "That was us."

"And there's us," said a ragged-looking young man with long dirt-colored hair. "We were a Boy Scout troop and a girls' hiking group. When the Hammer hit we were all in the mountain. We had it better than most. We trade dried meat for some of what the Stronghold grows. I'm just visiting."

Maureen Randall said, "They're self-sufficient or close enough."

They were talking to each other rather than Monte now. His attention began wandering. He heard, "The atomic plant can't send current very far, but some cottage industry is growing up around it, and their products travel. . . ."

"Bay level is going down, good farmland out there. . . ."

"Comrade lives with Leonilla; they're the other two astronauts. Everyone's pregnant—"

"Yeah, *now*."

"We used up a stock of condoms when we had it, to keep the hungry mouths to a minimum. Big box of condoms from the Shire. Paid for with chickens and a rooster."

"The Shire isn't getting many children, are you, Hennessey?"

Monte was losing the thread.

"Global warming? No, man, the Hammer shattered our weather. . . ."

Now a sick-looking guy two chairs down was talking about the cannibals, how he'd hidden around their edges and raided their garbage sites after they'd passed. The old man in the big, ornate chair was just letting them talk.

Monte perked up when a refugee spoke. "I rode a wave onto Santa Monica Beach and up Wilshire till I wiped out. . . ."

Monte hadn't caught his name. He must have arrived at the Stronghold gate earlier than Monte, maybe this morning. He was dark-tanned and gaunt, used to be muscular, Monte thought. "Walked out of Santa Monica and Westwood, over into the Valley. I wasn't having much luck till I got to the Shire. I was looking for them, you follow? Because the surfers used to talk about a hippy who'd inherited a ranch and some money, and he'd invited all his friends there, and he'd take friends of friends too. I made for the Shire. It was all I could think of."

"They've been kinder to passersby since it dawned on them that they'd offended the Mailman." That was a guy named Mark.

The dark-haired girl next to him had sung some kind of song earlier. Now she nursed a baby. "Harry still won't stop there. They have to work to get their news." She laughed.

"Damned straight," Harry said. Hennessey looked glum.

"Well, they were nice enough to me. Not that they didn't work me, they did, but I smoked some weed with them, and they fed me, even if it was all vegetables—"

Mark asked, "Did you get laid?"

"Well, yeah."

"It's funny what those hippies know. They'll lecture you on hybrid vigor."

"And they gave me some letters for Harry. He brought me here. I've been told I get a meal and a stretch of rug. The meal was excellent, sir," to the man across the circle.

"The rest depends. What have you got to offer?" the old man asked.

"I can match any story."

"Where you been?"

The Surfer stood up and ran his finger over a map that half covered one wall. "I'm mostly guessing here. Up from Los Angeles, over the mountain. I was behind the Brotherhood Army most of the way, I think."

"I did that too," said the sick-looking guy two chairs over. "Followed them. They didn't know how to eat some of the food in the markets. I could hide in drainpipes."

"I didn't see anything of an atomic plant. Shire's here. Harry was here," the Surfer said, pointing. The old man in the big chair was nodding, not saying anything. Monte had been told his name. He was important, somehow.

"A bunch of us were surfing that morning, waiting for a wave off Santa Monica Beach. I knew when the Hammer hit: I saw something way brighter than the sun come down and split the sea. I got most of us turned around and paddling before the wave came over the horizon. I don't think anyone lived through it but me. I rode the shock wave when the wave hit the cliff. I was still on it while it ran down Wilshire as far as the Barrington Apartments. Then I couldn't get out of the way.

"I aimed for a set of glass doors on a balcony.

"I just grazed the top of an iron railing halfway up the Barrington B. Leaned back on the board and got it tilted up and smashed through the glass doors flat on. I didn't hit glass, I smacked against balsa and nylon. Hey, my nose was already bleeding; ears, too. But half the wave was still above my head, still smashing at the building.

So now I'm in a hallway in a surge of water I just can't fight. It takes me down to the far face of the building, and now I'm starting to get my breath back. Then *those* doors shattered and I spilled out into space. The water was two or three stories down by now.

"I grabbed a floating desk.

"It gets a little hazy. I think I hit my head on the desk, coming down. When the water started going backward, I grabbed a lamppost. Or maybe a parking garage railing a few stories up. When I could walk I was too wiped out, and crying because all the others were drowned. I couldn't do more than find a place to sleep.

"I made for a backpacker's store, but it was already looted. I had to put together my own package, doing my own looting.

"I'd heard of the Shire, a heaven on earth established by a rich hippie. I got there. Two nights. They worked me, farming rice. They let me wash and dry my clothes. Fed me lots of rice, but also bacon and eggs. I'm not sure if they'd have let me stay, they think I'm lucky, but they were so weird, man. And they told me about you, and about a village in the mountains. . . ."

The old man asked, "Can you drive?"

"Sure."

"Water in the San Joachin has been subsiding, so sea bottom that was out of reach is more shallow now. Looting underwater isn't good, but it's possible."

"I'm your man," the Surfer said.

"Then we all get our happy endings. We're the lucky ones. I'd have loved to see the lights go on in my living room again," the old man said. "Jellison, Senator Jellison. Wait now—"

The guy two chairs over wasn't just unhealthy. Good Lord, he was coming apart. The smell . . . not unpleasant . . . smell of dinnertime.

"I remember. They caught me. Pulled me out of the culvert. They boiled me," he said.

They'd said Senator Jellison died of a heart attack.

The Surfer said, "I hit the desk coming down. Banged my head. Are we all dead? All of us?"

And they were all looking at Monte. Monte struggled to speak . . . but agony ran through his limbs, and he screamed instead.

Tim Hamner was gaping at him.

"Cramps," he said. "Sorry. It was a long flight. You can't relax when you're flying a fanribbon."

Hamner said. "You okay now? We just let you sleep, but you could have the rug and a pillow."

"Yeah, thanks." He was trying to walk off the cramps. His calves wouldn't relax. "God I had nightmares. Dead persons all around me."

"Survivor guilt. Ashamed of being alive when so many are dead. We all get it sometimes," Tim Hamner said and handed him a pillow.

# THE MAN WHO OWNED THE FUTURE:

## Remembering Jerry Pournelle

### by Robert Gleason

**BACK IN LATE 1972,** when I was a young editor at Simon & Schuster-Pocket Books, I approached Robert Heinlein's agent, Lurton Blassingame, with an idea for a Robert Heinlein Reader. I saw it as a collection of short stories and novel excerpts along with some commentary by Robert on how he came to write some of the various pieces. Robert was and still is arguably the greatest SF writer of all time. Since I inordinately admired his writing, I really wanted to do the book with him. Lurton and Robert liked my idea, but Robert was busy at the time, and they put it on hold. Eventually Robert's second agent, Eleanor Wood, developed a book idea along similar lines, and I got to publish it at Tor Books, where I was editor-in-chief. The book was titled *Requiem*.

However, that first lunch with Lurton bore another kind of fruit. He had represented Frank Herbert's *Dune* and Robert Heinlein's *Stranger in a Strange Land*, and he told me at that lunch that he had a novel that equaled those two masterworks. A first-contact-with-aliens thriller, it was a true epic saga of spectacular proportions. He said there were problems in the first 200 pages though, and the story didn't take off until the reader met the aliens. He believed the other editors, whom he'd shown it to, hadn't gotten beyond those first problematic 200 pages; consequently, he'd received over twenty-three rejections. S&S-Pocket had even rejected it. Lurton said if he sent it to me, he wanted me to read at least half of the 1,200 page manuscript myself before turning in my lunch pail and not send it to a reader.

I promised I'd read the whole thing, and I stayed up till 3:30 in the morning for three consecutive nights, reading it for more than eight hours a night. I went to the office each following morning on less than three hours sleep, and while I was tired at work for those three days, I was also walking on a cloud. The book was easily the best SF novel I'd ever seen or heard of, let alone read. The authors were the only ones I'd ever come across who turned the aliens into plausible, intricately-nuanced viewpoint characters. The authors also created the aliens' culture in elaborate, in-depth detail and made their world come dazzlingly to life. No SF writers had ever done that, not to the degree that these authors had. The novel was utterly enthralling in every respect.

So I signed it up, and, of course, we fixed the first 200 pages. The book, which every publisher in New York had turned down, went on to sell millions worldwide. It still generates extraordinary sales forty-five years later. Robert Heinlein gave it the only blurb he'd ever given up to that point. He called it very simply: "The best science fiction novel I have ever read."

The book was Larry Niven's and Jerry Pournelle's *The Mote in God's Eye*. I desperately wanted to do another SF novel with the two writers. They proved in *Mote* that they could do aliens like no one else had done before or since, so I suggested that they invent some new alien viewpoint characters, create another alien civilization and have them attack the Earth. The authors could then dramatize how the nations of the world responded.

Niven initially resisted, saying alien invasion novels had been done to death. I argued that there had never been a good alien invasion novel, in which the aliens were viewpoint characters and where their cultures were fully developed. Jerry eventually got my point, saw the book's potential and talked Larry into the idea.

In Niven-Pournelle's plot synopsis, the aliens deflected an asteroid into the Earth's orbit, which, after it hit Earth, was supposed to destroy *Homo sapiens* in the same way that the KT asteroid annihilated the dinosaurs. The aliens could then take our planet over, unopposed.

I was fascinated with the asteroid and the catastrophic effects it unleashed. This was 1974, and I had never heard of such global cataclysms. The Alvarez hypothesis, which argued—and which today is almost universally accepted—that an asteroid had obliterated the dinosaurs, would not be made public until 1980, six years after Niven and Pournelle started their book and three years after it was published. So in 1974 very few people understood the apocalyptic consequences of massive asteroid impacts. My boss also recognized the potential for such a novel. I phoned Pournelle, shouting: "Stop the presses! I have a book idea that's going to blow New York publishing wide open! I want a novel about an asteroid strike!"

The two men explained, somewhat heatedly, that, while they liked both ideas, they'd already put a lot of work into the invasion novel and had given me a lengthy treatment.

"Okay," I said. "Let's do two books."

They agreed, and we decided to do the asteroid novel first. They changed the asteroid to a comet. The comet was essentially a super-gargantuan block of ice, inside of which were two super-massive bodies of rock and metal ore, and when the comet swung by the sun, its heat melted the ice. These two hard-rock mountains then rocketed toward the Earth at speeds four times faster than those of a mere asteroid. One of these Mount Everests hit the Atlantic, the other the Pacific. Cracking Earth's mantle, molten magma erupted straight up from the Earth's core, vaporizing zillions of tons of sea water. In the polar regions, the $H_2O$ came down as ice and snow, inaugurating a new ice age. In the temperate zones, it came down as saltwater rain, destroying the top soil. Humankind was effectively exterminated.

*Lucifer*'s *Hammer* is the most powerful novel I have ever read. I was haunted by it then, and I'm haunted by it now. It inspired me to write apocalyptic novels of my own, including *End of Days* and *Wrath of God*, which were both critically acclaimed, national bestsellers. It is fair to say that Jerry Pournelle and Larry Niven changed my life in a very personal, fundamental way.

These two books also changed their lives. *Lucifer* reached #2 on the *New York Times* list, and the alien invasion novel, *Footfall*, hit #1. They were now top *New York Times*–bestselling authors.

Jerry and I were friends for forty-five years, and I could tell a million wonderful stories about him. The two-week camping trip we took in the southwestern desert could provide a million all by itself. We set out in a Bronco jeep, armed with seventeen guns, two hundred pounds of ammunition and six cases of beer. We blew two tires—one in the Mojave Desert and one up in the San Carlos Mountains, where we had gotten lost. We were on a dried-up streambed and had to four-wheel-drive the Bronco along the outermost edge of a mountain. When we looked out of our left-hand windows, we were staring straight down into a vast, vertiginous void.

So when the tire blew, we had to change it there on the spot; otherwise, we believed, we would be stuck on that mountaintop for weeks, the area was that remote and sparsely populated.

Even though Jerry had done parachute jumps during the Korean War, he suffered from horrendous acrophobia, and his vertigo was too debilitating for him to squat on the brink of the precipice. Since the blown tire was on the cliff side of the streambed, I had to hunker down and lean backward over the cliff, while I changed it. The whole time, his eyes shut, Jerry held onto the front of my belt, sometimes with two hands. I cranked the jack, removed the lugs and replaced the wheel, while both of us trembled above the abyss.

In short, we had the time of our lives.

But if I had to take one thing away from my forty-five-year friendship with Jerry it would be something he said to Larry and me one afternoon in his house back in 1973. He was telling Larry and me about MIT's *Limits to Growth* study and how eventually the Earth would run out of natural resources, even as its population proliferated and that we had to mine the asteroids if we were to survive. He also talked about the dangers of comet and asteroid strikes and why it was therefore imperative that the human race expand into space in a major, permanent way. Otherwise, he said we would go extinct.

He suggested that afternoon that we do a nonfiction book entitled *So Our Children Will Not Curse Us*. In it, he would describe all the things we could do to make the world a better place. He then pointed out that books can do more than entertain. Books have the potential to transform for the better both humanity and the planet.

"Bob," Jerry said, "I only want to change the world. It's not too much to ask."

I was stunned by the audacity of Jerry's suggestion. He said that as writers and book publishers, we could strive to make things better. I'd previously been too modest to entertain such thoughts. Jerry not only provided me with the insight and much of the subject matter, upon which to base such books, he inspired me to think in those terms. He was always trying to improve our world, our species, our future. Always.

Another thing about Jerry, which I'd like to stress, is how funny he was. Larry, Jerry and I spent countless hours discussing possible book projects, literature, history, the state of the world, whatever, but part of the fun was that all three of us liked to laugh. Whenever one of us would make a humorous observation, Jerry, in particular, would be quick to develop the joke even further, to riff on it until it was genuinely sidesplitting. Falstaff once remarked on himself: "I am not only witty in myself but am that which is the cause of wit in other men," and Jerry made us all funnier. He was one of the most hilarious people I've ever known, and he had more important knowledge in his head than anyone I've ever known.

Jerry had been a legendary Cold Warrior, an expert on global strategy and at one point the top authority on the inertial guidance systems that for so many decades determined the trajectories of our ballistic missiles. But despite his military background—or perhaps because of it—he genuinely hated war and resented all the money the Pentagon spent on war's planning and execution.

"Think of all that Pentagon money that we squandered on boondoggles these last seventy-five years," Jerry used to say. "Had we spent it on education, on science and technology, on health and infrastructure, imagine what a different and prosperous country we would have today."

After the Soviet Union collapsed, he complained that his onetime Cold War allies in Washington were now trying to turn the US into an empire. He feared that that had been their goal all along and that we could not be both an imperium and a democracy.

He argued forcefully that America should stay out of Iraq. "To be an empire," he used to say, "you have to subjugate your people at home as well as your so-called enemies abroad. In that case, the

Patriot Act will only be the beginning. Far more repressive laws and oppressive policies will follow." He liked to quote from Robert Heinlein's iconic short story, "Logic of Empire," which Robert had written seventy-seven years earlier and which vividly dramatized that very point.

A true renaissance man, Jerry had at various times been a combat veteran, a learned scholar, a NASA scientist, an insightful historian, an intrepid explorer, an inveterate world traveler, an erudite journalist—among other things, one of our foremost computer journalists—a mesmerizing raconteur and an illustrious author. He'd read everything of importance; he'd been everywhere and had seen everything. He had truly experienced the world in all its wrath and wonder.

He suffered the curse of Odysseus—incurable curiosity—and everything fascinated him. Speaking of Odysseus, I believe Tennyson's lines from his poem about that Eternal Wanderer describe Jerry better than anything I've ever read. The words are Odysseus's, but they apply to Jerry as well:

*. . . I am become a name;*
*For always roaming with a hungry heart*
*Much have I seen and known; cities of men*
*And manners, climates, councils, governments,*
*Myself not least, but honour'd of them all;*
*And drunk delight of battle with my peers,*
*Far on the ringing plains of windy Troy.*
*I am a part of all that I have met. . . .*

Jerry Pournelle was indeed "a part of all that he had met." A man in full, he was also a man for all seasons, one who touched life at all points, and when he died, I do believe the gods broke the mold. One thing is for sure: We shall not look upon his like again.

Larry Niven once told me that those who dream the future, own the future, and if Niven was right, then Jerry owned the future in spades redoubled. In fact, people, like Jerry—who are so vital, so indispensable to changing the world and improving what comes after us—ought to live a thousand years. I say this knowing that in Jerry's case a single millennium would still not be time enough for him to see all his dreams, epiphanies and passions fulfilled. His vision was too vast and his soul too universal to be restrained by something as trivial as time.

Jerry, you were one of a kind. Goddamn it, we sure do miss you.

—Robert Gleason
Executive Editor
Tor/Forge Books
New York, NY
www.RobertGleasonBooks.com